IN THE SHADOW OF ZIAMMONTIENTH

MYTH OF THE DRAGON™ SERIES BOOK 01

MICHAEL ANDERLE

LMBPN Publishing
PMB 196, 2540 South Maryland Pkwy
Las Vegas, NV 89109

Version 1.00, November 2021
ebook ISBN: 978-1-64971-896-9
Hardcover ISBN: 978-1-64971-897-6
Paperback ISBN: 978-1-68500-503-0

THE IN THE SHADOW OF ZIAMMONTIENTH TEAM

Thanks to our Beta Team
Larry Omans, Kelly O'Donnell, John Ashmore, Mary Morris, Rachel Beckford

Thanks to our JIT Readers

Angel LaVey
Jeff Eaton
John Raisor
Larry Omans
Misty Roa
Tim Adams

If We've missed anyone, please let us know!

Editor
The Skyhunter Editing Team

To Family, Friends and
Those Who Love
To Read.
May We All Enjoy Grace
To Live The Life We Are
Called.

ZIAMMOTIENTH
ERYMUS RIVER
CITY OF TOLAN KEIRAN
(OLD CITY)
KILLZONE
NEW CITY
ZIAMMONTIENTH
AND SURROUNDING AREA

CHAPTER ONE

Darkness blanketed the city. The moon hung thin and low and did nothing to illuminate the thoroughfares. Occasionally, light would flicker from inside a bar and spill out into the streets.

The land rippled in the dark folds of rough hilltops and the jagged edges of rock formations almost invisible against the sky. A single road led through them and twisted as though it tried to evade the monsters that roamed toward the beast blotting out the stars.

That stretch of road was called the Kill Zone for a reason.

Few ventured there and fewer still reached the vast expanse of ruins at its end. These were barely visible on a night like this, but the campfires of a hundred tribes lit its square hollows and straight walls, and more pinpricks of light dotted the flanks of the mountain above.

The mountain dominated the valley and rose taller than the unbroken range that enclosed the area, but it wasn't whole. Some said it had always had two peaks and others insisted that it was once whole and a dragon had broken it in two.

No dragon prowled the valley now, but myriad monsters emerged from the mountain depths and hunted any foolish enough to dare the ruins or slopes above.

Those two peaks rose spear-like to threaten the sky and gave the mountain its name—Twin Spears. The ruins at its feet were known as Tolan's Doom, although the city's residents simply called it the Doom.

It was both a name and a prophecy for those who moved toward it.

The city overlooking the Kill Zone and the ruins at its end was a different matter. Known as Tolan's Waypoint, it marked the only entry to the valley and was the last chance for provisions for those stupid or desperate enough to venture farther.

Most came on the promise of treasure—and very few returned.

The monsters saw to that as they prowled through the devastation like soldiers on patrol. The Waypoint's walls and guards kept the brutes out of the city and from spilling into the plains beyond. But even in the valley's newest—and only—city, there were other dangers.

On nights when the moon was but a sliver, the rooftops became a highway. Shadows flitted over them.

Those of most concern were humanoid in form, their movement swift between the patches of dark thrown by chimneys or that pooled in angular valleys. Now and then, one would peer at the city walls to make sure the guards were facing out and not in.

The last thing those who ran the peaks needed was for the alarm to be sent to Dreamers' Corner. The guards patrolling this area were alert enough.

They didn't need a reason to be additionally vigilant.

Occasionally, one of the shadows descended to the gutter-line and their eyes gleamed with reflected light as they scanned the streets below. Most were empty but a few held patrols.

What those hiding in the shadows sought lay closer to the center of the section and not there, where the merchants and craftsman had set up shop.

One figure moved ahead of the others, slid down the roof pitches with ease, and used their momentum to leap the narrow streets dividing the buildings. Slender in build and dressed in dark but tattered clothing, the figure kept her cloak's hood low as she ran along the next roof ridge.

A disguised grunt was all that was released as she jumped from one ridge to the next.

The hood concealed her face, but the clothing did nothing to conceal her form.

The figure relied on the darkness to do that.

A close observer would have noted that it was a young woman who leapt from the closed shopfront of True Shot the fletcher's, to the still-warm slates of the Steel & Shields.

She paused and turned to survey the streets below, disappointed by their emptiness. No would-be adventurers were dossing in the streets or returning to the boarding houses set away from the more popular and expensive inns around Orcs' Head Square.

It was typical that on a night when they needed them most, the usual drunkards simply weren't around to hand their tithes and tips to those who needed them more.

The cloaked head moved to look down the street. "I guess we'll have to find the not so usual drunkards," she muttered, scampered up the weaponsmith's roof, and slid into the valley where the workshop roof joined that of the smith's living quarters.

She hoped none of the apprentices were having a sleepless night. It would only take one to realize that the soft sounds overhead weren't rats and for the smith to call the guard.

Moving silently, she ran along the ridge line, threw herself across the intervening street, and twisted in mid-air to reach the roof of the Clawed Cup.

When she landed above the kitchen gable, she dropped swiftly to her knees in case her movement had drawn attention. She rose into a crouch, pulled her hood lower, and moved to the shadows of the closest chimney.

This time, she didn't settle against it.

The Clawed Cup served meals late into the night and the ovens were still active. The sweet smells of roasting pig made her stomach grumble. Annoyed, she told her body to shut its whining down.

She looked back as her accompanying shadows descended the weaponsmith's roof to the alley below. A moment's wait was enough to confirm that they reached the street in one piece and undetected before she turned and ran half-crouched along the ridge line toward the tavern's entrance.

When she reached the front of the building, she dropped onto her belly, edged closer to the eaves, and peered over.

Her irises needed a moment to adjust.

Warm light spilled from the tavern's windows and sounds of rowdy enjoyment drifted up with the stink of ale and additional aromas of well-cooked food.

The young woman's rebellious stomach ignored her earlier command and rumbled. She swallowed against a sudden surge of saliva.

If she was quick—no, very, very quick—and lucky, they might all eat tonight. She only had to wait for the perfect moment.

The tavern door cracked open and bright light spilled into the street.

"And take your friend with you," Grunder shouted. "I've a good mind to call the Watch."

"No, no, no…" The voice that answered the barkeep sounded like its owner had enjoyed one too many ales. "Thatsh…" He paused for a moment before he continued. "It won't be necesshary."

A shadow swayed on the cobbles as the man who cast it was burdened by another whose arm he'd pulled over his shoulder.

Make that one dozen ales too many, the girl thought, her grin feral in anticipation.

Grunder had said "friend." Did that mean there were only two? She crossed her fingers.

The shadow solidified and was then eclipsed by the figures of two solidly built men. Both wore chainmail tunics, leather breeches, and sturdy boots. Neither wore helmets—not that it would make a difference.

From the look of them—and of the two who followed—they were professional soldiers, mercenaries who hired out to protect adventurers who wanted to ensure that they survived the journey into the Doom.

All wore belt knives and two had swords strapped to their hips.

One had a mace tucked crosswise through the back of his belt, and the fourth had an ax haft secured by a loop at his waist, the blade covered by a leather hood.

The girl stifled a soft groan and ducked her head in case they had heard it.

Her shoulders slumped. *Why does it have to be mercenaries?*

Unfortunately, they were still the best marks she'd seen all night.

A swift glance showed that the moon had almost reached its zenith.

They were probably the only marks she would see that night. Given the sounds rising from the tavern, the other patrons were likely to be there until dawn or would sleep on the tavern floor if Grunder let them.

She pushed to her feet with a sigh, retraced her steps, and stopped to mark the targets' trail before they wove out of sight. Her heart sank when she noted their size and selected one slightly taller than the rest.

The chances were he was the leader and now her responsibility.

Her gaze followed them as they turned away from Orc's Head square and along the road that would take them past Steel & Shields and possibly True Shot. Hidden in the shadow of her hood, a frown creased her brow. If they kept going that way, she had a very good idea of their destination.

Slowly, she moved forward and tracked their progress by their heavy tread and the jangle of their weapons. They reached the corner and continued, and the girl breathed a sigh of relief, hurried to the end of the roof, and increased her pace as she approached.

The mercenaries came into view, wove unsteadily past the front of True Shot, and continued. The girl smiled. There was only one doss house in that direction and she knew a shortcut.

After a low whistle, she stamped her foot hard on the roof, drew a deep breath, and raced forward. With a flick of her body, she hurled herself into a flip to adjust her trajectory to Steel & Shields' roof. She landed, glanced back to find the eaves, then reversed and dropped over.

A gasp came from below, followed by a hastily muffled moan as she hung momentarily, bunched her legs, and pushed off the wall. Ignoring the sound, she twisted her body as she dropped toward the rear wall of the tavern.

She struck it with flat palms and the balls of her feet, pushed off again, and turned to alight on the cobbles facing away from it. As she landed, she bounced into a roll that brought her to her feet, and two swift strides took her into the shadows along the smith's back wall.

"Kaylin!" Raoul's harsh whisper greeted her from the dark.

She snapped her head toward it and raised her hand for silence.

It was not enough to keep them in the shadows. They all wanted to hear what she had in mind and she knew she had little time. Instead of pushing them away, she gathered them close and crept into the shadows in a corner of the smith's yard.

"There are four of them," she said and watched her friends' eyes widen in alarm as she continued. "Most likely mercenaries, too."

"And the good news is?" Raoul asked and his concern edged his question.

"They're dead drunk." She smiled.

"That doesn't mean they'll have forgotten how to wield their swords," another of her friends retorted and she suppressed a sigh.

Trust Melis to point out the only real weakness in her plan. As she opened her mouth to reply, a deep baritone echoed down the street. They all froze, and the smallest of their crew jumped with fright. The fifth, Isabette, laid her hand on his shoulder.

"It's fine, Piers. He's singing."

"A...are you sure?" Piers whispered. "Because he sounds like an ogre with a bellyache."

"Pfft!" Isabette patted the cloth under her palm. "How would you know what one of those sounds like anyway?"

"I can imagine," the boy retorted in a hissed tone.

"Well," Kaylin told them firmly, "if they've reached the singing stage, it won't be long before they reach the sleeping or tossing their cookies stage. That means they will be very distracted. We don't have to tell them they're being robbed."

She drew a small belt knife and wiggled it at them.

"So?" Melis demanded. "They're mercenaries. What will we do if they catch us? It's not like we can do much to overcome them." She glared at Kaylin and pointed at Raoul. "A walking stick's no match for a full-on mace." Her finger moved to Isabette. "And a sling won't do anything if they can close the distance, and as for these..."

She drew her little knife and twirled it a few times, and the light barely created a reflection. "They can't get through anything more than leather and the blades are too short to do anything more than make the target angry."

Kaylin sheathed the knife and rested her hand on her hip.

"Liss, are you honestly telling me you're not fast enough to cut a purse-string and catch the coin before it hits the ground?" she challenged and the other girl narrowed her eyes.

"I'll have you know I'm one of the fastest Hands there is," she snapped and Kaylin nodded.

"I know," she reassured the girl, "and it's good to see you know it too. All we have to do is coordinate."

She turned to catch Piers and Raoul in her sights. "And you won't tell me you can't tag-team a drunk, singing mercenary as easily as you do an overweight inobservant merchant?"

The boys' eyes widened.

"Oh," Piers said as his eyes gleamed and his gaze darted to his brother. "We can do that, can't we, Ro?"

Raoul rolled his eyes. "Well, duh. That part we can manage just fine."

"And me?" Isabette demanded and Kaylin rolled her eyes. The girl was the closest to her in age of any of them and as close to her second in command as she was likely to get.

"Are you fishing for compliments, Iz?" she asked sharply. "'Cos I could remind you that you're two purses behind Liss and tell you I'm surprised you let her get so far ahead if you want me to."

"Mean." The other girl pouted. "You coulda said I could shoot a gnat out of the air or shatter a window pane at a hundred yards and was your best hope for a distraction."

Kaylin grinned. "I could do that."

A second voice joined the singing—a tenor if she wasn't mistaken—and her grin faltered. She fixed the other four with her sternest look. If the mercs continued with that racket, they were likely to draw an audience—or the closest Watch patrol, which would be worse.

"Don't make me remind you that Goss needs us. That if we don't get him his medicine, he might die."

They shook their heads, their narrow faces pinched with worry. She pressed her advantage.

"And do I have to tell you that none of us have eaten more than sweet stems for the last three days?"

At the mention of the wild delicacy that grew in any spare piece of soil it could find, her stomach rumbled and her mouth watered anew. She grimaced and hated herself for having to push them this way but without this effort, none of them would eat.

Kaylin swallowed when her nose reminded her of the food smells coming from the Cup's common room.

"We need to eat," she told them, "and none of us is strong enough to stand against one fully armed mercenary worth half a damn. We'll have to go in fast—quiet and quick."

She tugged the cloak shrouding Isabette's face and indicated the wraps both Raoul and Piers wore. "It's not like they'll see your faces and even if they did, they are probably too drunk to remember you anyway."

"Do you want to make a bet on that?" Liss demanded and Kaylin glanced toward the intersection from which the singing came.

"I have to," she told them softly. "Goss is relying on me—on all of us—and we're the only family he has. If we want to save him, we need to pull off a bigger score than the pennies we usually get."

She looked around and exaggerated searching for something she couldn't find. Finally, Isabette tired of her theatrics.

"What?" she asked impatiently.

"Oh… I'm looking for that handy noble not in their carriage and not traveling at a gallop—you know, like all the other nobles we've passed up."

"What other nobles?" Raoul sounded confused and she put her hand on her hip and cocked her head.

"Exactly!" She pointed to the boy. "I haven't seen one outside a carriage in weeks. How about you?"

Raoul shook his head and she imagined his cheeks reddening in the shadows.

Kaylin took a step toward him and lowered her voice to coax urgency. "Come on. I don't like my chances if I try it on my own, but with the four of you, I know it can work. I have the fastest hands, best-aimed sling, and the best team of light-fingers I've ever had the misfortune to meet—and they're all on my side. And I'd like to think Goss does, too."

"But...mercenaries," Liss protested and Kaylin laid a hand on her shoulder and shook her.

"Can you do it or not? Because you can head back and look after Goss if you want to," she suggested.

Melis' eyes flashed in the depths of her hood.

"I will not go back to that boy to tell him I've been sent to look after the carriage," she snapped in return. "He'd never let me live it down."

Raoul snickered. "I wouldn't either."

She turned on him. "So, you're in?" She snarled a challenge.

Surprise crossed the boy's face and his gaze shifted to their leader. She returned it and made sure he could see it was all his choice. He could join her and help his friend or not, but she wouldn't press him any further.

A third voice joined the chorus of mercenaries and clay shattered.

"It sounds like someone brought extras," she observed, "and they were deep in their cups already."

"Truly?" She couldn't blame Liss for the suspicious edge to her voice but she didn't have to pretend when she answered.

"Yup, they were almost fall-down drunk and looked like they have more than enough left to spend. We'd have what we need for the medicine and a good meal."

That, if nothing else, decided them, although Melis was a little harder to convince.

"How good a meal?"

Kaylin pointed at the Clawed Cup. "We could afford to eat there for at least two nights in a row and still have enough to feed ourselves for a week after."

"With no dishes involved?" the other girl persisted and regarded her suspiciously.

She sighed. "Not this time, Liss."

It seemed Melis still hadn't forgiven her for the time she'd snagged meals for them at the Cup and not managed to sneak them out before Grunder had caught them. At least the taverner had only insisted they do the night's dishes.

He could have called the Watch.

"This will keep our heads above water for enough weeks that we can be more selective about the next score."

"Promise?" Liss didn't give up easily.

Kaylin responded with her most sincere stare. "I do solemnly swear," she intoned.

The girl stared at her for a moment longer, then giggled. "Fine." She darted a glance at Isabette. "When the night's done, I'll be more than two pouches ahead."

"Says who?" the older girl challenged but in a whisper.

Liss melted into the shadows on the opposite side of the street and Isabette slid into the closest patch of darkness. Raoul and Piers vanished in her wake and left their leader to follow. She glanced ahead at the mercenaries and realized she'd made a horrible mistake.

The doss house wasn't the only thing in this direction, and her drunken marks showed no sign of wanting to end their celebrations. What if they had other plans?

She groaned as they turned right into a lane that would take them to the Windy Wizard. If they reached the tavern before the group could strike, all bets were off. The Wizard was a rougher establishment than the Cup and its patrons usually ended the night passed out on the floor since the bartender didn't care how drunk they were as long as they had the coin.

The rumors were that irrespective of how much coin they had when they collapsed, none of the Windy's guests had more than ten gold when they woke—and none of them could remember how much they'd spent. Nor were they ever in any condition to argue the fact.

Gossip also had it the Windy's barman drugged the last round of the night, but there was never any evidence of that either. Kaylin hurried her steps and vanished into the shadows Liss had chosen.

Every one of her crew knew the danger ahead and that they needed a large return on their efforts.

Goss needed it.

She chewed on her lip, unsure how much longer he'd last if they didn't succeed.

They might not have caught up with the mercenaries if the drunkest of them hadn't decided he needed to pee and couldn't wait.

He dragged his friend into the shadows of a narrow alley between a stolid stone two-story house with darkened windows, and what looked—and smelt—like a walled garden plot.

Kaylin knew she hadn't imagined the small patch of shadow that beat the two men into the darkened alley and she hoped Liss hadn't misjudged her mark. They would never hear the end of it if the girl ended up in a puddle.

She needn't have worried. The mercenaries didn't venture far and one propped his hand on the wall while his friend made sure he stayed upright. It was doubtful that either of them noticed when their purses vanished into the shadow.

If her focus hadn't been fully engaged by the remaining two, she might have smiled. Both men seemed a little more alert and cast their gazes up and down the street. Despite this, they weren't as vigilant as they might have been.

Neither of them noticed when Piers stepped behind the man who supported his friend and slid his knife in a long, thin line across the base of the belt pouch that hung over one hip. The damage wasn't apparent until they turned while one adjusted his trousers and the other pretended he was nowhere nearby.

Before either of their companions could remark on it, the one being supported burst into song—one of the bawdier favorites of men on a drinking spree.

The lyrics were usually butchered and the chorus would see them arrested if the Watch heard them, but that didn't matter.

One of those waiting chuckled and sang snatches of verse as he moved to support his friend's other side.

"There's a good place not far from here," the tallest of them remarked. "Clean sheets and girls who smell of lavender and roses—"

"Are the girls clean too?" one of the others asked.

"They bathe if that's what you mean," the tall one answered and the singing died. "And if you meant anything else, they've got a cleric on call for that."

The four of them exchanged glances and didn't notice the small, swift shadows who darted in, their small fingers moving from the gaping rents in belt pouches to the slight bulges in leather breech pockets. Small blades flashed despite being blacked to prevent it, but the men remained unaware.

Kaylin couldn't believe their luck.

If the wealth they carried was any indication, the four must have recently returned from a journey into the ruins. The bounty wasn't limited to coin either. Some of those pouches held gems and pieces of jewelry no merc could have afforded—at least not in the quantities they carried.

She was glad they'd reached them first. The five of them were doing the owner of the Windy Wizard a huge favor because she was sure the mercenaries wouldn't have been fooled by the suggestion that they'd spent everything.

There would have been a slaughter.

Her frown mirrored her inner caution. There might still be a slaughter if any of these four noticed the way their pockets and pouches were lightening. With a soft chirrup, she signaled the crew to stop. What she'd seen them take would be enough to cover Goss' medicine and she knew she hadn't seen everything.

The mercenaries had taken to singing again, inspired by the sound of the music that drifted through the Windy Wizard's doors.

One of the mercenaries caught sight of the sign. "I wonder why they call him that," he exclaimed and pointed at it.

"'Cos he'll be a bag o' wind like all his kind," another slurred. "Wizards are all talk and no action if you know what I mean." He snickered drunkenly.

One of his friends slapped a hand over his mouth. "Don't let any of them hear you say that."

The first shook his face free of the other man's grasp and glared at him through bloodshot eyes. He flung an arm out to indicate the street around them and almost took Isabette's head off.

She ducked under the sweep of his hand and slid into the shelter offered by a rise of stairs. Kaylin saw her huddle out of sight and breathed a sigh of relief. The girl had been lucky.

Or fast, she reminded herself. She was fast. This time, her friend had made her own luck.

The thought brought a rush of pride at Isabette's skill and she made the chirruping sound again. She hoped Raoul, Piers, and Melis got the message. At any moment, these men would notice that something was wrong and she didn't want any of her people in the firing line when they did.

"I don't see any wizarding types out here. Do you?" the mercenary demanded. His eyes narrowed. "You're making fun o' me."

"Oh no," his tall companion retorted. "I wouldn't dare."

"Yeah, you would." His eyes narrowed even more and his hands balled into fists at his sides. He staggered out from under his friend's arm but managed to keep his feet. "You do it all the time."

The other man saw the implied threat and clearly didn't want to spend a day in jail for fighting in the street.

"Fine," he conceded hastily, "but I always buy you a drink after, don't I?"

That got through to his companion. The first merc stilled or at least tried to. His hands remained fists as he swayed unsteadily on his feet and stared blearily into his comrade's face.

"You sayin' you owe me a shrink?" he demanded belligerently and blinked both eyes as he tried to focus before he corrected himself. "I mean a drink?"

"Yes!" the tall merc assured him hurriedly. He patted the space where his pouch should have been. "And I even have—"

He stopped and glanced at his belt.

"What?" Again, the drunker merc's eyes narrowed. "You're not going to try to tell me you're out o' gold, are you?"

The tall merc shook his head, placed a hand on his friend's shoulder, and pivoted slowly to scan the street. "Check your pouches," he snapped.

"You're making fun o' me," the very drunk man protested but his fingers strayed to where only the knot remained of the purse that used to hang on his belt. "Wait!"

He patted the empty space frantically. "Wheresh…ah…" He tried again. "Wherezit gone?"

Kaylin watched as he started to turn and she ducked into cover as his gaze passed where she lurked. She wished she could have at least scrambled onto the Windy's awning.

The drunk wobbled around and peered suspiciously at the street and its incumbent shadows. She held her breath for a moment, then exhaled slowly before she drew another one, this one sharp with surprise. As drunk as he might be, the merc's hand had settled on the hilt of his sword and drew her attention to the weapon.

Her eyes widened when she recognized the thick, short curve of the blade and noticed the gems sparkling on its hilt. That scabbard must have been specially made and the weapon was enough to cause a brawl in and of itself.

No dwarf would tolerate a drunk human carrying a blade like that

Or would they?

She frowned and tried to remember what she'd heard of dwarven smiths and who they hired out to. Would they believe that the man had commissioned the blade?

Kaylin studied what she could see of it beneath the mercenary's grimy paw. She studied the dagger like it was a steak dropped from the skies above complete with a gallon of ale.

If it was of dwarven make, it wouldn't even need to have come from the ruins. Someone would pay a fortune for it.

She glanced at Isabette's hiding place and withdrew slowly to a point that gave her a clean jump at the Windy's awning. A barrel provided a useful launch point and she vaulted onto it and used her momentum to propel her upward.

Her fingertips caught the awning's edge and she heaved to pull her chest up and over the top. A kick of her legs and wriggle of her hips took her the rest of the way onto the wooden surface and she was able to look at the dark hollow in which Isabette was hiding. A faint suggestion of movement caught her eye and she focused on the pale glimmer that was the girl's face under the hood.

Knowing her companion could see her, she gestured at the drunk merc. The glimmer blurred in what might have been a negative but vanished when he turned to face the darkness under the stairs.

Smart move, Kaylin thought, glad the girl had remembered the first rule of concealment—hide your face. A formless lump in a blob of shadow was always more interesting if it had a face. Without one, it was merely another blob and most people would search for something else.

She dropped into a crouch lest anyone be drawn out of the tavern and look in her direction. When the merc stumbled a few steps closer to Isabette's hiding place, she tensed but immediately relaxed when he stopped.

His face was still creased in a tormented frown but his gaze searched the façade of the building instead. A few steps away, his three companions had drawn together and now patted their pockets and the other places where they'd hidden their wealth. She noted the way one picked up the hem of his cloak and inspected it.

Was something...were gems sewn into the garment's edge?

Surprised, she made a note to check that when next she plucked a goose with similar finery. Wondering what Raoul and Piers thought of it, she scuttled across the awning and dropped swiftly to the ground on the other side.

Kaylin crouched in the shadows next to the tavern for several heartbeats while she estimated her chances of reaching the drunk and cutting the leather that secured the scabbard to his belt before he noticed.

Maybe she'd be better off if she simply wrapped her hands around the hilt and ran off with it? It couldn't be that heavy, could it?

She crept to the edge of the building, studied Isabette's hiding place, and caught sight of Melis as the girl moved swiftly from one shadowed place to the next when the drunk homed in on where she'd been. He came close enough to see that the suspicious patch of shadow was empty and swayed for a moment, a bemused expression on his face as his friends bickered.

"Are you sure you didn't leave it at the last bar we visited?" one of the mercs asked the tall one.

He glared at the speaker and pointed meaningfully at his belt. "Did you?" he demanded.

The man gaped at his compatriot when he registered that his pouch was missing. "But I…I…" His mouth opened and closed like a grounded fish.

"So how many taverns have we been to?" the third one asked and Kaylin hated the hint of sobriety that had crept into his voice.

She stabbed a finger at Isabette and then at the sword and gave the signal that said she needed a diversion. The girl did have a sling, after all. Silence greeted her request and she had no choice but to trust that she would do exactly as she'd asked.

Hopefully, Raoul and Piers had seen the exchange. The two were skilled in distraction. Granted, this was usually against targets a little less experienced than these but also those who were far less drunk. Whatever they cooked up, it would work. She was sure of it.

With infinite care, she inched forward to stand behind the drunk, who hadn't moved from where Melis had hidden before. That changed as she arrived and he turned his focus on his comrades. She moved with him and hoped fervently that Isabette was ready. The mercenaries already looked far more alert.

Kaylin hooked a hand through the belt and pulled it a little off the man's waist so she could inspect how the scabbard was attached. She decided it would be easier to slash the belt and pull the scabbard free and reached for her knife.

"Hey! Obard, what's that attached to your belt?"

She immediately let go but even drunk, the merc was fast. His large, meaty hand slapped over hers and pinned it in place. Fear sent a wave of cold over her skin and her mind raced.

Where was Isabette's diversion? For that matter, where were Raoul and Piers? What was Melis doing?

The merc's hand tightened on hers and she gasped as she raised her other hand, clamped it around his wrist, and clung to him as though her life depended on it.

"Help me." She gasped and continued in a small and breathless voice that grew louder as she spoke. "Please help me, sir. Don't...don't let them take me!"

"Wha—" The mercenary gaped at her.

Whatever he'd expected, this was not it. Kaylin pulled herself closer and glanced over her shoulder at the dark.

"Please..." She added a slight whimper to her tone and looked into his face, her eyes begging for help.

"What are you doing, girl?" one of the others demanded and she turned her eyes to him and released the drunk mercenary's wrist to reach toward him.

"I need your protection," she half-whispered.

Obard yanked her hand off his belt and pushed her away hard enough to make her stumble.

"Get off me, ya scrawny little rat!"

She yelped and remembered at the last minute to take the fall and not roll to her feet as she usually would. After all, she was trying for helpless.

He took a step toward her and she flinched and made a show of getting slowly to her feet while she stared at the dark. More determined than ever to have the sword, she took a step toward him but froze when he stamped his foot at her.

"Scram!"

Kaylin jerked as if in fright, hunched her shoulders, and looked at him like she was terrified. She knew Melis and Isabette were probably having conniptions in the shadows and Raoul had very likely smacked himself on the head with the palm of his hand before he slid his hand down his face to watch her through splayed fingers.

It didn't matter. The sword would pay for a month's worth of medicine for Goss and still feed them. They might even be able to afford a room in one of the doss houses, away from the rats of both human and rodent varieties.

Dammit! I have to get it.

"Get yershelf out of here," the tall mercenary snapped and stepped forward to stand alongside his friend. "Go find someone elsh."

"Yeah, we're off-duty," added the one who'd helped Obard keep his feet. He moved forward. "And we deserve the time off."

His gaze trailed over her as though taking notice of her for the first time.

Kaylin let her face crumple.

"I..." she began and felt her pockets as though searching for something.

Making a show of finding it, she pulled out one of the gold coins she'd taken from him and held it up.

"I...my parents can pay," she told them and watched their eyes light with greed.

The tall one stepped forward, snatched the coin out of her hand, and bit down on it. Satisfied, he stowed it in a pocket sewn into the back of his belt.

"Az a down payment," he slurred and lashed his hand out to wrap around her wrist.

He stooped so he could look her in the eye and stared into her face. It was all she could do to not pull away. He'd smelt bad enough when she'd snitched the coin from his pocket but this close, she couldn't avoid the stench of his breath.

"Sho…tell me about these bad people of yours."

The way he said it suggested that he didn't think anyone could be bad enough to worry them and she hated him for it. It wasn't that he was belittling her, necessarily, but this was how he would treat anyone who might go to him for help.

He was the one with the sword, dammit, and should be looking out for anyone weaker. She stifled a scowl and forced her face into worried lines. It wasn't difficult. His grasp on her wrist had begun to hurt.

"Please, they're…" she began and twisted her hand to loosen his hold. That only succeeded in making him tighten it and she hoped the others had picked up her cue. They needed that sword.

"They were right behind me," she told him and remembered to keep her voice breathless and to dart a nervous glance over her shoulder. "They were. I swear."

When she saw no sign of her crew, she continued and raised her voice in desperation.

"There's this girl 'bout my height with long dark hair. She was… She was wearing a cloak and these broken boots."

"Another girl," the other merc muttered.

Kaylin didn't like his tone as he nudged Obard in the ribs.

"And?" the tall man prodded.

"And a boy with black curly hair but mean with a stick." She drew closer to the leader, twisted her small hand in his shirt, and wondered if he'd notice if she slid her fingers behind his belt.

"Go on. How many of 'em were there?"

"Four," she replied promptly. "The other two are smaller but just as nasty. The little blonde girl is the worst, and the other boy might look innocent but…"

She faltered, not able to think of a single thing that would make Piers seem a threat. Instead, she lowered her voice and added, "He scares me worse than any of 'em."

"And why are they after you?" he demanded.

"They… It's my birthday," she told him and pointed at his belt. "Mother told me to buy something nice."

Doubt crept into the man's features and she knew she was losing him. The shops had closed hours earlier and he might be drunk but he wasn't as drunk as she needed him to be.

"They saw me on the way to the market and told me to hand it over, and—" Kaylin cast a desperate look at the street around her and raised her voice as a signal that her friends needed to do something. "And they've been following me ever since!"

He followed her gaze and then scanned the street and his companions did the same. Obard swayed so badly that she thought he would pass out at her feet. He squinted past her as the leader exhaled an exasperated sigh.

"Then where are they?" the merc demanded. "We can't protect you against something that's not there."

"They'll be waiting," Kaylin told him. "Thinking you'll go away and they can grab me. Don't let them!"

She begged as though the threat was real but being attacked by the mythical four wasn't the worst of her worries. It was not getting away from the mercenaries and then being found with something they recognized. The gods knew some of the trinkets she carried looked unique.

"Maybe you could escort me home," she babbled. "They…they won't attack while you're there. They're…they're cowards and bullies and would run if they had to face real warriors. Please…take me home."

That brought a leer to one mercenary's face. "Girl, I'd take—"

A stone streaked out of the dark and smacked him in the shoulder. He pivoted, a surprised expression on his face.

"Ow!"

Movement caught her eye and Raoul emerged from the shadow and slapped the cane menacingly against the palm of his hand. He might be slight in build but the surly cast of his features made him look older—and he was taller, Kaylin realized, and she noticed he was broader about the shoulders too.

"Hand her over," he ordered. "She owes us."

The mercenaries snapped their heads toward him.

"And what will you do about it, little man?" the mercenary leader demanded.

She used his distraction to slip her fingers into the pouch sewn on the back of his belt and pull the coin from its resting place. When she touched something else—something small and hard—she scooped it into her palm and was about to withdraw when she felt a smooth circular band.

It was almost too easy. She snagged it with her finger and pulled her hand away as the man released her other wrist.

"I don't know about him." Isabette's voice rang clear and cold from the opposite side of the road and a stone rattled off the chain mail covering the third mercenary's shoulder. "But I will put the next stone into someone's eye," she continued, "if you don't give her to us."

The man glanced at where the rock had struck him and then at the girl.

"You're mine, little pissant!"

She took the time to sling a second stone before she moved toward the alley. "And you're no one's, you oversized troll's turd."

With a roar, the mercenary bounded after her but stopped when another rock hurtled out of the darkness to strike him in the chest. "What?"

"Hand her over," Melis demanded and brandished her tiny belt knife in one hand while she flung a second stone with the other.

"Yeah! Troll turd!" Piers threw another small rock and this one struck the leader. "No one wants you."

Kaylin muffled a smile because she was sure that one had been meant to hit the same man Melis and Isabette had aimed at. The mercenaries were not amused.

The tall man gave her a disbelieving look.

"They're kids!" he exclaimed. "You're scared of a group of kids."

"That doesn't stop them kicking the stuffing out of me when I'm on my own," she retorted. "If they're so trivial, why haven't you gotten rid of them yet?"

He scowled at her but a stone hit his back and he spun angrily. "Right!"

Raoul made as though to move around him to reach her and the merc pulled his ax free and slid the hood clear. The boy paused and his eyes widened momentarily.

"He won't save you," he snarled and directed his glance at Kaylin. "He's as weak as piss."

She grimaced as Piers hurled another stone and it clacked off a stone wall in the dark.

"Weak as?" the younger boy asked scornfully and gave the man a derogatory glare and a rude gesture. "He *is* piss!"

"I'm gonna piss on you," the merc promised, hefted the ax, and took a step toward her friend.

"Oooh, I'm real scared," Isabette taunted and flung another stone.

This one struck the fourth merc in the forehead and he stumbled. One of his friends caught his arm to steady him.

"You go down because of a little girl and you'll buy me ale for the rest of the week."

"The Spears Deep, I will!" The other man rallied and the four of them moved to form a line facing their tiny tormentors.

Kaylin shifted so she was behind them but only one of them glanced back. Obard swayed and staggered and had to clutch one of his colleagues by the sleeve to keep himself upright. The man gave him a startled glance but otherwise ignored him and he held fast.

She saw her chance and took it, stepped close to him, and drew her belt knife. With two quick slices, she sheared his belt and cut through the waistband of his trousers, and a careful tug slid the scabbard free.

With her breath held and her muscles tense, she waited for Obard to feel the lack of weight at his waist. The man was fixed on the fight, however, and his knuckles had turned white where he grasped his colleague's arm.

This was her moment and she didn't wait any longer. She backed away carefully, then whirled and bolted to the shadows, slid beneath the stairs Isabette had found, and darted out and around them to the small pathway beyond.

As soon as she reached the next street, she whistled sharply and melted into the shadows again. Trusting her crew to make good their escape, she wove deftly through the darkness until she'd found a sheltered position.

A careful look around assured her that the coast was clear and she stopped. It took almost no time at all to unbuckle her belt and slip the scabbard on before she fastened it again.

Once it was secure, she scaled the nearest fence and pulled herself onto the roof of the house adjacent. From there, it was a relatively quick jog across the rooftops toward home.

Raoul heard the whistle and smirked. He leapt back out of the way of the axman's clumsy swing.

"You're not so bright, are ya?" He sneered and stooped quickly to scoop up a handful of dust.

"Kneeling won't sh…shave you, boy!"

"Then it's best if I stop, then, i'n it?" he quipped in response and flung the dust into the mercenary's face as he straightened.

It caught the man full in the face and put him off his next swing.

"Son of a tarting troll! You little pigshwillin'—" he exclaimed and covered his eyes with the crook of his arm as he stumbled back.

Raoul didn't wait for another opportunity. He bent hastily, snatched up a handful of stones, and hurled them at the man who faced Piers. They bounced off his head and shoulders and made him turn.

"I'll make a pin cushion out of you, boy!" the merc shouted as his newest adversary echoed Kaylin's short, sharp whistle.

The boy made an obscene gesture with his cane. He stayed long enough to see Melis grab Piers before he bolted. Isabette had darted down an alley with the other merc in hot pursuit, and the one Kaylin had taken the sword from collapsed face-first on the cobbles.

He was sure he heard a snore as he darted to the back of the Windy Wizard and vaulted the low wall that surrounded its rear yard.

The mercenary thundered behind him and his hands brushed Raoul's heels as the boy leapt from the wall to the tavern roof.

"Too slow!" he crowed as he scampered to the ridgeline and darted along it to make the jump onto the neighboring premises.

"Boy!" the man bellowed. "I'm gonna feed you to the orcsh!"

He turned, stormed back to the street, and sank a boot into Obard's ribs. When that elicited nothing more than a groan, he picked the man up by the scruff of his neck and slung him over his shoulder.

"Useless, good-for-nothing…" he muttered.

When he heard the heavy tread of more boots, he looked around furtively, half-afraid it was the watch. He sighed with relief when he saw it was Adam and Dev.

"Did you get them?" he demanded.

Adam hooked his ax into his belt and fixed him with a hard stare.

"Where is she?" he demanded.

"Where's who?"

"Don't play the idiot. The girl!" He spat in disgust and looked around. "Her parents had better make the trouble worth it."

The four mercs turned in different directions as if they had only now noticed the empty street.

"Maybe she got scared and hid," the mercenary suggested hopefully and pivoted for another slow scan.

Adam followed his gaze. He didn't see the girl but he noticed something else.

He placed a heavy hand on his comrade's shoulder and turned him roughly.

"What have you done with it, Boris?" he demanded.

"Done with what?"

"The sword." He frowned. "You know we don't steal from each other."

"I ain't."

"Then where is it?"

Before the other man could think of a reply, Dev uttered an angry oath. "That little bitch! I will have her hide if I ever find her."

His friends swung as one to stare at him. When he caught the looks on their faces, he scowled at them.

"Don't you get it?" he asked. "It's obvious, isn't it?"

"What?"

"She set it up. She weren't no damsel in distress and those kids weren't chasin' her."

"Huh?"

"They were her friends!"

"But—"

Dev patted his pockets dramatically.

"That can't be right," Adam muttered.

"Yuh think?" Dev challenged. "Then why don't you check where you stowed 'er coin? I'll bet you ten to the dozen it ain't there now."

"And if you're wrong?"

"Check it." The other man sneered.

Adam did so, then ran his fingers through the empty pocket a second time. His face paled, then glowed red, then paled again.

A giggle floated out of the darkness and they whipped toward it. Another followed and more laughter drifted out of an alley or perhaps off a nearby roof. Stare as they might, none of the mercenaries could pinpoint the source.

Adam turned an angry face to his friends. "I will gut them all." He snarled in impotent fury. "And then I'm gonna lay them out in the fields and let the orcs have 'em."

CHAPTER TWO

Kaylin didn't go in. She stopped in the valley where an attic window protruded from the roof of a dockside inn and scanned the street.

The sword's hilt poked her uncomfortably so she adjusted it but didn't leave her eyrie until she'd counted her friends home.

Only then did she descend to the street and slink through a gap in the ramshackle wall of the Riverdog's Rest. It had once been an inn but now, its floors were charred or soft with rot, and most of the lower floor was a single open space.

Beams still clung where the second floor used to be but no boards covered them and the rafters formed a cavernous roof overhead where the slates weren't missing.

The riverdog who'd owned it had run into debt and died in the fire that had destroyed most of the walls inside the building before they were extinguished. A blend of stone and brick, the outside walls had managed to contain the heat like a potter's furnace.

Even now, after all this time, the smell of old smoke and charred timbers permeated the ruin.

No one knew who'd done it but everyone thought they knew. It had laid a kind of taboo over the structure and made the older folk of the underworld squeamish about entering.

That hadn't bothered Kaylin and her crew. The exterior of the building was mostly intact and so was the roof. While it was admittedly echoey and disconcertingly hollow, it was better than the streets.

She and the others liked to call it home. With that thought in mind, she moved quietly through what had once been a storeroom. She skirted the gaping hole leading to the inn's old cellar and slid into a corner of the abandoned kitchen.

Some of the upper floor still clung there, and a shelf protruded from the wall and half-collapsed chimney to mark where the kitchen used to be. The counters were mostly intact, even if the top half of the wall had been scorched away. They served to cut the draft down and separate the smaller kitchen area from what had been the common room.

Worried voices greeted her as she pushed aside the old blanket they'd hung over the doorway. She slipped past it silently and paused to study her friends where they huddled around the small pit they'd made by prising one of the flagstones free of the inn floor.

A fire burned inside it, small and hot. With the opening to the common room covered by old sacks and the fireplace blocked by the same, the room was almost warm. Isabette and Raoul were the first to notice her return.

"Kaylin!" the girl exclaimed, half-scolding and half-relieved.

"You made it," she replied and allowed her concern to color her voice. "Thanks for the distraction."

"You scared the life out of us," Raoul told her sternly. "We thought you'd gone mad."

"Crazy, maybe." She grinned and unbuckled her belt so she could free the dwarf sword and its scabbard. "But I had a very good reason."

She crouched beside them and placed the sword on an open space of the floor. "Look at this."

They crowded around, oohing and aahing.

"This must be worth a fortune!" Raoul exclaimed. "Look at the gems in its hilt."

"And the gold," Piers added worshipfully. He glanced suspiciously at Kaylin. "Where do you think they got it?"

"I don't know." She shrugged. "And I don't care. Tomorrow, you and Melis will take it to Eloine and he'll give you all the medicine Goss will ever need."

They stared at her in wide-eyed surprise.

"Truly?" Isabette's eyes returned to the sword. "It's worth that much?"

"Tch! And more," Melis told her scornfully. "Eloine will get a bargain and he'll know it. We can't even check to see if it's magic."

Raoul gaped at her. "And how do you know all this?"

Her face flushed and she frowned. "I don't know," she answered shortly. "I just do."

It was a lie and they all knew it, but she hadn't run with them for very long and they knew she'd open up in time. For now, she needed to know she was part of the family and her skills were needed.

It was hard but Kaylin let the questions lie.

If the girl had wanted to cause trouble for them, she could have done it by now. The fact that she hadn't was a good indicator that she probably wouldn't. One day, she'd tell them why she knew so much about weapons and old trinkets.

It merely wouldn't be this day.

"Uh-huh..." Raoul let all the doubt of any brother show in those two syllables. He might not be related to Melis but he treated her like a sister anyway—a bratty younger sister.

Soft coughing issued from the back of the room and they all turned toward it. When it finished and the smallest member of their team didn't stir, Isabette turned stricken eyes to their leader.

"It's not too late, is it?" she asked and took a handful of coin from her pouch. "Eloine will still be up, right?"

Kaylin thought about it, then nodded. She turned to Raoul.

"I'll take Isabette to get us something to eat and drink. We're the only ones old enough to get into one of the taverns. You and Melis could take the sword and the rest of it to Eloine. The sooner Goss gets his medicine, the better."

"What about me?" Piers demanded and she fixed him with a stern stare.

"I need you to keep the fire going and make sure Goss stays warm. We took a big enough risk leaving him on his own for as long as we did."

The boy gave her a disappointed look and she squeezed his shoulder.

"One day, you'll be old enough to get into a pub and I'll be the one left tending the fire," she assured him and added, "I need to know Goss will be looked after while I'm gone. Can you do that for me?"

Piers studied her face for any deception before he nodded. "Will you be gone long?" he asked and she shrugged.

"I'll be back before dawn," she promised and he snorted.

"You better be, or I'll hafta send Goss out to find you."

She grinned at that, then squeezed his shoulder again. "Keep him safe, okay?"

He jerked his head in assent and shifted his gaze to where Raoul and Melis were sorting the haul into gems, coins, and trinkets. Kaylin followed his focus and watched as the two stowed various items around their bodies. It might not save them from a real shake-down, but it would stop them from having to show everything at once.

Hopefully, it might even allow them to keep something in reserve to sell to Eloine later. She hated having to send them out with even some of their treasures. The risks were enormous but what they'd acquired was no use to them if they simply hid it. Someone had to make the exchange and as kids, they would hopefully attract less attention.

She sighed and pushed her reluctance aside. They all had to do what they could and at least they wouldn't carry all they'd accumulated. For now, they'd be better off taking the blade and maybe the coins and some of the gems. She didn't know how much the medicine would cost but if they were short, they'd know how much to bring the next time.

Eloine had blanched when she'd told him what was wrong with Goss.

"Creepers Croup—and gone too long," he'd said, his face bleak. "You'd be better off putting him in the river. I could give you something to make sure he'd sleep all the way through. It'd be kinder that way—safer too."

He hadn't said anything more and she had been too afraid to ask him what he'd meant. The fact he'd even suggested it was a shock. She still didn't know how she felt about it.

"Can you get me the medicine or not?" she'd demanded, her voice rough with worry and uncertainty.

"Aye. I could," the man had agreed as his eyes narrowed suspiciously, "but could ye pay for it?"

"I have a job coming up," Kaylin had said. "A big one. It'll pay for a good supply."

She hadn't known what job at the time but Eloine hadn't asked.

Now, she hoped he'd believed her as much as he'd seemed to and that Melis and Raoul wouldn't come back empty-handed.

"Are you ready?" she asked and recognized that the roughness had returned to her voice.

Raoul finished wrapping the sword and looked at Melis. The girl nodded and her dirty blonde curls bobbed.

"We're ready."

"I am too," Isabette declared and the four of them came together and bumped knuckles before they turned to different exits.

Raoul and Melis took the storeroom and Isabette and Kaylin headed into the long-abandoned common room and the Rest's half-blocked front door. It took them only a few heartbeats to make sure the street was clear before they slipped into the night.

Kaylin's heart lifted as the river breeze touched her cheeks. It was pre-dawn cold but that didn't matter. She touched Isabette's arm.

"We'll get firewood too."

The moon had crossed the city by the time they returned. Kaylin had a sack slung over her shoulders to form a makeshift carry-pack, and Isabette had one slung across her front to support the wooden platter she held.

This was covered by a domed lid tied in place by two leather straps and the smell of roasted meat leaked out from under it. That didn't matter, though. They hadn't gone far to find their food and Dmitri and Cassia had been more than generous once she had produced five gold pieces and placed the stolen gem beside them.

"You come back tomorrow," Dimmy had told her after examining the gem. "It's too much to carry otherwise."

Kaylin had given him a worried stare but he'd smiled and patted her shoulder as Cassia pulled a sack from the storeroom.

"Come back," he told her reassuringly. "We owe you more food, yes?"

Although she'd been uncertain, there was no way in the world she would turn more food down. She only hoped Dmitri kept his word.

"A season's worth," Cassie had stated firmly. "You come back until the leaves start to change. You've paid that much." She paused. "Unless you want somewhere to stay?"

The girl stared at her, then glanced at Isabette. Her second in charge had gone still, her expression frozen in place. Kaylin cleared her throat.

"I'll discuss it with the others," she muttered and took the bag of supplies the woman slid across the counter.

Cassie nodded. "If you want long-term, there's the attic. The kitchen chimney goes right through it so it'll be warm. Dry, too."

She had no reply to that so simply nodded.

A room. A real room…it was too much to take in.

Dmitri and Cassie had steered them out the back door. "You can't be followed that way," the innkeeper had assured them and he'd been right.

No one had waited in the street beyond or slipped into the alley behind them when they'd turned to enter the narrow gap between what was left of the Rest and the warehouse next door. They'd ventured past the rubble and into the ruined common room with nothing more than the smell of the river to keep them company.

"Did you ever see so much food?" Isabette whispered as they

picked between fallen beams and broken floorboards to the charred remnants of the bar.

Her companion bit her lip and shook her head as a smile tweaked the corners of her mouth.

"And it's still warm," the girl squeaked, hardly able to contain herself. "Goss will get better so much faster eating like this."

She held the blanket aside so Isabette could maneuver the tray into the kitchen beyond and frowned when all she saw was Piers.

"Where are the others?" she asked.

The boy rolled his eyes.

"Sure, I'm fine," he snarked, "and Goss is too, for all you care. No one bothered us at all, not even that big thing you say is an owl. Oh, and I swear I heard squeaking coming from the cellar, but everyone knows river rats are only a myth. Everything's only apples."

Kaylin stared at him and Isabette smothered a giggle. The girl set the tray on a low bench formed by fallen stones and two broken boards and watched as he caught the aroma.

The boy crept closer. "Is that..." He swallowed convulsively. "Did you get real meat?"

"Mmhmm." Kaylin lowered her chin and her gaze wandered to the corner where Goss slept.

Piers caught her look and his face softened. "He's okay. I gave him an extra blanket and he settled again. We need to keep him out of the cold."

Kaylin stifled the urge to demand when he had become a healer. Just because he wasn't didn't make him wrong. The cough became worse when the air was cooler.

She moved to the pallet she and the others had built to raise him off the floor. He stirred as she approached and the movement triggered a fit of coughing. She picked up a rough stone bowl of water and looped an arm under his shoulder.

"Here. Drink," she ordered as soon as he opened his eyes.

"How'd you know?" he whispered and she gave him a secretive smile.

"I always know," she assured him.

"Becau…because that's not at all spooky," he muttered and tried to not give in to another bout of coughing as he took the bowl and drank.

He handed it back to her when he was finished.

"You calling me spooky?" she demanded in mock ferocity and he sniffed the air.

"Is that roast pork?" he asked and changed the subject.

"Nah," Kaylin told him. "The orcs would never allow it. I think it's mutton."

"Old sheep?" Piers asked.

"Well, it couldn't be a young sheep," she retorted. "They have too many mouths to feed at the Dockers."

"You're a sheep," Goss retorted.

She blew a raspberry and took the bowl when he passed it to her. "It takes one to know one."

He managed a tired smile as she settled the bowl beside the bed and let him sink back below the blankets. His eyelids fluttered as he tried to stay awake.

"Don't eat it all…" His words faded to a mumble when his eyes drifted closed again.

Piers stopped beside them with a plate in one hand and steel fork in the other.

"His timing sucks," the boy observed.

Kaylin shook Goss by the shoulder but the boy was a dead weight.

"You'd better eat that," she told Piers. "He won't wake for a while."

His face pinched into a frown. "I thought we would wait for the others."

She shook her head and tried to hide her worry that Melis and Raoul hadn't returned.

"Do you know how mad your brother will be if he finds out I haven't fed you by the time he gets back?" she asked and gave him a pretend look of wide-eyed worry.

"I'm not a puppy," he protested and she poked him.

"Are you sure?" she asked. "Because there are days I'm very sure you need to be kept on a leash."

Piers scowled. "You've been talking to Raoul again."

"Have you been raiding the temple orchard again?"

"Was not," he protested.

"That's not what Raoul said," Kaylin replied.

He flushed. "Raoul needs to keep his big mouth shut."

"Raoul was scared witless," she told him.

"I was only lookin'!" Piers snapped. "Seein' if the berries were in bloom yet."

"And?" she asked and watched realization dawn on his young face.

"You're after 'em for yourself," he accused and she laughed.

"Eat your meat," she said but he wouldn't be deterred.

"They'll notice if you pick too many," he warned and meant the priests and the fruit they grew in a small orchard on the temple grounds. He settled on his haunches and waved a piece of meat at her.

"They will," he assured her before he took a mouthful. His next words were muffled and twisted as he chewed. "You don't think they sell trespassers to the orcs, do you?"

She stared at him. The templars were scary folk and put far too much value on the berry trees that were their pride and joy, but traffick with the orcs? She shook her head and smirked.

"You're too small to sell to an orc. One mouthful is all you'd be."

"Half a mouthful," Isabette corrected and nudged Kaylin with a plate. "Here. You need to eat like anyone else. The last I looked, you were human like the rest of us."

"Who said you could look?" She flushed.

The girl grinned cheekily. "Believe me, I wish I hadn't," she quipped but blushed even redder than she had. "I didn't," she added hastily. "I wouldn't…it was only a joke…"

Kaylin chuckled. "Trust me. I'd have known." She gestured at the platter. "I'm not the only one who's human and there's more than enough there."

When Isabette cast a worried glance toward the door, Kaylin set her plate to one side.

"Hey!" the girl protested. "What are you doing?"

"Well," she replied, "if you don't eat, neither can I. It wouldn't be fair."

Her companion gaped at her. "But that…that's stupid."

"Uh-huh." She smirked. "It is, isn't it?"

Isabette stared at her a moment longer, then a reluctant smile tugged at her lips.

"Fine, I'll eat." She selected a few slices of meat and a roast potato from the platter and settled herself on another stone block near the fire.

With another worried glance at Goss, Kaylin moved to sit beside her and signaled Piers to join them. The boy caught the worried look on her face.

"He'll be all right," he assured her. "The others will come back with his medicine soon. That and the food will see him right in no time."

She smiled sadly at him.

"He wouldn't be sick if I'd taken better care of us," she told him and Isabette shoved her shoulder roughly. "What?"

"It's not your fault. You've kept us alive this far."

Kaylin bit back the reply that keeping them alive wasn't all she wanted to achieve, that she wanted them to have more of a future than merely fighting for the next meal. Instead, she shrugged and took a bite from one of the pieces of meat.

Her mouth flooded with saliva and her stomach clenched. Dimitri certainly knew his way around a kitchen. She closed her eyes, forced herself to chew slowly, and did her best to not moan out loud.

It was so good!

For several minutes, silence settled in as the three of them ate and savored the food. She cleared her plate and set it aside. Behind her, soft coughing indicated that Goss had woken and she stood and moved to his pallet.

"Will you stay awake long enough to eat this time?" she asked.

He gave her a weak smile.

"You sayin' you left me some?" he asked and scrunched his face in mock suspicion. "What's wrong wiv it?"

"Keep talking like that and I won't feed you at all," she quipped in return but he merely laughed.

Isabette stepped beside her with a plate of food and Kaylin helped Goss to sit upright and put one of their packs behind him for support. She made sure the blankets were tucked around him and rested the plate in his lap.

"Medicine's coming," she promised.

He nodded and didn't answer until his coughing fit had subsided and he'd sipped from the bowl of water she held to his lips.

"I'll pay you back," he promised and his gaze shifted from her to Isabette and Piers. "Every last coin."

"Pfft," the other boy told him. "You'll pay us back by getting better."

"Well enough to help you filch some of Averda's berries?"

"It's not the god's berries I'm after," Piers retorted. "I only want some of the fruit from his orchard."

"Did you ever think to ask?" Isabette challenged. "I'm almost sure they wouldn't turn you down."

"Korval tried that," the boy told her solemnly, "an' now, he's wearing priest robes. No way am I gonna ask."

"I'm not sure they'd take you anyway," she replied and studied him critically. "You're too scrawny."

"I won't always be scrawny," Goss interjected. "One day I'm gonna be as big as Raoul, you'll see."

He drew a breath to add more but his voice caught and another bout of coughing shook him. Kaylin caught his meal before he could drop it and waited until the fit was over. This time, when she raised the water bowl to his lips, he took it in his hands and drank from it himself.

She let it go but it was hard to not keep her hand under it in case it fell. He handed it back as debris rattled in the empty common room.

They all froze and his hands clutched the edge of his plate.

"Stay here," Kaylin ordered and picked up several large chunks of stone as she headed to the sacking that curtained the door. "Isabette, take the back way and go outside to the front."

The girl hesitated and she thought she might argue, but she gave her a short, sharp nod and vanished through the cellar curtain.

"Stay here," Kaylin repeated to the boys and picked up one of the heavier pieces of wood beside the fire. She handed it to Piers and added, "Look after Goss."

"Goss can look after himself," the patient protested as if speaking about someone else. "He doesn't need—"

His voice caught and he set his plate down hurriedly and tried to smother the next round of coughing with his hands. His face was flushed and she was sure it wasn't only embarrassment. The boy had been running fevers on and off for the last few days—the main reason why she'd risked the mercenaries.

He needed that medicine.

After another glance to make sure the boys were settled, Kaylin moved close enough to lift the sacking and peer beyond it. The sound of uneven footsteps reached her, but the remains of the bar blocked her view. Cautiously, she moved through the makeshift curtain and crept along the base of the bar until she could look around it.

The two figures who wove clumsily across the debris-strewn floor made her gasp with worry. She recognized Raoul's dark head and Melis's lighter one. What worried her was that he had one arm draped over the girl's shoulder and the other clutched around his middle.

The girl staggered under his weight and Kaylin hurried forward.

"What happened?" she demanded, slid her arm around the boy's waist, and flinched when he gasped.

"We were jumped," Melis snapped fiercely. They reached the bar and she and Kaylin maneuvered him carefully around it. She held the curtain aside and they got the boy into the warmth of their living space and helped him to his sleeping mat.

He groaned as they eased him onto it and his face beaded slightly with sweat as he leaned back against the wall. One eye was swollen almost closed and his cheek had begun to purple. His lip was split and that side of his mouth was puffy and bruised.

As she glanced at his knuckles, Isabette slipped soundlessly through the curtain from the common room. The girl's gaze traveled over the three of them and she put a hand on her hip.

"I see you started the party without me."

That brought a weak smile to Raoul's lips but he didn't answer. Isabette gave him a worried glance before she lifted the lid from the platter and started serving. Kaylin crouched beside the boy and looked from him to Melis.

"Who jumped you?" she demanded. "And where?"

He drew a breath and pressed his hand over his ribs. Melis patted his shoulder.

"I'll tell them," she said gravely.

To Kaylin's surprise, he didn't argue. Instead, he nodded and subsided against the wall. Melis squeezed his shoulder and settled onto the edge of his bed.

"It was Korbyn," she began. "Him and his crew were waiting for us when we got to Eloine's."

"But—" Kaylin started.

The girl held up her hand and she subsided and let her continue.

"Not all his crew," she added and darted a glance at Raoul, "but enough of 'em that we didn't stand a chance."

"Are you sure—" Kaylin tried, and Melis cut her off again.

"Yeah. We're sure. They were scattered around the shop with Korbyn at the counter with Eloine. I swear that useless troll's butt didn't say a word to warn us either—and he knew what we'd come for."

"Knew we were…coming, too," Raoul rasped, his voice so gritty with pain that the words didn't form properly. "Were…waiting…"

"Waiting for you?" Kaylin asked and they both nodded. "But they shouldn't have known we were coming."

"Shouldn't, couldn't, did," Melis snapped. "They let us get to the counter and pretended that they didn't care we'd come, but the minute Raoul asked if Elo had some time, they were on us like flies on dung."

"Knew we had…stuff." Raoul wheezed a breath. "Asked for it…st…straight up."

Kaylin reached toward him but he held up a hand to stop her.

"Later. Listen."

He glanced at Melis and the girl took that as her cue to continue.

"Korbyn asked us to show them our wares and said they'd be taking delivery." She flushed and her eyes burned with anger, her voice bitter. "Raoul told them we were there to do business with Elo and Korbyn said the bargain had changed so—"

"So I…asked him…to show us the medicine," Raoul interjected.

"And he said we wouldn't get that either," the girl added.

"Said I wouldn't…be doing business then," Raoul muttered. "Went to leave. Thought we could…come back later when they…were gone."

His face grew redder and for a heartbeat, Kaylin thought he would cry. He didn't but he swallowed hard and his voice cracked as he added, "Couldn't…stop them."

"You tried, though," Melis said and tried to comfort him. She turned to Kaylin. "You should have seen him. He pulled his cane and smacked the first guy to get close."

He snorted softly. "Didn't do any good."

The boy's face burned with shame and he lowered his gaze and refused to look Kaylin in the eye. Melis shoved him in the shoulder —hard.

"Didn't stand a chance, more like," she told him and turned a semi-defiant gaze to Kaylin and Piers since the boy had crept closer. Worry creased his face. "They came at us from all sides and Korbyn stood on the other side of the counter and laughed."

"Did…didn't use blades," Raoul added. "Only…sticks."

He drew a deep breath and winced, and Kaylin began to worry that something was broken.

"There were six of them," Melis told her. "I'm not sure why they thought they needed that many piss-ant troll-sucking cowards." She blushed and lowered her head. "I tried to get past them and out."

"Told you to," Raoul comforted her. "Knew we couldn't…win."

"I didn't want to," the girl answered shortly, "but he was right and we worked too hard to lose it all."

"Lost it anyway," he muttered glumly, his face still flushed. "Couldn't…keep them off."

He drew another breath, clutched his ribs, and wheezed painfully.

"They grabbed me and knocked Raoul down." Melis's eyes darkened as she remembered. "First, they worked him over good to teach him a lesson, then went over him extra careful."

"Didn't miss…a thing," Raoul put in. "They took it all." His face crumpled but firmed a moment later as he brought his emotions under control. "Even the sword."

"Yeah. They were real happy with that." Melis snarled her frustration and rage. "Troll-suckers."

For a minute, Kaylin thought the girl had intended to use another epithet, but her gaze had shifted to Piers and she'd changed it. She lowered her eyes and blushed crimson to the roots of her hair.

"They went over me pretty good too and took everything I had on me."

"Everything?" Isabette's voice was faint with shock. "All of it?"

Melis nodded and tears glinted in her eyes.

Kaylin's fury rose.

"And you think Eloine knew?" she asked, her voice tight with anger.

The girl stared at her with a closed expression. "He wasn't surprised when they moved on us and didn't try to stop 'em either."

"Did he say anything?" she asked. "When they were done?"

Raoul shrugged and winced when he remembered why he shouldn't. "Don't know. They…they threw us…out the front door. Said not to come back."

"I asked them what they thought they were doing attacking kids and they laughed," Melis protested. "They said they heard we were after something expensive and could pay." She flushed angrily and took a breath. "They said they decided they could save themselves some trouble and simply pluck the pluckers. Ass-faces."

Kaylin laid a hand on Raoul's arm and held him gently when he tried to pull away.

"It's not your fault," she told him firmly.

He shook his head and his face deepened in color.

"I shoulda fought harder," he replied. "Shoulda..."

"Against six full-grown men?" she challenged incredulously. "*Six?* What exactly do you think you should have done?"

"I...uh...I..." He fell silent and flushed again when he caught Piers watching him.

"You fought when you couldn't run," she told him firmly, "and you tried to give Melis time to run. You did what you could."

He caught her gaze, then broke it and looked away. She shook him gently.

"We won't always be kids, Ro. One day, we'll be able to hold our own."

"Against six?" he challenged and laughed bitterly, and she smiled ruefully.

"Maybe not six," she agreed, "but you might be able to break free of them long enough to escape."

"Or buy a friend some time," he added.

"And that friend might not be too useless to escape," Melis told him. "It's not all on you, you know."

"Nothing is on either of you," Kaylin declared. "I don't know why you both can't get that through your heads."

Raoul looked at her, his face bleak.

"We lost so much today, Kay. More than we're ever likely to make again."

"And now Korbyn knows we exist," Melis added. "Now, he and his Blackbirds will be on the look-out for us. They won't let us keep a penny of what we get if they think they can take it."

"No. They will leave us well alone," Kaylin told them, "and they'll give back everything they stole. I'll give them 'pluck the pluckers.'"

The others gaped at her but she ignored the looks.

"We'll teach them a lesson they're not likely to forget—and Eloine, too."

Silence greeted that statement, but she rose from her crouch, took the plates from Isabette's hands, and passed them to Raoul and Melis.

"Eat," she ordered, her face hard and angry.

"But, Kaylin…" Melis ventured in a small voice. "What will you do? They're bigger and older than us and they've been around much longer."

"Yeah, and there's more of 'em, too," Raoul added drily.

"They're right," Isabette interjected. "You go after the Blackbirds and they'll come at us twice as hard and no one will lift a hand to stop 'em." Her voice softened into pleading. "You know it's true—and we'll be in a worse place than we are now."

Kaylin shook her head.

"No, we won't," she told them decisively. "Now that they've plucked us once, word will get around. If we don't do something about it, Korbyn and his Blackbirds won't be the only ones we'll have to look out for. It'll be everyone looking for an easy mark and if that happens, we'll never get out from under it. We'll always be hungry, and we'll always be poor, and someone will always be working us over."

"At least we'll be alive," Melis pointed out. "You take on the Blackbirds and we might not even live for everyone to pluck."

"Nope," she said shortly. "We'll take 'em on and we'll be better off at the end. I'm not sure what I'm gonna do yet, but whatever it is, it'll be something that only comes back on me, not you. Whatever happens, you guys will be safe." Her voice dropped a note but the intensity was still there. "I promise."

Her eyes refocused as she looked up. "I promise," she repeated and looked at each of their faces. "You will all be okay."

Melis was the first to answer, but the expressions on the others' faces said she spoke for them all.

"Yeah?" the blonde girl challenged. "Well, if I had any gold, I wouldn't put it on your chances of succeeding."

Dawn was almost breaking by the time they slept. It was still light when Kaylin woke, and the brightness of the daylight showed through the gaps between the stonework and the roofline.

Midday, she thought, *or early afternoon.*

She rose quietly, pushed back the thin blanket that served as a cover, and lifted the lid on the platter. As hungry as they'd all been the night before, there had still been some left over.

Careful to make sure there was enough for the others, she took a piece of meat and stuffed it into her mouth. She chewed slowly as she prepared to head out.

The crew continued to sleep as she lifted a stone quietly from the floor at the head of her bed. In the hollow below, she'd stowed the only real weapon they had—an old belt knife taken from the street after a brawl outside the Clawed Cup.

It was a real dagger, deadlier than the smaller street knives they used for cutting purses. She slid the knife into her belt and concealed it beneath the folds of her cloak. A cautious glance confirmed that the others still slept, oblivious to her hiding place and the weapon she now carried.

All except one. As Kaylin breathed a soft sigh of relief, she heard the soft rustle of cloth and noticed a pair of bright green eyes watching her. She stifled a gasp as Goss swung himself out of bed and she frowned at him.

"What are you doing up?" she demanded, her voice sharper than she intended.

The boy smiled and coughed when he tried to laugh. He sat on the edge of his mattress, picked the water bowl up, and lifted it to his lips.

"I couldn't sleep," he told her when he set it down. "'Sides, I have to pee. Can't do that in bed. I'm ten, not two, and you guys worked too hard to make the mattress for me to ruin it."

He coughed again, softer this time, stood, and crossed the stone floor to stand in front of her.

"Why do you need the dagger?" he asked and dashed any hope that he hadn't seen the weapon or her hiding place.

"It's only in case I run into trouble," she told him reassuringly, shifted the stone into its place, and stood. "Last night was a good reminder of exactly how dangerous this city can be. Not all the danger is at the old mountain."

Goss nodded and shivered slightly even though the room was warm.

"Just…don't stab anyone you can get away from," he said, his voice soft as he turned toward the cellar.

He swayed a little unsteadily and Kaylin stepped alongside him a moment later.

"Are you all right?"

Her question brought another soft laugh and more coughing. He patted her arm and moved away slowly.

"I'll be fine," he told her. "It's not the kind of thing I want company for, anyway. Not girl company, at least."

She blushed. "That's not what I was asking. I can wake Raoul or Piers if you—"

"Please don't." Goss shook his head. "I feel a little weak, is all."

From the heat she'd felt when he'd touched her, weak wasn't all he felt, and Kaylin made a note to find some feverdim. Maybe there'd be some growing near the orphanage, or maybe she could creep into Mistress Florey's garden and find some there—if the mistress wasn't home.

She could be that lucky, couldn't she?

Concerned, she watched the boy cross slowly to the cellar door and resisted the urge to follow until she remembered she needed to take the same exit.

"I'm going out the back way," she told him gruffly and gestured to the opening on the other side of the storeroom when he gave her a worried look.

He nodded and started down the stairs but paused before he descended below floor level.

"That dagger…" he began and she tensed.

"Yeah?"

Goss's face reddened. "You're right," he managed. "Something needs to be done and I trust you to get it done—and not only because I need the medicine. If we don't do something, you'll have more than me being sick to worry about. Whatever you come up with, it'll be the best chance we can find."

Kaylin paused, her hand on the edge of the crevice they used as an exit.

"Thanks, Goss," she told him. "That…that means a lot."

She sighed, glanced at her feet, and shook her head before she looked him in the eye.

"I honestly hate that I have to do anything," she admitted finally when the frustration at their current plight finally got the better of her tongue. "This cannot be all there is for us. We live on the edge of the blade and survive from hand to mouth and for what? So someone bigger and nastier can push us over the edge? It can't be all there is."

He stared at her but she continued.

"There has to be a better way. We can't keep doing this or one day, we'll end up like Astor Korbyn and his crows."

"Blackbirds," he corrected and a slight smile played about his lips.

Kaylin glared at him in frustration.

"Blackbirds…crows…what's the difference if all they do is treat us like carrion waiting to be stripped clean?"

"You won't let that happen, Kay," he told her, his voice so full of confidence that she wanted to cry.

How can he be so sure?

She wasn't a mighty hero who could solve their problems with the flick of a wand or swish of a sword. There were days when she wondered if she would make any difference at all. She was only human and barely into her eighteenth year.

With effort, she didn't let her turmoil display on her face and he didn't appear to notice she'd gone quiet.

"Just like you won't ever let us get to be like Korbyn and his crew," Goss added. "You'd never allow us to be like them."

Again, his words made her want to break down, especially when she remembered the look on Raoul's face the night before. The boy had been ashamed and angry and frustrated and he hadn't been comforted by the fact there'd been nothing he could do.

"I might not always be able to control what you guys become," she said. "Look at Raoul. After last night, he's one step closer to becoming a killer and a thug like those who beat him up."

She paused when she registered the look of disbelief on his face.

"And not because he's a bad person," she added, "but because the streets are teaching him that killing and thuggery and not caring for those around you is what works."

Goss gave her a pitying look.

"That's not up to you, though," he told her. "Raoul will be fine and he isn't—if he chooses to go that way—it isn't your fault. That's on him because it'll be his choice. Living on the edge is only part of what happens when you're born on the streets."

"Yeah, but there's living on the edge and then there's living on the sharp edge," Kaylin protested, "and we shouldn't be forced to stay this way. We need to find a way to be better."

"Kay…I know what you're saying but folk like us, we don't always get to find a better way. That's for lucky folk or those with money. It's not usually for the likes of us."

He saw the refusal on her face and hurried on.

"Me, I'm one of the lucky ones. Me mam would have sold me to an orc for a snack if she could, and Melis and Raoul might as well have been born from the gutter for all they know about their families. Isabette's da was even worse and then there's you. How old were you when that street brawl took your folks?"

Kaylin lowered her head. She'd been five, maybe six, when a band of adventurers and a group of mercenaries had fallen out about the terms of a contract. They'd taken their argument to the streets as her parents were walking home, and they hadn't watched where they swung their swords.

That's what the Shepherds at Herders Gate had told her, anyway.

Goss continued relentlessly.

"The fact that we're all alive and found each other is a wonder in itself. It's more luck than folk like us usually find in a lifetime."

Another bout of coughing shook him and Kaylin glared.

"Well, it's not enough for me." She growled in frustration. "Merely surviving can't be enough."

He drew a breath as though he intended to argue and interrupted himself as he began to cough.

"Look at you, Goss. You need medicine," she told him. "We need to find a way to beat the streets at their own game. Otherwise, all we're doing is taking our time to die, losing a little of our lives every time something goes wrong. There has to be more to living than that."

"Like what?" he rasped and the faintest shadow of a smile curved his lips.

He wasn't mocking her or even mocking the idea that there was more. It was like he found the thought that there was more for them a funny concept. Seeing it only made her frown deepen.

"I don't know what it would look like or what it would cost," she responded finally, "but I know it's there. We only have to find it."

Goss blinked. "Hold that thought," he told her and disappeared into the cellar depths.

Kaylin thought about leaving while he was there but decided against it. He had looked as pale as a ghost and as unsteady as a drunk rolling home at sunrise so she leaned against the wall and waited for him to emerge.

She heard him before she saw him. His footsteps stumbled on the steps and his hand brushed the wall for support. Rather than run to meet him, she let him ascend at his slow, halting pace before she moved alongside him.

"Do you need a hand?"

The fact that he nodded and let her slide an arm around his shoulders was testimony enough that he felt worse. She didn't comment on it, though, exactly like she didn't comment on the fact his skin felt like it was on fire.

Kaylin walked him to his bed and helped him ease beneath the covers. Another fit of coughing shook him and she fetched him more water and stayed to watch him drink it.

"Kaylin..." he wheezed, handed her the empty bowl, and let her pull the covers close around him. "Sometimes, it feels like you want everything and not only for yourself but for everyone."

She cocked her head.

"And what does a little something like that cost?" she asked and forced a smile.

Goss shook his head.

"You get what you pay for." He groaned as she took the blanket off her bed and settled it over him. "To get everything..." His voice became a whisper as the fever took him to sleep. "It'll cost you everything."

CHAPTER THREE

With Goss tucked in and asleep, Kaylin eased out the gap in the storeroom wall.

She paused to make sure the road was clear before she slipped into the narrow street that ran up the side of the inn and trotted to the river.

Eloine had a chandler's shop facing the docks. His "real" job was selling everything the rivermen needed to supply and run their boats. Swathes of netting draped large stands at the front, while the shop's interior boasted candles, lanterns, iron hooks, and reels of fishing line.

Solid boxes for holding a catch and long iron needles for mending nets and sails also had a place, as did sailcloth and tar. The whole shop was a melange of scent and carried a little of everything a riverman might need.

The young woman made her way quickly and quietly along the boardwalk between the inns, taverns, shops, and the river. At this time of day, Eloine would either be inside the store—an ideal place for an ambush if the Blackbirds were still watching him—or he'd be out the front watching the river.

Kaylin didn't want to confront him in either location. She needed him in the small courtyard out the back where he had his stock delivered where there'd be less chance of their discussion being observed and interrupted—and not only because of the Blackbirds.

While Eloine's true calling was known in the Waypoint's underworld, it wasn't common knowledge outside it.

Some of his neighbors might suspect but that was all, and she wouldn't be the one to blow his cover. Still, making sure he was where she needed him would take planning.

She peered up and down the docks and listened intently. It took her a few moments to locate who she was looking for.

At this time of day, the youngest children living in the area were playing their games before their parents returned with the boats and demanded their help. They'd be ready for mischief and a little pocket money.

By the time she found them, she'd almost reached the chandler's shop. At first, there were only two playing a complicated game with multi-colored stones.

"What you want?" the little girl demanded when she came to stand beside her.

Kaylin dropped a brass penny into the middle of the stones.

"I have a commission."

The child's hand flicked out and moved fast enough to beat her brother's as she snatched the penny up and held it to her eye. Her brother thrust his hand out, palm up, and gestured for her to hand it over. The little girl took her time and Kaylin tapped her foot.

"I don't have all day," she told them and immediately regretted the words.

A shrewd look crossed the girl's face and her brother glanced up to mirror it.

"Need a rush job?" he asked, and she sighed and dropped another penny.

"I need you to mess the nets up out back of Elo's," she told them.

Twin grins lit their faces and as quickly disappeared. Both children rose to their feet and the boy thrust his hand out.

"Five brass," he told her. "Three for the job and two for the rush."

Kaylin sighed and counted out three more pennies. He flicked his fingers to indicate that she owed him two more.

"I already—" she began and his grin faded.

The hard, cold look she received was more adult than the child's years.

"That got you an audience," he told her. "The rest is for the job and the rush."

She thought about arguing but decided against it. Kids learned early and some grasped the nuances of street life faster than others, even if they didn't need to. Besides, arguing would take time and she didn't have any. She handed him another two pennies.

"Wait here," the boy told her. "You'll know when he's out there."

Kaylin frowned. He was sharp and had seen right through her request to the purpose beyond it. Again, she didn't argue and instead, she nodded and tossed them another two coins.

"If I like the job I won't ask for 'em back," she told him and the grin returned.

It was a risk to pay them a bonus before the work was done, but she reasoned that she wasn't likely to see them after, not if the job worked the way these things usually did.

She leaned against the wall of the nearest building and watched them race around the corner. The next few heartbeats would tell her if her coppers were well spent or wasted.

Thankfully, she didn't have long to wait. She heard piping voices—the boy and his sister calling to their friends—and a soft thump when someone hit the fence around the courtyard. More bangs and bumps followed and she knew the noise was deliberately designed to draw Eloine's attention.

A short silence followed before she heard the happy shrieks of children wreaking havoc as they played. At first, nothing happened, but a few moments later, a door crashed open.

"Get out of here!" Eloine roared. "You brats know you shouldn't be here. Lexi Lexison, your father will hear about this!"

Uh-oh, Kaylin thought. *It's time I wasn't here.*

If she stayed, the little br—entrepreneurs would be back to charge her more for Lexi getting seen. Maybe she should charge them for tips on how to not be recognized. Someone would have to teach them.

Yes, but it doesn't have to be you, she imagined Goss telling her and stifled a smile.

If not me, then who's gonna bother before one of them gets hurt? she asked him in her mind.

The imaginary Goss didn't answer and she moved around the side of the building, vaulted onto a window sill, and leapt across the narrow alley to another window ledge a little higher on the building opposite.

She pushed off again and twisted to reach the third-floor window of the building beside the chandlery.

After that, it was easy to make the final thrust that propelled herself across the alley to turn and land on the ridgeline of Eloine's roof. A multitude of footsteps raced past below her, accompanied by laughter and voices chattering in amusement.

"I thought I told her to wait here." The brother's voice floated behind Kaylin as she slipped over the ridge line and slid down the slates to the gutter.

A glance showed Eloine standing at the base of a stack of barrels and crates while he shook a broom at his vanished visitors. She assumed the children had fled up the stack and over the fence to escape him. Muttering curses and imprecations and still holding the broom, he turned to where several nets had been tumbled from their stands.

Well, that's got you mired, she thought, slid over the gutter, and dropped to land lightly and tumble smoothly. She rolled easily to her feet and stepped behind the storekeeper as he stooped to pick a length of net up.

"Eh?" he asked and straightened with the net in one hand and the broom in the other.

Kaylin didn't give him time to turn. She drew the dagger and laid the tip against his ribs.

"You and me," she told him. "We need to talk."

He snorted and started to turn. "About what?"

She angled the dagger so his movement pushed against the blade and made the point penetrate his leather jerkin and rough-spun shirt. He froze.

"How about who you've been talking to?" she suggested. "Let's start with that."

"You know me, girl. I don't discuss one client with another," he began and she prodded him with the dagger.

Eloine froze. "Hey. I didn't. It's not good for business, no matter how small or big the asker is."

That didn't make any sense to her. As far as she knew, he was a shrewd businessman and his bigger clients would pay well to know what his smaller clients were up to—enough, she believed, to make it worth his while.

"Uh-huh." Kaylin let all the doubt she felt show in her voice. "Pull the other one. It plays Shelleck's Shanty."

Eloine sighed. "Look, can we talk while I clean up? The little locals decided my delivery yard was a climbing challenge and they've left it a mess. I'd like it cleaned up before the night crowd comes to visit."

The night crowd, she thought. That wasn't a bad way to describe his shadier clientele.

"Fine." She stepped back and slid the dagger away from his ribs and out of his tunic.

No sooner had she stepped clear than he struck—or he tried to. The instant the blade was gone, he pivoted and swung the broom in a short vicious arc. She didn't wait for it to reach her but tumbled past the angry shopkeeper, came swiftly to her feet, and stepped behind him as he swung.

The movement put him off-balance, something she used to her full advantage. As Eloine registered her absence, she raised one foot, hammered it into one broad buttock, and caught him before he could regain his footing. The kick made him stumble forward to tangle in the net he still held in one hand.

Kaylin didn't give him a chance to recover. She bounded forward, shoved hard between his shoulder blades, and finished what the stumble had started. He fell forward and his arms flailed while the broom clattered to the flagstones as he tried to stop himself from landing face-first.

As quickly as she could, she grasped the net and dragged it up and over his head as she crouched over his back, then centered one knee between his shoulder blades and grabbed his hair with one hand. With the other, she slipped the dagger through the net and laid the blade against his throat.

"So…" she all but snarled, "tell me again about this policy of not talking about one client to another."

"I…don't…" he began and pushed against the stone in an effort to rise.

Kaylin hauled back on his hair, pushed down with her knee, and followed the movement with the knife blade. She had no idea how effective this would be until he froze.

She froze too, not sure what the slight shift of the knife had meant. Slowly, she eased the blade back but remembered to keep the pressure on his back and her hand tight in his hair. His gasped breath of relief told her she'd made the right decision.

"Your policy?" she repeated and added persuasively, "Tell me you didn't make an exception."

"I…I…uh…" Eloine began and his shoulders flexed.

Rather than risk cutting his throat by mistake, she moved the dagger away and bounced on his back to stop his latest attempt to rise. He flopped onto the stone again but she felt the experimental wriggle he made a short moment later.

With a scowl of irritation, she stowed the dagger hastily and grasped the net with both hands. As he pushed up, she yanked it under him to wrap a swathe of it around his head and pulled it tight. Using the leg not resting on his back, she shifted more of it around him.

"Are you sure you didn't forget?" she asked. "I've heard Korbyn has his ways."

Eloine stilled. "You don't understand, girl—"

Kaylin smacked him on the back of the head.

"I think I do," she snapped. "We need the medicine and we had the means to pay."

She caught his hair with both hands and bounced his head on the cobblestones.

"And you..." She snarled and thumped it on the stone again. "Told..." Again, she thrust his head forward. "Him!"

Although she was breathing heavily when she'd finished, she felt a little better. Eloine slumped beneath her but a soft moan told him he was still alive. He didn't try to get up.

It's less than you deserve, she thought and recalled the heat of Goss's skin. *If he dies, I'll make sure to deliver the rest.*

"But, I didn—" was as far as Eloine got before Kaylin smacked the back of his head with the flat of her hand. If it hadn't already been resting against the ground, it would have thunked on the stone again.

She leaned close to his ear. "You were the only one who knew about Goss and the medicine," she whispered. "The only one."

When he didn't respond, she held him by the hair and started to lift his head.

"All right. All right," he protested and she released his head.

With a groan, he lowered it onto the cobblestones and stayed there. She drew the dagger from its sheath and poked him in the ribs with it. He flinched.

"Well?" she demanded.

"You're as bad as they are," he muttered, and she poked him again, a little harder this time.

"Ow... Okay, I did tell them."

Kaylin twisted the dagger and he gasped, even though she didn't think it had done more than prod his shirt. "Why?"

"It didn't have anything to do with you," he answered and drew another sharp breath when she pushed the dagger a little deeper. "Not at first."

"Tell me," she pressed.

"It would be easier if you weren't cutting a hole in my hide," he retorted roughly.

She eased the pressure on the dagger and drew it out a little but not all the way. Goss would have been shocked. Eloine seemed to think it was an improvement.

His shoulders relaxed and he began to talk again.

"They came in the afternoon, just before the Dusk Bell when the gates close for the night."

"Who?" she demanded impatiently. She knew the Dusk Bell. It tolled at sunset to warn travelers that the gates were about to close and they had to reach them before the last light faded.

"Korbyn, two of his crew, and two of the Wardens."

"The River Wardens?" she asked, and he sighed.

"Girl, if you keep interrupting me, this story will take forever to tell and I'm expecting my first customer not long past sunset."

As a warning that time was short, it was effective. Kaylin poked him with a finger on her empty hand.

"You'd better hurry then," she told him.

He didn't bother to reply to that but went on with his tale. "He said he was consolidating his power and wanted to know when a crew might come in with a big score."

"And you thought it would be a good idea to drop us in it?" she asked in disbelief. "Even though you knew how much Goss needed the medicine."

"Honest, I wouldn't have," Eloine wheezed, "but he had two Wardens with him and one of them had sergeant's flashes on his shoulders. They weren't ordinary watchmen. Not both of them. And there he was shaking me down in broad daylight with them standing by and looking on. Looking impressed too, they were—and they ain't never suspected me for bein' what I was. I've never been so scared in my life."

"But why us?" Kaylin demanded. "Why drop us in it? Why didn't you simply make something up and then tell him they didn't show?"

"Because he didn't give me time to think," he told her and sounded desperate. "I was panickin'. I knew very well what he was tryin' to say. He was showing me he had contacts, that he was untouchable, that he could do business—and interfere with my business—while the troll-tartin' Wardens were present. And it was a threat."

"A threat?" she asked in disbelief.

"A threat, girl, like he was sayin' he's got connections and doesn't have to worry about the law now but that I did—that he could send the law through my business anytime he wanted and ruin me with a word. A threat."

"So you told him."

"I panicked. Only one crew was bringing in anything worth talkin' about. Believe me, if I'd had time, I coulda thought of something different but with the Wardens right there and his two goons standing right alongside me..."

Kaylin poked him.

"I tried to tell him 'bout my policy and to remind him it benefited him as much as anyone else, but they shoved me up against the back wall, cut me shirt wide open, and left a scratch right down my front until they had their dagger tip against something more personal."

She leaned closer to his ear. "I wish I'd thought of that," she whispered.

"Like I said, I panicked and I told him." Eloine's voice sounded broken.

"And the medicine?" she asked and hope bloomed in her chest. "Where's that? You've still got it, right?"

He shook his head and turned it from side to side without raising it from the cobbles.

"No."

"Why not?"

"Because Korbyn didn't believe me. The bastard said I was only tryin' to scam you, and..." His voice faltered.

"And?" she urged.

"And I got it out to prove I wasn't, that I had the medicine ready to deliver," he replied with an edge of disbelief to his tone. "I got it special, had to talk to the healers an' all and Korbyn he..." The man gulped. "He snatched it out of my hand with one hand and back-handed me with the other."

He drew a long, shaky breath.

"And?" Kaylin asked. Disappointment made her voice harsh.

Eloine's shoulders shook and the next sound he made sounded suspiciously like a sob.

"You lot m...may rob and kill each other all the time, but it used to be fences were respected and protected."

"Not anymore, it seems," she muttered and eased the dagger away from his ribs. She poked him with the finger of her other hand and added, "and my crew might steal but we're nothing like Korbyn and his Blackbirds."

"Pfft. All thieves are the same," he grumbled softly. "Looking out for themselves."

"In that case, then," Kaylin retorted and folded her arms, "I guess we aren't thieves."

She paused but remained on his back as another thought occurred to her. Almost regretful that she'd sheathed the dagger, she poked him again.

"How did Korbyn know when Raoul and Melis were coming? We'd only just made the hit."

"You think you're the only thieves on the streets at night?" Eloine asked almost scornfully. "You think I didn't have a good idea what had gone down and who'd done it?" He snorted. "It's not every night four mercs of the Red Talons are bested by children."

"Red Talons?"

"A merc company based in the Merchant's Quarter," he explained. "Those boys won't live that robbery down for a long, long time. It would be a story you kids could dine out on—provided you weren't too fond of having your heads on your shoulders."

"That still doesn't tell me how he knew to wait for them."

"Simple." He shrugged. "He clicks his fingers and these two kids come in from out front—orphans like yourself, except they look at him like he's life and death to 'em. As far as I can tell, he is."

"And how would you know that?" she asked scornfully.

"Because we got to talkin' while we were waiting," he admitted. "It turns out they each had a brother or a sister Korbyn was holding at the Rookery. Insurance, he called it." Eloine shook his head again without lifting it from the cobbles. "Poor little blighters."

"And?" she prodded.

"I know where you live, see?" he pointed out. "I had one of them watch until they saw your people leave. They ran here and the other one ran to let Korbyn know. He had business on the docks and was on his way over. He arrived before your two and the rest is history." He hesitated for a moment. "The boy..." he asked tentatively. "Is he all right?"

"He's hurting," she said shortly, slid off him, and stepped clear.

She'd almost reached the stacked crates and barrels when he called after her. "Hey... A little help here?"

Kaylin bounded lightly onto the first set of barrels. As his words reached her, she half-turned and glared at him.

"You're on your own until you apologize," she told him coldly and shivered when the Dusk Bell tolled.

Although the Dusk Bell had tolled, twilight reigned. Kaylin took to the rooftops and raced over ridge-lines and leapt narrow streets and alleys until she reached the southern edge of the city. There, set against the wall beside a small, narrow gate leading to the foothills, stood a large stone building surrounded by a thick stone wall.

One of the earliest structures in Tolan's Waypoint, the Herder's Gate Orphanage provided a home for the children left by the mercenaries and adventurers who headed into the Doom and never returned.

She perched on a roof overlooking the road leading to the narrow gate and the orphanage itself.

Children played just beyond the wall and kicked a makeshift ball made from strips of rags wound together. She watched them and let her eyes wander over the lamp-lit scene while she tried to hold the memories at bay.

They'd played that game when she'd arrived at the orphanage over ten years earlier. Some of the children had waved, others had stared, and still others had shrugged indifferently at her arrival. The next day, she'd run from them and hidden in a distant corner of the orphanage grounds.

Thick bushes surrounding the Glade of Contemplation had shielded her from prying eyes and from the children she'd outdistanced. When they'd given up their search, she'd remained in the sheltering leaves, her knees drawn to her chest and her arms wrapped around them.

Her eyes had burned with dry fury and she'd stared into the glade without seeing it.

The brothers and sisters of the Shepherd's Flock had left her alone —provided she came in for the evening meal. She'd needed time to adjust to the loss of her parents and they'd been kind enough to let her have it.

Kaylin stared at the twilit courtyard and the children and wondered how many of them had been told they'd "lost" their parents. It was ridiculous and one of the biggest things her younger mind had struggled to understand.

She hadn't lost her parents.

"It's not like I misplaced them or put them down and forgot where they were!" her younger self had screamed in pain and lashed out when her emotions strangled her ability to control herself. "It's not like I will ever find them again." Her lungs had heaved as she glowered at them. "They were taken from me, and I will never get them back!"

With that, she'd fled, raced through the gardens to the grove, and crawled into her hiding place. Once there, she'd cried herself to sleep, curled in the leaf debris as sobs racked her body. She'd woken to the soft glow of lamplight and the smell of a rich, warm stew and freshly baked bread.

"Are you coming out?" the sister had asked when she'd heard the girl stir. "I'm far too old to crawl through the shrubbery, you know."

Kaylin had peered through the leaves, relieved when she'd seen the sister alone. Sabine's dark eyes had met hers and the woman had given her a gentle smile.

"You must be hungry," she'd said and held the tureen up, "and I thought I'd share my meal with you. What do you say? Do you have time to keep an old woman company?"

Looking back, Kaylin had to smile. Sister Sabine had been much cleverer than anyone she'd ever met. She'd shared her meal and asked the girl if she would read to her the next day because "my old eyes aren't what they used to be."

That had led to her learning to read and to hours spent with the sister's calm, undemanding companionship.

She saved my life, she mused as the children were called inside. And it was true because she knew that without Sabine's intervention, she might have died. She'd been loved and her parents had worked hard to make their tiny house a home until one day, there'd been a brawl and they hadn't come back.

The Wardens had come instead.

They'd taken her to the orphanage and told her she'd "lost" her parents. It had been too much for a young girl to take in. Not even the funeral had seemed real, but Sister Sabine had stayed with her and drawn her out of weeks of solitude and fasting to a semblance of life.

Kaylin sighed.

The old woman had died a year after befriending her, and she had been left alone again. At least that time, she'd been able to say goodbye —and she'd stayed, despite resenting the sister who had taken Sabine's place.

As far as she was concerned, Sister Nadiya had a long way to go before she could even think about filling her predecessor's shoes. She'd hated her and her eight-year-old self had criticized everything the woman said and did. Nadiya had been the reason she had left—and she was the reason she had returned.

If anyone could make it possible for Korbyn to exploit the orphans as he did, it had to be Nadiya but first, she needed proof. She might dislike the woman for trying to force her path but part of her insisted that she prove the fact.

Another part of her disputed the need for it.

The sister had pressed her to help with the younger children and to consider joining the order as her sixteenth birthday approached, and she had refused. She'd loved Sister Sabine but hadn't found it in herself to share her beliefs. When Nadiya had suggested she join the order, she had run.

A bell pealed to draw her attention to the orphanage again, and she realized she'd sat there for longer than she'd thought. She recognized the stocky, balding figure of the man who stood at the courtyard door.

Brother Deodot had always treated her kindly and her heart lifted to see him still alive and well. It had been years since she'd last been there. She was also glad for another reason.

He was slightly forgetful or perhaps not able to concentrate on more than one thing at once—calling the children in to eat and then forgetting to lock the door after the last one had passed, for instance. It had been a trait she had used to her advantage on more than one occasion.

She'd learned to scale the walls and the rooftops so she could escape the orphanage's confines. Brother Deodot's unlocked doors had enabled her to leave on almost any night she wished and return undetected.

As soon as he'd closed the door behind him, she dropped off the roof she was on and swung off the eaves to cling to a second-floor window, drop to a ground-floor window, and then spring to the ground. After that, it was a simple matter to bound across the road and use a striding step placed halfway up the wall to vault her to its top.

Quickly, she dropped into the courtyard, hurried to the door, and tried the handle. Despite expecting it, she still exhaled a small breath of relief when it turned beneath her hand. She eased the door open and peered around it to make sure the interior was clear before she slipped inside.

The hall was as dimly lit as she remembered. Lamp oil and candles were expensive and used sparingly. She moved, wraithlike, through well-remembered corridors until she reached Nadiya's office.

She might not have visited it often once the woman had moved in but it had been a second home while Sabine had been there. Now, she tried the door carefully. When she found it locked, she pulled out the key she kept on a chain around her neck and unlocked it.

Sister Sabine had given her the key and she had never returned it. It had been the only thing of the woman she had and she hadn't wanted to give it up. Somehow, in the midst of Sister Nadiya taking charge, the fact she had it had been overlooked—or maybe her predecessor had never told anyone.

Either way, it didn't matter. What did was that she had it now.

Kaylin closed the door behind her and moved to the desk. It was as neat as it had been in Sabine's day and she had to begrudgingly admit that Nadiya kept as tidy a workspace. It rankled but wasn't as important as what she was looking for.

The neat stack of letters seemed a good place to start. Maybe Korbyn sent his requests in writing.

She found nothing in the letters. As she replaced the last one in its envelope, she studied the desk. A ledger sat to the left and curious, Kaylin picked it up and turned the first page. Names were listed down the left-hand side with dates and circumstances on the right, but the ledger seemed new. She'd have to look further if she was to find anything older.

That didn't stop her from leafing through it in search of names she knew. When she found none, she sighed and set it carefully back where she'd taken it from. A smaller notebook on the desk caught her eye and she reached toward it.

As her fingertips brushed its cover, she heard the hard rap of Nadiya's steps coming down the hall. The woman had never learned to walk quietly. Perhaps it was her time in the mercenary forces she was rumored to have served with, or perhaps she was simply too lazy to control her feet.

Kaylin had no time to decide which. She glanced around the room and looked for a hiding place as the footsteps drew closer. The hollow under the desk was visible from the door.

That's out of the question, she thought as her gaze shifted in search of somewhere else, but nowhere looked promising. Her heart hammered as the footsteps drew closer and she moved swiftly to stand behind the door.

She barely reached the position in time. A key rattled in the lock and the handle turned. When the door remained locked, the woman cursed softly and her key rattled a second time, this time more violently than before.

"Damned locksmith," she cursed, flung the door open, and stormed into the room.

Sister Nadiya strode to her desk and didn't notice when the door stopped short of thumping into the wall. Kaylin stood behind it, the handle clasped firmly in her fist. She waited until she heard keys rattle again and the clunk of a drawer being pulled violently open.

"Whores' cursed, son of a cess-pool sucking, troll-tarting, misbegotten corpse-spawn necromancer's seed," the sister muttered, her voice accompanied by the rattle of parchment being unfolded. "When I—"

She fell silent and the girl pushed the door cautiously a little away from herself.

Nadiya was bent over the desk and pulled an ink well closer with one hand while she held a piece of parchment down with the other. She was so preoccupied with what she was doing that she didn't notice when the lithe intruder moved quietly behind her.

"And now Ivera and Tomas," the woman muttered and dipped the quill into the well with hurried movements. "Of all the—"

When she saw the paired names on the parchment and heard another pair, Kaylin didn't hesitate. She drew her dagger and wrapped her hand around the woman's throat to pull her hard against her while she dug the point of the dagger into the small of her back.

"You bitch!" She snarled in suppressed fury. "Give me one reason to not stick you right here and right now."

CHAPTER FOUR

Nadiya stiffened but she reacted in barely a moment. She hadn't survived ten years as a mercenary by being at anyone's mercy. The hand at her throat lacked strength and maybe conviction, and the blade at her back wasn't held firmly enough to be a threat—not if she was fast.

That assessment took one heartbeat or maybe two. By the third, she had driven her elbow back and slammed it into the body behind her. After a soft whuff of lost air, the pressure on her kidney eased.

She used her elbow as a lever to push her attacker back as she twisted toward the blade to wrench herself out of the hold on her throat. Her opponent stumbled back as Nadiya half-turned to find the knife.

When she saw the dagger, she straightened her elbow and closed her hand around her attacker's wrist, slid her fingers onto the handle, and plucked it from her grasp. The young woman gasped as the sister thrust the dagger in her belt before she clamped her left hand onto the intruder's shoulder and grasped her opposite bicep with her right.

Her opponent stiffened and began to pull against it, but she stepped in close and dragged her hard against her as she stepped alongside her. She braced her outside leg and swung her inside leg back to sweep her attacker's feet out from under her at the same time as she shoved forward on her shoulder and pulled her arm.

The woman landed hard on her back and her mouth formed a surprised "oh" as she thudded on the boards. Keeping her opponent's arm trapped, Nadiya yanked the blade from her belt and prepared to use it. It seemed fitting to use an assassin's blade to end the attacker who'd intended to end her.

Stunned by this turn of events, the intruder stared at her with dark eyes wide with shock as she prepared to deliver the killing blow. Fear and surprise warred on her face and she stopped when she realized that she knew her assailant.

She might not have seen the girl in two years but she knew her.

"Kaylin! Serpent's Sting, girl! What are you doing here?" she demanded, her tone rough.

She didn't lose sight of the fact the girl had attacked her—clumsily, true, but with a dagger no less. It was not what she'd have expected, not even in the child's most rebellious moments, and that alone saved the girl's life.

"I'm sorry to interrupt your note-taking, *Sister*," the girl snapped and hissed the title like a curse. "We wouldn't want you to lose track of all the little ones you've sold to the Blackbirds, now would we?"

The older woman's eyes narrowed. Seconds from death and the girl still had spit in her voice. Nadiya released her arm, backed away a couple of steps, and kicked the office door closed as she did so.

"What do you know of the Blackbirds?" she demanded and tensed her body for another attack when her would-be assailant scrambled to her feet and put another couple of steps between them.

"I know you aren't fit to lick the dust off these floors, much less to stand as Sabine's replacement," she told her coldly. "I knew you were a bitch, *Sister*, but I didn't know you were a monster too."

The words stung but realization dawned, and Nadiya clenched her fist around the knife.

"And I never took you for an idiot," she snapped and flicked the dagger so she held the blade between her fingers before she tossed it end over end across the room.

It drove blade first into the doorframe and stuck there, quivering.

"I keep that list as evidence to present to the River Wardens, girl. It tracks what Astor Korbyn and his band of miscreants are doing. Honestly! Selling the children, Kaylin? Do you hate me that much?"

Kaylin watched the play of emotion on the other woman's face and almost felt sorry for her. The brief flash of hurt preceding the disappointment had seemed very real—and something of a wake-up call.

She forced herself to take a breath but kept a careful eye on the sister. For someone who'd had their life threatened at knife-point, she took things very well and her explanation…well, it made more sense.

After all, if she thought about it, Nadiya had been in charge of the orphanage for a very long time and she couldn't recall any siblings going missing when she'd lived there. Maybe she needed to take a little time to uncover a few more facts.

"So…" She paused for a moment to collect her thoughts. "You're telling me you have nothing to do with the Blackbirds using orphans as messengers."

"No," the sister answered firmly. "I only noticed…" She paused. "I don't know what I noticed. About a year and a half ago, there was an increased demand for siblings. At first, I thought it was sweet that the kids could be kept together. After all the loss they'd already faced, it never seemed fair when I could place a sister and not a brother, or a brother and not a sister."

Kaylin snorted and the woman paused.

"You don't believe me?" she asked and the girl struggled to keep the answer off her face.

She wasn't successful and another flash of hurt marred the sister's expression. It was followed as quickly by a look of great sadness and the older woman sighed.

"I might not be Sabine," she said tightly, "and I know I'll never fill her very big boots, but I'm not the monster you want me to be, Kaylin. I came here because I was tired of battlefields and dealing death.

Caring for children, especially those belonging to people like those I've faced in battle, seemed a good way to atone for the deaths I'd caused."

She studied her visitor with resignation. "You can believe what you like, girl, but I didn't discover what was happening to the children until..."

Again, she hesitated but this time, it wasn't because of the look on Kaylin's face. Instead, she seemed to be considering how much she could reveal. She surprised the girl when she crossed to the door and peered swiftly into the hall. When she was sure it was clear, she returned.

"This isn't to go beyond you," she said sternly, "but I...hired someone to follow some of the children." She shook her head. "I couldn't believe it when they told me they'd gone to the Rookery. The couples who came to adopt them could all be verified as living in the Merchant's Quarter. Only one came from the docks and they looked like a legitimate fishing family." Her expression darkened. "Let us say that I do not approve of their unusual catch."

Kaylin couldn't imagine she would if they were members of the Rookery. She snorted softly and wondered what the good sister would think of her and her activities. Again, hurt flared through Nadiya's expression.

"This won't work if we can't trust each other," the woman told her and she curled her lip.

"Did you know that Korbyn holds one sibling hostage against the other's good behavior?" she asked, and Nadiya's expression stilled.

"I didn't," she replied and turned to her list. She tapped her forefinger against the parchment. "But it makes sense. All these children were tightly bonded. It makes sense when the only person they have left in the world is each other."

"You're saying they didn't take every sibling?" she asked and the sister shook her head.

"No. There were some brother and sister pairs the couples weren't interested in. I couldn't work out why until you mentioned one being held against the other's good behavior. Now, it makes sense—and gives me a fair idea of who might be taken next."

Kaylin sidled closer and studied the list. One of the things that caught her eye was its length.

"So many," she murmured, and Nadiya hastened to enlighten her.

"Not all of those were adopted," she stated. "Some ran away."

"But kids run away all the time," she pointed out and the woman smiled wryly.

She flushed but Nadiya merely answered her observation.

"I know but usually, we can work out why. Most times, we let them go until the Wardens bring them back and then we try to give them a better reason to stay, but these..." She indicated three pairs of names. "These all disappeared with no trace, not even a sighting. I'd have thought the Wardens would have seen them by now."

"Not if the Wardens were working for the Rookery," she pointed out.

Nadiya stopped for a moment before she turned and gave her a sharp look.

"Are you saying..." she began and let her question go unfinished when the girl nodded.

"Yes. Eloine told me Korbyn brought two River Wardens with him when he came to threaten him."

"He what?"

Kaylin gave the woman a wide-eyed stare.

"Oh, didn't you know? Raoul and Melis were robbed when they took some trade to Elo—Blackbirds were waiting, and when I went back and asked Elo why—"

She stopped at Sister Nadiya's sharp intake of breath but the woman motioned for her to continue.

"Elo said he had no choice, that the Blackbirds have found some powerful friends and the River Wardens do as Korbyn orders."

"And you didn't think I might need to know this?" Nadiya exclaimed. "Given that I'm putting together a list to give to them?"

"I..." She closed her mouth, then opened it again. "I only remembered now," she admitted finally.

The woman's mouth twisted with regret. "And you were still making your mind up as to whether or not I was a monster," she stated.

Kaylin hung her head but again, the woman read her expression and sadness crept into her face.

"Of all the troll-tarting, shits-be-shaded, cavern-dwelling sphincter huggers," Nadiya muttered. "I will gut them like the piss-swilling, butt-sucking ass-crawlers they are." She glanced up and caught her visitor's look of surprise, and her face flushed crimson. "Please. Forgive me. It's a hangover from my mercenary days. I am truly sorry."

She snorted and saw another flash of hurt in the sister's eyes. Realizing she'd upset her, she drew a deep breath.

"It's okay," she said. "Don't worry about it."

The woman's face softened with relief and she looked at the list. Kaylin followed her gaze and saw her finger tapping the parchment. When she looked at the sister's expression, she noticed it shift from relief to thoughtful concentration.

"What can we do to stop them?" she asked and Nadiya raised her gaze.

"Do you want some tea?" she asked. "And are you hungry? I always find I think better if my stomach's not rumbling."

Tea and cake? she thought but brushed it away. If she wanted to beat Korbyn, she could do with help, and while she couldn't see what a sister of the Shepherds could do, there was only one way to find out.

"Okay," she agreed and flinched when Nadiya yanked the knife from the door frame.

The sister flipped the blade expertly and offered it, hilt first, to her.

"I take it you don't want to be seen here," the woman suggested. She stepped to the door and looked out into the corridor. "Why don't we retire to the private meeting room? You know the one?"

Kaylin nodded. Of course she remembered. She'd sat in the corner of it often enough when Sabine had been alive.

Nadiya peeked into the corridor. "I'll meet you there."

She didn't wait for a reply but stepped from the room and the hard strike of her boots on the stone floor echoed as she strode down the hall.

The girl waited until they faded, then checked that the corridor was clear. The sister was right. She didn't want to be seen at the orphanage. The Blackbirds had eyes everywhere and she didn't know where was safe.

Her journey to the meeting room was uneventful but she didn't sit at the small table. The room held too many memories. Instead, she paced silently in a quiet circuit as she studied her surroundings.

Nadiya hadn't changed much—in fact, Kaylin realized as she looked around, the woman hadn't changed anything that she could tell. Even the red velvet chair at the window was still in place. She stood and stared at it and recalled how many times she'd sought refuge on its padded seat.

It seemed an age before the sister returned, and Kaylin had taken a position at the chair and stared through a gap in the curtain at the street beyond the wall. It was empty but she still started when she heard the rap of heels in the hall outside.

The woman entered with a rattle of crockery from the tray she bore, and she hurried to the door to help her with it.

"Thank you." Nadiya smiled tentatively and the girl lowered her head, closed the door, and followed her to the table. To her surprise, the woman hadn't brought cake from the kitchens but several small pies, some savory and some sweet.

Nadiya caught her look and her smile grew warmer. "You haven't eaten yet, have you?" she asked.

She shook her head and swallowed the saliva that had pooled in her mouth.

"Good. Because I missed the evening meal and I'll think better when I've eaten," The woman put the tray down and lifted the teapot.

She poured the tea as Kaylin sat on the opposite side of the table. Neither spoke until Nadiya put the teapot down and sat.

"Eat first," she instructed as she picked a pastry up, and the girl scowled.

When the woman raised an eyebrow, her scowl grew deeper. She snatched a pastry from the tray, took a bite, chewed quickly, and washed it down with a gulp of tea. The hot liquid scalded her throat and she coughed.

The sister shook her head, finished her pastry, and sipped her tea while Kaylin caught her breath.

"So, what did you have in mind?" she asked, and Nadiya lowered her cup.

"I assume you want to get back what they stole?" the woman asked.

Kaylin nodded. Want to get it back? Regardless of what she heard there, that was exactly what she intended to do.

As if reading her mind, her companion smiled.

"So," she continued, "from what you've said, we can't rely on the River Wardens because they're getting paid off, which means their loyalty is only as long as Korbyn's pockets. If you can scout them while I get some community support—"

"What good will community support do?" she challenged and Nadiya gave her a sharp look.

"I won't only look for support, dear. I'm going for outrage. If I can create enough of a stink with the people, and if you and your crew..." Her mouth twitched with distaste as she continued. "And if you and your crew plunder them just before a payment is due, they'll be without the Wardens' support."

"But they'll only promise them more," she argued. "There's a lot a man will do for the promise, even if it can't be made to happen *now*."

Nadiya's face took on a cunning look. "That all depends on how widely known the robbery becomes."

Kaylin paled. "It only has to become known to those getting paid," she countered and the woman's smile became feral.

"Exactly," she agreed. "Trust me. They'll know the Blackbirds are out of coin but they won't know who took it or where the coin has gone. I'll merely pass on the information my sources tell me."

She stared at the sister in disbelief. "And they'll believe that?"

"Oh, yes," Nadiya told her confidently. "They've benefited from that information before and have no reason to doubt it—although this time, I might need to show them some proof."

Her eyes narrowed. "What kind of proof?"

"That blade I assume you took," her companion replied. "The dwarven one. Its owner's raised seven kinds of hell about it."

"But it's only been a day," she protested.

"Yes, and the Wardens have already asked me if I can find out who the thieves might be."

Kaylin drew a breath to protest but the woman hurried on before she could speak.

"You'll have enough extra to cover what it's worth. The Blackbird's treasury will have other items. I don't care what else you find but if you bring the blade back as proof, they'll believe me."

"But—"

"It has the added benefit that I'll be able to blame the robbery on Korbyn's crew or at least point eyes in their direction that would otherwise be looking..." Nadiya raised an eyebrow. "For you."

"Well..."

"And you're not the only ones they've threatened. If we eliminate their Warden support, it might be enough to drive them off. Or the Wardens could turn on them and hang them for the criminals they are," she added.

Kaylin picked another pastry up. She was hungry and she needed to think. This time, she ate more carefully, aware that she was being watched. The sister didn't press her, though, but merely lifted her cup and waited.

She would have been happier if Nadiya had talked and emptied the air of the silence that irritated her. Instead, the woman waited exactly as Sabine would have done. The knowledge didn't improve her temper, nor did having to admit what she said next.

"There's only one problem with the plan," she stated and the sister raised her eyebrows.

Instead of asking what that might be, Nadiya put her cup down, picked a pastry up, and motioned for her to continue.

She sighed. "I like the idea of plundering the Blackbirds," she assured the woman and paused momentarily before she hurried on. "But I don't know where the Rookery is and even if I did, there's a very good chance the Blackbirds have all kinds of protections in place."

Nadiya nodded but again, like Sister Sabine would have done, she signaled for her to go on. Kaylin lowered her head.

"And I wish I did," she added fiercely. "After what they did to Raoul, I want them to pay but—"

When the woman remained silent, she sighed. "But the others are afraid. They beat Raoul very badly and they're worried that if the Wardens turn against us—"

"Waypoint doesn't hang its children," Nadiya reminded her sharply. "The Shepherds see to that."

"But they might not see Isabette and me as children," she retorted. "We're not exactly little anymore."

"And the others are frightened that might happen?" her companion asked.

Kaylin nodded, her eyes dark with concern for her crew. "I'd tell them not to worry," she admitted, "but it's not the kind of thing they can shake, and if they head into a job with that kind of emotion, they'll get themselves killed. I like your plan but I'm not up for a suicide mission."

"What if I said I had an inside man?" Nadiya asked. "Would that change your mind?"

"It would certainly help the crew get over their nerves," she replied, "and it would give us a location. We wouldn't have to risk warning the Blackbirds by asking around."

"That's settled, then," the sister told her. "I'll talk to my contact and if you come back tomorrow afternoon, I'll introduce you to someone who can help."

CHAPTER FIVE

Kaylin let the crew rest that night but woke the next morning to Goss coughing. She scrambled out of her blankets, hurried to the boy's pallet, and offered him water.

"Go back to bed," he told her crossly when he could catch his breath. "I'm not a baby."

"You're welcome," she snapped in return, refilled the water bowl, and placed it beside him before he could protest any further.

He scowled at her, his fingers clenched around his blankets and his face pale.

"Go to bed," he ordered roughly. "You ought to be sleeping, not worrying about me."

She raised her hands in surrender and returned to her mat. She'd barely closed her eyes when another fit of coughing wracked him. He stopped her when she propped herself up.

"I'm fine," he croaked fiercely. "Go to sleep."

Reluctantly, she lay down again. Sleeping was out of the question. Goss continued to cough on and off throughout the morning and each fit sounded worse than the last. There was nothing she could do to ease it and he wasn't in the mood for help.

If she insisted, he'd only become agitated and his coughing would get worse. If he'd had the medicine when they'd planned, he'd be getting better right now.

Korbyn would pay, she vowed.

Even if Nadiya's plan didn't work and the Wardens continued to support the man, there were myriad ways she could make his life difficult. She could… She could… Her brow furrowed. What exactly could she do?

Nothing, except maybe pray to the gods that Korbyn's backside would break out in boils, or that he'd develop a terrible itch in places he couldn't touch, or that his skin would melt from his bones.

Goss coughed again, and she turned her head toward him. The boy propped himself up until the fit had passed and drank from the water bowl. She couldn't help noticing how it shook in his hands—and feeling that it was all her fault.

If she'd gone to see Eloine instead of sending Melis and Raoul, maybe she could have snatched the medicine and escaped with it. Except it had already been gone, she reminded herself. Well, maybe she could have gotten away with some of their loot or fought well enough for Raoul and Melis to get away.

Kaylin stifled a sigh and rolled onto her side, pulled her thin blanket over her head, and closed her eyes. If she didn't sleep soon, she wouldn't be as sharp as she needed to be in the afternoon's meeting. She drifted and finally slid into sleep, only to be brought fully awake by another round of coughing.

Goss cursed softly, no doubt feeling guilty at the thought of waking them and the idea that he was a burden. He probably felt guilty about Raoul too. She forced herself to lie still. Perhaps if the boy thought she was asleep, he'd settle sooner.

The light shining around the edge of the curtains at the door grew brighter and sleep refused to come. When yet another bout of coughing disturbed her, Kaylin got out of bed. Seeing his look of dismay, she gave him a reassuring smile.

"Nice timing, Goss. I'da been late for my meeting otherwise." She stooped to collect his water bowl and refill it. "It was on my way," she told him gruffly as he stuttered his thanks.

"Liar," he rasped and took the bowl, and she flashed him a brief grin.

"You're welcome," she retorted.

When she noted the pallor of his face and felt the heat of his fingertips when they brushed hers, she silently cursed Korbyn's interference. As much as she didn't like what it involved, if she didn't get the boy some medicine—and very soon—he might die.

Next time I see him, I will gut him like a fish, she thought. *And then I'll kick him into the river and feed him to the fish.*

She let none of that show on her face but gave the boy a grave nod.

"Tell the others to stay close to home. We have enough for another day's rest. I'll be back by dusk and hopefully, with good news."

Kaylin didn't wait for him to reply before she slipped through the curtain leading to the storeroom and through the gap into the alley. To her relief, she saw no sign that the Blackbirds knew where they lived or that anyone else was watching them.

Still, it didn't hurt to be careful. She took the fastest route to the rooftops and broke into a swift, sure-footed trot amongst the chimneys and valleys that would lead to the rear of the orphanage. Even with the children at afternoon classes, the grove and the gardens were still her best chance to enter the grounds and reach the building unseen.

The gap between the buildings opposite the orphanage walls and the walls themselves was much narrower there and she could duck into a nearby alley if someone came along before she vaulted the wall. When she reached one of the wider streets, she threw herself into a leap to the other side.

She landed firmly on the rooftop and continued across another street, scrambled up the pitch of the next roof, and glanced along the road leading to the front of the orphanage. Immediately, she froze and reviewed her plans.

Sister Nadiya stood at the front gate and looked up and down the street. She even peered at the rooftops as if she knew Kaylin's favored route. The girl frowned.

Granted, they'd never said exactly where they'd meet, but what made the sister think she'd be dumb enough to meet her at the orphanage's front gate? She turned, backed away a few steps, and bounded across the street again to move cautiously along the rooftops parallel to the orphanage wall.

The closer she got, the more suspicious she became. The sister hadn't struck her as being this stupid.

Maybe she's waiting for someone else, she thought and slipped behind a chimney when the woman glanced up. She gave her a few heart-beats' grace, then peered out from her hiding place. Thankfully, her co-conspirator's attention had returned to the street.

Kaylin moved more cautiously, slid down, and inched along a narrow valley where two roofs met. When she reached an alley, she moved to the ridgeline again. Soon, she'd have to go down to street level but she could check to make sure it was clear first.

Quickly and quietly, she paused at the top and dropped to her belly to peer over it.

When the street remained clear, she sighed internally and returned to the ridgeline. She backtracked to where a balcony overlooked the entrance to another alley. Once she'd ascertained that the road was clear, she dropped lightly onto the outer edge of the balcony and into the alley mouth.

When she peered out, she realized Nadiya hadn't seen her. The sister still stood at the orphanage front gate.

With a hasty glance at her attire, Kaylin smoothed the torn and dirty folds of her tunic before she stepped into the street. She watched Nadiya, sure the woman would notice her with the next turn of her head. As she passed under the shadow of the balcony, two men emerged from the alley opposite the orphanage entrance and the girl stilled.

The men didn't turn into the street but strode directly to the sister, their profiles clear in the bright afternoon light. She knew one of them.

Was this Sister Nadiya's so-called inside man?

Fear warred with curiosity and disbelief with hope. While she wanted to believe this was Nadiya's contact, she had her doubts.

Firstly, Nadiya had only mentioned one inside man. Why were two Blackbirds visiting the orphanage? Had they come to take more children?

Kaylin frowned and decided she needed a better vantage point. She turned quickly and trotted toward the alley, hoping neither the good sister nor the Blackbirds had seen her.

She reached the alley mouth and turned into it but she'd gone another few paces before she realized no one was coming after her. That couldn't be right. Nadiya must have been expecting her and she'd have caught sight of her as soon as she started to run. The Blackbirds too, for that matter.

Nothing drew attention like movement—especially to those whose survival might depend on it, like mercenaries and thieves. But if they'd seen her, why hadn't they come after her?

Both confused and concerned, she turned to a rickety staircase leading to a second-floor door. The overhanging roof was a short jump above it and she could pull herself up from there.

Kaylin moved quickly and quietly, sprinted up the stairs, leapt to catch the guttering with her fingers, and hauled herself onto the roof. After that, she made a short jump across the alley and raced to the one from which the Blackbirds had emerged.

This time, she didn't bother to look for balconies or stairs. Instead, once she'd confirmed that the alley was clear, she swung over the edge and pushed off the wall. She bounced from one side of the alley and back again until she landed on the cobblestones in a crouch.

Thankfully, her antics had drawn no attention and she trotted quietly to the end of the alley and crouched to slip close to the corner. She peered out at the two Blackbirds, who did their best to tower over the sister.

"What do you want?" Nadiya demanded and her cold tones carried across the street.

Kaylin thought she sounded more angry than frightened. She noticed how the woman's hand lowered to her belt as though she'd find a sword still there. The Blackbirds noticed the movement as well and snickered.

"What's the matter, *Sister*? You're not frightened, are you?"

The woman fixed him with a hard stare. "Should I be?"

When the other Blackbird stepped closer, Nadiya stiffened.

He smirked, his low rumble very audible from where Kaylin crouched. "We heard you been making lists and might be considering making a noise," he stated and stared menacingly at her.

His partner took up where he left off. "So we stopped by to tell you it won't do you any good and to mind yer own business."

"I see," she stated and her tone made it very clear that she saw and wasn't impressed.

"The boss thought it only fair to warn you there'd be uncomfortable consequences if you didn't want to listen," the first added.

Nadiya raised an eyebrow. "Oh, he did, did he? Tell me," she continued, "if what I'm doing won't do any good, why are you wasting time telling me? I'd find it out soon enough and it's only my time I'd be wasting then."

Anger flashed quickly in the men's faces. The second man swept his gaze over the woman's tense form before he stretched his hand out to chuck her under the chin with his finger.

"Because maybe the noise makes things a little more expensive for us," he told her and his voice hinted at other things.

He moved his hand past her shoulder to press his palm against the wall as he leaned closer.

Instead of moving away, the sister stood a little taller and her hands balled into fists. "Your expenses mean nothing to me," she told him sharply.

The Blackbird didn't look impressed. "Maybe..." He leered and scrutinized her speculatively. "Maybe we say it means we come back here and take our money's worth out of you, Sister, as compensation for the trouble."

Nadiya looked him in the eye and brought her face close to his.

"You come back here looking for compensation," she responded, her voice almost a growl, "and the only thing you'll collect is your teeth from the gutter."

Fury darkened the man's features and his free hand drifted to his dagger. Kaylin tensed in preparation to intervene if things turned violent. To her surprise, the other man laughed and gave his friend a playful slap on the shoulder.

"Our teeth!" He chuckled. "As if she could." He tapped the other man again twice. "Come on," he said before he turned to study Nadiya lasciviously, "there's enough woman there for the whole crew to take their expenses from and take our time while doing it. Losing our teeth won't come into it."

The other Blackbird leaned closer and breathed deeply. "And sweet into the bargain," he added and smiled at her. "Go ahead. Make your trouble. I could do with a little girl-time."

For a minute, Kaylin thought the sister might strike the man, but the first Blackbird pulled his friend away and they began to turn. She retreated into the alley and looked for somewhere to hide. An alcove beckoned, a narrow duck-in that led to a semi-hidden doorway.

What are the chances that they'll walk right past? she wondered, but the crunch of boots on cobbles warned her she was running out of time. She didn't wait any longer but slipped into the shadows in the alcove and dropped into a crouch.

As the footsteps approached, she curled close to the ground and tucked her face against her knees. She didn't know what lay beyond the door and there was no time to inch up the wall. All she could do was hope the Blackbirds kept walking.

Their footsteps crunched closer and she tensed. With her cloak hood up, she should look like another shadow. She hoped she looked like another shadow.

It would be too bad to have Nadiya face these bastards so courageously, only for them to discover she'd seen them. Given what they'd done to Raoul, she could only imagine what they might do to her. Remembering that—and what they had said to the other woman—her heart sank.

To think she'd gone back to believing Nadiya was on the other side! What was wrong with her?

The closest she could come was that she'd been so disappointed at the idea of losing the chance to avenge Korbyn's theft that she'd forgotten the woman was their only chance of doing that and of helping Goss. Foolishly, she'd almost walked away from that.

For what? Because she didn't like the woman who'd replaced her first true friend at the orphanage? She had to be better than that. From this point on, she needed to become better than that.

She listened to the footsteps of the two Blackbirds as they walked past the alcove and gradually faded. Only when they had gone completely did she raise her face cautiously to scan the alley. When nothing moved in the shadows, she uncurled slowly and trotted toward the orphanage gate.

To her relief, Sister Nadiya was still there, although she leaned against the gate post and appeared to be examining her nails.

"It took you long enough," she snapped when the girl arrived.

Kaylin ignored the snarkiness in the comment. "I saw the whole thing," she said, and Nadiya pushed off the post and turned to unlock the gate.

"So?"

"I've never seen anyone stand up to the Blackbirds like that."

Surprisingly, the woman blushed.

"It was nothing," she answered brusquely. "I've faced orcs who were bigger and minotaurs that smelt worse. Two thugs are child's play."

"They didn't look like child's play to me," she told her seriously. "You didn't have a weapon and they still backed down."

"They've been on the streets long enough to know when they need to be careful," Nadiya replied. "If they hurt me and drew attention from the North Wardens, Korbyn would have had their guts and even they weren't stupid enough to risk that."

"Still…" Kaylin began. She saw her companion tense and finished lamely, "It was very impressive."

Sister Nadiya snorted. "Impressive or not, they'll be back so we need to get this right."

She locked the gate behind them and moved briskly across the yard to lead her visitor through the foyer and up a small set of stairs at the side.

"What?" she asked and turned to look at the girl. "You thought I'd bring you in through the back?" When she saw the confirmation on her face, she laughed. "Have you forgotten the classrooms look over the gardens?"

Kaylin blushed. She had forgotten. If she'd gone in the way she'd thought best, the only approach to the orphanage would have led them in full view of the classroom windows.

"Besides," Nadiya added kindly, "it's almost summer and the weather's fine, so I ordered a week of instruction in the common herbs to be found in and around Waypoint. As you know, we have quite a fine collection."

That made her smile. The Shepherds did have a fine collection of herbs and supplemented donations with earnings from their sale. Not only that but a little herb knowledge would stand the children in good stead if they ever chose to follow a career in the market gardens or tried for an apprenticeship with the healers.

Nothing the Shepherds did was wasted.

"I'm more concerned that the Blackbirds knew about the list," the sister confided as they reached the top of the stairs. "Did you mention it to any of your crew?"

It was a logical question. The girl suppressed a small spark of annoyance and shook her head. If Nadiya hadn't said anything, it was only natural that she should ask if Kaylin had talked about it.

"It didn't come up," she told the sister. "They were still tired when I got back and I didn't want to get their hopes up until we had a plan. They would have asked too many questions otherwise."

Her guide nodded and checked the corridor before she led her along it to the meeting room.

"This way," she ordered and kept her voice low as they left the stairwell. Changing the subject, she asked, "Did they see you?"

"No," Kaylin replied. "I hid and they went straight past."

Some of the tension left the woman's body. "That's good," she answered. "The last thing we want is for the Blackbirds to discover we're working together. If they didn't see you in the alley, you made it in unnoticed. The streets were empty when we met."

She wanted to ask her how she knew but decided the woman would know. The gods knew she had watched the street sharply enough.

"They're quiet at this time of day," the sister added as though Kaylin needed a reason.

While she hadn't intended to ask, it was good to know. "And this informant?" she asked.

"Is one of the main reasons Korbyn must not know," Nadiya answered as they reached the door.

The meeting room was occupied when Kaylin entered and it was an effort to not stop and stare. The small figure seated at the table belonged to a girl who couldn't be more than Goss's age but probably younger.

She glanced at Nadiya and the sister smiled and gestured toward the table.

"Why don't you take a seat, Kaylin? I'll have the kitchens send something up." That comment earned her a sharp glance from both girls. "They'll knock," she told them shortly, "and I'll collect it from the door. You won't be seen."

Whether that comment was directed at her or the child, she didn't know, but she leaned back in the chair and turned to study the stranger. It was no surprise to be on the receiving end of a similar assessment.

Large brown eyes met hers and the girl didn't look away. Kaylin didn't try to break the contact. The eyes were the window of intent was what Sister Sabine used to say, and she had found it to be true.

"This is Kit." Nadiya seated herself at the table.

A world of pain swam in Kit's eyes, she decided, and didn't hold the wariness there against the girl.

Oblivious to these thoughts, the woman continued.

"Kit and her brother Jacques left the orphanage a couple of years ago."

The girl lowered her head but not before her face colored with embarrassment. Nadiya ignored the movement.

"Jacques believed the rumors about the coin to be made." Kit snorted and the sister gave her a sad smile as she continued. "Jacques didn't want to leave his sister behind and thought she'd be safer with him than without."

The girl stilled and raised her head as Kaylin looked around the room. "He ain't here," she said, her small voice sharp.

She glanced at her.

"I don't know where he is," Kit added as if she had asked. "He didn't come back."

Her voice broke and Sister Nadiya reached toward her but placed her hand on the table when the girl flinched. Kaylin frowned and glanced worriedly at the woman, and Nadiya resumed the tale.

"We knew Kit and Jacques had gone to join the Blackbirds. They weren't the first and they haven't been the last."

Kit's hand crept onto the table but Nadiya kept speaking.

"They found a use for Jacques in the gang's business. Korbyn sent him on errands but kept Kit at the hideout."

"Not out of the kindness of his heart, I take it," Kaylin stated and the child shook her head.

When she didn't say anything, Nadiya explained. "No. They put her to work as some kind of house servant—scrubbing pots, cleaning floors, and doing general kitchen work."

Kaylin hid a smile as Kit moved her hand to rest it over the sister's fingers. Nadiya paused to smile at the child, who met her gaze and kept her hand where it was. That meant something to the woman, whose face softened momentarily before it hardened as she went on with the story.

"Jacques was sent to collect information about the other groups, merchants, or anything else Korbyn had an interest in. As he became more trusted, he was given messages to carry."

"Packages," Kit whispered and darted a glance at both their faces before she lowered her head hastily.

"And packages," Nadiya confirmed. "But when he didn't come back from the last delivery, Korbyn gave orders that Kit was to be used as an example for the other messengers as to what would happen to their siblings if they should ever fail to return."

The child snatched her hand away, tucked both hands against her chest, and huddled in her chair. Again, that soft, fierce whisper floated out. "I ran."

Kaylin didn't blame her. The kinds of examples Korbyn believed in were enough to turn most stomachs and hers was no exception.

"How did you get out?" she asked. "Is there a way out? Doesn't he keep the place locked down?"

Kit nodded and looked up with wide, solemn eyes. "There is, and I used it when I worked out I was in trouble."

"And how—" she began, but the child continued.

"I came to evening meal and they looked at me…and…and I knew Jacques was out so I looked for him and he wasn't there. Ty and Birdie started coming toward me and Korbyn looked at the messengers' table and asked—"

Her breath caught and her face paled. Kaylin waited and wondered if Nadiya would intervene, but the sister sat silently and gave the girl time to gather herself.

"He…he said, 'Do you know what happens when a messenger fails to come back?'" Kit squeezed her eyes tightly shut and drew a quick breath. "I knew I was in for it then. Didn't need no one tellin' me how bad they were gonna get. I ran."

"But—" Kaylin began but subsided when she caught a warning look from Sister Nadiya.

Kit didn't appear to notice the interruption. She stared into nothing as if seeing events unfold as she spoke.

"There's a way out through the storerooms, see? I only had to make it to the kitchens and into there an' I'd be all right. They's too big to foller me, so I ran. Cook had no idea. I scooted right under his arm and into the pantry."

She caught another breath.

"Birdie's fast and he almost knocked Cook into his pot tryin' to get to me. I heard the clatter and Cook swearin' like he does when someone hides his salt or adds ten guests to a meal he's just done makin' and I ran faster. That Cook, he's got a mean temper, that one."

She paused, a faraway look still in her eyes, but Kaylin waited and Nadiya waited with her. After a moment, Kit continued.

"Ty almost caught me. Birdie's fast, but Ty—" She shuddered at the memory. "He don't stop."

She swallowed as if that could erase the fear in her voice.

"I went through the break and Ty tried to go through after. When he didn't fit, he started tearin' the boards, but I made it to the cellar before he thought to go to the door. I found the gap in the blocks behind the wine casks and was in and through it before they made it to the room and I was out at the canal and running before they—"

She gasped, clapped both hands over her mouth, and turned a fearful look to Nadiya.

"I didn't mean to—" she began and the sister took both her hands in hers and held them gently.

"Kit," she said softly.

The girl pulled back and shook her head in denial. "But I didn't tell," she protested and her voice faded to a frightened whisper. "I didn't."

"No," Nadiya told her firmly. "You didn't tell. There are many canals in Waypoint."

She tightened her hold and drew the child's hands toward her.

"If we're ever going to get rid of Korbyn, and Birdie, and Ty, we need to know where the Rookery is. We can't do this without you."

Kit closed her mouth and her gaze searched the woman's face for sincerity. Kaylin cleared her throat and the child snapped her head to stare at her.

"Will I fit?" she asked. "If I want to go and take every penny Korbyn has so he can't pay the Wardens off, will I fit?"

The child stopped pulling against Nadiya's hands. "You can't go alone," she whispered. "You'd never get it all out."

"I won't go alone," she told her. "I have four crew coming to help. I'm the biggest."

Kit gaped at her, then closed her mouth. "Why?" she asked. "What's in it for you?"

"Korbyn hurt one of my crew," she replied and let the girl see her fury at Raoul's injuries. "Now, he threatens my livelihood. The man needs taking down a peg."

"And I want my children back," Nadiya added, equally as fiercely. She hesitated. "That is…if they want to come back."

Kit nodded vigorously.

"They do. They want to come back. Most knows what chances they passed up when they left or got adopted out to the liars. They'd rather be back here with you than anywhere else. They—" Her face fell. "They's just too scared."

"Which is why we've gone to great lengths to keep you hidden," Nadiya reassured her. "As long as Korbyn thinks you're dead or trapped or whatever, he won't look for you here. And if he doesn't know you're here and talking to Kaylin and me, he won't suspect a thing, now will he?" She watched the young girl.

"S'pose not," she muttered.

"Guaranteed he isn't," Kaylin reassured her. "And wouldn't you like to make sure he's gutted the only way that matters?"

Kit pressed her lips together, extracted her hands from Nadiya's, and folded them in her lap.

"You can't make it true," she muttered and lowered her head. "Nothin' you can do's gonna undo that whore-lump."

Nadiya sighed, recognizing the signs. She turned to the other girl. "I'm sorry."

Kaylin looked from the sister to the child and frowned. "Don't be," she replied. "But…can I have some time alone with her?"

The woman's gaze sharpened and she wondered if she was afraid she'd harm the girl. To her relief, the sister rose from her seat and walked around the table.

"Be kind," she instructed as she leaned close to her ear.

She looked like she wanted to say more but didn't. Instead, she straightened, walked out the office door, and closed it behind her as she said, "I'll go see what's happened to our tea."

Kit didn't look up as the older woman left. She flinched when the door thumped closed gently and hunched tighter.

"You ain't gotta be scared o' me," she assured the girl and dropped into the patois of the street as she spoke. "You ain't."

Her companion didn't look up but Kaylin didn't give up.

"I came 'ere when I was just a little tacker. Me mam and me dad got done in a fight between mercs and an adventurin' crew and never came 'ome. Dumped me here, see?"

She paused, rewarded when Kit raised her head but dismayed by the girl's suspicion.

"So you knows the sister real well then, right?"

Kaylin rolled her eyes. This kid was even harder than Goss on a bad day.

"Nope. Never liked her. I thought she shouldn't oughta be trying ta fill shoes she had no right steppin' into."

That caught the kid's attention. "You what?"

"I told you already," she answered and leaned back in her chair as if she didn't care.

Kit straightened a little and stretched her hands out in front of her. When she did so, the pale ridges of scar tissue marking the girl's arms were visible.

"So, tell me again," Kit demanded. "If you're not so tight with the sister, how's you here? How's she told you I'm here?"

What she was asking was if Nadiya had betrayed her. Kaylin shook her head.

"I came here lookin' to put the sister into the Shepherd's arms," she admitted. "Two nights back. You know it?"

"She were upset two nights back," the girl admitted and rubbed a thumb over the scar tissue on her wrist. "Wanted to know what in all the troll-loving, goat-sucking arts of Melerus she'd done to deserve such hate." The little girl's eyes narrowed. "That be you?"

Kaylin stared at her. "She said all that?"

"All that an' more," Kit told her with a sly grin. "You want to hear?"

Did she? Kaylin decided she didn't and shook her head hastily. It was better she didn't.

"We got to an understanding," she admitted and the girl smirked.

"You're bettin' an awful lot on that," she said and Kaylin shrugged.

"It's my funeral."

Kit's smile died. "Could be if you get after Korbyn and the like."

"And my choice," she told her defiantly.

"Like it was your choice to be 'ere?" the girl challenged.

She lowered her gaze to the child's scarred wrists, then raised it to her face.

"Fate said I should come," she replied. "Was me who said I'd stay as long as I did."

"You and who else?" the child demanded and Kaylin smiled sadly.

"Sabine," she said. "The sister who was before this one. She brought me out of the black."

"How black?" Kit demanded, and Kaylin rolled her sleeves.

"How about this black?" she asked and revealed a set of scars much like her young companion's.

The girl stretched a forefinger out to touch them and traced the jagged tear line. "You thought what?"

"I thought crossing was better than staying," Kaylin told her shortly. "It took the sister to show me there might be more reason to stay."

Kit satisfied herself by tracing the second scar, then leaned back in her chair.

"You for real?" she demanded and lifted her lip in a sneer in response.

"I look like a ghost to you?" she asked.

The child cocked her head, turned it this way and that, then jabbed Kaylin's left scar with her fingertip and dug deep. The older girl yelped and pulled back to nurse her wrist.

"What did you do that for?"

Kit snickered. "I'm makin' sure you're real."

"Real enough," Kaylin told her. "I stayed here until I left—and I left because I didn't want to become a sister or a herb-wielder. I decided there was more."

Her young companion snorted softly. "Same as Jacques," she

pointed out. "And look where that got the two of us. Him—"

She had thought the girl would say "crossed over," but Kit's face crumpled and the girl raised both hands and pressed her palms to her face.

"Hey..." She spoke softly as though to soothe a fractious pony. "Hey. Ain't no need. We's here. You an' me. We'll take that Crow-Eater down. Make your brother happy. Yeah?"

"Yeah," the girl agreed, rested her elbow on the table, and raised her hand.

Kaylin reached across the table and clasped palms with her.

"Yeah."

They grasped each other's hands, squeezed to show fidelity, and released their holds. For a moment, neither of them spoke, then Kaylin ventured a question.

"You see a body?"

Kit shook her head and pressed her lips together.

"So how's he dead?" she challenged, and her companion's eyes filled with tears. "How?" she persisted, and the younger girl placed the heels of both palms against her eyes.

"He wouldn'a left me." Kit sniffed. "He wouldn'a."

The sob that followed was heart-wrenching and Kaylin guessed the girl hadn't given way to the sadness of her brother's loss. It was like a dam had broken.

"If he was still walkin', he'da come back," the child persisted through sobs. "He wouldn'a let me face them Blackbirders alone."

She hoped the child was right and that Jacques hadn't had a better offer and taken it and left his sister to bear the punishment for his lack of return. It wasn't something she could voice, however, so she moved around the table and was about to crouch beside the girl's chair when Kit came out of it.

Kaylin opened her arms and drew the child into them. "It'll be fine," she assured her. "You will be fine."

"Promise?" The voice came out muffled and Kaylin laughed softly.

"Well, she's not Sabine, but Sister Nadiya will fight the world to keep you safe," she told the girl.

"And you?"

"I'ma gonna take the Blackbirds down. Vengeance for your brother and my crew." She stepped back and stretched her arm out to show the scars on her wrist. "You heard of blood brothers?"

The girl looked warily from Kaylin's scarred wrist to her eyes and nodded.

"Well, we're something even better," she told her. "We're scar sisters. We didn't only bleed, we survived. That is something special, and never let anyone tell you differently."

Kit's eyes welled with tears and she flung her arms around her waist and buried her face in her tunic.

Kaylin wrapped the girl in her arms and hugged her tightly, holding her as she sobbed. They were still standing together when Nadiya decided they'd been alone for long enough.

She came through the door with a tray similar to the one she'd shared with Kaylin and ignored Kit as she placed it on the table.

"I thought I told you to be kind," she grumbled as both girls stared.

"I was," the older girl protested.

"She was," the younger agreed, slid out of the hug, and settled into her seat, her eyes on the pastries and fruit on the tray.

Nadiya gave them both a tight smile and began to pour the tea, and Kaylin returned to her side of the table. She chose a pastry from the tray, took a bite out of it, and waved it at Kit.

"Sho," she said around a mouthful of meat and crust. "You in?"

The girl had helped herself to two pastries from the tray, sandwiched them together, and taken a bite out of the end. Kaylin's question caught her with a mouth so full her cheeks bulged, and all she could do was nod.

"Eat what's in your mouth first," Nadiya ordered and placed a cup of tea before each of them. "Then talk."

But, as stern as she sounded, it was easy to see she was happy.

The girls did as she'd instructed, and Kit ate the rest of her pastries and picked up two more before she spoke again.

Her voice started soft but her conviction hardened as she continued. "You know the canal…"

CHAPTER SIX

"Where you been?" Raoul demanded the second Kaylin slid through the door to their lair. "You been gone all sodding afternoon and without a word as to where."

She opened her mouth but Melis cut her off.

"That's the second afternoon in a row," the girl observed tartly. "I take it he's a very pretty boy, then?"

She put a hand on her hip as Kaylin gaped at her, her discomfort not helped by the way Isabette tried to stifle a smile. Goss had been quiet when she walked in but he made a strangled sound and started to cough.

"I had a meeting," she snapped. "Had two meetings. One today and one yesterday." She gave Raoul a defiant stare. "Not that it's any of your *sodding* business."

"It is if they were business meetings," he retorted and she glared at him.

She shifted her gaze around the room. "Are you done?" she demanded. "Because I ain't seen any supper and I know we have enough."

Melis' expression shifted from sarcasm to worry.

"Well, we didn't," she replied, "and unless you're carrying more than your cut or have a plan for more, we still don't."

Kaylin gave her an easy grin. "Go get supper," she replied. "Take Isabette with you." She jerked a thumb at Raoul. "Troll ticker here hit the money. They were business meetings and I have news."

That caught their attention and they crowded forward.

"Spill!" Isabette ordered and her sharp tones revealed annoyance at being left out of the planning.

"Nope. Food first," Kaylin told her and borrowed a phrase from Nadiya's book. "None of us think well on an empty stomach."

"Go," Goss croaked tiredly from his pallet. "There's no reasoning with her when she's like this."

Melis pivoted on her heel and headed to the door. "Yeah—and I don't want to deal with her when she's in a mood. Better we feed her before we tell her no."

"No?" Kaylin asked. "But you haven't even heard the plan."

Isabette leaned close as she went past. "You're not the only one who's unreasonable on an empty stomach. Don't take it too badly. She doesn't want to go out in the rain."

"The rain?"

"Can't you smell it? We're gonna be soaked if we don't hurry," the girl responded.

Her second in command didn't wait for her to answer but followed Melis through the sacking and into the ruined common room. Kaylin watched them go and shook her head as they disappeared. When she turned back to the room, she found herself under the scrutiny of three very alert gazes.

"What?" she asked and caught Raoul's eye.

"Spill?" he suggested and she shook her head.

"You think Melis is unreasonable? I saw the look on Isabette's face when I said I'd gone to two meetings without her."

"Me, too." Piers snickered. "You and she are gonna have a talk later as soon as she thinks we're not listening."

"I'm very sure that will never happen," she answered. "You lot are always listening when you're not meant to. No privacy."

None of them looked sorry but Raoul tapped Piers on the shoulder and jerked a thumb at the door.

"Wood," he said. "There should be some old crates out back of most places, and we'll need to fetch it before it's soaked."

"But don't get caught," Kaylin warned them. "The way some folk are, you'd think the trolls-cursed things were made of gold."

They chuckled at that and vanished swiftly through the sacking. She felt guilty at not going with them but she'd only just returned.

She stared at the empty space and shook her head. If she worried about them it was only because they were family.

Speaking of worrying, she had a much larger concern. She turned to Goss. "How you feeling?"

He swung himself slowly off the pallet, began to cough, and flipped his thumb at her.

"I'm good," he croaked when the fit had passed.

"You don't sound—" she began but stopped when he held a hand up for silence.

When she subsided, he picked his water bowl up and took several cautious sips.

"I'll be back," he told her and moved to the cellar.

Kaylin nodded and resisted the urge to accompany him. Instead, she filled the time by tidying their small living space of the few pieces of debris they hadn't already shifted. When that was done, she settled on a stone and waited.

They weren't her blood but they were her siblings.

The smell of rain grew stronger and thunder rumbled overhead, which made her wish she'd gone to fetch wood with the boys. The Rest always got colder when it rained, even if the roof still held. A gust of wind curled through the room and she looked for where it could be coming from.

Goss was sick enough as it was. He didn't need the cold and wet to make him any sicker. That thought alone made her impatient to share her plan. The sooner they got his medicine back, the better.

He, of course, was the first to return but was accompanied by

Raoul and Piers. Their cloaks were damp and their arms heavily laden with wood stacked into two crates. Her eyes widened.

"Where'd you get those?"

"Back of the Dockers," Raoul told her.

Kaylin frowned. "What? Just lying around?"

"Nah. It was waiting tied up in a bow," Piers snarked and his brother nudged him.

If it hadn't been for the nudge, she might have believed them, but the gesture gave it away. She narrowed her eyes.

"What happened?" she demanded and Raoul's shoulders slumped.

He gave Piers a hard look as he answered, "Dimmie was waiting," he admitted. "I swear, we didn't go knocking and we were quiet, but he…he came out as soon as we collected the first crate. He said you'd overpaid or something and we was to wait while he got your change."

"Only he didn't come out with any change," Piers added. "He only brought an armful of wood with Cassie right behind him. They filled the crates an' she said the attic was still open if we didn't mind a bit of dust." He frowned. "What did she mean by that?"

"We haven't discussed it yet." Isabette interrupted from the doorway, "but she mentioned it to us as well. She seemed keen for us to be somewhere warmer."

The two girls set the platter on the makeshift table and shook their cloaks out.

"I see her point," Isabette remarked sourly.

"'Bout time we got to it," Melis added.

Kaylin sighed. "I was still thinkin' on it. I didn' want to move and then have to move out again."

"Fair call," Raoul agreed.

He grabbed some of the logs he and Piers had brought in and began to feed the fire. Goss pulled up another chunk of stone and huddled close to the leaping flames.

"The attic's not the only thing we have to talk about," Kaylin began once they'd started eating.

The rain outside grew heavier and the others nodded, although they didn't say a word while they savored the river chowder Cassie had sent. There were bread rolls in a basket to go with it. They were still warm and filled the small room with the smell of baked bread.

Kaylin paused and between bites of the soft, warm bread and mouthfuls of chowder, she told them where she'd been.

"But you hate Nadiya," Goss exclaimed through a mouthful. Crumbs sprayed into the fire and he covered his mouth hastily.

"Not anymore," she told him. "It seems she might be all right, after all."

Raoul's eyebrows rose and Isabette laid her hand on Kaylin's knee briefly. She ignored them both.

As she chewed, she looked at each of her crew. "She found us a way into the Rookery."

That floored them and she enjoyed another mouthful of stew as they gaped at her. It didn't take them long to recover and the questions came thick and fast.

"But no one knows…" Melis began.

"Are you insane?" Isabette demanded.

"Honestly?" Piers sounded intrigued.

Raoul narrowed his eyes. "And what did you want to know that for?"

Kaylin gave him her sweetest smile—the one she used just before she did or said something truly evil.

"Because we're going to get our stuff back and put them out of business," she told them and suppressed a grin as their eyes widened in disbelief.

Piers turned to Raoul. "She's completely flipped it this time," the younger boy muttered.

His brother nodded but he took another spoonful of stew and gave her a thoughtful stare.

Melis looked like she was trying to decide between arguing, waiting, and laughing. Kaylin couldn't decide which reaction would be better. Isabette merely arched her eyebrows.

"Well?" she asked when no explanation was immediately forthcoming. "I take it there's a plan."

"You know the Chapel of Ghosts?" she asked.

"Seriously?" Melis demanded. "That's where they are?"

The others shushed her and their leader continued.

"Yeah, that's where they are."

"And how are we meant to get into there?" Melis asked. "Apart from the fact that it's across from the graveyard with its rear wall on the Charney Canal, Korbyn's likely to have guards and all kinds of alarms rigged on the approach."

"Ooh, listen to you being all adventurery and stuff," Piers mocked. "'Alarms rigged on the approach.' This isn't some kind of battle, you know."

"Uh. It kinda is," Raoul corrected, "but I don't think Kaylin has a frontal assault in mind."

Kaylin shook her head. "Nope." She glanced at Melis. "That canal you mentioned—it goes right up to the back of the chapel and the Blackbirds have rigged a bridge through the back door."

"The one them priests used to chuck the bodies into the canal from?" Piers asked, his eyes as wide as saucers in a face gone as pale as milk.

"That's the one," she confirmed.

They all knew the stories about the chapel. Ten years earlier, it had been dedicated to Hrogath and offered cheap burials for the dead adventurers or mercenaries whose companies were too poor or stingy to give them a proper send-off.

It turned out the so-called good priests weren't priests at all but a small adventuring band that had cleared the catacombs beneath the chapel and seen a chance to make money for little work. They'd simply thrown the bodies into the river and trusted the swift water and treacherous current to carry them out of Waypoint before they surfaced.

The scheme had lasted as long as it took for the first heavy rain to fall. The water level had risen and dumped half a dozen bodies onto the streets where the canal joined the river flowing beside the docks.

Many unhappy friends of the dead returned to have a few discussions with the "priests."

"But what about the ghosts?" Piers asked, and Isabette smiled.

"I bet the last lot of ghosts were the Blackbirds making the most of the rumors," she told him and he glowered.

"Typical," he grumbled. "That's exactly the kind of sneaky thing they'd do too."

"Yeah, but they wouldn't do it instead of other things," Melis pointed out. "They're not stupid."

"Exactly," Kaylin told them, "which is why we won't go in through the graveyard or over the bridge."

"There's another way?" Isabette asked and she gave them a smug smile.

"There's another way," she told them and they shuffled closer. "There's a hidden entrance leading to the canal."

"The Ghosts' Path," Piers whispered, referring to the stories that said the dead thrown into the river had found a way to return to the chapel and haunt it.

"Pfft. I bet that was Korbyn too," Kaylin told him. "He's old enough to have taken advantage of the situation."

"And he doesn't believe in ghosts," Melis added and ignored the curious looks they cast in her direction. She returned them, then shrugged in response. "Well, I don't think he does, anyway."

"Well, whatever it was,' Kaylin interjected, "it's not there now. What is there is the gutter that runs beside the water for the sewermen—and a way into the chapel basement from the sewer tunnel that runs beside it."

"No way," Raoul murmured and she gave him a happy nod.

"Yes, way. There's a secret passage coming off the sewer tunnel," she informed them, "and I know exactly where it is."

"Nadiya?" Goss asked, and she nodded.

She chose not to say anything about Kit yet. The fewer people who knew about the girl, the fewer chances there were that someone could be made to reveal her escape. And the child deserved to stay off Korbyn's radar, especially after what she was about to do.

Siblings or not, she deserved that safety and it didn't hurt her crew to not know.

She finished her speech. "We can get in without them suspecting a thing and take everything not nailed down on a night when they're out of the Rookery."

"I'm in." Melis' voice was hard. "We'll hurt them exactly where it means the most."

"I hate to tell you, Liss," Piers commented cheerfully, "but I don't think Kaylin's planning on anyone being there for you to cut a few nuts."

Melis curled her lip.

"I'm not talking about their balls. I'm talking about their coin purses. If we hit those good and hard, they'll be hurting for months."

"As opposed to only a few days," his brother added, and Kaylin wondered when he'd ever experienced being hit where Piers had suggested.

She didn't ask and Raoul continued.

"I'm in too. It's about time we made those troll turds hurt. Payback."

"About that," Isabette interjected. "They'll be mighty pissed when they find out and the first thing they'll do is come after us."

"Why us?" Raoul asked. "They won't know who hit them."

"Firstly, you can't know that," she informed him, "and secondly, they aren't stupid. We're the last crew they stole from so it's only logical we'd want revenge. Thirdly, we're probably the only crew with folk small enough to get through this passage." She turned to their leader. "Am I right?"

Kaylin chewed her cheek in thought but soon nodded. Isabette might be quiet but she could think three ways at once when she had to. "What did you have in mind?"

"The attic," the girl replied and hurried on before she could reject the idea. "We get Goss into the attic before we leave. That way, we'll know he's safe while we work, and we'll have somewhere to hide that no one knows about when the job's done."

"What makes you think anyone knows about here?" Piers demanded.

Isabette gave him a pitying stare. "You thinkin' they don't?" she challenged. "The only reason they haven't come after us is we haven't pulled anything off worth taking us for."

"And the place is cursed," Piers added but his expression said he knew Isabette was right.

"So?" she told him. "We don't want to give them more of a reason to believe it's cursed. Anything happens to us and that's what will happen, but I bet you anything you like nothing will happen to those who come."

She made a good point and Kaylin was about to say as much when the girl continued.

"'Sides, we pull this off, we're gonna be able to afford the attic and we'll want somewhere warmer than here when winter comes."

"Winter's ages off," Piers said scornfully. He turned pleading eyes to his brother. "I still say the ghosts were more than only stories," he stated. "Stories have to come from somewhere, don't they? And the dead do rise if you neglect 'em. How do we know the noises were all Korbyn—or if any of 'em were him?"

Raoul slid an arm over the boy's shoulders. "We don't," he admitted, "but if there were ghosts, the Blackbirds wouldn't be living there or keeping their treasure there, would they?"

"Maybe they've made a bargain with 'em," Piers suggested as Goss began to cough again.

Raoul raised his arm and placed his hands on each of his brother's shoulders. "You don't have to come if you're scared," he said kindly, "but we've got to go."

"For vengeance?" the boy muttered sulkily. "That's a stupid thing to throw your life away on."

"To get our stuff back," Raoul told him firmly. "Because we need to eat and because Goss needs his medicine."

Goss put his bowl down and waved the comment away but he was still coughing and couldn't argue. His face reddened, but that could have been as much from the fit as it was from embarrassment at being a burden.

Kaylin watched him pick his water bowl up and head to the old cistern to fill it. The boy's shoulders shook with half-smothered coughing.

"Fine," Piers grumbled. "I'm in too, but we see a ghost and we all leave, right? Worse case, we pitch Goss into the temple orchard so the priests have to help him."

That brought a round of chuckles and even a few from Goss, although the laughter set off another round of coughing. This brought Piers to his feet and he snatched the bowl from the other boy's hand and steered him to his bed.

"You need to rest," he ordered and settled him under his blankets before he held the bowl to his lips.

"Not before we get him into the attic," Kaylin told them. She gestured at the firewood. "I know we only just got the wood, but a couple of nights won't hurt us and we can come back once we know the Blackbirds are gone for good."

"We're doing it tonight?" Melis gaped at her.

"The Blackbirds are out on some business," she replied. "Nadiya has a network."

"Hmmph. Typical sister," the girl grumbled. "Nosy as pack of goblins on a meat run."

"Be that as it may, it's the best time and we're going."

Raoul sighed and waved at the wood.

"We'll carry this back when we drop our gear," he said. "There's no point wasting it."

"And it'll be one less thing to point to where we've gone," Melis added. She finished her bowl, mopped it clean with the bread, and returned it to the platter.

One by one, the others followed suit before they bundled their things into makeshift bags made by their blankets.

"We go up and get settled," Kaylin told them, "and then we leave by the roof. That way, if anyone sees us go in, Dimmie and Cass can tell them we never left."

"Are you sure the stairs wouldn't be better?" Raoul asked and studied the wet slates beyond the attic window as they prepared to leave the dry attic. Goss was already settled on the pallet behind them.

"Only if you want us found faster," Kaylin told him. "We're lucky the back stairs come off the storeroom or we'da been done before we started."

"Fine," he grumbled but he didn't look happy at the sight of the wet roof beyond "Let's get out of here before it gets any wetter."

"I'll go first, then Isabette, then you, Melis, and Piers," she whispered. "We'll cross to Elo's and go to the ground from there. It'll be hard for anyone to tell where we came from that way."

"Harder," Melis corrected. "I'm very sure the locals already know."

"It won't matter in a week or three," she told the girl and slid out the window and down the roof below.

The others followed, and only Isabette needed steadying before they turned and scurried along the guttering and up the pitch. It was hard going and Kaylin soon abandoned her plan to cross more than the Docker's roof.

"It's too wet," she told the others after she'd signaled a halt in the valley where two corners met. "We'll have to risk it."

"It's not like anyone knows where we came from to get here," Melis reminded her and she nodded.

"Let's hope our luck holds," she agreed.

The water dripped off the cowls of their hoods as they proceeded carefully to the eaves and swung over. Glances up and down the side street showed that the rain was doing them a favor.

No one had ventured past the warmth of the inn's front door. Moving quickly and quietly, the five trotted along the docks until they reached the Charney.

As a tributary to the dockside river, it wound through Waypoint from the opposite side of the city and emerged from the surrounding ring of mountains to flow through the noble's quarter before it emptied into the bigger river.

Numerous sewer outlets emptied into it, relying on the sweeping current to take the effluent far away.

Kaylin found the access stairs the sewermen used and led the others down them. There wouldn't be any work crews on a night like this, but she peered cautiously up and down the Charney to be sure.

Not that she could see anything.

There were no lanterns and without the moon overhead, it was hard to see where they had to go. Only the slight glimmer of the path and the water's ravaging darkness gave her an indication of where the path was.

The rain now fell even harder and saturated her cloak and the tunic beneath. She shivered as the wind chilled her through the soaked cloth. If they weren't careful, Goss wouldn't be the only one who needed medicine.

She forced herself to focus on the narrow walkway that edged the Charney's swirling water and led the others in a swift walk to where a narrow footbridge crossed over. As she stepped onto it, she realized the water was higher than when they'd reached the bottom of the stairs.

Then, she'd been able to see a gap beneath the footbridge and the river. Now, the water lapped the base of the bridge and small jets sprayed over the top.

"Careful," she warned as she inched onto the slippery surface.

"You don't say," Piers snarked.

A soft thump followed and Kaylin knew Raoul had the youngster in hand. The kid always got mouthy when he was scared.

Not that she could blame him. She was scared too. Besides the fact that the stories surrounding Hrogath's Chapel ranged from creepy to bloodcurdling, the canal was no place to be in a thunderstorm. They'd all grown up with stories of people who ignored the weather and had been washed away.

"Hurry," she ordered as soon as they'd reached the other side.

Already, the rush of the water had increased in volume.

"It's not far," Melis assured them and pointed upward with a short stab of her finger.

They all glanced up and caught sight of the first gravestone slanted in a crazy silhouette above them. Kaylin shivered.

"This way," she said gruffly and motioned them into the shadows.

Before any of them could demand why they'd stopped, she pointed up and forward and noted the moment when they understood the danger. A sturdy wooden bridge spanned the canal ahead. One end of it rested on the opposite bank of the canal, but the closest side vanished into the wall that rose above the canal.

The Rookery Bridge. Kaylin wondered what they called it. The Perch?

She almost laughed at the idea but suppressed her amusement quickly. The bridge might look empty but it was probably not unattended. With even one sound out of place, the guards would emerge from their shelter to investigate.

Korbyn would demand no less. He might be sadistic but he wasn't stupid.

With her watchful gaze fixed on the bridge, she led the others forward. Nothing moved on its surface and they reached the space below its footings without hearing an alarm. She exhaled a relieved breath, only to stifle a gasp when a rough voice snapped from somewhere above.

"He's got to be kidding if he thinks any of us are goin' out in this."

"Yeah," another voice sneered, "and you can tell 'im that. He says jump and I'm jumping. A bit o' rain is nowhere near as dangerous."

"The cut might not be as big for stayin' back and guardin'," a third voice added, "but I'm not gettin' soaked."

As the words reached her, Kaylin realized they were coming out of a crevice above her.

It must open into the guard room, she thought and made a note to be extra quiet. Sound could as easily travel up as well as down.

She prayed that Nadiya's information was accurate. She had no wish to enter Korbyn's lair if the man was anywhere near home.

The way is too small to follow, she reminded herself. *They don't fit through the gap.*

Keeping that thought in mind, she rose to creep quickly along the gutter and tried to keep an eye on both the walls above and the Charney rushing not far below. Her boots sloshed through the water pooling along the narrow path, the sound of her steps swallowed by the roar of the canal.

Kaylin spared a glance at the river and then wished she hadn't. The sight of the water rushing past so close made her head spin and she put a hand on the wall and forced herself to look ahead to where the sewer entrance waited, but not before she noticed the water was lapping the edges of the path.

She wracked her mind and tried to remember if Kit had mentioned any other way out. Each sewer outlet they'd passed had formed a waterfall beneath their feet as they crossed the little metal bridges the sewermen had erected to cross from one side to another.

Each waterfall had come a little closer to their feet.

It was both a relief and a shock when they reached the entrance they needed. On the one hand, the water gushed out of it with such force that it struck the bridge and foamed as it flowed over it. On the other, they didn't need to cross and the maintenance path stood a little higher than the filth rushing past it.

"Don't fall in," she instructed and pressed one hand against the wall as she inched around the corner. There was no reply and she glanced back. The others were still with her and like her, they did their best to stay away from the outflow.

"Not far now," she whispered and stopped when Isabette grasped her sleeve.

Looking back, she saw four pale and frightened faces staring at her.

"We won't be able to come back this way," Melis stated in a hoarse voice and Kaylin nodded.

"If the water gets too high, there'll be another way," she assured them, "but we won't get another chance like this."

On that, they had to agree.

"We'll be quick," Raoul interjected. "Maybe we'll be fast enough to beat the rise."

They all knew that would probably not happen, but this was all they had so they said nothing but pushed on and followed Kaylin into the pitch dark of the sewer.

I wish I had a lantern, she thought but kept it to herself. She'd memorized Kit's instructions.

"Take sixteen steps," the girl had said, "and keep your hand on the wall. There's nothing wrong with the path so you don't need a light. You'll know when you get to it. You'll feel the gap."

The gap was what she was looking for now—if looking meant feeling blindly with her fingertips. She fretted that she'd miss it and her whole body became tense with anticipation. Her ears ached with the sound of the water bouncing from the walls around her, and her lips curled with distaste as her fingers trailed through something slimy.

Moss, she told herself firmly. *Nothing floats that high.*

She hoped she was right. The thought of anything else was intolerable. Her stomach twisted and she pushed the idea away hastily. She didn't have time for that kind of squeamishness. Right now, their sole focus had to be on getting in and out unseen.

To distract herself, she fingered the satchel she'd slung across her chest, glad Nadiya had mentioned the need for them to have something to stash their ill-gotten gains in.

It wasn't overly large but anything bigger would have been too awkward to carry and the ex-mercenary sister had been explicit in her instructions as to what items would be a bigger loss.

"Jewelry, coin, and anything that looks finely made," the woman had instructed. "Of the rest, wine bottles break and anything can be dropped in the river if you have time. It's a waste but it's better out of their hands than in them."

Kaylin had to admit the sister was smarter than she'd thought and infinitely more devious than Sister Sabine had ever been. She shuddered to think of what might have happened to her if Nadiya had been as black as her prejudice had painted the sister.

A few missing orphans would have been nothing.

As that thought crossed her mind, her fingers fumbled over a long straight slit in the stone wall and she stopped abruptly.

Isabette bumped into her, and she slapped a hand around to make sure the girl didn't fall into the sewer.

"I'm okay," Isabette assured her and a moment later, added. "Are we there?"

"I think so," Kaylin told her and heard the sibilance of her voice as she relayed the news to the others. It made it hard to focus on what she had to do next, but she managed. She was sure she could feel water lapping around her feet—more water, that is—and the idea of being trapped in the sewer if the rain became heavier and the water flow higher was enough to make her struggle to recall Kit's instructions.

"The latch is at your waist height," the girl had told her. "You need to wiggle your fingers into the crack until you feel it. Push down and hold it for two breaths and the door will slide open. Go through quickly, though, 'cos it'll roll shut on its own."

"And can it be opened from the inside?" Kaylin had asked.

Kit's face had twisted with scorn. "Course. How'd you think I got out?"

Hearing that had highlighted how stupid her question had been, and Kaylin had blushed.

She blushed again as she remembered it and her fingers found the latch as she had been told.

"Hurry!" she urged, slipped into the space beyond, and moved quickly forward.

Kit hadn't been joking. The space *was* narrow. If Kaylin had been any bigger, she'd have stuck for sure. She heard Raoul grunt and remembered the boy was almost as big as she was—and still growing. It wouldn't be much longer before he wouldn't be able to go on jobs like this one.

Hopefully, he had no growth spurt while they were doing this job.

Enjoy it while you can, she thought and wondered what Raoul would do as he got older. He couldn't be a thief forever, could he?

The thought made her angry and as she pushed along the narrow corridor, the cloth of her cloak and tunic scraped the walls. If the treasure room wasn't empty, they would be in trouble. There was no way any of the Blackbirds would miss that sound.

A grating rumble as the door closed behind them made her tense, but when no one cried out in alarm, she relaxed, glad she didn't have to push to the end of the passage and then go back in to trigger the lock. She was extra glad because she didn't want to leave anyone in the sewer tunnel for long.

Not with the water rising so fast.

The passage ended sooner than expected and she twisted out of it and slid along the rough wall of what had been the temple cellar. To her relief, the room was empty of anything but the amassed plunder of Korbyn and his Blackbirds.

"Woah..." Piers' soft whisper of appreciation was cut short when Raoul reached out of the gap and slapped a hand over his mouth.

The expressions on her crew's faces reflected the boy's sentiment, however, as they looked at the neatly stacked shelves and chests and the weapons racked along the wall. It looked like this was the most secure room in the building. Remembering the roar of the water in the sewer and the feel of it lapping around her ankles, Kaylin wondered how they would get out.

It would be ironic to come this far only to be trapped in the treasure room for Korbyn to pluck yet again. This time, he probably wouldn't leave any feathers for them to fly with. *And that's only if he doesn't roast us,* she thought morosely.

She didn't let her fears show on her face. The treasure room might be secure and their escape path probably blocked, but they did have one thing working to their advantage—no one expected them to be there.

That might give them enough of the element of surprise that they'd be able to escape before they could be caught.

Sure, and pigs can fly and cows give cream and apple tarts, Kaylin scolded and reminded herself of one of Sabine's favorite sayings. *Hope is not a plan.*

Well, Sister, that might be true but it's the only plan we have. Now, show me where they hid Goss's medicine.

It turned out they hadn't hidden it at all. The medicine looked like it had been tossed carelessly onto a shelf beside a crate of wine. A scattering of mostly copper and bronze coins lay around it.

As if the medicine isn't worth any more than that, Kaylin thought angrily and, with a cursory glance toward the stairs, pushed away from the wall.

As she did, she swore she heard the scrape of a chair and the stamp of boots and froze. A glance at her team confirmed that she wasn't the only one to have heard the sound. Both Raoul and Isabette had raised their hands as though reaching out to pull her back and Piers' eyes were wide with fear as he peered over his brother's other hand.

Melis scowled, her small body tensed as if for flight, although there honestly didn't seem to be anywhere she could run. Kaylin shuffled quickly to her place against the wall, crouched, and scanned the room for a hiding place. When she didn't see one, she looked at the passage from which they'd emerged and frowned when she saw nothing but a blank expanse of wall.

Raoul caught her look and followed it and his face creased with puzzlement when he saw the wall. He took his hand from Piers's mouth and reached past the boy to touch the space where the gap should have been.

His slight gasp made them all tense but none of them looked toward the stairs to see if it had been heard. They were too busy staring at where his hand vanished into what looked like solid stone. Well, that answered the question as to why the passage had never been found.

Kaylin could only assume Kit's passage from the kitchen storeroom was hidden the same way, but that wasn't a priestly trick. Nor did it fit with any of the gods she knew of.

She tried to shrug the thought away but her mind continued to struggle to remember what she'd read of such things. This kind of magic was more arcane, wasn't it?

"The Wardens are on their way." The gruff tones drifted down from the door.

"That what you saw?" the other voice asked.

"Yup." The answer was followed by a snort. "It's pissing down but those bastards are still coming for their payment."

A chair scraped back. "We got it?"

"'Course we got it." The first voice dripped with scorn.

Kaylin began to make urgent gestures with her hand to signal the other to return to the passage. They stared at her, then heard footsteps. Raoul caught hold of Piers and shoved the boy into the exit before he ushered Melis and Isabette through. He looked at Kaylin but she pushed him toward the gap.

CHAPTER SEVEN

Kaylin glanced hastily around the room while her mind shrieked a protest at the bad timing.

Her gaze fell on Goss's medicine and she bolted across the room, running as lightly as she could. She snatched the small bottle from the shelf and as she darted to the gap, she wished she'd thought to ask for a signal as to where the hell it was exactly. She could not afford to run into the wall.

Raoul's hand appeared out of the masonry and gestured frantically.

She grinned with relief, glad the boy had thought to do it.

The footsteps stopped and as keys rattled in the door leading to the cellar, she thrust herself into where she thought the gap should be. Her shoulder caught on the corner and she bit back a cry of pain and wriggled into the darkness beyond, relieved to feel empty space before her.

When Raoul's hand caught her arm and yanked her deeper, she almost yelped with fear. The two of them were about to move farther into the passage when they heard the heavy clump of boots on the stairs. They both froze and held their breaths as they listened.

Kaylin peered toward the storeroom and slid a hand over her

mouth to remind herself to stay quiet. She wanted to crouch low to the floor but the movement would have made enough sound to draw attention. Instead, she told herself that she couldn't be seen and that from the other side, the wall looked solid.

Still, she held her breath as a heavy-set man strode across the room toward the shelf that had held Goss's medicine. He didn't seem to notice it was missing and turned instead to the crate of wine set alongside.

After a moment's deliberation, he picked up two bottles and returned to the stairs.

They were paying the Wardens off with wine?

It made her wish she knew more about it. Maybe there was more money to be made as an innkeeper than she realized. She waited until the door clunked closed behind him and gave Raoul a gentle shove.

"Time to go," she whispered.

"But...what about the loot?" he asked.

She shook her head. "It's too risky with the Wardens here. We'll have to come back another night."

"And what about Goss?" Melis' sharp tone was only to be expected.

"I snagged his medicine before the Blackbird opened the door," Kaylin told her. "He'll be fine now."

"And paying Dimmy?" Isabette asked as they all edged closer to the door leading to the sewers.

"We'll be back here before we need to," she told her. "It won't be a problem."

"Promise?" the girl pressed with doubt in her voice.

"I promise," she assured her firmly.

"You need to tell me how to open this door," Piers demanded, "'cos I don't think you can reach from back there."

Kaylin rolled her eyes and told the boy what he needed to know to get the door open.

"Gotcha," he said and shifted to do as she'd said.

The dull snick as the door unlatched was followed by the faint rasp and grind as it opened and Piers' sudden whimper of fear. Before any of them could ask what the problem was, several shrill squeaks echoed down the tunnel. They were accompanied by a sudden rush of water and the brush of fur and press of bodies around their legs.

"Don't go out there," Raoul whispered, harshly. "Stay where you are! All of you."

Kaylin felt his body shift as he turned toward her. "The door shuts on its own, right?"

"Yes."

"Good. We're gonna need another way out."

She would have challenged the assumption but he was right. More rats slid past her feet, headed toward the drier ground in the treasure room or maybe even the stairs beyond, and the water swirled past her ankles.

"Stay in the passage," she ordered and was answered by Melis' fierce hiss of frustration.

"How will we get out then?"

"There's another passage," she assured her, "but it's invisible like this one."

"Oh, yeah?" the girl whispered. "And where does that one lead? Right into the Charney?"

"No, the kitchen storeroom."

"Pfft. Because that's so much better," Melis snarked.

"It's better than being washed into the Charney and drowned in shit," she reminded her as the door ground shut again.

There was a high-pitched squeal, followed by the crunch of bone, no doubt a rat that didn't quite make it. Kaylin forced herself to stay still until no more furry bodies forced themselves past her legs. The last thing any of them needed was a rat bite—especially since they wouldn't be able to take as much of Korbyn's wealth as they needed to.

Could they hurl it into the sewer? As tempting as that thought was, it was no longer an option. Firstly, the rats made opening the door too dangerous and secondly, the water was rising too fast. If they opened the door, the water would simply come in and take what it wanted—them included.

She edged into the treasure room, noticed how the rats had fled to the corners farthest from the light, and wished she could do the same. Voices drifted down from the guards' room, accompanied by the clank of mugs.

Kaylin wrinkled her nose. Sister Sabine would have had something to say about good wine being drunk by the mugful. She wondered how Nadiya felt about such things. Not that it mattered.

With one eye fixed on the rats, she signaled Raoul and the others over to the shelves and crept to the stairs. The door at the top was still closed, but the rats had made no effort to leave yet.

She reached the landing and crouched behind the door. The voices were still muffled, but they were audible.

"So Shacklemund's," stated the rough voice of the one who'd sent the other to fetch the payment.

Kaylin quietly dubbed him Chief.

"What about it?" That voice was new and she frowned. A River Warden?

With a shrug, she decided the owner of that voice was River Rat One. Glass rang against metal, and she assumed they were topping their mugs up. While she waited for the conversation to resume, she considered what she'd heard.

Shacklemund's... Shacklemund's... It took her a moment to remember where she'd heard the word before and when she did, she frowned. It was a safety deposit house, somewhere adventurers and mercenaries heading into the Doom left their gear and any wealth they didn't want to take with them.

Its full name was... Kaylin racked her brains. Shacklemund's... Shacklemund's Usury and Strongboxes. That was it. They did loans too. She rested her ear against the door and waited for the conversation to resume.

"What about it?" a new voice asked.

A second Warden? she wondered and mentally dubbed him River Rat Two.

"The boss has something in mind." That one she recognized. It belonged to the man who'd come down the stairs for the wine.

Wine Getter, she decided. She covered the ear not pressed against the door and tried to filter the conversation from the background storm.

Wood creaked as though someone large and heavy shifted in a chair not made for their weight.

"What kind of something?" Rat Two asked.

"Nothing too flashy," Chief replied, "but we were thinking not many of them what use Shacklemund's come back to get what they leave behind."

"Doesn't matter," Rat One told them. "Shacklemund's keeps it safe until the owner returns."

"Or a verified heir."

Someone snorted, then Chief spoke. "It's hard to verify an heir when no one knows they are dead."

"There are ways," Rat One replied. "Priests of Geredda."

Kaylin folded her arms over her chest and rubbed her biceps with her hands. The goddess of death was not a name to be invoked lightly. It seemed the Wardens thought so too.

"Not quite the folk Shacklemund's has been known to deal with," Rat Two replied hastily.

"Not yet," Chief responded darkly, but the Wardens brushed that away.

"This job," Rat One inquired, "what did your boss have in mind?"

"He wants to clear Shacklemund's a little space by removing what belongs to those he knows aren't coming back."

"And he could guarantee that, could he?" Rat Two sneered.

A muffled meaty thump and a scrape of boots followed.

"He could," Chief assured them.

"We have a list," Wine Getter added, and Kaylin wondered if that information had been meant to come out. "Most of what he wants wouldn't be missed."

"Most?" Rat One wasn't slow to detect the alteration.

"Most," Chief assured him. "There are one or two items he needs that might be missed, but only if their owners return from the journey they're currently on."

"And I take it that return's not guaranteed?" Rat One asked.

“Said the boss had a plan for Shacklemund’s,” Chief replied. “What he wants from you is information.”

“And?” Rat Two pressed.

“Compensation depends on quality,” Chief told the Warden. “Now...”

The shelves below Kaylin rattled and the voices fell silent.

“What was that?” Rat Two asked and she tensed.

She glanced at where the crew was working and saw Raoul lowering Piers to the floor. It looked like he’d caught his brother, who must have fallen. Both boys returned her gaze and looked worried, and Isabette and Melis had paused in mid-grab.

Kaylin focused on the noise she could hear coming from behind the door.

“Rats,” Chief said after a moment’s hesitation. “The rain must be washing ’em out of their nests.”

A brief silence followed and the conversation continued.

“What kind of information?” Rat Two asked.

“The usual,” Chief replied. “Guard times, watches, anything special you might discover guarding the entrances and exits. You know the drill.”

The way he said it, this wasn’t the first time they’d asked the guards for information on somewhere they wanted to rob. Kaylin wondered who and how many other establishments had found themselves the victims of a theft whose success they couldn’t explain.

Shacklemund’s, though, was a bold choice. And strong boxes belonging to someone who no longer needed their contents? That certainly had merit.

An idea sparked and started to form, but she set it to one side and slipped down the stairs to help clear more of the Blackbirds’ loot from their shelves. As she reached the bottom, another nervous query reached her.

“What was that?”

This time, neither she nor her crew had made a sound.

“I told you. It’s rats,” Chief snapped. “Look at the river. They’re only tryin’ to get out of its way.”

"Ghosts more like," Rat One replied and slurred his words slightly.

That brought a chuckle from Wine Getter. "The only ghosts here are us. All the others been laid to rest." He paused. "You okay? You look like you seen one."

Chief was more pragmatic. "Not getting' cold feet, are you?"

"No." The belligerent denial came from Rat One.

Rat Two was more assuring. "We merely want to make sure no one overhears the plan."

Wine Getter snorted. "The only ones close enough to hear anything are the rats, and they're more worried about stayin' dry than anything we might plan to do."

Kaylin looked around the cellar and noted the rodents crowded into the corners and the bulging bags and pockets. She signaled the others to approach and drew them into a huddle.

"We won't go out through the kitchens," she told them. "We'll use the stairs and the bridge. It's the quickest way."

Raoul opened his mouth to argue and she pressed a finger over his lips. She patted her still-empty satchel. "I'll fill this and then I need your help to get the rats moving. Those guys are scared of ghosts and know the rats are around. We'll use both to help us get past them."

"How will that work?" he asked. "You going to pretend to be a ghost and then what? They'll never fall for that."

Kaylin gave him her most evil smile. "They'll fall for it long enough for the rats to arrive."

"Pfft, as if they'll be afraid of a horde of rats—"

"Full well, they will." Melis surprised them by interrupting. "Many grown men are scared of rats. Do you know what a bite from one of them can do?"

"No..." Raoul stared at her as if she'd grown a second head.

"Well, I do and so do most of those who live near 'em. Trust me. They'll be scared."

He gave Kaylin a look of disbelief. "You honestly think this will work?"

Isabette thumped him on the shoulder. "It's the best plan I've heard all night—unless you want to try to get out the way we came in."

He shook his head. "No, but what about the kitchens?"

"I don't know how to get out of the kitchens or how many Blackbirds we'll meet if we try," Kaylin admitted. "This way, we only have to get past the four men on the gate and over the bridge."

That made sense to the boy. He glanced at the creatures and his face paled. "I guess we could simply try pokin' em."

"Lanterns," Melis said matter of factly. "Rats don't like fire. They might attack us if we try shifting 'em with sticks or blades, but they'll move away from the lanterns."

Kaylin nodded. "You're right on that. I've got to—"

Isabette leaned closer and pulled the empty satchel's strap over their leader's head. "And me and Piers will fill this. You haven't had time to look at what's here and we have. We know where the best pickin's are."

She opened her mouth to protest, then closed it again.

"You should fill your pockets, though," Piers suggested.

"I'll keep watch," Raoul said, "then come down and help with the rats."

With their roles decided, the five of them locked gazes briefly and hurried to their tasks. It didn't take Kaylin long to fill her pockets with enough coin and gems to make them bulge, or for Isabette and Piers to load the satchel and hand it to her.

In the meantime, Melis had walked around the room, unhooked the four lanterns hanging on the walls, and placed them in the center of the storeroom before she took her place beside Raoul on the stairs.

Seeing her, Kaylin realized she'd lost track of the conversation. She hoped Raoul had been listening because whatever the Blackbirds planned to do at Shacklemund's, she wanted to be there before them. Their plan couldn't work if the loot had already been taken and there was no way she wanted them to be able to replenish what she and the crew now risked their lives to take.

Not that it seemed to have made much of a dent. If the sewers hadn't been so flooded, she'd have told the crew to help her to dump the rest into the river, but they couldn't risk opening the door. Who knew how far the waters had risen now?

She lifted one of the lanterns and hefted it to catch Raoul and Melis's attention.

"Are we ready?" she asked when they'd joined her.

"I still don't know how you'll get them to go upstairs," Raoul grumbled.

"Well, first, I'm going to open the door," she told him. "Then, I'm gonna jump down here and chase the closest group of these little blighters up the stairs. I need you three to stop them from going to the other corners. You got it?"

They nodded but their faces revealed the doubt none of them voiced.

Kaylin didn't wait for any of them to decide to argue but hurried quietly up the stairs, turned the handle, and pulled it wide open before she bounded off the stairs and tumbled to land gracefully on the floor.

She pivoted and ran toward the closest huddle of rats as she swung a lantern in front of her. The closest ones snarled at her and shied away from the flame to scurry farther into the corner.

With a haunting scream, she swung the lantern again. She struck one of them and lamp oil splashed and the light flickered. The rodent squeaked in alarm and bolted out of the corner, which panicked those around it. It ran halfway across the cellar but was confronted by Raoul's lantern.

The creature shied away and changed direction to scamper toward the stairs, the only path not blocked by humans. At the same time, she shrieked again in the best imitation of a banshee she could.

From overhead, the sound of furniture toppling reached her, along with a shout of alarm.

"Haunted! I told you."

She didn't wait to hear more but hurried toward the next corner of rats. With the panicked rodents now streaming up the stairs, she assumed it wouldn't take much to convince the others to follow. When they saw what she was doing, Melis, Raoul, and Piers followed her example.

Faced with fire and seeing a way to higher ground, the rats fled.

They swarmed up the stairs and erupted into the corridor beyond like a furry river.

"Rats!" The cry held enough shock and terror to convince everyone that the plan would work.

Kaylin didn't hesitate. "Now!" she ordered and the five of them raced up the stairs after the rodents.

The corridor was empty but sounds of chaos came from every door opening onto it.

"Rats!" The violent explanation preceded the clatter of pots and pans from what could only be the kitchen. Outraged squeaks followed.

"This way!" she instructed, turned away from it, and ran the short distance between the treasure room and the guardhouse.

The four men inside were incoherent with fear, their gazes fixed on the creatures that massed around them. They swung their swords at the vermin and shouted in wordless panic. One leapt onto the table and kicked and swiped at anything that tried to follow—and increasingly alarming endeavor as the rats had noticed the remains of the men's late-night supper.

The two Wardens had backed against the wall and danced frantically as the panicked rodents tried to claw up their legs. The roar of the river made the scene even more chaotic, but Kaylin gestured at the open door and the bridge beyond.

"Go!" she shouted. "Go! Go! Go!"

The crew sprinted to the door, but their movement drew the attention of the Blackbird guards and the Wardens.

"What are you doin' here?" Chief roared.

She recognized the voice but didn't stop to answer as she pushed Melis and Isabette ahead of her. "Go!"

The man stepped toward her, Raoul, and Piers and kicked at the rats as he moved. Piers shouted in fright as a particularly large rat shrieked at him. His hasty retreat brought him in grabbing range of the Blackbird.

"No!" Raoul shouted and darted forward to shove the man away from his brother.

Caught by surprise, the Blackbird fell and landed heavily in a squirming knot of rodents. Raoul grabbed Piers and dragged him toward the door and the man screamed and thrashed as he tried to regain his feet.

The indignant creatures bit and scratched him in return.

Kaylin gave them a horrified look and bolted after the boy, almost glad of the rain. She was surprised when she met him on his way back in with the two girls hot on his heels.

"Korbyn!" They gasped and bolted past her, and it took only one glance into the rain-slashed night to understand what they meant.

Coming over the bridge and emerging from the rain like too-solid ghosts, Astor Korbyn and his squad of Blackbirds were returning to their roost. She turned on her heel and ran, trying to remember where the chapel stood in the graveyard.

"Get them!" he roared after her as she raced through what had been the chapel itself.

She fled through the open space, glad to discover the number of rats grew less and her passage was unimpeded. The same could not be said for Korbyn and his Blackbirds, however.

Outraged squeaks and cries of alarm and horror rose behind her as the thieves reached the guard chamber with its seething mass of vermin.

"I'll have their blood!" The leader's threat rolled after them, accompanied by the sound of sword strikes and more high-pitched chitters. "What were you doing up here?"

Kaylin reached the other side of the chapel and bolted into the rain as she heard the first heavy steps racing after her. This time, she was grateful for the weather. It would help her and her friends hide and maybe they'd reach the graveyard's edge without any of them being caught.

She pushed aside all thought of the countless traps and tricks Korbyn might have laid on this side of the Rookery, turned sharply out of the chapel's door, and sprinted into the nearest avenue of broken crypts and headstones.

This was where she needed to be stealthy rather than fast because movement would draw the eye more than another shadow among the stones. She only hoped the others remembered it. The last thing she wanted was to have to tell Goss that Korbyn had one of his friends.

The boy blamed himself enough as it was.

"Do you see them?"

"No. They must have gone to ground."

Those voices sounded too close and she peered cautiously toward the door. A dozen Blackbirds stood on the chapel portico. One had brought a lantern that he now shone into the dark, the fancy kind enclosed on three sides with mirrors inside it to focus its light into a strong beam.

Kaylin ducked as the beam swung in her direction. She pulled herself tightly against the gravestone she'd chosen as her first hiding place, scrunched into as small a ball as possible, and kept her face down and hidden in her cowl as the light passed.

"See anything?"

"No. We're gonna hafta go out in it."

"We know where they lair?"

"We can ask come morning but the boss wants 'em tonight."

Grumbles greeted that remark but none of them argued. Kaylin peered out from behind her gravestone long enough to see them moving down the steps before she ran toward one of the ramshackle crypts. When no one called out behind her, she paused briefly to remember where the nearest street was and chose her next piece of cover.

Twice more, the lantern stabbed through the darkness and twice more, she froze to become one with the shadows as the light illuminated empty paths through the storm.

Thunder boomed overhead and the rain continued.

At one point, she rose carefully out of a crouch and was looking toward another crypt when she heard a boot scrape over stone. She dropped instinctively into the shadows and waited for the inevitable shout of discovery, but only the soft crunch of boots reached her.

It grew louder as she huddled, miserable, wet, and shivering, in the shadow of the crypt. The footsteps stopped, then moved up the crypt stairs as though their owner peered inside. Kaylin held her breath and waited.

"We could stop and wait it out in here," a gruff voice suggested.

"I'll pretend you didn't say that," another responded. "The sooner we finish this row and get back, the better."

The footsteps moved reluctantly down the stairs and onto the path, and she curled into a ball and kept her head down as they moved past.

"You know he'll only send us out again."

"Even he will work out they're gone and he's better off hunting them in daylight."

"They won't be out in daylight. They're thieves like us."

"They're kids and bound to make a mistake sooner or later."

Kaylin pursed her lips. *It's nice to be underestimated,* she thought but didn't honestly appreciate the fact. *Kids, are we?*

It was all she could do to not leap out from behind the crypt and try to stab one of them.

The operative word being try.

She couldn't afford that kind of pride. It made more sense to hope the Blackbirds would continue to underestimate them and that her friends were much closer to the edge of the graveyard and escape than she was.

As soon as the men had moved far enough to become indistinct figures in the rain, she darted across the path behind them, slid into the cover of another crypt, and waited to see if she'd been noticed. The footsteps didn't falter and she risked peering after them.

Neither man looked back and the lantern shone its revealing light ahead of them. Kaylin used the light to see if she could tell how close she was to the outer wall. She watched it march over headstones and grave mounds, reflected from crypt walls and fallen blocks, but didn't see what she was looking for.

As the two Blackbirds moved farther from her position, she continued her journey away from the chapel. If she kept going in the one direction, she'd eventually reach the perimeter. Whether she'd get there without being caught was another matter.

With another glance in the direction the men had gone and a hasty scan of the area around her, she chose another point of shelter and moved quickly toward it. While she saw nothing through the rain, that didn't mean the graveyard was empty.

She scurried forward, reached the rear wall of another crypt, and scuttled into the shadows. As she turned so she could scan the graveyard for more of Korbyn's crew, she reversed carefully. Her foot struck something soft and a muffled "oof" sounded from near her ankles.

Before she could move away, a hand lashed out and wrapped around her leg. She bit back a scream, shook her leg loose, and twisted as she drew her belt knife and focused on the shadows.

"Kaylin?" Raoul's quiet tones made her breathe a sigh of relief.

She dropped into the shadows. "Where are the others?"

"Right here," Melis snapped. "You're the only one we're waiting for."

"Uh-huh, and I thought I told you to get out of here."

"We couldn't exactly leave you behind." Piers's whisper confirmed the boy as the lump she'd run into.

"We need to go," Isabette interjected urgently. "They're coming."

As if to confirm her words, lamplight slashed through the dark.

"This way," Raoul directed. "I'm sure I saw the gates."

"But won't they be waiting?"

"Most of them are search—"

"This way!" the cry made them all peer around in search of its source. "I heard 'em."

"Go. Raoul, you know where the gates are so you lead," Kaylin instructed. "Piers, you go with him. Melis, you and Isabette go next."

"What about you?" Isabette asked.

"I'll be right behind you."

"Uh-huh. Like the last time?"

"I promise. Now, go!"

Boots crunched closer.

"Are you sure?"

Kaylin peered toward the source, barely able to make out the silhouette of a man who moved cautiously through the rain.

"I tell you, I heard 'em." He sounded like he was on the other side of the crypt.

She tapped Raoul on the shoulder and signaled him to go. He reached behind him and caught his younger brother's arm.

"With me," he whispered hoarsely as Isabette and Melis paired up.

The two boys raced to the next stone and then a crypt, and the girls followed. Kaylin stayed long enough for them to get clear and bounded after them to settle in the shadows beside them.

"How much farther?" she asked.

"We're almost there," Raoul told her. "Only—"

He fell into silence as bootsteps splashed through the mud—several bootsteps coming at a steady jog. When they'd faded, he peered around the edge of the crypt behind which they huddled. He spent several heartbeats squinting through the rain, then looked at them.

"They're heading to the gate," he whispered.

"And this time, we won't have rats to help us distract them," Melis commented, her tone worried.

"Maybe there's a gap along the fence," Isabette suggested and added, "It's not like they're taking much care of the place, is it?"

She had a point.

"How many were there?" Kaylin asked.

"A half-dozen," Raoul replied. "I don't think Korbyn's very happy with us."

"You think he knows who we are?" Melis asked.

"I think it's a good thing we moved our doss," he replied, "and I don't think we're gonna want to go too far from it for a few days either."

More footsteps splashed past and they fell silent.

Kaylin indicated for them to move farther from the gate and they rose and began to thread carefully between gravestones and crypts. They'd gone a dozen paces when a shout went up from behind them.

"There! I swear it."

"You've been seeing things all night," someone retorted.

"This time, I know I saw them—skulking among the gravestones like a pack of ghouls."

"You'd better hope not," someone answered roughly. "Ghouls is the last thing we need right now."

"That way, I tell you."

Isabette and Kaylin exchanged glances and they all looked toward the gate. Their mistake was obvious the second they turned their heads. The crypts gave way to what had once been neatly laid out rows of graves, which provided a clear line of sight between where they'd strayed and the clustered forms at the gate.

On the other hand, they could now see the low wall surrounding the graveyard and the pitted, rut-filled track that ran the length of its inner circumference.

"Run!" Kaylin shouted as a beam of lamplight speared through the darkness.

They'd barely begun to move when Raoul stepped into its path and dove quickly behind a stone. His attempt to avoid it was too late. The damage had already been done.

"There!"

Kaylin raised her head in time to see the cluster break apart and several forms move toward them.

"Run!" she repeated, lunged forward, and grasped the boy by the arm. "Come on! They've seen you."

Raoul grabbed Piers and shoved him forward. "Find us a gap!" he ordered. "Hurry!"

The younger boy scrambled to his feet, dodged around headstones, and splashed through puddles where the ground had subsided over coffins. Melis dashed after him.

"I'll help."

"Iz, go with them," Kaylin ordered and hauled Raoul up. "Come! On!"

He glanced at where the Blackbirds had started down the perimeter track, then at Kaylin and staggered after her. Ahead of them, Piers ran diagonally over the grave beds. The boy had almost reached the road when he uttered a sharp exclamation of surprise and vanished into the ground.

"Piers!" Melis shouted and flung herself toward him as he threw his hands up over his head.

Isabette dove after her and Kaylin and Raoul changed direction to reach them. They arrived as Melis and Isabette hauled Piers, choking and spluttering, out of a water-filled hole. The boy thrashed and gasped and what had happened was very evident.

Not all the graves were full—or old—and water had filled one that had been freshly dug. She wondered who it could be for and then decided she didn't want to know.

Leaving Melis and Isabette to hand the boy to his brother, she raced to the wall.

Her appearance on the clear ground of the track raised shouts from the direction of their pursuers, so she ran faster. The wall had once been solid but now, stones had broken free to litter the ground around it and water had carved gullies at its foot,

Kaylin raced along its edge until she found a gap—or almost a gap. She glanced back and saw the Blackbirds' lanterns bobbing closer. Ignoring them, she bolted toward her friends and waved frantically to beckon them.

Isabette saw her and changed direction to meet her. The others followed and Kaylin stopped. She'd turned and was about to return to the gap when Isabette uttered a yelp of pain and fell. Raoul pushed Piers toward Melis and stopped and the Blackbirds divided into two groups.

Half of them continued down the road and increased speed despite the uneven ground. The other half diverted from the track toward where Raoul tried to drag Isabette to her feet. Kaylin ran to meet the two younger members of the crew and directed them to the gap before she hurried to see what had happened to Isabette.

She arrived in time to hear Raoul pleading.

"Get up, Iz. Get up. You don't want to be caught by the likes of these."

As she skidded to a halt beside them, the boy dragged Isabette's arm over his shoulder.

"She tripped," he reported. "Was so busy lookin' at you she hit the headstone and—"

Kaylin didn't wait for him to finish. She noted the fallen headstone and way Isabette had fallen and guessed the rest. With no time to waste, she dragged the girl's other arm over her shoulders.

"This way," she ordered and didn't dare to look back. Already, flashes of lantern light illuminated the blocks around them and she didn't want to know how close Korbyn's people were to catching them.

Isabette groaned.

"Wake up, Iz," she ordered. "We need you to run."

"Stop right there!" The command rang out not twenty paces away but none of them obeyed.

If anything, they ran faster when the girl came to her senses enough to start moving on her own. Melis and Piers were waiting for them on the other side of the gap and Kaylin shoved Isabette through and pushed Raoul after.

"I'll catch you up," she promised and pivoted toward their pursuers.

"Are you crazy?" he demanded.

"No, but I need to know you're through."

As she spoke, Raoul caught her arm, pushed through the break in the wall, and dragged her after him.

"Thank me later!" he shouted as rough hands tried to catch her tunic.

Her satchel scraped against the wall and she tugged it to her as she came out of the gap like a cork out of a bottle.

"Don't stop!" Melis ordered and led them into a nearby alley, although that was too generous a name for it. The space between the warehouse and the shop beside it was barely wide enough for Raoul and Kaylin to fit but they didn't stop.

If they found it this tight a squeeze, the Blackbirds would find it impossible. Kaylin worried that the thieves would move around the building in time to meet them on the other side, but that wasn't to be.

Melis stopped a third of the way along and nudged two planks aside to lead them into a storeroom and then into a kitchen and up a flight of stairs.

"We can't make it across the roofs," Kaylin protested after one look at Isabette's pale face and rapidly purpling forehead.

"We aren't takin' the roofs," Melis retorted and she didn't stop until they reached the attic space.

Kaylin said nothing as she and the others followed the girl through a series of attics where solid timber walls didn't exist and the sound of the rain drowned out the quiet squelch of their footsteps.

"You know someone could follow us for miles," Piers observed and glanced at the trail they'd left.

"They hafta know we're up here first," Melis answered defiantly and continued. "Last one, and then we're gonna need ta be real quiet. Shandy Croker don't like visitors coming unannounced."

"Shandy?" Kaylin hissed in protest. "You don't mean—"

"Shutup—and yes, I do. Ain't no way Korbyn's men are goin' to be disturbin' the Witch of Waypoint, is they?"

"How do you even know—" Kaylin started but the other girl shook her head and held a finger over her lips to demand quiet.

She pointed to the floor. "We need to be real quiet," she reiterated as she stretched toward the trapdoor at her feet. "You got me?"

They all nodded. Kaylin weighed the chances of getting caught by the witch with what might have happened if they'd been caught by the Blackbirds and still found it a better bet.

Piers had his doubts.

"She doesn't eat children, does she?" he asked after he dropped into Raoul's arms.

He'd been the last—and none of them knew how they would close the trapdoor after them to hide the fact that they'd been there. Raoul clapped a hand over his mouth as lamplight flared yellow.

The voice that followed made Kaylin gasp.

A gruff comment shattered the silence. "Not if they pay a toll."

Kaylin pivoted and swept an arm out to push Melis and Isabette behind her. She took one look at the solidly built figure before her and fumbled in her pockets to withdraw three of the gems. With a deep breath, she dared to look into the witch's eyes.

"For your trouble, mistress," she said and held them out. "We…we didn't mean to wake you."

"I'll bet you didn't," the witch replied and scooped the gems from her palm.

She held them up, turned back, and held her hand out.

"Two more," she ordered. "One for each life I'll spare, and then a third for the fact that I'll forget I ever saw you pass."

The girl gulped and dug three more gems out.

After another brief examination, the witch nodded briefly and tucked her payment into a pocket in her skirts.

"I'll unlock the side gate for you," she said. "There's an alley opposite. It should take you right to the docks."

Kaylin's jaw dropped but she closed her mouth quickly. The woman gave her a knowing smile and beckoned for them to follow. Still a little stunned, the girl cast a glance at the others and was relieved to see they were as surprised as she was.

None of them said a word as the witch ushered them out into the rain and pointed to the alley.

"Safe travels, little ones."

Perhaps it was simply relief, but Kaylin thought it sounded like there was a hint of caring in the old witch's words.

"As if we had a journey of any kind ahead of us!" Piers exclaimed. "And she never said she didn't eat children, only that she wouldn't eat them if they paid a toll."

Goss listened to them and smiled as they shared the adventure again. He had begun to look much better. The color had returned to his cheeks and the coughing fits came less often. The medicine, warmth, and extra food were making a difference.

"Not that it matters," Isabette told Piers and she scowled at Melis, "but we will never take that way again."

"Never say never," the other girl told them darkly. "I said that once and look what happened."

That sobered them, so Kaylin rifled in their joint stash, pulled out several oranges, and tossed one to each of them.

"Remember to carry some kind of payment on you," she instructed. "It might have been gems this time but I think she'd accept a reasonable cut of whatever you were carrying as long as you were polite."

"Polite?" Raoul scoffed. "You weren't only polite. You was scared shitless!"

"Uh-uh." Piers came to her rescue. "She stepped out in front of all of us and even pushed Melis behind her."

"I was scared, though," Kaylin admitted. "I honestly didn't know if she'd take what I offered."

"Are you kidding?" Raoul demanded. "Those were good gems."

"But who says gems are of value to a witch?" she retorted and he fell silent.

"You mean…they might not be?" he asked.

"Who knows?" She shrugged. "Don't witches deal in potions and ointments and salves and such?"

"That's healers and wizards," Melis corrected, "but that's what Shandy sells in her store."

"So she's a healer?" Piers asked and the girl shrugged.

"Who knows. All I know is she must have been in a real good mood or we'da all been much sorrier for waking her."

"She didn't look like she'd been sleeping to me," Piers noted and they all looked at him.

Now that she thought about it, Kaylin realized the boy had a point. Shandy had been fully clothed and her booted feet had rapped the floor as she'd led them out. She held her hands up.

"I don't want to know," she told them. "We're lucky Melis recognized a way out, is all, and that it ended as well as it did."

"Sister Nadiya is happy," Isabette noted quietly. "She said to thank you for the donation and to let you know she would use it to make sure the younger ones had what they needed and the older ones had 'more choices.' Whatever that means."

Kaylin blushed and recalled why she'd left the orphanage—and some of the things she'd said on the way out.

"I know what it means," she replied, "and I'm glad she's taken that path."

"You going to explain?" Melis asked and tilted her head.

She smiled. "Eat your orange."

The girl smirked, finished peeling the fruit, and dropped the peels carefully into a small wooden bowl sent up by Cassie for that purpose. They were still in the attic—it was warmer for one thing and also more secure, simply from the point that no one knew they were there.

Cassie and Dimitry made sure of that.

"You want to know what else I heard?" Isabette told them. "Nadiya said most of those who were with the Blackbirds came back—even Jacques."

"Really?" Kaylin's heart lifted and she tried to play down how much the news meant to her.

Isabette gave her a small smile that said she saw right through the act.

"Yup. It seems Korbyn told him his sister would be killed if he didn't get back on time, so when he was jumped by a rival gang and stuffed into a Warden cell, he was beside himself. When he got out, he heard she'd disappeared and went into hiding. He only came out when he heard the others had gone back to the orphanage."

She smiled.

"The sister said he was surprised to find Kit safe and sound and the two of them are staying there to get their adult training. She also said to tell you before that happened, a carriage visited the Rookery and took Korbyn away for a while."

Her eyes grew round and in hushed tones, she added, "While he was gone, the Wardens came and raided the place. They took everything that weren't nailed down and arrested anyone they could catch."

"No… That's some serious double-cross," Raoul muttered and Isabette nodded.

"When Korbyn got back," she continued, "he went into his office and hasn't been seen since."

"Not just that," Raoul added from the gossip he'd heard, "he's lost several men to the gallows. It seems they were caught doing one thing or another and the Wardens wouldn't give 'em back."

"Do they ever?" Kaylin asked and he stared solemnly at her.

"They do if you have enough coin."

"And Korbyn doesn't have enough coin," Kaylin said with satisfaction. To be truthful, the Wardens must have asked for a large amount. They had taken a fair amount of coin from the treasury, but she couldn't believe they had done enough damage if Korbyn was willing to trade it for his men.

She guessed there was always a price the man was not willing to pay.

"No," Isabette agreed. "I wonder why that would be."

They all laughed at that.

"Know what?" Piers said, having finished his orange. "I'm still hungry."

"Sure, you are," Melis teased him. "Let me guess—you think we've still got some of Amri's hard candy stashed somewhere."

He regarded her with hopeful eyes. "Well, we still do, don't we?"

They all looked at Kaylin and she sighed, went to the box, and pulled out the last six sticks of Amri's dragon-claw candy.

"This is the last of it," she told them and they moaned with disappointment.

"Are you sure?" Melis asked and looked around. "I could have sworn we had more."

She chuckled. "We did have more—three days ago."

Isabette sighed. "Well, then. I guess it was good while it lasted."

"Yup." Melis sighed, bit the end off her stick, and pulled it into her mouth so she could take her time with it.

Kaylin wished she could do the same, but the truth was it was hard to deal with the candy and talk and she had decided it was time to see if the others were on board with what she had planned next.

"So," she began, tried to sound casual, and failed.

That immediately drew their attention.

"So...what?" Melis asked around a mouthful of candy.

She blushed. The idea had sounded good in her head but now that she was about to say it out loud, she wasn't so sure. Still, it would haunt her if she didn't try it and there was only one way to find out what the others thought.

Determined to voice it, she took a deep breath.

"So, with the Blackbirds stony-broke and crippled, there's a void in the Riverside," she pointed out.

Isabette's face took on a wary look. "And?"

"And I'm thinking we could fill it with something better," she told them. Immediate denial formed on their faces, only to be smoothed into wary curiosity.

"What kind of something better?" Melis asked warily.

"One that can look after the community instead of preying on it," Kaylin told them. "One that protects people instead of hurting them."

"But isn't that what the River Wardens do?" Piers asked and Raoul shook his head.

"No," he told his brother, "Come on, Piers. I thought I taught you better than that. You know the only people the River Wardens look out for is the River Wardens."

"They didn't used to," he grumbled, and Raoul wrapped his arm around the boy's skinny shoulders.

"I miss him too," he said.

"And mam," Piers murmured, and his brother tightened his arm and his face hardened as he pushed the sadness away.

"I like it," Goss pronounced quietly.

He was seated close to the kitchen chimney, enjoying the warmth coming from it.

Kaylin threw him a grateful glance and looked around at the others.

"So, are you in?" she asked and after a slow exchange of glances, they shrugged and nodded.

"I take it you have a plan," Melis prodded and she blushed.

"Now that you mention it," she replied, "I might have one."

"And the plan is…" Isabette probed and started to sound a little impatient.

"Perfect," Kaylin told her. "It's perfect. There's good money to be made and not much chance of getting found out."

"It sounds too good to be true," Raoul mocked, but Goss shuffled forward to sit in the circle and watched her intently.

She leaned forward and the others crowded around her.

"Have you ever heard of Shacklemund's Usury and Strongboxes?" she asked.

"I've heard of it," Melis admitted. "It's the place where adventurers and mercenaries stash their stuff while they go into the Doom to get more. Your plan had better be perfect because if they catch us, they'll make the Blackbirds look like the nicest of nursemaids."

"It happens to be perfect," Kaylin explained, "because we won't take anything from the living so no one will know it's gone."

"We won't?" Isabette sounded confused. "Not that it matters, though, because we'll still be taking stuff that doesn't belong to us and the Wardens still think of that as stealing, so if we get caught…"

She didn't have to finish that sentence. They all knew what the Wardens did to thieves.

"Pfft! Who cares what the Wardens think?" Kaylin asked. "Besides, it's not stealing when you think about it, because the owners are dead. They will never come back for it and their relatives don't even know they're gone."

"But what if they do come back?" Piers asked nervously.

"They won't," she assured him. "And why should all that money go to waste sitting in some boxes if no one will ever come for it?"

"But how do you know?"

"Because I did some listening." Kaylin waggled her eyebrows. They looked at her with no smirks. *So much for theatrics.* "Shacklemund's stores things in order, which means the oldest boxes either belong to the most famous adventurers or to the dead ones. Those are the ones we'll get into."

"It makes sense," Goss agreed, "but how do we get into them? Shacklemund's has a reputation for being able to keep things safe. If they couldn't, we wouldn't be talking about them now."

"That's a good point," she agreed, "so we'll take our time and do our research. After all, the owners won't come back for their stuff so it's not like it's going anywhere. Also, we don't need to worry about eating or sleeping somewhere safe until next spring, so we don't have to rush."

She looked at their worried faces and smiled. "Are you forgetting that we've done this kind of thing before?"

Their faces said they were trying to think of exactly when she was referring to, so she gave them a hint.

"Exactly like we did at the Rookery, we've infiltrated numerous places—and came out again."

"Yeah," Melis agreed and smiled as something crossed her mind. "You remember Costa's Trinkets?"

They did and the memory made them laugh.

"Or that time we had to get that chest off Scaby's ferry." Raoul chortled.

"I thought we would have to swim for sure," Melis admitted and her eyes widened at the memory.

"And then Raoul took the boat—"

"Oh, Olmand's heart, that was a close one, wasn't it?"

"So, do you think we can do this?" Kaylin asked when the laughter died down.

"Sure, we can," Melis assured her. "It's a long way from the river. For once, we won't have to worry about drowning."

"Or getting wet," Piers muttered sourly and made them laugh.

"Only if we don't go on a night when it's raining," Raoul added.

"I'll have you know that rain saved all our butts," Kaylin told him.

"And you saved ours," he reminded her. "If you hadn't thought of using the rats—"

“And you saved mine when you pulled me through that gap,” she countered. “They’da caught up with me for sure.”

“The sister would have been upset if I let that happen,” he told her.

“And we couldn’t upset the sister,” Isabette finished.

“So… We’re good?” Kaylin asked.

Melis gave her a happy grin.

“Shacklemund’s won’t know what hit them.”

CHAPTER EIGHT

Two days later, Kaylin, Goss, and Melis watched from a distance as Isabette and Piers followed another mercenary through Shacklemund's front doors.

It hadn't been their imagination. The River Wardens were more alert and the crew didn't want to risk running into those who'd been at Elo's when the Blackbirds had robbed Raoul and Melis.

Because they couldn't guarantee that, they'd decided to not send the two of them on any of the scouting missions where the Wardens might be—like the street outside Shacklemund's, for instance.

"The security is crazy," Melis muttered for what must be the hundredth time as the doors closed behind the latest group. The flash of light that illuminated the door's edges was easy to see if you knew what to look for, and the sigil etched into the stone beside it was hard to miss. "How will we get past that?"

"Well, I didn't plan to use the front door," Kaylin replied.

"And we won't visit in daylight," Goss added before he gave her a concerned look. "Will we, Kay?"

"No," she reassured him. "We will most certainly not tackle this place in daylight."

The doors opened again and Isabette and Piers reappeared, each in the grip of one of Shacklemund's guards.

"Don't come back," the man holding the girl ordered and released her shoulder as he pushed her into the street.

"And the same goes for you," the other one added and let Piers go with a gentle shove. "You've got no business here until you're older."

The boy stumbled forward, then noticed that one of the nearby Wardens had seen them and leaned toward his partner. He didn't wait to determine if either of them would do anything else and bolted to weave between the other pedestrians before he darted down a narrow footway between two businesses.

Isabette merely shrugged and turned in the opposite direction. For a moment, it seemed as if she hadn't noticed the guards, but the girl turned into the street running alongside Shacklemund's outer wall, crossed it, and walked into the closest shop.

Kaylin smiled. Her crewmate would walk from the front of the shop to the back and vanish over the fence into the alley or yard behind it, or she'd find a route onto the roofs.

Either way, by the time the two Wardens who moved toward the shop reached it, the girl would be long gone—and more than likely without the shopkeeper seeing her.

She tapped Melis and nodded to Goss. "It's time to get some sleep," she instructed. "We'll be back tonight."

"Seriously?" Melis challenged. "Haven't we seen enough to know we'll never get inside?"

"You know Kaylin," Goss said comfortingly. "She never gives up. She'll find a way. You'll see."

Kaylin wished she had the boy's confidence. He might be right about her never giving up, but finding a way? That was what tonight was for. If she didn't find it, she would have to look for something else to fuel her takeover of the river docks.

But it won't be force, she promised herself. *We need to offer folks something better than that.*

They returned to the inn and she blew out a breath of tension she had held when Piers and Isabette met them part-way there.

"We can't do that, again," Isabette told them. "We got through the door all right and into the waiting room, but that was where it got weird."

"How weird?" she asked.

"Well, firstly, only one of the mercs we followed had anything to deposit. We stuck close like you said but not close enough to make the mercs suspicious. I think until Shacklemund's guards moved in, they thought we were there on business like them."

She looked at Piers for confirmation and the boy nodded.

"I thought so," he agreed. "I don't know what tipped the guards off, but we was listenin' and lookin' like you said, and we were fine for...I don't know...maybe three or four customers to take their stuff to the clerk."

Kaylin's interest sharpened. "They don't go to their boxes with their stuff?" she asked and the two shook their heads.

"No. They put it on the counter and the clerk takes a parchment and writes down exactly what they're putting in," the girl told her. "Or he draws it or something. I don't know, but he turns the parchment around for the person to check and asks if that looks right, and only when they say it does, is everything transferred to a Shacklemund's box and carried out by the guards."

"That's... The mercenaries put up with that?" Kaylin asked incredulously. "Doesn't anyone complain?"

"I only heard one complaining," Piers replied. "The guard looked at him and said it was the best way to keep his stuff safe. If no one knew what the layout was or exactly where a box was put, they'd have a hard time findin' it, wouldn't they?"

"And what did the mercenary say to that?" she asked as they swung into the alley behind the Dockers.

"He said he'da liked to see the arrangement, and this adventurer behind him laughs and tells him that's the charm of it. No one knows the exact arrangement so no one can plan on stealin' it."

"The merc still didn't like it," Isabette added, "but he shut up quickly when the adventurer stopped laughin', asked him what his problem was, and suggested he was maybe planning a raid himself."

"Yeah," Piers agreed. "That shut him up good and proper. He said it weren't nothing like that, only that he was used to making sure his goods were secure himself."

"And what did Shacklemund's say?" Kaylin asked.

"They said..." Piers let his words peter into silence as they reached the Docker's back door.

None of them spoke again until they were safely in the attic and settled around the tray of bread, meat, and cheese Cassie had sent up with them.

"So," Kaylin stated and prodded Piers to finish his answer. "Shacklemund's?"

"They said they used to let people see where and how their stuff was kept but someone abused the privilege and retrieval specialists were expensive." He frowned. "What's a retrieval specialist?"

"It's a thief you hire to get your stuff back from a thief," Raoul told him and chuckled. "No one asks 'em where they learn their skills or checks to make sure they're only usin' 'em for official retrievals, but there's at least one office in Waypoint."

"They do dungeon crawls and ruin diving too," Melis added and they all stared at her.

"The things you know." Isabette studied her friend, only half-teasing.

"It's not hard to figure out," Melis answered. "You probably knew it but didn't remember seein' it."

Somehow Kaylin doubted that, but she didn't press the point. They'd found Melis curled in a corner of the Rest one morning, her eyes red and swollen and bruises purpling her cheek and arms. She'd never told them what had happened or where she'd run from, but she'd pitched in without being asked so they'd let her stay.

The others looked at the girl and Raoul shrugged.

"If you say so, Liss."

"So, you didn't get any farther than the front?" she asked and Isabette rolled her eyes.

"Haven't you been listening?" she demanded. "No one gets any farther than the front desk. Not the adventurers, not the mercs, and certainly not the likes of us."

Kaylin frowned.

"Did you see if there were any locks on the doors the guards went through?" she asked.

The girl shook her head. "Yep, exactly like the doors and gates on the outside—those heavy locks that are hard to pick, and there's something else too. The guards have to stop and wait for a few heartbeats before they open."

"And they close right behind 'em," Piers added. "I couldn't see why or how, but they look as solid as the outer doors."

"You could hear the locks being turned too," Isabette added. "They lock 'em from both sides."

"That will make it hard to get in," Melis observed. "Last I looked, none of us had the ability to shove our hands through solid blocks of wood to pick a lock."

"Yeah, but the outside guards can't do that, either," Raoul pointed out. "That means they have some other way of getting through."

"Or that the outer doors aren't locked on the inside when the guards are outside," Piers added.

Kaylin sat back on her haunches and alternated bites of bread and meat as she thought.

"I'm gonna need to take another look at it tonight," she decided. "There has to be something I'm missing."

"Apart from all the treasure they got stored inside, you mean?" Isabette teased. "Because they have a ton of good stuff if what we saw going in was anything to go by. It's not only gold. There's magic trinkets, rare potions, weapons..."

She paused and her eyes took on a wistful look.

"There was this one guy. He brought a crossbow in—the sweetest thing you ever did see. Silver inlays and gems." She licked her lips. "But it was the wood that made it."

Piers snorted. "Made it," he muttered, "'cos crossbows are made of wood, right?"

She ignored him.

"It was kind of peachy and gold and…and it had a soft glow about it." She sighed and her eyes snapped back to the present. "Anyway, there's treasure like you wouldn't believe kept at Shacklemund's, and if we can ever get inside it and out again without getting caught, we'd never have to do another job—and I mean, like, *ever*."

"That kind of stuff, though," Raoul stated thoughtfully, his eyes dark with worry. "I mean, if you're talking magic like that, you're talking magical protections and traps and…" He paused. "Shacklemund's ain't never been broken into, has it?" he asked. "'Cept that one time they needed the retrieval specialist?"

The crew looked at each other and shrugged.

"If someone went in after they got their stuff back, we've never heard about it," Melis answered. "Why?"

"I'm thinkin' there has to be a reason for that," Raoul told them.

"It doesn't mean we can't be the first," Kaylin reminded them. She finished her sandwich and dusted her hands off. "Time to sleep," she instructed. "We'll take a real good look around it tonight and make a decision tomorrow."

"As long as it isn't another suicide run," Melis told her tartly. "The Rookery was only one step short of a horrible disaster."

"And look where it got us," she reminded her. "Blackbird free. Now, we have to offer something better."

She looked at their faces, met their eyes, and held their gazes until they nodded, then watched as they rolled into their blankets and settled down to sleep. Finally, she did the same and drifted off to the soft buzz of conversation that wafted up from the inn below.

Dusk found them on the rooftop overlooking Shacklemund's front door. This time, they all huddled together and peered over the ridgeline at the street below. The storage center closed its doors as the last light faded from the sky, but it wasn't until the lamps had been lit up and down the street that anyone emerged.

"There they go," Isabette murmured as the day clerk stepped out.

He was accompanied by four guards and chatted amiably with the two closest to him as they walked down the street.

"I wonder what happened to the others," Isabette murmured as the small group disappeared around a corner.

"What d'you mean?" Kaylin asked.

"She means there were a dozen inside," Piers replied beside her, "and we're seein' only four."

"Maybe they sleep inside," Melis suggested.

"Or they're on the first shift," Raoul interjected.

He stifled a yawn and Melis elbowed him in the ribs.

"It's time you woke up," she told him sharply. "We can't have you falling down on the job."

Piers snickered. "We're on a roof. He'd better be awake."

Raoul responded with a muffled groan. "I don't need two of you."

Kaylin glanced at Isabette. *Two of them?*

The other girl rolled her eyes, which made her wonder what she'd missed because it was clearly something. She frowned but pushed that thought aside as not important for now and studied the front of the big storage center.

"We need to split up," she decided and Melis gave her a look that said she already knew that. "You and Isabette take the back. Raoul and Piers take the street to the right, and Goss and I will work down the left."

"So who's watching the front?" Melis challenged.

"I think we've found out about all we need to know about the front," Kaylin retorted and Goss groaned.

"You know better than that, Kay," he admonished her. "I'll take the front. You're big enough and ugly enough to handle the left on your own."

She stared at him. That had been the most she'd heard the boy say in a long time.

"Fine," she agreed. "I'll take the left on my own and you'll watch the front—and by watch, you'll stay on the roofs and well away from it, understood?"

His mouth moved in a quick smile and he nodded.

"Loud and clear, boss girl."

"And don't call me that," she snapped.

Melis giggled. "Yeah, she'd much rather be known as the bossy girl."

The others chuckled and Kaylin shook her head.

"Get to work," she told them "We've only got until dawn."

She wondered if this was what being a good leader meant. If she didn't treat her crew like Korbyn and instill fear, would she get nothing but sass from her people? She'd have to work on that problem some other time, though.

"You've only got until dawn, you mean," Melis sniped. "We don't have to work out how to get inside."

"No, but you do need to have a report for me when you get back," Kaylin answered, "or I'll want to know why."

For a moment, she thought the girl would ask her what she would do about it if they didn't, but she merely smirked at her and rolled her shoulders in an elaborate shrug.

"Whatever you say, boss girl."

She didn't wait for Kaylin to reply but slid down the rear of the roof, leapt lightly over the alley behind the tavern where they were perched, and scrambled up the slates on the other side. Isabette darted Kaylin an apologetic look and hurried after her.

"Come on, trouble," Raoul said, addressing Piers, although his eyes never left Melis's silhouette as the girl darted across the rooftops before she descended to cross the street. To Kaylin, he said. "She doesn't mean anything by it, you know."

"I know," she assured him, although she knew no such thing.

Melis was prickly at the best of times, but lately... She turned to ask Raoul what he thought but the boy had already started across the roofs with Piers trailing behind.

"It'll be all right," Goss assured her and she gave him a brief nod before she followed a path down the roof to the ground below.

The alley behind the tavern was quiet, and she hurried along it unobserved and emerged a block up from Shacklemund's. She doubled back until she found a way onto the roof opposite the left wall.

The locks weren't the only thing they had to worry about and neither were the guards, although they were a concern. No, the main problem she could see was the amount of light around the building, even at night.

A coach lantern hung on either side of every door, and more lanterns were positioned along the wall, spaced far enough apart that the circles of light they cast overlapped. There weren't any shadows near an entrance into the building.

As if that wasn't bad enough, the sigils she'd noticed carved into the stone beside the entry door glowed at night. When she ran her gaze over the building, she realized they were present at each and every possible entrance or exit—and that included the few windows set into the upper floors of the building itself.

"There has to be a way," Kaylin murmured and crept along the roofline until she saw one of the Shacklemund's guards patrolling the street.

She settled into a shadowed valley between two peaks and watched the man approach one of the wrought iron gates leading to a walkway between the buildings beyond. At first, she thought he would check it like he had the one farther down the street but instead, he looked carefully in either direction before he raised one hand and made a swift gesture in front of the sigil.

It dimmed and she held her breath.

Now what?

The guard lowered his hand and glanced up and down the street again. As soon as he was sure it was empty, he looked at the buildings opposite and waved for someone to approach. Whoever they were, they must have hesitated because he made the gesture again.

After a brief pause, the soft scuff of light steps on the cobbles could be heard. She held her breath until a young woman tripped into view. The guard held one hand out and she took it and let him draw her close and kiss her lightly on the lips as he reached behind him and opened the gate.

Kaylin wrinkled her nose as the man wound one arm around the girl's waist, drew her past the gate, and closed it softly behind him.

Some people!

He held the woman close with one arm and repeated the gesture he'd made outside with his free hand. It was hard to focus given that the young lady was untucking his shirt, but Kaylin managed—although she was blushing furiously by the end of it.

It helped that the sigils outside the gates lit up as soon as the gesture was complete and the guard repeated it to enter the building closest to the gate. Again, the sigil outside the door faded, only to re-light a short time later.

It's interesting that it can be re-set from the other side, she thought, *but it makes sense.*

She stared at the building and wondered what it was.

A barracks? she thought but decided the guard would look for somewhere more private. *An empty storage room, perhaps? A stable?*

She looked around for the obvious traces of horses in the dirt. *Does Shacklemund's have stables?*

Whatever it was, if the guard was seeking a quiet place for a tryst, he'd have to emerge again—and before anyone noticed he'd been delayed on his patrol. She settled down to wait, her questions unanswered.

The moon had risen and Kaylin began to think she'd have to move to a different valley when the sigil dimmed and the couple appeared. The lady's hair was tousled and the guard's jacket still unbuttoned, but neither seemed to notice. She wound her arms around his neck and pulled him into a passionate kiss.

Seriously? the girl thought and her mouth twisted with distaste. *You couldn't have waited for a better time? Like maybe when you're off-duty?*

It seemed not because when the woman went to break the kiss, the guard recaptured her lips and kissed her again. A distant bell chimed and the couple drew apart guiltily. The guard made a hasty gesture at the sigil on the door behind him.

He needed two attempts to get it to set again, and Kaylin watched his fingers intently. *I wonder what happens if he gets it wrong a third time?*

While he didn't oblige her by doing so, she noted the pattern his hand made before the sigil lit up.

Like that, is it? She frowned and her fingers twitched as she ran through the gesture in her mind.

As he turned to face the outer gate, her gaze sharpened. This time, she was sure she'd caught the right movements. She waited as he ushered the woman into the street and stopped to button his jacket and straighten his clothes.

When he'd made himself presentable again, he followed her through the gate and waved goodbye as she tripped across the street and disappeared between the buildings, one of them from which Kaylin was watching.

The girl didn't try to see where she went. She was too busy watching the guard repeat the gesture to bring the sigil to brightness and this time, her hand traced the same path through the air before her.

She wondered if the others had noticed the same thing and watched the guard walk away.

He appeared several more times that night, although a different man took his place shortly after the moon reached its zenith. She marked the time. If midnight was when the guards changed their shift, they'd want to make their entry either an hour before or an hour after but no closer.

It would give the guards going off shift time to make their reports and leave, and the guards newly arrived to settle into their patrol. She thought about that for a moment, then decided it might be better to strike early in the morning rather than in the late hours of the night.

Wasn't that when people were at their least alert? Kaylin hesitated, tried to remember where she'd heard that piece of advice, and shrugged when she couldn't. It didn't matter. She and the crew were used to operating at those hours. Maybe there would be guards who weren't and if she could get the sigils open, all the better.

She moved her hand and repeated the gesture as closely as she could remember it. The air sang softly over her fingers so she tried it again. She'd almost perfected it, she was sure, but almost wasn't good enough.

Kaylin scrabbled in her belt pouch until her fingers closed over the worn piece of chalk she kept there. It was useful for leaving markers for her crew and stood out better than those made by charcoal. It might not be as good as the carvings, though.

She gazed across the street and focused on the sigil. It was deceptively simple in design but she wouldn't take any chances.

Carefully, she made the first line, then referenced the mark again. Its glow made it visible even from this distance, and she found the next stroke easier to produce than the last. It didn't take her long to finish a rough sketch and when she compared it to the gleaming beauty across the street, she was satisfied.

It might not be perfect but it would do. She repeated the gesture the guard had made and smiled with satisfaction. This felt better, she decided. Somehow, her hand felt more sure.

She made the gesture again and then a third time.

The fourth time, she noticed that the sensation of air moving over her finger came from more than the night around her.

That's odd, she thought, repeated the gesture, and focused on the sensation that passed over her fingers as she did so. *There's something here.*

Her vigil on the street below forgotten, she made the gesture again. This time, she was sure and she slowed the movement when she repeated it and paid close attention to what was happening with her fingers.

It was nothing different than when she learned how to pick-pockets.

The pressure tugged at the muscles of her little finger. Kaylin relaxed her digit and let it shift until the pressure eased. The next time she made the gesture, she moved her little finger into the position before it started.

Now that she'd noticed it, she felt it in other places and shifted her index finger a little higher, paired it with her ring finger, and curled the finger beside her pinky as she circled her thumb the way the pressure wanted it to go.

Light flared briefly, twined faintly around her hand, and disappeared.

Kaylin glanced nervously into the street to see if anyone had noticed but the thoroughfare remained empty and the guard had only just turned the corner. She made the gesture again, slower this time and with more focus on where she placed her finger.

She stared at a third sigil—one she'd carved out of the air in front of her.

"No waaay," she whispered as it disintegrated into glowing motes of light.

Even when it had faded and no sign of it remained, she continued to stare at where it had been.

She might have found a way in—if she could only do it again.

Energized, she moved a little faster, still focused on maintaining the right finger movements, and paid attention to any shift in the current of air over her fingers. Again, the sigil appeared in the air before her.

A giggle filtered out of her throat and she clapped her hands over her mouth, bounced her feet on the slates in excitement, and didn't care that she smudged the sigil she'd drawn there.

She no longer needed it.

Unbelievably, she had found a way past the magic protecting Shacklemund's gates and doors.

CHAPTER NINE

Two nights later, when cloud shrouded the moon, Kaylin dropped into another alley. This time, she had the rest of the crew with her and each one carried packs slung over their shoulders. These looked ridiculous on the smaller members of the crew, but she had argued that they were better than trying to drag heavily laden sacks if they had to hurry.

"Are you saying we'll get caught?" Piers challenged her and Melis had answered before she had had a chance.

"Nah, she's sayin' we're goin' to have another close shave," the girl declared. "Ain't that right, Kaylin?"

If she hadn't caught the sly smile on the girl's face, she might have taken offense. She did, however, and managed to curb the sharp retort that suggested Melis stay behind. Instead, she smiled sweetly.

"I'm saying I won't take anything for granted," she said and indicated the room around them. "And this way, we won't need to unpack it. We can simply stuff it in a chest as is."

It was a good point and they knew it, but Melis still had something to add.

"We gonna have to unpack it to sort out what's what," the girl declared and Isabette had come to Kaylin's defense.

"True, but this way, we only have to unpack one at a time."

That had decided them and all six had donned their packs and used belts to pull the shoulder straps together on the smaller members of the crew. It had been enough to stop the packs sliding off as they climbed to the rooftops.

Fortunately, the seamstress who had provided them wasn't likely to associate the purchases to a possible late-night alternative acquisition engagement.

The group navigated the rooftops, which made a faster journey than taking the streets and soon, they were huddled in the alley opposite Shacklemund's wrought iron gate.

"Are you sure this is the best way in?" Raoul asked and studied the interlaced ironwork.

"There were locks on the doors the guards used behind the clerk, weren't there?" Kaylin asked, and both Melis and Piers nodded.

"The hard-to-pick kind," the boy confirmed and Kaylin tossed Raoul a challenging look.

"I don't know about you but I haven't gotten to a point I can get through one of those. How about you?"

He flushed slightly and shook his head. "No," he admitted.

"And I don't see any locks on that gate, do you?"

Again, he shook his head. "You had better hope you can get into the vaults once we get into the yard," he told her.

"That should be the easy part," she replied and ignored her misgivings as she checked the street for the guard.

"Is there any chance lover boy will be back for some after-shift recreation?" Raoul whispered.

Melis and Isabette made hushing noises and Kaylin shrugged.

"I guess there's only one way to find out," she answered and darted across the empty street.

When she got there, she was dismayed to see a keyhole set in the center of the ironwork. She hadn't noticed the guard using a key before he pushed the gate open.

With a frown, she turned to face the sigil. Making the same gesture as the guard, she was still stupidly surprised when it worked. The sigil dimmed and a soft click from the gate answered the question of how they would unlock it.

She gestured for the crew to join her, pushed the gate open, and slipped inside. As soon as they were through, she repeated the gesture to activate the sigil again.

"There's no point in letting the guards know anyone's been here," she explained and darted along the edge of the building closest to the back of the main structure.

The others didn't answer.

This had been an argument they'd had in the attic and one they'd finally agreed on—if somewhat reluctantly and only because Goss had shown he could make the gesture needed.

It was a feat none of the others could get exactly right and Kaylin was worried about what might happen if they got it wrong in front of one of the wards.

They'd spent two days working on the gestures before they'd finally admitted defeat. As dexterous as the crew was when it came to sliding their hands into and out of pockets, they didn't seem to have the knack for whatever the gesture needed.

It didn't matter how many times she tried to explain what they had to do, they merely became more confused and none of them had been able to determine why.

"It's because it's magic," Melis had snarled in exasperation. "Only those tied to the house are supposed to be able to make it. No one else."

That had drawn more curious looks from the others and the girl had raised both hands to ward them off.

"Oh no. You don't need to know how I know. You only need to know that none of us is supposed to be able to make the sign that turns the magic on and off."

"But Kaylin and Goss—" Piers began and the girl had given the two of them the dirtiest look possible.

"Yeah, and doesn't that make you wonder why?" she'd demanded.

Deciding there was no purpose in antagonizing the girl, Kaylin had changed the subject.

"I don't know how I can do it," she'd admitted, "but I'm grateful I can and even more grateful that we have Goss as well. That way, if anything happens..."

Goss had laid a hand on her arm. "Nothing's gonna happen to you, Kay. You've planned this as best you can and we're the fastest Hands around." He looked at the others and challenged them to say otherwise. "Are you in?" he asked and held his fist out.

"In," Raoul and Isabette snapped and bumped their fists to his.

Piers and Melis had followed suit soon after.

Getting into the building was easier than expected. Following the wall of the outermost building, they reached a second iron gate under a stone arch. This one led into a small courtyard garden. Kaylin peered through, then deactivated the sigil.

"I can see a door into the shop," she whispered and Raoul and Melis bumped fists in victory.

Goss crowded close to her side and they moved swiftly around the courtyard's central fountain, brushed against bushes and flowers, and left a trail of scent behind them. None of them paid it any attention and she repeated the gesture to open the rear door into Shacklemund's main building.

A set of stairs led to the right and they glanced at each other before descending. The sound of a door opening and closing followed by the sound of soft voices almost made them freeze. Kaylin tugged on Raoul's sleeve and Goss poked Melis and they hurried silently and swiftly down the stairs.

Footsteps sounded above them but didn't follow. The walkers paused at the rear door and she tried to remember if she'd locked it again and whether or not the fact would be obvious from the inside. There was no time to worry about it, however, as they reached the bottom of the stairs.

She signaled that they should take the centermost hallway and follow it to the end but stopped when she found a second stairwell. Surely the oldest treasures would be stowed the deepest? She nudged Isabette and pointed at the stairs, then looked at the others.

They hesitated, then shrugged so she moved first.

The stairs led to a small atrium with a single door—one that had not one but four sigils, two on either side. None of them matched the one she was used to.

Raoul drew a sharp breath and Isabette grasped her arm as if to stop her from doing something foolish. Kaylin shook her off, her gaze already fixed on the symbols around the door. Her fingers twitched as she studied them and made the first movements each might need.

Again, air flowed over her skin and again, she felt an indistinct pressure move her digits to new positions. Some of that flowed up her arm and subtly altered the position of her hand. She took a step forward and her gaze flicked over the sigils once, twice...thrice.

Where the one on the outside was shaped like a diamond with a series of diamonds patterning its center, these seemed odd. Kaylin frowned. They were diamond-shaped but their edges were smoother and their corners were different.

All were rounded but some looked like they'd had a bite taken out of them but there was no pattern. No bite was adjacent. She moved closer to the door, her focus drawn to the lines swirling through the middle of each.

They looked like they should join.

She chose one and started to make the gesture that felt most correct but stopped when she sensed something off in the air that moved over her skin. With a frown, she tried a second one, but tension ran over her skin and she stopped.

After a moment, she raised her hand and waved them in front of the remaining two. When she felt the tension ease, she stopped and began a new gesture. The light in the sigil flared and died but Kaylin barely noticed. Only one line had connected with the dented corner.

She glanced at the remaining sigils and chose the one with a dented corner connected by two lines. This time, there was no tension and no resistance when she moved her hands. Her fingers flickered with light and moved faster as she completed the gesture.

Wariness tugged at her mind, part of her aware that she skirted the edge of danger and one wrong choice of sigil would result in an alarm. Maybe choosing the next one incorrectly would drop the floor from beneath them or the heat she felt in her mind would be nothing compared to the heat that would sear the flesh from her hands if she made a mistake with the fourth one.

Each time she completed a gesture, the sigils flared with extra life, then faded—and each gesture was more complex than the last and took longer to complete. Kaylin moved through each one and paid careful attention to the pressure on her hands, her arms, on each of her fingers, and even the tension in her knuckles.

The pressure curled her fingers in unexpected ways and sweat dampened her collar and back. Fine tremors made her skin shiver and muscles shudder. By the time she reached the fourth sigil, she moved her hands more slowly and tried to stop them from shaking out of the pattern.

"Control," she muttered, moved her finger in response to the delicate frisson of pressure, and flicked through the last of the movement with a precise snap. "It's all about the control."

To her relief, the final sigil blinked out and the soft grind of a well-oiled mechanism rumbled through the chamber.

The vault door slid open before them as she lowered her hands, her breath coming in short huffs. For a moment, no one moved before Raoul uttered a softly jubilant whoop and slapped her on the arm.

"Nice work," he told her and the impact of his blow shook her out of her frozen state.

She started as they hurried past her.

"Look for the chests with the thickest layer of dust," she instructed and Melis gave her a scornful glance.

"Are you telling me the maid doesn't make it down here to clean?" she asked and Kaylin rolled her eyes.

"No, but the dustiest ones are the oldest and so least likely to be opened and checked."

"But don't clean the top of 'em when you find 'em," the girl snarked. "We wouldn't want anyone to realize they'd been touched recently, right?"

Kaylin ignored her. If there was one thing she'd learned about her, it was that she got snippy under pressure and arguing wouldn't do any good.

"They'll probably be at the back," Goss stated, tapped Piers' shoulder, and led the way down an aisle.

The others followed and moved between racks of chests until they reached a rack standing against a solid stone wall.

"Gotcha," Piers whispered and studied the chests on the lowest shelf.

Kaylin followed his gaze and noted the thick patina of dust on them. She also noted the large padlock on the front of each and sighed. No one had said it would be easy.

Of course, it wasn't that hard either. A small sigil shone from the center of each lock—a small, familiar one. When he saw them, Goss smiled and made the gesture needed for the outer gate in front of the closest one. He glanced happily at Kaylin as the lock snapped open.

"I remembered," he whispered and the gleam in his eyes made her smile.

"You did," she agreed. "Now open the ones over that way and I'll take these. Only the dustiest, got it?"

"Got it," he told her and they opened half a dozen of those closest.

"Motherlode," Raoul whispered.

"Don't just stand there admiring it," Melis snapped. "Get to work. It won't leap into your backpack on its own."

So saying, she slipped her pack from her shoulders and began to fill it. She lifted bags of coin and checked their contents before she stowed them and set one back in the box.

"Copper," she noted and curled her lip in scorn.

"Take it anyway," Isabette told her. When the girl gave her a look that questioned her sanity, she added, "Well, it has to be here for a reason."

Melis studied her as if searching for any sign the girl was making fun of her before she put the purse in her pack.

"Take the jewelry," Raoul instructed. "It's more valuable weight for weight...and any weapons...or anything that looks magical...and..."

"Do I look like I'm stupid?" Melis retorted as she took out a belt with two daggers on it.

"Do I have to answer that?" he whispered in reply.

Melis didn't bother to reply and she didn't put the daggers in her pack, either. Instead, she strapped them onto her waist and leaned into the chest to see what else she could find.

"Is this… Is this a wand?" Piers asked, his voice tinged with awe. A moment later, his voice was striving to create a coherent sentence. "Are these…all…wands?"

Kaylin turned to see him holding up a leather roll like one used for cook's knives. Instead of containing blades, however, this one held several foot-long lengths of…well, not all of them were wood.

"Don't take them out!" she snapped. "You don't know what they'll do."

The boy paled and almost dropped the bundle, but Raoul leaned forward and took it from his hands. Careful to not let his fingers brush the thin rod-like lengths, he rolled the leather and fastened it before he handed it back.

"Good find, Piers."

When the younger boy took the roll and stowed it gingerly in his pack, Kaylin turned back to the chest she was slowly emptying.

Although emptying is too strong a term because there's no way I'll fit all that in here.

She cleared the chest carefully from the center to one end. When her pack was full, she set it to one side and filled her pockets until they bulged.

"Maybe one more thing," she murmured and scanned the scatter of objects left at one side of the chest.

Coins had spilled from pouches, along with some odd-colored stones, but it was the flare of red that caught her eye. Peering closer, she saw what looked like a ruby except that this one was the size of her thumb and attached to a band by a network of gold and silver threads.

She might have left it behind but Raoul's words echoed in her head.

Take the jewelry. It's more valuable.

Kaylin wrapped her hand around the gem to lift it out. When it didn't come, she leaned into the chest to get a better grasp and gave the ruby a firm tug. This alone would make sure none of them had to worry for a year. Maybe two?

It came loose with a sudden click, followed by a resounding boom.

Lightning flashed and another rumble followed. A burst of acrid green smoke billowed from behind the chest, accompanied by a stench that made her eyes water.

"Oh, kreck," she croaked, grasped her pack, and hauled it over her shoulders. She waved her hands to move the smoke and gasped before she rasped, "Go! Go! Go!"

The others didn't wait for her to finish. They snatched their packs up and staggered toward the front of the vault.

Raoul grabbed Piers and half-hauled and half-leaned on the boy as they raced to the door. Piers caught hold of Goss and Melis and Isabette stumbled, coughing and choking, after them.

Kaylin lurched behind her crew and gagged as her stomach roiled. The weight of the pack dragged her off-balance but she reeled on her feet, crashed into the racks that bordered one side of the corridor, and clutched a shelf for support.

The others shuffled ahead of her and she hoped the door to the vault stayed open.

She wasn't sure she could make it through the gestures required to deactivate the sigils a second time—not without a night's rest between. When she reached the door, it wasn't closed, thankfully, but she glimpsed the heels of Isabette's boots disappearing up the stairs.

Coughing against the bitter burning at the back of her throat, Kaylin staggered forward. Tears streamed down her face as the smoke burned her eyes and her stomach cramped.

"Who in all the hells puts—" She tried to think of a description for the stench clawing at her nose and throat and failed. "*That* in a treasure vault?"

A shout echoed down the stairwell and she almost tripped on the next step in her hurry to escape. To her relief, the others hadn't stopped, even if they moved more slowly than she'd like.

"Go!" she shouted. "I'm right behind you. Go!"

It wasn't entirely true but her words had the desired effect. Isabette and Melis picked up the pace and didn't look back to see how close she was. She teetered over the last step and carved a drunken path to the door leading to the courtyard with its fountain and beds of sweet-scented herbs.

Memory of the smell made her hasten her steps. From the corridors behind, she heard the rattle of boots and more shouts. The metallic clatter of an alarm bell added to the cacophony, and she willed her legs to move faster.

The explosion and smoke had left her feeling sick and her legs rubbery and uncooperative. She wove to the door and clutched the lintel to stop herself from falling down the slight step leading into the garden. When she looked up, she saw Raoul reach the gate and look back.

"Hurry!" he called and urged Piers through.

The younger boy obeyed but Goss looked back and his eyes widened in alarm. He'd slipped into the garden before Raoul could stop him and pushed between the girls.

"Run, Kay! Run!" he screamed and she glanced over her shoulder.

At the sight of a large armored body hurtling through the door, panic coursed through her legs and she managed a spurt of speed as Isabette doubled back and caught Goss' arm.

"Let me go!" he shrieked as Melis stopped Piers from darting past Raoul and kept the boys moving.

"Come on, Iz!"

Kaylin raced forward and yelled at her second in command. "I've got him. Go! Get them out of here!"

Iz released Goss as Kaylin reached them.

"You have to get the gate!" she shouted and the boy turned and fled.

She ran after him, heard the thunder of footsteps behind her, and knew she would be too slow. The backpack of treasure and the after-effects of the smoke were slowing her. If she reached the gate, she'd be luckier than she deserved.

If any of them got away, they'd do better than she deserved. Unless they could reach the alley in time to get onto the roofs, they would have to try to find their way through unfamiliar streets while being hunted.

Goss met her as she raced out of the garden. Raoul, Piers, and the girls were with him—and none of them needed to explain why they'd returned. Kaylin could hear those pursuing. She didn't stop running but changed direction and took them along a path that ran beside another building.

If she had it right, it would take them to the far end of Shacklemund's property and there had to be an entry there somewhere. She was almost right. It led them to a wall with another wrought iron gate set into a stone wall. Another sigil—a familiar one—gleamed beside it.

Kaylin stumbled closer to it and forced her hand to remember the necessary movements while Goss watched anxiously. She'd barely completed the maneuver when the first guard emerged from beside the building.

"Go," she ordered and pushed Raoul toward the gate. "Go!"

He took one look at their pursuers, saw the second and third guard emerge, and grasped his brother. Melis grabbed Isabette and the four of them raced through. As they passed, Kaylin noticed a thick wooden lever protruding from the wall and glanced up.

Above them, set into the stone of the overarching wall, she saw the bottom edge of a portcullis and knew what she needed to do to buy them time to escape.

"Go!" she ordered when Goss hesitated. "I'll be right behind you," she told him.

He turned and was about to go through the gate when she grasped the lever. The movement caught his eye and he cried out in alarm.

"Kay! No!" He started to turn back and she let go of the lever and slipped the straps of her pack from her shoulders.

"I have to," she responded harshly, took the two steps that separated them, and shoved the pack against his chest.

Using her momentum, she pushed him away from her, then lashed out with her foot. It landed squarely against the pack and propelled the boy out and into the street beyond. As soon as he was beyond the wall, she didn't hesitate. She dove at the lever and yanked down hard to bring the portcullis crashing over the gap.

She pushed unsteadily to her feet, turned to the gate, and wrapped her hands around the thick iron bars. On the other side, Goss picked himself up off the cobbles. She pointed at the pack with a brief, sad smile.

"Use it to become something more than only a thief," she ordered.

Footsteps crunched the gravel behind her and her smile vanished.

"Now, *please*… Run!" she yelled as a guard approached her from behind.

CHAPTER TEN

Kaylin arched her back and tried to straighten it despite the pull on her arms. She held the position for a few minutes, leaned her head back against the stone cell wall, closed her eyes, and suppressed a groan.

Breathing hurt and her chest ached, but at least she'd stopped coughing.

That didn't negate the fact that she was chained to the floor of a cell in some...some fancy house at the top end of town—and she didn't know if her crew had escaped. She had a horrible feeling that, despite her desperate act with the portcullis, they hadn't gotten far.

The idea brought tears to her eyes and clogged her throat with grief.

If they'd been caught, where were they?

She'd had only enough time to see Goss take to his heels before one of the guards had hurled himself into her, hammered her against the portcullis, and pinned her there while they secured her hands.

A firm hand had grasped her hair and collar and she'd been spun away from the gate. A second hand had taken hold of her belt and she'd been part-marched and part-carried into Shacklemund's, past the fountain, and past the opening to the stairs and the vaults below.

They'd taken her to a private meeting room she assumed was one adventurers might use to visit their treasure. There, her situation had become worse. She'd been thrown into a seat and the table in front of her pushed to one side.

"Who are you working for?" That had been easy to answer.

"Myself," she admitted.

At first, they hadn't believed her.

"Not possible. Who trained you?"

"The streets," she told them.

"Not lock picking," they countered. "Magic."

"No one."

A gauntleted slap had followed, then a reprimand—but not for her. She might have laughed if she wasn't seeing stars and tasting blood.

"She can't answer anything if she's not conscious."

"And there's no point in getting answers if they can't be believed."

"We need to know how long she's been at the Academy and who her master is."

That had made her laugh, and her soft chuckle had drawn their attention.

"What's so funny?" the one who had told the other not to slap her asked.

"Ain't got no master," she replied.

The next slap had been followed by a backhand that had spun the chair, and she'd seen a brief span of dark before she woke upright as someone wiped blood from her chin.

"Master!" a voice snapped at her.

The demand made Kaylin start and she almost toppled the chair as she threw herself away from the face that rasped questions inches from her own.

"Master!" it repeated and someone steadied the chair and braced it in place as she tried to scramble back.

"Not your master," she muttered. "Not..."

The guard turned away with an exasperated sigh.

"I don't believe she's smart enough to curl a sigil," he began as she tried to focus on his clothing.

Chain mail over a slate-blue tunic—collared, slate-blue tunic, dark-gray or blue trousers, boots with blue flashing. Kaylin knew those colors… She frowned and tried to concentrate on their significance while the guards argued.

"You saw her."

"It doesn't mean I can believe it."

Her mind snapped to the guards when they both turned toward her. The questions came thick and fast after that.

"Who's your master?"

"How long have you been at the Academy?"

"Where did you receive your training?"

In response, she had stared blankly at them and watched their faces grow redder and redder with frustration.

"Speak, girl!"

She started at that and regarded them with as fierce a glare as she could produce. Of course, she was sure it had them quivering in fear. If she had the energy, she would have laughed at her private joke.

"Well?"

"I don't know what you're talkin' about," she told them and swallowed hard. "I don't…have a master."

The upraised hand made her flinch. She scrunched her eyes shut, hunched her shoulders, and tensed as she waited for the blow to land. When it didn't, she opened her eyes slightly and flinched again when she realized she was eyeball to eyeball with one of the guards.

No…not guards… Well, yes, guards, but not any guards. These were knights… Spear Knights…Lance Knights… Knights of the Twin Spears, the…the Lances Jumelles.

Shacklemund's had Knights of the Twin Spears as guards?

"Oh, troll turds," she muttered. "Why?"

"Why what?"

"Why are you here?" she asked the face in front of her.

The guard leaned his forehead against hers and prodded her under the collar bone with a single gauntleted finger.

"It's. Our. Job," he rasped.

"You're not doing a very good one, are—" she began but yelped when the chair tipped.

She twisted or tried to, but her hands and feet were attached to the chair—which stopped a hand-span from the floor. The knight followed her down and his face filled her view as he leaned over her.

"Who. Is. Your. Master?"

Kaylin turned her face away and closed her eyes.

"Told you, ain't got no master and I don't know what troll-spawned academy you mean. Wanted a future for my crew."

"By stealing?" The shout was a roar and she jerked in fear.

"From the dead," she whispered, "who don't need it."

A hand curled itself in the front of her tunic and jerked her upright, chair and all.

"Fine, then who helped you? You must have had a friend. A trainee wizard…a young man, perhaps?"

Kaylin snorted at that.

"No?"

She shook her head.

"Truly?" he pressed.

"No one helped me," she told him and added bitterly, "No one has ever helped me."

"Are you sure?" The hold on her shirt had tightened.

"Yeah. No one helped me. I'm very sure I'da remembered if they had," she snapped.

"Someone from the Academy must have helped you." The knight's grasp tightened and he shook her, chair and all. "Who was it?"

"Don't know." She gasped and the shaking stopped.

"You don't know their name?" he asked and placed the chair down.

"No, troll-tart. I don't know what you're sucking well talkin' about!" she shouted at him.

He released her tunic abruptly and shoved her back. This time, the chair didn't travel very far. One of the other guards caught it.

"What d'you think?" the first guard asked.

"I'm starting to think she hasn't a clue," the other one replied.

Kaylin quietly dubbed him Chair Catcher and the first one Loud

Mouth. It helped but she still flinched when Loud Mouth pivoted to face her. This time, she didn't close her eyes.

"I told you, I don't know," she insisted. "Ain't got a clue. Don't know any wizard trainees. Don't know any Academy. Don't know why you think I even needed help."

Her voice rose in frustration and angry tears filled her eyes. Embarrassed by the emotion, she lowered her head, surprised when neither of the guards said anything. Instead, Loud Mouth had tugged on his companion's sleeve and drawn him out of the room.

She hadn't heard the conversation, but only one of them had returned—Chair Catcher, she was relieved to note. He didn't say anything but settled his rump against the wall and stared at her. While she did her best to ignore him, she found it unnerving to be the center of such concentrated attention. She was about to say something about it when the door opened again.

Chair Catcher came to sudden attention and Kaylin raised her head to see who deserved such a response. The dark-haired woman was as tall as Dimitry and solidly built—muscled but not heavy. The girl frowned and studied her as she stalked into the room, her blue-gray eyes unsympathetic as she scrutinized the prisoner with a hard expression.

Despite her sudden rush of concern, she returned the stare and tried to ignore the polished silver of a steel breastplate in favor of the stern face above it.

The woman didn't waste words in greeting but moved directly into the cell, followed by six guards—six young guards, Kaylin realized when she glanced at them—and Loud Mouth greeted Chair Catcher with a subdued nod. Both men looked anxious although they did their best to hide it and, when she caught the woman's words, she had an inkling why.

"I don't see how she could have made it into the compound without someone helping her," the woman said, her face hard with disapproval. "If there was no one else, one of you..."

The younger guards had been followed inside by several older ones, all wearing plate instead of the chain mail worn by her original captors. Fear haunted the younger guards' expressions and they exchanged worried looks with each other as the captain continued.

"None of us can come up with a single alternative as to how they made it to the central vault."

Kaylin saw Loud Mouth pale and remembered the impact of his gauntleted hand against her face. It was very tempting to agree with the woman that she'd indeed had help. She could have them guessing for days.

All she had to do was hint that she'd received assistance from one of the guards on duty and they'd be at each other's throats to discover the culprit.

Chair Catcher's throat moved as he swallowed hard. His face paled as though he faced his worst fear and saw no way to defeat it. His dark eyes and unruly dark hair reminded her so much of Raoul that she almost felt sorry for him.

What would it be like, she wondered, *to have a secure job, a future, and then lose it because someone had been smart enough to get into somewhere you'd been guarding?*

And what would she do to make sure it never happened to her friends?

She watched them for a little longer and listened while the woman asked them if they were sure they knew nothing of how the girl had gotten past the sigils.

"It's not a matter of whether one of you are guilty," the woman continued matter of factly, "but which of you and how many are involved."

A soft gasp drew her attention.

"But..." Loud Mouth began, "we'd—" He turned to include his fellows in the statement. "None of us would betray the trust—"

His blue eyes were wide with worry and his skin the color of milk.

Kaylin might have laughed but she'd never seen a grown man, even a young grown man look so frightened. It was as if they faced the gallows with her.

Or something far worse, she thought as she scrutinized their faces, *but what could be worse than being hanged?*

She considered saying something but decided the woman would find out soon enough. Instead, she contented herself with watching and learning as the captain worked through the guards. It was good to have something else to focus on instead of her pain but it still wasn't enough.

A cramp pinched her triceps and she twisted and tried to relieve her aching muscles. A small groan escaped her and the woman paused. Kaylin froze and raised her head enough to see what was going on.

All that happened was she caught the captain's glance and watched her turn her attention to the older men.

Knights? she wondered as the woman dismissed the guards.

"Captain."

"Yes, Captain."

Kaylin saw relief flash through the harried expressions on the younger men's faces but didn't let that distract her from the woman. One of the older men remained and closed the door after the guards and their escort, and she froze as they turned their attention to her.

"What d'you think, Ademar?" the woman asked and they both studied her.

The girl stared in return and tried to hide the bite of the rope at her wrists.

"She doesn't look old enough to be the cause of so much trouble," Ademar replied.

"But?" she asked.

His eyes gleamed with a brief purple light before he sighed.

"And yet she is."

The woman gave him a sharp look and her gray-blue eyes narrowed. He cast another look at the prisoner.

"And she knows it," he added. "Don't you, girl?"

Kaylin lowered her gaze and pressed her lips together so she wouldn't be tempted to speak.

That last had been spoken with quiet certainty, a statement, not a question. He didn't need her to confirm it. Whatever magic he possessed had already shown him the truth. She wondered if it would be enough to keep the young knights out of trouble.

The woman snorted.

"Well, whatever she knows, she'll tell it soon enough. Take her to the chapter house for a more thorough interrogation."

"Yes, ma'am."

The woman studied her again and still didn't seem impressed by what she saw. Her mouth curled in distaste and she pivoted and left the room.

Ademar stepped forward and took a set of cuffs from his belt before he untied her hands. The movement sent pain lancing up her arms and she winced.

He pursed his lips.

Chapter House? she wondered, then remembered the Knights had their own way of naming things. Some said it came from elvish and some from wherever the order's founders had come. Whatever it was, she didn't understand what most of it meant.

With her hands secured, he took a soft cloth bag from his belt and dragged it over her head before he pulled her to her feet and marched her out. The bag was of a soft, dark cloth that clung around her nose and chin and she began to breathe faster. When she tried to shake it clear of her face, he clamped a hand over her shoulder and shook her.

"You'll be able to breathe," he stated, "but if you keep trying to get rid of the bag, you'll find it harder."

Kaylin stilled and bit back the command to explain.

Some things, she decided, *are better left a mystery.*

And if it involved having trouble breathing worse than she was dealing with already, she didn't need to know that badly.

After a short carriage ride, she'd been steered through a gate and into another building, where Ademar guided her unsteady progress down a long set of stairs to a cellar that smelt of stone and damp.

The drop in temperature made her shiver but he didn't seem to notice.

"Sit," he instructed once he'd guided her through another door.

He pushed on her shoulder and she let her legs fold and settled on the floor. The bag remained over her head as he positioned her hands palm-down on the floor and shackled her wrists to keep them in place.

At first, Kaylin had wondered how that was meant to stop her from making the gestures she might need to open a lock. It wasn't until she tried to lift her hand from the floor that she understood. The shackles protruded from the wall at the right height that lifting her palms from the cold stone once they'd locked around her wrists was impossible.

The knight noticed. "I'd relax were I you," he told her and lifted the bag from her head.

The dim light of the cell made her blink and she drew a shaky breath of relief. The air was cool and there was nothing else in the room save her guard.

"Where—" she began but he shook his head.

"That is not your concern," he told her. "If the captain wants you to know, she'll tell you."

"Captain?" She licked her lips and swallowed to moisten her mouth.

The guard snorted softly and left the question unanswered as he rose to his feet and closed the door behind him.

Kaylin watched him go and suppressed the part of her that wanted to ask him not to leave. She flinched as the door thumped shut and leaned her head against the wall. Why wasn't she at the Wardens?

Why wasn't she being told how long she had until her appointment with the gallows?

Had her friends been caught too?

She swallowed and pushed the idea away. If they'd been caught, it would have been leverage and given that they hadn't been mentioned, she could only hope Goss and the others had made it safely to the attic.

Suddenly weary, she closed her eyes to try to get some rest before whatever came next started. That was when she discovered exactly how uncomfortable she would be.

The shackles held her arms close to the wall and pulled them slightly back until her forearms began to hurt. She tried to ease them by stretching against the restraint but there was no play in the solid iron.

Soon, the pain spread into her biceps and burned in sharp tweaks along her muscles until it reached her shoulders and crept into her chest and back.

This was why she now tried to stretch her torso, even when she had no hope of taking the pressure off her hands. Her wrists were a mass of pain and her fingers had begun to ache by the time the cell door opened again.

The captain entered—the woman—and she'd come alone. She also carried a tray that held a bowl, a mug, and a large bread roll. Kaylin's mouth watered at the sight of it, but she kept her gaze on her captor's face.

She'd waited for the interrogation to start and for someone to arrive with the tools they might need to force her to confess the truth. Warily, she scanned the tray as the woman put it close to her but didn't see anything designed to give her pain. She raised her gaze to watch the knight as she settled beside her.

"I am Captain Jocelyn Delaine of the Chevaliers des Lances Jumelles," the woman said, "a captain of the Twin Spears Knights."

Kaylin remained silent and continued to stare. The smell of stew made her mouth water and she swallowed but refused to look at the tray. Perhaps Captain Delaine would eat it in front of her.

"You must be hungry," the captain surprised her by saying. She leaned forward, made a simple gesture with one hand, and the shackle on the wrist closest to her popped open.

When the woman moved to her other side and repeated the gesture, the girl made herself watch. While she might not be able to repeat it with her hands bound, she could try to remember it in case she needed it later.

Her captor's eyes gleamed with amusement but she said nothing and merely freed her wrists from the shackle and massaged them gently. Kaylin hissed softly as the motion sent pain shooting up her arm but she didn't pull away. Her muscles unknotted beneath the captain's touch and while she anticipated more pain to follow, she wasn't in any condition to resist.

When the door opened a second time, the knight moved to the tray and picked it up as Ademar and Loud Mouth walked in carrying a small table between them. Chair Catcher followed with two wooden chairs, which he placed on either side of the table.

"Come on, girl," Delaine said and put the tray on the tabletop.

Kaylin watched as the three men retreated to the door and left the room before she drew her feet under her slowly, stood, and rubbed her arms.

"What now?" she croaked, and the woman indicated the food.

"You drink something for your throat and eat something," she told her with a gesture at a chair.

The girl glanced briefly at the door and noticed the shadows of someone waiting outside—the two guards, she guessed—and sat where the captain had indicated.

Delaine relaxed and Kaylin felt as if she'd passed some kind of test.

As much as she wanted to, she didn't touch the food on the tray but clasped her hands together in her lap and hunched while she waited for the next blow to fall.

"Eat, girl," was not what she expected to hear, but the woman nudged the tray toward her. "You'll think better on a full stomach."

She frowned. Where had she heard that?

The memory eluded her and she glanced at the captain's face.

Her captor was older than she'd first thought. Crow's feet edged her eyes and her gaze...she shivered. Those eyes had seen death and perhaps even ordered it. She could imagine them watching dispassionately while her orders were carried out. Abruptly, she pushed the tray away.

Part of her wanted to demand that the woman get on with the interrogation, that she ask her questions or do anything except sit there with that exasperated look on her face. The knight remained statue-like as she studied her prisoner's face.

Finally, she sighed and stretched across the table.

Kaylin shoved her chair back, preparing to dodge a blow, but the woman merely lifted the stew from the tray and picked the spoon up.

"It's not poisoned," she stated, dipped the spoon into the bowl, and stirred its contents.

As the girl watched, she took a spoonful, blew carefully to cool it, then ate it. When she was finished, she put the bowl and spoon on the tray again.

"Eat."

When Kaylin still hesitated, she gave another sigh, broke the roll in half, and tore a piece from it. With her gaze on the prisoner's, she ate the piece she'd taken, picked the mug up, and took a sip.

"There," she said, put the mug down, and leaned back in her seat. "Now, will you sit and eat?"

The smell of the food and her rumbling stomach brought Kaylin back to her chair and she curled her hand around the bowl and began to eat. After the first mouthful, it was all she could do not to bolt the food down.

She took rapid spoonfuls and alternated them with a bite of bread and a swig of water from the mug. While she knew her actions and her manners—what few she knew that mattered—weren't pretty, she was too hungry to care. Besides, if this was how they wanted to poison her, she decided it was at least tasty and probably more enjoyable than a noose.

The knight didn't say anything until she was on her fourth spoonful and had slowed a little.

"You know," the woman began, "none of us can explain how you and your crew got into Shacklemund's if none of you are Academy-trained and none of our guards helped."

"Truly?" she asked, the word muffled by the bite of bread she'd taken.

"Truly." The knight smirked.

Kaylin chewed rapidly and gulped water to clear her mouth.

"I don't know how your Academy could have helped but it took us days to work it out."

The woman arched her brows and Kaylin blushed and hid her embarrassment by taking another spoonful of stew.

"All right... It took me days to work it out and I'd almost given up, but I thought we'd try one more night of watching how the place was guarded."

She paused to take a bite from her roll and finish it with a mouthful of water.

"You know, I did get help from the guards," she added but hurried on before the captain could say anything. "But not directly. See? I was watchin' from the roof."

Again, Delaine's eyebrows rose, but she didn't try to speak. She merely placed her elbows on the table, clasped her hands together, and rested her chin on her knuckles. Kaylin continued and drew the memory out.

"I saw him open the gate. He...made this movement with his hand and the light went out." She looked up to meet the knight's eyes. "Like this."

The woman didn't try to stop the repetition but watched it with the intensity of a cat hunting sparrows in the square. As the girl completed the final movement, she interrupted.

"You learned all that from seeing him deactivate the sigils only once?" she asked and caught her as she took a mouthful of stew.

She shook her head hastily. "No," she mumbled and swallowed quickly. "He had to come out again."

"So you saw it..." She turned her head slightly to the side and left the question in the air between them.

Kaylin thought about it. "Four times."

"Four?"

"Yes." Her mouth pursed as she tried to think of something she'd missed. At the moment, her memory was still somewhat fuzzy.

"But...was that it?"

She took a bite of bread and shook her head as she chewed.

"I started to see if I could make the sign but it was hard to focus so I drew the sigil on the roof and practiced making the signs in front of that."

The knight's jaw dropped. "And that worked?"

Kaylin frowned. "Kinda. It was weird but as I made the movements I'd seen the guard do, I could feel this pressure on...no...*in* my fingers. Anyway, it was like the air was pushing my fingers into different positions and they felt right—better than what I made on my own so I did them that way."

"And the vault?" Delaine asked.

She took another mouthful of stew and a bite of bread and chewed thoughtfully.

"Well," she said when she'd swallowed, "I looked at the sigils and practiced the moves I thought I should make. But those were supposed to be done in a set order, see?"

The woman nodded, her face a mask of patience. "Yes..."

"I couldn't tell which one should go first but when I started on the wrong one, it was like the air burned over my skin and my hands were tense, so I moved my hand over each one and hovered it while I looked at it. When I got to one that felt right, I started the gesture."

"It was that easy?"

Kaylin shook her head in disagreement. "There was nothing easy about it. For one thing, I didn't know the sigil. I had to work it out there. It was a good thing I'd had that time on the roof because it meant I could feel the changes the sigil wanted to see and I went slowly enough that I could move my hands and fingers the way it wanted me to."

Astonishment colored the knight's tones. "Are you saying the sigil directed you?"

She shrugged. "I don't know what else could have, but those last two..." She shivered. "Those last two wanted me to move more than only my hands and they took a long time to make. I didn't think I would ever get through them."

Delaine leaned back in her chair and studied her with such an intense stare that the girl thought she was trying to see inside her head. She took another spoonful of stew, watched the woman warily, and waited for whatever she would say next.

A padlock pounded onto the table beside her bowl and she jumped.

"Show me," the captain ordered and ignored her startled glance.

Kaylin looked from the padlock to the knight and back again. A sigil glowed softly in its center. It was new but there was something familiar about the way its lines flowed.

With a shrug, she put her spoon down and stood, her gaze fixed on the padlock even when the knight tensed. Slowly, she moved her hand through the air and mirrored the sigil.

Cool air touched her fingers and pressed against them until she altered their position in response. The sigil gleamed more brightly in places but dimmed when she stilled her hands and curled them into fists.

When it had returned to its original brightness, she began the movement again. This time, she moved her fingers through the new positions. The sigil flared as she made the last motion and the lock popped open.

Delaine frowned but Kaylin sat and studied the captain's face as she dipped her spoon into her bowl. When it came up empty, she looked into the bowl and carefully scraped every last piece of stew from its sides. When there was nothing more, she used the last piece of bread to wipe it clean.

Still, her captor didn't say anything and she began to worry as she picked her mug up. She sipped slowly so she had an excuse to hold it.

It helped her to hide her nerves. The knight was thinking hard and the fact that she didn't know what was in the woman's head frightened her, perhaps more than anything else that had happened so far.

When the captain leaned forward again, Kaylin put the mug on the table but kept her hands wrapped firmly around it. She met her gaze and waited for her to speak. The knight's next words gave her even more reason to be afraid.

"What not many know about Shacklemund's," she said, "and even fewer know about us, is that we mark every piece of treasure stored there with a tracking hex."

Fear washed through her on a wave of cold and her heart sank.

The knight gave her a dispassionate look as she continued.

"So if your crew still has it, they will be found—and that's assuming they haven't been found already." She leaned forward. "We will arrest them and we'll take anyone stupid enough to shelter or trade with them—and then they will join you waiting for trial in the dungeons of Waypoint's Wardens."

Kaylin closed her mouth and swallowed against the sudden dryness in her throat. She tightened her hold on the mug until she thought the pressure from her fingers would crush it.

Her captor's stare didn't waver.

"As I'm sure you are aware, the punishments for theft are many and varied, but given what you stole..."

She had a brief flashback of Melis strapping the daggers to her waist, Raoul rolling the wands in their leather covering and stowing it in Piers's pack, and of the gemstones, bags of coins, and the jewelry.

Her face went numb as the blood drained from her skin, and the knight's lips creased in a brief humorless smile.

"The penalties you and your crew receive will be among the harshest ever seen, especially since you robbed the most secure vault in the city. It is not something that will be let go of lightly. An example will have to be made."

Kaylin propped her elbows on the table, raised her mug, and rested her chin against the rim without shifting her gaze from the captain's face.

"The very best the youngest of you could hope for in consideration of their ages would be time in the inner dungeon. The oldest of you will most likely hang—and if you're lucky, that's all you'll do. There are many preludes to death."

The girl recoiled and lowered her face so her chin rested on her chest. She held the mug so tightly it was a wonder it didn't shatter, but she wasn't a warrior or a dragon. Breaking heavy metal mugs with her bare hands was beyond her.

She'd known she would probably hang, but thinking of Goss and Piers in the dungeon knifed with unbearable anguish. Her hands tightened with the pain of it and she almost wished the mug would burst. She hunched her shoulders to stop them from shaking and suppress the sob that threatened to tear from her chest.

Pressing her lips together helped to fight the urge to cry, and squeezing her eyes tightly shut put a temporary stop to the tears.

The only thing that stopped the dam from bursting was the idea that if that was truly what the knight intended to let happen, she'd probably be in the Waypoint dungeons already—with whichever members of the crew they'd managed to find.

From what she could tell, the knight captain didn't seem like the kind of person to waste time in gloating. She hoped.

After a very long interval of silence, Delaine continued.

"Now, I'm willing to place all the other members of your crew—who my men swear are your age or younger—into a place of foster, if..."

Kaylin raised her head.

"If you will agree to be seconded by the Chevaliers des Lances Jumelles for training at the Academy as a mage."

The girl stared at her and the pallor of her skin accentuated the darkness of her eyes.

"You want what?"

Delaine pursed her lips. "You heard me."

She shook her head. "I'm no mage and I don't know nothin' 'bout this Academy or being seconded—" She pushed her chair back and placed her mug firmly on the table as she rose to her feet.

"It's the only way," the captain persisted gently. "You take mage training and I'll take care of your friends."

Kaylin turned away from the table. "But I'm not a—I know nothing about magic."

"Exactly," Delaine agreed.

"And you owe me nothing," she told her and turned. "This training—it's expensive, isn't it? I mean, you Cheval...Chevals will spend a ton of money on me." She pointed an accusing finger at the captain. "You...you're rewarding me for trying to rob you blind. You can't do that."

The knight placed her hands on the table and rose, and Kaylin skittered back and only stopped when she felt the wall behind her.

"No one tells the Chevaliers des Lances Jumelles what we can and cannot do," the woman announced and her voice rolled across the cell like thunder. "We choose who we second and where and you need to be in the Academy." She softened her voice but didn't move from behind the table. "We are helping you."

Kaylin tried to reverse farther away and curled in on herself when she couldn't.

"And there's that," she protested. "You can't be helping me. No one helps me," she protested. But was she arguing with the captain or herself?

"Sabine did," the captain retorted tartly and the girl froze before she raised her head and uncoiled slowly.

Delaine continued before the girl could say anything. "And the Shepherd only knows what she would say to see you now."

Aghast, she stared at the woman, who pressed her advantage.

"What would she say to see you throwing your life away because you were too afraid to accept help when it was offered?" she demanded and added, "What would she say to you throwing away the lives of your friends because you were too proud to accept help when it was offered?"

"But..." Kaylin protested softly, "I don't deserve—"

"To die?" the woman asked bluntly. "To be lashed, hung, drawn, and quartered in Orcs' Head as an example of what happens to those who steal from the dead? To see your friends beaten and brutalized before the trapdoor's dropped?"

The girl sank against the wall and slid down to sit at its base, her forearms draped over her knees as she stared at the knight.

"This Academy...it's expensive."

"Oh, yes," Delaine assured her. "Only the wealthiest of Waypoint's families can afford to send their children to it."

"And...and it's powerful."

"That is true." The woman frowned.

"So, it's an opportunity." Delaine nodded. "And...and the others get to live if I go." This time, Kaylin wasn't asking. To the knight, it sounded more like the girl was listing an argument for.

She nodded to confirm it. "They get to live and be looked after in a home instead of having to try to survive on the streets."

Kaylin clenched her teeth and the muscles in her jaw jumped at the tension, then she struggled to her feet. The woman stopped her with a single word.

"But—" She resumed her seat and the knight continued. "But you have to see the training to its end. You have to graduate."

She raised her head. "And if I don't? If I decide it's not for me?"

Delaine quirked her eyebrows and smiled but it disappeared quickly when she replied.

"You don't get to decide," she told her. "If you quit the school or 'decide it's not for you' and run away for that or any other reason, the trial and sentences for your attack on Shacklemund's will be reinstated and you and your friends will suffer the consequences of your actions."

Kaylin stared at her, not seeing the knight but running through the alternatives. It didn't take her long to identify the only true option she had—for her friends' lives and her own.

"I don't have a choice, do I?" she asked and even to herself, she sounded bitter.

The captain snorted. "Oh, you have a choice," she assured the girl. "I'm not saying it's a good choice or even one you want to make, but it is there."

That earned her a wry smile.

"Fine," the girl stated and her companion had almost relaxed when she added, "I'll go on one condition."

The unexpectedness of it startled a chuckle out of the knight. "I would point out that you're hardly in a position to negotiate," she commented, "but I think I have the measure of you enough to know that it is hardly enough to stop you. Go ahead."

Kaylin moved closer, stopped when she was halfway between the knight and the wall, and kept the table carefully between them.

"My crew," she continued resolutely, "should be placed with Sister

Nadiya at Herder's Gate." Delaine raised her eyebrows and the girl continued. "I know the sister will look after them better than I could."

The knight hesitated, aware of the girl's gaze as she considered what Herder's Gate had to offer against her other options. She gave the prisoner a measuring look and caught her anxiety and vulnerability beneath the determined expression she wore.

Finally, she agreed. "Done!"

CHAPTER ELEVEN

Kaylin waited. The knight had agreed but she still stared at her over the table. When the woman hadn't spoken for longer than she could bear, she broke.

"What?"

"You look like you've been living in a gutter for the past year," Delaine told her with a disapproving sniff. "And you smell like it too."

She folded her arms. "Funny you should mention that—" she began but her companion didn't let her finish.

"And like you said, the Academy is expensive and so is seconding. You might not think you deserve it and we might only be doing Waypoint a service by getting an untrained mage off the streets before they can do any damage, but you have to look the part."

"You what?" she exclaimed. "I don't—"

"Are you backing out of a deal made in good faith?" the captain challenged.

Kaylin gaped at her. "I never... I said... I..."

It didn't take her long to realize she had essentially agreed to anything that might happen from this point forward—and the crew's survival still hung on her actions, no matter how insulted she might feel. She closed her mouth and satisfied herself with giving the knight a murderous glare.

"So what will you do about that?" she challenged and the woman responded with a bright smile.

"Me?" she answered with a short laugh. "I won't do anything about it except hand you over to those with the time and know-how to deal with street rats like you."

"I am not a—" Kaylin began and her face burned. She stopped when she realized that a street rat was exactly what she was—and had been ever since she'd slipped over the orphanage wall and left it behind.

"You were saying?" her companion prodded and the girl folded her arms across her chest.

"You have a plan?" she snapped.

Delaine made a point of scrutinizing her and her expression said she didn't like what she saw. The girl set her jaw and returned the stare. There might not be anything she could do about the embarrassment that flamed across her skin but that didn't mean she would run.

After everything they'd gone through and the trouble she'd landed them in, her crew didn't deserve to have her abandon them now. Not to mention that she was the idiot who had decided to take that one last gem.

The Academy, whatever it entailed, was a small price to pay for their lives and Sister Nadiya would make sure they came to no harm.

With that in mind, she met the knight's eyes with a steady gaze and waited. That earned her a small nod, and Delaine turned toward the cell door.

"Come," she ordered.

Kaylin suppressed a snort. As if she could or would do anything else.

She followed cautiously, aware that she now moved into grab range but decided she'd been there all along. When she stood at her side, the woman opened the door and led her into the corridor.

"She's with me," the captain told the guards on the other side, "and on Lances Jumelles business."

When the name rolled off the knight's tongue, she wondered if she'd ever get used to hearing it or learn to say it. She assumed she'd have to if the Chevaliers seconded her. Someone at the Academy was bound to ask who her sponsors were.

Not being able to say their name might attract more trouble than she needed.

Kaylin rolled her eyes. *Who am I kidding? I already have more trouble than I need.*

She followed along the prison corridor and noted that some of the doors had small windows set high in the center and that all these windows were barred. The knight led her past these and into a reception with a solid wooden desk behind which another knight sat.

Dark-haired and dark-eyed with a face weathered by the sun, the woman rose to her feet as they entered. Her gaze flicked across Kaylin in professional assessment as she addressed the captain.

"Captain Delaine."

"Lieutenant Morgan. This is Apprentice..." She glanced at Kaylin.

"Kaylin," she replied.

The knight waited and finally gave her a hint as to what she wanted. "Your surname, girl."

She froze. While she had a surname, it had been so long since she'd heard it used that she'd forgotten it or had left it behind in the tumult of memory that had followed her parents' deaths.

"I..."

It wasn't a place she wanted to visit and the captain looked like she didn't want to wait. Kaylin looked around the room in search of inspiration but found nothing.

Boots, Table, and Chair all seemed too mundane and she didn't want to be known by any of them anyway.

"Well, girl," the woman pressed. "Surely you know your own name."

She stared at her, then her eyes flicked to the woman behind the table and the answer seemed obvious.

"Knight," she answered firmly and dared them to make something of it.

Delaine's brows rose. She replied without inflection. "I guess not." She pursed her lips and looked at her colleague. "Apprentice *Knight* will stay with Matrons Otila and Taragood for the next couple of days."

Lieutenant Morgan nodded, flicked a heavy ledger open, and made the appropriate annotations.

"No belongings?" the lieutenant asked with a frown.

Delaine's mouth twitched. "Most of what she had didn't belong to her and she's wearing the rest."

Kaylin blushed and looked at her feet. Part of her was embarrassed by the fact she'd been caught as a thief and the other part was angry that the profits of the robbery had been so easily taken.

She remembered Delaine's words. *We mark every piece of treasure stored there with a tracking hex*. Of all the dirty tricks, that had to be the worst. Where was the fairness in tracking the loot? It felt unprofessional. Or perhaps too professional?

"Thank you, Captain. You can take her out now."

As if anything could stop her, the girl thought wryly but kept her face blank as she glanced from one to the other.

"This way, girl," Delaine ordered and Kaylin wondered what the point of having a name was if no one used it.

She didn't bother to ask but used the journey to get an idea of where she was and how it was laid out. If things didn't work out, maybe she could escape.

With a grimace, she stopped that thought in its tracks. For one thing, the only sanctuary she'd have with both the Chevaliers and the Wardens after her would be outside Waypoint's walls—and there was no way she could survive that without extra equipment.

What was it? Late spring? The time of year when the monster tribes were at their most active around the city, hoping to catch travelers who moved through the pass or made the journey to the Doom.

Kaylin shivered.

As if that wasn't enough, she had to consider her friends. Even if she could find them and get them out of wherever they were being held—and she now had no doubt they were being held—they deserved a better future than having to take their chances in the wilds.

She thought of Goss and imagined him still ill with no medicine and no chance of finding any. And Raoul and Piers, or Isabette and Melis in the forested hills she'd seen beyond the walls—or in the Kill Zone between Waypoint and the Doom. She shook her head.

No, even if she could free them, she wouldn't be able to keep them alive beyond Waypoint's walls, let alone offer them a future.

Their best chance was for her to keep her bargain with the Chevaliers, go to the Academy, and take whatever learning it had to offer. Maybe in a couple of years, she could think about leaving but until then, this was her life.

The knight drew her to a halt and she realized she'd been too lost in her thoughts to take as much notice of her surroundings as she'd intended.

She vaguely recalled a walk to the ground floor where they turned right at a wide cross corridor and moved through a set of heavy double doors into another twisting stretch of hallway and a room at the end.

Kaylin looked around. She'd never imagined a room like this could exist.

Dark-gray stone paved the floor and reflected the sunlight from the windows that stretched across most of the end wall. Beyond them, she could see garden beds full of flowers intersected by paths of white. A fountain peeked out from behind a small copse of fruit trees and her heart ached when she thought of Goss.

The boy would have been fascinated by the fruit forming on the branches, while Melis and Isabette would have been more interested in the tapestries that draped one wall and the books and items on the shelves of the large bookcases that stood along another.

Piers would have been drawn to the food being served to the older folk seated around several small round tables, and Raoul to the scarred men and women eating it.

Kaylin let her gaze travel to where a large banked fireplace stood at one end of the room. Several women sat at a table before it. They looked up as Delaine paused at the door and one waved her hand in greeting.

"Joss, sweetie!" a gray-haired woman called and struggled to stand from the table.

Sweetie? Kaylin snuck a sideways glance at the captain.

The knight pursed her lips. "I've brought you a distraction," she stated, put her hand between the girl's shoulder blades, and pushed.

She resisted and the push became a shove that made her stumble two paces forward. The gray-haired woman seemed to notice her for the first time and bustled closer.

"Well, what have we here?" She glanced at the table. "Rhodda, Creswyn, come and see."

Two other women rose from the table to join her, and a third pushed her seat back.

"Forgotten as usual," she grumbled.

"Not forgotten," the first woman told her cheerfully. "I merely didn't want to scare our recruit by shouting Dagger across the room."

The word resulted in a chorus of scraping as chairs were shoved back from tables and weapons drawn. Kaylin might have bolted for cover if Delaine hadn't grasped the back of her shirt and held her steady. A crossbow bolt whipped past their heads to thunk into the wall behind them.

"Ambrose!" the captain scolded and glared at a large man who stood next to a sideboard at the back of the room. "How many times have you been told to not bring your crossbow to the meal table?"

He gave her an unrepentant grin. "As many times as I've almost shot some unsuspecting serving maid or visitor?" he asked.

"And where did you hide it this time?" she demanded.

Ambrose shifted his gaze from her angry face to the ceiling.

"Oh...I don't know..."

"Don't give me that," the captain snapped, but the gray-haired woman chuckled.

"He coulda hidden it down his trousers for all you know," she suggested.

Delaine gave her a look of disgust and the woman added, "Well, it's not like there's anything else down there."

Kaylin looked from one to the other, then back at Delaine.

The captain caught her glance and shook her head. She surveyed the room sternly and cleared her throat. "You all know Dagger is Matron Steele's first name, but every time—" She glared at them. "Every time one of you shouts it, we get this!"

Rueful laughter sounded around the room as weapons were sheathed.

"And not one of you is supposed to be armed." Exasperation tinged her voice.

"We're Chevaliers," Dagger replied and moved closer. "It's kinda expected."

Kaylin noted strands of silver gleaming in her dusty-blonde hair and creases around her eyes and mouth.

"*Ex*-Chevaliers," Delaine retorted.

"Retired Chevaliers," the gray-haired woman corrected. "I trained you. Remember?"

"Aye, and me," interjected a balding gentleman as he lifted a chicken leg from his plate. He waved it at her as he continued. "Something you shouldn't forget. Chevaliers are always armed. We might be retired and some might think we're in our dotage, but we're still Chevaliers."

He took a savage bite from the chicken leg as though to prove a point and followed it with a hefty swig from the mug beside his plate. All around him, others returned to their meals except for the women.

They closed on the latest arrivals and Kaylin tensed.

"Like I was saying," the gray-haired lady repeated, "what have we here?"

"This is Kaylin Knight," Delaine declared. "We're seconding her to the Academy."

She drew breath to continue, but the older woman cut her off.

"The Academy?" She squawked and studied the girl in disbelief. *"This?"*

Kaylin glared at them and was duly ignored. It seemed her ability to glare suffered when directed at those in their dotage.

"In *this* state?" another challenged, her faded red hair streaked with white and her blue eyes bright with indignation. "You can't do that."

"And when did you plan to take her?" the gray-haired woman demanded.

"You might want to rethink that," the fourth woman suggested as she ran a critical eye over the recruit's thin form. "She looks like something the rats refused to touch."

Kaylin's glare turned into a scowl and she wondered what her chances were of shrugging free of the restraining hand and reaching the garden. The hold on her shirt tightened and she pressed her lips together.

"Enough!" Delaine snapped and the four women turned their attention to her.

The redhead folded her arms and raised an eyebrow, while Dagger put her hands on her hips and tapped her foot. The gray-haired woman and her friend both swung toward the captain with annoyance on their faces.

"As I was saying, this is Kaylin Knight and the Chevaliers des Lances Jumelles are seconding her education at the Academy."

A soft snort carried from the tables. "Good luck with that."

"I know you're not particularly fond of the masters," the gray-haired woman stated, "but is there any particular reason why you thought an undernourished, flea-infested street rat should be set among them?"

Kaylin's face burned but she wiped it of all expression and waited for the reply.

"This undernourished, flea-infested street rat disarmed the sigils in the central vault at Shacklemund's," the captain told them. "*Without* setting the alarms off." A soft murmur rose around them as she added, "And she did it with no training or assistance whatsoever."

The girl snuck a glance around the room and realized she was the center of attention.

Now, she wanted nothing more than for the floor to open up and swallow her, but given that it wouldn't happen and she couldn't flee, she stood frozen to the spot.

"Did you, girl?" the gray-haired woman asked and she managed a single nod.

"And all on your own?" the redhead demanded.

Again, she nodded.

"With no help from the Academy?" The blonde woman sounded like she couldn't believe it.

Kaylin shook her head.

"She doesn't even know what the Academy is," Delaine told them and the fourth woman snorted.

"And a good thing, too. If she did, she'd have never agreed to go."

The captain tensed. "Be that as it may," she responded, "she has agreed and she needs to be prepared."

Like I'm some kind of meal, Kaylin thought and waited for whatever came next.

The gray-haired woman conducted another slow scrutiny. "Well, there's no disputing that. What did you have in mind?"

Delaine gave her a smug smile. "I remembered you'd had some experience with that, Matron Otila." She loosened her hold on Kaylin's shirt. "And your friends can help you."

The old woman frowned. "Where did you say she was sleeping?"

"Her quarters are still being assigned," the captain informed her. "We don't expect her to be here for very long."

"The girl will still need a room to come back to."

"I doubt it. She'll have her hands full catching up to the others. Our reasoning is that she'll live at the Academy for at least a year."

"Hmmph. Well, she can have a cot in my quarters," Otila declared. Delaine gave her a predatory smile but the old woman continued before she could speak. "But not before she's been thoroughly cleaned and deloused."

The captain released Kaylin's shirt and stepped away.

"I'll leave her in your capable hands then," she commented but stopped when Otila raised her voice.

"I take it all the necessary items have been sent to my quarters?" she demanded.

"They're about to be. I'll have them delivered to your sitting room."

"*Our* sitting room," the redhead grumbled and Dagger sighed.

The knight's smile grew a little wider. "I'm thankful for your understanding, Matron Steele," she added and gave the recruit a stern look. "Do as the matrons ask. I'll come to collect you for supper."

Kaylin nodded. *Supper?*

She glanced out the window and realized the garden was lit by morning light and that she and the crew were usually sound asleep by this time. It might be normal hours for the Chevaliers and their retirees but it was way past her bedtime.

The realization brought with it an overwhelming urge to yawn and she wondered how the rest of the crew were doing, if they'd been caught and how long before, and where they were being held.

Madame Otila poked her in the chest and gave her finger a look of distaste.

"I'm sorry?" she said and the old woman frowned.

"It looks like the dirt's gotten into your ears, girl."

"That's not a surprise," the fourth woman muttered. "It's gotten into everywhere else."

The girl blushed but Dagger came to her defense.

"Now, Creswyn, it's not a bad thing for her to imitate a walking mullock heap. She's less likely to be bothered that way."

Walking mullock heap? She lowered her head and glanced at herself. *How bad am I?*

"I'll leave her with you then," Delaine stated and turned.

Kaylin glanced at the captain's feet. *Why hasn't she gone yet?*

As if to answer her question, the knight yawned and shifted farther away. "I have reports to write." She drew a breath as though she considered adding more but said nothing. Her boots struck the stone in determined steps as she left the room.

Fully aware of the scrutiny she was receiving, the girl waited, her gaze fixed on the floor. Finally, Madame Otila sighed expressively.

"Well, I guess the cards can wait," she stated and headed to a door set in one corner of the hall. "Come along, girl."

She walked away and Kaylin followed. The other women fell in around her as though they were her bodyguards—or perhaps guards escorting a prisoner.

Conversation rose behind them and she realized the hall's occupants had been more interested in her than she'd thought.

It made her wish Delaine hadn't revealed her skill with sigils—not that she understood why everyone thought it was such a feat. She'd seen them, copied them until she had them right, and performed them.

And as for the ones in the vault...well, they'd simply been variations, hadn't they?

This time, she paid more attention to where she was going, surprised to see men and women wearing the garb of healers coming and going amidst younger men and women dressed in the leather jerkins, heavy cloth tunics, and breeches of Chevalier trainees.

Otila noticed her curiosity. "Some knights retire to their families," the gray-haired woman explained.

"But some of us don't have any family we'd care to retire to," Dagger added, earned a glare, and ignored it.

"And some of us retire only in name," Creswyn added and gave the blonde Chevalier a sour look.

"Most of us retire because we don't have a choice," the red-haired knight told her. "Old injuries or plain old age mean we'd be more of a liability than an asset in the field."

"And in the training halls," Otila remarked, "although we do still have our uses in the classroom."

"There is that," Dagger admitted as their leader stopped outside one of the doors in the corridor.

"Here we are."

Kaylin followed the elderly Chevalier inside, surprised to find herself in a comfortably furnished sitting room from which four doors opened into four separate quarters. The old woman crossed to a fifth door in the rear of the room.

"We're old enough to warrant our own washing space," she explained and led her charge into a stone-floored chamber dominated by a single large tub at one end and twin privies separated by low half-walls at the other.

"Age has its privileges," Otila told her, "and the Chevaliers like to boast that they can provide for their own."

It was an extravagance Kaylin associated with the rich and she hadn't realized the order was this wealthy.

She stared at the washroom.

"Those still serving share their amenities with a larger group," Otila told the shocked recruit, "but this is how they thank us for our service."

The girl stayed near the entrance, aware of the three women who remained on the sitting room side of the door. Dagger stood at the door, while Rhodda and Creswyn had stopped beside bookshelves on either side of the washroom entrance.

"They'd prefer us to spend time in the gardens," Creswyn explained, "but they make sure we have enough to keep us occupied if we do not."

It's like cleaning street urchins up, Kaylin thought and turned her attention to the steaming tub that dominated the corner of the room.

Dagger closed the door to the suite and startled the recruit when a locking bar dropped into place with a thunk. She noticed the girl's startled flinch at the sound.

"Privacy," the older woman explained. "Unless you want one of the patrons to walk in while you're getting clean."

"No, I'm good," she told her and fidgeted as she waited for Otila to close the bathroom door. Instead, the woman exhaled a sharply impatient breath.

"Well, don't just stand there, girl. It's time you got out of those dirty things and into the tub. Someone will be along soon with fresh clothes."

Kaylin moved closer to the tub and expected the matron to leave. Not only did Otila stay exactly where she was, however, but the other three entered the washroom as well.

"Well, hurry up," Creswyn exclaimed and wrinkled her nose. "We don't have all day and Joss expects you to be presentable by dusk."

Dagger snorted. "That woman always did demand miracles."

"Even as a trainee," Rhodda commented dourly, "although usually of herself."

"Well, she's graduated to demanding them from her elders," Otila told them sourly before she fixed Kaylin with a determined stare, "and we'd better deliver."

Deliver what? the girl wondered as the old woman's look turned even more steely.

"Now, will you get out of those clothes on your own or do you need some help?"

"Help?" she repeated, shocked at the suggestion. "But...aren't you going to leave while I—"

The old woman raised her hands and made three short, sharp gestures in the air. She executed them so crisply and cleanly that Kaylin thought she could see symbols burning in their wake. In the next moment, the seams of her tunic and trousers unraveled and they fell in a tumble of filthy cloth.

"Hey!" She tried to clutch the shreds but to no avail.

"You said you needed help," Otila responded, a look of false innocence on her face. "Now, about your boots."

She raised her hands again, and the thought of losing the only pieces of footwear she had made her temporarily forget she was naked.

"I can manage," she assured the matron hastily and stooped to pull her boots from her feet.

"You call those boots?" Creswyn challenged and regarded the worn footwear with a jaundiced eye.

Kaylin set them carefully to one side. If there was one thing she'd learned on the streets, it was that her feet were the most important assets she had. Protecting them from injury was paramount to getting anything else she needed.

She'd liberated these from the rear workshop of Hobmason Chitairy when she'd snuck through an open window in the attic and proceeded to the ground floor to find a pair that fit. Interrupted before she could find anything, she had fled into the back room, where these boots had sat, newly completed, on the end of a bench.

It had felt like a match ordained by the gods, and she hadn't hesitated to pull them on and leave her worn and holey shoes in their place. The uproar that had erupted behind her had been nothing short of spectacular, and she'd taken to the roofs to escape.

When she looked at them now, she felt a pang of sadness.

They looked nothing like the well-polished product the cobbler had mourned losing. If she were honest, the soles were almost worn through and she was overdue another raid on Hobmason's. It had been something she'd planned to do before summer. Or perhaps she had hoped to pay for a pair after the success of one more hit.

"You leave them be," Kaylin ordered the woman and Creswyn snorted again as the young thief fixed her with a warning glance. "I mean it."

"Mean it all you like," Otila interrupted, "but mean it from the tub."

She stared at the woman. "I—"

"Oh, for goodness sake!" Dagger exclaimed and before the girl could register what she intended, the older woman had scooped her up and dumped into the steaming water.

Her yell of surprised outrage was lost in the resounding splash and the protests that followed, and she resurfaced spluttering and coughing. Her flailing hands sent suds and water to soak the already wet matrons as they glared at the blonde woman.

"What?" the matron asked as Kaylin's hand found the side of the tub. "She intended to argue and we don't have time."

"You filthy troll!" Kaylin began, only to be pushed under the water again.

"Manners never go astray," Dagger stated when she surfaced a second time, "and you need to get clean."

A sponge hit her on the side of the head and bounced into the water.

"You do know how to wash, don't you?" Creswyn asked and her tone suggested that she didn't expect her to have the faintest clue.

"I know," the girl muttered. She felt like she was getting a lesson in cleanliness from the four grandmas from Mount Doom itself.

"Good," Otila declared and flicked her fingers to indicate that she should go ahead. "And hurry."

Kaylin looked around for the sponge and her search was interrupted by an exasperated sigh.

"Stand up, girl."

She snapped around and found herself face to face with the redhead. Rhodda waggled a sponge and she tried to snatch it from her hand but the matron pulled it out of her reach.

"Turn around," she instructed. "I'll do your back while you do your front."

For a moment, she thought about arguing but Dagger hovered at the edge of the tub and she decided against it and complied. She turned and her gaze searched the water for the other sponge.

"Sit," Rhodda instructed and rolled her up sleeves.

"You just told me to stand," Kaylin protested in confusion.

"That was before I got a good look at how filthy you truly are. I will need more water. Now, sit."

Kaylin sat and her skin brushed against the sponge as she sank into the water. She snatched it before it could vanish again and began to wash. The feel of the other sponge being applied to her neck and shoulders made her jump but she forced herself to focus on what she was doing.

It wasn't until there was a knock at the door to the suite that she turned her head and caught sight of Rhodda leaning against one wall of the washroom while she moved her hands to direct the sponge from a distance.

"What?" the woman challenged her as Matron Otila bustled out of the washroom to answer the door. "Have you seen how much dirt you were wearing under your tunic?"

Kaylin blushed harder. Now that she looked at herself, she saw how filthy she'd become. It wasn't like they'd had too much opportunity to wash at the inn, and the river was too deep and dangerous for swimming.

She tried to think back to when they'd last washed and realized a midnight splash in the overflow barrel at Steele & Shields was the only one she could recall. That had been… She frowned and tried to think how many nights had passed.

It hadn't been long after the first snows, and the barrel had steamed slightly from the heat of the furnace behind the wall. She, Isabette, and Melis had taken turns to use the tea towel they'd stolen from an unattended washing line to rub away the most accessible grime.

A whole tubful of water to herself was more luxury than she had dreamed of in a long time.

"Now, we can deal with that nightmare you call your head," Otila declared and returned to the room carrying two baskets.

"Finally," Creswyn stated, plucked a square of soap from a basket, and pitched it in the recruit's direction. "Catch!"

When she saw the block hurtle toward her face, Kaylin dropped the sponge to catch it and her wet hands fumbled as they closed around it. The soap became slippery and she splashed frantically before it escaped her grasp and vanished into the tub.

"You'll need to scrub yourself again," Rhodda told her. "This time, use the soap. That should get rid of the rest of it."

The rest of what? the girl wondered as she felt around in the bottom of the tub for the elusive cleanser.

"Rub it on the sponge," Rhodda instructed, "then clean yourself all over and rinse it off."

As if she didn't remember what soap was. It had merely been a very long time since she'd seen any.

Two years, said a little voice in her head, *or more.*

It wasn't what she wanted to hear. She found the soap and scrubbed. Across the room, Creswyn had taken two flasks from the basket and hummed as she mixed their contents in a small bowl. When she was done, she passed the bowl to Dagger.

"Sit still," Dagger instructed and approached the side of the tub, her mouth curled with distaste. "We need to wash your hair."

Kaylin paused in her scrubbing. *Say what?*

The woman patted the side of the tub. "Over here."

She regarded her uncertainly and saw the matron's mouth tighten. Rather than risk being grabbed and dragged closer, she decided to do as she'd been asked and shuffled to sit against the side of the tub.

"Hold still."

Instinctively, she froze but flinched when the woman tipped the contents of the bowl carefully over her hair. Cold liquid flowed over her scalp, and the scent of lavender, rosemary, burdock, and elderflowers enveloped her senses. It was cut by a sharper tang of apple cider and vinegar and accompanied by the feel of someone massaging the mixture into her scalp.

Kaylin almost sighed with contentment except she didn't want to relax. Dagger moved to help Otila unpack the rest of the basket. A pile of towels and clean clothes were placed on a wooden bench positioned against the rear wall of the bathroom. It was followed by a series of brushes, combs, and other instruments she didn't recognize.

Possible torture instruments for cleaning her?

She stared but was distracted when she realized that Rhodda and Creswyn stood side by side and made kneading movements with their hands and fingers.

"What?" Creswyn demanded and the movements of her hands mirrored the feeling of fingers on her scalp. "If you think I'll touch you when you're like this, you do not realize how much I detest filth. Now, duck your head and rinse."

Rinse? Her hair? Some of her confusion must have shown on her face because Dagger made an impatient sound and took two strides to the tub.

"Like this," the woman snapped, pushed the girl's head briefly under the water, and rubbed furiously at her scalp.

For the third time that day, Kaylin surfaced with a gasp.

"Hush!" Dagger instructed as she started to speak. "Let me see the damage."

Damage? She stilled as the matron combed her fingers through her hair.

"And again." The warning gave Kaylin enough time to take a breath before she shoved her under the water a second time.

When she pulled her up, Dagger looked at the others.

"I'm not sure it'll be enough," she stated.

"I'm clean, aren't I?" she challenged and the woman shrugged.

"You're clean," she confirmed, "but your hair is a problem."

"Problem?" She wasn't sure if she wanted to know.

"Yes," Dagger confirmed. "When was the last time you washed it?"

Kaylin gave her a blank stare and Otila sighed.

"How about brushed it?" she asked and the girl blushed.

"It's been a while," she admitted, gathered her hair into a bundle, and squeezed the excess water from it.

"Well, at least we got all the lice," Dagger stated and rapped her on the shoulder. "Time to get out."

The girl looked at her.

"It wasn't a suggestion," the older woman told her and Kaylin sighed in recognition of the unsaid 'or else.'

Standing up was harder than she remembered. Her body felt like it weighed more getting out than it had when she'd been tossed in—and she didn't like the fact that four pairs of beady eyes studied her like she was a prize pony at a show.

"You'd look much better if you'd stop scowling," Creswyn commented.

"I'd feel much better if I could get clean in private," she retorted.

"Why? Because you've done such a great job of that before?" Rhodda snapped in return.

Otila pointed to a stool that had been placed in the middle of the floor between the tub and the privies.

"Sit," she ordered. "Let us look at your hair."

Kaylin firmed her jaw and thought about arguing, but she saw Dagger's body tense and decided she didn't want to be sat on the stool by someone else. She'd rather do it under her own steam.

"You're very strong for—" She stopped, mortified by what she'd been about to say.

Dagger laughed. "What? For an old lady?" she teased and the girl blushed to the roots of her hair.

She decided not to answer that and instead, stalked to the stool and settled herself on it. The four women followed and surrounded her as they studied her hair.

"She was crawling," Creswyn exclaimed in disgust.

"Well, she isn't now," Otila declared and pulled something from Kaylin's scalp. She pinched it between her fingernails and wiped her hand on her skirt.

The girl winced.

"Sit still, girl," the matron admonished and took a comb from her pocket. "Let's see if we can untangle you."

Kaylin wanted to ask why the untangling couldn't wait until she was dressed, but she didn't dare. She flinched when the comb caught a snag and Otila stopped abruptly. The matron tried again and this time, pulled firmly against the tangles.

"It's impossible," Creswyn muttered and left the room to return with a comb in hand.

Yes, most certainly torture instruments!

Now, two sets of hands pulled and tugged at her scalp and neither of them made any progress. It seemed that no sooner had they set the comb against her head and started to draw it through her hair than they encountered another tangle.

"Let me try," Rhodda insisted and Otila handed her the comb.

To Kaylin's surprise, the woman didn't try to comb from the top of her head down. Instead, she began at the ends of her hair, combed a few strands loose, and worked up. It seemed she was making progress until she hit a particularly tightly meshed clump.

She yelped as the comb came to an abrupt stop and yanked her head to one side.

"Quit yammering, girl," Dagger snapped as Rhodda apologized.

The four of them persisted for several more long, painful minutes until Otila and Rhodda snagged at the same time and the girl decided she'd had enough.

She slid out from under their hands and took the embedded combs with her.

"No more," she declared, untangled one of the combs, and placed it on the shelf with the brushes.

As she moved her hands to the other one, the women approached and she backed away to the shelf behind her.

"I said no more," she reminded them. "You are done messing with my hair."

"We'll have to cut it," Dagger observed and ignored her.

Kaylin stared at her with wide eyes. "Didn't you hear?" she challenged. "I said you are done."

Otila pursed her lips and shook her head. "I'm afraid that's not how it works, dear. Joss tasked us with ensuring that you are presentable enough to attend the Academy." Her gaze swept the girl's body critically and she tutted. "I'm afraid you're a long way from that. Oh, you're clean, but Academy-worthy?" She shook her head. "Not by a long shot."

Dagger's jaw dropped but she closed it abruptly. "And I thought I was the brutal one," she muttered.

"You are—until someone's dumb enough to get Tam started," Creswyn mock-whispered in return.

Kaylin looked from one to the other. "I mean it," she warned and Otila slashed her hands through a short sequence of movements.

Her body seized and she fell back against the bench.

"You're gonna have to get her to bend her legs," Rhodda commented and Otila shrugged.

"It's not like she's a board," she argued. "I thought we'd put her on the stool and bend them for her."

"This would be so much easier if she'd do that for herself," Creswyn remarked as they closed in.

Otila shrugged again. "She had the chance to do it and she didn't. Now, it's up to us."

Do I get a say in this? Kaylin wanted to ask but found she couldn't move her jaw to argue either.

She was surprised that her body remained rigidly out of her

control but that her limbs bent easily enough when the four older women moved them. Soon, she was seated on the stool with her back ramrod straight and her hands on her knees as they discussed the problem of her hair.

"To be honest, I don't think it's seen a comb anytime in the last century," Creswyn declared.

"And it wasn't likely to either," Rhodda added.

Sure, and why don't you say what you all feel? the girl thought but couldn't get her voice to work. She sighed and continued to sit rigidly at attention as the four matrons discussed their options.

"You know what it has to be," Dagger declared after another round of debate, and she stalked to the bench and picked a pair of scissors up.

Kaylin tried to scramble to her feet and succeeded in going nowhere.

Otila glanced at the implements in the other woman's hand and tsked.

"It's always blades with you, isn't it?" she asked and the blonde woman grinned.

"Dagger by name," she replied and the others chuckled.

"Hold still, girl," Otila told Kaylin. "It's the only way."

She sat perfectly still—but not because she had any other options. The spell held her that way and made her remember the rumors she'd heard about the Chevaliers—that they weren't merely knights. They were mage-knights.

She groaned—silently—and stared straight ahead as the scissors clicked and snipped and the hair fell away from her head. When they were finished and she could feel air moving against her scalp, Creswyn crossed to the basket and returned with a small bottle.

"Lavender oil," the matron stated and tipped a little onto her head. "It's good for soothing the bites and encouraging healing, and ginger to encourage growth."

The scents mingled and Kaylin blinked at the sharp blend. The oil soothed her scalp and Creswyn's fingers were strangely relaxing as they worked it into her skin—not that she'd ever admit that, of course.

Matron Otila released her spell with a snap of her fingers and Dagger caught the girl when she rocked on the stool.

"It's time we got you dressed," Rhodda declared as a yawn ambushed Kaylin and the girl tried to clap her hands over her mouth.

"Thief, right?" Dagger asked when she noticed it.

She blushed to her non-existent hairline. "Not anymore," she muttered.

The woman rolled her eyes. "What I meant is you were a thief and aren't used to being awake at this hour."

"Not to mention that you were brought in last night and couldn't have had much sleep in the cells," Rhodda added. "The fuss! It woke me from a thoroughly good dream, too. Now, I'll never get it back."

"There was a fuss?" Creswyn asked and the others laughed.

"Says the woman who can sleep through a troll raid." Otila snickered.

"I'd had a day of killing minotaurs," Creswyn protested. "Filthy cow-headed ass-lickers."

Kaylin stared and Dagger burst out laughing.

"Be careful, Cressy, or you'll shatter any illusions the apprentice has about us retired knights."

"We're knights, not priests," Creswyn snapped in response. "Useless tits."

The girl was so busy staring that she started when Otila thrust a towel into her hands.

"Dry yourself, girl. You won't get any clothes until they won't be saturated from touching your skin."

She shook her head and set about the task, reveling in the towel's fluffy softness. When she turned to see what the others were doing, her gaze fell on the pile of dark hair on the floor. The sight made her raise her hand to her head and her fingers lightly traced the smooth skin she found there.

It was as if she hadn't fully understood the meaning of the weight falling from her head. As she stared at the long strands curled on the floor, the impact hit her like a physical blow. She'd always had long hair and remembered her mother brushing it.

With a frown, she ran her fingers over her scalp. Now, she had none.

It was like she'd left a piece of her soul behind or like a portion of herself had been shorn away and discarded on the floor—like her life and having a choice of what she wanted to be. Her eyes welled with unbidden tears and she raised the towel hastily to her face before she rubbed it over the rest of herself.

"You're done." Otila's voice broke into the turmoil that rolled through her head. A hand rapped her arm. "I said you're done."

Kaylin blinked, saw the outstretched hand, and laid the towel in it.

"You need to get dressed in these," the matron added and handed her a set of dark-blue robes.

She wrinkled her nose and the woman chuckled.

"The dyers had a good supply of woad when the Academy chose its colors. They got a bargain and the apprentices got blue."

With no other choice, she took the robes and pulled them on, grateful when the women helped her to draw them down and settle them around her.

"There!" Otila stated with such pleased satisfaction that Kaylin couldn't be angry at her for the treatment she'd received. She couldn't even be upset about the pile of hair although the sadness remained.

"Don't forget the tabard," Creswyn added, hurried to the bench, and returned with a pile of creamy-white cloth.

She shook it out and handed it to Kaylin and again, the girl was being helped by four pairs of hands.

"There! Now, don't you look the part," Otila declared and stepped back to admire their handiwork when they'd pulled the last fold into place.

Even Creswyn looked happy with what she saw and Dagger beamed with quiet pride. Rhodda studied her critically and gave her an approving nod, and she was given an inkling of what it might be like to have four mothers all trying to prepare her for the next major step in life.

Having already lost two, she wasn't sure how to feel about that.

"Come. Come, come, come," Otila insisted, tucked her hand

through the apprentice's arm, and pulled her out through the sitting room and into one of the four rooms that opened off it.

The other women followed and their excitement rose as they hurried after her. Kaylin let herself be guided to stand before a full-length mirror in one corner of the room.

"There!" Otila repeated and turned her so she could see her reflection. "What do you think?"

In truth, she didn't know what to think. The young woman who stared at her looked clean and healthy, even if she was somewhat on the thin side. Her bald pate accentuated her wide dark eyes and sculpted cheeks, although the dark-blue of her new robes highlighted the bruises under her eyes.

The image made her pause. She hadn't looked at herself in a real mirror in years and had to satisfy herself with half-caught glimpses in windows and puddles—or, perhaps, she hadn't wanted to see her street-rat self more clearly.

Her reflection was not at all who she had thought herself to be and she wondered if she could live up to the one in the mirror.

CHAPTER TWELVE

Captain Delaine approved. She arrived as they emerged from Matron Otila's chamber.

"Ah, good," she said and ran her gaze critically over Kaylin. She smiled at the women. "The masters will take her on advisement." Her face wrinkled with distaste. "As if the support of the Chevaliers is not good enough."

After a short pause, she added, "Tonight." Otila's smile of satisfaction faded.

She returned the captain's gaze. "You're taking her now?"

Delaine responded with a curt nod.

"But it's just past time for the noon meal," the matron protested, "and I'm sure no one thought to give her breakfast."

That stopped barely short of an accusation and Kaylin's stomach rumbled in agreement.

"And I doubt she's slept since yesterday afternoon," Dagger added.

The captain shrugged. "I'll have the kitchens make some sandwiches but we need to leave now or we won't be behind the Academy's walls by sunset. She can sleep in the coach."

Otila's lips pursed in disapproval but the knight wasn't finished.

"I've had the quartermaster locate a pair of boots that should fit and another two robes and tabards. The Academy will provide the rest." She paused and a glint slid into her eyes as she added, "It is, after all, what we pay them for."

None of the women had an answer for that. Delaine looked at their disapproving faces and her expression softened.

"I did not expect the approval to come so soon either," she told them. "But since it has, we shouldn't keep the masters waiting." Her gaze swept over the girl again and she smiled approvingly. "You have wrought quite a transformation. Thank you."

"Thank you," Kaylin added, not sure what else to say.

Her throat clogged and her voice was husky. Leaving the women suddenly seemed like leaving four mothers she hadn't expected to be provided with, and she wished she'd had more time to get to know them.

They appeared to be about the same age as Sabine had been when she'd first been placed at Herder's Gate.

I wonder how many of them will still be here when I come back, she thought and hoped her studies wouldn't take too long and she'd get to see them when she returned.

Otila stepped close and clasped her hands in hers.

"Take care, child," she said, "and work hard. I know you'll make a wonderful mage."

The others followed.

"Make sure you bathe regularly," Creswyn stated, "and don't forget to eat. It's easy to do when you have exams."

"And look after your hair when it grows again," Rhodda added and surprised the girl by hugging her. "Don't let any of those Academy brats give you trouble about where you've come from."

She moved away and Dagger stepped into her place.

"Do your best," the woman advised, "but most importantly, don't forget where you came from. The skills you have now can still stand you in good stead for the future. Sometimes, the ability to move unseen and stay out of sight is as important to your survival as how well you can fight or cast a spell."

Kaylin might have asked how that could be but the others nodded in agreement.

"Sage advice, as always," Captain Delaine noted and nodded at Dagger. She placed her hand on the young apprentice's shoulder "We have to go."

"Thank you, again," Kaylin murmured as she followed the captain from the room.

"Come back safe." She managed to smile in reply before the door closed behind her and the women were gone.

"The carriage is waiting," Delaine told her and lengthened her stride as she led her along the hall they'd passed through that morning. "And I have your boots."

Her boots? The comment made Kaylin realize she was barefoot—and that there hadn't been a sign of her boots or any of her other clothes by the time she'd climbed out of the tub.

Those old... Still, as annoying as it was that they'd disappeared her only pair of boots, she couldn't be mad at them.

She sighed and Captain Delaine smiled.

"They tend to have that effect," the woman said quietly and, as though offering some reassurance, added, "Don't worry. You'll see them again."

Kaylin nodded and followed her into the kitchen where the knight ordered sandwiches for two.

"Until Tam mentioned it, I hadn't realized it was past lunch," she said when she caught the girl's look. "We'll eat in the carriage."

If that was the case, she hoped it wouldn't take them too long to reach the conveyance. The smell that rose from the cook's basket made her mouth water.

She followed Delaine through unfamiliar halls and rooms until they reached the stable courtyard, in the center of which stood the carriage. As they moved toward it, the knight pulled a towel off a hook beside a trough.

"I'll replace it," she said shortly, "but you'll want to wipe your feet before you put them into your new boots."

Despite her words, the stable yard was relatively clean and the girl managed to not step in anything more disgusting than a puddle. She was still shaking the water from her foot when the captain guided her into the carriage.

"You should watch where you're walking," Delaine told her unsympathetically and pulled the door closed before she banged on the roof to signal the driver to start.

The carriage jolted forward and Kaylin swayed as it made a wide turn before it bumped into the street beyond. She wriggled forward in her seat, peered out the window, and tried to work out where she was in Waypoint.

"North-west side," the knight stated when she noticed her frown.

"I don't recognize it," she admitted and her companion smiled.

"How often have you visited?"

She snorted and lowered her head. The truth was she'd never been across the river that separated the wealthier north-west sector from the rest of Waypoint.

Delaine read her face and nodded. "I thought so." She leaned back in her seat and watched while the girl gazed at the passing scenery. Finally, she opened the basket into which the cook had packed their lunch. "Hungry?"

The sight and smell of the sandwiches made Kaylin lose all interest in the city outside the carriage window. She accepted the thick bundle that was hers, opened it, and breathed in the scent of fresh, warm bread, cold meat, and cheese.

For a moment, she simply sat and looked at it, and the captain leaned closer.

"Do you want me to take a bite? To prove it's safe?" she asked and her eyes twinkled. The girl shook her head rapidly and swallowed hard against the saliva pooling in her mouth.

Delaine laughed, unwrapped her food, and began to eat, her attention on the world beyond the carriage window. Kaylin took a bite at the same time as the captain did and they ate in companionable silence while each one stared out of their respective window and didn't say a word.

The young apprentice studied the buildings they passed. Most were barely visible beyond tall stone walls but she caught the occasional glimpse of elegant front gardens beyond wrought iron gates, of pillars and marble, and thick vines and statues, and wondered that this part of the city was so different than the ones she was used to.

When the carriage slowed, she snapped a glance at her companion.

"The city gates," the captain stated as though that explained it all, and Kaylin stared at her in alarm.

"You didn't know?" the knight asked. "Truly didn't know?"

She shook her head. "I don't know anything about the Academy." She paused and sipped from the flask she'd been given. "It's outside the city?"

Delaine nodded, finished her sandwich, and wiped her hands on the napkin that had been used to wrap the sandwich. She rinsed her mouth with water from her flask and pulled two more neatly wrapped packages from the basket.

"Cake," she said succinctly and proceeded to unwrap hers.

Cake? Kaylin hastily followed suit and paused when she saw the creamy golden slab inside.

"Cook must think you're starving," the woman noted.

The carriage inched slowly forward, then stopped, then moved again. A rap on the door followed, and the knight set her cake to one side as she answered it.

"Business?" the guard demanded.

"Chevaliers des Lances Jumelles," she replied. "An Academy secondment."

The guard looked past her and his gaze traveled over Kaylin and noted her robes and tabard.

"Will you return tonight?" he asked and the woman shook her head.

"No. Early tomorrow."

"Very good, ma'am." He nodded and stepped back to address the coachman. "You can go."

The carriage jolted forward, and Delaine settled in her seat. "What did you want to know?"

"About the Academy?" Kaylin asked and her companion nodded. "They'll teach me about magic, right?"

Again, she nodded.

"And that will take time," the girl responded thoughtfully. "I guess what I most want to know is what I need to know."

"To fit in?"

"To fit in and to succeed. As I can't leave if it's not working, I need to know how to make it work," she declared.

"That's a good question," the knight told her. "I wish it was as easy as merely attending to your studies and keeping your head down, but it won't be."

Kaylin thought of her days at the orphanage. More than one of the other children had been jealous of her relationship with Sabine and made her life difficult as a result.

"It never is," she replied.

"Good, then you'll know that not everyone who befriends you wants to be your friend, and that is as true of the nobility as it is of the streets. You can't take anything or anyone at face value. If someone asks you to do something, make sure you know what they're asking—and what the consequences are of doing it."

"You mean they might ask me to do something that's not allowed?" Kaylin asked.

"It has been known to happen," Delaine told her, "and I don't want you caught."

"But why—"

"The students vie for the approval of their masters and sometimes, it's easier to make someone else less favorable than to do the work to earn the approval legitimately. And sometimes, they do it to lessen a rival's standing."

She took another sip from her flask and looked out the window as the carriage raced through the low foothills surrounding Waypoint. It was disappointing to find that people could be as unkind to each other off the streets as they were on them.

"Tell me about the study," she stated and decided she'd deal with each situation as it arose. "How do you know I'll be any good as a mage?"

Delaine gave her a pitying look. "I know how difficult those sigils are to deactivate—even for a mage trained in the signs they need to make. You can't help but be anything else."

"But Goss could—" Kaylin stopped abruptly at the interest in Delaine's eyes. "I didn't mean—"

The knight uttered a short laugh. "Don't worry. I won't pull your friend out of the orphanage."

She felt a wave of relief until the woman added, "But I'll ask Sister Nadiya to keep an eye on him for potential secondment. The Chevaliers could always do with more good knights."

The girl wrapped her arms around herself and looked out the window. "I'd rather you left him alone."

"Why? Because having a powerful organization looking after him would be a bad thing?"

Kaylin blushed. When it was put that way, her resistance sounded petty.

"I only wanted..." she began but trailed off when she couldn't work out how to say what she wanted to.

"If it helps, we'll let him decide," the knight offered.

She turned in her seat when she remembered the so-called choice she'd had to make. Delaine caught the look on her face and burst out laughing.

"A real choice," the knight added, "with options that don't involve being hung or seeing his friends die. How does that sound?"

The girl wanted to say it sounded fine—and how come the knights hadn't come up with the idea and looked for them sooner. The answer was, of course, that she and her friends hadn't done anything to attract their attention, but she couldn't help thinking looking for promising candidates was something they should be doing.

After all, she'd targeted Shacklemund's with the idea of giving her crew the opportunity to not be thieves for the rest of her life. What would have happened if the knights had been out there doing the same?

Aware that the woman was reading her face, she turned her gaze to the window again.

Their carriage had started to climb and her gaze drifted to Waypoint far behind them. Shadows had already crept from the cliffs surrounding the bowl to deepen those existing between the hills and stretch a wall of dusk toward the city.

The sight made her shiver, even as the broad band of Waypoint's river reflected the afternoon light and the smaller tributaries glinted in their race to join it. For a moment, she imagined she could see the Dockers' Den with the fishing boats coming in to dock, but from this distance?

Kaylin shook the idea away as the fit of fancy it was.

That didn't stop her from searching the eastern wall for the squat shape of the orphanage and she wondered if her friends had been handed into Nadiya's care.

Maybe I can write a letter, she thought and almost laughed. *Well, look at me being all fancy already.*

But the idea stuck and made her realize that she didn't know how sending messages worked. She thought about asking the knight but a glance showed her the woman was dozing. Her shoulders were propped in the corner where the carriage wall met the seat and her chin rested on her chest.

She added messages to the list of things she'd have to learn about. Given the distance the Academy seemed to be from the city, she didn't even know if they were possible. What message service would run this far—and take the risk of attack from the monsters roaming the valley?

It seemed logical that the only missives traveling between Waypoint and the Academy might be official ones, so she pushed the idea aside. She missed her friends—and she would miss them more when she got to the Academy.

There'd be no Isabette quietly assessing the alternatives, no Melis taking a situation to the extreme to make them see the possibilities in front of them and dare them to try, no Raoul checking the angles and making them remember their group's younger members. Kaylin sighed, blinked against the sudden sting in her eyes, and focused on the view.

Now, she looked at more than only the city and the life she'd left behind. She tried not to think about everything she'd lost. Sure, she'd had to sacrifice to save her crew—and herself—but it was a future. Maybe even a good one if she only gave it a chance to be.

The carriage followed a curve in the road and Waypoint slid from view to be replaced by the towering cliffs that made up the walls of the bowl in which the city sat. Between lay a jumble of hills that gradually grew taller until they vanished into the base of the cliff wall. None of the closest were as tall as the one the carriage now climbed.

"The Academy's at the top." Delaine's voice cut through the carriage's dim interior. "Of Seledryl's Mount. It's the highest point within a day's ride of Waypoint. The founders built it on the foundations of some kind of ruin."

"What kind of ruin?"

Her companion shrugged. "It was before my time but if I had to guess, I'd say it was a monastery or maybe a fortress of some kind. The adventurers who cleared it said it was the best vantage point for watching over Waypoint and the valley entrance. The mages said they needed the isolation for training, and the Chevaliers rotate a garrison here to watch over both the city and the Academy."

It was the most Kaylin had heard her say about her destination and she stared as it sank in. The woman gave her a brief smile.

"The garrison keeps to the outer precinct, except when it's training with the Academy or meeting for other discussions."

From the way the woman's brow darkened, she guessed the other discussions were rarely pleasant. She also assumed the knight wouldn't tell her what they were about.

"What happens next?" she asked, and Delaine gave her a look that said she thought she'd already answered that question.

"You work hard to graduate," she replied shortly.

"No," she corrected. "What happens after I graduate?"

"That will depend on your proficiency, but the Chevaliers will be able to give you a few options."

"And if I don't want to work for the Chevaliers?" she asked.

Again, the woman's brows rose but she still had answers. "There will be several options you can take depending on your results," she answered and her tone indicated that the topic was closed.

Kaylin returned her attention to the window, relieved to see the view had opened up. Now, instead of being dominated by the cliff wall, it showed the vast forest that cloaked most of the bowl. The carriage took another turn and the view changed to bring another mountain into view—the Twin Spears.

Legends claimed that it had once been a single peak surrounded by myriad streets of a teeming metropolis of elves and humans. They also said the people of the city had delved too deep into the mountain and woken a mighty dragon, a beast so large and so ancient that it had torn the mountain in half and destroyed the civilization at the feet of the massive peak.

Where the dragon had gone after its rampage, no one knew, but it hadn't been seen for over three hundred years and the valley had grown wild and verdant in its absence. She let her gaze travel over the soft contours of the forest canopy and rolling hills between the Spears and the Mount and noticed the orange dots of campfires becoming visible in the dusk.

Humans might huddle behind walls but the monsters did not. Kaylin wondered how long it would take until those closest to the Mount noticed the carriage. She hadn't seen any guards when she'd climbed aboard.

The conveyance began to slow, and Delaine straightened.

"We're here," she said as if the girl couldn't have worked that out for herself, then bent to lift something from the carriage floor. "You'll need these."

She took the boots the knight was holding and noticed the socks sticking out the top.

"Thank you," she responded and put them on. To her surprise, they fit.

"We had your old pair to work from," the captain explained when she caught her expression. "It took a little time but we found replacements."

Kaylin resisted the urge to ask what had happened to the old pair. Technically, she had stolen them and since her permission wasn't given, they were stolen a second time.

They were, however, replaced with something a little nicer.

The carriage came to a halt a moment before she heard muffled greetings and it rolled forward again. A shiver rippled through her, excitement that she'd arrived and fear at what might come next. She was being given a chance many would envy.

All she had to do was make the most of it.

In the short time it took the carriage to move from the main gate, through the outer courtyard, and into a second courtyard, the sun slipped from the sky. She watched as the gray light of dusk gave way to full dark. As soon as it did, the area was lit by a soft blue glow unlike any lamplight she had yet seen.

When Delaine treated it as normal, Kaylin followed her out of the carriage and stopped to stare at the scene around her.

The courtyard walls were a brilliant white stone and the blue light emitted from two crystals set on pedestals on either side of the stairs leading into a cavernous building.

"Close your mouth," the captain ordered, "and grab your trunk."

She had a trunk? She turned quickly. The coachman had descended from the driver's seat and placed a small trunk onto a two-wheeled moving dolly. She hurried forward and reached him as he finished fastening two straps to hold her luggage in place.

"Here you go, Apprentice," he said and turned the dolly's handles so she could take them. "Good luck." He winked.

"Th...thank you..." Kaylin stuttered but he waved her away and directed her to the captain with a good-natured flap of his hands.

She returned to where Delaine was waiting and followed her up the stairs, the dolly bumping along behind her. The woman didn't look back and she struggled to keep up, but she reached the top of the steps only a few steps behind her guide.

Two people waited inside the portico. One wore the same blue robes and white tabard as Kaylin. The other wore robes of deep red, his collar edged with white and blue thread. His narrow features were carefully bland as he watched the two of them approach.

"Conseiller Roche," Delaine stated by way of greeting, "this is Apprentice Knight."

The man snorted and his gray gaze raked the girl from head to toe, his expression one of distaste.

"So, I see. This is Apprentice Vaux. She'll show Knight to her room." He sniffed disapprovingly and returned his attention to the captain. "There, she'll find that everything is ready for her to commence her studies despite the indecently short notice we've been given."

Delaine gave him her most professional smile.

"A fact of which the Chevaliers have taken note and are deeply appreciative," she assured him.

"Deeply?" The conseiller's eyes sparked with momentary interest before he continued. "Well, be that as it may, I will be her magical advisor while she is here and my time is precious."

He turned to Kaylin. "I might have come out late to ensure your safe arrival and I might be your academic advisor, but do not take that as permission to pester me with every tiny thing you think you need to know. Here, we encourage independence of thought that should emerge as a student's willingness to find their own answers in minor matters. Is that understood?"

Dumbfounded at the hostility in his tone, she nodded quickly. Roche met her eyes.

"We expect you to speak when spoken to, Apprentice, and the correct term of address for students is 'Magister.' Understood?"

She started to nod, caught herself, and managed to say, "Yes, Magister."

It came out half-choked and she cleared her throat and prepared to try again, but he gave her an abrupt nod and turned to Delaine.

"Now, if there is nothing else?" he asked.

"I take it my accommodations are also prepared?" the captain asked in frosty tones.

"Of course," Roche replied, "although I doubt you'll require guidance to find them."

"Certainly not," Delaine replied.

"Unfortunately, you arrived too late to join us for supper," he added, "but as you know the Academy's routines, Captain, I assume you've already prepared for that."

"Of course," Delaine answered and her voice took on an edge as she repeated his earlier response, "we would not expect the Academy to alter its routines for mere guests."

He looked sharply at her. "You'll find that our guests are taken care of as circumstances dictate, but we expect our students to follow a stricter regime."

"I see," the knight replied. "Thank you, Conseiller." She nodded to Kaylin. "I'll leave you in the conseiller's hands. Do your best," she ordered crisply and pivoted on her heel before the girl had time to respond.

"Vaux, you know what to do," Roche snapped as the captain

descended the stairs. "See her settled and make sure she arrives at tomorrow's classes on time."

Apprentice Vaux clasped her hands in front of her chest. "Yes, Magister."

Kaylin didn't know what to think. Magister Roche's idea of a welcome left a lot to be desired. Was it because she'd come from the streets? Did the magisters even know her history?

She watched the man leave, aware that the other apprentice did the same. The girl didn't move until he turned right at the next intersection and vanished out of sight.

"Mirielle," she said and extended a hand in greeting. "I'm in the room across from yours."

That caught her attention and she accepted the hand and clasped it briefly.

"Kaylin," she replied.

The girl frowned. "I'm not familiar with your family," she observed. "Which part of Waypoint are you from?"

"Riverside," she answered without thinking, then blushed.

Mirielle patted her arm reassuringly. "That's okay. I'm sure the magisters won't hold it against you."

She snorted and glanced in the direction in which Roche had gone. The other apprentice followed her gaze.

"Oh, don't mind him," she insisted, "He's always like that—even if you have his support."

Kaylin stared at her and wondered what support she was hoping to receive but Mirielle turned.

"Come on," she instructed with a gesture to the right. "Our rooms are this way."

"This is mine?" Kaylin asked when the girl pushed the door to a small room open.

Inside stood a single bed, a desk and chair, a bookcase, and a wardrobe with two drawers in its base and a key in the door.

"Of course," Mirielle told her. "What did you expect? That we'd all sleep in one room?"

She nodded. "Something like that," she replied and thought how it had been at the orphanage.

The girl lowered her head and smiled. "The families would never stand for it," she explained. "Their precious children having to share? They have a hard enough time accepting that we only get something like this."

"I thought you only got to come here if you had an aptitude for magic," she remarked and the other girl chuckled.

"That would be something, wouldn't it?" she whispered, stepped aside, and gestured for her to go first. "If the people who had a chance at making magic got to study it?"

Kaylin shrugged. "Isn't that what the Academy's here for?"

"Supposedly," Mirielle told her, "but if a family is willing to pay a penalty fee, the Academy will take a well-connected student with little or no aptitude for a semester. If they don't show any magical ability during the first set of Trials, they're sent home."

"But—" she started, then stopped. What had Captain Delaine said? Keeping her head down and working hard might not be enough and she should watch who she trusted?

"It's not what I expected," she finished after a pause.

"That's what everyone says," her companion confided, "although usually for different reasons."

She pointed to a bare patch under the window in the far wall. "Your chest can go there and the dolly will fit in your wardrobe. That's where I'd put it because the door can be locked."

Kaylin thought about putting the entire chest in the wardrobe but decided against it. Firstly, it was too heavy to lift and secondly, the chest itself had a lock. She shuffled it off the dolly and into position before she took the key out.

Someone had threaded it on a stout leather thong, which she slipped over her neck and tucked the key out of sight under her robes. Mirielle watched her and nodded approvingly before she pulled another key out of her robes.

"This one's for your room," she stated and handed it to her, and Kaylin took her chest key out and threaded the other one onto the thong. She could add the wardrobe key later.

It struck her that she hadn't seen anyone else since her arrival.

"Where is everyone?" she asked.

"Probably studying." The other girl gestured at the papers and books stacked on her desk and the end of the bed. "You should probably do the same. You have so much catching up to do."

Kaylin sighed and regarded the piles with misgiving. "Do we need to know all of this?" she asked, and Mirielle gave her a disapproving frown.

"Of course," she replied. "That'll give you the basics so you can understand what they're talking about in class."

"But I thought they'd teach us," Kaylin protested.

The other apprentice put one hand on her hip and cocked her head.

"I don't know what it was like with your tutor or training academy but here, the teachers' only real job is to provide you with information and the occasional practical demonstration. You have to stay motivated and on top of your studies or you won't be able to put it together and then, you'll start drowning."

"And this is the beginning material?" she asked and tried to not sound as daunted as she felt.

Exactly what had she agreed to?

"Of course, and it'll be harder for you because you've come in a few weeks behind the rest."

"Is that where a conseiller comes in handy?" Kaylin asked and wondered if helping her catch up came under Magister Roche's idea of something she could pester him with.

Mirielle shrugged. "If you can catch their eye, sure, but fair warning—who you've been assigned to means nothing. All the magisters care about is what you can do for them. If someone makes a magister look good and happens to show up the students of another magister in the process, that student is set. They will keep feeding that goose as long as the eggs keep coming out gold."

It took her a moment to work out what the other girl meant, then she remembered the story about a magical goose and how it was killed out of greed.

"At least they do keep feeding it," she noted. "What do the other geese do? The ones whose eggs are the ordinary kind?"

"Study like all the minotaurs in the valley are after them," Mirielle told her, "and hope we pass our Trials when the time comes. Failing means we have to start at the beginning—and then only if we showed enough magical aptitude and can afford it."

She looked over her shoulder and took a step away from the door.

"Which is why I'll leave you now and go back to my room to study. Pyromancy is sweaty, uncomfortable work and I hate it, but if I can't light candles with a snap of my fingers or ignite a bonfire with a single word before the week's up, I'll never stay on track for my Trials." She took hold of the door and drew it closed as she left. "Good night—and good luck."

"Night," Kaylin muttered as the door clicked but the girl didn't reply.

She sighed and sat on the bed, perched carefully beside the books. The bookshelf stood empty on the other side of the room but tiredness dragged at her limbs and the bed was comfortable.

For a minute, she was tempted to stretch out beside the pile but Mirielle's words haunted her so she didn't. Instead, she decided she should take a look at what she needed to know and determine what order she needed to stack them in on the shelves.

In the end, she had to stand up to be able to both reach the shelf and transfer the contents of the pile onto it. Honestly, how much reading did they think she'd get through in a single night? And why did she have to read anything anyway? All she had to do was see it and she could work it out for herself.

What did she need these books for?

She looked around the room. When she'd been at Herders' Gate, a timetable had been pinned to the wall outside the dining hall. She hadn't seen anything like that pinned to any of the walls she'd passed on the way to her room but it seemed logical that there should be one.

Fortunately, there weren't many places to look and she found it in the middle of her desk.

Kaylin knew what it was as soon as she laid eyes on it. She set it neatly to one side, put the rest of her books on the shelf, then opened her trunk and transferred her robes and tabards to the wardrobe and the rest of her clothing to the drawers.

Someone had also stowed a small journal, an inkwell, two quills, and several sticks of charcoal in a small leather satchel. She wondered what it was for and why anyone would think she'd need a journal. The half-dozen sheets of parchment and matching envelopes were self-explanatory and she was glad to see them.

At least someone had thought she might want to send a message, although who they thought she might want to send one to was another question.

When everything was neatly put away, she picked her timetable up and settled onto her bed. With the pillow plumped behind her, she peeled her boots off and tucked her feet under her. She might not be able to read everything on her shelf in one night but she could at least start with the books she'd need for the next day's lesson.

It didn't take her long to confirm the three books she needed, so she got up and stacked two on the desk. She'd almost hopped onto the bed again when the window caught her eye. The curtains were closed but she was curious to see what lay beyond them.

Kaylin lifted half of the curtains back and peered cautiously out at a network of walls and courtyards. Beyond that lay a night-cloaked landscape dotted by the familiar orange lights of myriad campfires and in the distance, one shadow towered taller than the rest.

In the darkness, the mountain's jagged peaks rose above the distant opposite rim of the valley and looked like the crossed blades of a pair of spears in silhouette. The sight captured her attention and her heart raced in her chest.

One day, I will go there, she thought and tasted the truth of the thought. Maybe, when she graduated, the Chevaliers might let her be part of an expedition into the mountain depths. She stared at the mountain for several long moments, then let the curtain fall.

If she'd needed a reason to succeed, that was it—not because she needed to prove herself or justify the Chevaliers' secondment but because she wanted to go somewhere and "there" would be to the Doom itself.

And if she ever wondered why she tried so hard, all she had to do was look through her window and the Twin Spears would be outside, rising heavenward to remind her.

She tugged the curtain into place and adjusted the lantern before she settled against her pillow to read.

CHAPTER THIRTEEN

Kaylin woke to frantic hammering at her door. She'd fallen asleep, her book in her lap and her head and shoulders propped in the corner. As she bolted upright, her door burst open and Mirielle hurried in.

"Oh, good! You're dressed," the girl exclaimed. Her gaze fell on the book. "And you've been studying. Excellent."

She wanted to tell her she'd only now woken up but the girl was in too much of a fluster to notice.

"Come on," she urged. "You're not the only one who needs to get to class. Where's your timetable?"

"Class?" she asked blearily. Her limbs felt like lead and she had difficulty keeping up.

"Yes! Wait—" The girl's eyes narrowed. "Have you had breakfast?"

Kaylin's blank look gave her the answer.

"Ugh. Right. You only just arrived. What am I thinking? Why," she exclaimed in exasperation, "did Magister Roche do this to me?"

"He thought you could handle it?" she asked and received a frustrated glare for her trouble.

"Satchel," the apprentice snapped, turned to the door, and unhooked a large leather satchel from the back of it. She thrust it into the other girl's hands. "It looks like you've already got your books together. Do you have a journal of some kind?"

"Sure," Kaylin told her and retrieved her journal from her chest.

"Not the ink. The charcoal is faster and won't spill," Mirielle told her. "Show me your timetable."

She studied the document, checked the books Kaylin had placed near her bed, and picked up the one she'd dropped. "Good. All there. Now, come on. You're not the only one who needs to eat."

Kaylin tried to catch up to the girl's constant prattling. "I thought you—"

"I didn't remember until I saw you—and remembered you hadn't had supper. Come on." She hurried to the door. "Don't forget to lock up."

She hurried after her, stopped, stepped back, and locked her door before she scampered to catch up. Mirielle barely gave her time to catch her breath and the halls were crowded.

More than one of the students in the corridor turned to watch them and Kaylin caught whispers of "new girl," "baldy," and "too scrawny to have come from anywhere good," as she passed.

Her guide didn't stop or slow and she was hungry so ignored everything.

Other whispers followed—"her robes" and "looked like she slept in them" along with "probably can't afford to have someone do them." If Mirielle heard them, she didn't show it and soon, they arrived in the dining hall.

"You can take as much as you like," the girl told her, "but we don't have much time so I'd suggest the bread rolls. You can slip any extra in your pockets."

Pockets? Kaylin felt down her robe and discovered there were, indeed, pockets.

I wonder how much I can hide in these?

You could take the thief out of the slums but you couldn't stop her mind from wondering.

Her companion chattered on, oblivious. "Or you can try those pastries. They're not for me but meat in the morning was never my thing."

Meat? She followed the girl's pointing finger and snatched a couple of pastries as they moved on.

"And these are too sweet."

Sweet? Another two rolls followed before they took a mug of tea that smelled of oranges and cloves.

"This is the best pick-me-up there is," Mirielle said and led her to an empty space at one of the tables.

"Those seats are taken." The voice intruded as Kaylin put her tray down.

"Tessa..." Mirielle began, but the other girl interrupted.

Dark hair held back by a dark-blue headband crowned a set of piercing blue eyes that glared as she spoke. "Don't you 'Tessa' me," the girl exclaimed. "You know the rules. Only nobility sit at this table."

The other girl stabbed the handle of her fork toward Kaylin. "And she's not nobility."

"Says who?" Mirielle challenged.

"Says her haircut, the fact she doesn't look like she's eaten properly for a long time, and the way she's been seconded late in the term. She's a charity case."

"She was delivered by Captain Delaine herself," Mirielle replied and the girl only sneered.

"See? Like I said, a charity case."

"And she's from a Riverside family."

At that, the girl laughed sharply. "There are no families in Riverside," she pointed out, "unless you're trying to include criminal families as a form of nobility and I doubt she qualified for any of them."

The girl flushed, but Kaylin placed a hand on her arm.

"She has a point, and I'm no criminal." Her face burned as she said it but it was true.

She wasn't a criminal, not anymore.

The other girl crowed in triumph. "See? A charity case—and she'll probably be gone before the Trials even get here."

Kaylin left the table and found a seat at another. The students seated there didn't tell her the seat was taken but they left as soon as she sat. It wasn't quite the same but it was still rejection. She kept her eyes on her plate, ate quickly, and sipped the scalding tea.

"You don't need to look after me if you don't want to," she told Mirielle when she sat beside her.

"Two things," the girl replied. "One, if the Chevaliers seconded you, you should be here. They wouldn't have put you here otherwise—and that means you have talent. Two, if Magister Roche thinks I'll reject this task because the others laugh at it, he has another think coming."

"Will he be happy if you succeed?" she asked and her heart sank at the idea that she was merely another way for Mirielle to earn the magister's favor.

"I don't know," the girl answered. "He might want me to abandon you, both so you give up because you're on your own and because it'll give him an excuse to ignore me some more. Or he might want me to do what he asked and make sure you have a good start so you have a tiny chance of succeeding because it would amuse him to see a 'charity case' succeed where another magister's student fails."

"Another student from a better family?" she suggested and her companion gave her an evil smile.

"Exactly. If you out-perform a student from a wealthier family, particularly one like Tessa whose family asked for her to be assigned a different magister, you'll increase his prestige at the other magister's expense."

"A kind of 'I told you so,'" Kaylin observed bitterly.

"You can look at it that way if you like," Mirielle told her, "and let yourself get caught up in the politics of this place. Or you could take the opportunity you've been given and prove you have every right to be here."

She set her cup down and glanced at the timepiece on the wall.

"We have to go or we'll be late." She grabbed her tray and Kaylin picked hers up as well. Once she showed her where to leave her tray, she led the way into the halls.

"Your first class is elements of magic. It's basic but essential. I've got pyromancy at the other end of the building, so I'll show you where your second class will be and meet you at the dining hall for lunch, okay?"

Kaylin nodded, and Mirielle increased her pace.

"This one," she declared as they passed an open door, "is where you need to be right now, but..." She hurried on and expected her to follow. "This one," she announced after she'd turned left and arrived at a door halfway along the next corridor, "is where you'll need to be next—magical geometry."

"Sigils?"

"Something like that," the girl agreed. "Now go or you'll be late—and try to ignore the others. You're new, they're curious." She rolled her eyes. "And gossip will be rife."

She was gone before Kaylin could respond and left her to return to the first classroom on her own. She made it, but barely, and most of the other students had arrived before her. This meant she had an audience and that the teacher noted her presence.

Although she waited for the woman to say something, she merely smiled in a tight-lipped way, glanced past her to the door, and waited until a melodic chime reverberated through the classroom and halls. The door closed on its own.

The teacher looked at the assembled students and pointed a finger at a solidly built boy with mouse-brown hair.

"Name the three dimensions of magic," she commanded.

The answer was given without hesitation. "Experience, logic, and emotion."

Her finger moved to indicate a second student. "What is the dimension of emotion?"

This time, the answer was more hesitant but it was still correct. "The intent of the spell, the way the caster...feels?"

The magister frowned. "Feels about what?"

The finger moved to a third student.

"About the outcome. What they hope for and what they hope to feel when the spell is done."

The magister's lips thinned as though she'd hoped to catch them out but she nodded. "Correct." Another student was asked a question and provided the answer. This time, Kaylin realized she knew the answer since she'd read it only hours earlier. Likewise, she knew the next answer.

"Experience?"

The chosen student answered incorrectly and the finger moved to indicate Kaylin.

"Magical concepts based on or shaped by the caster's experience," she answered and the teacher's brows rose.

"And why are these three dimensions important?" she demanded and gestured to her to answer this question also.

"B…because they form the basis of magical geometry so are used to determine the words and gestures required for a spell to be cast."

The teacher stared at her and her heart sank. Judging from the silence around her, she had the answer terribly, terribly wrong.

"And you know this how?" the woman demanded as though the answer was a direct affront.

"I…it's in the text…Magister."

"Very good." The woman nodded. "It's nice to see you found time to study between your arrival and breakfast."

The class snickered and she reddened, although she couldn't work out what she'd done at breakfast that was so entertaining or why having studied should be a cause for laughter. The magister clapped to command their attention.

Kaylin kept her face to the front but watched what the other students did from the corner of her eye. Some pulled journals and charcoal pencils out while others sat and stared at the teacher like they were listening. No one opened their books.

She took her journal and charcoal hastily from her satchel and waited for the teacher to speak. Her actions drew whispers and giggles from a small group of students to her right but the woman ignored them.

Frowning slightly, she began the class.

For Kaylin, it was as if she'd been given the keys to something she'd discovered by accident. As the magister talked, she understood why the gestures had worked and began to feel the edge of new possibilities.

Carefully, she noted what was said so she could check it in her text later. What had Magister Roche said?

"We encourage independence of thought that should emerge as a student's willingness to find their own answers in minor matters."

She wondered if the theory of magic was considered a minor matter or if it maybe was simply the basics of magic. Perhaps he had referred to everything she was able to discover for herself, while he only wanted to be bothered by the big questions.

It was hard to understand so she decided to ask Mirielle over lunch.

"Any questions. All the questions," the girl answered when Kaylin brought it up. "The magisters don't like to be bothered."

"So...what good are they?" she asked and lowered her voice to a fierce whisper.

Mirielle looked around to see if anyone had overheard and relaxed a little when none of the students at nearby tables showed any sign of interest.

She leaned close to Kaylin to answer.

"Like I said last night, the magisters are only interested in things that advance them and whatever projects they're interested in. You doing better than a wealthy student whose parents chose a different magister will be of interest to Roche because it will make the other magister look less capable and mean that their projects are less likely to get support."

"So?" she whispered in response. "What good does that do me? I promised the captain I'd do my best, but I don't know if I'll be able to pass if my teachers don't...you know, teach."

"Oh, he'll help you," Mirielle assured her, "but only once he's sure you'll be good for his career. As soon as that happens, he'll offer pointers and tips and maybe even special tutelage."

"Special tutelage?" Kaylin almost forgot to keep her voice down. "You mean he'll withhold information until he thinks I'm worthy?"

The other girl reddened. "Well, yes, because that's how it works around here. The magisters only support the students who will bring the most benefit to them. They are the ones most likely to be hired by people like the Chevaliers, or to get a court position in their homelands, or be picked up by one of the better mercenary companies."

"I thought students who got those positions did so because they were good enough, not because some mage decided they were useful to have around."

Mirielle shook her head. "I'm sorry to burst that bubble," she said. "Trust me, it was a shock for me too when I found out."

Kaylin wanted to beat her head on the table. "It seems so stupid. Why wouldn't you support the best students you have and work with the rest to help them become as good as they can? You'd get more respect and support by doing that than by promoting the next or least best of your students simply because it would make their parents like you."

"The magisters need funding to support their private research, or their hobbies, or even to bring in the little luxuries they think they're owed, and it's the parents who have the money."

"But—" she began and her companion held her hand up.

"And by putting someone in a position of importance, you can call in the favor. Since they'll either have to rely on you for advice or feel obligated to repay you, they'll put in a good word when you need it."

Kaylin stared at her in shock before her mouth opened and shut a couple of times with nothing coming out. "That's sick," she stated and the girl shrugged.

"It's the way it's always been," she replied. "Sure, you need to be good at your classes and that will get you noticed and maybe helped, but everyone has something else to offer."

She frowned and was about to say she didn't think she had anything else to offer when Mirielle continued. "Even you," she said.

"No. I'm nothing special," she argued and shook her head. "I only

—" She shrugged, not sure how to continue. "What would I have to offer apart from becoming a good mage?"

"Status," Mirielle replied. "If you succeed, he'll show the parents of wealthier students why they should have chosen him instead of the magisters you'll defeat. And he'll be encouraged to help you succeed as you start to do that."

"Oh…" Kaylin wasn't sure she liked the idea of being praised for a skill simply because her hard work would make someone else look bad.

She took another mouthful of meat and vegetables and chewed while she thought about it. The other girl took one look at her face and patted her shoulder.

"On the bright side," she said reassuringly, "if you do succeed, it'll be because you've worked hard to develop your skills."

A soft snort close by made them realize one of the other students had overheard them. He caught their startled glances and sneered. "I wouldn't let it bother you," he said to Kaylin. "No one can work that hard."

He didn't wait for them to reply but sauntered past to take a seat two tables away.

Her eyes narrowed before she looked at Mirielle. "Who did you say his magister was?" she asked and the girl giggled.

After lunch, Mirielle showed her where her final two classes would be held and promised to meet her in the dining hall for the evening meal.

These two lessons continued in the same format as the earlier two, except they focused more on the practical side of magic—somatics and paraphernalia.

Kaylin's problem was that she hadn't had time to read up on either of them and she doubted her teachers would be tolerant of mistakes, a point that was proven shortly after.

"If you make that gesture," the magister snapped when she tried to guess the emotional element for lighting a candle, "you're likely to set yourself alight."

Magister Cantrell—she remembered the woman's name—scowled at her and her words brought hastily smothered giggles from behind her and the indistinct mutter of, "She'd do all of us a service if she did," from a knot of girls whose robes appeared to be made from a higher quality cloth than most others.

"And speaking of service," the magister said coldly and turned to the group.

The girls paled. One or two of their mouths dropped open and another dug her elbow into the ribs of a fourth girl. It was as good a signal as to who had spoken as anything else, and the teacher focused on her.

"Celia," she stated and the girl paled.

"Y...yes, Magister?"

"Why don't you show Apprentice Knight how it needs to be done?"

"But...but, Magister..." the girl began and the woman raised her brow.

"Yes, Apprentice Stoverson? Is there something you wanted to add?"

The girl gaped and her mouth moved soundlessly until she finally gathered her wits.

"No, Magister."

"Then begin."

The apprentice hesitated and her gaze darted left and right as she looked for help from her friends. When none was forthcoming, she closed her eyes, drew a deep breath, and made three hasty sweeps with her hand.

The teacher caught her wrist before she could finish the third.

"I think that's quite enough," she instructed. "It's obvious that Apprentice Knight wouldn't be the only human candle in the room."

The girl glared at Kaylin as though her failure was all her fault, but the woman hadn't finished.

"However, whereas she has the excuse of arriving late last night and having to prepare for other classes prior to this one—which I hear was adequately done—you do not. I will speak to Magister Gaudin about your lack of preparation and practice."

Having delivered her judgment, the magister turned to a small cluster of students on the other side of the room.

"Apprentice Derevax," she commanded and a tall boy with pitch-black hair and chestnut eyes stepped forward. "If you please."

He clasped his hands beneath his chin and acknowledged his teacher with a slight bow of his head before he moved his hands through the required gestures. Kaylin watched with hungry eyes, aware that her fingers twitched at her sides as she followed what he did.

On the magister's desk, a candle sprang to life and the woman gave a pleased smile.

"Very good, Damon," she all but purred in approval. "That is, indeed, the only candle that should be lit."

Kaylin barely paid any attention to the exchange. She kept her hands at her sides and her eyes to the front, but her focus had shifted from the room and those around her. As she made the gestures in her mind, she felt the movement of an invisible breeze over her fingers when she thought them through the movements Damon had made.

She wasn't aware that the magister had addressed her until the woman stood directly in front of her.

"Apprentice Knight!" the woman snapped, her voice whip-lash sharp against Kaylin's ears. She startled and took a hasty step back when she saw how close the woman was.

Magister Cantrell peered curiously at her. "I'm wondering where your mind was that you did not hear me speaking to you from the front of the class."

"Oh." Kaylin blushed. "I was thinking, Magister...about...about how to light the candle."

"Really?" the teacher stated, her voice full of doubt. "And?"

She flicked a sideways glance at Damon. "I...I think I can do it now."

That brought a look of disbelief from the teacher and scornful giggles and whispers from around the classroom.

"You do?" the woman challenged.

Kaylin nodded vigorously. "Yes, Magister. Now that I've seen which gestures are required—"

"You hadn't seen them?"

She blushed. "I'm sorry, Magister. I didn't have time to read the book."

"The gestures aren't in the book, Apprentice. I've only shown them in class."

This immediately made her want to know how the woman had expected her to make them but she bit her tongue. Judging by her interaction with Apprentice Stoverson, there was more at play than only the lesson. She made a note to ask Mirielle how the Magisters Cantrell and Roche got along—and who Apprentice Stoverson's magister was.

The teacher's voice intruded and demanded her attention.

"However, if you think you can repeat Apprentice Derevax's achievement, be my guest."

She stepped aside so the girl could see the candle on the table.

Kaylin stared at her, and the magister gave her a small superior smile and snapped her fingers. The flame went out and she waved her hand at the now lightless candle.

"Go ahead, Apprentice."

"Yes, Magister," Kaylin said despite a mouth gone dry.

What had she done to herself?

A small sound drew her attention and she glanced over to see Celia watching her, her lips twisted in a small derogatory smile. That was all it took. She clenched her jaw and stepped forward, settled her gaze on the candle, then stopped and refocused on the gestures she'd seen Damon make.

With her hands raised, she visualized the movements and her fingers twitched as they tried to recall the shapes they needed to make. When she was sure she knew what to do, she moved her hand slowly along the paths in her mind so she had time to make adjustments if she needed to.

The faint pressure guided her fingers into slightly new positions but she was sure she'd made the gestures correctly by the time she lowered her hands to her sides. Soft gasps rose around her and she opened her eyes.

The candle was lit.

Kaylin glanced at the teacher, who wore a look of chagrin and begrudging admiration on her face.

"I see it will not take you long to catch up," Magister Cantrell told her before she turned away. "Today, we'll build on this simple gesture." She gestured at the girl to sit.

She returned to her seat, all too aware that she was being watched, and was glad when the class was over—although that didn't make the next one any better.

When Kaylin walked alone to the dining hall, she knew she was being watched and heard the whispers that followed her down the corridors.

Some conversations were obvious.

"She lit a candle on her first day," whispered a student from her somatics class to another student she didn't recognize.

The response was an amazed, "You lie!"

Others were bare snippets and made her wonder where the students were getting their information from.

"I heard she used to be a thief on the docks. Got caught making a run on Shacklemund's."

"So...she's either stupid or insane?"

"Could be both."

Others weren't quite so obvious and carried a faintly threatening undertone.

"If she thinks their sponsorship guarantees she'll make it past the first Trials, she's got another think coming. So much can go wrong when you don't have your magister's favor."

Still others were dismissive.

"She's no use to anyone. She'll give up when no one helps her."

Rare conversations seemed focused on other more pressing matters.

"I've got to do something to win the magister's favor again. If I don't make it through the next Trials, my father's going…"

One group of girls were more concerned with appearances and made no effort to hide their derision when she walked past.

"You'd have thought she'd have tried to hide her baldness."

Other groups were focused on school politics.

"She's so arrogant. Did you hear she showed up Gaudin's latest pet? Made her lose face in front of the whole class."

Snorted laughter followed. "Well, she won't be here for long then, will she?"

If she was honest, she didn't know who Gaudin was or who might have shown up whom, but the incident with Celia sprang instantly to mind. What had Magister Cantrell promised? That she would speak to the girl's conseiller?

Kaylin's heart sank. The magister had looked particularly pleased to be able to do that.

If she hadn't caught the glances accompanying these words, she might have gone on blissfully unaware, but life on the streets had given her a strong perception for when she was being watched and these halls were full of eyes. She hurried to meet Mirielle for the evening meal, surprised when the girl met her at the door and rushed her through the serving line.

"What is it?" she asked as she was all but thrust into a seat at a corner table. "Why—"

"Hush!" the other apprentice ordered and pointed a commanding finger at her bowl of stew and bread roll. "We'll talk about it when we're in your room and not before."

The girl refused to say anything more but ate quickly and alternated spoonfuls of stew with bites of bread. It wasn't fancy fare but it was filling, and they matched each other mouthful for mouthful while students ebbed and flowed around them.

Even there, she was under observation.

Some walked toward their table, only to abruptly change course before they reached it. Others made a point of walking past and looking at them as they proceeded. It made eating uncomfortable, especially since she couldn't help getting ready to defend herself.

She'd identified her tray and mug as her best weapon options, and that was only if she couldn't upend the table and escape in the confusion. Given her street experience, she was very sure she could outdistance any pursuit and reach her room before they caught up to her.

The only problem was Mirielle. The girl didn't look like she could fight her way out of the orphanage's fish pond let alone anything else and the numbers would be against them. What if one of the "better bred" apprentices decided to threaten the girl?

To her relief, no one did anything more than give them a vindictive stare, and that was from Celia. Kaylin tightened her hold on her mug's handle and had begun to regret the potential loss of her tea when one of Celia's friends plucked the girl's sleeve and drew her away.

"What was that about?" she asked but Mirielle stood and lifted her empty bowl. "Come on," she urged.

She gave her bowl a hasty swipe with the last of her bread and followed the other apprentice. More than one face turned to them as they returned their dirty plates and left. She felt as though the entire room was watching them and found it hard to not look back.

Her glare hadn't worked on the four Grandmothers of Doom at the barracks, but she could give it a try.

The almost irresistible urge to give them the universal finger rose but she decided against it. As far as she could tell, she hadn't done anything wrong but she had crossed some invisible line and still couldn't work out what it was.

Mirielle knew, though. She was sure of that.

The girl walked briskly and deftly avoided groups of students while giving the impression that she hadn't noticed them. Kaylin admired her skill as she tried to keep up. Her companion said nothing as she led the way to their rooms.

She was about to take the last corner when she came to a sudden halt and then led the new girl through the junction. Kaylin was immediately curious to know what was going on and she heard raised voices.

"Magister Wanslow will hear of this!" said the shrill treble of a younger student.

"Then Magister Wanslow will replace what you've lost," a cold female voice replied.

"He…he won't. He said next time would be the last time he'd help me. That if…if I couldn't hold onto my materials I needed to learn to be more cautious."

"He sounds much smarter than I've been led to believe then," the female taunted.

The gloating she heard in those tones made Kaylin turn. She took a step in the direction of the voices but Mirielle lunged back and clamped both hands around one arm to yank her forward and away.

"Not now," the girl admonished in almost a hiss, "and not them. We'll find out what's happened shortly."

That seemed unlikely. The rate at which the girl dragged her down the corridor meant they wouldn't find out a thing. But the girl's hold on her arm remained vise-like and she followed.

They took the next corridor and entered through a door into a comfortably furnished room.

What is this place?

Kaylin looked around, trying to identify what the room was meant to be. On the one hand, it looked like it wanted to be a library or a study hall, but the unornamented sofas and armchairs set around small round tables hinted at a sitting room or parlor.

"Welcome to the common room," Mirielle whispered but even those hushed tones drew shushing rebukes from different corners.

A half-dozen students were bent over notes and books.

"We're allowed to study here," Mirielle told her in a whisper that was barely louder than a breath. "Anyone can borrow the books but they have to read them in this room. They can't take them out."

Kaylin wondered what stopped them from forgetting and taking one of the tomes back to their rooms.

"They're warded," the other girl explained as though reading her mind. "Spelled so they prevent the bearer from leaving with them."

She raised her brows.

"There are only a few copies of each one," her companion added. "No one is allowed to have them for long. It's fairer that way."

Fairer for who? she wondered since the rest of the Academy system didn't seem too worried about the principles of fairness.

Mirielle skirted the edge of the room for about the length of a corridor and opened another door carefully. She followed and her fellow apprentice's plan became clear. If she'd worked it out correctly, their journey across the common room should have brought them to their corridor again.

Her guess proved correct when Mirielle led them into the top section of the corridor that would take them straight to their doors.

"Hurry up," she whispered, but Kaylin risked a glance down the junction and caught sight of a group of six students facing off against each other.

Before any of them could notice her, Mirielle returned, grasped her by the sleeve, and dragged her around the corner to her door.

"Are you crazy?" she demanded in a whisper.

"That looked like Celia," Kaylin retorted in almost a hiss of indignation, "picking on… I don't know…someone else."

"Get us inside before she comes looking," the other girl urged.

Kaylin didn't like being rushed and she didn't like running away, but she unlocked her door and let Mirielle herd her inside.

"Why would she do that?" she asked as the girl closed the door behind them.

"Because you're new? Because she can? Because you showed her up in Magister Cantrell's class?" her companion demanded in a harsh whisper.

Kaylin noticed she'd flipped the catch to lock the door too. Surely, the other students wouldn't invade someone else's room?

When she remembered what the other apprentice had told her about locking her trunk, she revised that idea. It seemed they did.

Footsteps sounded in the corridor outside and Mirielle froze and placed a hand on Kaylin's arm and a finger on her lips.

The footsteps stopped outside her door and the handle turned, jiggled, and turned again. Celia's irritable tones broke the silence.

"Are you sure you saw her?" she demanded.

The mumbled affirmative was barely audible and Kaylin couldn't identify the voice. Hardly surprising, given how new she was.

When the handle rattled again, Mirielle placed a finger over her lips and only removed it when the footsteps moved away. She stayed quiet a little longer and a second set followed the first.

Kaylin raised her eyebrows and her companion mirrored her expression. Only when the last of the footsteps had faded did she speak.

"Now she's got something to prove—and seeing as she can't prove it in class, she'll do it by taking every opportunity to make life awkward for the students of the magisters who are most opposed to hers."

"Who is Magister Gaudin anyway?" she asked.

Mirielle rolled her eyes. "Only one of the most powerful conseillers in the Academy and one of Magister Roche's worst enemies. Trust me, if Celia can make you look bad, she'll gain a huge standing in Gaudin's books and everyone wants to have a huge standing with Gaudin."

"Even the ones who aren't his students?"

"Her!" the girl whispered savagely. "You truly don't know anything, do you?"

"I only arrived last night," Kaylin reminded her. "You should know. You were there."

"I know," she replied and her expression showed both sympathy and chagrin. She sat on the end of the bed. "Look. Let me explain something to you."

Kaylin dumped her books on her desk and leaned against the edge. "Go on."

"The magisters have their special areas of interest and each one needs to be supported. But the Academy has its own aims and agendas, which are linked to the interests of those who send their children here or the companies that send their people for training. It needs to keep them happy if it wants to have enough funding to run."

"So?" she encouraged. The thought uppermost in her mind was that the Academy sounded rather like the orphanage, except it didn't get donations from people who wanted to help the poor.

"So the magisters each have projects they support and projects they want to see go ahead, but the funding's limited and they have to prove their pet projects are the best."

"Let me guess—they do this by having the best students," Kaylin stated.

Mirielle nodded. "They do, and not only academically. If they have a student from a moneyed background whose parents are willing to donate, or if their student is 'better' than another student in some way, they have a greater chance to get the support they need to see their projects moved ahead."

"So, I'm something of a bust for Magister Roche then," Kaylin conceded and Mirielle chuckled.

"No one wants to say no to the Chevaliers, but the knights are less known for donations than they are for bringing interesting artifacts and books from expeditions into the Twin Spears, which is never guaranteed."

"So why did he take a chance on me then?"

"Because he was the one on duty when Captain Delaine's message came through and he knew no matter how much he argued, he'd end up with whatever student was coming. It was better to do it sooner rather than later and keep the fuss to a minimum. There'd be less chance you'd be noticed that way."

Kaylin snorted. "Well, I blew that one, didn't I?"

Mirielle couldn't help a small giggle. "Yeah... You kinda did, but you did show up one of Magister Gaudin's pupils and you performed well in Magister Cantrell's class, so it was a good kind of notice."

"And a bad one," she observed caustically.

"Unless you planned to fail." The girl shrugged. "You were bound to upset someone sooner or later."

"So tell me what the students get out of it?" she asked. "Apart from a good education, because I honestly think you'll only get that if you find it on your own."

"Mostly on your own," her companion corrected. "But the main thing a student gets from a magister's support comes when they graduate."

"If they graduate," she pointed out darkly.

"True," Mirielle agreed, "but if they graduate with a magister's support, they're more likely to be hired out to one of the better adventuring companies or find a position in a noble's court like I said before."

"So?" Kaylin asked.

"So they're less likely to have to take a position with a mercenary troop that will probably get them killed."

"Like those who go to the Doom?" she asked and recalled how many had gone there so they could explore under the mountain. She couldn't help glancing toward her curtained window.

"Exactly," the girl said, followed the direction of her gaze, and frowned in puzzlement at the closed curtains.

Kaylin thought about showing her the view, then decided against it. She wasn't ready to share that, yet—and she certainly wasn't ready to share the idea that she wanted to visit the Doom and the Spears. Not yet.

Mirielle pushed off the bed and moved cautiously to the door.

"I have to go," she told her. "I need to prepare for tomorrow's classes." She flashed her a smile. "You'd better do the same. After today, people will have expectations and the magisters who don't like Magister Roche are more likely to try to show you up in class. And then there are the other students. If you can't fight, you'd better not carry anything valuable on you outside the room—and keep your door locked."

Kaylin nodded and concealed her anger, trepidation, and sadness behind a serious expression.

The girl hesitated, and Kaylin thought she might return and hug her. She relaxed when she settled for a sympathetic smile instead.

"You'll do fine," she said. "Meet you for breakfast tomorrow?"

She nodded. "Sounds like a plan."

Mirielle unlocked the door and opened it cautiously only a crack before she slipped quickly into the corridor and pulled it closed behind her. Mindful of the girl's words, Kaylin locked it behind her and returned to her desk.

Before she sat, she opened the curtains so she could see the Spears, adjusted the lamp, and made herself comfortable to check her timetable and select the next day's texts. It was a good thing she was used to getting by on little to very little sleep—and that Sister Sabine's tutelage had ensured she knew how to read.

Kaylin moved the books to her desk and read until the lamp burned low and the first glimmer of dawn lightened the night sky.

Mirielle's thunderous knocking woke her the next morning—and for many mornings after—and the weeks soon eased into a familiar routine—breakfast, classes, lunch, classes, dinner, study, and sleep. Throughout it all, the constant politicking permeated every aspect of Academy life.

Ignoring barbed comments from the magisters and not responding to the ever-present snark from their students became a habit, as did dealing with the conflicts arising in the corridors. At first, Kaylin didn't interfere and soon learned that nothing was ever as it seemed.

An apparent aggressor could merely be someone retrieving their goods or delivering a little justice, and she certainly did not want to interfere with that. She also hoped she could get her head around the politics enough to avoid the worst of it.

There was no way she wanted to fall foul of the magisters enough to be expelled from the Academy—or to fail. Her friends needed her to stay so they could have a future, and now that she was there, she wanted to stay. She wanted to succeed and perhaps repay some of the trust Captain Delaine had shown her.

She didn't see much of Mirielle, only at meals and sometimes in the common room when they needed to access the library, but that was okay. While she missed Isabette and Melis's chatter and the banter of her crew, she was able to cope with it by burying herself in her study.

Magical geometry fascinated her and the theory wasn't as boring as she'd thought it would be—or as hard. Then there were the potions and the paraphernalia, and the gestures and verbal components. There was so much for her to get her head around and she knew she was missing things.

Unfortunately, she simply didn't know what—and she didn't want to bother Magister Roche with things he'd think she should have found out herself. What she wanted was to impress him enough to prove she was worth him paying attention to and more importantly, worth supporting. She would only have one chance to do that.

After the first four weeks, Roche had to give her a status report and let her know how she was doing. She was fairly sure he would do that under duress and that if he didn't have to see her, he wouldn't.

"Well, it sucks to be him then, doesn't it?" she muttered and worked through the last pages of the physical aspects of geometry.

She was looking for a better way to determine the gestures needed to create any particular spell but the chapter was no help.

"And it sucks to be me too," she added and glared at the page in frustration.

So far, she hadn't found a single thing that would make it worth him paying her any attention. Nothing!

And time is running out.

"I need a bigger library," she said to Mirielle. "There's nothing here."

The girl swept her gaze along the stacked shelves and gave her a disbelieving look. "What do you mean?"

"I mean all of this is stuff I can learn in class and none of it looks like…like something I can't."

"What would you want that for?" Mirielle asked.

"I want to prove I'm worth the magister paying me some attention," she whispered in return after she'd glanced around to make sure no one was there to hear her.

Her caution was justified when her companion echoed her movement and lowered her head.

"You'll want to go to the other library for that—the big one the magisters use."

"There's a bigger library?"

The other girl sighed. "Sure. Come on."

Their destination was well away from the student dormitories, and Mirielle looked around nervously as they left the central block of classrooms behind them. The halls became better appointed, the carpets beneath their feet richer, and the walls lined with tapestries or adorned by large paintings.

Here and there, in small niches, stood elegant tables of rich, dark wood and narrow display cabinets that held ancient statues, old weapons with the nicks still etched into their blades, and odd-looking artifacts. Kaylin glanced at them as they passed but her guide didn't stop.

The farther they went, the more the girl hurried her steps. Kaylin settled for mapping the route in her mind using the artifacts and tapestries as landmarks. She could always return to them some other time.

By the time they reached the tall, ornate, double doors leading into the library, both girls were a little short of breath. She scolded herself with the reminder that she'd been able to travel longer distances with less effort when she'd been on the streets. It was something she would have to address.

"Here we are," Mirielle told her in a hushed whisper and she got the impression the girl didn't visit often.

She was surprised when her companion walked in with her.

"You wanted to visit too?" she asked, relieved that her trip hadn't taken Mirielle away from her plans.

"I'd forgotten," the girl admitted, "but you raised a good point about impressing the magister so I guess I'll do some extra reading, too."

Kaylin smiled. "Let's see what we can find."

Their search took them deep into the stacks and late into the night, and they had to scramble to their rooms in time to read the next day's lessons.

That didn't stop them from visiting the next night, or the one after, or even the night after that. They changed their process and returned to their rooms after the evening meal, read the next day's texts, and hurried to the library to read late into the night.

Neither of them said much but sat in companionable silence as they worked through their books of interest. Sometimes, they'd discuss what they'd found in hushed tones over breakfast to fuel ideas for what they wanted to research later that night.

Kaylin's journal started to fill with notes from the texts, ideas from the notes, and references to books she needed to look for. Two weeks later, she found a reference to *Kristemar's Collection of Magical Theory.*

Kristemar had been interested in comparing the similarities and differences between elven and human magic and was said to believe that the elves had more efficient methods of establishing geometries in the first and second dimensions. *Kristemar's Collection* was reputed to take those beliefs and expound on them.

Unfortunately, when she looked for the text, she couldn't find it. After she couldn't see it on the shelves or on the return carts, she decided to ask the librarian.

"Kristemar's Collection of Magical Theory, you say?" the librarian asked, his voice unnaturally loud.

She nodded. "I wondered if the Academy had it and if I can borrow it."

"I see..." He didn't look like he saw at all.

"I've checked the shelves and the return carts but I couldn't find it," she explained, "so I wondered if it was here—and if it was if you could show me where."

"Uh-huh..." The man continued to stare at her.

"I... If it's been borrowed, I'm happy to wait until it's returned if you can tell me when it's due..." She let her voice trail off at the look on his face. "So..." she prodded when he continued to stare at her without saying a word.

The librarian frowned.

"Do you have a note from your magister stating you are permitted access to this book?" he asked after a moment's hesitation.

Kaylin blushed, even though she hadn't done anything wrong. "I don't," she admitted and lowered her voice. "I hoped to use it to show my magister that I'm making good progress—*notable* progress."

Her response startled hastily suppressed laughter from him and he made a shooing motion with his hands.

"Get away with you," he said and chuckled at her embarrassment. "That book isn't for the likes of you. First, you need to get your feet under you."

Annoyed at his presumption that she didn't know anything, she scowled at him. He repeated the shooing gesture, arched an eyebrow, and dared her to challenge him.

She was tempted but decided it wouldn't help to start a scene and returned to Mirielle.

"Don't ask," she muttered when the girl raised her eyes from her book.

Kaylin lifted her journal from the table and studied the other entries. "I'll be back."

While she might not be able to find *Kristemar's Collection,* there were at least a half-dozen other texts she could read. Maybe the book would be back on the shelf on another day. She took her journal with her, scanned her notes, then glanced at the shelves.

Her gaze roved over the students scattered among the tables between, but one young man—and the book he was reading—caught her eye.

She froze and stared, not sure she should believe her eyes.

Kristemar's Collection of Magical Theory was right there in the library. The librarian either didn't know what he was talking about or he was being deliberately obstructive. Kaylin knew which one she thought it was but it didn't matter.

After all, she'd found the book she needed. All she had to do was ask the boy if he minded her borrowing it for a very short minute. After a deep breath, she approached and studied him as she drew closer.

He looked like he was about the same age as her. His dark hair was pulled back in a neat queue and his dark eyes were serious. All in all, she decided he had a kind face—a kind, gentle-looking face. Surely he wouldn't mind if she borrowed the book for a short while and maybe copied a few lines of text from it to keep her studies moving forward.

She stopped at the table's edge, looked down at him, and waited until he glanced up.

"Hi, my name's Kaylin," she said, introducing herself. "I...um, I've just started here and I was looking for this book to help me with my study. Is it... Do you think I could borrow it for a little while?"

He simply stared at her so she hefted her journal.

"It's only that this other text mentions it and I wanted to... I wondered if it was okay if I took a couple of notes. I only need to go over the section to see what Kristemar says about elves and how they established geometries in the first and second dimensions. I wouldn't keep it for very long. Maybe a couple of heartbeats?"

His gaze didn't waver as she stumbled through her request. Hearing herself say it, she thought it sounded more like an imposition—like she was over-reaching or worse. She twined her hands together and twisted them nervously while she waited.

The boy didn't reply and his expression didn't change. It retained the same studious look it had held while he'd been reading. At first, she thought it was because he was shy, but a small sound escaped him—a laugh, she realized, but not the kind she might have expected.

This laugh wasn't kind, or endearing, or even tolerant. It was mocking, proud, and cold, and his face became infinitesimally harder. She froze her expression and tried to not react to the sound while she waited for a reply. Still, he did not respond.

When he continued to stare at her with the faintest trace of mockery on his lips, she decided she'd had enough.

"So," she pressed, "can I please read it? Only that one section."

Shuffling and suppressed whispers made her look around and she realized she'd drawn the attention of the other students—not what she'd intended. She caught a brief glimpse of Mirielle staring at her and her friend looked shocked.

Kaylin ignored her. She decided she could ask Mirielle what she'd done wrong later. No doubt there was something she didn't know and some invisible line she'd crossed. Well, too bad. The guy could at least give her an answer.

"I know where it is thanks to the citation in the *Sorciere Bibiliolex,*" she assured him and clasped her hands around her journal in an attempt to keep them still.

Finally, he spoke. "Ummm....no." He chuckled and glanced at her before he returned his attention to his book.

Her temper rose and she caught hold of it before it got the better of her. "So you're in the middle of some important research, too, huh?" Kaylin asked and tried to sound sympathetic.

He looked at her and smirked at her discomfort.

"Ummm...no," he told her, chuckled again, and focused on the book.

When she didn't move, he flicked his gaze to her face and made a slight shooing motion with his fingers before he shifted slightly to turn his back toward her. She stared, shocked at being dismissed like some annoying child.

As he pivoted the chair, she decided she'd had enough.

She caught the back of the chair, stopped him, and grasped him by the robes to turn him to face her. It was the same kind of move she'd used on Raoul when the boy was being particularly difficult—or Piers or Melis, come to think of it. The glare she gave the unfortunate boy was the same one she used on any one of them when they were being difficult.

"Look," she stated, her tone almost a snarl, "I'm new here and I don't know who you are. And honestly, I don't care because, so far, you've been the most ignorant, self-important jerk I've encountered in this place, and that's saying something."

Someone gasped nearby and the distant whispers renewed.

"What I'm asking would only cost you a few minutes of your time and you've made it clear I'm not interrupting anything important. So what I don't understand is why you refuse to help. More than that, though, I don't understand why, if you chose to say no, you had to be such a tit about it."

The boy stared at her, then he smiled. When she glared at him, he started to laugh.

"Do you get off on being a turd?" Kaylin demanded and the laughter turned to a chuckle.

"Some of us need to do the extra," she continued, not understanding what he found so funny, and the chuckle became an open-mouthed guffaw.

That was too much for her fraying temper. She released his robes, stepped back, and slapped him. All her annoyance was put into the swing and the resulting impact cracked through the library like a whip and the laughter stopped.

Gasps ensued, and the whispers ceased. A sense of utter stillness descended.

It was broken by one person—Mirielle. She raced forward, wrapped her hand around Kaylin's arm, and held it tightly enough to hurt.

"It's time to go," she whispered and dragged her friend away from the boy and the tables as a bustle of movement occurred toward the front of the library.

The apprentice didn't hesitate. She dragged her into the shelter of the stacks and hauled her along the narrow corridors between the shelves to take her around the study area and past the now-empty front desk.

"What exactly is going on over here?" the librarian demanded behind them and his stentorian tones carried through the double doors and into the corridor beyond.

Mirielle increased her pace, pulled Kaylin into the first side corridor, and didn't let go as she dodged into a second. The librarian's voice followed them and his next question faded as they took the second turn.

"What was that unholy noise?"

Kaylin had no doubt that the other students would fill him in and she stopped resisting her companion's pull on her arm.

"Do you know what you just did?" the girl demanded when she'd locked Kaylin's door behind them. Her voice rose in fear and frustration. "Do you have any idea what you've done?"

"Slapped an asshole who thoroughly deserved it?" she retorted. "Perhaps released a little frustration on someone who desperately needed it?"

Mirielle stamped her foot and balled her fists at her side. If her head could explode, perhaps the pyromancy student would accomplish it soon.

"You started something with Sylvester Ozanne!" she snapped.

"I showed a jerk that he couldn't get away with being a jerk," she told her.

"You dove head-first in a manure heap and started pulling the poop in over yourself," her companion all but snarled. "That is not a family you want to mess with."

"I wasn't messing with a family," she protested. "It was only one boy—and an arrogant jerk of a boy at that. Now, will you calm down and tell me who he's supposed to be?"

"Who. He's. Supposed. To be?" Mirielle exclaimed and her voice rose in disbelief. "He's Sylvester Ozanne, only the eldest son of the wealthiest, oldest family in Waypoint."

"So?" Kaylin asked.

"Ugh!" Her friend rolled her eyes. "Don't you remember anything? Students offer the magisters certain things that gain their favor, one of those being money and another one being able to influence important decisions." She stepped in close and poked her chest. "Remember that? Remember how it's kind of important to not make life difficult for your magister? How you're supposed to try to win your magister's favor?"

"Uh…" Kaylin began to see what had upset the girl so much. "Is there anything else I should know?"

"Yeah, because slapping the son of one of the most powerful, influential, wealthy families in the city isn't enough for you. How about you slapped one of Magister Hadrienne Gaudin's most favorite students and she will not be pleased?"

Her face grew cold. "You mean Magister Gaudin who is our magister's..." Mirielle nodded and she stuttered to a halt. "He won't be very happy with me, will he—"

"*Us*," the girl whisper-shrieked as she jerked a thumb at herself. "He won't be very happy with *us* because I'm still responsible for showing you the ropes."

She drew a shaky breath.

"And you've just slapped the favorite student of his major rival who also happens to be one of—if not *the*—most powerful magister in the Academy—and not only magically but politically and...and where it counts for getting her projects approved and put into practice. You are almost as big a...a...*tit* as Sylvester!"

She turned away abruptly, took two steps toward the door, and stopped as Kaylin began to apologize.

"I'm sorry," she said. "Truly, truly sorry. I didn't know..."

Her words trailed off as Mirielle spun and she froze as she stalked to stand in front of her and leaned into her face.

"Well, that won't matter now," the girl told her brutally, "because *now,* Apprentice Kaylin Knight, you have been marked. Everyone who is anyone will know they can abuse you with impunity because none of the magisters will do anything to them if they do."

"But—" she began and thought that surely Magister Roche would be forced to intervene, but Mirielle dashed that idea with her very next words.

"And that includes our magister," the girl snapped. "He will be too busy doing damage control for his favorite students and his projects to have any time for you. In *fact,* you'll be lucky if he doesn't decide to punish you for what you've done to set an example for the rest of us."

Mirielle took a step back and spread her hands helplessly. "I can't help you," she stated simply. "I truly can't. I will try but there isn't much I will be able to do."

"Then don't," Kaylin told her. "Don't get caught trying to help me. That's—it wouldn't be fair for them to go after you too and they will."

The girl pursed her lips and stared into her face before she shook her head.

"That's not how friendship works," she told her. "How it works is this. You'll be hunted or ignored. There will be no middle road and anyone who speaks to you or sits too close will be tarred with the same brush."

"That's exactly my point," she exclaimed. "You can't stay near me. You need to stay away. I'll be fine. It's not like—"

She'd been about to say it wasn't like she hadn't been on her own before, but that wasn't entirely true. Almost the same night she'd left the orphanage, she'd found Goss, and then she'd had Melis and Piers and Raoul shortly thereafter. Between them, they'd faced and survived through more trials than she imagined the students at the Academy had.

Even in the orphanage, she'd had Selene. That wouldn't be the case now. If she sent Mirielle away, she wouldn't have anyone. She would truly be alone.

And maybe that's for the best. That way, the only person I can hurt will be myself.

"Besides," the girl added, her face pale, "I'm already marked."

"But how?" she asked. "You didn't do anything. You di—"

"I got you out of there before the librarian arrived," she told her and cut her off. "If I hadn't, you'd be facing Magister Gaudin right now and maybe even be having your room cleared out as she shoved you out the front door."

"But—"

"And don't tell me they'd have to take you to Waypoint because you should already know that's not how it works. She'd dump you out the front gate and expect you to find your own way. After all, there's a road."

"But the orcs—" Kaylin protested in a strangled tone.

"Oh, yes," Mirielle agreed, "and don't forget the minotaurs. They're all out there, especially at night. You wouldn't reach the bottom of the hill let alone the city gates. It would all be a very tragic accident."

"Well..." Kaylin tried to find something positive. "At least you'd be safe."

"Pfft," The girl waved a hand dismissively. "Safe? I'm the one who spent the last two weeks in your company. I won't be safe anywhere after this. If I was lucky, Magister Roche might intercede and say I wasn't responsible for your actions and should be allowed to continue my education here. And if I was *very* lucky, I'd even be allowed to pass."

"What do you mean be allowed to pass?" she demanded. "Are you saying you can be good enough and still not pass your exams?"

The idea shocked her but her companion nodded. "Oh, yes. There's a very good chance I could study my backside off and still fail the Trial, and then I'd have to leave."

"But why?" she asked. "Don't you get to start over?"

Mirielle gave her a pitying look. "That only happens if you can afford to start over. You might not have to pay the enrollment fees a second time but there's the re-enrollment fee and all the tuition fees... and all the materials...and the cost of boarding...and—"

Kaylin put up a hand. "Wait! You have to pay for your room too?"

Her friend nodded. "And your food. That's why it's so expensive to come here. It's too far from the city for day students, not that they would allow it anyway." She sighed. "There's no way my family can afford to have me start over."

She straightened her shoulders and looked her in the eye. "No, if I fail, that's it. I get to go home and either marry well and have a horde of magically inclined children or I can join one of those less-reputable adventuring outfits and try to build my magical skills that way."

"It's not much of a choice," Kaylin told her, and Mirielle managed a watery smile.

"I don't know, most of the less-reputable outfits are simply poor. Even the big ones started out that way. I'd luck in on the bottom floor."

"You wouldn't choose to get married?" she asked. "Find some handsome young noble guy to lose your heart to?"

"That wouldn't be how it happened," the girl told her. "My dad would choose the 'right' guy but not the right guy for me—more like the right guy for him and his business interests, someone well-connected and wealthy who wouldn't mind having a failed mage as his wife." She snorted. "Knowing my luck, he'd send our kids to the Academy and they'd graduate just fine. I'm not sure how I'd feel about that."

"You'd manage."

"Yeah, but I'd be scared someone would connect them to me and punish them for what I did, and that wouldn't be fair."

Kaylin grasped her friend's shoulder. "You won't fail," she reassured the girl. "You work too hard and pay too much attention to what you're doing for that." She gave her a gentle shake. "I'm sorry I put you in this position," she said, "so this is what I'll do. We won't meet for meals anymore. You'll go on as if what I did was the last straw."

She held a hand up when Mirielle opened her mouth to protest.

"We'll still talk here if you can get in without being seen, but that'll be it. I will stay away from everyone and find a way to impress the magister during my status report."

"But—" the other girl began, and she placed a finger over her lips. Leaning forward, she gave her a swift hug and turned her toward the door.

"Starting now," she said sternly. "It'll be all right, you'll see."

Mirielle hesitated, drew a breath as though about to say something, then nodded and let herself out. From the look on her friend's face, Kaylin knew she doubted her plan would work.

At least she was willing to give it a try.

CHAPTER FOURTEEN

The test was going well—but it was also going poorly. Kaylin knew it and she hoped she'd be able to impress Roche by pointing the second aspect out by showing that she knew where both her strengths and weaknesses lay.

The first test had been a rapid-fire quiz to do with the theory of magic, but after five minutes of grilling her, he had moved on to the more practical aspects of her education. Potion-theory preceded three swift tests involving the identification of potion ingredients, the analysis and identification of potions, and the brewing of a useful tincture used for healing cuts and abrasions.

A similar test on magical paraphernalia had followed, and she'd unjumbled the components for six different apparatuses and assembled the equipment, all while being bombarded by questions regarding their use to enhance the casting of spells. Most had been covered in class and of those that hadn't, she was able to deduce the answer with a few stumbles but no outright mistakes.

If the magister was impressed by her ability and application of her learning, he didn't show it.

"And now," he said, "perhaps the most important aspect of being a wizard—the actual casting of spells."

He set a candle on the desk. "Light it."

Kaylin did so and recalled her first class with Magister Cantrell and how the woman's attitude had soured toward her since the incident in the library. She hadn't been alone. Even the most easy-going of the magisters had distanced themselves.

On the one hand, they hadn't savaged her in class like some of them, but by the same token, they hadn't given her a chance to shine either. At least she hadn't managed to upset any of the other masters by showing their students up.

She sighed.

"Are you paying any attention?" Magister Roche demanded and she started and realized she'd become lost in thought.

"I'm sorry, Magister."

"Is something on your mind, Apprentice?"

Surprised, she looked at him. She was about to tell him exactly what was on her mind when he continued.

"Or is it that you're stalling because you're incapable?"

A flash of anger replaced her surprise. "Incapable of what?" she demanded.

"Creating a spark of light bright enough to dazzle a man?" he snapped. "Or should I be led to understand your limit lies in lighting candl— Oh! Son of—" His arms jerked to his face and he patted his forehead. "What do you think you're doing, girl?"

Kaylin stared at him in shock. Her spell had been perfectly cast.

"I didn't see anyone else, Magister. I thought you wanted me to prove I could dazzle your eyes."

"Of all the fool— As if I would ask that." He snarled his irritation and held a hand over his face.

"But you said—"

"I *said*, did you want that to be my understanding?" he retorted belligerently, lowered his hand, and dabbed gently at his teary eyes.

"But doesn't that mean you wanted me to prove I could?" she asked, bewildered by his anger.

"Do I look like I wanted you to prove it?" he demanded, "Or to prove it on me?"

Now that he mentioned it, he had looked surprised when she'd cast the spell.

"Never mind," he grumbled. "We know you can cast instantaneous spells with some aplomb, but can you hold the magic and still have it do your bidding?"

"Well—" Kaylin began, only to be cut off.

He blew the candle out and the office became dim.

"Provide me with a glow for the count of three," he ordered. "We'll see."

She drew a deep breath but resisted the urge to exhale and admit defeat. What he was asking was almost beyond her and she knew it, but she also knew she could achieve it on very rare occasions.

Drawing her focus inward, she found the sense that enabled her to feel the magic directing the movement of her fingers when she tried to learn the somatics for a new spell. This time, she would have to draw the magic out and hold it.

Kaylin closed her eyes and imagined a soft glow emanating from a point in the empty air before her. When she opened them, the glow was there, a mere pin-prick in the air but bright enough that she could see Magister Roche's features clearly.

Slowly, she expanded the glow from a mere dot to something more the size of a quail's egg and called more magic so the light spread to the farthest corners of his office. He stepped closer and Kaylin held the light as long as she could but when she blinked, that was all it took.

The light went out.

"Hmmph."

She saw her opportunity.

"As you can see, Magister," she began, and his gaze sharpened with displeasure. Despite this, she continued, "As you can see, I can perform instantaneous spells without much difficulty but I have more difficulty with sustaining a prolonged emanation."

Roche responded with a heavy sigh but she rushed on before he could tell her to stop.

"I believe this is partly because my third dimension—the dimension of emotion—is significantly stronger than either my experience or logical dimensions."

The man snorted and again, she pressed on.

"I believe I can make the necessary adjustments to compensate for this while I strengthen those dimensions if you would write me a note so I can access *Kristemar's Collection of Magical Theory.*"

He stared at her and she swallowed.

"In the library," she added as though he needed the extra information.

Roche's eyes narrowed. "Is this the same text that led you to have an altercation with Apprentice Ozanne?"

Kaylin opened her mouth to respond but it was the magister's turn to continue without giving her a chance to speak.

"Because if it is, you should be more than pleased to know that the incident and that text has gotten you blacklisted with every magister in the Academy. *All of them,* as in *no one* is willing to touch you with a barge pole let alone be seen helping you."

He glared at her.

"Did it not occur to you how having one of my students attacking one of Magister Gaudin's students would look to the rest of the magisters?" he demanded.

She took a breath to reply but he continued. "Did it not occur to you what the effects of your behavior would be on my career, or my position, or my standing? Both in the school and in circles beyond?"

He circled her once before he came to stand in front of her.

"Do you have the slightest clue how difficult you have made my position?" He waved a remonstratory finger in her face and continued, his voice rising, "Oh, *no,* my dear Apprentice, you did not and now?" His voice softened. "Now, you are on your own."

Kaylin stared at him.

"But you're supposed to be my conseiller, my...my teacher! I've been sent here to learn and as hard as I try, there are some things I cannot learn on my own."

"It's something you should have thought of before you attacked a fellow student."

"He was being a troll-titted ass-wipe!" she retorted.

His arm raised as if he had started the horses racing. "And there it is, the gutter-snipe some idiot deity thought should be granted magical ability."

Her eyes burned. "Well, at least I have some, unlike some of the students you allow to buy their way in."

The magister raised his eyebrows and took a step back. "And then there's your complete unwillingness to understand how things work in the real world—the one situated above the gutters and the thieving grounds you're used to playing in. And your attitude."

"My attitude is fine when people are doing the right thing by each other," Kaylin replied. She was about to say more but decided she'd gone too far as it was. It wasn't easy, but she took a firm hold on her temper and pressed her lips together, an act that drew a thin smile of amusement from the magister.

"Ah, now see? She can learn to hold that wayward tongue of hers, not to mention that temper." He tutted. "Such a pity she didn't learn sooner."

"I was too busy trying to keep up with my lessons," she told him but kept her tone soft despite the anger vibrating through it. "As Captain Delaine expected."

"Yes, well, I'm sure she expected many things," Roche replied tartly, "and I'm afraid she'll be sorely disappointed. But far be it from me or any other magister to second guess what the good captain sees in you."

Kaylin gasped but closed her mouth with a snap and let him continue.

He shook his head at her and wagged a finger in disappointment.

"No, far be it for any of us to do that. The captain's reputation precedes her and as much as we respect her, it would be unwise for any of us to tell her what we truly feel about her latest pet project. While she might think your talent is enough to warrant the extra training, many of us cannot see the advantage in training a student of your extraction."

She blinked and swallowed against the sadness that threatened to clog her throat and fill her eyes with tears. He'd as good as said she wasn't worth training because she was poor, a nothing from the streets? Talent and a willingness to work weren't enough?

Despair washed over her and she tried to not let it show. She fought to cling to the fact that Captain Delaine had seen some worth in her, enough to risk her reputation on her talent and willingness to work. She'd try to keep that in mind the next time she felt like slapping some manners into someone who thoroughly deserved it.

As she thought that, she realized she was upset but not sorry and she wondered what Delaine would have to say about that. She didn't dare contemplate what Sister Sabine might have suggested. Neither thought was helpful, so she pushed them to the back of her mind and tried to concentrate on what Magister Roche was saying.

"But she is not here in the Academy and is only lightly attached to the periphery of the world in which it exists." He drew a breath. "And as such, her influence is not as strong as those with more powerful connections, such as the Ozannes, and it is certainly not as strong as someone with a powerful influence who dwells within the Academy's world." He sighed. "No, your precious Captain Delaine and her Chevaliers do not hold the same level of threat as the likes of Magister Gaudin."

"But—" Kaylin began and intended to point out that he was respected and an influencer in the Academy world.

"So," the magister rambled on and ignored her interruption, "my advice to you, Apprentice Kaylin Knight, is that you keep your head down and do your best to be unremarkable and unremarked on and perhaps, in a few years, the other magisters will forget your hideous lack of judgment."

"Years?" she squeaked.

Roche nodded, his brow creased by a thoughtful frown.

"Years," he confirmed, "although I doubt Magister Gaudin will ever forget or forgive since the intolerable boy complained to his parents about having to study in a public space where he could be exposed to the likes of..."

His frown grew deeper as if he was trying to recall the exact words Sylvester had used.

"Ah, yes," he exclaimed. "He complained about being exposed to the likes of gutter trash that felt it could not only occupy the same space and speak to him but thought making false claims about its understanding of letters, numbers, and magic gave it the right to touch the same books he did."

Kaylin's jaw dropped and it crossed her mind that a slap hadn't gone far enough and a closed fist followed by a good kicking might have been more effective.

Sure, she scolded herself, *more effective in getting you kicked out.*

"Regardless," the magister continued, "you need to keep your head down and, while Gaudin might not forgive, she may become otherwise occupied for a while and distracted by other matters once Apprentice Ozanne passes his final Trials in two years."

Like it's a foregone conclusion, she thought and her lip curled with scorn.

Roche caught her expression and chuckled softly.

"Yes, the boy will pass his final Trials and he is good enough to do it on his own merit so we will not be forced to endure his presence any longer than we might otherwise have had to. You, on the other hand, have a great deal of study ahead of you if you are to pass your first Trials, and where a student like Ozanne might be permitted his mistakes, you will be granted no such leniency."

He glanced pointedly at the clock on the wall and then at the door. "You'd best make the most of the time you have left."

"Without your help," Kaylin muttered resentfully.

"You're still here, are you not?" he asked mildly and she glared at him. He spread his hands. "I have done all I can, I'm afraid. To spend more time than this is to place more important things at risk. As I said, you're on your own, dear."

"But you're supposed to be my conseiller!" The protest burst out of her before she could rethink it.

Roche shrugged, his expression one of mock apology.

"Try seeing it from my perspective, dear," he replied coolly and all apology disappeared from his face. "If you leave here, fail, or even die in some horrid…mishap, I will still be here and have to do my best to keep my head above water. There is no benefit for me to put myself out to aid you, no matter what title I've been given."

"Unless I succeed," Kaylin pointed out wearily and added with a touch of bitterness, "but you don't seem to consider that a possibility."

The man gave her a long look. "Honestly," he replied, "I'm afraid I can't afford to have such fanciful optimism."

"Now, get out."

At Roche's gesture, Kaylin left the office. His farewell rang in her ears and made her face burn with shame.

She hurried out and lowered her head to avoid the pitying stares from the students waiting in the outer office. The silence behind her was as deafening as it was telling and she fumbled at the door before she fled into the corridor beyond.

Sometimes, when a student—no matter how disliked—faced something the others feared, there was nothing to be said. Not at the moment in which it was witnessed, anyway. No doubt there'd be a slew of whispers later.

For now, she simply wanted to be somewhere no one else was and she didn't feel like going back to her room. The deities alone knew she'd spent enough time confined there in the last few weeks.

And all because that little troll's ass had thought he was too good to share a book with her. It horrified her to think he would one day occupy an office where he could influence something important. She shuddered and longed for the touch of a breeze and the freedom of open air around instead of walls, and she hurried to where she'd seen an outer courtyard.

It was a fortress, right? A citadel of sorts? Surely there had to be gardens somewhere or even an outer yard between the walls. She remembered seeing a turning space for carriages on the way in but didn't try to find the entrance.

Gardens should be farther back or central.

It made her wish she'd looked up how such things worked or explored more, although there hadn't been much time for that. With the magisters kept busy giving status reports over the next few days, that would change.

She'd intended to use the time to study, but maybe finding somewhere beyond the view of other students would be a good idea too. It had been weeks since she'd been outside and she'd been so busy, she hadn't even thought of it. There must be a garden there somewhere.

It could even be a vegetable patch. The Academy didn't get all its vegetables from Waypoint, did it?

That was another thing she realized she should have known a long time before. Worst case scenario, if she knew the delivery schedule, it would make it easier to get to town if she ended up being thrown out —and that had to be better than trying to walk.

Kaylin finally descended to the ground floor and the main entrance, then turned deliberately away from the turning circle and followed the wide hallway to a large, airy ballroom. It had large windows looking out onto the paths and greenery of a formal garden. White gravel paths intersected garden beds and flowers topped stone-lined garden beds that peered out from the shade of trees or around the corners of walls.

The burst of heat when she exited the ballroom came as a surprise, and she realized that while she'd been focused on impressing her magister, the season had changed. The late spring of Piers' berry-watching days had given way to summer.

Not that it mattered. The shady interior of the garden offered more than only shelter from the tensions of school. It would cut the late-afternoon heat as well and maybe that heat would mean fewer students would be likely to try to find her.

That would be good, she decided. She needed time to recover, time as far away from the confines of hallway and classroom as she could manage—and the garden looked like the perfect place.

Kaylin didn't hesitate. She resisted the urge to run, pulled the door closed firmly behind her, and hurried across the wide patio beyond and down a set of stairs.

Half-expecting someone to call to her, she didn't slow until she'd put several turns between her and the patio before she stopped and drew a deep breath.

If she looked up, she could still see the walls of the Academy buildings rising around her but they were more like distant cliffs or hills surrounding a hidden valley. There were numerous trees and bushes to hide how close they were.

The garden was quite large and birds flitted between the trees.

Insects buzzed and droned among the leaves and flowers and a sense of peace flowed over her. Kaylin looked around and noticed that she'd come to an intersection where the garden walls formed a circle and the paths radiated away from her in four directions.

Benches were set in alcoves in the walls and two large trees spread their shade between them. She heard the sound of running water and turned toward it. The walls grew taller around her and she reached a set of steps that descended into a long wedge-shaped valley. At one end stood a grotto surrounded by rocks and lilies and small pockets of grass where private picnics could be held.

Vines draped the walls to conceal a slightly different colored stone. The stark white of the Academy walls gave way to gray marble intermingled with the rougher red of granite. She drifted along and smelled the floral scents of paths covered with multi-colored gravel and lined by ferns, lilium, and the drooping branches of willows and weeping cherry.

Small berry-bearing bushes formed clusters and the bright fruit gave her cause to think of Goss and the reaction he'd have to this. The thought made her smile and for a moment, she imagined him and Piers playing one of their stupidly complicated games through the garden beds.

It would probably involve fruit being eaten and thrown in equal measure, along with considerable good-natured jostling and cursing. A heartfelt sigh wrenched from her chest and her eyes blurred again.

Kaylin dashed at them with her hand and attempted to clear them as she looked around for somewhere to sit—somewhere a little hidden where she wasn't likely to be seen and discovered. The deities knew she'd had enough of being noticed to last her a lifetime.

She strolled around a bend and at the edge of a grassy clearing overlooking the grotto, she froze. It was too open and the clearing on the other side of the small pool and the stream running through the valley's center too exposed.

Reluctant to retrace her steps, she moved forward slowly until she saw a narrow trail leading behind the thick, grass-like leaves of a lily that stood taller than she did. With a nervous glance at the clearing on the other side, she stepped around the plant and into another niche.

It was partially hidden by the lilies, with a bench set along the vine-shrouded wall and only two narrow trails leading in and out.

There must be another path there, she thought and observed the second path cautiously.

As the sense of peace grew stronger, she sighed and moved toward the bench. This was what she needed.

The vines drew her attention and she wondered if they'd always been in the valley or if they'd been brought from somewhere else and by whom. Hadn't Captain Delaine told her the citadel had been cleared of monsters and then repurposed as a training place for wizards?

Kaylin brushed her hand over the vines and the fine web of veins in them. Their leaves were shaded an almost translucent green and she noticed the long, many-twigged sprays of green buds hiding amongst them.

Summer and they have yet to bloom? And what would Goss make of that?

The rock surrounding this part of the garden was a blend of red and gray and the granite and marble complemented each other. She dropped onto the bench and let her gaze rove the wall opposite. The vines didn't shroud all of it and the patterns drew her eye like nothing else around her.

Patterns? She leaned forward and her focus sharpened when she realized she was staring at more than clever masonry and there *were* patterns in the stones. They were half-hidden by the creeping vegetation but they were there.

After she'd listened carefully for sounds that would indicate the approach of another person, she stood. The marks she'd noticed were close to the ground where the vines were thinnest, but as she crouched to examine them, she realized they extended up the wall. They also looked vaguely familiar.

Kaylin took her journal from the satchel hanging at her hip, retrieved a piece of charcoal, and started to sketch. The first symbol was easy and the sense of familiarity grew stronger, but she still couldn't recall where she'd seen it before so she drew the next.

Sometimes, the vines were in the way, but she discovered that by crouching side-on to the wall to pin them back with her knee, she was able to see the inscriptions. It was as she brushed the vines back that she saw the symbols above her and more above them.

"What are these?" she whispered, sketched as rapidly as her hands would let her, and took care to keep the symbols in the same order as they appeared on the wall. She was determined that if she could work out what they were, she'd be able to study them wherever she was—and maybe even ask someone about them if she needed help.

She snorted. "Fat lot of good that will do you," she muttered and flicked through her journal to see if she'd made any notes that could give her a clue as to where she'd seen them before. Fortunately, she didn't have to look very far.

There, amidst all the notes she'd made on the existence of an elven theory for more efficiently combining elements, she found one of the symbols she'd copied from the wall.

Kaylin sat back on her heels and frowned from the note in her journal to the corresponding symbol on the wall.

These are elven!

Her heart leapt.

These inscriptions are elven. She peered closely at the walls and noted the different colored stone and slight crumbling where the edges met the mortar. *And this is older than the walls close to the ballroom.*

Are they older than the citadel, she wondered as she traced them up the wall, *or were the walls replaced or repaired with white stone?*

Or had they been covered with a thin layer of the white?

These thoughts chased themselves through her head as she knelt and stared at the inscriptions, her journal balanced on her knee.

And if they're older than the citadel, does that mean the citadel was built over an even older ruin?

"Did the adventurers go that deep?" she murmured. "Do some of the older buildings still exist under the citadel?"

She turned to a fresh page of the journal and scratched another hasty note.

What's in the basement?

It was a good question and she straightened out of her crouch and let the vines fall to cover the wall. When they didn't quite hide all the symbols, she rearranged them carefully with the toe of her boot and made a note to see if she could find a spell that would allow her to enhance plant growth. With that, she could make sure none of the magisters stumbled across the symbols and erased or hid them from sight.

"That would never do," she muttered and voiced a saying often used by Sabine. "Not until I've worked out what message they hold."

When she was happy with the way the vines fell, Kaylin tucked her journal into her bag and noticed how the light had faded since she'd made her escape. While it had been after lunch when she'd left Magister Roche's office, it was almost certainly close to supper.

Her stomach rumbled to confirm her guess, and she looked around for a way out of her refuge. Rather than return the way she'd come, she took the second exit and stepped onto a slightly wider trail close to the wall.

This time, the vines fell to form a thick curtain over the stone and she resisted the urge to pull them aside to see if any more of the symbols existed behind their concealing fronds. She was hungry and needed to find out how to access the lower portions of the Academy.

Did it have a basement? A...a wine cellar? Maybe an underground pantry or something, she reasoned as her mind worked through the possibilities.

The idea of an underground pantry made her pause for only a moment before she increased her pace, relieved when the trail led upward to the main level of the garden. It grew darker as she climbed and lights sprang up along the trails to illuminate the paths and the surrounding vegetation.

Rocks glowed and lanterns flickered to life. Small chains glittered in the trees and light glistened and refracted from odd angles. Kaylin smiled at the magical atmosphere that came with it and relaxed until the entrance to the ballroom came into view.

"Here we go again," she murmured and felt like she stepped into a hostile land as she walked up the steps and through the doors.

The dining hall was crowded when she entered and there was no sign of Mirielle. She wouldn't have sat near the girl anyway but it was still a comfort to know she was there. Not seeing her hit harder than she'd expected.

As she went to collect her plate, she was jostled by another student. At first, she tried to ignore them but she was shoved twice in rapid succession and stumbled. She glanced around and her gaze settled on Tessa, Celia, and Sylvester's grinning faces.

"Supper's over," Celia told her. "There's nothing left."

Kaylin glanced at the servery and saw the waiting meals.

A strong hand seized the back of her robes, hauled out of the line, and thrust her toward the door.

"You heard the wizard, *girl,*" Sylvester snapped and his dark eyes gleamed with anger. "There's no food here for *you.*"

She staggered back, felt a hand on her satchel, and jerked the bag out of Tessa's hand and pulled away. Sylvester's next push caught her off-balance and shoved her out the door.

When she tripped and landed hard on her rump, instinct kicked in and she twisted to the side, used her momentum to roll to her feet, and stood facing the door. None of her three tormentors were in sight but the dining hall doors were closed and she had no doubt she would find them locked.

Hungry, frustrated, and her face burning with humiliation, Kaylin stood in silence and glowered at the door. After a moment, she looked up and down the corridor and tried to decide what to do next. She intended to have something to eat and there would be nothing Sylvester and Gaudin's other favorites could do about it.

Common sense told her that an entrance to the kitchens existed somewhere.

Kaylin moved along the corridor and turned in the opposite direction to the one she'd usually take to reach the dormitories. The kitchens were easy to find. Logic dictated that they would be close to the dining hall and that the staff would have a way to access them that didn't take them through the common area.

What she hadn't expected was for the staff to have a dining room close by and she almost fainted when she caught sight of several magisters descending an ornate flight of stairs positioned to one side. She kept walking and hoped none of them would call her out. Her skin tingled with the weight of their gazes but she didn't look back.

If they didn't recognize her, maybe they'd leave her alone. And if they did recognize her, maybe they'd continue to pretend she didn't exist. It wasn't as though she had traveled out of bounds or there was a curfew on the apprentices' bedtimes.

Try as she might, she couldn't think of a single reason why they might try to stop her. It was still a relief when they continued, reached the bottom of the stairs, and walked through an equally ornate set of double doors, and she didn't relax until they were out of sight.

The kitchens were only a few feet farther on. The doors opened onto the corridor and staff bustled among benches, fireplaces, ovens, and stovetops. Food was set out to be carried to the student's servery and she slipped through the door and picked a plate up from a stack of clean ones opposite a sink full of dirty dishes.

She gathered cutlery in the same way and proceeded quickly through the bustle of staff to the quieter section on the opposite side of the counter. Trolleys waited to be loaded but those tasked with that assignment weren't there.

Maybe they're making deliveries, she thought but didn't wait to find out. She served herself quickly from several trays and stopped in front of a neatly sliced pie. Usually, she'd have come back for dessert and she didn't want to stack it on the plate with her main meal.

On impulse, she picked the pie dish up and moved forward beyond the kitchen in search of somewhere quiet to eat her ill-gotten gains. Her heart raced and a fierce joy surged through her. It had been a while since she'd had to steal to survive and while she doubted the school would share her exuberance, she felt elated.

It was good to be able to look after herself again, good to not be bullied out of another meal and not to have to rely on the charity of others to be fed. She smiled, her elation tinged by regret.

This was not how it was supposed to be.

Her gaze fell on a plain wooden door with a simple latch and she turned into it. Being so close to the kitchen, it could be a pantry or a broom closet.

Or the way to a cellar, she corrected herself as she walked carefully down the stairs and into the lamp-lit depths below. At least she'd get to eat in peace.

Kaylin reached the bottom and discovered it was less a cellar and more like an access to them—and that there were several.

She was about to enter the first door she came to when she thought that would be the one to see the most use. After all, it made sense that the room closest to the stairs would store the most commonly called-for items.

If she hid there, she'd have the greatest chance of being found. Determined to avoid this, she continued down the hall and debated how many doors she'd have to pass before she had a good chance of not being disturbed while she ate.

The sound of footsteps on the stairs behind her made the decision for her, and she tried to dart through the closest door. It was locked and she grimaced and leaned against it, hoping her attempt hadn't made any noise.

Kaylin almost panicked when the person drew closer. Judging from the sound, she didn't have time to reach another door and there was no guarantee it would be unlocked even if she could. Without much time to think of a way to get out of sight, she slid the pie onto her forearm to free one hand and cast the simplest unlocking spell she could think of.

When the lock clicked, she shoved through quickly and pushed the door closed. Worried about what would happen if it was found unlocked, she cast the spell again. The pie wobbled but she was fast enough to finish the required gestures and steady it before it fell. Her breath held in the silence, she waited.

The footsteps drew closer and keys jangled.

She resisted the urge to bolt down the stairs, knowing the sound of her steps would carry. Instead, she waited and hoped whoever it was would choose another door. The keys rattled followed by a sharp thunk as a lock disengaged, but it wasn't the one she stood beside.

Someone hummed a dance tune and boxes thumped and grated as they were moved around. After what seemed an eternity, the door closed and was duly locked, and the footsteps receded. She waited for a full count of twenty after they'd faded from hearing before she proceeded cautiously to the bottom of the stairs.

The girl didn't bother to go much farther but perched on the lowest step and made short work of her stolen food.

Supper there had never tasted so good!

When she had finished, she set the empty dishes aside and took a moment to look around. A single lantern burned in a niche in the wall and closer inspection revealed that it had been recently filled. She debated leaving it and making her own light, then remembered she wouldn't be able to hold the required magic for long.

Rather than be left in the dark, she lifted the lamp from its bracket and took it with her. She noticed almost immediately that the stonework shifted from white to gray halfway down the wall. Kaylin swung the lamp low and searched for signs of the red-colored rock, certain that this was her best chance to find more of the inscriptions.

Wine racks partially obscured the wall on one side and shelves stacked with crates and boxes covered most of the wall on the other, but the cellar started beside the stairs and seemed to go forever.

Driven by curiosity, she hefted the lantern and trudged forward.

In addition to the racks and shelves lining the wall, others jutted out at a ninety-degree angle. She made a point of peering down each one to be sure she hadn't missed any corridors or stairwells. It was hard to tell how long she spent moving forward before she heard the door to the stairwell open behind her.

Huddled behind some shelves, she looked back, surprised to see the light from the stairs was a distant beacon. It reminded her that the lantern would as easily be seen by anyone reaching the bottom of the stairs and quickly, she snuffed it out.

"Where in Agalon's name is the thrice-damned lantern!" The question echoed down the cellar in an angry bellow.

It was followed by the clatter of shattering dishes and another startled shout.

"Gustum! Have you been eating on the sly again?"

"No, sir. I've not had my supper yet." Dishes rattled. "And I'd never take a whole pie. Whoever did this probably borrowed the lantern and was much hungrier than me."

"Are you saying we feed you well enough to fill that pit you call a stomach?"

"I might be."

Another clatter followed as though someone swept the debris aside with their boot. Kaylin stayed as still as the cobbles beneath her and lowered her head, grateful that she'd extinguished the lantern. Silence followed before the sound of footsteps retreated up the stairs.

She waited as she'd only heard one set of steps ascending. They returned shortly after, accompanied by the bright light of another lantern.

"Do you think they're still here?" Gustum asked.

"Nah," the first voice answered. "They couldn't have sat that still for so long. I'da heard them."

He was right, she realized. If she'd moved, he would have heard her, so she hadn't. She might be a little rusty on the physical activity side but she hadn't lost her ability to stay still.

A little impatient, she forced herself to listen as the two went about their assigned task and finally took some dried goods and a crate of

"Gaudin's favorite" up the stairs. The lantern was left with a "Let's see how long this one lasts" and the door locked carefully behind them.

Kaylin remained motionless for several long heartbeats and listened to the silence and the shuffle of furtive movement in the dark.

Furtive movement? She stiffened but didn't let the sound panic her into movement.

It came again and she realized it hadn't come any closer, nor seemed to move from the bottom of the stairs.

Well, this is a problem, she thought and wondered if there was another way out of the cellar. If they'd put a watch on the stairs or even where the cellar came out in the corridor above, she would be caught for sure.

She glanced around and assumed there had to be a second way out. Unfortunately, she didn't know if she could find and reach it before she was missed at breakfast the next day.

Not that I would be missed, she grumbled internally, but the dark part of herself laughed. *Except by those who want to have a piece of you.*

It was right, she acknowledged. Having ousted her from the dining hall once, Gaudin's favorites would no doubt want to repeat the feat. She stifled a sigh. It seemed she would have to sneak her meals from the kitchen more often.

Maybe having a lantern of her own wouldn't be a completely bad idea.

Kaylin lost track of how long she waited in the dark but every time she thought of moving, she'd catch the surreptitious rustle that told her she still wasn't alone. She had almost convinced herself that it was close to dawn and it might be better to get caught than be trapped in the cellar for an entire day when the door opened again.

"Anything?" the first man asked.

"Nah. It's as quiet as the grave. Whoever it was is long gone," a new voice answered.

"Did you check the other door?"

"Did *you?*"

"Good point. No one's seen anyone coming from that way, so you're probably right and they're long gone."

This time, she gave the count until forty after she'd heard two sets of footsteps leave. When silence persisted, she lit the lantern and waited for a reaction that thankfully didn't come.

At least she now knew there were two exits.

That the staff know about, her inner voice reminded her. *And if this place is as old as you think it is, there are bound to be more.*

"I have to find them first," she reminded her inner voice. "There can be as many undiscovered exits as you please but if I can't find them, they won't do me an ounce of good."

Having given herself a stern warning, she began to walk on and shined the lantern down each space she came to. The farther she went, the fewer boxes and other items were on the shelves, and some of those looked like they'd been left there and forgotten.

It took her longer than she could count before she saw the stairwell partly blocked by empty shelving, and she only saw it because the darkness was in stark contrast to the gray wall behind the racking.

"Well, it's not a way out," she told herself and slunk forward.

She hesitated briefly and took the time to peer into the space and make sure it wasn't a sheer drop into nothing before she slid through. It was, indeed, another stairwell, narrower and darker than the one leading into the cellar and with a slightly different smell. She stepped down it, glad to have the lantern.

The air was cool there and a little musty, exactly the opposite to the air in the garden.

When she remembered the open sky and the smell of freshly turned earth, flowers, and vegetation, Kaylin felt a short burst of longing, which she suppressed.

"Tomorrow," she promised herself since there were no classes and the magisters would all be busy with their status reports.

The stairs led to another underground storage area but unlike that on the level above, this one hadn't been used in a long time. A thick patina of dust coated the shelves and floor and no well-tended lantern waited in the niche at the foot of the stairs.

She moved forward and held the lantern aloft in both directions in an attempt to see what the cellar contained. It was another big space so she reasoned that there had to be more exits. Also, it was fairly deep so the likelihood of there being an unblocked level was small. Still, she lived in hope.

And logic. She lived in logic, too.

With that in mind, she turned to her left and moved carefully along the shelf, keeping an eye out for another gap behind the racks. Up or down, she didn't care. She also looked for the tell-tale indentations of elven symbols carved in the wall. It wasn't a stretch to assume they'd be in the farthest reaches of the cellar if they were anywhere.

The farthest reaches could house other things, too, her inner voice reminded her. *Just because the adventurers cleared the citadel decades ago doesn't mean it's still clear. What if they missed an entrance or—*

Or what? Kaylin challenged it. *If they didn't miss any entrances, there's no way anything else can have entered here, is there?*

Not unless something dug a way in, the voice countered and Kaylin refused to listen to it.

Honestly, it was something of a downer.

She swung the lantern along one wall, hoping to find an exit. When she saw nothing, she moved to her left and followed the wall around and tried not to think of the possibility that this area might not be visited often enough for the magisters to know if something had burrowed in from outside.

The thought didn't bear contemplation. Surely there were precautions in place?

It was something she intended to check. Maybe next time Captain Delaine came to visit.

And since when does she ever do that? the voice asked.

Shut your cakehole, Kaylin told it. *Now make yourself useful and look for a way out. Preferably one not being watched by the staff.*

She wondered if it was possible.

There's only one way to find out, she thought as she continued along the line of the wall.

This portion of the cellar had walls made almost entirely of red stone with a scattering of gray blocks between. Some of the sections close to the door had the white stone common throughout the Academy's upper floors, and she guessed they'd been repaired prior to the shelves being used to block the stairs.

The shelves ran out to leave bare stone and she remembered what she'd come for.

With a step closer to the wall, she held the lantern up to scan above and below as she moved through the dark. She'd started to think she'd made one enormous mistake when her eyes caught an irregularity in the stonework.

Kaylin placed the lantern on the floor, knelt beside it, and brushed away the film of dust coating the stone. The symbol beneath made her catch her breath and she fumbled with the satchel to pull her journal clear.

This symbol was new.

With trembling fingers, she sketched it, moved to the next stone, and checked those above and below them. It didn't take her long to realize she would need more than one night—and to remember that it had already been late when she'd arrived.

She seized her curiosity with a firm grip, tucked the journal into her satchel, and raised the lantern. There had to be another door somewhere.

There was one, although it took her a little longer to find than she liked and it had rust on its hinges and would need oiling before it could be opened. She studied the rotting planks that comprised its surface. Or she could simply kick it in.

"Later," she told herself and looked around. "First, you need a way out."

The cellar ended in a blank wall and she was sure she saw the shapes of other inscriptions ridged beneath the dust. She pressed her lips together and resisted the urge to settle in front of it and spend however long it took to sketch what was there. Instead, she turned away and continued along the wall until she reached the next corner.

"If I was going to put a door anywhere..." she murmured and noticed vertical grooves running up the stone.

Kaylin stepped back and moved the lantern up until she saw what might be the lintel and the glint of metal set in a hollow at waist height. The hinges, when she dusted them, looked old but not rusty.

"Maybe it's been forgotten," she told herself, reached into the hollow, and lifted the metal ring she found there to give it a tentative twist.

It started to move, then caught, so she applied more pressure. At first, it didn't budge and she had begun to consider the possibility that she'd have to return the way she came in when it shifted under her hand.

She grunted and twisted harder and the handle shifted. With a grinding clunk, the door moved.

"Push or pull?" she wondered and did both. More dust showered around her but she ignored it.

The door opened onto a stairwell that went up instead of down.

Kaylin exhaled a soft sigh of relief and pulled the door closed behind her before she ascended the stairs. To her surprise, they reached a small, blank-walled landing and made a sharp-right-angled turn before they continued their vertical journey.

"Well..." she murmured and apprehension sent a thrill of uncertainty through her.

There was only one choice, though—go down or go up. She already knew what was down. All she could hope was that up would take her to an exit she could use. The climb felt interminable but the stone shifted from red to gray to white and she pressed on.

After two more landings and another turn, she couldn't even begin to picture where she was. She hoped she hadn't found a convenient shortcut into some magister's private rooms—or into the Chevalier barracks, although that wouldn't be anywhere near as bad as the first.

When she finally saw the door at the top of the fourth landing, she choked back a sob of relief, muffled the sound with her hand, and came to a complete halt before she hurried forward to seize the handle swiftly. Not even the thick cobwebs adorning the nearest corner deterred her.

She almost grasped the handle and turned it, but all the caution she'd learned as a thief kicked in and she made herself stop. What had she always told the others?

Listen first. You wouldn't believe how many times that's saved me.

Hopefully, she didn't need to be saved from anything now.

Kaylin drew a deep breath, released it slowly, and listened. When no sounds greeted her, she turned the handle and relaxed when it made barely any sound. No noise warned her that the next room was occupied, but she eased the door open with care and relished the rush of fresh air as she peered cautiously into the space beyond.

It was empty except for sheet-covered furniture and boxes. From the patina of dust that covered everything there, the room hadn't been used in years. An uncurtained window caught her attention and she hurried to stand against the wall and outside its frame.

She didn't need to be seen by anyone looking up.

That was also an unfounded fear as the window looked out over the valley. The only living things who would have seen her were the monsters roaming the night and they wouldn't tell anyone where she was.

Satisfied that she'd be safe, she leaned forward and looked for the mountain.

It was a little to her left but it gave her something to judge her direction from. She was at least in the same wing as her room. All she had to do was find a safe route to it and hope no one saw her. She moved quickly and quietly, returned to the door, and pulled it closed.

There was nothing she could do about the neat row of footprints she left in the dust on the floor but it hadn't been disturbed in forever, so there was a chance no one would see them until she was long gone. After a glance at the window, she hurried to the only other door and repeated her cautious exit.

The corridor beyond reminded her of the dormitory hallways below her, and she tried to picture where the stairwell was relative to the mountain she saw from her window. Using that to guide her, she turned left and felt weak with relief when she found it.

Although the floor below appeared as deserted as the one she'd just left, it was cleaner so she couldn't be certain it wasn't occupied.

Instead of stepping out into it, she followed the stairs down one more level and breathed a happy sigh when she recognized the painting opposite the landing.

This was her floor and it was completely deserted.

After one more glance to make sure it was clear, Kaylin moved swiftly to her room and let herself in. The figure slumped over her desk made her gasp but she relaxed when she realized who it was. She locked the door behind her quickly, hurried forward, and put the lamp down beside her friend.

"Mirielle!" she exclaimed in a hoarse whisper. "Why aren't you in bed?"

The girl sat bolt upright and stared wildly into her face for several heartbeats.

"Wha— Where were you?" she demanded but kept her voice to a furious hiss.

"I…uh, needed some space," she told her, then glared at her friend. "But never mind that. What are you doing in my room? I locked the door when I left."

Mirielle blushed. "I was worried."

"And?" Kaylin prodded.

Her companion sighed and pulled another key from her pocket. "I…I borrowed your spare from reception."

"What? Why?"

"I was worried, okay? I waited until she left for supper and I borrowed it." She paled. "The only problem is I don't know how I'll get it back."

She rolled her eyes. "Why don't you keep it?" she suggested. "That way, you won't have to risk getting into trouble the next time you want to check on me." The words made her pause. "Why were you checking on me anyway?"

"I heard your meeting with the magister didn't go so well. At least…at least, that's what some of the girls who saw you come out said. They said you looked upset and they…they heard shouting."

Kaylin arched her eyebrows. "And did they say what the shouting was about?" she asked.

Mirielle shook her head. "They said they wished they had because it sounded like you'd seriously upset him and he's famous for being able to say all the things we wish we were allowed to." She shrugged. "They would have only added it to everything else they're saying—or exaggerated it to make it sound worse."

She sat on the edge of her bed and pulled at her shoes. "He said I was on my own and that even if I kept my head down for the next two years, Magister Gaudin isn't likely to forgive me."

"She isn't," the girl confirmed and asked a second later, "What will you do about it?"

The question made her think about the symbols she'd seen in the basement and she decided it didn't matter if she had to keep her head down. She would be too busy deciphering the elvish writing to have time for much else anyway.

"I guess I'll keep my head down and do my best to not stand out in class. It's not like the magisters go out of their way to ask me anything anyway."

Mirielle responded with a short giggle.

"That's because they know you'll have the answer and make someone else's student look bad if they do. None of them want that to happen because they'd be in as much trouble for giving you the chance as they would be if they supported you."

Kaylin stared at her. "So you're saying I'm completely on my own —that no one will give me a chance to prove myself in class?"

"Or to make a mistake," the girl told her and pointed out the bright side. "The only way you'll get in trouble is if you mess up a practical because then they'll know you haven't been studying."

She thought that over, then crossed to the window, glanced out, and compared the position of the mountain from her window to how it had looked from the room above. Now, she was sure she knew where the room was and it gave her some comfort.

Mirielle stifled a yawn. "I'd better get to bed," she said. "I'll see you around?"

"Sure." She nodded and managed a tired smile for her friend. "But

I'll be studying very hard from now on to make sure I don't slip up in the Trials, so don't be surprised if I'm difficult to find."

The girl shrugged and yawned again. "It'll be fine," she reassured her, "and if you need a break from the dining hall for a while, let me know. I'll bring you some rolls or pastries or something."

It was her way of letting her know she'd heard about what had happened and Kaylin was grateful.

"I'll do that," she promised, "but I don't want you to get into trouble for me."

"I won't, but I don't want—" Mirielle exhaled sharply and fixed her with a firm look. "You're not alone, okay?"

Kaylin pressed her lips together and felt a familiar prickle at the back of her eyes. If the girl saw her cry, she would be even more worried than she was now and she wouldn't get a moment's peace—and she would need it.

She lowered her head, nodded, and swallowed to clear her voice before she managed a soft, "Thank you."

Her companion gave her an uncertain look before she was overcome by another cavernous yawn. With a flip of her hand, she unlocked the door and let herself out into the corridor. Kaylin was about to lock the door when she heard Mirielle's key rattle in the lock and the girl's footsteps crossing the hall.

With a smile, she flopped back on her bed and closed her eyes.

Although she had intended to turn the lantern down, she fell asleep instead and woke to the sound of students chattering and laughing as they passed her door. She lay still and listened carefully but none of them stopped, so she relaxed and tried to gather her thoughts.

In the end, her plans were simple. She'd return to the basement with her lamp, some candles, fresh charcoal, and her journal, and she'd spend the day copying the symbols.

If she took enough food to last her the day, she could return for supper before she headed to her room to study what she'd drawn. She was reasonably sure she'd be able to measure how long she spent in the basement by how long it took the candles to burn.

At least she hoped she would.

This plan went smoothly despite her misgivings. Even the dining hall was mostly deserted and she guessed Sylvester and Gaudin's other favorites all had their status meetings or had found something better to do.

Pulling the wings off butterflies, she thought uncharitably and loaded both her plate and her pockets.

On her way to the dormitories, she found a broom closet and took a cloth and a broom with her for the climb to the upper chamber and her time in the basement. It would make clearing the dust from the symbols easier and help to wipe her footprints away.

If anyone went into the deserted room, they'd only see clean floors, not a direct trail to the stairwell. The day proceeded quietly and she returned with more symbols than she could hope to translate in a night—which didn't stop her from trying, of course.

She went to the library late and skirted the book stacks so she encountered almost no one as she searched for the books she needed. Elven theory might be hard to find but some thought language texts were essentially harmless.

They were helpful and Kaylin's understanding of elven symbols grew in leaps and bounds.

When classes resumed, she changed her routine so she covered her lessons during her meal breaks before she disappeared upstairs. Some nights, she visited the basements and others, she went to the library to decipher what she'd found.

She ate quickly and slept little, but her growing pallor and the dark circles under her eyes were put down to her desperate need to pass the Trials and the stress of being an outcast. On her third week of studying in the basement, she ran out of symbols and basement.

With nothing else to fill her time, she turned to the rusted door and used lamp oil to loosen the hinges enough to force it open. After she'd worked it a few times, she got it to open and close with only a little stiffness. It was good enough.

Kaylin made sure she could open it from the inside, pulled it closed, and began her descent. The farther she went, the more it became clear that the hill had always been a place of learning. The red stone smoothed as she entered another room and she soon found more of the symbols she'd been studying.

Now, however, they were intermingled by other simpler shapes and designs. These looked more like stick drawings than elven letters and she had never seen the like.

"What language is this?" she wondered and her words echoed softly through the dark but didn't worry her. Often, she needed to hear herself to help protect her sanity.

No one answered and the silence didn't change. The lamp flickered and she drew a candle from her satchel, lit it, and dripped a pool of wax to stand it in. Once it was secure, she dusted the wall and sat before it to stare at the pictograms.

They looked familiar and she felt like they made sense from the point of view of harnessing the dimensions. She focused on the pictures but didn't try to analyze them. Instead, she simply let her mind rove over them and decipher the patterns she hadn't consciously picked up.

Something from her earlier lessons rose to mind, and she tilted her head to study the pictogram that had triggered the thought. It had been a practical lesson focused on the three basic positions for the hand before moving to each finger.

"So, there's a fourth position," she murmured and moved her hands through the patterns. "And a fifth."

She stopped and worked through the three positions she'd learned from Magister Cantrell, then added the two newer ones. As she did so, she slowed her hands and waited for the familiar buzz that came whenever she tried to learn a new spell.

For a moment, there was nothing, but it soon arrived to apply light pressure to her fingers as she moved them through the combinations she'd learned in class with the new hand positions as a basis. The candle had burned to a stump by the time she was finished and only its unsteady flickering alerted her to the need to return.

"Tomorrow," she promised herself, scrambled unsteadily to her feet, and gathered the candle stub and her lantern. She almost forgot her journal but remembered at the last moment to scoop it and the charcoal into her satchel before she returned to her room.

That night, when she slept, she dreamed of candles, flickering hand movements, and of her fingers curling and cramping through a range of new motions. Somewhere close to dawn, her dreams faded and she slept safely ensconced in the darkness.

CHAPTER FIFTEEN

It took her days to understand what one small section of the wall was trying to tell her.

This was mostly because she tried to read the other sections when she had difficulty with the one she'd started with and then had to start again. Only by going back to the beginning of the sequence was she able to determine what she'd gotten wrong.

"Oh..." she whispered and tried again.

It took her several more attempts before she thought of trying to apply what she'd discovered to the spells she already knew.

"Oh..." she said again when she attempted to use one of the new hand positions to light a candle and melted it to a stub.

"Oops." She giggled but the surge of power had made her remember how much trouble she had sustaining spells and she wanted to see if it made any difference to her ability to create a prolonged effect.

"I should have brought a pebble," she told herself when she thought of enchanting something to provide magical light.

Eventually, the other students would notice that the supply of candles in the hall closet was dwindling and they'd put a watch on it and she'd be cut off from her supply. It would be much better if she could create a light spell strong enough to study by so she didn't need a candle or a lantern.

The thought of light spells reminded her of the effect she'd tried and failed to create at her status interview. She'd made the gestures using the second hand position to incorporate the physical dimension and that had been her strongest option. When she'd practiced using either of the others, it had resulted in a brief spark. At least with the second position, she'd been able to keep the glow alive for more than a blink.

"More like two eyeblinks," she told herself and shook her head. "But if I maybe use this..."

She twisted her hand to the fourth position and felt the faint breeze alter the spacing of her fingers and the angle of the bend. This time, the light flashed brighter for a brief moment before it died.

"What was it again?" she asked. "Emotional, physical…experience."

With a frown, she lowered her hands to her lap and thought about what those three terms meant. She knew the emotions she felt when she wanted light or drew on it, and she knew the physical aspects she wanted to draw on, namely light and heat, but experience? What did that have to do with it save to feed her understanding of the other two?

Again, she let her gaze drift over the pictograms but this time, she tried to study how they related to the three aspects of magic. If these truly were elvish runes and the elves had a more efficient way of combining the dimensions, perhaps the pictograms were an elven teaching tool.

Maybe, if she tried to see what dimension they related to, she might be able to understand how to combine them.

"And if I was a teacher," she whispered as she pushed to her feet, "I'd try to ensure my students knew the gestures relating to each dimension and the effect they wanted to create before I got them to combine them, which means…"

Kaylin lifted the broom and set to work. It took her an hour or more to clear the entire wall.

"I should have done this to start with," she stated and walked the length of it. She sneezed from the dust and waved her hand in front of her face.

The vertical expanse was divided into sections, each one surrounded by a decorative border that consisted of yet more pictures, but the pictograms showing the gestures she needed drew her attention.

They were arrayed in columns and each one took up a section of wall. The basic movements for each dimension were stacked one under the other, starting at the top. Beneath them were several sequences combining each of the two different dimensions and showing the results.

The last few rows of stone portrayed the results of all three—and the different results and slightly different combinations wrought.

"This is magic," she whispered and her mind bubbled with excitement as she saw what she'd previously missed.

From the array of pictograms before her, she could see she'd started in the middle of a learning sequence and not the beginning. She chose a section of wall, worked down it, and copied each segment of pictograms one under the other into her journal.

When she reached the bottom, she realized that not only had the first three sets shown the different combinations of hand and finger positions that could be used, but each of the subsequent sets showed the possible combinations and their results.

"I've been trying to light candles using a *plant* spell?" she asked and shook her head at herself. "Well, that was bright." She thought a moment. "No pun intended."

Instead of chiding herself, she turned her attention to the first spell sequences in each wall section and took some time to work out what the results were meant to be.

"Think," she told herself. "If these are used to teach the basics..."

She ran her gaze down the wall, then along it, and compared each set as she went. What she found confirmed her suspicion and she nodded.

"Then these will all be similar to the basic spells we're using now, so one of these might light a candle, and another might heal a cut finger, and another might..." She rested the tip of her finger against the leafy stem shooting from the ground. "Be for growing plants."

Kaylin moved to the last section of pictograms and studied them carefully.

"So, if I was an elf and I wanted my students to create light without burning the forest down, what would that look like?"

She cleared another section of wall, then a third lower down before she found it.

"Of course it looks like rock." She tapped one pictogram. "Or a circlet...or a necklace...or a ring... What's wrong with simply making a ball of light and floating it along behind yo—oh."

At the base of the wall was a stick finger with a hand held before its face and a glowing dot floating before it.

"So, that's an advanced spell, huh?"

Kaylin looked up the line of enchantments and gestures leading to the floating glow. While it was tempting to skip all the others and try starting with the last spell, she'd been at the Academy long enough to not only know that was a bad idea but to be wise enough to not try it and have the self-control to not jump ahead.

They might have well put a sign up that read, "Here be a way to kill yourself if you are either ignorant or impatient."

With a soft sigh, she focused on the beginning and worked on perfecting each and every gesture shown in the pictographs. She was so focused that she forgot to keep track of the time and emerged from the stairwell as the rest of the students began to stir.

Her heart sank when she realized she'd gone through the night and had a full day of classes ahead of her. She moved into the corridor and kept her head down to avoid drawing any attention. When she decided she'd best change her robes before breakfast, she turned toward her door.

The other students flowed around her, all too interested in what they needed to do before the day began to pay her any attention. Kaylin breathed a tiny sigh of relief, pulled her key from around her neck, and glanced up as she neared her door.

A blue-robed chest blocked her view and a hand settled on her shoulder to grasp it painfully as she was turned and pushed into a wall.

"Early breakfast, was it?" a voice asked and she froze. "We've been waiting for hours to speak to you."

Kaylin recognized Sylvester's voice and scowled.

"Hours," Tessa agreed.

She honestly doubted it. Hours meant they would have been up before the breakfast rush and somehow, she didn't think they had it in them.

Sylvester's hand tightened on her shoulder and he shook her.

"What do you have to say for yourself?" he demanded. She merely looked at him. "Well?" he roared, irritated by her silence.

His frustration made her smile and he pushed her again.

"Don't you smirk at me, you little bitch."

Her cheeks heated and she pressed her lips together, which did nothing to stop the smile showing through. He saw it and shook her again.

Kaylin thought about punching him but remembered what had happened the last time she'd touched him. It crossed her mind that he was looking for an excuse to report her again. Then it occurred to her that he could report her anytime he pleased because no one would believe her, no matter what the truth was.

That fact stood out above all else. She kept her hands firmly on her satchel and knowing the other students wouldn't see what she did, she stamped hard on the boy's instep. The movement drove the heel of her boot into the arch of his foot and he yelped in pain.

As his hands loosened with surprise, Kaylin twisted out of his hold and turned to the stairs. She wove rapidly between the other students and darted up the stairs, relying on the fact that everyone was heading down them to get to the dining hall or class. She didn't bother to look back but bolted to the corridor above.

Running lightly on the balls of her feet, she grasped the first door handle she came to and slipped inside. A glance showed her a neat sitting room with doors opening from either side. Not sure if she was being pursued, she took the closest one and found herself in a small study—a small currently unoccupied study.

How long it would stay unoccupied was another matter and one she didn't have time to consider.

"That could have been worse," she told herself as she clawed under the desk and scrambled as far back as she could.

Breathing hard, she fought to silence the sound and calm herself. As far as she knew, she wasn't out of the woods. If Sylvester and his cronies worked out she'd gone up instead of down, they'd soon discover the door was unlocked. Her best hope was to be quiet enough that they decided to not search the room. She wondered what she'd done to draw their ire this time and couldn't think of a single thing.

She'd done her lessons competently but not spectacularly and didn't think she'd shown any of them up. Certainly not Sylvester because he wasn't in any of her classes, but the others… She frowned and shook her head.

No, she was very sure she hadn't done anything more than answer the questions the magisters had been forced to ask her in order to argue that they'd attended to her education. None of them had given her an opportunity to prove herself better than either of the girls currently in pursuit.

So why?

Footsteps thundered up the stairs on the other side of the wall and Kaylin tensed and listened to see if she could tell which way they were going. She lost track of them when they slowed. She drew a deep breath, held it, and exhaled slowly.

At least she was no longer breathing like a horse at full gallop.

I shoulda known better than to put myself in here, she thought and tried desperately to recall the room's layout. Was there somewhere better she could have hidden?

She couldn't recall any but her gaze caught on the legs of the office chair and she looked cautiously out to see if the room was still clear. She hadn't heard the door open but that didn't mean she hadn't missed it.

When she saw no one, she pulled the chair closer so it looked like it had been pushed in. It wouldn't save her but it might mean Sylvester and his friends didn't bother to check under the desk. When she had it drawn in as close as she could, Kaylin withdrew to the deepest reaches of the hollow and settled in to wait.

Her answer came soon after with an altercation at the door.

"Apprentice Ozanne! What do you think you are doing?" The outraged tones were matched by swift footsteps and the rattle of crockery on a tray.

"Magister," Sylvester replied in oily tones. "I did not think this room was occupied."

"Which still begs the question as to why you are on this floor, Apprentice. I'm sure Conseiller Gaudin would disapprove."

Kaylin held her breath and her ears ached with the effort to hear what came next. The mention of Magister Gaudin was a warning and could mean whoever was speaking had enough power in the Academy to warn one of her students away.

Sylvester evidently thought so because he gave ground.

"I'm sorry to have intruded, Magister Lorama."

"And you will be late for class," the woman pointed out. "These are my rooms and this floor is reserved for teaching and research staff only. If you don't waste more of my time, I might even forget I saw you—or you might owe me a favor. It depends."

A hasty shuffle of feet was followed by the sound of footsteps beating a hasty retreat down the stairs. Kaylin slumped against the back wall and closed her eyes momentarily. She opened them in a flash when she heard the handle turn and the rattle of tray and cups as the magister entered.

It was only a matter of time before the woman decided to sit at her desk and she gnawed her bottom lip as she curled into a crouch. She held her breath and listened as the magister moved into the sitting room.

The tray rattled as it was set down and the woman's steps retreated. Kaylin moved cautiously to the front of the desk. A door thumped in the apartment and she prepared to move.

If the door stayed closed past the count of three, she would take her chance.

It did and she pushed the chair back and scampered to the door. There, she hesitated out of sight of the sitting room and waited for any sign that her presence had been noticed. When the opposite door remained closed, she raced to the apartment door, opened it with silent speed, and slipped through.

It was harder to shut it quietly but she managed, her hands shaking and slick with sweat as she raced to the stairwell and hurried up quietly. If Sylvester and the others would be late for class, she might have a chance—a very small one, granted, but it was worth a try.

She raced along the corridor but instead of taking her secret path to the cellar, she used her knowledge of the floors below to navigate the deserted upper floor and find a second stairwell. With no one to hinder her progress, she descended at speed and raced past the staff level and down to where classes were held.

Magister Cantrell had her hand on the door and was about to close it when she slipped beneath her arm and into the nearest vacant seat. She sat and fought to bring her breathing under control as she pulled her journal out with shaking hands. If her luck held, the woman would disregard her precipitous entrance.

Thankfully, the teacher closed the door and proceeded to the front of the classroom as though the Academy's least favorite student's entrance was of no consequence. When the girl glanced at her, she surveyed the class as if she didn't exist, and that was all Kaylin wanted.

She was a ghost, invisible to the magisters and ignored by the students, and she was bone tired. That was not tired enough, however, for her to miss the look Celia darted at her from the other side of the room. It promised trouble and maybe violence, so she made sure she was the first out of the door and halfway to her next class before the other girl emerged.

By the end of the day, she could barely stay awake. Not only had she spent a night learning new gestures and motions, which was exhausting enough, but she'd spent the day on the run.

Everywhere she turned, someone was watching her.

Kaylin reached the dining hall but not the table before her tray was whisked out of her hand and flung against the wall. She escaped the attack that followed when she scrambled under a table and scooted out the door and into the kitchens, where she put her thieving skills to good use to pilfer another meal and find a quiet corner to eat it in.

As much as she wanted to, she didn't try to visit the cellar that night but studied for the next day's lessons and let herself sleep. The next day, she resumed her routine of classes, meals, cellar, and study and hoped an early return had beat Sylvester to her door.

She'd barely closed her eyes when her doorknob rattled. When she heard the sound of a key sliding into the lock, she knew she'd been betrayed. The door was flung open and the boy strode into the room.

Kaylin made it out of bed and onto her feet before she was grabbed and shoved against the window. Sylvester thrust his face against hers.

"You need to leave," he snarled, "while you can still walk."

She grasped his wrists.

"Why?" She gasped when he shook her.

"Because…you…don't belong here," he stated and shook her again.

"I belong here as much as—" she began and he released her collar and backhanded her across the face.

The blow landed with enough force that she fell sideways, her head ringing, but she forced herself to keep moving. She slammed one hand on the top of her bed, continued to turn, and folded under his next attempt to catch hold of her. Without a pause, she twisted along the edge of the bed to reach the door.

Unfortunately, Sylvester hadn't come alone. As she straightened and darted toward the corridor, Tessa stepped into her path and Celia moved up beside her.

"And where do you think you're going?" the girl demanded and pushed her back into the room.

Kaylin caught sight of a face that peered cautiously around Mirielle's door on the opposite side of the corridor. She thought the girl might come and help her but her face disappeared and the door closed.

The action caught her unawares and she stumbled, and

Sylvester's foot swept across her ankles and knocked her to the floor. He set his boot squarely in the center of her chest and pushed her down.

He leaned forward and put his weight on the foot that trapped her.

"You shouldn't be here," he told her, "and the sooner you realize you don't belong and leave, the easier it'll be for everyone."

She wanted to protest that the only person it would be easier for would be him, and that was because he wasn't smart enough to do any better on his own. He bounced his foot against her chest, which made it hard to breathe never mind deliver a smart retort before he stepped over her and left.

The boy paused at the door and held a familiar brass key up.

"Next time you're asked to demonstrate something in class," he told her and waved it menacingly, "make sure you get it wrong. If you don't, I'll be back to show you why."

Kaylin pushed onto her elbows and watched him leave and her chest heaved as she caught her breath. Her head still rang and the side of her face ached. When Sylvester kept walking and Celia and Tessa fell in behind him, she let herself sag onto the floor.

She spent the next few minutes staring at the ceiling before she turned her head to see if Mirielle would emerge now the others had gone. When she didn't, she looked at the ceiling again, then stood slowly.

Now, it looked like she truly was on her own.

It took her a long time to work out what to do and in the end, she decided the simple methods were the best. After a brief search, she found three door wedges and used them to jamb the door closed when she was inside.

She also made sure her trunk was locked at all times and that anything of value was left inside it, whether she was in the room or not. That only left the classroom situation.

The magisters were sure to ask her questions, even though they didn't want to, and she didn't want to be paid another visit. She also didn't want to deliberately fail—or to succeed.

After Sylvester's visit, she didn't bother to go to the dining hall for breakfast. Something told her he'd only be waiting and she'd lose another tray of food to a wall. Instead, she wandered into the gardens and followed the wall until she found the back of the kitchens and the delivery entrance.

Given that she was an apprentice, she decided she would no longer bother to sneak in. She simply walked up the stairs to the loading dock and let herself into the kitchen. Unruffled, she fixed the first servant with a look that dared them to speak and stalked to where the breakfast pastries were cooling.

She leaned on the wall beside them, took one, and ate it.

A cook glanced at her and she stared back in her best imitation of the way Magister Roche had looked at her when she'd raised her voice to ask if he was her magister or not. The man looked away and Kaylin took another pastry and ate it.

When the warning bell rang for class, she took three more and sauntered back the way she'd come. Not a single voice was raised against her and she reached her classroom with a full stomach and in good time.

Her mind whirled as she put the pieces together. The students were mostly from powerful families. No one wanted to be noticed by the powerful and no one wanted to stand out and be noticed. The magisters were afraid of Magister Gaudin, but they were also afraid of Magister Roche and, to a lesser extent, the Chevaliers.

No one wanted to draw attention from any of those parties—not the students, not the servants, and not the magisters. Kaylin thought about that and wondered how far any of the magisters would push it if she didn't cause any trouble but simply didn't cooperate.

Was she so undesirable that no one wanted to touch her? While she was used to being in the shadows and hiding as a thief, was that the best solution for this situation?

Magister Cantrell seemed like a good place to start, both because she wasn't aligned with either Gaudin or Roche and because she was the first teacher of the day. And who else was better to help her in her rebellion than Magister Gaudin? If only by reputation.

She waited for the magister to start her morning's experiment. When the woman began her morning's round of questions, Kaylin tensed and darted Celia a nervous look, which the magister couldn't help but notice.

"We'll begin by revising yesterday's gesture," Cantrell stated and worked her way around the class. Kaylin waited for her name to be called and didn't answer.

"Apprentice Knight?" The teacher's voice sharpened with annoyance and Kaylin raised her head and gave Celia a cool stare.

The magister followed the direction of her eyes, then looked back at her.

"The gesture?" Magister Cantrell repeated but the girl pasted a look of complete serenity on her face and fixed her gaze on the far wall.

With pursed lips, the woman stalked closer to stand directly in front of her. "Apprentice Knight," she began, "I demand to know what is—"

She shifted her gaze to look directly at Tessa, gave the magister another pointed look, stared at Tessa for another three heartbeats, and returned her gaze to the wall.

The teacher studied her face for a moment longer, then decided that maybe she didn't need an explanation—especially not one that could involve one of Magister Gaudin's favorites needing disciplinary action. She moved to the next student.

It was all Kaylin could do to not laugh out loud.

She waited until Magister Cantrell was focused on the next pupil and watched her interactions as she moved around the room. She couldn't quite suppress the movement of her hands as she observed the gestures the other students made and noted the corrections. At the same time, she also suppressed the desire to demonstrate the variation she'd learned from the cellar wall.

Now is not the time.

Not with Tessa watching her like a hawk.

The girl caught the twitch of her hands and a satisfied smirk curved her lips. Kaylin fought to keep her gaze on the magister and pretend she hadn't noticed. It was harder to not ball her hands into fists and take the three steps she needed to be close enough to punch the smirk off her face.

Instead, she maintained a bland expression and endured the rest of the lesson.

Shadows. No one looks in the shadows.

The tactic worked for the other magisters, and she wasn't sure whether she should feel pity or scorn.

The first duty of a teacher is to the welfare of her students, she thought fiercely. *Not to a political agenda.*

Irritation and anger made her moody and she was glad to escape to the kitchens. This time, she positioned herself beside the bread racks and was surprised when one of the kitchen hands set a plate of sliced meat and cheese beside her. The look he cast in her direction was almost her undoing.

The second he saw he'd caught her attention, he flicked a hand at the plate to indicate that it was hers and walked away. The only time he returned to her corner was when he came to fill the racks with bread.

That simple kindness was enough to make her throat thicken and swallowing difficult, as was the mug of water that appeared beside the plate when she almost choked on her bread.

It wasn't only the unexpected care that caused it, but the idea that they should care at all. Didn't they know who she was? That she was a pariah?

That helping her was a bad idea?

It was as if none of that mattered in the kitchens and while no one spoke to her, she didn't feel rejected. The feeling was difficult to handle and she longed for the sometimes salty camaraderie she'd shared with Melis and Isabette and the boys. At least they'd wanted her around.

Kaylin left as soon as she'd eaten her fill, dropped the plate into the sink on the way out, and arrived early at her next class. With a simple sweep of her hand, the door unlocked. Kaylin entered, locked it behind her, and pretended not to notice when the teacher arrived and found her waiting inside.

"Apprentice Knight!" Magister Theobold began but the other students had started to arrive and he didn't ask her to explain.

Her trick of glancing at one of Magister Gaudin's students and remaining silent worked with him as well, and she didn't know whether to feel relieved or sickened that one person or one small enclave of people held such power over so many others.

Still, it wasn't something she could fight alone and until she solved that problem, it would be better to devote her energy to increasing her abilities and working out how to win people to her side. Once there were more of them, they could work out how to fight back.

Maybe. But fight she would. For now?

Shadows.

She focused on her lessons and on staying ahead of Magister Gaudin's chosen students. The first part was easy, the second less so. As the weeks progressed, she kept up her routine of class and study and spent her time in the cellar, her room, or sneaking into the farthest reaches of the library.

It became a little easier once the magisters had accepted she wouldn't answer any of their questions. While the latter brought some relief, she didn't want to think of what it meant for her status report. Nor did it keep Sylvester away from her door, although he wasn't able to force his way in.

Kaylin became used to being alone but it was hard for her to not feel lonely, and she couldn't wait for the time she graduated and could see her friends again. These thoughts were always at their worst when she was at her desk, trying to study despite the sound of companionable laughter passing in the corridor outside.

To stave them off, she opened the curtains and used the sight of the Twin Spears rising against the night sky as a reminder of why she was there. She felt a faint sense of displacement when she caught sight of the trees closest to the Academy.

"Since when was it this close to autumn?" she murmured when she noticed the faint dusting of yellow that said the seasons were changing. She didn't think she'd been at the Academy that long. It seemed… She sighed, stared into the night, and reminded herself of her main purpose.

"You're here to learn," she said aloud. "To find a future better than any you had a chance at before. You're here for a reason. You were given this chance for a reason."

Her sanity appreciated the communication.

That was the truth of it and she had no doubt that the Chevaliers had a very good reason for wanting her in their ranks. She didn't want to disappoint, even if she still wasn't sure she wanted to join them. Maybe she would be better off at court. At least there she'd have a chance to help control the influence of people like the Ozannes.

With a heavy sigh, she stared out the window at the ruddy glare lighting the city at its feet. The Doom or Tulon's City—whatever folk wanted to call it—had been a major center for civilization hundreds of years before, one that might be even older than the Academy's cellar.

What secrets might she find there?

Kaylin stared at the barely visible outlines of walls fringing the base and wondered what it would be like to go and see. Surely it wouldn't be that much different to exploring the deserted buildings or the Blackbirds' graveyard?

And she was more capable now, able to cast sustained effects and more complex spells. With the right team, anything was possible.

For a moment, her head danced with images of her and a team of warriors and knights walking through the ruined city. She led them, saw the threats that lay around them before the monsters could strike, and hurled spells with startling accuracy to end the attacks before they could begin.

Ancient buildings opened before them, old libraries, a museum of artifacts that had survived the pillaging of countless others, and the imposing doorway said to lead beneath the Spears themselves. Kaylin sighed. If there were still treasures in the Doom, what greater rewards might lie in the mountain deeps?

She had started to imagine leading her new crew through those doors when a timid knock almost startled her out of her chair. With a quick breath, she steadied herself and waited. If it was Sylvester, she didn't want to confirm she was there—assuming he hadn't heard the rattle of her chair at his knock.

After a few heartbeats of silence, the knock came again. This time, it was accompanied by a thready, breathless voice.

"Kaylin?"

She stilled and the voice spoke again.

"I'm alone. Please talk to me."

It was the "please" more than the assurance that Mirielle was alone that brought her out of her chair to answer the door. The claim could have been a lie but it didn't matter. There was something in the way the girl had asked—a sadness and a need.

Quickly, she pulled the wedges from beneath the door and eased it open a little.

"Kaylin!" The exclamation held the hint of a sob and a world of relief. The girl pushed forward and she didn't have the heart to hold the door against her.

At the same time, she couldn't help remembering seeing her retreat and close the door across the hall as Tessa pushed her into Sylvester's reach. And the key—the horribly familiar key Sylvester had waved in her face to show her how he'd gained entry. Anger flared in her chest.

"What do you want?" she demanded and peered past the girl into the corridor.

Exactly as Mirielle had promised, it was empty.

The girl didn't answer. She rushed past, perched herself on the farthest edge of the bed closest to the wall, and clasped her hands in her lap as she raised a tear-stained face to watch her. Kaylin didn't press but closed the door, secured it, and shoved the wedges in place with more force than she needed to.

"Like I said," she repeated as she straightened. "What do you want?"

"I..." Mirielle began and it was obvious that she had been crying as her eyes were swollen and red-rimmed and her face was splotchy.

Her anger faded. "What's gone wrong?" she asked, and Mirielle burst into tears.

"I'm sorry!" she wailed, "so, so, so...sorry. I didn't... I couldn't... He came and he... He—" She burst into a fresh round of tears and stretched her fingers out as she wept. "I didn't want to stay away."

Kaylin bit back the angry retort that whether she wanted to or not, that was exactly what she had done. Instead, she sat beside the girl and let Mirielle take her hands.

"I didn't know what to do," she whispered, sniffed, and released her hands to dash tears from her eyes.

"What's going on, Mirielle?" she asked in an attempt to get her to talk about why she'd come.

The girl cast a nervous glance at the door.

"I... That is, a few of us have noticed how much you've learned..." She sniffed, gulped, and continued "Without te...teachers or any help at all."

She wanted to ask her whose fault that was but looked at her lap instead. It was the only way she could hide her expression as she fought to get her anger under control. When she didn't say anything, Mirielle went on.

"You...you've been at the Academy for less than six months and you're already performing like a second-year student."

Kaylin looked at her with a puzzled frown on her face, and the girl responded with a short laugh that bubbled with misery.

"Don't look at me like that. You are, even if no one's had the courage to tell you so. You're doing very well. Much better than I am." That last part was added in a voice so soft that she had to strain to catch the words.

"What's wrong?" she asked when the girl fell silent.

"I can't do it," Mirielle told her. "I'm afraid I'm going to fail."

"Fail what?" Kaylin asked. Being shut out of everything left her lost at times.

"Pyromancy," her companion whispered. "It's supposed to be my specialty. That's what they told me, but I...I can't. I've tried and I've tried but the spell simply won't work."

The last word spiraled into a wail, which Mirielle cut short with a sudden embarrassed snap. "I'm sorry," she said. "I should never have left you to face them on your own."

Part of Kaylin wanted to agree but the sensible side of her said, "Honestly, what could you have done?"

She wanted to acknowledge that the girl had more to lose than she did but that wasn't necessarily true. Captain Delaine hadn't said what would happen if she failed through no fault of her own.

"That doesn't mean it was right."

"No," she couldn't help saying, but Mirielle seemed so miserable that she decided not to make things harder for her and changed the subject. "What spell?"

"What?" The girl looked confused.

"What spell?" she repeated. "Which one can't you get to work?"

"Oh..." Mirielle frowned. "I'm...we're supposed to be able to produce a floating ball of flame and hold it long enough to boil a small pot of water."

"You what?" she asked and her companion hurried to explain.

"They...they hang these small cauldrons from a wooden pole set too high above the ground for you to rest the fire under them, so you...you have to make the fire off the ground—which is harder than it sounds. Then, you have to hold it under the pot and keep it going long enough for the water in the cauldrons to boil."

"You do?"

"And...and if you can do that, they make you conjure the fire at the edge of the room and move it to the pot and hold it there until the water boils."

Kaylin pressed her lips together to hide her smile, but Mirielle saw it anyway.

"Oh, you can laugh—" she began but her friend raised a hand for silence.

"I'm not laughing at the test," she reassured the girl. "I'm smiling because I've worked through that spell."

"You have?" Mirielle asked. "When? I haven't worked through it yet and I'm a year ahead of you."

She thought about telling the girl where she'd gained her knowledge but decided against it and put a hand on one hip. Her raised brow prevented any more questions. "Do you want to know how to do this or not?"

The girl gave her a look that said she wanted to push the point but she decided she wanted help with the spell more. Mirielle sighed.

"Okay, how do you do it?"

Kaylin looked around her room at the piles of paper on her desk, the books stacked in the wooden bookcase, and the blankets and sheets on the bed.

"How about we go somewhere less flammable?" she suggested and her companion smiled.

"That would probably be a good idea." She giggled and it was good to see her looking happier. The happiness soon faded, however, and she asked, "But where can we go?"

That made her pause. As much as she wasn't ready to tell the girl where she was getting her lessons from, she also wasn't ready to reveal her secret path to the cellars.

"How about the grotto?" she asked.

Mirielle thought about it. "I guess we can make it," she agreed and slid off the edge of the bed.

Kaylin led the way to the door and peered into the corridor to make sure it was clear.

"Come on," she whispered and led her through the students' common room and along the corridor to a set of stairs that would bring them out closer to the ballroom entrance.

"How do you know this?" the girl asked and she gave her a sheepish look.

"Weeks of trying to get to class without running into any of Magister Gaudin's students. I've been told to keep my head down, remember?"

Mirielle blushed and her eyes sparkled with sudden tears. "Kay—"

"Come on," she said and cut her off. "We're almost there."

It took them several minutes to slip through the gardens and down to the grotto with its stone walls and glistening pool.

"It's so pretty here at night," Mirielle whispered, and Kaylin nodded.

"It's prettiest when there's no one around," she told the girl. She gestured at the pool and added, "This should stop us from setting anything alight."

Her companion giggled. "Including the garden. Can you imagine what Magister Lorama would say?"

"Lorama?" she asked and Mirielle blushed.

"You won't have met her yet. Once you get to the next level in potions, you'll have the option of taking herb lore and she's the magister for that."

"And what do the other magisters think of her?" she asked and recalled the way Lorama had spoken to Sylvester.

"I don't know. She doesn't seem to have any special students."

"But why not?" Kaylin was intrigued. "Doesn't she have projects she needs to advance like the rest of them?"

"I...I don't think so," Mirielle answered. "I think she likes to be left alone...to look after her plants." She glanced around nervously. "Is it hard?"

"Is what hard?" Kaylin asked.

"This spell?"

She almost pointed out that Mirielle hadn't been able to master it but decided that would be mean. The girl had found it difficult enough to approach her in the first place.

"Some of the gestures can be a little tricky," she said, "but I find if you move your hands like this for the physical dimension..."

It didn't take the girl as long as they'd feared for her to learn the hand gestures, even if she'd been puzzled by the way Kaylin broke it down as her ball of fire lit and danced.

"But why do it this way?" she asked.

"Because they're part of a whole," she explained. "If you get one part wrong, even a little, you'll affect the rest. By practicing each part separately, you can work to combine them more smoothly."

Mirielle's gaze sharpened. "Like that elven text?"

She struggled to keep her face blank. "How would I know? I never got to read it. Magister Roche wouldn't sign the note for me and you already know Sylvester wouldn't share."

Her companion lowered her head. "Kaylin, I—"

"So show me that sequence again," she ordered to avoid another apology. "I think your emotional was a little off."

Mirielle closed her mouth with a snap and her face flushed as she did as instructed.

"Good. You're almost there," she encouraged. "Maybe make it so your hand travels almost flat when you push away from yourself and try to keep the movement smooth. I've noticed if you jerk or hesitate, the fire flares."

The girl repeated the gesture and floated her ball of fire around the grotto cavern until Kaylin told her to stop it over the pool.

"I think you've got it now," she said.

"Yes," Mirielle agreed. "It's so amazing that you can do this—make those connections. I mean, it's so simple once you know it but it takes someone to *show* you, sometimes."

Kaylin blushed. "I'm glad I could help. Now, do you remember how to cancel it so it doesn't explode?"

"It can explode?" Her companion's face paled.

"You didn't know?"

The pictograms had been quite explicit. Canceling any form of energy spell had to be done in such a way that the energy flowed smoothly into the environment. If canceled too early or too abruptly, it tended to end more dramatically.

"Maybe they rely on you starting the spell and letting it burn itself out," she commented.

"At least for the early stages," Mirielle said. "I've heard they do more next year."

Kaylin flashed her a happy grin. "Well, now you'll be ahead."

The girl looked worried. "I'm not sure that's a good thing."

"If enough of us do well in class and we aren't someone's favorites, maybe things will get better."

"Or we'll be chosen to be some magister's pet," Mirielle muttered bitterly.

"Pfft. Without the kind of money or influence people like the Ozannes have?" she asked. "I think you're fairly safe from that ever happening."

Mirielle's mouth dropped open and a look of hurt flashed across her face. Kaylin cocked her head. "Well, it's true, isn't it?" she challenged. "You've gotta laugh at it or you'll simply break."

Now where have I heard that before? she wondered and remembered Melis saying it, usually after she'd pointed out some painful truth to one of the others. It wasn't that the girl didn't care, merely that she didn't care to waste time easing someone through it when there were things that needed to get done.

"I'm sorry," she said. "I didn't mean to be so harsh."

Mirielle closed her mouth. "Well, it's true, isn't it? And maybe you're right. Maybe if enough of us excel without patrons, we can change the way things are."

She didn't sound convinced, however.

"About this fireball," Kaylin said, "you need to release the heat gently. Think cooling thoughts if you wish. Like this…"

She conjured a floating orb of fire and took her companion through the process of cooling and releasing it.

"Oh… It's the opposite," the girl whispered and made the gestures with a slow precision that banished the fire with a hiss of steam.

"I like that," Kaylin told her. "Most dramatic."

Her companion smiled. "Thank you."

They walked to the dormitory in companionable silence and Mirielle's hands moved as though she was going through the fireball spell in her mind. Kaylin caught the twitches and the distant look on the girl's face and took care to steer her up the stairs and into the ballroom.

As they walked, she thought about the idea of more students excelling without patrons. There must be other students who were struggling, others who didn't have the courage or who didn't know how to approach her.

Or who are too afraid. I wonder how many of them only need a little help like Mirielle and won't get it because they don't have the connections.

By the time they'd reached their doors, Mirielle looked much happier.

"I think I've got it now," she said and flung her arms around Kaylin in a brief hug. "I'll see you at breakfast."

She put a hand on her arm. "Can I ask you something?"

The girl paused. "Sure..." she said, unlocked her door, and pulled her inside, "but not out here."

She closed the door behind them and crossed to her desk, took her journal out, and jotted some notes. "What did you want to know?"

"Do you think..." Kaylin began, then paused. Now that she was about to put her idea into words, it seemed both silly and a little arrogant. Who did she think she was, offering help to the others like she knew it all?

I don't know it all, she told herself fiercely, *but maybe I know enough to help.*

"Think what?" Mirielle asked.

"That anyone else might be interested in that kind of help?"

"Being shown, you mean?"

"Yes. I...well, maybe?" She nodded.

The girl put her charcoal pencil down. "Are you crazy?" she asked and Kaylin's heart sank. "Of course there are others. I can think of at least a dozen who could do with the help—if you were interested in showing them, that is. I mean, we haven't exactly been—"

"It's fine." She waved yet another would-be apology away.

After all, apologies wouldn't help to fix things. They could only do that by moving forward.

"You could start a study group," Mirielle suggested after a moment's pause. "You know, something to help the mal-educated in this school."

"Mal-educated?"

"Yeah—like maltreated but to do with how they're treated badly in a learning sense. Kind of a combination of the two."

"But...how would I even begin?" Kaylin asked her. "It's not like anyone will talk to me."

"That part I can handle," her companion told her. "You'd have to try to think of a safe space for us to use."

They met in the gardens as the leaves turned gold, red, and yellow. At first, it was only one student, a boy who looked skeptical and wary and still rubbed his eyes as he slunk through the grotto entry. Kaylin heard him arrive but continued to look at the wall.

More carvings were hidden behind the ferns at the back of the pool and she wanted to take a closer look at them but now wasn't the time, not with Mirielle standing at the edge of the pool. Sure, the girl was watching the fish in the dimly lit depths but she knew she was watching her too.

When Nex arrived, Kaylin pretended interest in the water flowing out of the wall. She listened as Mirielle greeted him.

"Hi, Nex. She's over there."

She was sure she was being stared at and her face reddened. For the life of her, she couldn't make herself turn.

"I can see that, but..." His voice dropped from a whisper to a hiss. "What's she doing?"

Mirielle chuckled. "She's being shy. Why don't you come over and say hello?"

Kaylin assumed that was a suggestion to her and turned to face them. It took her seconds to realize the other girl had been speaking to Nex.

"Hi," she said gruffly, then remembered why she was there. "What can I help you with?"

The boy froze. His face turned crimson, then pale. "Uh..." he began and flashed Mirielle an uncertain look. "I—"

He glanced at the girl again.

"Ugh..." Mirielle rolled her eyes. "What Nex wants to ask you," she said, "is how to make a pebble hold a light."

"Like a candle?" Kaylin asked and the boy took a step closer.

"But without the flame," he told her. "And we're not supposed to make it heat up either."

"His keep exploding." The other girl giggled.

Nex gave her a dirty look but he shrugged as he turned to Kaylin.

"Like she said, mine keep exploding. They glow and they get hot and then they either explode or melt. It depends on the type of stone."

"Magister Abravi has given him the kind that melt," Mirielle informed her. "She says it's better than someone getting a shard of rock in their eyes."

"And I broke Ylaine's glasses," Nex admitted his face flushed. "Magister Cantrell—"

The girl laid a sympathetic hand on his shoulder and gave Kaylin a pleading look.

"I don't suppose your studies have taken you to something that might help?" she asked.

She smiled, relieved that the boy's question brought her to one of the first sections of wall she'd covered.

"What's the dimension you're using for the light?" she asked and looked around for a stone.

Nex proved as fast a learner as Mirielle had been and equally as puzzled as to why Kaylin broke the spell down into dimensions before she combined the gestures.

"That...that was seriously helpful. Thanks," he said finally when he held a small glowing pebble in his hand. "It's not even hot. Feel!"

Mirielle had taken a step back, which left Kaylin to pluck the stone from his hand.

"Chicken," she quipped.

"And not ashamed to own it," the other girl admitted, tucked her hands under her armpits, and made flapping motions.

Nex snickered but his smile faded when Kaylin handed him the stone.

"Nice job," she told him and swept the fragments from some of his earlier attempts into the pool.

He blushed, then looked into her face.

"Thanks," he said.

When he opened his mouth to say more, she held her hand up to stop him.

"You're welcome," she said. "But…don't tell the magisters where you learned it from, okay? Tell them you did some extra study in the library and things clicked for you."

"Yeah," he told her with a touch of sarcasm. "That's exactly what happened."

She handed him another stone. "Now, do it again."

When Nex returned the following night, he brought two friends. Mirielle brought another one and they gathered around Kaylin like she held the secrets of the gods. More glow-stones were needed, another ball of fire, and someone had to be able to turn water to ice without shattering the mug around it.

She divided them into groups. She set Mirielle to showing the student who needed to create a ball of fire and worked with Nex to make sure he had a solid grasp of how to light a stone. The other students watched with awe on their faces.

"So fast," one murmured.

"She makes it look so easy," another replied.

"I…think I can see what she did," the third one stated without any confidence at all.

"Nex," Kaylin called and caught the boy's attention. "You take Kamil and Leona. Make sure you show them the basic moves for each of the dimensions first, okay?"

"I remember," he told her and led his two students to one side of the pool.

"Mirielle…" Kaylin began, but the girl had already drawn her own conclusions.

"I'll take Kendall," she responded with a sigh.

"Well, don't if it's too much bother," the other girl snarked. "I can always fail the Trials on my own."

Mirielle caught her by the arm and dragged her to the water's edge. "There you go, thinking the worst of someone without giving them a chance to help you."

"But you—"

"I'm nervous," she snapped. "Okay?"

"Fine," Kendall grumped. "But don't let me set myself on fire."

"Why do you think we're this close to the pool?"

"Oh…very funny. I am *so* amused."

"Don't mind her," the last student said and caught the look on Kaylin's face. "She's always like that when she's scared."

"I'm not afraid," Kendall sang in protest but the student rolled her eyes.

"I'm Sula," she said and held her hand out. "It's nice to meet you."

Kaylin accepted the gesture and clasped hands briefly. The girl looked at her and worry pinched her heart-shaped face.

"Can you help me to not shatter the glass?" she asked. "I…I can make the ice fine, but every time I do, it shatters the cup."

"You have to get the magic to recognize the cup's boundaries," she explained and recalled how much difficulty she'd had when she'd first encountered the spell. "Once you do that, the water will freeze and the cup will be fine."

"But…how?" Sula asked, her soft query barely short of a wail.

"So, you remember the physical dimension…" Kaylin began and took her through the first of the gestures.

Word spread quickly and more students came. Some shivered as the wind took the leaves from the trees. It was getting colder and everyone began to worry about the end-of-year exams.

One or two of them were in their third year at the Academy, older siblings of those in Mirielle's level, but most were from the same level as Kaylin's friend. The first student from her level arrived in the third week.

She was leaving Magister Cantrell's class on magical theory when someone tugged at her sleeve. When she turned, she saw the earnest face of one of her peers.

"Can I have a word?" the boy asked and she nodded and glanced past him to where Celia moved purposefully toward them.

"Follow me," she ordered, "unless you want to discuss it with Celia listening."

The boy paled and his freckles stood out on his face. "No," he answered hastily. "Lead the way."

Kaylin took a left turn and then another, darted into a stairwell, and ascended quickly.

He followed. "That's the staff level," he whispered as they reached the landing on the next floor.

"We aren't stopping here," she told him shortly and guided him up another floor, along several corridors, and down again.

No tell-tale echo of footsteps followed them, and she descended to the gardens.

"How can I help you?" she asked when she'd brought him to one of the secluded study spots near the grotto.

"I'm Luka, by the way," he told her and flushed. "I heard you…uh, maybe could help me do better with my spells?"

Kaylin shrugged. "Sure. What do you need to know?"

Luka's weakness was in the emotion and experience dimensions. The first was a surprise but the second not so much. They were all young and without much experience to draw from.

"It's all of them," he told her. "I can't seem to get the gestures right. I can remember the commands fine, but I can't draw all the energies together in the right way. I'm not hopeless. I know what I'm meant to do and see but I can't make it work."

"Yet," Kaylin told him. "Why don't we start with the things you need to know for class and pick up anything else you're missing on the way?"

"Now?" Luka looked worried. "But it's lunchtime!"

"Right," she said and stood. She'd been ready to teach him in whatever time they had before the next class but they both needed to eat. "How about we meet here between the last class and supper?"

She'd been about to suggest they meet after supper, but she had study she needed to do for the next day, or she would help everyone else and still fail herself. It wasn't that she'd be asked questions the next day or that she didn't have enough pictographs in the basement to keep her busy. It was simply that she needed to keep up.

How could she hope to help the others if she didn't know what they were meant to know from their studies? How would she even know what gaps the pictographs would help with most?

Luka gave her a look of relief and raced away toward the dining hall. She reminded herself that as helpful as she was, most of the students who came to her still wouldn't stand up for her if Sylvester and his cronies attacked. She might receive the occasional nod of greeting in the corridor but she was still very much on her own—merely not completely so.

The weeks went from four to six, and the trees grew bare. Kaylin was busier than she'd been at any point she could remember. She bounced from taking classes to giving them, to meal times to more classes, and then maybe a little study of her own, either from her texts or down in the basements.

Sleep became a rarity and she struggled to stay awake when she was alone. She also started to miss things—like Sylvester waiting in an alcove whose plant stood to one side.

"I thought I told you to make sure you didn't get it right," he said accusingly, caught her wrist, and squeezed.

She twisted away and managed to reach her room far enough ahead of him to shove the wedges under the door before he could force it open. She hadn't come out until Mirielle had knocked and told her all was clear.

"What's wrong?" the girl asked as she rubbed the tears from her eyes.

"I only—" Her voice caught but she drew a breath and continued. "I can't keep up."

Mirielle frowned. "You are doing a lot," she reminded her.

Kaylin shrugged. "I know and it's getting too much. I don't know how I'll get through without letting anyone down—or failing myself."

"Is there anything I can do to help?" her companion asked.

"I don't know," she replied. She stopped and considered it, stared past the girl, and tried to think of something she could give her to ease the load. It was hard. Mirielle didn't know about the pictographs or the basement, so it wasn't like she could teach herself any of the new spells.

Kaylin thought about that. Why couldn't Mirielle teach herself? It wasn't like she had anything special when it came to smarts. The gods only knew Melis and Isabette had made that point painfully clear.

"How about I show you something instead?" she suggested.

"Sure..." her companion answered and peeked into the corridor. "You mean now? Because the coast is clear if you're asking."

"Of course I mean now," she stated.

"Sylvester had to study or something and Tessa and Celia are busy or asleep. Now is ideal."

"It's late," Kaylin pointed out. "Are you—"

Mirielle fixed her with a worried look. "You don't have to show me."

She stilled. Of course she didn't have to show her, but only if she wanted to try to keep going as she had been, which she didn't. She didn't think she could, and if Mirielle could teach herself, maybe she wouldn't be the only one.

It was merely that she was afraid that by sharing her secret, she'd give it away—and that she'd lose access to the pictographs if the magisters ever learned of their existence. Some of her fear must have shown on her face because her companion laid a hand on her shoulder.

"What is it?" the girl asked. "Are you sneaking into the forbidden section of the library or something?" She made an evil face. "Or are you sneaking into the magisters' quarters and sucking their secrets out of their brains while they sleep?"

That made her smile. "Nothing that brave," she told her and headed out the door. "Come on."

Their first stop was the garden. Kaylin led her friend along the paths and up the steps to the little alcove above the grotto.

"Do you see these?" she asked, brushed the vines aside, and showed the girl the elven symbols on the wall.

Mirielle conjured a small ball of white light and guided it over the stones.

"That's elvish," she murmured, lifted more of the vines away, and studied the symbols before she looked at her. "Do you know what it says?"

She pulled her journal from her bag. "Some of it," she admitted, "but not all. There are some letters here that aren't in the books upstairs."

"See?" the girl whispered triumphantly. "I knew you were in the forbidden section."

"Nope," she retorted. "The language section isn't forbidden."

Mirielle stared at her, then turned to the symbols with a smile. "Well, that explains it, then. Some of these are magical symbols. You won't find them in the language texts because they're not part of the regular elvish language."

"And you know this how?" she asked. "Given that elven magic is in the forbidden section."

"Only the parts the magisters don't show us in class," the girl retorted. "They've shown us the elven symbols for water magic, fire magic, and lightning." She pointed to some of the symbols Kaylin hadn't been able to decipher.

The third was almost self-explanatory and it still didn't explain to Kaylin why there was a picture of lightning in a garden.

Unless it wasn't always a garden, she thought.

Smiling at her friend's excitement, she glanced around, then said, "That's not all I wanted to show you."

Mirielle straightened and dusted her robes off before she pulled the vines carefully into place.

"Show me," she ordered, her voice crackling with excitement.

Kaylin led her quickly to the ballroom and up the nearest staircase, and paused when she heard footsteps moving along the corridor on the staff floor. As soon as they'd died away, she continued swiftly to the landing and onto the next floor to lead her friend to the room with the hidden staircase.

"What's so special about this room?" the girl asked.

She gave her a puzzled look, and Mirielle waved a hand around to indicate the dust-laden drop sheets covering the nearby furniture and the clean floor.

"Well, someone's taken the time to clean in here," the girl observed. "I bet if we went into the room next door, the whole place would be covered in dust, the floor included."

"Funny you should mention that," she remarked and pulled the broom and dustpan out from behind a wardrobe.

"You did that?" Mirielle asked. "But why?"

Kaylin stowed the broom in its hiding place and swept aside the curtain that covered the door.

"Because otherwise, my footprints would have led people straight to this," she explained and her companion gaped.

"Where does it go?" the girl asked, and she gave her a secretive smile.

"That's what I have to show you." She didn't say anything more but ushered her through the door and pulled the curtain across it before she closed it tightly. Mirielle waited and observed the precautions with wide eyes.

"So…no one knows about it?" she asked, and Kaylin shook her head.

"But the stairs go past the teachers' floor so we have to be quiet," she warned, "and I don't know who else's room they pass, okay?"

"Okay," her companion responded. "They might hear us through the walls. Gotcha."

Kaylin conjured a floating light and led them down the stairs.

"Is that why the candles started running out?" Mirielle asked when they reached the bottom.

"And why the kitchens were complaining about a missing lamp," she confirmed.

"That was you? I thought the magisters would have a fit. They warned everyone in the upper classes about the storerooms being out of bounds and suggested that anyone wanting a midnight snack only had to ask."

Kaylin grinned. "The midnight snack wasn't me and I only used the storerooms once—at supper time, after Sylvester and his friends threw my food away and kicked me out of the dining hall."

Mirielle blushed. "I heard about that."

She sighed and tried to shrug it away. "Well, it's behind us now. Come and see what I found here."

"Where are we, anyway?"

"Somewhere under the Academy," she told her. "I found these stairs in the kitchen basement, hidden behind some shelving."

"Did you ever think they were hidden for a reason?"

"Yeah, but I couldn't think of one. If the citadel was cleared of monsters, why wouldn't you seal off any stairs you didn't want to use? Or maybe why wouldn't you want to keep them clear in case you wanted to make use of the space for yourself?" She walked out of the stairwell and into the basement she'd cleaned. "It seemed weird until I found these."

Mirielle started to follow but stopped a few steps inside the doorway. Her mouth dropped open in awe as she stared at the closest pictograms. She put a hand on the stone as if to feel the etchings as much as see them. "This isn't elvish."

"It's not elvish script, sure," Kaylin agreed, "but I get the distinct feeling it's still elvish. Look at these. They show each of the gestures perfectly." She indicated the wall but the girl wasn't listening. She scrutinized the border surrounding the closest section of wall. "What?"

"Well," her companion told her, "all I can say is it's a good thing you found them and not me because I wouldn't have been able to make any sense of them from a magical theory standpoint."

"You wouldn't?"

Mirielle shook her head and directed her glow closer to the border.

"No. All I'd be looking at is the story," she said, her voice soft as her gaze roved across the walls.

She directed her glow to another section of the border and studied it carefully.

"Story?" Kaylin asked, confused.

"Yes," Mirielle murmured and traced her fingers over the cuts and grooves that comprised the area in front of her. "The story in these carvings."

"Really?" She moved closer.

"Mmmhmm. See?" She pointed to one of the figures. "Here, they're learning fire magic."

She moved her finger down the wall.

"There! There's the first one. See? They had that little lizard thing as a pet and it showed them that cave. They're carrying some kind of flaming wand when she comes out. And here..." Her fingers glided over the carvings. "Here, he—no *she*... She's taken on her first student."

The girl giggled. "See? Here she's putting him out and there, he blew their hut up. These are so clever. I think she's smoldering...and then he puts her out!"

She chuckled.

"And that brings in the water mage..." Her face lit up with delight. Halfway up the wall, she paused. "Where does it begin?"

It took the two of them a half-turn of an hourglass to find the beginning of the story and follow the border that ribboned around the edge of the room. As they traced the tale, they watched the elves encounter magic for the first time, study it, learn it, and teach it—and then write it down.

First came stone blocks and walls, then scrolls and parchment and rolled pieces of hide, and finally, books, massive tomes that were carried to a citadel on top of a large hill at the edge of a valley encircled by cliffs.

"That's here!" Kaylin exclaimed in a loud whisper.

She clapped her hands over her mouth and glanced nervously at the doorway as though her voice could travel up three flights of stairs to the ground-floor level.

"It can't be here," Mirielle argued. "If it was here, we'd be learning much more magic instead of the same old stuff we know is everywhere else."

"Maybe the magisters don't know," Kaylin suggested. "Or they haven't found it yet."

"Pfft. If they haven't, they're not looking very hard." The other girl scoffed.

"No, I'm serious. Why wouldn't they teach it if they knew? Why wouldn't we take classes in these rooms or be encouraged to study in them if the magisters knew these drawings were here?"

She stared at the story in the border again.

"I honestly think this *is* the place and that the citadel those adventurers found was where those mages had their library. We have to find it."

"But if it was that library," Mirielle argued, "why didn't we ever hear about it being found? A find like that would have been talked about everywhere."

"Like these pictographs were?" Kaylin challenged.

Her friend frowned. "I don't know..."

"But it's worth looking for, right?" she suggested. "In case it *was* missed."

Mirielle looked at the pictographs and the storied borders surrounding them and nodded. "If we had those books..." she began.

"Exactly!" she agreed softly. "If we had those books, we'd never need another magister. We might not even need to go to class. We could give ourselves classes, study at our own pace—"

"It could change everything." The girl looked at her friend.

Their eyes met and sparkled with the possibilities opening up before them.

CHAPTER SIXTEEN

"Do we tell the others?" Kaylin asked when they were back in her room.

Mirielle thought about it.

The girl was quiet for so long that she added, "If we tell them, there's a greater chance they'll slip up and accidentally tell someone else, but I worry that if we don't tell them, they might not do as well as they could."

"Don't." Her friend shook her head. "Firstly, because they'd only be able to make as much sense of those things as I did and it wouldn't help."

Kaylin stared at her.

"Secondly, if you tell them, someone will find out and the magisters won't be happy with students traipsing past their floor or through the kitchen cellars to get to the basement. There's too great a risk that even if the others don't say something, they'll still get caught going to and from. Most of them aren't as careful as you."

She raised a brow. "As used to sneaking around, you mean?"

Mirielle blushed. "You know that's not what I meant."

"I know." She gave her a small smile. "I was teasing you."

"Not nice," her friend responded with a mock frown.

They were silent for a moment while each considered the alternatives.

"You know," Mirielle said after a moment, "we could show them the symbols in the garden and tell them we think those are clues that there's something more, but we need more clues to find it. Maybe the classroom in the basement is just that. It tells the history and shares the basics but doesn't say where because everyone knew."

Kaylin groaned. "Of course! Everyone was alive and studying beside the library. They didn't need directions. That makes so much sense—but that doesn't mean there wasn't a sign."

"Or it means that each section of the garden had a specific purpose," the other girl added. "What if those symbols on the walls are part of another lesson—maybe for more advanced students?"

"Or older students," she replied thoughtfully. "If they used pictographs for the very young or the very new, it would make sense that they used words for those old enough to be able to follow written instructions."

"Or the people moved the rocks to where they were needed when they were rebuilding the place," Mirielle suggested and sounded thoroughly defeated.

Kaylin pushed her shoulder with her fingertips. "Don't be like that. I don't think they moved that much."

The girl nodded, then yawned. "What time is it, anyway?"

"Time we were both sleeping," she told her. "We've got a full day of class tomorrow."

The other students were excited by the fact that there were elven symbols on the Academy grounds. Some of those in the more advanced classes were even a little offended that the magisters hadn't told them they existed.

"What were they thinking?" one demanded. "This is exactly the kind of knowledge that should be shared!"

Kaylin shrugged. "Maybe they didn't know—"

"Yeah, and dragons give milk to their young and don't tear entire mountains apart because someone stole their treasure." The student scoffed.

"Now, now, Nikolai," Mirielle began and fixed him with a firm look. "You know what we mean."

"Yeah, I know." He ran his hand over the back of his head. "But it's...it's so frustrating, you know?"

He knelt beside the runes. "Even from what we've been given so far in class, I can almost understand what they were trying to teach here."

"You can?" Kaylin stared at him. "I can only get the words that have nothing to do with magic."

Nikolai grinned sheepishly at her. "Yeah, I forget you've only had access to what's in the language section. Look. See this symbol? It means a water spell, and this one is something to do with magical growth."

He frowned at the next symbol along. "It's my normal elvish that's not so good. Do you know what this one means?"

She knelt beside him, pulled her journal out, and opened it to the first page she'd made inscriptions on. "Increase?" she suggested. "Or maybe provide?"

The others huddled around until, by the time night came and magic lit the garden, they had a vague sense of what that corner was meant to teach.

"This would have been so much easier if they'd written it all down." Nikolai groaned.

"We think they did," she told him. She swept her arm toward the rest of the garden. "We think there's a library somewhere here that no one's ever found."

He stared at her in disbelief. "You don't think someone else would have found it if there was? You don't think the magisters already know?"

"Well, if they do, why aren't they teaching us properly?" Mirielle challenged.

"Maybe they're saving it for their special students."

Kaylin shook her head. "I don't know what those guys are like in the more advanced classes, but the way they cast their spells is the same as what's demonstrated in class—mostly—and the one or two different movements I've seen are nowhere near what's on these walls."

She stopped when she realized she'd almost slipped up and told them about the pictograms. Thankfully, none of the others seemed to have noticed. They'd all turned to look at the walls or through the gap to the path where other alcoves could be seen or guessed at.

"You don't think they've changed the layout?" another girl asked. She was younger and in Kaylin's class. "That each gardener who's come here has done something different?"

"I don't know," a third student answered. "Some of these stones look very old. Maybe they can't be bothered to shift them."

"We're in a school for mages," the other girl retorted. "You don't think they couldn't use a little magic to move these where they wanted them?"

Kaylin's heart sank. The girl had a point. She looked around at the walls and the stones and wondered how many of the alcoves and paths were in the same place or formation they'd had when the elves had occupied the citadel.

"Nah," Mirielle told them. "If they knew this was something the elves had built, they'd have kept the gardens the way they were and searched themselves. If we aren't being taught the kind of magic Kaylin found, the magisters don't know about it."

"Or they know and they're keeping it to themselves," Nikolai argued darkly. "Why would they train mages who might become more powerful than themselves?"

"Because having a powerful mage indebted to you is advantageous?" the other girl suggested.

"They've got that now," he pointed out, then sighed. "You know what? I'm with Kaylin on this one. If the magisters have moved the stones or found the library, we're out of luck, but if they haven't…"

"Then this could be a way forward for us," the girl finished for him.

The two locked gazes and Kaylin saw them come to an agreement —a unity of purpose that didn't need words to express.

"Right," Mirielle said. "I'll take the next alcove."

"And we'll take the one after," Nikolai added and the girl beside him nodded.

"We'll take the walls alongside the paths," Nex interjected and his two friends stepped closer to him.

"You might be seen," Mirielle warned.

"We'll say we annoyed Magister Lorama," the boy retorted, "and she has us looking for..."

"Cerel shoot," one of the older girls provided. "It grows in rocks and this is the right time of year for it."

They all looked at her.

"What?" she asked. "She mentioned it in class, so anyone who knows their herbs could find it and the magister won't ask any more than that."

"But what will they do if they're asked what it's for?" Mirielle challenged.

"That's easy," one of Nex's friends replied. "We're gonna ask them how in the Karista's troll-infested ass are we meant to know?" He caught their shocked looks and shrugged. "It's not like the magisters ever tell us what they want these things for."

They all laughed at that and headed into the garden, each one determined to find something that might point to the library's location.

Their days settled into a new pattern, and Kaylin began to teach small classes before breakfast as well as after supper.

She ran from class to class and slipped into the kitchen for meals until the head chef finally kicked her into the dining hall again. That came as a shock and she joined the line at the servery almost in tears. To her surprise, she was left alone.

This time, Nex's tray was thrown into the wall.

Ignoring Mirielle's light touch on her arm, Kaylin set her tray down. "Hey!" she shouted. "Leave him alone."

She didn't make it halfway across the room before she was shoved back. Her knees caught on a bench and tripped her. She landed hard, rolled under the table, and scrambled out the other side to race forward in a half-crouch to where she'd last seen her student.

With only a few paces left to the door, someone grasped her collar and hauled her upright.

"And I thought you had no friends." Sylvester sneered and pushed her against the nearest wall. "It looks like your bad influence is spreading."

Kaylin twisted out of his grasp and moved to the door.

To her surprise, he let her go.

She reached the corridor as Nex was marched toward a stairwell.

"You're going to tell us what the sudden fascination is with the garden," one of his escorts said, and she recognized Stokan Baldervick, one of Sylvester's cronies.

"I like the flowers," Nex snapped in return.

"Sure you do," his other escort sneered. "Why? Because they're the same color as your eyes?"

"Last I looked my eyes weren't pink," her friend retorted. "No, I like them because they smell better than you do."

"Oh, crap," Kaylin muttered and started to run.

Stokan swung a fist at the smaller boy's head and Nex ducked.

He threw his hands in the air and slid out of his robes as he landed on his knees. The bully's fist connected with his other escort and their victim scrambled to his feet and ran. Stokan's friend didn't think. He simply reacted and returned the punch with interest as Kaylin caught up.

She slid between them, scooped Nex's robes up, and raced after him as the boy turned sharply right into the kitchens. Judging by the startled shouts ahead of her, he didn't stop. She ran headlong after him.

"Which way?" she demanded and was answered by startled fingers pointing toward the service entrance.

"Help us," she whispered and began to run again.

Behind her, Stokan roared in frustration. A whine answered him, but she didn't stop to listen. She took the exit and called to her friend.

"Nex!"

She caught a glimpse of bare skin disappearing along one of the paths leading to the grotto and followed.

"Nex!"

The boy didn't stop and she soon lost sight of him amidst the twists and turns of the paths. At first, she despaired of finding him, but she continued to search and moved to the grotto, then hunted through the hidden alcoves.

"Nex?"

The sky had grown fully dark by the time she found him and ice fringed the night air.

"Stay out of here!" The sharp whisper issued from the next junction. "I'm…I-I don't have my robes."

"It's kinda why I'm here," Kaylin replied softly but stopped to one side of the opening. "It's freezing. Do you want me to throw them to you?"

"Are you serious?"

"Yes. So, shall I?"

"Oh, no! By all means, hold onto them while I try to decide between dying of embarrassment and freezing to death."

Kaylin snickered. "Well, if that's the—"

A hand snaked around the corner, latched onto the robes, and ripped them out of her grasp.

"Smart assed, troll-titted…" Nex began.

"Hey!" she whisper-shouted back. "At least I brought them to you."

She heard the rustle of cloth as he replied. "If it wasn't for you, I wouldn't be in this mess."

"Sorry. What can I—"

The boy appeared in the junction. "No," he told her. "I…I'm sorry. That wasn't fair. It's not your fault I showed Celia up in class this morning."

Kaylin couldn't help it. She laughed. "You didn't."

Her reaction made him smile and he lowered his head. "Yeah, I did. I'm sorry."

"Why? I'm glad you could but—"

Footsteps crunched on the stone path and Nex grabbed her arm and pulled her into the alcove. He laid a finger against his lips and dragged her behind him. Together, they crouched close to the ground and hoped the shadows would be enough to hide them.

"Nex?" Mirielle whispered through the darkness. "Kaylin?"

He was about to move forward but Kaylin placed a hand on his back and shook her head.

Mirielle spoke again. "Nex?"

A second voice joined hers. "Well?"

"They're not here. Even you should be able to hear that."

Her response was followed by the sound of a slap.

"All I can see is someone who is not helping me."

"You want help?" the girl demanded. "Why don't you go running to your magister and leave the rest of us alone?"

Another slap sounded sharply in the silence. "Where are they?"

"I don't know," Mirielle wailed. "I can't see them. Can you see them?"

"You said they'd be in the garden."

"I did *not!*" she shouted. "I said I didn't know where they were. You didn't believe me."

The rustle of cloth that followed ended in a thump and a soft "oof" of pain. A second grunt followed before someone walked away. Kaylin and Nex waited until they'd faded and they heard someone stir on the path outside.

A soft groan followed, and Mirielle swore softly.

"And I wouldn't help you if I could!" She snarled quietly and they heard the scrape of her shoes as she got to her feet. "Scharted asshole."

Nex glanced at Kaylin, his eyebrows raised, but she didn't stop to reply. She skidded around the corner. "Mirielle?"

Her hurried whisper was answered by a laughing sob. "So, I stopped in time, right?"

"You did. You crazy girl." She wrapped her arms around her friend and drew her into the alcove. "Are you okay?"

Mirielle dashed a hand at her eyes. "Me? I'm fine. How about you? Is Nex okay?"

The boy stepped out from behind Kaylin. "Yeah." He gave Kaylin an embarrassed look. "She looked after me."

"She does that," the other girl noted as she reached into the pockets of her robe and pulled out a flattened bread roll from each. "Oh..." She held them up. "I tried to bring you supper. Gram caught me on the way out of the ballroom."

Kaylin took the rolls and passed one to Nex.

"They're a little flat." Mirielle looked apologetic. "I think I landed on them."

With a firm look at her friend, Kaylin took a deliberate bite. "It tastes fine to me," she mumbled through a mouthful of crumbs, relieved to hear Nex crunch into his.

"Thanksh," he said and crumbs blurred the word.

Mirielle heaved a sigh of relief and went to sit on the bench in the corner. "I thought they'd given up on the bullying," she said.

He shook his head. "I don't know about either of you, but it's gotten worse—for us, at least. Ever since we started doing better in class."

Kaylin blushed and hung her head. "I'm sorry."

He caught her arm. "Don't be. I won't fail my Trials now and that's thanks to you. If they can't handle it, that's on them."

She frowned and touched the bruise darkening Mirielle's cheek. "This," she said, "is on me." She glanced at Nex. "We need to think of a way to stop you guys from being beaten up."

"What about you?" he asked.

"I was doing okay," she told him, "and I'd been able to avoid them, but there are so many of us now. We won't all be able to stay out of their way."

"They don't go after you if you're not alone," Nex told her, "but Cal and Logan wanted to study more before they ate and I was hungry."

He took a bite of his flattened bread roll as if for emphasis and didn't continue until he'd chewed and swallowed. With a small smile, he lifted the rest of it in a salute to Mirielle.

"Thanks for this."

The girl managed a smile in return.

"Fine," Kaylin stated. "From now on, none of us go anywhere alone. We walk in pairs or more if we can."

"Everyone?" Mirielle asked and she nodded.

"Everyone," she confirmed. "Even the older ones like Nikolai and Sula."

"They will love that," the girl commented and Nex grinned.

"They might. I think Nik likes Sula."

"Ugh." Marielle rolled her eyes. "Like any of us have time for that."

"Regardless," Kaylin told them. "Spread the word. We have to try to keep the others safe."

"Smart," Sylvester murmured as he watched Kaylin cross the ballroom and slip out into the garden. Four other students followed but each one entered from a different doorway and took a different path into the garden beyond.

He stood in front of a mirror, his blue eyes sharp with interest as he monitored the girl's comings and goings. A fine layer of snow rimed the ground but too many footsteps marked it to be of use.

The apprentice sighed. It was a pity that the garden didn't permit scrying to the extent he needed. Something there prevented him from seeing or hearing anything clearly.

While he could pick up impressions and almost recognize the locations, he couldn't make out words or determine exactly where he was. It was most frustrating.

He went to his magister to ask what he could do to fix it.

"Now why would you try to scry someone in the gardens?" Magister Gaudin asked when he broached the subject, and he blushed.

She gave him a tight-lipped smile. "A girl? Really, Sylvester? I'd thought you were above that kind of thing. You should have more important matters on your mind if you get my meaning."

He did. The magister had made it no secret that she expected him to secure a court position.

"Not that kind of girl, Magister," he replied and struggled to keep his tones calm.

A little of his frustration must have shown because she had arched an eyebrow in interest.

"Then which girl would you be referring to, Sylvester? I doubt there is anyone who can rival you. Not with my help."

"Knight, Magister. She is using something in the school to gain access to a specialized area of knowledge."

"And what makes you say this?"

"Because she's not the only one. She is sharing her knowledge with others."

"Some of mine?" Gaudin asked and Sylvester shook his head abruptly.

"No, Magister."

"Then whose?"

"No one's, magister," the boy replied, and she started to relax. "And therein lies the problem."

"How so?" Gaudin demanded.

"They're…" He flushed. "They're getting good, Magister, and are able to answer questions they should still struggle with without outside help. They're even ahead of some of us."

"You?"

Sylvester shook his head. "Not yet," he admitted, "but I'm afraid that if it continues…" He shrugged and let her finish the thought.

"I see." She'd looked pensive. "Do you have any idea what it is?"

"No, Magister. I thought maybe it was one of the other magisters helping her in secret—"

Gaudin shook her head.

"They wouldn't dare," she stated and cut him off. "Exactly like they won't interfere with what you and the others do to discourage them." She smiled a thin smile of satisfaction and added, "Not a single one wants to face the consequences of testing me with that."

He relaxed a little. "Then I don't know what she has access to, but she meets with her students in the gardens almost every night."

"And does what?" the magister demanded.

"That I do not know," Sylvester told her. "I cannot scry them clearly when they're out there, especially not once they enter the grotto's valley."

"Yes," Gaudin acknowledged. "That location has always been resistant to scrying and we've never discovered why."

She turned to her desk, rearranged the inkwell and pens, and shuffled the papers on its surface, aware that he was waiting for her to dismiss him. The boy honestly was a pain.

Still, he was a useful pain. She sighed.

"Continue to keep watch on them, and if you find they do have access to something special, take it from them and bring it to me. I shall be most interested."

He straightened. "Yes, Magister."

"Now, I suggest you get back to your studies and practice that variation I taught you earlier. You need to be ready to advance to the next stage of your studies and I fear you still fall a trifle short."

Sylvester blushed but acknowledged her with another brisk, "Yes, Magister. Thank you, Magister," before he wheeled from the room.

Gaudin waited until he'd closed the door behind him and sank into her chair. So the girl had discovered something "special" to assist her, had she?

Well, it couldn't have been one of the elven texts they'd discovered shortly after their arrival. Only a handful of the magisters knew of those. It was why their students did so well—and why the texts they had allowed into the library were only accessible with a note.

Ostensibly, it was to ensure that only students who could "handle" the knowledge had access to it but in reality, it was an excellent way to ensure that only the right kinds of students could use the advantages there to advance.

She would have to call the others together. If what Sylvester said was true and the child was spending more time in the gardens, she had almost certainly found the inscriptions Lorama was supposed to have hidden with plant life.

"Although I doubt even she is capable of deciphering those,"

Gaudin muttered. "Still, better safe than sorry." She pushed her chair back.

At least the idiot child hadn't started talking about a hidden treasure of elvish scrolls and books. That would have been harder to deny —especially if the girl thought to ask the Chevaliers. Captain Delaine might think to look up the records from the expedition that had been with the mages when they'd found the small collection of writings hidden in a corner of the ruins.

If the brat from the streets had caught wind of that, she'd bear watching.

"Why don't you tell me what you've found?" Stokan demanded.

"I don't know what you're talking about!" Sula's voice rose in defiance and fear. "I haven't found anything."

Kaylin began to run. How had the bully found her on her own? And where was Nikolai?

As if to answer her question, Nikolai yelled a protest. "Get your hands off her!"

"And what will you do about—" That was as far as Stokan got before a fist thudded into flesh.

It was followed by a thump and Nikolai asked, "Are you okay?"

Kaylin skidded around the corner as Sula replied, "Yes. Where were you?"

"I'm sorry. I had to get rid of Sylvester and Avrik. They followed me out of the library."

"Let's not do that again," the girl suggested and her voice shook. "They're getting worse."

"Agreed," Nikolai stated as Kaylin came up beside them.

"Are you okay?" she asked, a little breathless from her run.

The girl nodded but his eyes remained dark with concern.

"Next time, I'll set his robes alight," Sula muttered and he chuckled.

"That would be better than me breaking my hand on his face."

At their feet, Stokan groaned. Sula kicked him and stamped on his back as she moved over him and down the corridor with the other two on her heels.

"Any sign of it yet?" she asked, meaning the library.

Kaylin shook her head. "There are days when I wonder if it's even real."

The girl stopped and turned to face her. "Don't say that. I believe in you and I think you're right. The symbols all point to there being something more here. We *will* find it."

"Not if we find it first." The voice cut into their conversation as Sylvester stepped out of a nearby classroom.

He relished the look of shock on their faces and moved forward.

"You had to slip up sometime." He sneered. "And now we know to keep looking. Whatever you think is out there, we'll find it first—and when we do, we'll burn it to the ground."

"Why?" Kaylin asked. "What if it's something you could use to be a better mage?"

Sylvester snorted. "Why would I want something else," he demanded, "when the magister gives me everything I need in order to excel?"

"You don't know that," she retorted. "You don't know what she doesn't give you. How do you know she isn't holding something back to make sure you never learn enough to be a better mage than she is?"

His jaw dropped and he looked stunned. For a moment, she thought she might have gotten through to him, but he laughed.

"You have a good imagination, I'll give you that," he told her and continued down the corridor.

Kaylin had almost relaxed when he stopped and turned to look at her.

"But how *you* can imagine you belong here, I don't know—and I'll make sure you understand that."

This time, he turned and kept walking. She stared after him until he entered a stairwell and vanished.

"Come on, Kay," Sula told her. "Don't listen to him. You belong here more than he does."

"We haven't heard the last of this," Nikolai remarked and both girls rolled their eyes.

"Yuh think?" Sula asked but he missed her sarcasm.

"I don't think," he replied. "I know."

A day later, Nex bolted out of the ballroom and raced to the garden. Behind him came the thunder of half a dozen sets of boots and he put on a spurt of speed. He might have made it if it hadn't been for the rumbling ball of mud and rock that rolled out of the ballroom porch and pounded into his back.

The force of it shoved him forward and made him lose his footing and land hard on the cobbles. The projectile exploded, dissipated harmlessly into its component parts, and showered him with dirt and pebbles. He gasped for breath.

With a groan of pain, he picked himself up and staggered forward, only to be knocked down with a flying tackle by one of his pursuers. His hands smacked into the stone for a second time and he swore he heard something crack.

He didn't have time to investigate what it was before he was rolled onto his back and a fist whipped at his face. Nex moved his head and the hand impacted with the cobbles. That was followed by a cry of pain and a look of such fury that his heart quailed.

He was in for the beating of his life, and he knew it.

"Two can play at that game!" Kaylin's furious cry caught him by surprise, but not as much as the ball of light that picked his assailant up and threw him into the side of the porch.

He didn't have time to see what happened next, because two sets of hands caught hold of him, yanked him off the paving, and dragged him to the garden entrance he'd aimed for.

"Come on!" Mirielle urged. "You're almost there."

Almost where? He wanted to ask but couldn't catch his breath. His arm ached and his stomach roiled. What had just happened?

"Did you get him?" Kaylin demanded.

"Yeah, but someone's gonna want to know where that force ball came from," Mirielle quipped.

Force balls could glow? Again, the boy wanted to ask. Instead, he was hauled into the grotto's confines and pushed onto a bench.

"Show me your arm," Kaylin commanded. He held it out to her and yelped as pain seared in his wrist.

"I need it to write with," he protested and yelped again as she took hold of it gently.

"I know," she told him, "so let's see if I understood this next part correctly."

The healers said nothing when they brought Nex in until they saw his arm.

"What happened?" The initial question was immediately followed by, "Who started the healing?"

The boy looked at the floor and remained silent. He flinched when one of the priests touched the arm but still wouldn't be drawn on who had either caused it or tried to mend it.

"You know this kind of bullying isn't tolerated here," one of the healers said.

Kaylin barely contained a snort at that and hurried away and scowled when she caught sight of Celia and Tessa slinking into a side corridor.

"As if that would stop me from seeing them." She growled softly and Mirielle settled her hand on her arm. "It's okay, I promise I won't—"

Her sentence cut off as a burst of light spun out of the corridor. She dragged her friend prone and sheltered her under an arm as the light hissed overhead. It missed them but pounded into a large vase set on a table in a niche.

The resulting crack as the pottery shattered brought another two healers into the corridor.

"What is going on here?" one shouted and Kaylin raised her head slowly.

"Someone cast a force sphere at us," she said and pushed cautiously to her feet. "We ducked."

The healer watched them rise. "So I see. Did you see who it was?"

"No," she told her. "We were too busy ducking."

"Well, if it happens again and you do see who does it, please tell me." She frowned. "Is this incident related to the one that brought Apprentice Florin to us?"

"Nex," Mirielle whispered at her puzzled look. "She means Nex."

The woman's lips thinned. "Yes. Apprentice Nexar Florin."

"Oh..." Kaylin shrugged. "I'm sorry. I couldn't say."

The healer gave them a look that she said she didn't believe a word either of them said and returned abruptly to the clinic.

Mirielle exhaled a long sigh of relief. "That was close," she said.

Kaylin nodded.

"I don't remember seeing anything about shielding—do you?" she asked.

Her companion paused, then shook her head. "No. Why? Do you think we'll need it?"

"I think it's something we should investigate." She pursed her lips. "When is it usually taught here?"

"Third or fourth year," Mirielle answered, "but I don't think it's taught to everyone."

"Well," she declared. "That will certainly change."

Things became worse as the days progressed. Moving in groups was no longer a guarantee of safety—and more vases were lost. Kaylin explored other routes through the corridors and upper floors and found different ways into the garden. She also arranged with the head chef for some of the students to collect sandwiches from the kitchen entrance.

"It's not safe for them in the dining hall," she said the first time she asked.

"Now, Apprentice, I find that very hard to believe."

When Stokan, Gram, and Tessa tried to remove Nex, Sula, and Abigail from the food line, no one came to intervene. The three of them resisted and their fully laden trays were thrown across the room.

"You should have left when you were told to," Tessa stated as fire rolled between her hands.

"You can't throw that in here!" Nex exclaimed as he backpedaled, and the girl erupted.

"Don't you tell me what to do!" she screamed and hurled the perfectly formed fireball after him.

He snatched a tray and swatted it away, but his assailant and the other students in the line ducked and the fiery globe of magic sailed into the kitchen. A dull krump was followed by the clatter of pots and pans and several loud curses.

Sula and Abigail grabbed Nex and dragged him out the door before the head chef entered the dining hall and the shouting started in earnest. The next day, Tessa was absent from class.

"What happened?" Kaylin asked when she saw Nex.

"Tessa tried to fireball me at supper."

"And?" she asked. "Because you're still here."

"Well, I used a tray to deflect it and Abby and Sula got me out of there." He lowered his voice even more. "I think it exploded in the kitchen."

She stifled a sudden chuckle but it came out as a snort and he had to hide his smile.

"I guess it is kinda funny when you think about it," he admitted.

Neither of them smiled when Magister Wanslow addressed the class.

"There was an incident in the dining hall last night," he stated and his gaze roved over his students.

His forehead creased into a frown as it passed over Kaylin, Nex, and Abigail, but he focused his attention on the class and his voice rose angrily as he continued.

"I should not need to remind you that casting harmful magics at your fellow students is forbidden in this Academy." He paused but only momentarily and his voice rose from a shout to a bellow as he went on. "It is *particularly* forbidden *in the dining hall!*"

Kaylin's eyes widened, but the magister wasn't finished.

"The other magisters and I have fielded complaints from the kitchen staff since last night's little altercation and from the healers since last week. It seems that, in addition to having a vase broken outside their clinic, they've treated numerous spell-related injuries over the last week."

He continued to glare and Kaylin and Nex exchanged glances.

Magister Wanslow didn't appear to notice but he didn't stop either.

"This has to stop. You have not been brought here so that you can attack other mages. You are not war mages, nor are you the only magically inclined students in the valley. The school has more applicants than it can possibly accept for any one period of enrollment. Penalties for using your magical abilities in this way are being considered."

This only made her wonder why they hadn't been considered in the past. Surely there had been other incidents?

"Never," Magister Wanslow added, "in all my years as a magister, have I seen the like!"

Well, that answers that question, then.

"There has never been an incident like the one we saw last night in which a student—*a student*—has caused such distress to others, and any further incidents will be met with the gravest of consequences."

"He means expulsion," Nex whispered and Kaylin glanced at Magister Wanslow with alarm.

To her relief, he wasn't looking at her friend and Nex wasn't the only one talking. The entire class had erupted into a chorus of whispers. She sat still and silent and let the class bubble around her, but she was more than aware of the glances cast at her.

The magister gave them a few minutes and clapped his hands.

"And now," he told them, "it's time to discuss one of the more advanced aspects of magical theory."

Another week passed and the magisters had become more vigilant. The so-called severe consequences Magister Wanslow had warned of didn't materialize, but Kaylin was sure it was because the worst perpetrators were Magister Gaudin's chosen.

She ordered her pupils to lay low and meet in their rooms. The first snows had fallen and the garden was getting too cold for classes. She tried to decide if this was the right time to introduce her students to the basement but wasn't sure how much longer it would remain a secret if she did.

With these thoughts on her mind, she descended to the basement to see if there was something in there to help in their defense.

"Surely they had something their students could use to defend themselves with," Mirielle stated after they'd walked the entire perimeter of the room.

"Maybe there's another set of stairs," Kaylin suggested and they ascended to the cellar above.

Another hour of searching had led to them almost being discovered and they hurried down to what Kaylin had started to refer to as the Teaching Room.

"There's nothing," she said after she made another circuit of the room.

"What are we going to do?" Mirielle asked. "Nikolai and Sula couldn't find any references to shields in the library—and they said they didn't dare ask the librarian because Magister Gaudin's students were following them the whole time. They didn't want to give them any ideas."

"That was smart of them," she told her. "I hate it when bullies are smart." She sighed and began to walk around the room again. "So there aren't any shielding spells here...but that doesn't mean we can't make one up."

Her friend gaped at her. "What?"

"I mean," Kaylin replied and stood in front of the spell that allowed them to conjure an orb of water, "look at it. Water stops things." She moved along the wall. "Earth stops things." After another step, she paused and frowned. "Light…" She shook her head. "I'm not sure how that would work."

Mirielle shrugged. "Me neither, but go on."

She gave her a dark look. "You're being sarcastic now, aren't you?"

"Me?" the girl asked in a mock innocent tone she recognized all too well.

How many times had she heard that from Melis or Isabette…or even Raoul? Oblivious to her thoughts, her companion continued.

"No. I'd never be sarcastic about you trying to do something no student has ever tried before. You're an entire half-a-year student and fully capable of making up your own spells."

Kaylin gaped at her.

"Well," she said, "why don't you tell me how you feel, Mirielle? Is there anything else while you're at it?"

"Well…no…"

"Are you sure?"

Mirielle waved at her friend. "No, go and do your impossible thing," she told her exasperatedly. "And hurry up. We haven't got all night. The others will wonder where we are."

"I gave them the night off," Kaylin said.

"Yeah…" the girl replied, "but that doesn't mean they'll take it."

"Oh, for pity's sake! I can't do this as well as look after them," she snapped.

"Then don't," Mirielle responded.

"What?"

"I said don't. They're old enough to make their own decisions and we need you to come up with something. So come on."

She clapped twice, dropped cross-legged to the floor, and pulled her journal out. "I'll do some studying while I wait."

For a moment, Kaylin stared at her before she turned to the wall. It took her a while to work out which gestures she had to alter but she managed.

"It won't be pretty," she warned and took her friend through the motions.

"Nothing with you ever is," Mirielle told her and she frowned at her. "Aw, come on, Kay. I didn't mean it like that."

She managed a tired smile.

"Do it again."

While she worked with Mirielle, Kaylin tried to think of a way to end the bullying. If it continued as it was, none of them would reach the Trials, let alone pass them. The problem kept her occupied over the next few days as she made sure each of her students knew the variations to create shields of water and earth.

Through it all, they continued to dodge attacks from Sylvester and the rest of Magister Gaudin's students. Slowly, a plan started to form in Kaylin's mind.

Given how personal it had become, there was one thing that might put an end to the battle. She decided not to run the plan past Mirielle as the girl would only try to talk her out of it. Instead, she waited until she had a class relatively on her own.

At the end, she made sure the others left ahead of her and ignored their questioning looks as she indicated for them to go. As soon as they were headed to the dormitories, she moved toward where the more senior students had their lessons.

She didn't know his timetable, but she assumed she'd find Sylvester easily enough—or he'd find her.

The corridor began to fill with students, and she used them to gauge if she was moving in the right direction. When she was certain she'd found the right section of corridor, she leaned against the wall and waited. As she'd predicted, he was one of the last to emerge and his gaze settled on her almost as soon as he stepped through the door.

His mouth curved into a mocking smile.

"Well, well, well," he began and his gaze flicked up and down the corridor in search of her friends. "Look who thinks she's good enough to come visiting the senior school."

Kaylin pushed off the wall and moved toward him, aware of Gram and Stokan standing one on either side of him.

"What's the matter?" she asked. "Are you too scared to face me on your own?" She put one hand on her hip and made a show of not being afraid. "Don't dare stand in the same space as me without your bodyguards?"

She arched an eyebrow as she came to a halt in front of him. He was as tall as she remembered but not that much taller than she was. He looked at her and she made a point of meeting his eyes.

"We need to talk," she informed him and glanced deliberately at the two boys on either side before she added, "In private."

Sylvester stilled, and she forced herself to keep her gaze locked on his. It was harder to not say anything while she waited when all she wanted was to goad him, but she managed. Finally, he nodded.

"This way," he ordered, pivoted, and led her into a side corridor and an empty classroom.

Warnings clamored in Kaylin's skull when he gestured for her to precede him, especially when Stokan and Gram moved to follow.

Are you crazy? Getting yourself trapped in an unfamiliar classroom with three of them? her internal voice screamed.

She tried to soothe it but it was hard when her heart beat like a bird trapped against a window.

"Not you." Sylvester's voice startled her and she turned in time to see him stop his friends at the door. "Stay here. If I need you, I'll call."

Stokan gave him an uncertain look. "But...she's trouble."

Sylvester stepped forward so he stood chest to chest with the other boy. He thrust his head forward until his forehead was almost touching Stokan's.

"Are you suggesting you don't think I can handle one little street rat on my own?" he all but snarled and his friend backed away hastily.

"N...n...no, Mr. Ozanne. I'd never—"

From the fear that marred the boy's features, Kaylin believed him. She wondered what kind of power Sylvester had to make someone from a fairly powerful family so afraid. *And what is it with the Mr. Ozanne, anyway?*

She didn't ask and decided Sylvester probably wouldn't have

answered if she had.

Instead, she moved across the classroom in search of a space that would give her room to dodge and run if she needed to. Failing that, she wanted nothing in her firing line if she needed to cast.

Nowhere was ideal and she settled for a space that put a desk between her and the older student. Sylvester closed the door behind him and crossed the room. He noted the desk with a condescending stare and a sneer, then pushed it out from between them.

"You wanted to speak to me?" he asked and settled his rump against the back of the chair tucked into the desk behind him. His lips curled in mockery. "In private."

Kaylin fought to keep her face blank and her temper under control. "That's right. This situation has gone too far."

"Me pointing out how much you don't belong, you mean?" he asked.

"You refusing to acknowledge that having money doesn't make you a mage."

The retort was out before she could stop it and his eyes narrowed.

"I take it you came here to talk about something more concrete than making ridiculous claims," he replied coldly and she straightened.

"We need to end this ridiculous war," she told him, "before someone gets hurt."

"Oh?" he challenged.

"Or expelled," she added. "In case you hadn't noticed, you and I aren't the only ones in the firing line and you're not exactly immune."

He made a dismissive gesture with his hand, his expression bored. "I take it you have a plan?" he asked and pretended to stifle a yawn.

"I take it you're interested."

"I love a good laugh," he drawled. "What did your fetid little mind come up with?"

"A duel," she said promptly and he pushed off the chair.

Kaylin took two hasty steps back but he did nothing more than straighten and give her a sharp stare before he glanced around the room to make sure they truly were alone.

"What kind of duel?" he demanded and kept his voice low.

"A magic duel," she returned in equally quiet tones. "If I win, you and the rest of Magister Gaudin's students leave those who come to me for help alone."

"Do you know what will happen if we're caught?" he asked, his tone almost a hiss.

She raised an eyebrow and settled both hands on her hips.

"We'll both be expelled," she told him with quiet satisfaction, "because not even Magister Gaudin can protect you from a rule that is so embedded in the Academy's founding constitution."

"And *when*," he snapped in a fierce whisper, "did you get the time to look up the school's founding constitution?"

"When?" She snorted. "When I was looking for a way to keep my people safe from the assholes who follow you."

He smiled. "And you think you can defeat me in a Magus Duel?"

"Yup."

The idea amused him. "Truly?"

"Very much so," Kaylin replied. "Why? You don't?"

"I know you can't,' he replied.

"Prove it," she challenged.

"With pleasure." He snarled his derision. "We'll duel in the basement below the wine cellar. Do you know it?"

Kaylin couldn't quite keep the shock off her face and Sylvester smiled.

"You do know it," he said thoughtfully, "and now, I have to ask myself how."

He studied her through narrowed eyes and she hoped she hadn't given away the secret of what lay below.

"If you mean the basement just under the wine cellar," she told him and tried for casual, "then, yes, I know it. Where do you think I've gone to get away from you?"

His lips curled in disdain. "And I thought it was the grotto and the garden," he told her. "Now I know where you've been hiding, perhaps I'll take care to pay it more attention. What do you think?"

She didn't try to hide what she thought. The idea appalled her. The level they were referring to was the same one in which she'd found the rusted door leading into the Teaching Room. If he saw it open and decided to enter, it would be nothing short of disastrous.

"That only leaves us with the question of when," he said and she refocused hastily. "I'd prefer it to be before the Trials and maybe even supper. That way, not only would my studies not be interrupted, but I wouldn't have to endure the indigestion I get from seeing your face at every meal."

Kaylin stared at him, not sure how to reply to that, but he hadn't finished.

"It would also mean the staff would be busy in the kitchen and less likely to intercept us on the way to our little date. After all, I'd hate to miss our dueling deadline because I was detained by the wait staff."

The way he said it, the wait staff barely registered as human and she felt a surge of resentment.

"Tomorrow, then," she told him, "straight after class."

Sylvester smiled and she wondered what she missed.

"What?" she asked.

"I'm starting to wonder why you're in such a hurry. Are you afraid I'll have too much time to practice? Or maybe you're worried the word will get out and the whole school will turn out to see your defeat? What is it?"

Given that he looked directly at her when he asked, she decided she'd better give him a reason.

"That would be it," she said. "The fewer people there the better."

His eyebrows arched. "Oh? What are you hiding, I wonder?"

"Nothing. But if too many people come, the magisters will hear about it and it'll be a very short-lived battle, won't it?"

"Fool!" Sylvester sneered. "Who do you think will be capable of casting the obfuscation each duel requires?"

Kaylin froze. "I assumed there was some kind of item we used."

"There is," Sylvester admitted reluctantly and it was her turn to sneer.

"There isn't," she told him scornfully. "Do you think I'd come to you with this if I didn't know the rules and how the duel worked? The reason they're banned is because they can be invoked by an accumulation of power."

With her attention fixed on his face, she saw that this piece of information was new to him.

"Oh?" she asked in mock shock. "You didn't know? You, the great Sylvester Ozanne, didn't know how a duel like this worked? It's a ritual and must be powered by no fewer than three wizards other than the combatants."

"Four, then," he stated and recovered quickly. "We each bring four of our people."

"Can we get them to the basement without anyone seeing?"

"Well, you got there, didn't you?"

"I have the necessary skills," she told him. "You?"

"I have enough skill to get me through," he assured her and she arched her eyebrows again.

"Do you?" she asked. "I didn't take you for a sneak thief."

"Whereas I," he told her smarmily, "have known exactly from whence you have sprung, which is all the more reason why I should be the one to send you back there."

"Oh, so you had dealings with the Blackbirds, did you?" Kaylin challenged and caught the slight widening of his eyes that confirmed she'd hit her mark. "I wondered where your family got its wealth. Not so squeaky clean then, are we? Or was it only you? Needed to supplement our allowance, did we? Got bored doing the right thing, did we?"

She watched Sylvester go from pale to puce and waited until the color faded to normal.

"Four," he repeated through clenched teeth. "For each of us. And tomorrow, we meet straight after class in the basement below the wine cellar. No magisters, no authorities, and only you, me, and our four supports." He laughed snidely. "After all, you'll need someone to carry you out when I'm done."

"Deal," she told him. "Four supports, you, me, no magisters, straight after class tomorrow in the basement below the wine cellar. If I win, you and every other magister's pet leaves the rest of us alone."

Kaylin moved toward the door.

"Wait!" Sylvester commanded and she stopped and turned slowly to face him.

"What?" she asked.

"We haven't agreed on what I'll get when I beat you," he stated and she resisted the urge to move away again.

She fixed him with an impatient look. "Well?"

"You admit you were never good enough to be a mage and declare the Chevaliers were sorely mistaken when they seconded you. You leave and never return to study magic here again."

"Deal!" she snapped before he could add anything else and spun away from him.

After all, the Academy wasn't the only place she could study magic.

He took two long strides and caught up with her, grasped her by the arm, and turned her to face him.

"I will enjoy this," he told her and smiled like they were exchanging pleasantries.

Kaylin shook her arm free. "I doubt it."

Sylvester seized her before she could walk away. "But I will," he assured her and smiled in the falsely pleasant way of his. "I will prove once and for all why you don't belong here."

She tried to wrench her arm free but his hold was too tight. He leaned in close.

"For years to come," he told her and released her with a snap of his hand, although he kept his face close and his gaze locked on hers. "They'll whisper how I sent you out of here, crawling and begging."

For a second, she simply stared at him, then she laughed. "You?" she snickered and saw the scorn diminish in his eyes. She pressed her forehead momentarily to his. "You can dream about me crawling all you want," she told him and bared her teeth in a ferocious smile, "but tomorrow night?"

She pulled her head away from his and looked into his eyes.

"It will be you begging when I show everyone that being a magister's pet doesn't mean you're a real mage."

CHAPTER SEVENTEEN

By the time they reached the basement, the rusted door leading to the Teaching Room was closed. Kaylin had made doubly sure it couldn't be opened the night before by wedging it tightly from the other side, after which she'd made the trek from the upper floor to the Teaching Room and up the stairs.

She hadn't tried getting to it from the kitchen cellar because she assumed Sylvester would have a watch in place in case she tried to set something up. After all, that's what she would have done. She wasn't sure he hadn't, but given that he hadn't known about the ritual, she wasn't sure he knew how.

Let's not be complacent, she told herself and guided Nex, Mirielle, Sula, and Nikolai past the kitchen staff and into the storage room.

It came as both a relief and a surprise when she wasn't stopped by either the staff or a magister.

So he will go through with it, she thought and wondered if she wasn't making a mistake. What if he'd betrayed her? He could have told Magister Gaudin and had her waiting for them when they arrived.

"He wouldn't," she assured herself and tried to ignore the sharp retort in her head. *How much are you willing to bet on that?*

She could imagine what Melis would have to say about it.

"Well, it's too late now," she murmured, stooped through the shelf, and made the final descent.

Sylvester had already arrived but only two of his supports were there.

Kaylin caught the impatient glance he tossed at the door at her arrival. She also saw the irritation and disappointment in it and guessed she hadn't been the person he was waiting for.

"At least someone can arrive on time for their beating," he sneered.

"And someone arrived early," she quipped in response, not at all daunted by the color that crept up his neck and stained his face.

A clatter came from the top of the stairs and they all turned to face it. Kaylin gestured her crew to move into the cellar and out of the direct line of sight of the doorway. When he saw her signal, her opponent jerked his chin to indicate that Tessa and Gram should follow them.

"I take it we're not doing this right here?" Kaylin asked and he shook his head irritably.

"No, around the corner and toward the end. I'm not stupid."

She said nothing but reversed away from the stairs. Sylvester, on the other hand, stood and glared at them as though they'd personally offended him. He either knew who was coming or he didn't care, and that worried her.

He saw the new arrivals before she did, and he wasn't impressed. "You're late," he snapped. "She's already here."

Why that mattered, she didn't know, but she watched as Celia and Stokan hurried into the room. They looked at Sylvester and glanced guiltily in her direction. He gave them a scathing look and stalked toward the far end of the cellar.

"I wanted to have this place swept before we began," he told Kaylin, then shrugged and a mocking smile lightened his features, "but it doesn't matter. I'd rather see you crawling through the dirt. It's what you deserve."

She caught her temper and held it back to one simple retort. "Scared, are you?"

His smile became pitying. "Not of you."

They turned the corner and reached the cellar's end. He looked at Stokan and Celia.

"Tell me you at least had the sense to block the door to the kitchens."

They nodded hastily. "Exactly like you said," the boy reassured him. "No one will come down here until you're done."

As if I don't matter, Kaylin thought. She hated the small sense of relief she felt at knowing the battle wouldn't be disturbed but wasn't sure what would happen if the kitchen staff discovered the door was blocked.

It's better to not think about it, she told herself.

"Did you bring it?" Sylvester's voice brought her back to the present and she turned to see what he was referring to.

He looked directly at her.

Kaylin nodded and pulled the slender book out of her satchel. His eyebrows rose in surprise.

"Is that it?"

She waved the book at him. "I told you, it's a ritual."

"I thought it would be a device," he replied.

With a curt nod, she opened the book and flicked through the pages. "There are those too, but I couldn't find where they were kept or even if any are held at the Academy."

"And...you knew this before you challenged me to the duel. Right?"

"There wouldn't have been any point in challenging you if I hadn't," she answered.

"So...you have all the ingredients for the ritual?"

Kaylin gave the boy a look that asked him if he was as stupid as he sounded and his face tightened.

"Of course you did," he answered but sounded more scornful than ever.

She raised an eyebrow. "You can always back out." She waggled the book at him. "If you don't feel you're up to it."

"I could," Sylvester murmured and looked like he had begun to consider it.

For a moment, she simply watched him and wondered if he'd take the bait. She was disappointed to see the slow, mocking smile form on his face.

"But then my side of the bet would be forfeit and I know my people expect more of me than that. You, on the other hand, operate under no such constraints."

Mirielle gasped, but Kaylin laughed. She had begun to get a feel for how the boy operated and mock her as he liked, she had seen the faint rise of color that had stained his cheeks and throat. She smirked.

If he was thin-skinned enough to let a laugh get to him, he wouldn't like it when her spells got through during the battle. And the more she got under his skin, the more likely he was to lose his temper and make a mistake.

Her smile widened and Sylvester glared at her.

"While I'm sure you find yourself very amusing, I have some important business to attend to—"

"What, did some of your Blackbird friends escape the Wardens and need to hide under your skirts?"

His face paled, then reddened, and his fists clenched at his sides. He froze for an instant before he cleared his throat.

"I have nothing to do with those thieves," he snarled.

"So what thieves do you have things to do with?" she asked.

It was almost too much for the boy, and he stepped forward with his hand raised. He might have backhanded her then and there if Stokan hadn't caught his arm.

"Let's not give her any grounds to claim cheating," his friend murmured.

His words echoed through the cellar and he blushed.

"Yes, let's not," Kaylin told them. "I'd rather wipe the floor with you fair and square."

"The only thing you'll wipe the floor with is your tongue," Sylvester snapped. "Now quit stalling and get on with it."

"You'll trust me with setting the ritual up?" Kaylin asked.

"No." He sneered. "I will watch you set it up and then you'll pass the book to me so I can make sure you've done it properly."

Kaylin refused to take any offense. With a shrug, she turned to the circle of floor she'd chosen at the rear of the cellar.

"That's fine by me," she informed him and used magic to light the torch she settled in a sconce.

As it flickered to life, she caught sight of familiar indentations beneath the dust and regretted the haste of her earlier visit to the cellar. What else had she missed?

And more importantly, did Sylvester know of them? Was this why he'd chosen the cellar? Because there were elvish markings on the wall? Did he know how to read them?

She made a note of where they were and dismissed the indentations from her mind. They'd already been there for a very long time and the dust layered over them indicated that they hadn't been disturbed for a couple of years. He probably didn't even know they existed.

If he had, who knew what he would have done? Kaylin shrugged mentally. This wasn't the time to worry about that.

She opened the thin journal in her hands, went over the instructions again, and turned to her opponent.

"Where would you like to stand?" she asked.

"What? Why?"

"Because I need to draw the sigils in the center of the dueling area and to do that, I need to know what space you want to fight in."

The young scion took several paces forward and looked around. To her, it looked like he was checking his position relative to the exits and she wondered why he thought he needed to do that.

"Here," he told her after he took a couple of paces back and checked his line of sight to both doors.

Kaylin nodded and walked to where he stood. He watched warily as she stopped in front of him and took ten careful paces back before she marked her position on the ground.

"What are you doing?"

"I have to start ten paces back from you," she explained and took five paces forward. "Which means the sigils must be drawn here.

"And do I need to draw some of these sigils?" Sylvester demanded.

"You will," she told him, marked the centerline, and extended it across the cellar floor.

He strode forward and snatched the book from her hands. "Let me see that."

With a small shrug, she retrieved the necessary chalks from her pocket. She didn't spare Sylvester another glance as she marked the spacing for each sigil and drew the first one on the floor. Shortly after, he added his first sigil and glanced constantly at the book as he did so.

"You think you're smart, don't you?" He sneered at her when they were finished but Kaylin shook her head.

"If I were smart, I wouldn't be down here dueling you in the first place," she told him. "This has to be about the stupidest thing I've ever done."

"As stupid as trying to rob Shacklemund's?" he asked slyly.

Her eyes widened but she decided not to give him the satisfaction. As far as she knew, not even Magister Roche knew the full details of that particular folly from her past—although Captain Delaine had never promised that would be the case.

Kaylin had merely thought it logical that the Chevaliers wouldn't want it known their latest secondee was a thief. Had she been wrong?

She studied the sigils, then looked at Sylvester. "Are you ready?" she asked.

He glanced at the floor, then at Tessa, Celia, Stokan, and Gram.

"I have to show them the gestures," he told her. "I take it your people have been suitably drilled?"

He turned away when she nodded. She'd made sure Nikolai, Sula, Mirielle, and Nex could create the necessary gestures. They were simple and it hadn't taken any of the young mages long to master them. The same could not be said for his people.

Kaylin waited with her friends while they watched the five go through the movements.

"I didn't think it was that hard," Mirielle whispered, her eyes wide as she saw first Celia, then Stokan fumble through the first one.

"Me neither," Nex muttered.

They fortunately kept their voices low enough that they didn't carry.

Slowly, Sylvester's group gained mastery of the movements.

"You've practiced hard for the last six weeks," she reminded them, "and you're familiar with many of the basic movements we aren't taught. I think it's helping us learn new somatics faster."

"When you're done discussing your secrets..." Sylvester had returned. "Some of us are ready to duel."

Kaylin held her hand out. "I'll need the book," she told him.

His lip curled into a sneer. "And what if I say no?"

"Then you'll prevent the duel from continuing, which would put you in—" She stopped as he shoved the book into her chest. "Thank you."

She opened it to the correct page, studied the words and gestures again carefully, and held it up so he could see it. "Have you got it?"

"Yeah, I've got it. Shall we?"

He gaped at her when she stowed the book in her satchel and secured the flap.

"You mean...you don't need it?" he asked.

Kaylin met his gaze. "I need it," she told him, "but only to return it to the library on time."

"The...the library?" he asked in a strangled whisper. "Do they know you're studying dueling?"

"No," she told him and allowed herself a small smile. "If you have a close look, the section on dueling is a very small portion of the chapter on cooperative magic, which is a subject for next semester. They probably think I'm reading ahead."

"But, but..." Sylvester sputtered.

She gestured toward the sigils. "Shall we?"

Without waiting for an answer, she moved around him and took her place at the center of the line she'd drawn. He came to join her and stepped carefully over the chalk marks to stand opposite. Their eight assistants moved forward to stand four in a row behind each of them.

"Ready?" she asked, and a murmur of assent greeted her, even though Sylvester rolled his eyes. "On the count of three. One..."

She raised her hands, ready to create the first gesture.

"Two."

Opposite her, Sylvester mirrored her movements and the four apprentices behind him did the same. She tried to not wonder what her people were doing and pushed all thought aside as she prepared herself for the sequence to come.

"Three."

Their hands moved almost in unison but the slight dissonance wasn't enough to upset the magic. It was almost as if the person who'd designed the spell had created it with student mages in mind and that made her wonder what its origins were.

Had it been used as some kind of teaching tool in the past?

If so, that would explain why it was in a basic text for cooperative magic, but if it was, what was its purpose?

The air shimmered as she completed the first gesture and uttered the second verbal component. Sylvester's voice was clear but his features began to blur as though a mist rose between them.

As they completed the third combination of gesture and verbal component, the boy faded almost completely from view, and not because they both took the requisite five paces back to reach their respective starting points.

By the time they spoke the fourth word and made the fourth gesture, all she could see of the young mage were his hands as they made the required movements. Once it was completed, they vanished and so did everyone else.

It was like standing on a small island surrounded by mist, and Kaylin couldn't help glancing around in amazement. The instructions had said this was the effect they would have, but to see it was startling.

"Te'embra!" Sylvester's voice cracked through the space, his utterance the component of an unfamiliar spell. His hands were visible momentarily as they slashed through the motions required to harness the magic.

She dropped onto her knees and rolled to move away from her

starting space before the air around it sparkled with a network of lightning. Rather than think, she drew on the first spell that came to mind and pulled moisture from the air until myriad water droplets filled the space he should have occupied.

In the next moment, he surprised her when his hands appeared opposite her.

"Shost!" The word seemed to crackle and a glowing ball swept toward her.

Kaylin flattened herself on the floor.

"Barda!" she snapped as the projectile swept over her.

Colored light flashed and danced as she bounded to her feet and took two large steps to the right.

"Tonal!"

A soft boom of thunder followed at floor level but she was already casting.

"Kep!" she called and fire bloomed a little to the left of where she'd seen his hand.

"Firisk!" His response came as she stepped sideways and back.

"Tonal! Barda! Te'embra! Shost!" she cried in rapid succession.

"Avark, bostila te'embra, ka'arna!" he retaliated and she was torn between watching his hands to learn the ones she didn't know or moving.

This time, she chose to go left, then again, and finally, to crab forward quickly. A glowing ball of flame spun circles in the space she'd occupied. She thought Sylvester's voice sounded a little ragged and his syllables not as crisp as they had before, almost like he was in pain or out of breath.

"Te'embra, te'embra, te'embra. *Bardatonal!*" she shouted and lit the mist opposite with small displays of lightning over the three spaces she thought it most likely he would move to. The last combination was called the second she saw his hands fumble through the beginning of another series of gestures.

The hands vanished, and Kaylin drew another breath. She was about to repeat the lightning sequence when she saw Sylvester's hands.

"Avark!" he bellowed and fire appeared before her. "Avark, avark, avark. Tonal. Barda!"

"Helda, helda helda, slura," she replied but didn't bother to move as the fire arced into her space.

It didn't reach her, though, as the shield spell she'd learned and then taught so her people could protect themselves from the magisters' pets came in handy. Three fireballs cracked into the shields, while the first met the element of water and both spells imploded with a soft hiss.

"Tookro!" followed, but she was already in motion.

A mailed fist came into being and hammered on one of her shields, then into the space where she'd been. It was followed by three more. Each destroyed another shield before they battered in different directions.

One headed toward her and Kaylin took a single step back to let it pass.

Silence followed the attack as she tried to decide what to do next. The trick was to predict where Sylvester would move to and attack him with another spell—one that would knock him to his knees or make it hard for him to cast.

That would mean making it difficult to speak. Kaylin smiled. It might have been a little while since she'd seen him—or he, her—but that didn't mean she couldn't make the next spell count. She assumed he was probably waiting for her to cast so he knew where to target but that didn't matter.

She needed him to cast so she could see where to aim but to do that, she'd have to cast first, which would mean he'd know exactly where she was. Somehow, she needed to think of a way that would let her put him off-balance and maybe force him into making a mistake.

"Sluraheld," she murmured and water cascaded into her space and moved away from her to coalesce into a watery veil between her and her surroundings.

As expected, Sylvester's hands appeared and slashed through a familiar sequence, then ended in one of the new ones.

"Te'embrakarna!" he snapped and lightning danced up and down the outside of her shield before it pounded into it and tried to spin through the space.

I'll give him this, Kaylin thought. *The boy's a quick study.*

Until that moment, she hadn't seen anyone else combine the simpler charms except herself.

That didn't matter, though. Now, she knew where he was and the next trick she had was something she'd bet he hadn't seen, given that the only time she'd seen it had been on the wall downstairs.

"Slurashiel," she said and extended the gesture that designated the area her spell was to affect.

The elven translated very roughly to "watery heart" and caused a mild depression to fall over those in the area targeted. As soon as the gesture was complete, she took the part of it that designated area and slid it into her favorite cantrip.

"Bardafrisk!"

This time, instead of targeting one specific point in the space she thought Sylvester had stepped to, it spread and the colors didn't simply burst into harmless flashes. Frisk was the command for the bedazzlement she had so adeptly shown to Roche.

The sparkling colors filled the same area the sadness had, twinkled benignly into being, and flared in a series of overly bright bursts. Sylvester's answering flurry of fire orbs came in quick succession.

Poorly targeted, they simply flew around her.

"Tookro," followed with a burst of six shining fists and each hammered a different straight line.

"Helda." Kaylin chuckled, brought a shield into play, and used it to deflect two of them from their path. She tried to guesstimate where the rest of Sylvester was based on his hands.

"Shost-tonal!" she ordered and incorporated a stop point and a wider spread into the gestures to give the force orb direction and the boom of sound an area to effect.

She waited long enough to catch a flicker of hand movement and responded with a rapid series of lightning curtains. This spell didn't do much but it stung where it touched skin and made it hard to focus.

She blanketed the area with as many as she could before she saw Sylvester's hands appear.

The second they did, she laid another barda of colored lights over him and followed it with a frisk flash coupled with myrad-shiel or confused heart. Finally, she dropped another slura of water and called, "Te'embra," to bring another curtain of lightning into play.

For a long moment, nothing happened. The mist swirled around her, undisturbed by her opponent's hands or voice, and she hesitated and peered into the shifting white.

"Avark!" The command jolted out of the darkness and Kaylin caught a flicker of flame, but it didn't cross the space between them. It simply flared and died as she drew breath to retaliate.

The next words she heard were as unexpected as they were welcome.

"You win."

She stared in shock as the sigils on the floor flared and died and the mist vanished. Mirielle's happy shriek broke the silence that followed.

"You did it!"

Elation swept through Kaylin but was pushed aside quickly by a sense of apprehension when she saw her opponent crouched on the floor. She started toward him as his four friends noticed his plight and came forward hesitantly.

"Sly…" Stokan began but Sylvester put both palms flat on the floor and pushed to his feet.

Celia was the first one to reach him and caught the boy's arm and pulled it across her shoulders to steady him. Kaylin moved closer and he raised his head, his face a mask of pain and anger.

"What do you want?"

"I'm making sure you're okay," Kaylin told him shortly.

"A likely story," he sneered. "You're here to gloat like everyone else."

He tried to straighten, grunted, and wrapped an arm across his stomach.

"We'll take you to medical," Tessa whispered as she stepped closer to support him from the other side.

"Are you as stupid as you look?" He snarled and directed his anger at the girl. "Medical will ask questions and I don't want to explain how I was in a mage duel—which I shouldn't have to remind you is an *illegal* activity in this school."

"But you're—"

"And Magister has made it very clear that the next one of us to cause her any political discomfort will have a very short career as a mage, has she not?"

Kaylin's jaw dropped. The magister had said that?

"Something not even I am immune to," Sylvester added and glared from Tessa to Stokan and Gram and back again.

She closed her mouth with a snap when he swung toward her.

"And if you think this is anywhere near over," he told her with suppressed fury, "it's not. It's only the beginning."

Shocked, she tensed before she drew herself to her full height. "Don't you remember our terms?" she demanded. "This is very much over. I won, and neither you nor your magister pet friends will do any more bullying. Those were the terms."

Sylvester favored her with a pitying smile. "So they were," he agreed, his voice oily with sarcasm, "but I don't see anyone who can possibly enforce them, do you?"

He stared at her, daring her to contradict the truth, but she smiled.

"You need to read the rest of the chapter," she informed him, "where it says the conditions of the duel must be upheld or the duel-breaker's mark will emerge on the cheeks and forehead of the duelist who breaks the agreement."

"If that happens, I will personally see you take responsibility for your part in this affair," he croaked in response.

"Which will have the same result as if you went and told the magister what you've done, wouldn't it?" she challenged. She tapped the top of the satchel. "Did I also tell you that the duel-breaker's mark appears on the faces of your seconds as well?"

Tessa, Stokan, Gram, and Celia exchanged worried looks.

"Come on, Sly," Stokan urged and took Tessa's place. "Let's get you upstairs. I'll find you some supper."

"And a brandied tea," Tessa offered.

They gathered around Sylvester and Kaylin felt almost jealous. It was fleeting because she immediately felt Mirielle's presence at her side before Nex, Nikolai, and Sula pressed in close. Together, the five of them stood and watched as her opponent was supported to the second set of cellar stairs and guided carefully onto them.

As soon as they were out of sight, she released the breath she hadn't realized she'd been holding and dropped her hands to her knees. Nikolai ruffled her hair.

"That was a hard fight," he commented and she drew a deep breath and straightened.

"You could say that."

"I am," he told her proudly. "You'll have to teach me that trick where you combine two of those cantrips and come up with something...uh..."

"Unique," she finished for him.

"I noticed Sylvester did it too," Sula stated. "Do you think it's something the magisters teach their favorites?"

"Nope," Mirielle told them. "Did you see the look on his face when Kaylin pulled the first one out of her hat? It was like someone had smacked him in the head with a block of wood."

"And then he tried it for himself," Nikolai added. "Whatever else he might be, Sylvester's no slouch when it comes to learning new ways to manipulate magic."

"Yeah." Kaylin sighed. "It's such a shame it's been wasted on an ass."

The others chuckled and Mirielle slapped her on the back.

"Shall we?" Nikolai asked and jerked his chin toward the door. "Do you think it's clear?"

He took a step in the direction of the stairs and held his hand out to Sula as he passed. Kaylin managed a small smile as the girl took it. She was about to agree to go with them when a flash of light caught her eyes so she waved them on instead.

"You guys go ahead," she instructed. "I need to catch my breath."

"I'll stay with her," Mirielle told them when they looked concerned. "We'll let you know as soon as we're clear."

"Well, if you're sure," Nikolai told them. "We'll see you in the dining hall or the common room, whichever you decide to get to."

"Dining hall," Mirielle told him firmly. "I'm starving."

They all laughed at that and the two girls waited while the others left. As soon as they were out of sight on the stairs, she drifted slowly to the farthest corner, seeking the elusive spark of light.

"Kay?" Mirielle asked, and she nodded.

"Yeah, I'm fine."

"I did not mean are you okay," her friend corrected and swatted her on the arm.

She staggered under the weight of the blow and the girl hurried to steady her.

"Liar," she mocked, but Kaylin would not be deterred. She moved on until she reached the faint glimmer on the wall. It was already fading under a patina of dust.

"I missed these the last time I came through here," she murmured, knelt, and traced her fingers over the grooves.

The dust came off to reveal the faint glimmer of another elven mark.

Mirielle made an unintelligible sound and wandered away, but she paid her no mind. She assumed the girl already knew what she was interested in. Whether or not she stuck around to help her uncover them was another matter.

Supper was on the line after all.

Despite her thoughts, Kaylin continued to wipe the dust off the markings.

"You know that's disgusting, don't you?" Mirielle asked and nudged her with the bristled end of a broom.

"Where did you get that?" Kaylin asked.

"Well, duh. It is a storage cellar. Someone has to clean it. Ergo..." She poked her with the end of the broom again.

This time, she grasped it above the bristles and jerked it out of her hands.

"Fine. Thank you for the broom."

"You're welcome," Mirielle retorted mockingly and hefted another broom. "Now show me where you want me to sweep."

"You see these indentations here?"

The girl nodded and studied the sections of the wall on either side.

"It looks like it's only this corner," she said, and they set to work. It didn't take them long to get the dust cleared.

"Woah!" Mirielle breathed. "You sure know how to stop a party."

"I'm very sure that wasn't me," Kaylin told her. "The only traces of stray magic that came in this direction were from our very good Apprentice Ozanne."

"Yeah, but I won't tell him that, will you?"

"No." Kaylin chuckled and set her broom aside.

She took the torch out of its bracket and brought it close to where the sigils gave way to pictographs.

"Do you see this?" she asked.

Mirielle came closer to study what she saw.

"These are very similar to sparkles," she said and named the spell by what it was called in the textbook but repeated its verbal component, barda. "And look what you can make it do," she murmured and took her journal from her satchel.

The other girl sighed. "Do you want me to get supper and bring it down here?" she asked. "We could make it a picnic."

She shook her head. "This shouldn't take too long."

Her friend snorted. "Famous last words."

Kaylin smiled at her friend's skepticism, turned to the wall, and copied the sequences as quickly as she could. What she wanted to do was start working through the gestures and verbal components, but she didn't dare.

If Sylvester came back or if one of the magisters learned of the duel, what she'd found would be immediately visible to them.

Torn between speed and accuracy, she tried to write faster.

Mirielle turned her attention to the story in the border, which displayed the path of discovery and teaching like the walls in the chamber below. The two of them remained silent for some time before the other girl gasped.

"Oh!"

Kaylin raised her head. "I'm almost done," she reassured her friend.

"No. It's not that. It's... There's something under the carvings we can see."

"What?" She stood and brushed her knees off as her companion pointed to the area that had caught her eye.

Faint traces of light limned the ridges of each carving and made the images stand out, but more than that, another picture appeared to shimmer below the stone. She tried to touch it but her finger stopped on the wall's surface, while the picture continued beneath it.

"That's... Does that look like a library to you?" she asked.

Mirielle nodded, her eyes shining with excitement. "And that looks like the tower."

She nodded. The tower housing the Academy's library stood behind the grotto and rose above the gardens, while the Academy's walls hemmed the gardens' edge.

"No wonder it takes us so long to get there," Kaylin muttered when she considered the distance she had to trek to visit the tower. Seeing it only made that distance more obvious. She'd heard there was more of the citadel beyond the wall and that the tower was central, but the students didn't go there and she hadn't found an entry to it.

It seemed logical that there was something to be found in the outer section—the one between the Academy walls and the outer walls of the citadel itself—and that area was the domain of the Chevaliers. Some days, she wondered what went on in the other side but most days, she was too busy studying to even think about it.

Now, though, she wondered if more carvings might be found—more learning areas—and if the underground reaches of the Academy bypassed the tower and the walls. If they did, what other secrets could be hiding in the citadel's depths?

"Now why didn't we think of that?" she muttered and glanced at the newly revealed spells, then at the underlying picture. She wasn't sure what she was looking for, only that she'd know it when she saw it.

Mirielle watched her work and shook her head.

"You know you'll have to teach me how you do that," she stated, and Kaylin nodded.

She tried a spell devised to reveal hidden objects but tweaked the gestures so they related to images. Although she wasn't sure what the movement was for messages, given that most of what was on the wall was picture, it was worth a try.

The image shuddered.

"Do it again," Mirielle urged, her eyes wide. "I think I can see it."

Kaylin glanced at her friend, then at the picture, and saw nothing significant. It made her glad the girl was with her. She had more sense of story than she did, so maybe she'd pick up what the images meant.

Obeying her friend's instruction, she cast the spell again. This time, she focused on having the pictures reveal their secrets rather than wondering what the effect would be and obeyed the faint traces of pressure on her hands and arms as she made the gestures. It was like her intent altered the nature of the spell and the magic tried to show her the changes she needed to make to achieve it.

As she completed the gestures, the images moved and slid into each other with a shudder that made the library settle into the tower and disappear. She frowned and tried to determine which point it had vanished into.

"Now what?" she asked but Mirielle clapped her hands.

"You've got to be kidding me," she cried.

"What?" Kaylin demanded, exasperated.

"They hid it above where our library is now."

"Seriously?"

"Yup," her friend answered and her eyes sparkled with delight.

She started to laugh and Kaylin joined her before she turned away from the picture to study the walls around her. A flash of movement beyond the shelves closest to the stairwell caught her eye and she stared.

"That's—" she began but Mirielle sprinted past her.

"I'll get him!" she cried. "You need to find it and save what you can before they get to it."

Her friend was gone before she could protest.

For a few heartbeats, Kaylin stood frozen before the words sank in and she began to run—not to the stairwell where the girl had pursued Sylvester's spy but down through the hidden door to the Teaching Room. From there, she raced through the walls to the deserted upper corridors where her footsteps wouldn't attract any attention.

She had to get to the library—the elven library—and she had to do it before any of the magisters caught wind of her success.

CHAPTER EIGHTEEN

It was late. Kaylin hadn't realized how long she'd taken to copy the drawings and then work out the magic required to reveal the hidden meaning of the wall. She only saw it when she passed an old clock in the corridor and saw the time.

So late—how did it get to be so late?

At least it explained the tiredness she felt. She'd had a long day of classes, fought a mage duel, deciphered another wall, and learned some new spells that she'd cast to reveal an illusion hidden in the wall.

She bolted to the end of the wing and then darted quietly to the magisters' floor on the assumption she'd be far less likely to be seen traveling those corridors than if she tried to use the student and classroom levels. Besides, it wouldn't be for long. There must surely be another set of stairs leading up sooner or later.

The hallway was deserted and she moved quickly and cautiously over the thick runners on the floor and used the skills she'd learned on the streets of Waypoint. She also pulled a mist of magic around her, a simple spell that would blur her presence and trick the eye of a casual observer.

While she wasn't sure how it would work with magisters, they were mostly human and it was late and humans, whether they were magisters or not, didn't function too well this late at night. She stifled a yawn. Hells deep, she didn't operate too well this late at night—not like she'd used to.

Despite her weariness and the late hour, she was able to draw on the reserves she'd had as a thief. She moved silently down the halls, listened into the dark, and stepped into alcoves or crouched in the shadows near the walls when she heard a door open ahead or behind her. The magisters were more active than she'd expected.

Three walked into the room of a fourth, their voices raised in greeting as they closed the door behind them. As soon as the corridor was quiet again, she moved swiftly past the room, not at all tempted to listen to the lively conversation happening within.

Another time, perhaps, she thought and wondered if there would truly be an advantage in learning their secrets this way.

I'm sure Mirielle could come up with something.

Kaylin heard footsteps in a stairwell when she reached the corner where the building turned to run parallel with the outer walls and knew she still had two-thirds of the distance to go. With only seconds to spare, she slid into another alcove, pulled the hood of her cloak low over her face, and lowered her head to watch them pass.

She couldn't recognize either of them from the hems of their vermilion robes or the brief flashes of their boots but she was relieved when they kept walking and shifted slightly to watch them vanish into two separate rooms.

As soon as the hallway was clear, she checked the corridor around the corner and hurried swiftly along it. The farther she went, the quieter it became. Some of the doors looked like they needed a fresh coat of paint and the tapestries and pictures that hung on the wall had cobwebs in the corners.

Don't any of them live this far along? she asked herself and stopped when she noticed a set of stairs that climbed up as well as down. Despite her earlier hopes, she hadn't been able to find anything beyond stairs that ended with the landing to this floor. Now, she regarded the ascending stairs with suspicion.

I have nothing to lose, she decided after she'd worked out the odds of the floor above leading directly to the library or if she'd be better off following the magister's level a little farther. *Let's hope the entrance isn't from the library.*

The corridor above led to another blank stone wall.

Kaylin stared at it, shook her head in disbelief, and retraced her steps. She didn't return to the magister's floor or stop on the dormitory one but descended to the classroom level and hurried along the deserted corridors. A sense of urgency pressed in around her but the late hour worked in her favor and she soon stood in front of the library's double doors.

After a glance over her shoulder, she pushed through the doors and hoped the librarians didn't work all hours and that she didn't meet anyone sneaking out after a late night of study. She knew some of the seniors worked long hours, especially those without a magister's favor.

To her relief, the library foyer was as empty as the corridor behind her. She moved immediately to a shadowed corner where she closed her eyes and tried to picture the image she'd seen in the cellar. When she had as much of it fixed in her mind as possible, she opened her eyes and raised her head, and her heart sank when she realized where she had to go.

"I wonder if it's locked," she muttered and moved swiftly to the door leading to the librarian's office. It was, but she'd long since mastered the simple cantrip for opening most locks. It was a much simpler spell than those she'd needed for deactivating the sigils outside Shacklemund's.

With another furtive glance behind her, she pulled the door wide enough to slip inside and closed it carefully after her. The librarian's office was more a communal room with three or four private spaces at the back.

Kaylin walked through it quietly and looked for any sign that someone had decided to work late. She had no idea how much time Mirielle's pursuit of the spy had bought her so she moved quickly to the back offices and sighed when she discovered a narrow corridor to one side that led to a storeroom.

"Now, if I were an ancient elven wizard," she murmured, "where would I hide a secret passage leading to a hidden level?"

It didn't take her long to rule out the three offices, since the only one with a broad enough wall had a window set in that wall to show a view of the gardens.

"That's too narrow for a passage," she concluded and tried her new spell for revealing things hidden. She aimed it at the rear wall and came up with nothing but plain stonework.

The spell made short work of her search through the other two offices. The only things hidden that she revealed were part of the desk and a wall cabinet, and she didn't have time to investigate any of the four compartments that glowed briefly.

Another time, maybe, she promised herself, not at all sure that she'd ever find the need.

With only the corridor and the storage area left, Kaylin moved swiftly through the narrow passage. Her heart sank when she saw that the space it led to was almost as large as the library itself. Rather than waste time in the most easily accessible parts of the room, she hurried to the back and tried to relate where she was with where she thought the thickest walls might be.

She stopped about halfway down and threw the first seek hidden spell.

The attempt brought no result, not even when she moved it higher, lower, or close to the floor.

"Weird," she muttered and noticed that the stonework there wasn't the pristine white the Academy's new occupants had chosen but more of the gray and red blocks found in the basement and older parts of the garden.

Maybe there was a section of wall with more of the older stone. It wasn't like she'd find a secret tunnel to an elven library in areas of new construction. If that were the case, the stone would have to reach the ceiling and if it didn't, it wouldn't matter if the passage was there or not.

The new work would mean the magisters had found the library and plundered it already.

With that in mind, Kaylin conjured a small ball of light and floated it to the ceiling. She moved deeper into the room, keeping the orb close to the wall while she looked for an area where the gray and red blocks rose uninterrupted to the ceiling. It felt like an age before she found it and even then, it was only the narrowest strip of wall. The rest was concealed behind the floor-to-ceiling high stacks of books.

Why aren't these on the shelves? Kaylin wondered and fought the temptation to inspect the stored titles more closely. Instead, she moved to the wall and cast her show hidden images spell.

The sudden gleam of pictographs and elvish runes startled her.

"Oh..." she murmured, studied the carvings, and caught a secondary shimmer beneath them. "Well..."

This time, she chose show hidden messages and was surprised by the ripple of golden light that flowed over the images in the stone. The carvings faded and a series of sigils rose to take their place—or perhaps the carvings sank and the sigils came to the surface. She couldn't decide which.

They were both new and not. Kaylin recognized most of them from the Teaching Room and portions of the others were related.

"What were you trying to tell us?" she mused. "Who were you hiding your library for?"

The sigils didn't reply but she hadn't expected them to. Instead, she drew her journal out and sketched them quickly in the order they had appeared on the wall rather than the order in which they were written. That made much more sense.

They'd appeared in a way that demanded the reader prove themselves.

"How..." She muttered and moved from the sigil that made the demand to the next. "Oh..."

With a frown, she moved on to the next one.

"Well, yes, I can do that...I think."

She copied the others and stepped out of the niche before she turned to face the sigils and their silent demands.

"I can show you an understanding of the three dimensions," she informed them softly. "Whether that understanding is enough...well, that is for you to decide."

Of course, they did not reply but she didn't let that deter her. Instead, she took the first dimension.

"Experience," she announced quietly. "I don't have much of it but such as it is, I share with you."

Kaylin knew this kind of magic was as much about intent as about spell work, so she focused on the events that had made up her life thus far.

"Community," she told them, "can be found in the lowest walks of life."

She drew on her experiences with the crew, their shared meals and dangers, and their shared dreams.

"And it can be found at higher levels, too," she continued and pulled in the memories of her time at the Academy and the loneliness of being an outcast. These were followed by the community of need she'd founded in which she and the other bullied apprentices had drawn together to learn from and teach each other.

The first sigil filled from the bottom up and shifted from emerald to gold as she finished the gestures that represented community, need, and mutual assistance. She gave it a brief smile, then moved to the next one.

"Logic," she told the sigil and saw the brief flare of light that acknowledged her choice, "and how experience feeds it."

It flashed again and she inclined her head toward it as though it could see the action and cared.

"This then," she told it, "is the logic of the situation in which we find ourselves."

She made the movements for teacher, neglect, and the lost and fed the intent of showing the logical consequences of her experiences interlinked with those of her fellow students. Experience had shown her that when people in power neglected their responsibility to care for others entrusted to them, those neglected by them could either fall or fight.

She filled her intent with memories of the students finding a way to care for themselves and each other's needs and used the gestures for mutual support, to search, elven, ancient, and knowledge to represent their activities over the last few months. She added pain, harm, self-taught, and healing.

After a moment's thought, she threw in fear and another mutual support when she considered how she and the others had sought the elven texts so they could teach themselves when the magisters refused to do so despite the fact that it was their sworn duty. She thought of how their neglect had led their students to replace them with the texts they needed to complete their education and watched the sigil fill from blue to silver and finally settle to gold.

The third sigil wanted more. It wanted the link between logic and emotion. The one above it wanted the link between emotion and experience, and the one positioned outside them so its midpoint sat where the two sigils met wanted the emotion itself.

Kaylin took a deep breath. Emotion had always been her strongest dimension but she was thankful for the way the last few months had taught her to temper it with the other two. Now, she had a chance to answer the riddle correctly.

She drew on the emotions of loss and hopelessness from her first days at the orphanage. From there, she built into it the rebellion and resentment she had felt when Sister Nadiya had seemed to dictate the path she should tread with no concern for her desires. Finally, she added the determination to succeed on her own.

Those threads were easily woven into the determination she'd felt to protect her friends after the failure of their raid on Shacklemund's. They built naturally into the logic of her helping her fellow students to master their courses despite the magisters' neglect and blatant favoritism. Memories of that unfair treatment fed the feeling of frustration she felt at being compelled to learn this way and see others forced to do the same.

"They deserve so much better," she told the sigils. "I am no magister. None of us are. Together, we do our best but what if our best is not enough? It is our experience that gives us the ability to push on. The logic that we can do it if we must drives us toward our goal, both in spite of and because of our emotions. Our frustration feeds our determination and defiance."

The third, fourth, and fifth sigils gleamed amber and raced quickly to gold before they shifted to join into a single loop that slid to overlap and intertwine with the other two. Finally, the three interlinked with a potent snap and a pictogram formed in the center of each before another series appeared where they interlinked.

Kaylin studied them and a tiny laugh escaped her.

"As you command," she told the wall when she recognized the pictograms and the order in which they needed to be performed.

She gave the circlet a tiny bow, moved through the gestures it asked for, and pronounced the elven word for each as she went. They flowed together and magic swept out of the pattern and past her to the center of the room, where it spiraled upward in a shimmer of silver.

Her mouth agape, she could only stare as it swept to the ceiling and lit another series of sigils she hadn't noticed.

And why would I? she thought as the patterns illuminated and ceiling stones separated soundlessly before they extended into a stairway that floated to the doorway newly formed at its top.

Kaylin gasped.

She had found the library.

CHAPTER NINETEEN

Kaylin approached the stairs slowly. They hung with no apparent support but looked as solid as the walls around her, although limned in a faint blue aura. She glanced at the door, then stepped onto the first step and rested a trembling hand on the balustrade.

When nothing happened, she took a second step and then another and her heart beat faster with excitement. It looked like she was the first to find the library and decipher the runes on the wall. Mirielle must have caught up with the spy and delayed them.

Not sure how long her reprieve would last, she rushed up the last few steps and came to an abrupt halt before the door. It was made from a rich, dark-brown timber reinforced with metal bands that shone black against the surface. The handle was also black.

Not sure what to expect, she placed her hand tentatively on the handle and gave it a firm twist. It turned easily in her hand and the locking mechanism responded smoothly. The door swung open on silent hinges and she stepped into the cavernous space beyond.

It was empty except for the dust and a few tattered cobwebs.

A little disbelieving, Kaylin took several steps into the room and pivoted to inspect her surroundings.

Massive stone shelves stretched from floor to ceiling to form hollow columns and broken corridors. The same stone shelves lined the walls as well. Dust lay in a thin layer of gray over everything like a drifting shroud.

The cobwebs waved in the breeze created by the door opening but nothing scuttled over them.

Her footsteps echoed hollowly as she crossed the floor. She turned her head to look in all directions for the wealth of knowledge that should have been there—the books and scrolls that should have filled each shelf with learning—and her heart sank with every step.

Slowly, she moved through the empty aisles and wanted to weep with disappointment, and rage at the unfairness of having solved the riddle and found no prize. Not willing to believe their search had been in vain, she refused to give up and eventually, she stood somewhere in the center and stared at a dozen volumes arrayed on a shelf.

Unable to believe her eyes, she approached them and stared hungrily at the elvish script written on each spine. She recognized some of the characters but not others. They made her realize how much she had yet to learn and she wondered why these, of all those that must have been there, had been left.

That reason became all too clear once she was close enough to drift an orb of light across them.

The books were old as she'd expected, but what she'd not expected was for them to look like they would crumble to dust the second they were touched. With bated breath, she stretched a finger out, poked one, and almost sobbed with relief when it held together.

Kaylin withdrew her finger, blew on the tome, and extracted it from the others slowly and carefully. She held her breath as she opened it gently. It was everything she had hoped for. The elvish script was mostly clear, even if the pages were yellowed and stained, and the diagrams were undamaged.

She closed it carefully and slipped it into her satchel.

The next book was in much the same condition but seemed to be less about magic and more about weather cycles and plants. Sometime in the past, it had suffered water damage and the ink was blurred and smudged in places. It wasn't so much that the entire book was a loss but sufficient that it would take time to determine whether it contained anything they wanted.

With a frown, she slid it onto the shelf and looked around. There must surely be more in there than what she'd found

Kaylin turned away from the shelf and looked around the chamber.

There must be more.

With a sigh, she moved toward the nearest wall, glad to see it was made of the same red and gray stone that denoted the older parts of the citadel. Maybe this wasn't the library in the inscription and there was another secret chamber where the books were kept.

She wove another spell, asked it to reveal what was hidden, and this time, she held it. She'd finished inspecting one area and moved the spell to another section of the wall when a voice interrupted her concentration.

"It is disheartening, isn't it?" Magister Roche asked.

His words made her gasp and she dropped the spell. He noticed the lapse and tutted quietly, but his gaze roved over the shelves as he continued. "How much we've lost."

He sounded almost as disappointed as she felt and she turned toward him.

"Where did it go?" she asked when the shock of being caught faded enough for her to focus on the most important question. After all, there was nothing she could do now. "What happened?"

"We don't know." The magister shook his head sadly. "It was almost all gone by the time the mercenaries cleared the citadel, well before the Academy was first established." He gestured at the central shelf with its pathetic collection. "What you see here is the sum of the magical knowledge upon which the Academy is founded."

Kaylin ran her gaze over the collection of worn and ratty tomes. "That's it?" she asked, horrified by the thought. "That's all of them?"

"Well, we've certainly taken and expanded the theorems and built on the principles, but yes, our basic conceptions of magic all start here."

"You knew?" she asked, meaning not only the elven concepts of magic but the library itself.

"Oh, yes," Roche assured her and his words rolled confidently around her. "We knew. How else do you think we can control the knowledge? Even with what we held back, we were able to produce students whose magical capabilities were far greater than most others in the kingdom."

"But what about when they left?" she asked.

"We made them swear to not teach others what we had taught them and warned them of the dire consequences that would follow if they did. Most were more than happy to comply." He cocked his head. "I'm not sure we could have the same assurance about you, could we?"

"But why would you forbid them from teaching other mages to be better at their art?" Kaylin was aghast. "Why wouldn't you want Academy mages known for being able to improve the skills of those they work with?"

Again, Roche tutted. "My dear, you are far too idealistic and naïve. If we did as you suggested, why would anyone want to come to us to learn? All they'd have to do would be to take their secrets from our students and we couldn't have that, could we?"

"But what is the value of an education you can't share?" She couldn't understand, no matter how much she wrestled with it.

"Patronage, dear girl," he told her. "We give our students the skills to excel beyond the walls of the Academy and any new knowledge we might gain, and we give them the support they need to achieve their goals as their careers progress."

"You bribe people to do what they want," she exclaimed.

Roche gave her a condescending smile. "My dear, we do more than that."

"What? All of you?" Kaylin asked and the smile broadened.

"Of course, dear. This would hardly work if some of us disagreed with the procedure, now would it?"

Magic vibrated around her and she pivoted, surprised when the air glimmered around the end of one of the bookcases. It settled to silver and Magister Wanslow appeared, his face set in disapproving lines.

The next bookcase over shivered with light and Magister Theobold came into view.

"What—" Kaylin began and Roche's expression filled with pity.

"We don't do these things alone, Apprentice. When action must be taken, we act as one to secure our victory."

Alarmed, she looked from one to the other, then along the bookcase ends surrounding her as one after another, the magisters dropped the veils of invisibility they'd waited under. When she looked at their stern faces, she felt a rush of fear.

Now that Roche had revealed so much of their power and their plans, there was no way they would let her... She paused. Let her what? Stay? Leave?

Live?

As if he read her mind or perhaps the sudden pallor of her face, her magister continued.

"And therein lies the pity," he told her, his voice a little sad. "We use the knowledge in these tomes to maintain our power base and leverage the cooperation of others in power both within and without the Academy, which I am sure you'd have worked out."

He sighed and gave her a sorrowful look before he continued.

"As I'm sure you've now deduced, we cannot let you return to the student population with what you've discovered. You'll have to be removed, I'm afraid."

"What..." she asked softly around a lump in her throat. "What do you mean?"

"I mean your education is at an end," Roche told her.

Kaylin pivoted, intending to hide amongst the shelves and move to the door.

She managed two steps as the magisters cast the spells they'd prepared while Roche had held her attention. A moment later, she registered the impact of the first two spells and was out before she fell.

Kaylin woke to the rumble of wheels. Her body swayed with the movement of the surface she was seated on and her head ached. She opened her eyes slowly and discovered she was not alone.

It took her a few heartbeats to work out she was in a carriage and a few heartbeats more to make out the features of the magister sitting in the opposite corner. She hadn't met Hadrienne Gaudin in person and had never been this close to her before.

She wriggled and tried to straighten from the slumped position in which she'd woken, and the magister tilted her head.

"So you're awake."

It was a statement and not a question, so she didn't bother to answer. Her feet felt heavy and she registered the metal bands that weighed heavily on each wrist. As she shifted, chains rattled but that wasn't the worst of it.

Her mouth was dry and blocked. Kaylin tried to work her jaw and tasted metal. More pressed her lips against her teeth and held her tongue down. Panicked, she tried to raise her hands but they were stopped short by a jerk of the chain that vibrated the chains at her bare feet.

Where were her boots?

"I'd sit still were I you," the magister advised and her gaze remained fixed on her face until she stilled.

A chill raced through the girl as she returned the mage's stare and fought to bring her breathing back under control. Oblivious to the struggle within, the coach continued and she knew with a sinking heart that it wasn't taking her anywhere good.

The magister watched her for a little longer before she stretched across the space between them.

Kaylin flinched instinctively and the woman responded with a small, tight smile.

"Lean forward," she instructed and after a moment's hesitation, the girl complied.

The jangle of keys was followed by the release of the pressure that banded her skull and the gag over her head was removed. Gaudin set it to one side and leaned back.

"Roche begged for your life," she said with casual disdain, "and we have agreed to grant him his request." She paused and studied her prisoner with hard, cold eyes. "I hope you throw all that groveling away by being foolish enough to try to escape."

Despite the faint hopefulness in the woman's voice, Kaylin knew better than to make the attempt. She didn't have a hope of getting out of the carriage while she was shackled and chained and as tempting as it was to try to scorch the sneer off the magister's face, she knew the woman was waiting for her to try.

After all, she only needed one excuse.

"I think you're all overreacting," she replied and the magister's eyes widened. Unperturbed, she continued. "I don't understand what all the fuss is about. Why all the favorites? Why share the knowledge with some and not others?"

She leaned back in her seat and would have folded her arms across her chest if she hadn't been chained. "I don't understand why you can't let others learn from the books. It's not like you have anything to lose."

Gaudin's eyebrows rose in surprise, although she suspected that had more to with being addressed in such a way by a student and less to do with what she'd said. She watched the magister's face and decided it was a shame that one so beautiful and talented could be so narrow-minded and cruel.

"I don't even think the library is truly gone," she added and startled the woman again. "I think if you all stopped squabbling long enough to look for it, either in the Academy or anywhere else the elves used to be, you'd have a real chance to recover much of what's been lost."

Gaudin gave a startled laugh. "Do you honestly believe that?" she demanded.

Kaylin nodded. "Yes. I believe there's a wealth of knowledge waiting to be found."

"And you think the magisters are the ones to find it," the woman concluded.

She shrugged. "If you were truly interested in building the Academy and developing its students' abilities then yes, I do."

"It sounds like considerable work for something that doesn't get me any closer to what I want," the magister retorted with a scornful laugh.

Her words reminded the girl of something she'd heard in Waypoint, only it had come from someone talking about members of the Waypoint underworld.

They only look out for themselves.

She sighed, and Gaudin's laughter died. When the woman spoke again, her voice was more serious than she'd yet heard.

"I suppose you're wondering what we plan to do with you." Kaylin nodded and curled her fingers around her knees. Gaudin noticed the movement and her mouth twitched. "Spell's End," she told her.

She said it in such a way that the name was supposed to mean something, but she had never heard it before. The magister caught her lack of understanding and frowned.

"Spell's End," she repeated. "Surely you've heard of it?" The woman sighed when she shook her head. "Not that it matters," she said, "but it's a correctional facility for wayward wizards."

Apprehension formed a dull weight in her chest while she waited. Gaudin read the expression on her face and her mouth twitched into a fleeting smile that vanished as she continued.

"Once you are there, the wardens will move through your mind, cleanse it of its ability to cast magic, and remove any memory of the spells you have learned or any other knowledge you might have gained pertaining to the art."

Kaylin's jaw dropped but the magister didn't seem to notice.

"Or until they've managed to turn your very fine mind to mush." She tutted. "I'm not sure why Roche pleaded for your life when death would have been more of a mercy but there you have it."

The young apprentice closed her mouth, frozen by the sheer barbarity of what she had heard.

Again, the magister read her expression and this time, her smile was full of satisfied mockery. She lifted the gag and slipped it over

Kaylin's head, tightened it with deft familiarity, and patted her cheek.

"Spend these last few hours," Gaudin told her as she settled into her seat, "with the understanding that soon, everything you worked so hard for will be gone forever and you won't remember it at all."

CHAPTER TWENTY

Kaylin kept her eyes closed. Firstly, she didn't want to look at the magister or the interior of the coach and be reminded of what was going to happen and secondly, she didn't want Gaudin to see her cry.

The thought of losing her magic was unbearable.

She pressed her lips together and tried to find something else to focus on. The rumble of the coach wheels was a constant but with the blinds drawn, she couldn't even look out to watch the country passing by. She didn't know if Spell's End was inside or outside Waypoint or if the Chevaliers would know what had happened to her.

And what would happen when they discovered she'd vanished from the Academy? What would they be told? Would the magisters simply say she'd run away? If so, what would happen to her friends?

After a while, she opened her eyes and considered asking the magister to...what? The thought gave her pause. Gaudin had already made it clear that Roche had begged for her life and they'd decided to turn her brain to mush instead. What would they do to her friends?

Would they believe them ignorant of what she knew? And what would they do to Goss if they discovered he also had an aptitude for magic?

Kaylin closed her eyes and her mouth and decided it was better for her to risk the Chevaliers' mercy and that maybe—somehow—they would learn that she'd been sent away in disgrace and not fled. Failing that, she would have to think of a way out of the coach and hope she could reach Waypoint and the Chevalier Chapter House in time to save her friends.

Tears threatened to rise and she squeezed her eyes shut, hoping to cut the flow off before Gaudin had the satisfaction of seeing it. The mage would never understand that she wasn't crying for herself but for the fate of her friends.

Perhaps it would be better if she focused on the sound of the wheels, after all.

Their rumble was almost soothing as long as she didn't think of where it was taking her.

It was also surprisingly loud too. She focused on that and tried to hear the sound of the horses pulling it as she imagined the jingle of harnesses and the clatter of shoes on stone.

Was the road dirt or stone? And why was everything slightly muffled?

Aside from the winding trail to the Academy, there was only one road she knew of and it ran north to south from the Doom to Waypoint. She couldn't tell which direction the coach was moving in. The road to the Academy was cobbled through the foothills and up to the school, but the road to the Doom was hard-packed earth.

So which one was she on? Dirt or stone?

Kaylin listened harder and tried to discern the difference, but all she became aware of was a faint hissing sound as if the wheels were brushing against something.

The rumble and hiss grew louder but the sound of hoofbeats became clearer. She frowned when she realized that many horses were pulling the coach and more seemed to be moving closer.

How was that possible? Now that she was attuned to it, she thought she could hear hoofbeats approach from behind and move around the coach.

Since when were coaches pulled by horses on either side?

As she dismissed the thought as ridiculous, Magister Gaudin gave an exclamation of annoyance.

"By the gods, what is it this time?"

As she spoke, the coachman called soothingly to the horses and the conveyance came to a juddering halt. She opened her eyes but Magister Gaudin had already unlatched the door and kicked it open.

The woman didn't look back as she stepped out. Snow crunched under her feet as she landed.

Well, that explains the hissing.

"What," the magister began, "is the meaning of this?"

A murmured response greeted her as the carriage door swung closed, but the girl caught a glimpse of milling horses and a flash of blue.

An apprentice from the Academy?

Kaylin frowned. She hadn't known any of them could ride—or who would be allowed to if they could.

Voices rose in anger beyond the carriage door, the magister's one of them, but the others were too indistinct and not loud enough for recognition. Whoever it was, they had the woman's attention and had certainly earned her ire.

She wondered if now was the time to stage an escape and swiveled to nudge the door closest to her. It was no surprise to find it locked. With a sigh, she swiveled to face the opposite wall.

Maybe she could hear what was going on if she worked at it.

The spell to amplify sound was beyond her, so she concentrated on using the ears she'd been born with. It didn't help much, though, and all she could do was hope it was someone who'd been sent to investigate the coach and that they'd get around to opening the door soon.

A heated conversation continued for several minutes more and Gaudin spoke less as another voice continued to speak even more forcefully to her. Kaylin wondered who it was and if they realized what kind of trouble they were bringing down on themselves. Despite this, she waited and tried to disregard the hope that pushed through resolutely.

The voices stopped and the carriage door was flung open abruptly, the figure coming through it dressed in chain mail. Kaylin startled, and the figure lifted its head and cursed softly when it saw her.

"Orc's teeth, girl! What have you gotten yourself into this time?"

As if the magisters being selfish troll toads was anywhere near her fault.

Kaylin tried to glower at the knight but couldn't. She was too busy trying not to burst into tears at the sight of her. Captain Delaine took one look at her, spoke a single word, and snapped her fingers as she did so.

The shackles fell from her ankles and around her wrists. A sudden snick at the back of her skull signaled the release of the gag, and she raised trembling hands to the metal straps that encircled her head.

"Let me," the knight ordered and lifted the gag away gently before she hurled it through the carriage door behind her with more anger than she'd ever shown.

Delaine held her hand out. "Come on," she ordered. "This is your stop."

Alarm flashed across Kaylin's features and the captain looked chagrined.

"I meant this is where you can get out, not that you'd reached their intended destination," she explained softly. "Come now. We can't hold them forever."

She took hold of the extended fingers and let the woman guide her out of the carriage and down the step. Aside from a sharp gasp of surprise, she didn't complain when snow closed around her bare feet or object when her rescuer pushed her slightly behind her and turned to face the magister.

"You can go now," the captain told the mage. "Your duty to the Academy is done."

Gaudin blanched. "But—"

"I don't advise a delay," Delaine informed her coldly.

From the look on the magister's face, she had more than a delay in mind. Kaylin had never seen anyone look so furious. She looked ready to burn the world to the ground or as if she'd like to set a few knights on fire.

The captain, on the other hand, looked like she could counter anything the woman could throw at them and return it with interest. As she glanced from one to the other, Kaylin realized the knight hadn't come alone.

Three Chevaliers in gleaming breastplates and mounted on armored mounts pressed around the mage, while another held the horses pulling the coach. At the shuffle of hooves behind her, the girl glanced around and realized that another two were in striking distance although one of those held the captain's horse.

Kaylin looked at Gaudin and was relieved to see the magister back down. The woman's gaze flicked over her before they zeroed in on her rescuer.

"I'll handle things from here," the captain stated, her voice cold and hard and the words more of a dismissal than the one she'd given before.

"You have no idea what she's done," the magister snapped, and Delaine gave her a tight smile.

"Whatever it is, it is now a matter for the Chevaliers to handle, not the Academy."

"You—" Gaudin began but stopped abruptly when the other woman raised a hand to shoulder height.

"A *Chevalier* matter," she repeated firmly and swept her other hand out in a gesture that indicated the open coach door. "If you please."

The magister opened her mouth but thought better of the attempt and closed it again. She mounted the coach step and turned as if to speak before she changed her mind again and stepped inside.

Delaine moved as if to close the door for her, but the woman yanked it closed with a crash. Furious banging from the inside of the coach signaled the driver forward, but it wasn't until the Chevalier who held the horses had glanced at the captain and received a nod that he was able to drive forward.

Kaylin stood silently behind her rescuer as the coach turned in a slow and careful arc before it returned to the road and set off the way it had come.

Dirt, Kaylin noted, as they watched it dwindle into the distance. *Muddy dirt.*

Following the direction it had taken, she saw Waypoint's walls rising in the distance.

"They'll bypass the city," Delaine observed. "Otherwise, they won't make the Academy by nightfall." She laid a hand on her shoulder and turned to face her.

"I was able to get you released to my custody but you're not out of the woods yet."

"I didn't run away," she blurted and the knight smiled and squeezed her shoulder gently with her gauntleted hand.

"I know."

"But I still can't go back," she concluded and read the truth in Delaine's face.

The woman's mouth twisted with distaste, her voice a mixture of anger and regret. "No."

"My friends…" she began. "I didn't run away."

That brought a smile to Delaine's lips. "No," she agreed, "you did not."

"And I didn't quit," the girl declared, anxious that she understand.

Again, she squeezed her shoulder. "No, you did not." The captain straightened and stared in the direction the coach had taken. "And I will honor my promise to keep your crew safe and in the care of Herder's Gate until they reach their majorities and can choose their own path."

She relaxed at that, but the woman had not finished.

"It is you who poses the greatest problem," she continued, unhooked a pouch from her belt, and held it out. Kaylin heard the chink of coin. "What you've done at the Academy is… It will take some time to smooth out. This should be enough to get you through the valley and into the southern kingdoms where you can start a new life."

"Away from the Doom?" she asked and Delaine smiled.

"Away from Waypoint and the Doom," she confirmed and shook the coin pouch.

Kaylin accepted the bag and raised her gaze to Waypoint's walls before she pivoted slowly to find the coach had stopped on a short rise and she could see Tulon's City crowded around the base of the Twin Spears. She let her gaze follow the base of the mountain to the split peak.

"Roads can go two ways," she said and turned to her rescuer. "Can't they?"

The captain studied her face, then raised her gaze to take in the city and the mountain. She closed the girl's hand around the pouch with a heavy sigh.

"I'll take you to Waypoint," she said, "but you'll need to be out of the city by first light—preferably a long way out. Understood?"

She nodded, unable to stop the smile that rose to her lips, even though she tried to stifle it.

The knight saw it and shook her head although she allowed herself a smile.

"My friends," the girl began.

"They'll be fine," Delaine assured her. "I promise you, they'll be fine."

Kaylin shook her head.

"No, I know you'll take care of my crew. You promised—" Her smile faded and concern filled her face. "It's my friends at the Academy who I'm worried about. They're good people and I don't know what will happen to them. I…I only tried to help them because the magisters wouldn't and—"

Her voice shifted closer to tears and she drew a breath. The captain placed her hands on her shoulders and stooped to catch her gaze.

"Don't you worry about your friends," the Chevalier told her. "I'm not done with the magisters yet."

She raised her head, surprised at the fierceness in the captain's words. Delaine caught her look and gave her a grim smile.

"Oh no," she continued. "Thanks to a little bird, I know exactly what happened. I was able to get here in time and now, I will put a word about the Academy's practices in a few of the ears I hold and explain that if the magisters hadn't been so busy playing favorites, *you* would have never had a reason to find the repository. Then I'll ask pointed questions about the wisdom of allowing one institution to hold the secrets it has so far kept, among other things."

The look of satisfaction on her face was such that she wondered exactly how long the knight had waited to be able to shift the hold the Academy had worked so hard to establish. From her expression, a reckoning was coming—and it had been a long time in the making.

She might have felt pity for the magisters if they hadn't caused so much grief. Now, she only hoped the Chevalier could protect those who'd come to her for help from the repercussions such a power shift would bring. At least she had the basics of being a mage and maybe her friends would be treated a little better by the time the captain was through.

"Come," Delaine ordered and broke into her thoughts as she signaled for her horse. "I'll drop you inside the city gates. I trust you know your way from there?"

When she nodded, the woman fixed her with a stern stare

"Remember, in and out and be as far from the walls as you can by dawn. Understood?"

She mounted and caught the girl's nod before she extended her hand.

Kaylin took it and was hauled up behind the saddle.

"Hold tight," Delaine ordered and barely waited for her to comply before she wheeled her horse and headed to the city at a gallop. Her squad fell in around them.

The gates opened before they reached them, and the Chevalier galloped through and traveled several blocks before she turned into a quiet side street and helped her passenger to slip to the ground. She pointed to the coin pouch the girl had tucked into her belt.

"Once you've spent it, get out of the city," she ordered. "But understand this—once you are out, whether you go north or south, you can't return for at least a year. If you come back before then, not even I can keep you safe."

Once the knights had gone, it took Kaylin a few minutes to get her bearings. The South Gate was closest to Orcs' Head Square so she turned and trotted quickly toward it. Mistfire's wasn't far from the Cup and she was familiar enough with the area to find it with no difficulty. She stopped before its open oak doors.

Never in her wildest dreams had she ever hoped to be able to shop there. Okay, maybe in her wildest dreams, those she never shared with Melis or Isabette.

She drew a deep breath, bounced up the stairs, and took a few paces inside. A little overwhelmed, she almost turned and went outside again, but she knew she couldn't. She reminded herself of what Delaine had said.

The order had been very clear. She had to be as far from the walls as she could by dawn break.

That meant she had to be finished before the Dusk Bell tolled because once that happened, the gates wouldn't open until morning and she'd never be away in time. After another deep breath, she rested her hand on the coin purse hanging at her belt and marched to the counter.

She hadn't expected the clerk to notice her or even speak to her, but his head snapped around at the sound of the door closing behind her and his eyes sharpened with interest.

"And how may I assist the Academy today?" he asked.

Kaylin looked over her shoulder and her heart raced at the thought that the magisters had discovered her already. She realized that no one was there—no red-robed figure determined to drag her back to the Academy, no blue-robed apprentices, and no Wardens.

A puzzled frown on her face, she turned to the man. He looked as confused as she felt.

"Unless," he stated uncertainly, "you're not here on Academy business." He gave her a worried look. "You're not thinking of running away, are you? Taking on the Doom and the Spears on your own?"

His words startled Kaylin into a laugh and she moved a little closer.

"Not on my own, I'm not," she told him, "but the Magister told me to..." She frowned. "What was it he said? Oh...I was to outfit myself as befitting an assistant about to accompany her magister on an important errand to Tolan's great city."

She did her best to imitate Roche at his most pompous and the man laughed in response.

"Very well," he said but his smile faded. "And I assume your master sent the gold you'd need to do such a thing?"

Kaylin patted the pouch at her belt. "He did," she admitted when the coins jingled, "and he gave me a list and a budget and told me not to go over it. 'Equip sensibly,' he ordered. 'I'll not have you looking like some idiot noble playing at adventuring mage.'"

"He didn't mince words, did he?" The clerk sounded suitably affronted on her behalf. "Well, let me see four of your gold and we'll get started."

Four gold? Her eyes widened but she pulled the purse off her belt and hoped Captain Delaine knew more about what she'd need than she did. She opened the strings and removed the first four coins she found, both relieved and alarmed when they were all gold.

After a moment's hesitation, she retrieved a fifth and blushed as she laid it on the counter.

"If...if it's okay," she told the clerk, "can I add a little extra to get something that will last longer?"

He looked at the coin and then at her face and smiled reassuringly.

"I'll see what I can do." He swept the coins off the counter and studied her appraisingly.

"Tell me, how finicky is your master about robes?"

She frowned thoughtfully. "I don't think he cares as long as the clothing looks presentable and isn't covered in lace and sprinkles."

The clerk chuckled. "Right. No lace and no sprinkles," he said. "Like the Academy, Mistfire's has a certain reputation to uphold."

Kaylin exhaled a breath of relief but the clerk had another question.

"And blue?" he asked. "Is that something else we can ignore?"

"Certainly," she replied. "The magister wants us to be taken seriously, so I assume he would prefer colors and styles that would allow us to blend in with the company without mimicking its uniform."

"Well, given that I don't know what company you're traveling with, you should be relatively safe from that."

He led her to a corner of the store where cloaks, tunics, and jerkins hung in a rack along the wall and shelves held neatly folded piles of sturdy trousers and undergarments. Belts hung in a row at the end of the shelf.

"These," the clerk told her, "should last you for any journey, although I'd strongly recommend a second set so the first may be laundered—and three pairs of socks. You will, of course, need to speak to a cobbler about footwear."

His last statement reminded her that she was barefoot and she silently cursed the magisters for taking the second set of decent boots she'd ever had in her life.

"Now, if you'll excuse me, miss, I need to take your measurements."

It was an odd experience to be measured and given the choice of colors and clothing that fitted. She did as he suggested and took two sets of clothes.

"You'll need a pack to carry them in," he observed, "and a sleeping roll, water flask, flint and tinder, a lantern..."

The list went on but he seemed to know where everything was kept and very soon had a neat stack of what he termed "adventuring necessities" piled on the counter. Kaylin regarded it with concern.

"Don't worry, miss," the clerk told her when he completely misinterpreted her look. "I haven't forgotten the food or the means to eat it with." He paused and gave her a quizzical look. "And will you need cooking equipment, or will the mercenaries take care of such things?"

"I..." She thought about it and wished she knew a little more about what lay ahead of her. While she wanted to have the means to cook if she needed to, she didn't want to be weighed down. "Maybe only enough to make the magister a cup of tea or something quick to eat if the mercenaries are busy?"

The clerk cast her an odd look but returned swiftly with a small kettle and pot.

"These should do you, then," he told her. "The kettle will hold two cups of water, and the pot should feed two if one of you isn't a big eater."

Kaylin made a face that suggested her magister might be exactly that and he laughed.

"You can always make a second serving," he told her. "The next size up is for four."

"This will do fine," she told him. "It's only to supplement what's supplied, anyway, and he can always send me for another if he doesn't agree."

"There is that," he agreed.

He turned his attention to what she already had and appeared to work through a mental checklist.

"Only the supplies now," he told her and hefted the flask. "And I'll fill this from the water we have here. It will save you having to stop at a river."

She nodded and he sighed as he placed the flask on the counter.

"Look," he said, "if you're thinking of doing what I think you are, all I can suggest is don't. Nothing's so bad that you need to head into the Doom on your own."

Although she wanted to tell him he had no idea what he was talking about, he read the look on her face and continued.

"For one thing, the road between here and there is full of orcs, minotaurs, and goblins. The first will make a nice serving wench out of you and when they get bored, will either eat you or sell you on. The second will sniff you out in a heartbeat and simply eat you, and the third—"

He shuddered. "They come in hordes or scouting parties, and if they don't eat you, they'll put you to whatever use strikes their fancy and food isn't the worst of those. You could end up anywhere—or in any number of pieces."

Kaylin didn't bother to deny it. "So, how do I avoid that?" she asked and he stilled. His gaze went from concerned to grave.

"Well, given that you aren't arguing that your magister will be traveling with a band," he told her, "I'll have to assume you've got a real good reason to go."

She nodded, her eyes shadowed when she remembered Captain Delaine's warning.

"And I need to be gone before the Dusk Bell," she told him, "so any advice is welcome."

He nodded, moved away momentarily, and returned with a short, sturdy dagger in a sheath.

"Fine," he began, lifted her belt, and threaded the sheath onto it. "First, you'll need to get through the Kill Zone. Like I said, it's teeming with goblins, orcs, and minotaurs and I wasn't exaggerating. They're every bit as nasty as I made them sound. Worse even."

Kaylin nodded to show she was listening and he continued as he placed the dagger and belt on the counter.

"You'll hear minotaurs coming, so get out of the way. Goblins… well, when you see one, a dozen more will be close by, and orcs only stop chasing you if they have something better to do. You'll need to avoid them if you can."

"Any tips on how?" she asked.

"Since they're most active at night, you should be smart and hole up by dusk. Since you're traveling mostly on your own, you stand a better chance of getting across unnoticed if you're careful and stay off the beaten track. Maybe move parallel to the road but not on it since that's what they mostly watch."

He pulled a map out. "I assume you have another couple of gold for a good map."

She dug into her pouch and passed the coins to him.

His forehead wrinkled with concern and he looked at them, then at her. "Will someone miss these?"

Kaylin shook her head. "No. I have a patron."

"Like you had a magister?"

Her lips curled with distaste. "I had one of those too, but the patron who sponsored me to the Academy is also sponsoring this trip."

He gave her another wary stare and she hoped he wouldn't ask who it was.

Instead, he said, "And you don't want to say who they are because you're worried about some political shenanigans going wrong for them."

At the look on her face, he gave a mirthless chuckle.

"Don't worry, girl. You've mentioned the Academy and you're wearing their garb. It's not hard to work out the rest." He swept the coin off the counter. "And it won't be something I want to be involved in, so let's get you kitted out and on the road." He sighed again. "I merely wish you were going in the other direction—or is that not an option?"

"It's an option," Kaylin admitted, "but the Doom is where I'm going and I need to leave soon."

The clerk shook his head, stowed the equipment in her pack, and paused when he reached the clothing.

"I suppose you need to change?"

She had planned to do so once she'd left the city, but if she could do it there, all the better. When she nodded he pointed to a door leading to the back of the store.

"I'll get your rations." He held a hand up as she reached for her coin purse. "It's covered, and I'll throw in an extra flask of water. Hurry, now, or you'll miss the cobbler. He likes his supper early."

Kaylin hurried and caught his eye as she emerged from the changing room. He smiled when he saw her bare feet and waved a pair of socks at her.

"I kept these out. You'll need them when you get to…"

"Hobmason's," she told him and hoped the remaining coins would stretch to cover a pair of boots from there. She didn't like the idea of stealing another pair from the poor man. One had been more than enough.

The clerk nodded and helped to settle the pack on her back.

"When you get to the Old City," he told her, "find the Final Rest. It's an old inn but more like a small fortress, and it's where you'll find mercenaries and adventuring companies and a modicum of shelter."

"Final Rest, fortified inn," she repeated. "Got it."

She turned toward the door.

"You'd best hurry," the clerk told her kindly. "The gate shuts at the Dusk Bell and you have little time."

"Thank you," she replied and moved swiftly out the door.

Hobmason Chitairy's was a few buildings down and she arrived as the man reached the door. He was about to close it anyway when he glanced down and saw her feet. She tapped the pouch at her belt and he sighed.

"I won't make you a pair on the spot," he warned and glanced at her feet again. "And you'll need to tub those before they go anywhere near the merchandise."

Kaylin was about to ask him what he meant by that when she caught sight of a tub of water set beneath a bench.

Tub them. Right. She nodded and hurried to the bench.

A cloth hung from the counter nearby and she took it and proceeded to dip each foot into the tub and wash it clean. The water wasn't warm, but the cobbler returned with a steaming kettle and poured it in.

"I'll get a better fit if your feet aren't frozen through."

She didn't know how true that was and she didn't care. He was waiting with a dry towel by the time she'd finished cleaning her feet. She dried them and he gestured to a seat and lifted the boots he had put on the counter. As she settled where he'd indicated, he took a towel from his belt and passed it to her.

"I take it you have socks."

Kaylin nodded and retrieved them from the pocket she'd shoved them into.

"Good." He grunted briskly. "Get them on and we'll see how good my eye is."

She obeyed, a little put out when he rose to his feet and crossed to take another pair of boots from the shelf. Halfway back to her, he paused.

"It is boots you're lookin' for, isn't it, miss?" he asked. "Only given the way you're dressed, I thought—"

"Yes, boots, please," she assured him. "I have a fair walk ahead of me."

"Nowhere too interesting, I hope."

"The Kill Zone," Kaylin told him and when his face fell, she hastened to reassure him. "I'll be fine."

"You'll be food is what you'll be," he corrected as he fitted the boots to her feet. "Stand."

Kaylin stood.

"Sit," he instructed, removed the boots, and replaced them with the second pair. "My eye's not as good as it used to be. Stand."

Again, she obeyed.

"Now, walk to the end and back."

Puzzled, she complied, aware that the man's gaze studied her every step.

"That'll do," he said when she returned. "Five gold."

She opened her pouch and pulled out another five coins, amazed that Delaine had given her so much. All she could think was that the captain knew her business.

The coins vanished into the pocket on the cobbler's leather apron and he scrutinized her for a long moment.

"Will that be all?"

Kaylin nodded and lifted her pack. The boots felt good on her feet and she couldn't help but smile when she moved. He helped her with the pack and he led her to the door.

"Thank you for your business," he told her as he ushered her out into the street.

She jumped when the door closed firmly behind her but wasn't surprised to hear bolts rattle home. With a small smile at the firmness of the gesture, she hurried down the step and turned toward the gate. She'd spent more time at the provisioners and cobbler's than she'd realized.

Already, the sky had faded to soft purples and mauves and the shadows were lengthening. There wasn't much time before the Dusk Bell. She increased her pace to a brisk jog and hurried to the South Gate, her boots crunching in the snow.

CHAPTER TWENTY-ONE

Kaylin reached the gate moments before the Dusk Bell tolled. The Wardens gave her curious looks but let her pass.

"You know it's coming on dark soon?" one said in warning and she gave him a firm nod.

"I know it," she told him and tried to keep her voice hard, daring him to make anything more of it.

"Right. As long as you know the gates won't open until the Dawn Bell," he replied and she nodded again.

"I hear you."

She turned to leave and another asked. "Urgent message, then?"

"Something like that." She shrugged, her expression set.

Rather than wait for them to ask any more questions, she turned and walked into the gathering dark. It had taken everything she had not to run. That would have drawn suspicion and there was enough of that as it was.

The darkness closed around her as she followed the road. As soon as a fold in the hills blocked her view of the gates, she broke into a jog. "Be as far from the city walls as you can by dawn," Delaine had said and she intended to be.

At war with those orders, however, was the merchant's advice to be holed up by dusk if she were smart.

"Well, no one said I was smart," Kaylin murmured and hoped the humanoids would be hunting farther away from Waypoint's walls. Maybe there was some kind of patrol that came out of the city or maybe the goblins and orcs liked to stay out of bowshot of the walls.

"However far that is," she muttered and kept her pace steady and her gaze fixed on the road.

At first, it was easy to see and then it was easy to find because of the way it formed a thin line between the snow-covered forms of the rocks and bushes lining it. When she looked up, she found the moon and decided if she could keep going for half the night, she should have traveled enough distance to begin traveling during the day.

There was another reason she should avoid the road, and it wasn't only the marauding monsters. She realized that if the magisters decided to send someone after her, they would also use the road.

"Yet another reason for me to not be on it," she decided and scrambled to the top of a rocky escarpment. She didn't stand on the ridgeline based on the simple logic that it would be akin to standing on top of a roof in the city. It would make her easy to see and would draw attention.

No, if the rules of sight worked the same way in the Kill Zone as they did in the city, she'd be better off lying flat on the highest point or not protruding above it in the first place. With that in mind, she crept to the top of the rocks and lay on her belly to survey the land ahead.

The road from Waypoint to Tulon's City—or the Doom—wasn't straight. Its makers had done their best to take as direct a path as they could, but the land was more a series of rolling hills than an open plain and sections of rock that simply wouldn't give way.

The route twisted and turned and took the smoothest path or the most possible path and not necessarily the most direct one. As she looked down on it, she traced it through the hills and noted when the snow faded and clear terrain began.

Curious as to why that might be, she followed its winding route into the ruins of the Old City and tried to work out where the Final Rest might be. As she did, she noticed the dull orange glows of the fires that indicated where the humanoids had camped.

It made her wonder how many of them belonged to orcs and how many to goblins or minotaurs or whatever else roamed the valley night. She shifted carefully and looked at Waypoint.

The city's walls were still too close for her liking, but the number of fires gave her reason to pause. She wasn't sure how far the monsters roved from their encampments. Did they stay close or did they go in search of camped travelers? What was her best option?

As she thought about it, Delaine's words haunted her. *Be as far from the city walls as you can by dawn.*

What did the Chevalier captain know that she did not?

More like what did the magisters promise to do as soon as the next sun rose?

She swiveled and checked the land ahead, still very perturbed by the number of fires she saw.

Kaylin looked again at the ruins and tried to make out which of the buildings might be the Final Rest. There was only one that looked like it might be described as a fortress.

"And it might not even be them," she muttered. "For all I know, orcs build fortresses too."

Still, it was the only aim point she had and a direct path to it took her across the road and into a valley, then up another hill. Stare as she might, she couldn't see anything resembling a campfire, so she chose the top of the hill beyond the road as her next stopping point and noted the shape of the rock formation at its peak.

That would do as a landmark until she reached it. Once there, she could choose another. She took one last look at Waypoint, surprised to see it wasn't as far behind her as she'd thought, perhaps only a couple of miles.

"Another reason to be away from the road," she muttered, then studied her rock formation and the ground ahead before she slid from her perch and carefully descended the side of the hill.

The moon cast a dull glow behind the thin layer of clouds overhead. It slid out from behind them and lit the countryside. While not a full moon, it was bright enough for her to see by and still give her a chance to remain unseen.

"A chance," she reminded herself and crouched beside a scruffy, waist-high bush to survey the land around her. When nothing moved, she focused on the outcrop and rose from her hiding place.

The journey that followed was punctuated by many such stops. It was one thing to travel through a landscape of rooftops and streets in a city where her worst fear was embodied in a Warden's uniform or a rival thief, but there?

She only had stories to go on, tales overheard in taverns and from clusters of mercenaries as they passed in the street—and the advice of the clerk in Mistfire's. Kaylin's ears ached with trying to decipher every small rustle and scuttle and she started at the clatter of each stone she dislodged.

When she reached the road, she stopped again. This time, she listened for more than only monsters. If Delaine needed her to be away from the city, it was very likely that the magisters had threatened to hunt her through the Kill Zone. And if the Chevalier believed the magisters would wait for morning, the woman was more naïve than she gave her credit for.

Yet again, she found shelter in the shadow of some of the scattered shrubbery. She listened for hoofbeats or even the lighter tread of a human on foot although she didn't believe anyone the magisters hired would be that foolish.

"Unlike me," she muttered and reminded herself that pursuit or not, she wasn't alone in this region.

While there might not be many—or any—humans, there were more than enough other things to make up for it. When she was sure nothing would see her, Kaylin chose another point of shelter on the other side of the road and sprinted into it.

Once there, she caught her breath, peered both ways along the road, and tried to see into the shadows beside it. Again, when nothing moved, she looked for her landmark and trotted swiftly toward it. The moonlight faded and a light snow began to fall and she shivered.

What had the clerk at Mistfire's said?

"You'll be holed up by dusk each night if you're smart."

"It's one thing to know what's smart," Kaylin grumbled, "and entirely another to be able to do it."

She reached the base of the hill and scurried up the ever-increasing slope until she reached a small upthrust of rock. Hunkered in its shadow, she looked back the way she'd come, glad to see her footprints slowly disappearing.

Nothing moved at first.

A glance toward Waypoint assured her that the road remained

empty so she turned her attention to the countryside between her and the city.

Her searching gaze revealed only the tracks she'd left behind.

Satisfied that nothing was trying to sneak up on her from that direction, she shifted her attention farther from the road to the hills and shallow dips of ground between it and the forest that edged the Zone.

The trees unnerved her, not only because she'd never been in a forest but because there were so many of them so close together. It was like they waited in ambush and outnumbered her by several hundred to her very solitary one.

"Dumbass," she scolded herself. "It's not the trees you have to worry about but what's hiding among them."

As if to prove her words, she caught the flicker of something large moving along the forest's edge—several big somethings, she realized when she took the time to look. Kaylin crouched closer to the ground. The distant figures looked small but when she compared them to the trees at their backs, the reality was clear.

They're huge, she thought and remembered these weren't the only things in the Kill Zone. There could be more and perhaps closer to where she was hiding. Her gaze scoured the ground between the trees and the road, then flicked to the half-dozen huge forms that ventured slowly into the mostly bare crowns of the hills.

Without a doubt, they were moving toward the road.

She glanced at the rock formation she'd chosen to move to.

Her initial goal had been to reach the highest point of the hill she could without climbing and choose the next point, but the sight of the creatures made her rethink her plan. Maybe Mistfire's clerk had a point.

With another careful check to make sure nothing was close enough to see her, she crept up the hill and stopped only when she reached the base of the outcrop she'd used as a landmark. Another glance at the big creatures on the forest's edge revealed that they'd left the tree line.

They moved easily and trotted steadily toward the road. As if aware of their size, they traveled the floor of a valley, careful to watch the ridgeline and stoop when it dipped. She squinted while she studied them, as frustrated by the lack of light as she was grateful for the dark.

Along with the limited visibility, she would have to trust the dull gray-brown of her cloak and clothing to conceal her. She studied the rock face above her and tracked the faint lines of ledges and cracks in the stone. It looked easier to climb than the side of a house, even with the snow.

Fortunately, that assessment proved correct, and she soon reached the top. Lying flat on the rocks, she belly-crawled across to peer over the ledge. She'd camp on top if she had to, but she'd rather be below the skyline because she had no idea how well the monsters could see.

Her careful study of her surroundings revealed a ledge overlooking the valley on the other side of the hill and she was glad she hadn't pushed on in the dark. If she had, she might not have seen the cliff before she went over it. It wasn't tall as cliffs went, but it was high enough to provide a sheer drop into the gully below.

When her eyes couldn't penetrate the darkness below, she used her ears. Kaylin heard the sound of running water and the thought of a long, thirst-quenching drink and refilling her canteen almost tempted her from her perch. If shadows hadn't concealed the floor of the valley, she might have acted on that idea but for now, she decided against it.

Beyond the stupidity of climbing down the cliff in the dark, there was the even greater stupidity of climbing down one when you couldn't see what was waiting for you at the bottom. She certainly had no desire to become some monster's plaything or next tasty treat.

The way the big creatures from the forest had moved suggested that they could see in the dark. They hadn't walked cautiously or haltingly through the night but had moved as swiftly and surely as she did in the day.

She lowered herself carefully down the cliff and settled onto the ledge.

Almost immediately, she wished she hadn't. She couldn't see the top of the formation—or anything that might climb onto it and use it as a perch the same way she had. The reality was that she'd have no idea of any threat coming from that direction until it dropped onto her head.

Still, the likelihood of that happening was almost nil, and she pushed her fear aside and explored her new perch as best she could. At least she couldn't be seen against the sky down there and with the color of the clothes she wore, it was likely she couldn't be seen easily against the rock.

She made a note to thank the clerk if and when she ever returned to Waypoint. He *had* known what he'd been doing and she wondered if he'd been a mercenary before he'd taken to provisioning them. It would make sense.

Kaylin sighed. Now, she wished she'd asked, but she'd been so wrapped up in her problems that she hadn't thought of it. She also wished she'd thought to eat before she left—maybe some bread and meat from the Cup—but there hadn't been time.

With a sigh, she slid out of her pack, rested it against the cliff face beside her, and leaned back against the rock. Her rations were on top and the flask had been hooked to her belt. She ate slowly but didn't like her chances of getting the sleeping roll out without losing something over the edge.

In the end, the cold won. The cloak served its purpose and kept the snow off her and she'd bought winter weight, but the garment had its limits. Very carefully, she unpacked her belongings and placed things against the base of the cliff so she could extract her sleeping roll. The rock formation blocked the worst of the wind but did little for the snow.

She positioned it on the rock and slid into it—not to lie in it but rather to sit against the rock wall and pull it up and alongside her face. It immediately made a difference and she leaned against the pack and the cliff and stared into the night.

"Avark-bostila," she whispered when the cold continued to bite.

The combination summoned a small orb of fire and encased it in force that stopped it singeing her. She bent her knees and set the combined ball beneath them.

It took a while before she warmed up enough to dispel the spell, but she used the time to study the country around her.

The hill opposite was smaller and the moon peeked briefly through clouds now and then to set the snow covering the shrubs and grasses aglimmer. She looked past it and watched shadows move in the terrain beyond while she listened to the world around her. No sound came from the top of the outcrop and she drifted into a light sleep.

Kaylin was woken by the sound of something moving around the side of the rocks. Its heavy tread crunched over the stony ground and it came to a stop several yards to her left. She froze and didn't dare to move.

Her mind worked frantically as she tried to remember how far along the cliff the ledge stood. Was she far enough away from the side that she couldn't be reached? She thought so but it was poor comfort.

Something drew a deep questing breath and followed it with several curious sniffs. A series of rumbling grunts preceded more sniffing. She imagined feeling the air move and tried to work out if she could get her pack on without alerting the creature to where she was.

Unfortunately, she remembered that she'd have to put everything inside it again before she could go anywhere and she pulled the sleeping roll tighter around her. She would simply have to sit very, very still and hope whatever creature was out there grew bored and left.

Another series of grunts and sniffs was accompanied by the sound of boots—or was it hooves?—that scraped the stone and dislodged a few pebbles to bounce over the cliff. They rattled and clattered into the gully below and she forced herself to remain motionless and breathe quietly.

What if it could climb? Or could see her through the dark?

She glanced up and was relieved to see the moon was no longer above her. It also meant she had difficulty seeing even the detail on her pack, but maybe it guaranteed that she wouldn't be seen by whatever was scenting around the rock.

Kaylin waited and held her breath again when the sniffing seemed to have moved closer as if the creature had leaned around the edge of the rocks. It was an effort to not look. She knew nothing drew the human eye faster than a face and she wasn't sure she wanted to find out if that were true for monsters also—especially when she had nowhere to run.

Something shrieked—angry or fearful, she couldn't tell—and the monster at the edge of the outcrop stopped in mid-sniff. The cry came again, and she thought the sound might have held meaning. Was it more of a command than a cry of fear?

After a moment's silence, the sound of footsteps moved ponderously away from the outcrop. She didn't relax until she heard the buzz and chirp of insects resume. She hadn't noticed them or even that they had gone, but now that they'd returned, she realized they were there.

Maybe they go quiet when something big and nasty is around or when there's something dangerous.

It was a strange thought, but she remembered how rooms fell quiet when certain types of adventurers or mercenaries entered and wondered if it might be something similar. Powerful adventurers caused a momentary lull unless those already occupying the space thought the newcomers might not be dangerous.

Those silences were only broken when the mercenaries or adventurers had settled at a table and were focused on their food.

It must be the same out here, she decided and made a note to pay attention to the noises in her surroundings. *Silence means danger. Gotcha.*

She wondered what Melis would have made of it and decided the girl would have given her the look that said she had finally worked out something her friend had known all along. *Smartass,* she thought with a pang of loneliness.

Alone and in the dark, she missed her crew more than ever.

Kaylin exhaled a slow, shuddering breath and realized she had drawn herself into a crouch and that her dagger was in her hand.

Idiot! she scolded herself and slid the small weapon into its sheath. *You might not be a full mage but you have had magical training and you'd be a fool to not use it.*

She checked the sky and settled against the rock. When the sky began to lighten and the shadows retreated from the touch of the sun, she packed her belongings and slid the pack onto her back.

Rather than descend, she returned to the top of the formation and again lay flat to observe the land around her. Movement at Waypoint's gates caught her eye and she watched a half dozen riders leave and trot in her direction.

They stuck to the road but seemed to be looking for something.

"Or someone," she observed as they drew closer and their heads turned to survey the surrounding countryside.

They wore a mixture of heavy leather armor and chainmail, and their horses were protected by barding of the same materials. She could hear it jingle as they came closer.

Mercenaries.

Kaylin thought about getting off the escarpment and running farther from the road and into the hills, but she was certain the movement would give her away. There was no cover on the flat surface of her perch and her time dodging the Wardens had taught her that movement drew attention. Rather than rush into action she might regret, she lay still and waited while she studied them.

They're looking for someone, she decided and wondered if the Academy had sent them.

No wonder Captain Delaine had told her to be as far from the city as she could get by dawn. It almost made her regret her decision to stop for the night until she remembered the dark ungainly shapes that had traveled out of the forest.

The clerk's advice had been good and maybe there was more speed to be gained by patience.

It was a long while before the horsemen rode past and their path showed her how far she'd traveled from the road. She wondered if they had trackers among them—or perhaps rangers—and if she'd left a trail clear enough for them to follow despite the snow.

With that in mind, she tried to locate the point where she'd crossed the road at. Was it on the flat part of the rise? Or maybe there, where the bushes crowded close to the road?

She shook her head, unable to recall moving through that many bushes.

The riders continued and neither slowed nor stopped. Kaylin decided they either didn't have trackers or she hadn't left enough of a trail for them to notice and follow her.

Or it's been obscured by other footprints, her unhelpful inner voice suggested.

Kaylin shushed it and looked at the city. She frowned when a second set of riders emerged. These behaved in a similar fashion to the first except for one thing. Instead of staying on the road, they spread out and left three to follow the usual route through the Kill Zone while the others traveled parallel to it several horse-lengths distant.

The sight made her chuckle.

"Yeah, good luck with that," she murmured when she recalled the way the road twisted and turned through the undulating terrain.

Their presence meant she had to wait a little longer and she divided her time between observing the two groups and finally, a third. The last riders moved at a walk and appeared only when the second had reached the section of road parallel to her hiding place. By that stage, they'd returned to the road or traveled a scant few yards from it.

She sighed heavily.

"Third time's the charm, right?" she whispered and wondered if anyone would notice if she wriggled to the ledge and took care of a more pressing need.

In the end, she waited before she descended from the escarpment on the side she'd scaled it and relieved herself in the relative privacy of some bushes.

"No one ever talks about that part of adventuring," she muttered in disgust, glad nothing had stumbled across her while she'd been busy.

Kaylin skirted the hill, kept it between herself and the road, and discovered a small stream that flowed out of the gully at the cliff's base. It took only a moment for her to refill her water bottle and rinse her face and hands. That done, she chose a second marker and moved on.

As tempting as it was to run, she couldn't do that and watch in the direction of the road and remain alert for monster camps. She couldn't remember seeing any fires close to where she was now, but that didn't mean the nocturnal creatures hadn't set up camp while she was sleeping.

They were nocturnal, weren't they? Or did they have night and day shifts?

Several hours later, when the sun had passed its zenith and began its descent toward night, she asked herself whether they truly existed.

The landscape had remained empty, and even though she'd still been able to see the horsemen from the top of her second and third markers, she'd seen nothing bigger than a bird moving through the tufty grass, isolated stands of stunted trees, and scattered bushes.

Now and then, she'd glance at the not-so-distant forest and suppress a shiver. She wanted to think of it as a wilder version of the garden at Herder's Gate or the Academy but her mind wouldn't accept it.

It's not natural, her other voice muttered. *There shouldn't be so many so close together.*

And yet you've seen it in the distance all your life, she scolded it.

There was a wall then, it retorted, *and it looked like the surface of a very big lake. Peaceful.*

Kaylin remembered the large forms that had emerged from the trees the night before and shivered.

Not so peaceful, she corrected and her other voice agreed.

She continued to walk but had to remind herself of the dangers said to rove the area. It was hard to believe the stories when she saw nothing to prove them. Maybe the snow had kept them away or in their camps.

From the fourth checkpoint, she watched the last group of riders enter the ruins on the outskirts of Tolan's Doom. They slowed, then moved off the road and into the shelter of some semi-solid-looking walls.

Camping for the night, she decided and assumed she should do the same. After all, if mercs who looked as seasoned as these did stopped before dark, she should probably follow their example.

Her next checkpoint was another cluster of rocks that were neither as high nor as wide as the first and she studied them critically. *Maybe I'll be lucky and it'll be safer than it looks.*

While the location fortunately didn't have to prove how safe it was, she was able to find a hollow at its base surrounded on three sides by towering boulders and concealed by thick brush. As she wormed through the vegetation, she discovered the bushes had thorns and wondered if she could light a fire.

"Fires have smoke." She sighed and used another force-encased fire orb to keep herself warm.

To her surprise, she slept better on the ground than she had on the rock ledge despite waking twice to distant cries. They were similar to the one that had distracted the sniffer and once, she thought she heard hooves moving over the stony slope outside. Nothing stopped to investigate her hiding place, however, and she spent the night unmolested.

Dawn dragged her out of her bedroll and she shivered a little from the cold as she got ready for the day. With her bedding stowed in her pack, Kaylin ate another small portion of her rations and emerged cautiously from her hiding place.

Again, the countryside appeared empty so she climbed to the top of the escarpment and tried to determine which of the buildings in the Doom might be the Final Rest. Now that she was closer, she had her doubts about being able to find it but it wasn't difficult.

The ruins were...well, ruined, and the Final Rest was not. Its walls rose above the remains of the city around it, a mixture of dark stone and wood and their tops flat save for the low battlements along their perimeter. From where she sat, she thought she could make out figures keeping watch and noted the glow of small fires in the shelters at each corner.

It looked safe.

Now, I only have to reach it and hope no one's waiting for me when I do. She touched the coin purse at her belt. Although she had a little left after her visits to the outfitter's and cobbler's, she didn't know how long it would last her.

Again, she was glad of her mage skills.

While she didn't think she'd get a position as a full mage, she knew the Academy's reputation would stand her in good stead. She might be able to find a mercenary company willing to take her on as an apprentice. That was her hope, anyway.

Kaylin drew an imaginary line between her position and the walls and scanned the ground between her and her destination. While there was nothing directly on her route to the inn, she noticed faint columns of smoke not far to either side.

They reminded her of the mercenaries and she looked toward the walls she'd seen them disappear behind the night before. Sure enough, the horsemen were emerging and she noticed that all three groups had come together at the camp.

This time, they divided into two groups. Half moved deeper into the Doom toward the inn and the other half headed toward Waypoint.

Again? Well, I guess they're thorough if nothing else. Maybe if they find I'm not there, they'll stop looking and go home.

Of course, she'd have to watch the road as well as the country around her again and with this in mind, slid off her perch and set off toward her first landmark for the day. The snow gradually faded from the land around her and the air felt a little warmer. When she looked back, she realized she'd been descending since she'd left Waypoint.

The snow became patchy and then almost non-existent, and she breathed a sigh of relief and continued her journey. At first, the countryside seemed as empty as it had the day before and she allowed herself to relax a little.

A short while later, she rounded an outcrop of rocks and noticed two small figures scratching in the dirt of an open patch of ground. They were child-sized and if it hadn't been for the outsized ears on either side of their heads and their gray-green skin tones, she might have mistaken them for children.

They poked at the dirt with short spears, their heads close together as though discussing something important. Kaylin came to a rapid halt and began to back away, but their ears twitched and they raised their heads, and their wide yellow eyes gleamed when they saw her.

As one, they raised their spears. She reacted instinctively and conjured a shower of flashing light in their faces.

"Bardafrisk!"

One of the goblins shrieked in surprise and danced back and away from the lights. The other dropped his spear and flattened his ears against his head as he clutched his eyes.

"Utseza!" they shrieked almost as one. "Utseza!"

She threw the spell again and glanced at her marker to gauge the distance to it. The goblins took to their heels and cries of "Utseza!" rang in their wake.

As she watched them flee, the Mistfire clerk's words echoed unbidden in her mind.

When you see one, a dozen more are close by."

"Oh, crap." She drew a breath and began to run.

A spear whistled through the space she'd stood in a moment before. She ducked instinctively and jinked to the left.

"Helda!" she commanded to drop a shield at her rear as another spear arced over her head and a third flew through the line of her original path.

Behind her, voices shrieked and gibbered but the only word she could pick out was utseza and she made a note to ask what it meant—when no more of them were chasing her, of course. When she got to the inn, she assured herself.

The bushes ahead of her rustled.

"Avark!" she shouted and her fingers flashed through what she hoped was the right sequence of movements.

She couldn't be sure and didn't have time to slow and check. A tiny globe of fire launched out from her fingertips and whatever was in the bushes uttered a startled squawk. As she passed the source of the sound, she caught the fleeting impression of a flat, gray-green face, large ears, and yellow eyes. Also, she realized smugly, of fire and hasty hand movements when the goblin's tattered clothing caught alight.

Kaylin didn't stop to make sure it wouldn't pursue her. She quickened her pace, located the marker, and tried to steer a little toward it. While fairly sure she wouldn't be able to stop and climb it so she could choose the next one, if she could keep it at her back, she could maybe stay on course until the goblins stopped chasing her.

"They do stop, right?" she had asked the distant clerk so she at least knew they wouldn't continue in endless pursuit. "You only said the orcs kept chasing you. You never told me if goblins were the same, only that there were always more of them."

As she cursed her oversight in not asking the man for all the information she could, she sprinted forward. The goblins' cries sounded farther back but now and then, something would thump into the path behind her or clatter off a rock as she ducked around it, and she knew they had not given up.

Her lungs began to burn and her legs ached with the effort required to propel her forward under the extra weight of the pack. She wondered how many spears she'd find hanging out of that when she was finally able to stop.

The goblins, unfortunately, managed to move ahead of her.

Somehow, they found a way around her so when she topped the rise of another low hill, she could see them coming in at either end of the low valley between it and the next hill.

"You said it was orcs!" she shouted and thrust a hand toward the closest group flanking her. "Tonalavark!"

More shrieks greeted the spell, momentarily drowned out by the low boom that accompanied the fire orb she launched at them. She decided that hadn't created enough havoc and tried the variation she'd seen Sylvester use on the other group.

"Tonalka'arnal!"

She followed that with "Helda!" and raised a shield in time for more spears to clatter off it. It wouldn't do her any good, however. As she half-ran, half-slid down the bare slope to the valley floor, she caught sight of movement at the top of the next rise.

Since when were there so many?

Shrieks were replaced by shouts of impending triumph, and Kaylin took the next slope at a diagonal. She hoped to either slide between the group coming over the top of the rise and those that tried a pincer movement from the bottom or to reach a cluster of rocks at the foot of a low escarpment.

If she was very lucky, she'd be able to bounce to the top of one of the outcrops and maybe find a ledge to jump to that would put her out of goblin grab range. She tried hard to ignore the tiny voice that reminded her that any such leap would not put her out of spear range.

There had to be a limit to how high they could throw, right?

Yes, but whether or not you can reach it is another question, the voice warned but it was silenced by a sudden roar.

It was accompanied by the rumble of hooves and the ground shuddered underfoot. Stones rattled down the slope and the goblins froze. She glanced over her shoulder but continued to run.

Where she had come from, stopping led to unpleasant consequences. If the little bastards stayed still long enough, maybe she could get clear.

A second roar triggered a fresh wave of goblin screams. Some shrieked in terror and others in pain, and she almost stopped. The creatures closest to her were no longer interested in what she was doing. Instead, they all stared beyond her.

As much as she wanted to see what they were looking at, Kaylin wanted to get away more so pressed on. The screeches grew louder after another bellow. This time, when she glanced over her shoulder, she saw giants.

No, not giants, but...were those cows walking on their hind legs while they pounded goblins with their fists?

She gaped as the beasts crammed the smaller creatures into their mouths and crunched down on them.

The goblins closest to her turned, ran, and vanished over the rise and out of sight.

Good idea. She bounded onto the closest pile of rocks.

With disconcerting clarity, she remembered the sniffing and snorting she'd heard on her first night into her journey. Had that been a minotaur? Were these minotaurs?

Kaylin landed and scanned the escarpment for a potential handhold.

There's no way they won't notice that, the little voice in her head snarked.

I won't be there for long, she retorted. *I'm going up and over and down.*

And hope you don't run into any gobbers on the other side.

"Shut up!" She gritted her teeth, pushed off the outcrop, and caught hold of a ridge in the rock. Her feet scrambled for purchase but found it in the many cracks and crevices and she pulled herself up.

The roars and shrieks continued in the valley, and she threw herself flat on the ridge top and twisted to get a better look at what was happening. More importantly, she needed to see if her flight had been noticed by any of the big brutes that approached at the other end.

She almost wished she hadn't.

With her panic abated, she now recognized the minotaurs from the pictures she'd seen on bounty posters and the descriptions she'd heard from mercenaries at the inns and taverns she'd snuck into. These were busy battering as many goblins as were in reach.

Those creatures that had escaped the valley had scattered. She could see the signs of their passage as bushes and grass tussocks shook or as small groups of them raced across open patches of ground. They didn't appear to remember that she existed.

Kaylin exhaled a slow breath. It looked like she'd escaped.

She lay there and caught her breath as she watched the minotaurs in their hunt for a little while longer before she slid along the top of the outcrop. When she noticed that it ran a little farther along the edge of the next valley, she moved into a crouch and half-ran, half-walked to the end.

From there, it was a short drop to the ground, which she only made after another careful look around. The fires at the inn burned more brightly now and she was able to make out what looked like another high point of rock two valleys over.

With this as her next landmark, she remained low and moved as quietly as she could toward it.

Soon, she would have to stop for the night, but she required more distance between her camp and where the minotaurs were feasting. She doubted the goblins would be out hunting that night but wasn't willing to take any chances.

She wanted to be up high and sheltered where she could gain a good idea of what waited for her when the next day's journey began.

CHAPTER TWENTY-TWO

Mostly, there were more goblins—a scouting party the next day and a small group of raiders the day after but none the day after that. There were other things, though. Kaylin moved more cautiously and had realized that while patience might not mean speed, it almost certainly meant living to see another day, which was preferable.

She remembered what Dagger had told her at the Chevaliers' chapter house.

"Do your best," the old woman had said, "but most importantly, don't forget where you came from. The skills you have now can still stand you in good stead for the future. Sometimes, the ability to move unseen and stay out of sight is as important to your survival as how well you can fight or cast a spell."

Wise words, Captain Delaine had called them, and she had to agree. Instead of moving with caution through the Kill Zone, she now moved with caution and with magic.

How many times had she used magic to cloak her movement through the halls at the Academy or through the gardens? How many times had she used a simple cantrip to dull the sound of her steps on the stone paths of the garden or the wooden floors of the corridor above the magisters' floor?

Too many, given that it should never have been necessary, but it was a skill that would stand her in good stead now as it had then. She cursed her stupidity in neglecting it when she needed it most and was even more grateful to the learning she'd gained from her pursuit of elven magic.

Kaylin drew on her ability to blur her outline or dull the noise her boots made on the stony ground. She tapped into the skills she'd learned while sneaking into the upper stories of taverns or small local businesses as a thief. These helped her to move quietly using the cover offered by the terrain around her.

While there were no walls to hide behind or gardens to shelter in, there were rock formations that were easier to climb. The bushes and grasses did the same job as any rose bush or clump of delphinium.

She'd been an idiot and was lucky to have survived the first two days without being eaten or worse, but she'd be an even greater fool if she pushed her luck too much.

Her precautions didn't mean she traveled without incident, only that she had a better chance of not walking into another group of foraging goblins or other creatures.

They weren't foolproof, though.

Twice, she used the thief staple of tossing stones so they clattered and drew attention away from her location. Once, she used a spell to recall the rumbling echo of minotaur hooves to drive the scouting party in another direction when one of their members looked like they'd found her trail.

On another occasion, she used both stones and a conjuration of dancing lights to draw the attention of a group of minotaurs away from the path she'd taken to reach her latest campsite. The big, bovine-headed monsters showed a real preference for hunting at night and she soon understood what she'd seen on her first night on the trail.

They seemed to like sheltering in the forest or deepest gullies during the day.

It made Kaylin glad that she hadn't followed the first stream she'd crossed to its origins. Who knew where that first group of shadows had ended up?

With them constantly in mind, she made sure to camp high up. She wasn't sure about goblins but she was fairly certain that minotaurs didn't climb that well. Her logic was that as long as she stayed out of grab reach or the range of a questing spear, she'd be safe from them camped on top of one of the outcrops scattered around.

The only time that approach had almost landed her in trouble, it hadn't been minotaurs or goblins. It had been with something much larger than either.

She'd completed another leg and reached the checkpoint after a roundabout journey around a narrow valley and across a sparsely vegetated plateau. The Doom was hidden by a slight rise in the ground and a low ridge of rock, and the sun had begun to drop.

Kaylin hurried forward, eager to reach the top of the checkpoint in time to try to strike out to one more before she stopped for the night. The ruins weren't far off and she almost expected to see some kind of derelict structure each time she crested a hill.

When she didn't, disappointment twisted through her and she wondered if her journey would ever end or if she was doomed to travel day after day while the city never came any closer. Maybe she was moving in the wrong direction and didn't know it.

Idiot, she scolded herself. *It's getting closer. You only have to keep moving. See?*

The reprimand spurred her on and she hauled herself up the last part of the ridgeline—and very nearly let herself fall again. There, seated on top of the rock with its tail stretched along the edge of the ledge and its back to her, was the largest lizard she'd ever seen. Easily, she thought in bemusement, two or more horses in size.

Blue-gray scales with streaks of gray-brown and gray-green made it surprisingly difficult to see where it stopped and the rock began. It also helped the creature blend in with the sky and the hillside beyond.

How does it do that? she wondered and tried to keep her breathing soft and quiet. It became harder to hold her position but she didn't want to risk either climbing onto the rock or to the ground below.

From her position at the edge of the ledge, she thought it was looking out over the road leading into the city. Its head was up and it seemed to study the distant fires and shadows in the ruins.

Kaylin held her breath, not sure whether to run, hide, or stay where she was. She braced herself so she could rest her elbows on the rock and make the necessary gestures without falling, then blurred her outline and drew a little of the gathering shadows around herself.

The lizard shifted and she stared as she counted six long-clawed feet. She held her breath as its head moved as though it scanned the surrounding landscape for danger.

Curious despite the very real possibility of danger, she wondered how good its hearing was or if it relied more on sight and sense.

Its tongue flicked in and out as though tasting the air, and she readied herself to drop below the level of the ledge and then to the ground. She doubted that she could outrun it but maybe it wouldn't like the drop and would have to take another route to reach her.

Six legs! She imagined it loping up behind her and launching into a pounce. *I bet it could take down a minotaur if it wanted to.*

The huge head swung away from her and its tongue quested for more scents on the late-afternoon air. Dusk was closing and she didn't want to spend the night anywhere near it.

Bardatonal. She didn't say the word combination out loud and wondered if the magic would work without the sound or if the silent motion of her mouth and her loud mental intent would be enough.

There was no way she wanted to draw the lizard's attention. The creature was easily the size of a wagon or maybe a small carriage. It probably needed six legs simply to hold itself up.

Kaylin forced her attention away from its size and tried to focus on the spell. She'd used the gestures to increase control and duration and wove them into the spell. On the piece of hillside opposite the creature's perch, a soft boom rang out.

Rock rattled and a burst of color flashed into being. The lizard's head jerked around and it hissed softly. It shifted its body forward and its tail followed. She adjusted her grasp hastily and ducked below the ledge as the appendage swished past the space where she'd been.

She struggled to hold the spell where she'd last seen it as the rock vibrated beneath the heavy tread as the beast descended. The tail swept over her again but she risked peering over the ledge to see where it was going and what had happened to her lights.

To her relief, they were still there even though the lizard was not.

Kaylin caught sight of its tail disappearing over the other side of its perch and she hauled herself up cautiously until she could creep to the other side and see where the creature had gone.

She'd been right. It did move fast. She might not have seen it in the gloom below if it hadn't been for its rapid movement through the grass tufts and shrubs and even then, she only caught blurs of it as it bounded toward her flickering spell lights.

Satisfied that she was now alone, she glanced left and right and noted the gap between the rock pile she had climbed and the next escarpment. It was no wider than what she was used to between houses and she scrutinized the other side to identify the handholds she'd need. Still crouched, she moved toward the gap and drew the lights along the opposite slope as she did so.

When she reached the gap, she looked for the lizard and saw it pounce at the lights. She whisked them up out of its reach and made a short gesture with her hand to wave them higher before she made the jump.

As expected, it was an easy distance to cross and she landed hard on the other side but found her grip and held on.

When she looked at the opposite slope, the lights had vanished but it didn't matter. The lizard had chosen to look for them. It zigzagged across the opposite slope while it turned its head from side to side.

Kaylin crouched low on the rock and looked for a way that would let her work around it. This would take her slightly off course but if it meant she wouldn't become lizard lunch, it would be worth it. The sun touched the far rim of the valley and she frowned.

She had to stop for the night but she also needed to be a good distance away from there. There was no way to know if the beast would track her scent when it reached its perch the next day or even if it would return, but she wasn't willing to risk either.

With a sigh, she focused on another outcrop of rock and hoped it wasn't the home for a second lizard—or the temporary look-out point for a goblin tribe.

Honestly, she'd be glad to be out of the Kill Zone.

It took her two more days, during which she narrowly escaped discovery by another minotaur hunting party and two more goblin patrols. Once, she had to change her route to avoid what looked like a large camp of goblins. It took her farther around the ruins than she'd planned, but she reminded herself it was for the best.

Her logic told her that if most of the humanoids preyed on travelers, they'd be found closest to the road.

She reached her first tumbled wall halfway through the seventh day and her heart skipped happily.

"The Doom," she whispered and savored the way it sounded coming out of her mouth.

Kaylin stifled a relieved giggle as relief flooded through her. She was almost home-free.

Caution kicked in and she pushed down the exuberance that threatened to make her race through the ruins and focused on what lay ahead of her. She moved through the skeletons of long-abandoned buildings and avoided the tumbled stone blocks of another world and time.

Vines grew in shrouds to soften their outlines but dragged the walls apart even as they held them together.

As she worked through the weeds and bushes that had pushed through the paving stones and cobbles, she avoided other things too. Bones were plentiful, some bleached by the sun and others held together by rotting rags, and rats skittered through tumbled piles of debris and refuse.

Halfway through the afternoon, when the ruins were closer together and the ground between them paved with broken cobbles, she climbed a crumbling arch and looked for the inn.

It was certainly closer but she didn't think she'd reach it before dusk. She peered at the stone floor of what had been a kitchen or perhaps a sitting room and startled rabbits and rats darted across the room. When she looked over the ruins, she noticed the flare of half a dozen small fires and the ruddy glow reflected on broken stonework of a dozen more.

Voices carried on the afternoon air. Most held a guttural note, a few gibbered in the higher register she now associated with goblins, and none of them spoke Common. It was time for her to seek shelter for the night.

Kaylin looked for a way to avoid returning to the ground but didn't see one. What she did notice, however, was that some of the buildings still had one or more floors left relatively intact.

Her arch didn't reach any of them, however, and the weight of her pack prevented her from attempting the leaps she was used to making to cross such gaps in Waypoint. Reluctantly, she chose a route leading to a square of floor above the rest and descended.

Nothing impeded her passage and soon, she had reached her goal.

It was the highest point in the ruins that she could find and wide enough that she could spread her sleeping roll and still have ample room between herself and the ledge. Confident that she couldn't be seen from above or below, she slept.

She woke shivering as the world paled to gray. The sun had painted the sky in flares of pink and yellow, and furtive rustling told her she was not alone. She rolled swiftly out of her bedding and looked around to see who or what might be sneaking up on her.

At first, she found nothing but a moment later, she saw the rats. They'd scuttled along the narrow bridge of wall that connected her perch to a section of vine-shrouded flooring lower down. She drew her dagger with one hand and began to move her other hand through the first gesture of the fire orb spell.

"Let's see how well you like when I set your whiskers alight," she muttered.

The rodents paused and all stared warily at her. They seemed to come to a decision and continued to watch her as they pivoted on the wall and scurried to the shelter of what must have been their den.

"I'm lucky they didn't eat me in my sleep," Kaylin muttered, shoved her sleeping roll into her pack, and retrieved a ration bar. With a frown, she added, "Or steal my rations."

She glanced around the ruins and noted the soft, gray curls of smoke that rose here and there. Her gaze drifted in search of the walls of the Final Rest and she was relieved to see them looming much closer than they had the night before.

If she hurried, she could reach them by lunch.

That thought buoyed her spirits and she bounced across the stonework to land firmly on the ground. After a moment to reorient herself, she pivoted toward the walls of the inn and trotted forward.

With a small frown, she tried to recall if she'd seen any smoke coming from this direction and thought not. Still, she couldn't be too careful. She moved quickly along what had once been a narrow street before she reached a point where the walls on either side had collapsed and rubble blocked her path.

Carefully, she took note of where she was and where she wanted to go next before she turned through the closest doorway. Hopefully, it would lead her past the walls hemming her in and out to another street.

What she didn't expect to find was a small encampment of orcs.

She didn't even register what it was until she'd looked past the dying glow of the embers to the sleeping rolls crowded between the fire and the six-foot-tall remains of the walls on the other side.

A moment later, she noticed the orc leaning against the opposite wall cleaning his sword. Unfortunately, he saw her at the same time.

His eyes widened and she noted the mish-mash of leather and metal armor he wore and made an abrupt about-face. She darted through the door and was halfway to the last cross-street she'd passed before the first orcish shout reached her ears.

Kaylin didn't recognize that word either. Not that she needed to recognize it. The shouts and clashes that followed made it very clear what was happening.

The orcs were waking and pulling their armor on and they were very excited about something.

She knew the something could only be her and pivoted as she reached the corner to make a sharp right turn. Hopefully, her memory served her correctly when she didn't recall seeing any other exits except the one she'd entered by. Several projectiles whistled past the corner behind her and metal struck stone in a series of clatters.

Another attack followed immediately, this time from the wall on the opposite side of the street.

Instinctively, she looked up and realized that while she didn't remember seeing a way onto the level above the orcs, there was one. They ran along the open floor above her and fired huge bows that looked like they were constructed from bone and horn.

Kaylin ducked and more arrows streaked over her head. She bolted to the corner of the street, intending to cross into the alley opposite, but a storm of arrows filled the space between her and the opening and she turned right again. Behind her, the sound of heavy boots pounded across the cobblestones and something much larger than an arrow sailed past her to bounce off the wall opposite.

She glanced toward it and her eyes widened.

A spear? Seriously? Like arrows weren't enough?

Panic flared and she summoned a burst of speed. Another spear sailed past as the first of the orcs made the turn behind her. Bootsteps sounded above her when the orcs on the next level gave chase. She hoped they would stop when the floor ran out.

A momentary silence was followed by a heavy thump and a grunt from behind her.

It sounded like one of the big lugs had leapt from the roof and landed on her heels. Kaylin resisted the urge to turn her head and see. Instead, she jinked closer to the wall and was rewarded with a swooshing sound beside her.

The noise continued as a small ax spun past her end over end. It ran out of momentum and thunked on the cobbles and she sprinted past it. The orcs were no longer firing at her from the rooftop, so she tried to dart across the road.

She'd only moved two paces to her left before three or four spears sailed past.

These guys are either lousy shots or they're not trying to hit me, she thought and glanced up in an attempt to see past the buildings to where the Final Rest might be. She still felt like she was going in the right direction but she couldn't be sure.

More arrows whistled past. These went high over her head and she resisted the urge to duck and roll. The sound of boots gaining behind her helped with that, but not with the urge to see how close her pursuers were.

Kaylin glanced over her shoulder, not surprised to see that the orcs were much closer. They were taller than she was and unlike the goblins, they ran with smooth easy strides that ate the ground beneath them.

She snapped her attention to the front and decided she didn't want to watch. What she wanted to do was run and find a way to go somewhere they didn't want her to be—preferably without getting shot for her trouble.

The Mistfire man's words came back to haunt her.

"They'll make a nice serving wench out of you and when they get bored, they'll eat you or sell you on."

Serving wench? She had the feeling he'd sanitized that because of her age or her gender, or a combination of both, and she didn't want to find out what he truly meant. Not in person and not by personal experience.

She learned how fast the orcs could move when a dozen of them stepped into the street ahead of her.

As best as she could deduce, they'd sprinted into the alley she'd been dissuaded from, raced her along the back of the buildings opposite, and cut in ahead of her. At least she hoped they'd sprinted. More to the point, if they'd sprinted and were able to out-distance her, did that mean those behind her hadn't even tried?

Kaylin looked for an escape. So far, she'd resisted the urge to duck into any of the doorways beside her. She did that now and pivoted abruptly to leap the rubble-strewn steps and bolt into the space beyond.

What she was looking for was an exit—which was exactly what she didn't find.

A shadow fell across the floor and she didn't have to look back to know she was in trouble. She glanced around again and noticed an empty window, a partially collapsed internal wall, and a ruined staircase too high to reach but which drew her attention to the partial floor above.

She took two long strides that ended in a leap as she stretched upward, not to the dangling stairs but for the top of the wall. Her fingers caught and the orc behind her roared, but she didn't hesitate. Her boots scrabbled for purchase and she hauled herself to the top of the uneven surface.

Once there, she didn't stop. Instead, she ran along it, kicked off, and aimed for the remains of the second floor and the broken wall leading to the street beyond. Her practice in the city paid off as she dropped the short distance to the cobbles, rolled to her feet, and broke into a run.

Before she'd jumped, she'd caught a glimpse of fortified walls with what might have been human faces peering over the edge. If that was the Final Rest, she could attract the guards' attention.

What? her inner voice demanded. *Do you honestly think they will help?*

Kaylin didn't bother to answer but she hoped they would. After all, what was the inn's reputation worth if it couldn't protect the people who came to it for shelter?

Surely they wouldn't let her die at the gates.

Shouts erupted from the cross-street as she bypassed the sprinters' blockade. She laughed and raced toward the inn, knowing she couldn't waste the tiny lead she had. While she didn't know what the orcs had been doing while she'd made her escape, she was very sure it wasn't baking cakes and sharing candy.

She imagined she could hear boots pounding through the streets to either side and ahead of her and tried to increase her pace. Her aim was to turn right and head toward the inn when she reached the next intersection, but she realized she hadn't imagined the sound of bootsteps.

Like he'd leaned against the wall and waited for her, the biggest orc she'd ever seen stepped around the corner. He wasn't that much larger than his fellows but he'd timed his appearance so that she was in grab range.

Kaylin didn't stop to think.

"Myradshiel!" she shouted, wove the appropriate gestures with her hands, and thrust them toward him.

He recoiled, dropped the unwieldy blade he'd held, and raised both hands to cover his face, but not before she saw tattoos bent and twisted by a pale gray scar that stretched from temple to chin. She tried to dart past him, aware now of the thunder of boots from the other end of the street leading into the intersection.

The sprinters hadn't wasted any time in their pursuit.

As she drew alongside him, the orc lowered his hands and shook his head as he looked around. His eyes lit up and his jaw dropped into a savage grin when he saw her. She threw herself into a roll and fumbled for the dagger at her belt as she came to her feet. Unperturbed, he stooped toward her.

Without thought, she simply reacted and slashed reflexively at the center of his face. Her blade scored his forehead and nose in a deft swipe.

Her adversary recoiled with a roar and clutched his head, but she didn't stop. She'd caught sight of the narrowest of gaps between two stone walls and hoped the orcs had discounted it as too narrow.

It might be too small for their great bulks but it wasn't for her. She slipped inside it as he recovered and began to bellow orders. Shouts answered him and the boots changed direction. She wiggled faster. The gap was a tight fit, even for her, and she hoped there wasn't another route that would allow her pursuers to reach the other end before she did.

She made it through, only to be greeted by footsteps coming hard in her direction. A glance confirmed that the orcs had known of a shortcut through the ruins and were closing fast.

Kaylin bolted along the street as she looked for some way to escape.

A low section of wall created a path to a first-floor ledge and another formed a narrow bridge to a second story. The sight of the inn rising above the rubble three streets over made her pause, and an arrow whirred dangerously close to her head.

The scarred orc roared and he sounded furious and frustrated. One of his comrades barked a protest, which was followed by the sound of a fist smacking flesh and what might have been a cringing apology.

The next arrow that streaked past her was much closer and she ducked.

She glanced at the wall again, ran across another section, bounded across a small gap, and dropped to a lower part. The orcs tracked her from the ground and cut through buildings and down sidestreets she hadn't thought led anywhere.

Spears clattered against the stonework below her feet and arrows whistled past but missed when she balked and leapt from the top of one wall to another. The attacks threatened to throw her off-balance and she slipped and dropped into a crouch to steady herself. The orcs shouted in triumph and started to close in on her from the ground.

Kaylin had to admire them. The ruins were their home and they knew its ways well. She thought they'd catch her when she had no choice but to drop into an alley as they turned into it. This time, she noticed a crack marring the stones at the top of the wall and cast another spell on the fly.

"Bardatonal!"

It was easier the second time around and her fingers flowed through the gestures as she directed the magical energy into the loose stones while she ran. Behind her, a sharp crack and a rattle of stones culminated in a clatter when the wall caved in. Frustrated shouts rose behind her and she raced on.

Her flight along the walls had taken her one and a half blocks. The collapsed wall bought her another block before the orcs raced into the road behind her. She could hear them closing and managed an extra burst of speed as she lunged out of the street leading to the road around the base of the Final Rest's walls.

"Hey!" she screamed. "Hey! Open up!"

She sprinted to the gates, half-expecting them to open and half-expecting them to stay closed. Either way, she didn't slow but barreled directly toward them. More arrows whistled overhead, and she swore she felt something slam into her back. Other arrows swarmed in the opposite direction when they arced out from the wall and into the leading rank of orcs.

Her pursuers came to a sudden, juddering stop. Their boots slid on the cobbles as they halted and their attention alternated between her and the guards on top of the wall.

"Kill her!" The shout rang out from behind her as she careened into the still-closed door.

Kaylin could hear people moving on the other side and the grating noise of timber scraping as something heavy was lifted, but she didn't know if they would be in time. Determined to fight for her freedom, she turned to face the orcs.

It was instinctive to reach for the dagger at her belt, but she remembered that the blade wasn't the best weapon she had. With an effort, she moved her hands away from her belt and wove a shield sigil in the air before her.

"Helda!" she snapped and moved back toward the gate until something stopped her from stepping any further. It held her off the gate's surface and applied pressure to her pack.

The scarred orc pushed to the front of his troops.

"Kill her!" he repeated, took the bow from his back, and nocked an arrow.

A spear launched from the wall and she thought the orc leader was about to pay the price for his pride, but one of the others leapt forward, extended a shield, and knocked the spear aside. He paid for his intervention with his life when two arrows pin-cushioned his head and another spear skewered his middle.

Their leader drew the bow as one rank of orcs stepped forward and extended their shields to provide cover for their comrades in the second rank. Those orcs had drawn their bows but they weren't sighted on the soldiers on top of the wall.

They were all aimed at the young girl who faced them defiantly.

Kaylin wondered if her shield would stop them all and what the logistics would be for conjuring a second. The shield floated in front of her as she tried to decide between an attempt to conjure a larger shield or if she should try to blind the archers with flashing sparkles.

In the end, she didn't get to decide. More arrows launched from the wall, along with more spears, and lightning flashed. She darted a glance at the sky and saw nothing. No clouds marred the blue of a late spring day and no storm wind blew.

But the lightning came anyway. It scythed from the heavens, sizzled into the double rank of orcs, and flung them outward. At the same time, the gate opened and she was jerked inside. She lost her balance as she was thrown back and two soldiers slammed the gate closed again, while four others dropped a massive beam of wood into place.

From her position on the ground, she saw a tall figure in dark-blue robes with long hair that formed a halo of white around his head. In one hand, he held an enormous black staff but the other was upraised and empty.

He spoke in a cacophony of sound and thunder boomed.

Panic erupted outside the gates and she pushed slowly from the cobbles. The soldiers ignored her and raced to return to their posts on the wall, even though the sound of running footsteps indicated that their help wasn't needed.

She was breathing hard from her run and felt more than a little bruised from her hard landing on the cobbles as she limped toward the stairs.

There had to be someone she could thank for her rescue.

CHAPTER TWENTY-THREE

The guards weren't interested in Kaylin's thanks. When she climbed to the top of the wall, she was greeted by one of the two who had dragged her inside.

"You shouldn't be up here," he snapped.

"I only—" she started but he cut her off.

"Get off the wall and out of the way." He growled impatiently and lowered a hand to the hilt of his sword. "We've got enough trouble as it is without you underfoot."

She stared at him and he turned away abruptly to focus on the ruins. Irritated, she looked around to find another guard to talk to. When she located the other one who'd rescued her, she moved toward him.

It took her a few strides to realize the mage wasn't where she'd last seen him.

But I wanted to talk to him. Sure he couldn't have gone too far, she swept her gaze around to try to locate him.

Kaylin caught sight of the wizard as she reached the guard, who was as happy to see her as the first one had been.

"What are you doing up here?" he demanded. "You shouldn't be here."

"I only wanted to say thank you," she told him, "for what you did back there."

He shrugged. "That's our job, which is why we're allowed here and you are not unless we ask you to come."

"Fine, well—" Her response was cut short when the guard took her by the shoulders and spun her.

"Get off the orcs-be-damned wall, girl," he ordered and shoved her toward the stairs.

She stumbled, then realized she had no idea where she was meant to go and glanced at the guard. He'd already turned his attention to the ruins so she approached one of the others.

The man's attention was fixed over the walls and he held a bow loosely in one hand, but his focus wasn't so taken by the sights beyond that he didn't notice her approach. As she moved closer, he pivoted to face her.

He didn't say anything but watched her warily. She saw the tension in his frame and stopped a few paces distant.

"I just got here," she began and he jabbed a finger at the main building inside the walls.

"Go and start spending money," he snapped, "or else I'll boot you back to your admirers."

At his words, she glanced at his face, then at the wall. Without asking for permission, she took two quick steps and peered over the edge. The archer moved with her but didn't try to stop her or boot her into the ruins.

As Kaylin looked down to see what had happened to the orcs who'd pursued her, he raised his bow, fitted an arrow to the string, and drew it. She ignored him, too intrigued by the scene below.

The orcs were still there. Most of them were dead and those who weren't looked like they were dying. The big orc with the scarred face moved among the warriors, nudged one with the toe of his boot, and stooped to inspect another.

The one he nudged didn't move and after a brief inspection, he drew a heavy-bladed dagger and cut the throat of the next. She gasped at the sheer brutality of it and the orc glanced up at the wall.

Blood had dried in a messy line from his forehead across to his other cheek.

Scarsnout, she thought—she'd considered Scarface as a nickname but corrected that now—and felt a quiver of fear at his glare.

Whatever she wanted to call him, he didn't look happy—or like he would forget her in a hurry. She shivered as he returned his attention to his warriors.

Dividing his attention between the walls and his troops, Scarsnout inspected each of the orcs left in the open area in front of the walls.

He killed some and searched others to take pouches from their belts or other small items from their fingers or throats. Each time he moved to another, he cast another nasty look at the walls, glared at the soldiers, and scowled venomously at her.

Finally, he lifted one of the warriors from the ground and dragged his arm across his shoulders. He darted another look at the wall as he turned toward the ruins. His face promised murder for anyone who'd opposed him and her in particular.

Kaylin watched him leave and knew he wouldn't give up. She would have to be very careful the next time she entered the ruins.

The archer watched them go, then glared at her. "Get. Off. My. Wall," he ordered harshly and she looked at him in surprise.

The look on his face was as bad as some of those Scarsnout had cast at her.

Huh. I wonder what I did wrong this time. She turned abruptly on her heel.

"Thanks for your help," she called over her shoulder, although what help and how much thanks she owed him weren't clear. It merely didn't seem right to leave the wall without saying something.

He didn't reply and when she glanced at him, he had already returned his stare over the wall, his bow held loosely at his side. Not only did he not look at her, but none of the other guards did either.

Well, I guess that shows me. She sighed inwardly and moved down the stairs to the courtyard below.

The main building looked similar to the inns she'd seen in Waypoint but more defensible. Instead of large windows at the front, this inn had smaller windows with heavy storm shutters that could cover them. These were being locked open now that the trouble outside had settled.

Kaylin caught the curious glances directed at her but she was quickly dismissed. It was almost as if she was like any other adventurer who visited the inn. The idea was strangely comforting. After all, a year was a long time and she hoped to fit in.

Fat chance, her inner voice mocked but she pushed it away and walked inside.

Two steps inside the door, she came to a sudden stop. While she'd been in taverns before, this one was different from several perspectives. The first was the noise, and not because it was noisy but because of the multiple languages being spoken. The second difference was in the customers.

In Waypoint, patrons were almost always human. She'd seen a few dwarves like those seated at the bar and some of the tables, and while the majority of the others were human, there were other races, too.

She drew a deep breath to steady herself and resisted the urge to turn and walk out the door. Although she didn't know any of the faces around her, she recognized the kind of person who wore them.

These were men and women used to fighting and killing as part of their living.

Some of them would probably have no qualms about taking her life if they thought there was enough profit in it. Judging by the way they scrutinized her and turned back to what they were doing, she didn't offer any kind of monetary incentive, nor was she worth their time.

That's not a bad thing, she told herself and forced her feet to start moving toward the bar.

The innkeeper had glanced up when she entered and gone back to serving his customers, but he glanced at her now and then. It was probably best to not keep him waiting.

Kaylin let her gaze wander around the inn as she crossed to the counter. The humans seemed to come from all corners of the world.

Some stood at six feet and others were shorter than a dwarf. As for dwarves, she found them fascinating.

She tried not to stare but she hadn't known they could vary in race as much as humans. They were all shorter than the average man and all heavily muscled, stocky, and bearded, but while some tended to pale or bronzed skins and beards in shades of red and brown, one seated next to the wall at the fire was noticeably different.

He was slighter in build than his fellows with a head of coal-black hair and swarthy skin. While he carved meat from a small haunch on a platter beside his plate, he observed the rest of the inn and its occupants warily with dark eyes. She got the impression he hadn't been at the inn much longer than she had.

The biggest difference, however, was the number of monsters in the inn. Her head snapped around in a hasty double-take when she caught sight of a large bull-headed man seated on a chair in one corner.

He was comfortably propped and drank quietly from an enormous jug.

The sight made her uneasy. The last time she'd seen a minotaur anywhere near this close was when a herd of them had pursued a tribe of goblins, trampled them underfoot, or picked them up and shoved them screaming into their mouths.

And speaking of goblins... Her gaze drifted to the other end of the inn, where four of the small, bat-eared creatures were seated around a table shaking and rolling several small colored bones in a complex game like dice. Coins were piled in front of each and some had small gemstones lying next to those, but their wide yellow eyes were fixed on the bones.

Their small brows were furrowed in concentration and one would occasionally snap a comment at the others.

These were either greeted with mocking laughter or equally fierce replies before the bones would be rolled and counted. Once the score was discussed, the coins would change hands and occasionally, a bone would be pushed across the table.

Kaylin reached the bar and the innkeeper bustled closer.

"New?" he asked and smiled at her wide-eyed nod. "Do you need a room or will you sleep in the commons?"

The question caught her by surprise, but Kaylin followed the sweep of his outstretched arm to look through a set of double doors leading into a large room filled with rows of bunks. After a nervous look around the taproom, she shook her head and decided she didn't feel safe sleeping with the company she saw.

She was about to ask him the price of a room when something shattered across the room.

Her startled look revealed a dwarf—almost as tall as she was but at least two of her across—who glared at the chest of a human warrior. The man looked at him with a broad grin on his face.

"A pox on your mother," he said.

The dwarf poked him in the center of his armored belly. "What did you say about my mother?" he demanded, his voice rising.

"I said she'd have to fetch a stool and ask real nice," the man retorted and swept his gauntleted hand down in time to deflect his opponent's short, sharp punch at his groin.

"She wouldn't go near a hoary piss-wipe like yersel'. Ye're not good enow!"

The warrior placed his hand on the dwarf's helmet and stepped back, keeping his opponent at arm's length.

"But you're sayin' she's in the business," the fighter teased, "and I don't hear you denyin' she'd need a stool."

"Are you callin' me mother *short*?"

From the way he said it, Kaylin thought he might find that comment more insulting than the other suggestion. The tables cleared around the two of them and hardened mercenaries picked their meals and drinks up carefully and moved well away.

All except the goblins.

One of the shifty-looking creatures cocked his head to look at the potential combatants, then shrugged and returned to his game. It was almost as though the creatures didn't think anyone would dare to interrupt them.

Kaylin watched in near disbelief as the bones rattled onto the tabletop and another complex round of calculations began.

The bones were passed to the next goblin and shaken and in the same moment, the dwarf stepped in, seized his tormentor by the waist, and lifted and hurled him back. The warrior gave a startled shout and landed with a thunderous crack on top of a table.

One of the goblins twitched an ear but its gleaming yellow eyes never left the bones being sorted and it happily took possession of the coins pushed to it shortly after.

When the dwarf picked a chair up, a low round of "ooh" rose from the watching crowd.

"That'll be an extra gold," the barkeeper shouted and shook his head.

"And worth every ounce!" the stocky fighter roared and swung his impromptu weapon as the warrior placed a hand on the neighboring table and pulled himself to his feet.

The chair caught the man across the upper arm. One of its legs shattered on his pauldron and the other snapped over an outsized bicep.

This time, the warrior roared.

Some of the patrons snickered and others held their hands out to receive grudging payment from those closest to them.

The warrior bellowed again and the dwarf roared in response, scooped a chair up from behind him, and brought it down in an overhead swing.

Its target looked up and caught it to halt its descent.

With a belligerent grunt, the dwarf bounded forward and jackhammered both feet into his opponent's chest. The man's breastplate rang with the sound of hob-nailed boots and Kaylin swore she saw it crumble.

When the heavy boots rebounded and thumped onto the inn's floor, the short attacker still brandished the chair.

His opponent wrenched it out of his hands and the dwarf lowered his head and charged.

He bumped another patron, whose ale sloshed down the front of the man who stood beside him. Fists swung and the brawl spread as others joined the fray.

She jumped when a heavy hand nudged her shoulder.

"If you intend to stay," the innkeeper shouted in an attempt to be heard above the brawl on the other side of the room, "you've got to at least pay for a meal if not a bed."

"How mu—" Her question was cut short by another resounding crash from behind her and they both looked to see what had happened.

The dwarf had caught the man around the waist and propelled him onto his back to destroy another table. He landed astride his taller opponent and hammered his head with both fists.

"That'll be two gold!" the proprietor yelled but his protest appeared to have gone unheard.

"And you!" he shouted at a female fighter, who'd lifted another man and was preparing to throw him. "Four gold if you break another table this week."

She laughed and hurled the man, and the resulting crack made Kaylin flinch. Across the room from her, the warrior rammed one of the chairs at the goblins' table.

It tilted sideways and back and the occupant responded with an outraged screech. The sound sent chills down Kaylin's spine. Now there was a sound she recognized.

She didn't have time to dwell on it, though. The two opponents continued their fight, oblivious to the trouble they were about to unleash on their heads.

Another goblin was launched from his seat when the warrior's feet lashed out. The dwarf stepped forward and upended the table to shove it out of his way.

All three goblins shrieked in fury, and doubtful glances were exchanged between those patrons who hadn't joined the ruckus.

"Enough!" the innkeeper thundered and his voice rolled like a death knell across the inn.

Some of the fighters paused but for most, the fight continued unabated and the goblins now joined in. Rather than keep it to a brawl, however, the little monsters simply drew their daggers and forced the two initial combatants to fight as a team to defend themselves.

The innkeeper pulled a horn from under the counter and blew a series of three clear notes. Immediately, the fighters froze. The goblins exchanged glances and backed away but one of them gestured at their opponents in a way that promised trouble later. Around the inn, other fights ended quickly and those involved sat at nearby tables.

When the door to the inn burst open and a squad of guardsmen entered with cudgels and nets at the ready, the dwarf was straightening one table while the warrior stacked the remains of another against the wall.

The goblins had picked up the scattered pieces of their game and were setting things up for another round at another table.

The guards' leader looked at the innkeeper, but he shook his head and gestured at the miscreants now cleaning their mess.

"You!" the guard leader bellowed, and dwarf and man looked around. "Come on!"

"This is your fault!" the short fighter shouted and stabbed a short stumpy finger at his adversary, their brief cooperation forgotten.

"It's more like your mother started it," the man retorted and the dwarf charged.

It took the guards several long minutes to separate the two and subdue them enough to drag them from the inn, and Kaylin stared open-mouthed as they did so.

"So what will it be?" The voice at her elbow made her jump. "Room or commons?"

"How much for a room?" she asked.

"A small one?" the innkeeper asked. "And only for the night?"

"Yes," she answered. "To both questions."

She decided she could always pay for an extended stay if she had enough coin but she wasn't willing to count what she had in the public arena of the bar.

"Wise choice," the innkeeper told her. "Seeing as you're new here, it'll be five copper. The usual price is a silver."

"A night?" she asked and he nodded.

Kaylin pulled a coin out. It gleamed gold in the lamplight and he swept it quickly out of sight.

"Do you want a meal?" he asked as he placed her change on the counter. She nodded and he slid a coin out of the pile. "Ale?"

Again, she nodded.

"Dark or light?" She frowned in confusion. "The ale?" he explained.

"Dark?" She shrugged.

"If you're sure."

"Yes."

"Pint?"

She responded with another nod. It seemed safer than saying "whatever's normal." One look at the folk around her said there wasn't a normal.

"Will you eat at the counter or at a table?"

A glance around revealed a couple of empty tables positioned against the inn walls where she could hopefully sit undisturbed. She chose one and pointed. "There?"

He smiled and his dark eyes twinkled. "There is fine. Here's your ale. I'll bring your food when it's ready."

Kaylin nodded, took her mug, and threaded between the other patrons to the table.

To her relief, it remained empty until she arrived. She slid across the bench seat to the other end, wrapped her hands around her mug, and sipped tentatively. The brew tasted bitter at first but a fullness of flavor followed and the bitterness mellowed.

It was surprisingly good but made her head buzz, so she placed it on the table in front of her and waited for her meal. With nothing else to do, she used the time to study the other folk around her.

Like she'd thought before, most of them looked like adventurers rather than mercenaries.

She watched them over the rim of her glass, careful to try not to let them catch her staring. There was considerable variation in how they dressed and the weapons they carried. Kaylin tried to guess what each one did from what she could see.

A man who stood at the bar not far from the goblins, for instance, looked like a hunter of some kind. Or an archer, she amended, although he wore leather armor and carried a long sword in a plain but sturdy leather scabbard, and she couldn't see a bow.

Maybe he'd left it in his room.

As she wondered where it might be, he glanced up and looked around with a slight frown until he caught sight of her. She lowered her gaze hurriedly but not before she caught a glimpse of hawkish features, sharp gray eyes, and a well-tanned face.

Thankfully, he gave her a brief smile and shook his head without any indication that he'd taken offense and returned his attention to the monsters and their game.

Two women in sturdy chain mail, leather leggings, and boots, left their table to approach the bar. They held an animated discussion about food with the proprietor and pointed at items pictured on the chalkboard.

Sometimes, their questions were answered with a shake of the head and at others, with a sharp retort. She couldn't hear exactly what was said from where she sat, though.

They finally chose their evening meal and sauntered to their table and Kaylin wondered if she'd ever be as tough-looking as either of them.

Both gave her a cool look as they passed, their blue eyes curious, but their expressions warned against any attempt at conversation. She didn't know if she'd passed or failed their assessment when they looked away, but she was more interested in the weapons they carried.

Both wore a short, curved blade on each hip and a bandolier of short, straight blades across their chests. They had long hair but it was hard to tell how long when the tails of their braids disappeared below the collar of their armor.

At first, she thought they were sisters but despite their eyes, their faces were different and their hair color wasn't the same.

One was auburn, her features slightly more rounded and her lips fuller than those of her friend whose features were narrow and her lips thin. Both moved like a street cat stalking pigeons in Orcs' Head Square.

As her gaze roved across the bar, Kaylin looked for the wizard. She'd seen him on the wall and searched for an older man, bearlike in build.

Surely he'd come into the inn after the battle.

It took her several long moments to find him and when she did, she was surprised to see he was much older than she'd expected. His eyebrows were silver, as was his beard, and his long hair blended with the silver-white fur that trimmed his cloak. Even seated, she could see he was massive—at least by human standards.

The minotaur still dwarfed him, however.

He smoked a long-stemmed pipe, his empty plate pushed to the edge of his table and a large mug in front of him. A tall jug of ale stood in front of that, and he rested a book on the edge of the table, seemingly oblivious to the noise around him.

Kaylin wondered if he was looking for an apprentice and if, after his display on the wall, she dared to think she was good enough. While she was still contemplating the problem, a soft voice interrupted her.

"Easy there. It's all right. You're safe. See?"

She swiveled in her seat toward the sound and stared as a woman stroked the scaly face of a small lizard that peered out from under her short-bobbed hair. The creature made a soft chirruping sound and she tutted softly and cut a small slice of the juicy-looking meat on her plate.

It cocked its head as she offered it the tidbit but held it a little out of its reach. The small creature looked around the inn and tilted its head from side to side as it assessed the shift in the movement of the people around it.

"See?" the woman crooned and waggled the meat.

The lizard crept out from under her hair to perch on her shoulder and Kaylin stared in fascination. It had a narrow face with shrewd, intelligent eyes and was about the size of a small falcon.

Still wary, it inched forward and took the meat neatly off the point of her dagger before it rested a forepaw on the side of her head and looked around the room. The woman cut another slice and reassured by what it saw, it crouched on her shoulder with its tail draped down her back and wings neatly furled on either side of its spine.

It was the prettiest creature and she wracked her brains trying to think what it was called. Iridescent scarlet scales glittered on its body and a double row of purplish-red plates protruded from its spine. A small set of horns curved back from its forehead and its eyes were a startling green flecked with gold and silver.

Now that she'd seen it, she noticed others. Some fluttered from the rafters, bribed by meat or pieces of fruit. One refused to go anywhere near its owner until a serving maid carried a slice of pie out. She screeched and dropped the plate when the creature leapt from the ceiling and landed in the center of it.

"Kvask!" an older gentleman scolded and lifted the plate, lizard and all, from the floor. "You know better than that."

That brought soft chuckles from the others at his table, and Kaylin had to smile.

"I've never seen a drakeling like a cherry pie the way yours does," one of them commented softly and pretended to reach for the plate.

The creature bridled, arched its back, and flared its wings as it hissed and snapped at the intruding fingers.

"He's usually much nicer mannered," the older adventurer protested and earned more good-natured ribbing. He rolled his eyes. "It's not like the mage who gave me the spell to call one gave me another spell that enabled me to choose a well-mannered one."

"Pfft! I don't think even the mages know how to do that," one of the female adventurers told him as she scratched the chin of a slender cat.

The feline and the drakeling stared at one another, and the cat slunk onto its owner to seat itself in the crook of her arm, although its bright green gaze remained fixed on the small lizard. It merely paused in its feast to stare balefully at the feline and only returned to its food once it was sure the cat had settled.

Magic. Kaylin wished Captain Delaine had been able to retrieve her journal from the Academy. Hadn't she seen something to do with animals in the Teaching Room?

She hadn't paid it much attention since none of the magisters at the Academy had shown an interest in the uses of magic to tame animals and it hadn't been relevant in any of her classes. That hadn't stopped her from copying all the inscriptions from the wall and deciphering what elvish script and symbols she could.

If she could only remember them.

With her eyes closed, she tried to remember what the sequences had looked like while her fingers twitched as she thought about the gestures. A solid thump on the table beside her elbow told her that her meal had arrived, and she jerked upright with a gasp.

"Thank you," she mumbled, but the serving maid had already turned away and swung her hips as she maneuvered between tables to deliver the next meal.

The arrival of her food drove all thought of enspelling a drakeling from Kaylin's mind, at least until she'd cleared her plate. After that, it was both easier and harder to think of the gestures associated with creatures. As she contemplated the problem, she realized she'd forgotten the basic principle of intent.

After all, she knew the movements and some of the syllables for the spells associated with creatures, but surely there would be an element of friendship in there. Logic insisted that it should be something that symbolized the bond she wished to create together with the component to show she was interested.

For instance, if she wanted to draw a drakeling to her as an adventuring companion, she would have to be able to offer it protection—and maybe express the intent to protect it. If she did that, she'd have to acknowledge the need to feed it, look after it, and a host of other things.

Did the little lizards communicate?

She looked around. They looked intelligent enough and some of what she saw being said to them showed that they at least understood the meaning behind what was spoken, even if they didn't understand the words themselves.

Her fingers twitched and she wrapped them around her still mostly full mug of ale, lifted it, and took a thoughtful sip. It tasted better this time around.

What would she have to do to get a drakeling interested in establishing a bond?

Kaylin sipped again, then took a deeper draught, put the mug down, and settled her hands in her lap. There weren't many mages in the inn—or any she could see, given that the bear-mage had left his table and disappeared—and she didn't know how people would react to seeing her practicing magic.

Especially once she reached a point where the drakelings started to respond.

If she reached that point.

Having worked out what she thought would draw their attention, she decided she should write it down before she forgot. When she reached reflexively for her satchel, she remembered it wasn't there and also hadn't been on her when she'd woken in the coach with Magister Gaudin.

My notes! Her heart sank in despair. What had the magisters done with her notes? She'd had her satchel with her when she'd found the library, but it had been latched closed. Would they have searched through it or simply taken it away?

And did they know she'd drawn the Teaching Room's instruction in her notebook? Or would they merely brush it aside as the random scribblings of an all-too-nosy student?

She hoped they'd dismissed it and left the satchel unopened with the rest of her belongings but even if they had, she still wouldn't get it back. She doubted Captain Delaine had thought to ask and even if she had, how would she know exactly where she had gone?

As she wondered about the fate of her journal, Kaylin realized she'd overlooked several very important items when she'd shopped at Mistfire's. She hadn't bought anything to write with or to write in. With a groan, she rested her head in her hands and bumped her mug, which reminded her it was there and still had ale left in it.

Kaylin picked it up, sipped slowly, and went through the sections of her drakeling spell again. It was hard to fix the gestures and syllables in her head without being able to write them down, but she tried and ran through them while she kept her hands under the table and the words under her breath. She watched the three closest drakelings as she did so.

At first, she thought she'd been mistaken or that she'd formed a gesture incorrectly or forgotten some essential syllable.

She frowned and was about to repeat the sequence when a woman spoke.

"What is it, Asper? What's the matter?" asked the warrior who'd reassured her drakeling immediately after the fight.

A querulous chirp answered and Kaylin looked over her shoulder. The red lizard sat tall on its mistress's shoulder, its head turned in her direction. It seemed to be asking her if she meant what the spell had promised.

She hid her shock under the questioning look she directed at its owner.

The woman blushed. "He's not usually like this," she said and answered the unspoken query. "Ignore him."

That last instruction was spoken in the sharp tones of an order and the girl nodded. The woman cut a small piece of meat from her meal and waved it under the drakeling's nose until reluctantly, the little creature turned away.

Kaylin shook her head and picked her ale up, as much to hide the relief that trembled through her hands as anything else. She glanced around the room over the rim of the mug and realized that the other two drakelings also seemed alert and curious.

Fortunately, they didn't look directly at her but darted inquiring glances around the room as though searching for something. She breathed a sigh of relief. While she was fairly sure the adventurers would overlook one curious drakeling who stared at her, she knew they wouldn't overlook all three.

She stifled a yawn and realized that her flight from the orcs, the excitement of her arrival, and the strain of creating a casting were taking their toll. Weariness swept in and she was almost ready to fall asleep where she sat.

Ruefully, she drained her mug and stood slowly. She approached the bar and caught the innkeeper's attention.

"I need my key," she told him and stifled another unbidden yawn.

He nodded, took a key off the rack on the wall behind the bar, and tossed it to her.

"Up three, turn left, then take the first right. It's the fourth door along. The number's on the tag if you're not sure."

Kaylin nodded but he'd already turned away to respond to yet another demand for more ale.

She walked carefully to the stairs and tried not to step on the comatose forms left by the brawl. No one else seemed interested in them so she assumed this might be normal for the inn.

What have I gotten myself into? she wondered as she ascended the stairs, her tread light and her heart excited.

Whatever it was, she was glad to be there.

Now, all she had to do was work out what she could do to make the most of it.

CHAPTER TWENTY-FOUR

Kaylin's first course of action became obvious when she counted her coin the next morning. She hadn't been able to the night before but dawn had brought a sliver of light through the narrow window at the end of her tiny room.

She looked around and wondered if the space had once been used as a storage closet.

There was barely enough room for the narrow cot positioned along one wall with the chest tucked at its foot. A simple test showed the key for her room fit the lock on the chest.

Her frown faded as she shrugged. At least it was warm, if only because of the chimney running up one wall. It didn't have a fireplace of its own but the inn's fires rarely went out and the radiated heat was enough to take the chill from the room.

Apart from the chest, the only other storage was a single long shelf tacked along the wall above the chest and bed. The other wall was bare and barely far enough from the bed to allow her access to the window.

When she'd entered, she'd set her lantern on the bare window ledge, almost grateful for the absence of curtains. She used the edge of her cape to rub the glass pane and peered out. The view made her realize that the inn was constructed along similar lines to the Academy.

Separate from the walls, it formed a square with a small courtyard in the middle and a well in the center of that.

"At least I know where the water comes from," she murmured and felt slightly comforted by the idea that they weren't reliant on water being transported through the Kill Zone for their supply. If things got tough, they'd at least have that in their favor.

She noted the stables along the rear of the inn and the small, square kitchen garden tucked along the opposite wall. The door beside it opened and a man in an apron stepped out and moved between the rows of greens as if inspecting them.

The cook?

Kaylin shrugged. From the size of the garden, she didn't think fresh vegetables were in great supply. That was probably one of those things they brought in from Waypoint. With a sigh, she moved away from the window and counted her coin.

It was depressingly meager. She had maybe enough for another two or three nights but only if she didn't eat more than one meal a day. Her stomach rumbled in protest and she laughed softly at its timing.

"Well, we have our work cut out for us," she told it. "You need to be filled and I need to find enough treasure or salvage or whatever the adventurers use to live on to get the coin to fill it."

For a moment, her spirits fell and she wondered if this would be another life of desperate scraping to make ends meet. Would they open the gates for her if they knew she didn't have the coin to pay?

"Why did I come here?" she asked in frustration as she tucked the coins in her purse. She sighed. "Because I wanted to find an elven library," she replied in answer to her question. "The lost library of Tulon."

When she said it out loud, she realized it sounded ridiculous. *And you sound like every other starstruck adventurer who's ever gone to the Doom,* she concluded and waved the thought away.

The difference between her and any other adventurer who'd come calling was that she would succeed. She ignored the little voice that reminded her this was something every adventurer before her would have said, tied the coin pouch to her belt, and emptied her pack onto the shelf above her bed.

Everything except the rations and water bottle went there.

"I don't know how much space I'll need," she muttered, "so I'll give myself as much as possible."

She took her key, locked her door behind her, and hoped it proved more secure than her room at the Academy. She didn't want to think about what would happen if she came back to find everything gone. Some inner voice tried to protest that she should do more, but concern and irritation drowned it out.

Once she found her feet and dealt with the more immediate problems, she'd make time to think a little more clearly. She trotted down the stairs to find the innkeeper sweeping the taproom.

"You're up early," he called, and she approached him.

"I'd like to have the same room for tonight if I can," she told him and dropped one of her remaining gold coins into his palm.

When she'd counted them earlier, she'd decided it would probably be a good idea to have more of the smaller coins in case she needed to purchase other things elsewhere. While she had no idea what those might be, instinct told her to be prepared and avoid flashing gold coins and this seemed to be the safest way to acquire change.

He held it up. "This'll buy you the rest of the week," he said, "with a simple meal and a mug of ale at the end of the day. Are you interested?"

Kaylin nodded, and he bustled to the bar to pull out a heavy ledger and put it on top of the counter.

"Key?" he asked when she followed him. She frowned at him and he sighed impatiently. "I need the number and I'll hold onto the key while you're out in the city. That way, I know exactly where it is and when you get back in. Don't worry," he added at her worried look. "Your room stays yours as long as it's paid up and if you don't come back, I take your gear and store it. You get a year and a day before I send it to Shacklemund's Store for Lost Items. You won't lose anything."

He held his hand out. "Now," he said, "key."

From the look on his face, this wasn't something he'd negotiate, so she handed him the key and hoped she could trust him.

"Name," he demanded, placed the key beside the ledger, and dipped a quill into a bottle of ink he had tucked under the counter.

"Kaylin."

"Any surname?" he asked.

"Knight," she added reluctantly.

He nodded and penned it in. "Next of kin?"

"What?"

He sighed again, even more impatiently. "Do you have anyone who should be notified if you don't come back?"

"Oh." She blushed and thought about that.

Did the Chevaliers count? Or Sister Nadiya? And if she did die, would anyone be able to get a letter to her friends and let them know? Did she even want them to?

In the end, she decided it was better to give him one name rather than five, and that only one name would matter.

"Captain Jocelyn Delaine," she stated. Since the captain had given her a time limit for staying out of the city, the woman might expect her to let the Chevaliers know when she returned—or if she wasn't going to. After all, she still didn't know what their agreement entailed now that she wasn't at the Academy.

"Of the Chevaliers?" The innkeeper's surprised tones interrupted her thoughts.

Kaylin nodded. She caught herself before she could say the captain was the reason she was there in the first place and decided that was probably more information than he needed, especially as she didn't know who else he might speak to.

After a brief pause during which he studied her face, the innkeeper wrote the captain's name in the next of kin column. The speculative look on his face made her glad she hadn't added anything else.

"You're not—" he began and she shook her head.

"I'm here on my own," she told him hastily and closed her mouth so she wouldn't say more.

The man was looking far too curious as it was. She hoped he could keep a secret.

He finished his notes, then pushed the book out of sight.

"The gates close at sunset and don't open again until dawn," he told her brusquely. "You'll need to be back before dark and ring the bell if they stay closed when you get here."

There was a bell? She frowned and tried to remember if she'd seen it. Then again, she hadn't seen much during her chaotic arrival.

The innkeeper stepped out from behind the counter and picked his broom up.

"Don't get eaten," he told her by way of goodbye and she recognized that she'd been dismissed and headed toward the door.

Don't get eaten? Exactly what does he think I'll be doing out there?

It was maybe better than being told to be careful and she thought about that for a moment. *Or go get eaten.*

It seemed logical that the areas closest to the inn and along the route to Waypoint would have been picked clean, so she moved deeper into the ruins. The first thing she wanted to do was to find a high point from which to get a feel for the city. What did most adventurers do there, anyway?

Did they go straight into the tunnels and mythical treasure vaults of the Spears? Or did they hunt humanoids through the rubble to keep the area around the Rest monster-free?

She shrugged that last thought away. The evidence didn't support it. There'd been large numbers of humanoids roaming the ruins when she'd come in.

Still, if the adventuring companies did go straight into the Spears, that would mean there were numerous unexplored spaces in the city itself. Whether or not they'd be monster-free, however, was another question entirely.

To fulfill her first goal, she looked around for a high point somewhere near the inn that would allow her to get a good look at the city. She had moved maybe a mile from the inn's walls before she finally saw one. The more she searched for a vantage point, the more she was reminded that Tulon's City had been a great metropolis. It almost hurt to see how badly it had fallen to disrepair.

Disrepair? She snorted softly. *As if being destroyed by a dragon is the same as being destroyed by neglect and time.*

A story of a dragon sundering the mountain and destroying the city below was certainly more interesting than time and weather doing the same over hundreds of years.

She found a length of wall that ascended in ragged sections to form steps. It was three floors in height and the remains of each floor stretched tenuously over wide broken spaces open to the sky. She used a pile of rubble as a springboard to bound onto the first level.

It shifted under her feet but didn't tumble until she leapt off.

Kaylin landed in a half-crouch and moved forward immediately, using her momentum to fuel her next jump up as she vaulted from the first level to the next. That required a little more effort and she paused at the top and took a moment to survey the nearby streets.

Ahead of her and a little to the left, the buildings looked somewhat more intact. Tucked in close to the mountain's feet, some even looked like they'd been excavated into the mountainside.

There, she thought and studied what she could see of the dilapidated structures. Grass had grown onto where their roofs had been and large boulders and rocks were piled over some sections of the buildings.

It looked like several sections had been destroyed by landslides.

Maybe there, she amended and scrutinized what she could see before she focused on the next section of wall. It was one thing to think she could see what she needed but quite another to be sure. She ran along the wall top and scaled the next tumbled-down section to reach a point where she could see the ruins better.

What caught her eye was the number of humanoids moving through the broken stonework of the city although they weren't gathered in hordes. Most traveled in groups of two or three and only one group numbered five or more. Those headed toward the edge of the ruins and carried bows.

A hunting party, Kaylin decided and watched them carefully until the distance between them and her was obscured by rubble from buildings that formed canyons and gullies of stone.

The more she observed the city, the more she realized how alive it was.

A rich tapestry of odors drifted to her. The smells might be smoke at one moment, then dust lifted from a wall to be carried along with perhaps the smell of plants as well.

The streets and ruins were more than merely bare walls and roads of rock. Grass had split the ancient roads and small bushes had found space to put roots down and grow into thickets. Others dotted the ruins in isolated clumps and the vines seemed to be the most prevalent.

They clung to every wall and sometimes covered entire sections. Their leaves softened the outlines of some buildings while they only formed isolated patches of green on others. Once or twice, she thought she saw a tree and wondered if the forest would claim the abandoned dwellings.

Faint tendrils of smoke rose here and there. She noted the dun to brown colors of hide awnings tucked into the hollows formed by the empty shells of walls that still stood where the inside of the building had long fallen to decay.

The ruins were still a city in their own right, its composition different but the essence similar.

With a firm mental note to be careful, Kaylin proceeded along the wall until she could see the buildings that had caught her eye before. Although she focused hard, she didn't see any sign of a camp of either adventurer or monster, and the closest smoke column was a block away.

Either the buildings had been picked clean or they'd been overlooked. If she was honest with herself, she didn't think the latter was likely but she hoped nonetheless. If she wanted to be able to afford to keep her tiny broom closet of a room, she would need to find something.

It was simply that the idea of wasting time looking in the wrong places was almost paralyzing.

"It's better to waste time than to not look at all," she told herself firmly and ran her gaze over the route she'd need to take to reach the location. While it looked easy enough, she remained cautious.

She wondered what kinds of businesses or homes would have been constructed close to the mountain's feet. Had they been wealthy? Or had the wealthy lived higher up?

Waypoint got humid in the middle of summer and she couldn't imagine this place being any different. If that were the case, then the wealthy had almost certainly made their homes higher up where the winds blew to keep them cool.

That left the question of who might live at their feet. Was it the place of the poor? Or of merchants who dwelt close to their patrons? There was only one way to answer that question. She lingered long enough to use her eye to map a path across the top of the ruins before she started toward her goal.

Kaylin kept watch for other likely places between and intended to drop down to them as she journeyed. She was rewarded when she discovered that the houses abutting the mountain weren't the only semi-intact structures along the way.

Remembering the orcs from the day before, she moved carefully through the ruins and took paths along old walls and sagging stone floors until she reached the broken flags of what had been an ancient hall.

At least, she thought it had been an ancient hall. It might have merely been the lower floor of a large house with wooden walls, but there was nothing to confirm if she was right or wrong. The flagstones that comprised the floor were mostly intact but grass had pushed through and blocks of stone formed impromptu rock formations around its edges.

She wove to one of these and crept through a door-shaped gap across the space between this ruin and the next.

It was half-buried in a slide of rock and stone that had settled against the mountain's flank and crushed the house beneath. The walls adjoining the landslide were intact, however, even though the doors were missing and the shutters gone from the windows.

After a hasty survey of the immediate area, she slunk through the closest doorway. She stopped a few steps inside, let her eyes adjust to the gloomy interior, and wished she'd thought to bring her lantern.

"Idiot! Sestila," she scolded and conjured a small floating ball of light.

On the upside, she could move it through the building ahead of her and it would save her the cost of a candle or lamp oil. On the downside, she would have to remember to sustain it or it would go out and leave her in the dark unexpectedly.

To her relief, nothing had made its home in the building's depths. There was, however, little left to show what it had been used for. The location didn't feel like a home. It felt more like a storefront or the public area of a craftsman's workshop where they met their clients.

Of course, there were no furnishings to confirm if the feeling was correct or not so she moved deeper toward the back, where the landslide had come down. She couldn't help but wonder how many had been caught there and died working their craft.

"Probably none," she told herself. "It's not like they wouldn't have had some warning."

Her guess proved partially correct and she caught the glimmer of metal near benches of stone. She moved the light, unwilling to go closer to the hollows and niches that formed deeper patches of darkness in the shadows.

Her fears proved unfounded when she registered that the hollows were cupboard shelves and that not all of those shelves were empty.

"I wonder if they pay for metal?" Kaylin picked up a metal bowl covered in a patina of age. She proceeded carefully along the shelves and gathered some odd-looking tools, three metal mugs, and a slightly crushed jug.

The metal might have been silver or pewter, she couldn't tell, but apart from the jug, the tools, mugs, and bowl looked in almost usable condition. She wondered how much they were worth—if anything—as she continued her search.

Would they be enough to pay for another few days at the Rest? A week? She looked around the room to see what else might be available before she put the found items into her pack and cinched it.

When the light revealed nothing more than dust, she left but paused inside the ruin and looked into the daylight beyond to allow her eyes to adjust before she stepped out. The wait revealed that the street was still deserted, and she hurried to the next building along.

Each structure had a slightly different feel except for a vague sense of loss and desertion. A metal vase lay on the floor in one at the right distance for it to have fallen from a long-decayed bedside table. Another had an ornate lamp base, and a third had scattered pieces of cutlery in what might have been a dining room.

As she searched, Kaylin caught glimpses of what life might have been like in Tulon's time, and it reminded her of the knowledge once developed and stored inside the city's limits.

This was not merely some old city of ruins. It had been an advanced city whose ruins included farms and ranches that now decayed slowly under the forests in the valley.

She'd overheard stories about the magic of the elves—that the city had been a center of learning for an empire and that a great library had been built as a central repository for it. Not all the talk in the tavern the night before had been about the brawl or the food on offer.

Some had been conjecture on what might be found once they entered the doorway leading beneath the mountain. One mercenary group had been adamant that treasure was more important than some moldy old tomes.

It had certainly sounded like she needed to go into the mountain to find the library. Perhaps it held books that would continue her learning, enough so that the magisters, may the captain take their tongues, wouldn't be so quick to tie her up next time.

She could dream.

Kaylin sighed. "First things first," she told herself. "Food, shelter, and a safe place to return to."

It was calming to know she could secure her room while she was away and that her friends would know if she did not return.

The thought reminded her that she should ask about whether a journal was available to purchase and paper so she could write them a letter in case she didn't make it out. She wanted to write her drakeling spell down for a start.

While she waited for a moment in the shadows to look around before she emerged from another of the partially collapsed ruins, she noticed it was close to midday. The sun rode high in the sky and the day grew steadily warmer. She decided she needed to take another look at her surroundings and studied the walls.

"Maybe it'd be better if I tried from the second floor." She shrugged and entered the next house. This one leaned drunkenly against its neighbors and its walls contained gaping holes that were matched by piles of rubble around its base.

If going into the mountain made you an adventurer, what did spelunking into the buildings in the rubble of a city make you?

She considered that thoughtfully. "An adventurer with brains," she concluded. If raiding Shacklemund's vault had taken a while to plan and focus on, this mountain was so much more so yes, she would be careful.

Judging from the stone counter running the length of the back of the room, this had been a shop of some kind. Her spirits lifted. Maybe something special was hidden amongst the debris or out in the back.

Later, she decided as she looked around and allowed her eyes to adjust enough that she could check the darker shadows. *First, we check for others.*

Once at the stairwell, she noted the bolts where wooden stairs had originally been affixed to the wall. Going up was awkward, but she made short work of the climb to the next floor, grateful that the owners had built with timber either enhanced by magic or from a very durable tree.

Vaguely, she wondered what the wood was if only for the salvage value. Would this location earn her coin from someone with the ability to retrieve the lumber?

Kaylin padded swiftly across the floor, inspected the ceiling, and noticed half the level was open to the sky while a small corner of the attic space remained. She wormed cautiously up the broken sections of rock until she could look out over the area around her.

She couldn't help glancing at the cliff behind her but saw it was only a cliff and that the road leading to it disappeared under another tumble of rock. Maybe there'd be more buildings above and if they had belonged to the wealthier folk in the city, they might provide more valuable pickings.

With that in mind, she looked for the Rest and tried to mark the route between it and the rockfall. It wasn't easy and she wasn't sure if she could remember the way she needed to take once she was in the canyons and alleys at street level.

She studied the rockfall and the cliffs above it. Would it be worth it?

"Well, there's only one way to find out." She chewed indecisively on her lip. "But not today."

Her immediate need was to gather as much as she could so she had what she needed to secure her place at the inn.

After one more look at the route she'd have to take to reach what was hopefully the wealthier tier of houses above the rockslide, she dropped into the second-floor room and began to search to see what treasures might remain.

The upper floor had consisted of two rooms and a short corridor, and the stone support wall continued from the ground floor to the ceiling and what was left of the roof. It didn't take her long to go through them and she dropped down the hollow stairwell to the lower floor.

She landed lightly, crouched in the base of the stairwell, and listened to ensure that she was still alone. For a moment, she'd thought she'd heard something—some slight movement in the shop front—but she couldn't be sure. She waited for it to come again.

When it didn't, she moved to the corner and peered into the room beyond. The light in the street was blindingly bright but the sun didn't shine into the building. She peered into the room and tried to find the source of the sound.

At first, nothing caught her eye but after a moment she saw what looked like the tip of an iridescent tail flicking out the door.

A drakeling?

Kaylin's heart jumped. She'd fallen in love with the little creatures since she'd seen them the night before. She thought quickly and the idea of collecting more items to add to her stash warred with the idea of having one of her own.

What color had that tail been? Red? Orange? Bronze? It had vanished too quickly for her to tell.

She hurried to the door and peered cautiously out in time to see the little creature scamper into a building across the street. It *was* a drakeling, one with dark-red scales edged in bronze and she wanted it.

Without a moment to reconsider, she raced across the street and came to a quick halt outside the door the little creature had vanished into. She took time to catch her breath and force into a quiet rhythm before she slid through the entrance.

The urge to close her eyes in the street and open them once she was inside was strong but she resisted. It might have been the fastest way to adjust to the gloom but it was also the best way to not see anything that might be waiting for her.

It would be all too easy to run into a stone wall, trip over the rocks, and injure herself if she fell. Given what she'd already encountered in this city, that wasn't the best idea.

Kaylin entered the building and blinked rapidly to get her eyes to adjust. It took her a couple of minutes before she caught a flash of movement and the little lizard dropped out of the partially collapsed second floor to pounce on something on the counter.

It looks like this was another workshop, she thought and watched the drakeling explore the surface.

Rather than approach, she decided to see if the magic she'd worked out the night before would be enough to attract it to her.

Without shifting her gaze from her prize, she worked through the gestures with her fingers and realized she needed to tweak the intent.

This time, she wasn't trying to see if she could attract its attention. She was trying to draw it into being her friend or companion.

That required a slightly different approach. It didn't take her long to tweak the spell and she watched the lizard dart along the counter and in and around the debris on the floor.

Either it hadn't noticed her or it had decided she wasn't a threat and it didn't need to be afraid of her. Whatever the reason, it explored the room freely and occasionally tipped a stone onto its side to catch the beetles that raced out from under it.

The sound of the creature happily crunching on his catches made her smile as she cast the spell. She fed her memory of friendship at the Academy into the movement for experience, the idea she could provide it with food, shelter, and protection into the logic dimension, and her longing for companionship into the emotional side.

At first, it seemed to have no effect, and the creature launched into a lazy glide that brought it close to the door. She worried that the spell had scared it off but the drakeling didn't even look at her when it landed. Instead, it began to forage amongst the straggly grass and scattered rocks near the exit.

Kaylin furrowed her brow. Curious as to what she'd done wrong, she moved forward and cast the spell again but the little lizard continued its hunt, either oblivious to her efforts or uncaring.

It flipped a slightly larger rock and unleashed a torrent of beetles. As her spell settled around it, the lizard pounced into the middle of the largest group and slapped its paws this way and that as it snapped at the fleeing insects. It trapped some under its hind paws and lifted one, wriggling and scratching, with both forepaws.

As she stared at it in dismay, the creature tilted its head as if to catch her eye, bit the beetle's head savagely, and chewed in an almost defiant fashion.

For a moment, Kaylin had the impression the drakeling was laughing at her.

So it's like that, is it? She cast the spell again and focused on each intent and principle more intently. The magic she released felt stronger and she pushed it out to wrap the tiny beast with all the thought and power she could safely pull.

It had finished its first beetle and was digging the next out from under its hind paw when the spell settled. With an angry hiss, it dropped the beetle and its wings flared as it pivoted with a small bound.

It reminded her of a small and furious cat and she smiled. Sure that she had gotten through to it, she cast the spell again and reiterated her need for companionship and how much she would welcome its company.

The little creature launched from the floor and circled to the ceiling with several flaps of its wings. This brought it around to face her, and she wondered if the spell had worked. Her heart skipped happily but a second later, the drakeling folded its wings to its sides, extended its talons, and uttered a furious screech as it plunged toward her.

Kaylin ducked and it flew past her and banked sharply to avoid hitting the wall before climbing again. She straightened, confused by its behavior, and turned to follow its flight. When it folded its wings and dove toward her again, she responded with a startled cry.

She stumbled back and heard a hiss and a clatter as something streaked past her and into the wall beyond.

A spear?

The little lizard momentarily forgotten, she glanced toward the door. Scarsnout looked at her down the shaft of a long, barbed arrow. As she stepped back another pace, the orc tracked her with the bow.

She pushed aside all thoughts of the drakeling as panic surged through her. Remembering her journey to find the library, she used a simple spell to blur her outline and took another step as the orc released the arrow.

Her back met the wall and the arrow sang past her before it clattered off the stone.

"Avark!" she cried and her hands flashed in the right sequence to summon a small globe of fire.

At the doorway, her adversary drew his bow again.

"Barda!"

Light erupted in front of his face and burst into myriad colored sparkles and she bolted to the door at the back of the room. The orc laughed and another arrow whistled past her head.

"Barda! Avark!" she yelled as she dodged the arrows and a broken table.

Focus on a drakeling and get an orc arrow in your back for not paying attention!

As the fireball and colored light exploded behind her, she threw herself into a dive and tumbled through the ruin's rear door into a section of the building that hadn't survived the centuries well. Its roof had been wood and its walls had caved in when it bowed to pressure from the elements and time.

Another arrow flashed past her face and she lashed out with another string of colored lights and a fire orb before she hurdled a low section of the wall and bolted down a narrow street behind it. More arrows flashed past, each one closer, and she wondered how the orc could be so accurate when she was blurred. She also wondered what had happened to the drakeling.

Kaylin reached an intersection and ran right toward the Rest. As she rounded the corner, an arrow whistled past her and she jinked to the left.

"Barda."

Another chuckle rumbled behind her and she risked a glance over her shoulder.

Scarsnout had exited the building and drew the bowstring back for another shot. His aim didn't seem affected in the slightest by her blurring, although he'd stepped out of the area affected by the flickering lights.

"Shostom," she tried and paused to conjure a thin layer of haze between herself and the orc.

As soon as it appeared, she turned and ran and aimed for the road that would take her back to the inn. The hiss of the next arrow came with a sudden burning pain across her bicep.

"Troll's rocks!" she muttered, dodged to one side, and pushed into a sprint.

She ran for half a block before she registered the absence of a follow-up shot.

"Now what?" she asked herself and slowed so she could take the next turn and look back. "Crap."

The orc had forsaken his bow but not the chase.

In one hand, he held an ax and in the other, he brandished a knife. He moved toward her in the ground-eating lope the orcs had pursued her with the day before and grinned when he caught her gaze.

"Run." He snapped the command in a soft growl that swept down the road and shocked her into action. "Or die."

His laughter lapped at her heels as she renewed her flight. Kaylin ran and heard the sound of his steps grow louder as he gained on her. She glanced desperately up, looking for the Rest, and almost lost her footing.

The stumble cost her dearly and she heard the full-bodied swish as the ax swept toward her. She threw herself into a roll and the blade met empty air. As she regained her feet, she focused on the lower edge of one of the nearby walls and bounded up and onto it.

She didn't slow when her feet met its uneven surface but ran up and along. The ax rang viciously off the stonework below her. She didn't let that distract her and directed her attention to the floor above and the building opposite. The second floor still hung intact and all she needed was a little more height.

Although she desperately wanted to, she didn't dare to look down to see what the orc was doing. She knew what she would do if she were him, and the wall left her all out of places to dodge. Her only hope was to push forward with her plan.

Kaylin reached the small overhang she needed and launched herself across the gap, landed hard, and tumbled toward the wall to take some of the impact.

"Oof!"

The floor was uneven and littered with rocks and stones and she collected several more bruises, some grazes, and a scrape along one forearm. She barely raised her hands in time to avoid her head meeting the wall she'd used as a backstop.

"Remind me to not do that again." She hissed against the sting of her injuries and searched for the route she needed to get to the ground and reach the Rest's gates.

The orc's voice rumbled at her from inside the building below.

"I can hear you breathing," came the sing-song taunt. "Why don't you come down to pla-ay?"

Why is the orc who hates me so good at speaking my language? Seriously, did I piss the gods off at some point in my life?

She kept her mouth shut and brought her breath under control. An arrow sailed past the platform's edge but rattled off the wall above her. She gave it a startled glance and noticed the rope attached to it. A sharp tug on the other end jerked it back and over the edge.

It clattered onto the floor below, and she rolled into a crouch as she searched for her best way out of there—preferably one that didn't take her into view of one scar-snouted orc with a bow. She let her gaze follow the wall and noticed that it ran in a single line to abut with another semi-solid length of upright stone.

If she reached the end of that, she could drop to the road and the orc would have to go around. It might buy her enough time.

Another arrow hissed over the lip of the ledge and she rolled again. It struck the wall lower down and clunked beside where she sat. She stared at it, then quietly rolled one of the smaller stones onto it and nudged another onto the rope with her foot.

"Let's see what you think of that," she muttered and rose to her feet.

Another arrow skewered from below and she fell prone. Scarsnout chuckled.

"Here fishy, fishy, fishy," he taunted and the sibilants in his voice wrapped around the last consonants of the words.

The ropes on both arrows tautened.

Kaylin kicked out and tried frantically to roll another rock onto the rope of the second arrow and the orc chuckled again.

"Let's see what I've caught."

What he'd caught? It took Kaylin a moment to realize that the orc thought the second arrow had struck and that her struggles meant he'd snagged her.

I'd make far more noise if one of those had landed where you wanted. She snorted quietly and decided to take her chances.

The ropes jerked and she gasped when the arrows began to move toward the edge.

Scarsnout thought that was funny too.

Keep laughing, turd for brains. She pushed to her feet and moved quickly and cautiously onto the wall.

"Oy!" The orc sounded furious.

"Whoops!" She moved a little faster.

She had nowhere to go except over the wall if he fired at her now. Rock clattered and triggered a storm of oaths as he retrieved his arrows but she'd caused enough of a distraction for her to reach the road. If she did that, she might have the time to reach the Rest.

The wall seemed stable under her feet, so Kaylin risked running, careful to watch her footing. When she reached the end, she dropped to a crouch, pivoted, and slid over the edge. There were no handholds to move down to so she kicked out, twisted so she could see the pavement, and tucked into a roll as she touched down.

It wasn't a perfect landing and she added a few more bruises to the ones she'd already collected, but she didn't stop to dwell on them.

Without looking back, she found her feet and pushed into a sprint. Moaning in pain could wait for her tiny space she called home.

She'd forgotten orcs could sprint too and very angry orcs had extra fuel to burn.

A roar of frustration echoed through the ruins and footsteps pounded the pavement outside the building where she'd run across the walls. She gasped and tried to go faster but could soon hear Scarsnout's boots in the road behind her.

Rock cracked and crumbled as he gained and she skidded around another corner and saw the Rest's walls rising in the open space at its end. She bolted toward it, not looking back.

Her back itched in anticipation of feeling the orc's ax and her chest burned. Her backpack thudded painfully against her spine but stopping wasn't an option.

She would do something about the various objects digging into her spine next time.

Provided she had a next time. His steps were closer, his pants so close she could almost smell the humid reek of his breath.

For a moment, she was tempted to ditch the pack, but she needed what was in it to pay for food and board and she didn't want Scarsnout to profit from her hard work. Besides, slowing to ditch it would mean letting him catch up and he was far too close as it was.

The orc proved that particular truth seconds later when his ax swooshed through her cape.

Kaylin felt it catch and reached back to jerk the garment away from the blade. Cloth tore and he grunted in frustration. She continued to run and burst out of the street and into full view of the Rest's wooden battlements.

It was tempting to stop there but she remembered that the orcs had pursued her almost to the gates and didn't want to bet her life that Scarsnout wouldn't do the same. She was betting enough of her life as it was. What if the guards didn't let her in?

What if they decided she brought too much trouble to their door and decided she was too much of a risk?

"I paid for the room, dammit!" She snarled and ran directly to the gates, raised a fist to pound on them, and hesitated when she heard the sound of the bar being lifted. Rather than keep her back to the danger, she drew her dagger and turned.

To her surprise, her adversary had stopped at the entrance of the broad, clear area in front of the Rest. Fury darkened his face but his gaze was wary as he assessed the activity on the ramparts above her.

"Mine," he told her, looked her in the eye, and extended the ax toward her. "Mine," he repeated, shouldered it, and turned away to walk into the ruins.

The gate gave way behind her and she stumbled into the inn's forecourt. The two guards moved around her to close the gates and drop the locking bar in place.

"You took your time," one grumbled. "What were you doing? Blowing the big bastard a kiss goodbye?"

Kaylin flipped him the bird, unable to find the breath to speak. Now that she'd stopped, fine tremors ran through her muscles and her hands shook. She fumbled with the dagger as she tried to slide it into its sheath and it landed on the stone.

The guard chuckled as she picked it up and stowed it.

"Getting ready to go up against an orc with a dagger?" he said with a shake of his head. "Well, you've got guts. I'll give you that. Not too many brains but plenty of guts."

"Yeah," the other guard added, "and someone will spill 'em for her if she doesn't start using whatever's inside her skull."

He didn't add anything more but strode up the stairs to the ramparts. His partner followed him without a backward glance.

Still breathing hard, Kaylin inhaled deeply and stalked toward the inn's front doors. It was time to see what the proprietor paid for a pretty vase.

"The name's Clay," he told her when she called him sir. "Whaddoya need?"

Kaylin slipped her pack off her shoulders and hefted it onto the counter. "I have things to trade."

His eyebrows rose. "You do?"

She nodded, glad that her breath had finally settled.

Clay's eyes narrowed. "And what makes you think I'd be interested?"

Her face fell and she started to pull the pack off the counter but he placed his hand on top of it.

"This way," he ordered and jerked his head toward a door behind the bar.

She followed and took the pack with her.

The room she entered was a simple one, consisting of a table with a wooden bench on either side and walls lined with shelves of crates. Her eyes widened when she noted the items she could see and she matched them mentally to what she had in her bag.

The proprietor followed her gaze and gave her time to take everything in as he closed the door.

"Now," he said. "Let me introduce you to the trade around here. You done some in the city?"

"Waypoint?" she asked and he nodded.

"I've done a little," she admitted and recalled some of her more spirited discussions with Elo over the value of the various little trinkets she'd collected.

"Good." Clay's word broke into her thoughts. "Then you'll have an idea of how this works."

He took her through the base prices of the items she saw on the shelves and inclined his head at her.

"I pay more for something I have a customer for if it's in very good condition or if it's not the usual representation of its type," he added. "And if it's clean."

Kaylin frowned. "So I can come back then?" she asked and he smiled as he stood from his seat.

"You can but not during the evening rush. The times for trading are either very early, before lunch, or about now. Once the customers arrive, I'm too busy to deal. Now—"

As if to punctuate his words, the inn door slammed.

"Hallo the bar!" At the demanding roar, Clay spread his hands.

The barkeep jerked his chin at the pack as he headed for the door. "Bring it tomorrow," he told her, then added, "Baths are out back on the left near the stables." He trailed his gaze slowly over the dust and destruction of her clothes from the recent run-a-map of her morning's efforts.

"I'm not sayin' you need one, but..." His face was grim but there was a slight twinkle in his eyes.

Kaylin blushed. "Thank you."

He opened the door for her and she fled up the stairs to her room as the newcomers commented on her appearance.

"She's a bit below your usual standards, Clay."

"Do you want a room or would you rather spend the night outside the gates?" the proprietor retorted.

This brought a round of cat-calls and tutting.

"Now, now, now, there's no need to be like that." The second voice seemed to have swallowed stones as far as she could tell. "We all know your tastes run to—"

That sentence was choked off with a thump, but she didn't go back to see what it was about.

People would think what they wanted to think and nothing she or Clay said would change it.

Besides, if these were regulars—and they sounded like they were—they already knew about the trade room so they also knew what had been going on.

If they wanted to make it into something else, there was nothing she could do to stop it. Clay, on the other hand, seemed to deal with them well enough and it wasn't like he needed her help.

She hurried up the second and third flights and checked that the corridor was clear before she unlocked her door. Habits from being in the Academy died hard, and she locked it again as soon as she'd entered. She crossed to her bed, took her sleeping roll down, and spread it over the inn blankets before she tipped the contents of her pack on top of it.

"Clean, huh?" she asked herself and sorted the items into different piles according to price.

She studied it all carefully and sighed in frustration before she focused and inspected them with what she hoped was a sensible evaluation. "And I thought having to study was the worst thing to have to do at the end of a long day."

It didn't take her long to realize that she had probably enough to add another four nights at the inn with meals, and that was if some of the items were only worth the base price. When she examined them, she decided the lamp base and the vase might be worth more. And if he had a buyer lined up, that might add to their value.

"I can live in hope," she muttered, bundled all of them into her sleep roll, and placed it into the chest. She was hungry and now she'd had time to notice, she realized she stank and the smell was bad enough that it interfered with her ability to think.

She might have earned a few more nights at the inn but she wouldn't last very long foraging in the city if she couldn't handle one lone orc. An ambush seemed like the best way to deal with him, but how she could manage it was another matter entirely.

What wasn't an option was heading back to Waypoint and not only because the captain seemed to be adamant about the year—and frankly, Kaylin didn't want to know what magic she might have to confirm if she was gone or not. But she had an itch about the library. They refused to let her know about what they found at the Academy, but she'd be willing to bet there were old dusty tomes of knowledge somewhere still in the ruins or certainly below ground.

Not every book in the mountain would be from the old years. Some would be from wizards like herself who took them down on a trip and neither the book nor the wizard ever came up.

They wouldn't help a dead wizard in that case.

She'd think much better once she was clean and had eaten something, and by the time she was done, she'd know exactly how to deal with old Scarsnout.

"Mine, huh?" she asked belligerently as she headed across the courtyard. "We'll see about that."

CHAPTER TWENTY-FIVE

Kaylin was up before the sun had time to reach her window. It was still cold but she had the perfect plan—or one as perfect as she could get it—but it involved a little climbing and maybe borrowing the window in an empty room. Not even she could fit through the one in hers.

She'd taken a tour around the courtyard and a quick peek in the stables the night before. The stablehand had solemnly insisted that if she didn't have a horse she shouldn't be there, and she'd left before he could become suspicious—but not before confirming that there was no way onto the roof from the stables.

Her main problem was getting onto the ramparts without being noticed by the guards and she didn't want to leave by the main gate. She'd slipped out of the inn after her supper to inspect the space between the inn and the wall.

"Someone might be inclined to think you were up to mischief." The guard's voice made her jump.

"I needed a walk," Kaylin answered.

"I thought you had enough of one this morning," he returned, closed a hand around her bicep, and pulled her around. "And you keep looking up."

"It's nice to see how tall they are," she answered. "It makes me feel safe, you know?"

"And safer because we don't allow folk to wander inside at night," he told her firmly and pointed her in the direction of the inn. "The courtyard's usually quiet at this time of night. Take your walk over there." He released her arm and she moved in the direction indicated.

She assumed he was on the afternoon shift and wouldn't be up this early, but she wouldn't take any chances.

As quietly as she could, she wandered down the corridor until she reached a section where the doors were spaced farther apart. She assumed this was where the larger rooms were located, wove an unlocking spell over the lock of the one farthest from the stairs, and stepped quietly inside.

Why work with picks when spells did it so much cleaner? You could take the thief out of Waypoint but she landed on her feet in the shadows of the Doom.

The room was empty, its furniture shrouded by sheets. Kaylin closed and locked the door behind her and crossed quickly to the window.

That was also locked and equally as simple to open. What she'd noticed in her shortened walk from the night before was that the gap between the inn roof and the walls narrowed toward the back.

It was still a wagon and a half wide, but that was better than the two wagons' wide gap at the front. All she had to do was get onto the roof or a similarly high perch and leap across to the ramparts—and hope the guards were mostly concentrated at the front.

In case they weren't, she cast a spell to blur herself and looked carefully up and down the length of the wall she could see. It appeared empty except for the faint movement she could see at the front and was shadowed since the sun hadn't risen yet.

She clambered carefully onto the window ledge, looked down and around, and encountered the first problem in her plan—there was no easy way onto the roof.

"Plan B," she told herself, balanced on the edge, and pulled the rope out of her pack. "Let's hope we don't have to go to Plan C or things might get too interesting."

Once she'd made a loop and slip knot, she chose one of the poles that edged the inside of the ramparts and flung the loop around it.

It took a couple of attempts before she settled the knot over the post and pulled it tight, but with that accomplished, she dropped the rope out the window, snuck out of the room, and closed the window behind her.

Now, all she had to do was get to the rope before anyone discovered the incriminating evidence.

She refreshed the blur spell and added another to muffle the sound of her feet as she headed downstairs—exactly as she had when she'd negotiated the magisters' level at the Academy on her way to the hidden library.

To her relief, the bar was empty, although a bacon sandwich stood untended on the counter and she could hear voices in the kitchen, one of them Clay's. She didn't recognize the other but it didn't matter.

What mattered was that the taproom was empty and she could slip through it unseen to the courtyard exit.

The aroma of the sandwich convinced her that she could also take it on her way out and maybe offer to pay for it when she returned. After all, it wasn't like the bar was tended and she had time to order one.

She didn't give herself time to argue and with her breakfast in hand, she hurried through the courtyard and into the stables. Habit kicked in and she made sure to stick to the shadows and move quickly to the exit leading to the outer section.

Once there, she noticed the rear gates—closed and barred but something she wished she'd known about sooner. She didn't stop to check for guards, hastened to where the rope still dangled from the walkway, and pulled on it to check it was secure.

Reassured, Kaylin climbed it, hauled herself up hand over hand, and squirmed onto the walkway, where she stopped to retrieve the rope and drape its hastily coiled length across her torso.

A look from the wall showed her that she might have been too hasty. It was well-constructed and the closest ruins were four wagon lengths from its edges for most of its length. As her eyes adjusted to the shadow in the early morning gloom, she realized there was a half-constructed building below her with incomplete walls enclosing three sides.

The fourth side abutted the inn wall but was only half its height. That was still high enough to solve her dilemma. She padded toward the tallest section of wall, scrambled on top of the rampart, and slid over the edge.

Caution made her look down to verify that she'd calculated the drop correctly before she moved six inches to her right. After a deep breath, she let go and dropped. She landed hard but rolled, flicked herself over the edge of the second wall, and grasped it briefly with her fingers to slow her momentum before she kicked outward into a twist and landed in a neat forward tumble.

When she stopped, Kaylin remained in the crouch she'd ended in, glad her pack was empty and that the surrounding streets and ruins were as quiet as they'd looked from the top of the walls.

She considered whether any of the closest structures would have what she needed, but a quick search showed them to have solid floors where they had floors at all.

Wary after her experience the day before, she listened intently, then felt to see if her subconscious picked up any indication that she had been seen.

After a while, she shook her head, took a careful look around, and headed deeper into the Old City. What she needed was a basement—not because of what might be stored down there but because she needed a hole in the ground.

It took her most of the morning to find a location that looked suitable.

"One wrecked house with one wrecked basement," she murmured with satisfaction, "and it has a hole right about where I need it."

This was in the middle of the floor of the room above.

She patted her hands together to knock some of the dust off. "No digging required."

That would have been the easy part. The hard part was making it look like the hole in the floor didn't exist. She didn't have the time or the skills to weave a net that could be stretched over the opening and she hadn't had the chance to ask Clay if he had one in stock.

What would I have bought it with if he did?

Either way, she'd have been out of luck anyway. She looked around, pulled some of the ever-present vines from a nearby wall, and stretched them across the hole to pin them in place with some of the larger slabs of rock from the base of the walls.

That done, she took more of the vines and stretched them the other way to form a lattice-work strong enough to support a few of the smaller stones around the ruin. A scattering of dust helped to disguise the floor, but she knew it wouldn't be enough to fool a goblin, much less the orc.

She would have to create a spell.

Given what she wanted to accomplish, her intent, and her new experiences, she worked on the three parts of the spell. It took her about ten minutes and two failures before a small grin settled on her face.

A simple illusion smoothed the ripple of vines into a facsimile of the stone floor surrounding them and she nodded. The orc would be chasing her when he encountered the patch so it should be enough to fool him.

A soft niggle of doubt suggested that since he was able to tell that her limited range of spells wouldn't do him any real harm, maybe she was being overly optimistic.

Kaylin pushed it away.

The next thing the plan needed was to make sure Scarsnout took the route intended.

As it stood, rubble was strewn across the entire floor with no single way across being any better than the others. She needed to make the route into the trap the best way through.

It sounded simple enough but she had to do it without making it obvious.

Good luck with that, she muttered inwardly and studied the rubble.

The floor above had been mostly timber and supported by thick beams of wood. While the beams were still there and looked ratty and decayed, the boards were mostly gone. Like in so many of the other ruins she'd passed through, the stones from the slowly disintegrating walls had fallen haphazardly through them.

It took Kaylin at least an hour of cautiously shifting rubble to create a natural-looking pathway leading over her makeshift pit. She continued it on the other side so the endpoint wasn't as obvious and retreated to a sheltered corner to work out the last spell she needed.

While creating the illusion to get the trap to match the rest of the floor had brought her close to the edge of her magical skills, this next part would take her past it.

The whole plan rested on having Scarsnout pursue her into the ruin and chase her blindly over the trap.

Its success rested on him falling while she went over it. He wouldn't be fooled if he saw her make the jump across. The orc was too smart.

He might be furious with her for the loss of his comrades but he wasn't so angry that he would be blinded by it.

No, if she jumped, he'd jump, too—or he'd have enough of a clue to see through her illusion. She needed something more for him to not see her jump. He had to see her continue to run even as she cleared the trap.

That was harder to conjure. She didn't want to have the image of her running through the ruin to happen before she arrived so had to set a trigger for it. That part was relatively easy to accomplish.

The spell had to activate when she entered the ruins. Setting the area, she revised the gesture for start and drew on what she knew of mirroring to make the spell copy whatever she was doing when it was activated. After that, it was simple. It had to keep doing that until the illusion reached the edge of the area, regardless of what she did after it was triggered.

That result was not so simple to achieve.

Kaylin fumbled through a few different sequences until she was able to create a picture of herself walking over the pit trap and out the entry on the other side of the room.

The effort, both mental and the energy pull for testing, was exhausting but she was at least sure it would work.

If she was running instead of walking, the spell would show that. *Take that, you third-year students!*

She exhaled a sigh of relief, took out the bread she'd saved from her previous night's meal, and ate it. Once she'd swallowed it with a few judicious sips from her canteen, she set out in search of the orc.

After a moment's thought, she decided he was probably lurking around the main entrance to the Rest. It made sense so she headed in that direction but circled wide to approach the gates from well down the trail.

Her movements wary, she slipped from shadow to shadow and froze at every rustle until she knew its origin.

Sometimes, it was the breeze whisking between the buildings but at others, it was a party of monsters camped in a not-too-distant room or a group of goblins foraging. Most often, it was the furtive movement of some small animal seeking its breakfast while it tried to not become something else's food.

Slowly, Kaylin moved closer to the Rest's gates but took a zigzagging route through the buildings. At one point, irritated by the complete lack of orc, she scrambled into the ruins' unstable heights and looked around.

It didn't reveal Scarsnout but it did help her to avoid another goblin camp carefully concealed in a vine-draped overhang. She liked the better view she got from the walls so she proceeded across them while she scoured the ground below for the orc.

She'd almost reached the row of buildings opposite the inn when she heard a distinctive whistle and dropped into a crouch. An almost familiar barb-bladed arrow flew through the space she'd occupied and Scarsnout's familiar chuckle rippled through the buildings.

He didn't bother to taunt her and she didn't bother to wait to hear what he might say next.

She flipped over the side of the wall away from the arrow's origin and only remembered to roll at the last minute to absorb the impact of the drop. Already, she could hear the orc's heavy tread.

He moved at the easy hunter's lope the orcs had and was closing fast. Kaylin glanced frantically around the ruins she was in and tried to remember the path to her trap. Too late, she wished her search hadn't taken such a roundabout route.

His boots reached the opposite side of the wall and turned and she knew she was out of time. She raced to the opening farthest from him and vaulted over a low ridge of fallen blocks to reach the street beyond.

Small stones dislodged by her feet pinged against walls and generally made a ruckus as the two played a deadly game of orc and mage.

It was kind of like cat and mouse with a whole lot more death involved.

Across the building from her, he broke into a run—and not the usual easy lope he took when hunting her. Perhaps he was trying to cut her off from the Rest.

"Please, oh please be that," she whispered.

If his aim was to cut her off, he'd take a more roundabout route to reach her and first try to put himself between her and the inn. He might even think she'd panic and run blindly toward it.

If he did, she'd have more time to not only work out where she'd left her trap but to reach it.

When she heard him move along the street leading to the Rest before he started to cut in toward her, she ran faster. Her last two days in the ruins had given her something of a feel for their layout, and she tried to picture the path she'd taken that morning and her direction relative to both the inn and her current route.

She didn't stick to the roads but leapt through gaps in the walls and over tumbled piles of stone, dodged around walls, and ducked under vines with scant regard for whatever else might be there.

If she ran into a pack of goblins, would the orc chase them off by claiming her as his prey? She wished she'd known the answer to that before she'd started this chase.

Given the display he'd shown the night previous, Kaylin thought it likely. The memory made her run faster and she'd gained two blocks before he realized the inn wasn't her goal.

"Where are you running to, little mage?" he shouted. His voice echoed off the buildings and made several birds take flight.

Frantic scampering from the ruins around her suggested that the rabbits and rats were taking shelter to avoid being included in the hunt. She caught sight of the building she needed and angled toward it.

Behind her, stones rattled in the street and the sound of the orc gaining kicked her fear up a notch. Adrenaline pumped through her body.

It was tempting to stop running and give in to the inevitable. Every instinct said she'd lost, that she'd never outrun him, and she wouldn't get through the ruin in time.

She glanced back and drew a sharp, panicked breath. The orc was gaining significantly.

"Trolls—" She left the rest off because she had neither the time nor the imagination at the moment.

Finally, the broken doorway leading to her trap was in reach and she bolted forward, dove through, and imagined she felt the swish of the ax passing close to her back. Part of her head told her it wasn't her imagination but she ignored it and made the hasty gesture for start to trigger the illusion.

The sight of herself running full tilt directly at her was almost enough to halt her in her tracks, but the fear of the orc kept her moving. Her carefully laid plan was thrust aside now that he'd caught up with her so soon. She leapt the pit and sprinted across the relatively clear ground and wondered if Scarsnout would notice.

Scarsnout roared as she reached the other exit and slowed to look back. He swept his ax at the Kaylin running toward him, then fixed his gaze on the one who stood, winded, at the door.

"Your days are done!" he roared and raced forward, and she discovered her second mistake.

The orc was so much bigger than her that his stride covered more ground. It almost carried him over the pit to a safe landing. He fell half a stride short and his chest pounded into the side of her trap as he fell.

His reflexive grab for a handhold saw both dagger and ax skitter across the floor.

"You!" he roared and his face darkened with rage and outrage.

He began to scrabble at the side of the pit and angled his hands to get the leverage he needed to haul himself out. She watched in horror as he began to drag himself onto the flagstones

Too short of breath to get a word out, she drew her dagger and bounded forward.

Her frantic stab at his arm brought her into grab range and the orc snatched her arm and closed his hand around it. Her dagger clattered to the floor and she pulled away from him and tried to jerk her arm free.

The orc tightened his hold even though he'd started to lose the ground he'd gained and looked like he would fall into the pit.

Kaylin braced herself against the drag, faced with the dilemma of letting him haul her into the pit as he fell or pulling him out of it as she fought to get free. Not fighting wasn't an option, but his weight was too much and she began to slide toward the edge.

"No!" she shouted and used her free hand to try to push herself back. She jerked against his hold again but slipped faster. Frantic, she willed herself to focus on making the sigils needed to throw a spell but the sudden pain when his fingers bit into her other arm blew her concentration.

As she protested and struggled, a shrill cry filled the chamber and a small, savage shape plummeted from the ceiling to land on Scarsnout's face.

Still pulling against her captor, she gaped in surprise as the drakeling she'd seen the day before scratched and clawed the orc's forehead, his eyes, and his nose while he shrieked in protest.

With a startled shout, Scarsnout released her arm and tried to swipe the little lizard off his head. He lost his hold on the edge of the pit and fell into the basement below. The creature dodged his arm and flicked itself into the air as the orc plummeted into the darkness.

Kaylin scrambled away from the edge, breathing heavily, and her heart beat rapidly in panic as she rubbed her bruised arm. She tracked the drakeling's flight as it circled the room once and came to land beside her.

"Get over there and kill that thing!" The command seared through her skull in imperious tones, accompanied by an urge to grab the ax lying nearby.

It made her look toward the pit as a large green hand slammed down on the edge.

"Don't just stand there! Get it!" The pressure to snatch the ax grew stronger and was accompanied by the fleeting image of the weapon descending on Scarsnout's head.

She scrambled to her feet as the orc's other hand appeared on the edge of the pit. It was followed by a grunt and his bloodied face appeared. She didn't wait, snatched the ax up, and used both hands to swing it hard at his head.

He roared at her and struggled to heave more of himself out of the pit, but her blow was powered by both panic and desperation and the blade bit deeply into the side of his skull, shattered bone, and launched a spray of blood and brain onto the pit's edge and the rocks around it.

The orc's roar was cut short and he tumbled into the basement and took the weapon with him.

Kaylin had let the ax slip from her fingers and dropped to her knees for a moment before she scrambled slowly away from the pit.

She stared at the grisly evidence before she turned to her side and threw up.

CHAPTER TWENTY-SIX

The drakeling perched on a sun-warmed rock and watched her.

It was embarrassing, Kaylin decided, but the fact it was there meant nothing else was hunting her.

She averted her gaze from the mess near the edge of the pit, moved to sit on another rock, and met its gaze.

I wonder if he'll come now given that he stuck around to help me.

Since the little creature seemed amenable to friendship, she started the spell she'd designed for attracting drakelings. Her fingers had barely moved through the first sequence before it rustled its wings and hissed at her.

"I am not one of those stupid drakelings." This time, the voice in her head was adamant.

Kaylin stopped, her eyes open in shock. "You aren't? Then what… er, who are you?"

The creature preened. *"I am Wivre,"* he told her, his voice a light tenor with a touch of bass, *"and I am a dragon."*

She bit her lip in an attempt to hide her amusement.

He regarded her with blatant disapprobation. She believed the two eyes would shoot flames if they could. *"That was not a joke,"* he told her and sounded so offended that she wiped the smirk off of her face.

"I'm sorry," she sputtered. "It's only that…well, you're so small. I kinda expect something bigger when I hear the word 'dragon.'"

"Most sentients do," the little creature responded sharply, *"but the truth is that a dragon's size is dictated by the size of his prey and mine have been..."* He looked into the corners and crannies between the rocks. *"Rather small."*

Kaylin remembered his pursuit of the beetles the day before and dragged her pack off. As she rummaged through it, she asked, "So where did you come from?"

The dragonette cocked his head.

"The mountain," he told her. *"Most of my youth was spent in caves and caverns. I remember darkness and stone and eating whatever I could catch. The prey down there is mostly small and anything that is not small is not prey."*

"I can imagine," she commented as she retrieved the bacon sandwich she'd pilfered earlier.

"And there wasn't much of it down there," Wivre continued and ignored her interruption. *"So I kept moving and hunting, although avoiding the larger creatures meant I didn't reach the surface world for a very long time. I am, you might say, a little stunted for a dragon."* He sighed.

When she examined the little fellow, Kaylin couldn't help but nod. Wivre was stunted for a dragon, but it certainly made the perfect disguise.

Most adventurers would take him for a drakeling and either ignore him or treat him as one. If they knew he was a dragon, they'd hunt him as either a trophy pet or a living supply of magical components—or a not-so-living supply.

In her book, being small was probably more of a blessing for the young dragon than a curse. She was about to say so but the dragonette hadn't finished.

"When I found monster lairs, I was able to steal from their pantries to supplement my hunting and I grew a little larger, but not large enough to be more than prey to them. It wasn't until the tribe I was pilfering from went to war against another tribe that I was able to move past them and reach the surface."

He paused and she opened her mouth to ask him a question, but the little beast kept talking.

"Of course, I traded the darkness and tunnels for a world full of things that wanted to kill and eat me and where light revealed me more easily to my enemies." He preened a little. *"So I remained small, hunted small things, and became very good at being unnoticed."*

"So I see," Kaylin began, only to have Wivre cut her off again.

"Being small is not a bad thing," he said stoutly. *"It has kept me alive in a very hostile world."*

"So I see," she tried for a second time.

She unwrapped the sandwich and her mouth watered at the smell. It made her feel a little guilty about having taken it but she decided she needed it more. She looked at Wivre and thought he might need it too.

"I think we are even now," he announced and she gave him a startled look.

"Even?"

"Of course," he replied and his nostrils flared as his gaze darted to the sandwich in her hands. *"I felt so bad about distracting you, yesterday—and almost getting you killed by the orc—that I have been seeking a way to make amends. Today, you gave me the chance."*

He flexed his wings as though about to take flight.

"Wait!" she snapped and waved the sandwich. "Are you hungry?"

The dragonette settled his wings along his back and craned his neck to sniff at what she held.

"I don't eat bread," he told her decisively, *"but...what is that?"*

"This?" she asked and pulled a slice of bacon from the sandwich.

Wivre's nose twitched again. *"Thaaaat,"* he answered.

"Bacon," she told him and held it out, "with smears of lard."

"Meat?" he asked and hopped off his rock to take the slice from her fingers.

"From pigs," Kaylin explained.

"I haven't had pig," the dragonette informed her. *"They are too big. Too savage, too. Orcs get upset when you take their herds and the little ones —"* He shivered. *"No. Pigs have not been prey to me."*

"This one is," Kaylin informed him, took a second slice from the sandwich, and placed it in front of him.

Wivre looked from the bacon to her, then back at the bacon before he settled himself on his haunches and held the piece between his forepaws.

He tore a chunk out of it, began to chew, and closed his eyes in ecstasy. *"Delicious!"* he told her, chewed quickly, and pulled another chunk out of the slice he held.

Kaylin noticed him slip the toes of one hind paw over the edge of the other slice she'd given him and hid a smile. It was probably instinctive but she had no desire to offend him by telling him she wouldn't steal his food.

"Why are you here?" he asked suddenly and she ceased her inspection of the bread to stare at him.

"What do you mean?"

"You are young for a human—unless I am mistaken—and you are clearly here on your own so I have to wonder. Why are you here?"

"Ah, that's a long story," she replied and dropped another piece of bacon in front of him.

"I have more bacon," he informed her and ripped another piece off.

Kaylin found it strange to listen to a voice not interrupted by chewing as he scarfed it quickly and licked his claws before he picked the next slice up.

"So?" the dragonette pressed. *"Where did* you *come from? I have shared* my *history."*

In brief, she thought but decided there was no harm in exchanging stories with the little creature.

"Like you, I grew up mostly alone but with other humans around me. And like you, I took my food where I could find it."

"But not all the time," the little dragon observed and made her wonder if he could read minds.

"No," she agreed and shook her head. "I spent some time in an orphanage—"

Wivre gave her a quizzical look.

"A place where humans care for young humans who don't have parents," she explained.

"They raise them even though they are not their own?" the dragonette asked. She nodded. *"Then why did you leave?"*

"I was almost fully grown and I wanted something different than what those caring for me wanted me to choose," she explained.

"You wished to choose your own path." The dragon nodded as though this made sense to him. *"And did you know what that path was?"*

"Not at first," she told him. "I left the shelter of the orphanage and discovered it was hard to survive in the world without help. Soon, all I wanted was to find enough to eat and to feed my friends and—"

"You had friends?" the little dragon asked and she wished he hadn't made that sound as unlikely as he did.

This time, it was her eyes that narrowed. "Of course I had friends," she snapped. "I rescued them and helped them to survive, and they did the same for me."

"That sounds nice," the dragonette noted, his mind voice wistful. *"But it doesn't tell me what brought you here to the Old City."*

"Here?" She gave a choked laugh. "I used to wonder what it was like here but that is not why I came. I came because— It's complicated."

Did he raise one eyebrow only? *"And I haven't finished my bacon,"* Wivre reminded her and gave her a mental nudge to tell him the story.

She glared and took a large bite out of her now baconless sandwich. The drippings had soaked in, though, which left the flavor, and she sighed happily.

"And?" the dragon prodded to remind her that he was waiting.

Kaylin wondered if he could be bribed by stories to stay. As strange as he was, she enjoyed his company.

"Well," she told him, "one of my friends fell sick and we needed to purchase medicine for him."

It was surprisingly easy to tell him how she and the others had stolen from the mercenaries and she soon had the little creature chuckling at their antics. His amusement gave way to outrage, however, when she revealed how the Blackbirds had stolen from Melis and Raoul.

"Outrageous!" he snarled. *"Tell me you did not let them get away with such foul play."*

"We didn't," she said. "We discovered where they were lairing and snuck inside using a passage they did not know about."

The dragon settled, chewed his bacon, and listened with rapt attention.

"So you escaped and your friend received his medicine," he concluded happily, then gave her a draconic frown. *"But that still doesn't explain how you ended up here."*

"I wanted more for my crew," Kaylin told him. "I wanted them to be able to become more than thieves stealing to keep a roof over their heads and food in their bellies."

Wivre finished his last piece of bacon, cleaned his paws, and settled in front of her to bask in a stray ray of sunshine.

"And?" he demanded.

"I learned of a place where treasure was kept and even better, the treasure of the dead."

"The undead?" the dragonette asked and she shook her head.

"No, only adventurers who'd come to the Old City and the Spears to find their fortune but didn't return. I thought it wouldn't be stealing if I took what no longer belonged to anyone."

He made a slight raspberry sound to show her exactly what he thought of that logic, and she responded with a soft smile.

"Exactly," she told him. "It was still theft, but I decided our need was greater and so we went to the treasure vault of a place called Shacklemund's."

"And that was your first taste of magic?" he asked after she'd told him how she'd learned how to deactivate the first sigil.

"Yes." Kaylin smiled. "That was the very first time I'd ever tried to cast a spell, and it was... Well, it wasn't as hard as I'd thought it would be."

"Of course not," Wivre told her. *"You hold a great potential for magic—if you survive."*

She glared at him. "Do you want to hear the rest of the story or not?"

Wivre licked his paw. *"If you insist on telling me,"* he told her but showed no sign of leaving.

Kaylin sighed as though he was asking too much. "You know..." she began.

"Finish the tale!" he ordered imperiously and she chuckled.

"As you wish," she replied and related the disastrous events at the vault.

"That still does not answer my question," he stated when she'd reached the point where she'd been given the choice of going to the Academy or facing the severe punishments Waypoint enforced for thefts on the scale she and her friends had attempted.

"Are you sure you want to hear more?" she asked and received a fierce glare and a growl in reply.

"Just tell the troll's-butted tale!"

The young thief-mage wondered if tales were like treasure to the little beast. Until she told the full story, he would continue to seek more.

The affront in Wivre's tones made her giggle, but she told him about her arrival at the Academy and her discovery of elven magic and the establishment of the study groups in answer to the magister's blatant favoritism.

The little dragon was outraged.

"But they are the teachers!" he exclaimed. *"They...they have a duty."*

Kaylin wondered how the dragonette would know about duty or teachers but didn't want to digress. She had a feeling that if she didn't eventually give him the answer he was looking for, he might fly into a rage—and she didn't want her face to end up the same way Scarsnout's had.

"They didn't see it that way," she told him soothingly and he settled as she described the politics of power. That, at least, seemed to be something the dragonette understood.

"So I was given another choice," she concluded when she reached the point of her rescue by Captain Delaine. "I had to leave the city and stay away for at least a year while she made things safer for my return. She suggested going south, away from the valley and the mountain, but I—"

"You wanted to explore the mountain," Wivre concluded and added slyly, *"And maybe find more of that elven magic you'd had a taste of."*

"Exactly," Kaylin agreed. "I am guilty of wanting that."

"They were all around here once," he surprised her by saying, *"or so the legends go."*

Her eyes lit up. "I know, and that's why I came." She gestured at the ruins around them and those beyond where they sat. "There was a library here—a great library that held countless books on magic and spells." Her eyes shone. "That's why I'm here. I want to find it. I *need* to find it." Those last words held more power than she surmised.

"And become a greater mage than those who betrayed you?" the dragonette asked slyly.

"No, merely to become a great mage," she told him somberly, the longing in her voice clear for both of them to hear.

The little dragon cocked his head, raised a forepaw, and stared at his claws with studied intent.

"Well..." he began, *"for more of that meat you call bacon, I'd be willing to help you find such things."*

This creature was as devious as it was talkative. And that was saying a lot.

Their search began with Wivre turning his nose up at her closet-sized room.

"There is barely enough room to turn around in," he informed her, and Kaylin shrugged.

"If you want more room, we'll need to find more things to trade for it."

"Do you mean like those?" the dragonette asked and indicated the array of bowls, spoons, and lamp bases in the trunk at the foot of her bed.

"Of course," she confirmed. She frowned as she made the necessary calculations. "We will need four times that amount to secure a larger space."

"And breakfast," the dragon added, having sat in on her discussion with Clay after she'd paid for the missing bacon sandwich. *"Breakfast is where the bacon is."*

The dragonette had a point and she nodded. "We need—"

"Pfft." This time, the dragon's reply was accompanied by a hiss. *"If I help you find the items, will you negotiate a larger space and more bacon?"*

"Deal," she told him, "but we'll have to have the coin before Clay will allow us to upgrade."

"Which reminds me," Wivre added. *"Why have you not properly secured your hoard?"*

"My hoard?"

He replied by indicating the trunk with his foreclaw. *"Your hoard."*

"What do you mean by properly secured?"

With an impatient sigh, he raised a draconic eyebrow at her. *"You do remember the sigils at Shacklemund's, do you not?"*

"I do, but what... Oh..." Kaylin smiled. "I'll need to purchase something to write with."

"Or you could carve the sigil into the surface." Wivre cut her off and regarded her dagger meaningfully.

"I...but Clay..." she began to protest.

"The innkeeper will forgive anything if you have the gold to pay for it," the dragonette informed her. *"And we don't have to tell him. We can wait until he notices. You will need cleaning material also, if we are to get the best prices for our finds."*

She considered her dwindling supply of coins and studied the dragonette thoughtfully. "You know that will cost us, don't you?"

"Of course," he agreed, *"but the return will be worth it."*He watched her think his words over, then uttered a pitiful creel. *"Can we not eat while you think? The bacon is almost ready."*

Kaylin laughed and extended her hand for him to walk onto her shoulder. She emptied her backpack into the chest, locked it, and headed to the bar. Another bacon sandwich sat on the counter and she barely grabbed Wivre before he pounced on it.

"I take it you'll be wanting breakfast now you've got a drakeling of your own."

The dragonette bristled and she brushed a soothing hand over his snout.

"How much?" she asked.

Clay studied the two of them and shrugged. "Two copper, one for a sandwich and one for a plate of bacon on the side. I'll have no brawling at my tables."

"Brawling?" she asked and he chuckled.

"I've seen how much a drakeling can eat—and the way that one's eyeing my breakfast doesn't bode well for yours."

"I see." Kaylin risked a glance at Wivre, who did his best to give her an innocent blink before he stared fixedly at the sandwich.

"Two coppers," she agreed and hoped her companion could live up to his promise of finding enough leavings for a larger room and breakfast.

"We'll find twice what you need," the dragonette promised, *"and don't forget to ask about the cleaning materials."*

And a journal, she wanted to add, but she gritted her teeth, found a seat instead, and settled Wivre on the table beside her.

Clay frowned when he saw where the dragonette sat but he didn't protest.

"As long as he leaves nothing behind," he told them and she nodded and ignored the creature's offended look.

"I'm tempted to dump him a present for his mistrust," he grumbled. *"I am no drakeling to drop dung where I eat."*

"Then don't behave like one," she warned him. "Remember that he's only had bad examples to judge by."

This somewhat mollified the little dragon, who settled on the table. *"So where do you wish to start?"*

Kaylin was tempted to tell him that he was the one who'd said he could help her but decided against it. She'd only just earned his partnership and she wasn't sure exactly how far a continued supply of bacon would go to keep it.

"You know the first place we met?" she asked.

"The place I almost got you killed, you mean?"

"Where I let Scarsnout sneak up on me because I wasn't looking," she corrected.

"Because of me," he told her.

"Fine, because of you, but it's not entirely your fault," Kaylin reminded him and continued in a subdued voice before he could reply. "Anyway, that place."

"Yes," the little dragon acknowledged.

"Well, a rockslide has cut off a road that led up and I thought..." She heard footsteps enter the bar and lowered her voice a little more.

Wivre flicked his tail and growled at anyone who came too close as he listened.

"You may be right," he told her. *"I haven't explored many of the heights, but I remember seeing more of the metal objects we will need in the ruins up there."*

He paused as Clay returned and set two plates before them. One was full of bacon and he pushed it forward to rest in front of the dragonette's snout. The other held a bacon-filled sandwich cut neatly in half.

"If you want half wrapped for later, let me know," he told her kindly.

The question caught Kaylin unawares and she glanced at him.

"If that's no trouble..." she began.

He gestured toward Wivre's plate.

"I could also—" A small, savage growl rumbled from the dragonette, and he withdrew his hand with a chuckle. "Perhaps not, then."

She chuckled too and suppressed a sigh at the thought of Wivre eating the bacon out of her sandwich. Still, if that was the price she had to pay for getting closer to her goal, so be it.

This time, she left through the front gates and took a meandering route when Wivre informed her that two others had left behind them and seemed to be following. While they moved, she looked for a way to elude them and soon smirked and headed along a wall at a trot.

They gave up after she took to the wall tops to avoid several goblin camps and the dragonette gave the all-clear shortly after.

"Serves them right," Kaylin muttered when he told her the two had bolted toward the Rest's walls with a goblin pack in hot pursuit.

The little dragon snickered. *"I didn't think you had it in you,"* he admitted. *"That was almost dragon-like of you."*

"They were bigger than me—and older. They shoulda been lookin' for their own loot," Kaylin informed him.

"They'll get some coin if they stop to kill the goblins," Wivre answered. *"You don't need to feel too badly. After all, you did lead them to treasure."*

That observation made her laugh. "Not the easy-to-grab kind they were after, though."

She felt his mental shrug. *"Like you said, they were bigger and more experienced. They should have been able to handle a few goblins."*

"That was more than a few," she told him. "There were almost twenty of them."

"Forty," he corrected and brought to mind the Mistfire merchant's advice—*where you see one, a dozen more are close by.*

Kaylin broke into a trot that brought her to the almost intact ruins huddled at the mountain's feet.

"Up there," she said and gestured to the rockslide.

"It shouldn't be too hard," Wivre told her and took flight. *"Follow me."*

She complied and scaled the first layer of boulders with some scrambling and considerable cursing.

"You do know I am a young dragon," he told her.

"And your point?" she demanded and rubbed her stinging palms as she picked herself up from a slide down the rocks.

"Such language is not good for my delicate ears," he told her and barely suppressed his laughter.

"You stole from the pantries of underground monsters," she reminded him, "and I'll bet you got underfoot while making your escape. It's nothing you haven't heard before. Besides which, what did you say yesterday?"

The little dragon chuckled unrepentantly and flew along the edge of the slide.

"This way should be better," he told her.

"That's what you said the last time," she grumbled.

"Well, this time, I'm right."

They reached the top of the landslide and Kaylin crouched on one of the boulders and surveyed the city below to make sure nothing had marked her ascent and decided to follow them.

After several moments of observation, she'd seen nothing more than the usual small animals and smoke from humanoid campfires.

"They mostly come out during the early morning and late afternoon," Wivre told her when she remarked on the lack of movement. *"The light hurts their eyes."*

Remembering the size of the goblins' eyes, she realized that made sense but it didn't explain some of the others.

"And the orcs?" she asked.

"They prefer to hunt at night," he told her, then added, *"unless some foolish human walks into their camp and stares at them while they sleep."*

Her eyes widened. "You saw that?"

"It made it surprisingly easy to take their food," the dragonette told her unrepentantly.

"So you were following me?" she demanded.

"You were entertaining—and I never knew when you might make it easier for me to grab a quick snack."

"And now there's bacon," she concluded, and he closed his eyes momentarily and smiled happily at her.

"Yes, now there's bacon," he agreed and tilted his head to look at the sun. *"Is it time to eat?"*

"Not until we find at least two coppers' worth of treasure," she told him firmly.

"And then it'll be time to eat?"

"That all depends. The more we find—"

"The sooner we eat," the dragonette interjected, *"and the more bacon there'll be."*

"Smartass," she grumbled, but she reversed carefully off the boulder and approached the first semi-intact building with caution.

Wivre earned his bacon. Exactly as Kaylin had guessed, the buildings that had been built farther up had belonged to the wealthier residents of Tulon's City—and some of them had even been mages.

He entered each one first to make sure nothing was living inside that could endanger them, and she followed on his all-clear.

It made the search go more quickly if she didn't have to stop every few minutes to check that her surroundings were still safe.

"Humanoids don't come up here often," the little dragon told her as they sifted through the lower floor of what had been a wealthy household.

She nodded. They'd found the dining room and the mostly intact remains of a sideboard containing a few items that looked like they might be made of silver. The sun had reached its zenith by the time they'd finished poking through the rubble of the downstairs rooms and taken the stairs to the next floor.

"They had a library," she whispered when their investigation took her into a large room with decaying bookshelves lining the walls. "I wonder..."

"They were elves," Wivre told her. *"Almost all of them practiced magic."*

Kaylin wanted to ask him how he knew that if he'd spent most of his life underground and had only recently emerged, but the little dragon had flown to the highest shelf of one of the bookcases and now scruffled through the dust and debris he found there.

Some of the dust came over the top of the shelf like a dry waterfall and a few last puffs of sand trailed behind.

With a sigh, she chose a different section of the room where she was less likely to have dust and dirt "accidentally" kicked onto her head.

Their search of the room took them most of the afternoon and by the time Wivre remarked on the waning light, they'd managed to find a fancy scroll case—unfortunately empty—some barely legible scrolls, and a couple of books that looked like they could be read carefully.

"We need to go," the dragon insisted when Kaylin straightened from searching a cupboard set in the foot of a desk, *"and you promised me bacon."*

"You had your bacon at lunchtime," Kaylin told him. "For dinner, there will be roast—"

"Chicken?" Wivre asked hopefully.

"Or mutton," she told him and headed to the door.

"What's mutton?" the little dragon asked. A moment later he added, *"Is it as good as bacon?"*

Goblins, as Wivre had explained, liked hunting in the dusk.

Kaylin reached the gates at a dead run with a hail of spears in her wake and a half-dozen arrows protruding from her backpack. She was relieved she'd had something in it to stop them from penetrating her back.

"Next time, head back earlier," the gate guard commanded, "and try to not invite the whole damned city for dinner."

Wivre hissed at him, and he ruffled the dragonette's head but yanked his hand away from the answering snap.

He was still laughing as he mounted the stairs to continue his watch.

Breathing heavily, she turned and headed to the inn, glad of the few coins she had left in her pouch. Both she and the dragon needed a bath and she still had to buy the cleaning materials.

There was enough for both but not enough to cover the cost of a journal and a pencil.

With a heavy sigh, she hoped she'd found enough to cover that as well. She didn't want to try writing in the margins of the scrolls and books she'd found or to see if she could remember everything she read without making notes to make sense of it all.

What she wanted most was to see if she could read what she'd found, but a bath and feeding Wivre took precedence.

She looked at the water and glanced at her companion. This wouldn't be easy.

"You want me to go in there?" the dragon demanded when she showed him the newly filled tub.

Kaylin nodded, peeled her dirty tunic from her back, and decided she needed to wash at least one set the next time she came.

"Try it," she told him. "You'll like it."

He flew closer and perched on the rim to regard the water dubiously. *"Are you sure?"*

She was about to answer when someone banged on the door.

"There's only supposed to be one of you in there," Chloe called in a firm tone. "Open up."

"Why?" she asked.

"'Cos if there's more than you and that drakeling, you owe me another silver."

"There isn't," she answered but she crossed to the door and opened it so the innkeeper's daughter could see.

Chloe looked past her, around the room, and even peered into the tub as if someone might hide in the water.

"You never know," she said and stared suspiciously at Wivre.

"You know you can talk to me by thinking?" the dragonette told Kaylin when she had locked the door again.

He flitted to perch on the side of the tub and peered suspiciously at the water while she removed the last of her clothes. He was so busy studying the tub that he didn't see what she was doing until she stepped past him and slid into the water.

"What happened to your scales?" he asked and she burst out laughing.

"I don't have any. I'm human, remember?"

"Shell-less, scale-less..." he muttered and his tirade ended in a startled squawk when she scooped him off the side of the tub and dumped him in the water before she settled him on her knees.

"There," she told him and rubbed his scales with a rough cloth. "That's not so bad, is it?"

He tried a growl but it came out as a contented rumble when she found a particularly itchy patch on his scales and rubbed it vigorously.

"Tell me about this talking to you with my mind," she whispered.

"It's easy," he answered. *"You merely have to think it. Think of me and what you want me to hear or see, and that will be what comes into my head. It would be better for when we're in the city too."*

"Like this?" she tried and continued to clean his scales.

"Not so loud," the dragonette protested. *"Think...softer."*

Kaylin complied as best she could and they practiced while she washed the dust from his scales. By the time she had finished cleaning him, she found speaking to him this way much easier.

Pleased at having learned a new skill, she washed herself and let Wivre leave his perch on her knees to float in the water beside her with his wings outspread.

"This is nice," he told her. *"We should do this again."*

"Not every night," she responded. *"It costs a silver."*

"And if I find a silver's worth of treasure every day?" he wheedled.

She sighed. *"If you find a silver's worth of treasure more than we need, then fine."*

Kaylin stood, stepped out of the tub, and dried herself with the towel the inn provided. Wivre paddled to the edge and hooked his chin over it until she lifted him out and dried him as well.

Some of his scales seemed a little dry and she made a note to ask how much it would cost to buy a little oil for them. She'd noticed that some of the adventurers who owned drakelings poured something from small bottles onto the scales of their pets and had wondered what it was and why.

Now, she believed she knew the answer.

The thought made her sigh at the unexpected expense. No wonder owning a drakeling was considered a sign of prestige—they were costly critters to have and she doubted a single one of them was anywhere near the help Wivre was.

These thoughts occupied her mind as she ordered and ate dinner at a table in a far corner while she introduced her scaled companion to the joys of roast mutton and potatoes.

"It's not as good as bacon," he commented as he chewed on a mouthful of the expertly cooked meat.

Kaylin smiled and carved a small piece of potato. The drakeling's reaction was predictable.

"Not as good as mutton," he declared and refused to eat another piece, but not before he'd licked it clean of lard.

She shrugged and gave him another slice of mutton instead before she cleared her plate and studied him. *"So, what's next?"* she asked.

"As if you need to ask," he reprimanded her. *"Tonight, we clean our treasure and tomorrow, we turn it into even greater treasure."*

With a sigh, she pushed away from the table.

Cleaning would take her all night.

It didn't take all night, but the moon was high by the time she and Wivre had lined the shelves of her small room with gleaming metal objects. Most were silver in color but of those, Wivre assured her only a handful were real silver. The rest were silver-plated or some cheaper metal.

Kaylin grouped the real silver ones together. "We ask a higher price for those."

"And this," the dragonette told her as he pushed a slim metal band to the collection. *"It's tartalium."*

"Tartalium?"

"A rare metal, good for enchanting, although this is not enchanted."

"Maybe it was being prepared for enchantment," she suggested.

He gave the equivalent of a draconic shrug. *"Who knows what people were doing when the dragon tore their world apart."*

She frowned. First, she was getting used to the idea that the story of a real dragon tearing apart this mountain might have some reality to it and second, she wanted to ask if the dragon who'd torn the mountain in two had been his mother. It didn't seem like the right thing to ask, however, or the right time to ask it.

The little dragon was just settling into the idea of a partnership and she didn't want to ruin their chance to solidify that.

The next day, they bargained with Clay and she surprised him with her knowledge of the metals from which her items were made. A couple of times, he glanced at Wivre but the dragonette merely gave him a drakeling-like blink and started to groom his tail.

"How do you know so much, girl?" he asked when she pointed out that the lamp base was not only silver but of a higher level of craftsmanship than the rest.

The cincher had been when she'd pointed out the signature engraved into its base.

"Mage training wasn't the only thing I learned in Waypoint," she told him and resisted the urge to drop in the harsher tones of the streets. She would if she had to but the fewer people who knew about that part of her past, the better.

His eyes sharpened with interest but he didn't press her any further and she noticed he was far more direct in his dealings from then on. When they'd concluded their barter, he held the tartalium ring up.

"Find me more like this," he told her, "and I'll consider selling you a room."

Kaylin grinned at him.

"That sounds like a challenge to me," she began, only to have Wivre's voice intrude inside her head.

"Tell him to throw in a bath every night and you're sold," the little dragon advised and made her chuckle.

"Add a nightly bath in that room and you've got yourself a deal," she stated.

"Once a week," he retorted.

"Three times."

"Twice."

"Done," she agreed and added, "So, how many more?"

She indicated the ring with a jerk of her head and he frowned.

"If I said two dozen of that caliber with negotiating room to reduce the number for any of higher or lower quality?"

"Deal," Kaylin told him, "but it has to be one of the bigger rooms. I won't pay that much for something the size of my current one."

Clay smirked. "We didn't specify—" he began but stopped abruptly when Wivre rumbled a savage growl. He rolled his eyes. "Fine. It's a fair price for one of the larger rooms."

The little dragon settled onto his hindquarters and began to wash a forepaw. The innkeeper eyed him warily, then smiled.

"And I suppose you'd like breakfast and something for the road before you leave?"

Wivre uttered a happy squeak and bounced to his feet and this time, she rolled her eyes.

"So much for bartering," she muttered. "It's like the damned thing understands everything you say. I swear if it was half as intelligent about everything as it is worried about breakfast it could help me find these rings."

Clay chuckled, led the way into the bar, and gestured them to their usual corner as he went to speak to the cook.

"What do you mean half as intelligent?" Wivre demanded.

"Don't give me that," she retorted. *"You are acting too smart by half and forgetting that we don't want you known as a dragon."*

It took a few days for Kaylin to get used to the routine but soon, she and Wivre worked as a well-oiled team. They rose early to complete their barter before they left to look for more, then returned to eat and clean their haul before sleeping.

The days flowed into one week, then two, and some of the other adventurers began to notice their success. They also became something of a fixture at the inn, and adventurers began to recognize them in the evening, even though they kept to themselves.

It was amazing how far a nod, a smile, or a simple hello went to making the inn feel like home.

That recognition also brought dangers and she sometimes had to take to the walls and the upper level of the rubble to discourage followers. Not everyone wanted to do their own work to find what they needed.

At the end of the second week, they had enough to pay for a bigger room and she bought a journal and several pencils in different shades. Wivre grumbled that they should clean everything they found and sell it the next day, but she pointed out that they could store some and only polish what they needed.

"I need time to study," she told him and waved a hand at the small stack of books and scrolls she'd amassed. It was nice to have a bookshelf to stack them on and a desk to work at, but she hadn't had time to even look at them. *"What's the point of doing all this work if it doesn't get us any closer to our goal?"*

"Your goal," the little dragon reminded her acerbically.

"Fine, my goal then," she agreed and inclined her head. "What's yours?"

Wivre curled his tail around his forepaws and blinked at her. *"I... haven't thought about it,"* he admitted finally. *"Until now, my life has been focused on trying to survive. Then I discovered bacon."*

Kaylin chuckled. *"And baths."*

"And citrus-oil." The dragonette sighed and sidled closer. *"Speaking of which..."*

She rolled her eyes and took the bottle of oil from the shelf. *"Okay. Show me where."*

"All over?" he asked hopefully.

"Fine," she grumbled, *"but then I get the rest of the night off so I can study."*

"Deal," Wivre agreed and turned to show her where the itch was.

Having a human attend to your scales wasn't such a bad thing.

"Done!" Kaylin exclaimed a little while later.

She'd spread her sleeping roll on the floor and sat Wivre on top of it. There was no point in upsetting Clay's daughter by leaving oil spots on the floor. The girl was busy enough cleaning as it was.

His belly scales shined as she wiped a cloth over them to remove the excess oil, and the room smelt of a mixture of oranges, lemons, and limes.

"You missed a part," the little dragon muttered, rolled onto his side, and stretched on the sleeping roll.

"Did not," she retorted, capped the oil bottle, and rubbed the cloth over his side and neck.

The dragon did not reply and lifted his head lazily so she could rub around his chin and eye ridges. As she did so, he rumbled a sound that sounded remarkably like a purr.

It made her smile as she straightened and packed both oil and cloth into their chest.

"Now, I get to take a look at these," she told his semi-comatose form and took one of the books from the shelf. With her journal at hand, she settled into the chair behind the desk and lifted the cover gingerly.

To her delight and chagrin, the book was in elvish. She even remembered one or two of the words. The rest, though, were gibberish.

Kaylin heaved a heartfelt sigh and wondered if she could risk sending a letter to Captain Delaine asking for her journal. The problem was she didn't want to risk anyone from the Academy getting hold of it, and she didn't know how far the magisters' reach extended—or if Gaudin was still hunting for ways to destroy her.

"It's better to not risk it," she muttered, stared at the book, and wondered what her chances were of having Clay source her an elvish dictionary—and exactly how much he'd charge her to do it.

She scowled, then started to leaf glumly through the pages. At least it looked like it had something to do with magic. Now and then, one of the symbols would remind her of something on the walls in the Academy's basement and she'd stop to write it down.

When she grew tired of trying to decipher the symbols, she flicked through the book, looking for something to indicate what it was about—a diagram or a picture or something.

It would be annoying to spend all that time reading it only to find it had nothing to do with magic. Wivre's sudden weight on her shoulder and his voice in her ear startled her.

"You're either the fastest reader I've ever seen or you're looking for pictures."

"What?"

The little dragon protested her sudden jerk and dug his claws in so he didn't fall off.

"Ouch!" Kaylin exclaimed. *"That... How did you know I was looking for pictures?"*

"Because not many humans can read elvish," the dragonette told her forthrightly, *"and there isn't a human alive who can read it that fast."*

"Oh, yeah?" she challenged.

The dragon regarded her smugly. *"I doubt even an elf could read it that fast, ergo, you're looking for pictures."*

"I was trying to see what it was about," she whined and hated the self-pity that had crept into her voice.

The dragonette flicked his tail and it encircled her neck. *"Most people would do that by reading the words."* He snaked his head around to look her in the eye. *"Or is that the problem? You can't read the words?"*

She blushed. *"That's the problem,"* she admitted. *"I can't read the words and I need to be able to see a picture to know what it's about."*

While they'd talked, she'd flipped pages and found a diagram that confirmed her hopes.

"See? It is about magic!" Momentarily lost in happiness, she forgot about the dragon's questions.

Wivre hadn't. *"Yes,"* he acknowledged, *"but how do you hope to understand it if you can't read it?"*

"I had a journal which had a fair amount of elvish translated in it," she told him morosely, *"but it's... At least I hope it's at the Academy."*

"The magisters took it?" He sounded outraged. *"And you can't read this book without its help?"*

"Yes," she admitted forlornly and tried to close the book.

He leaned off her shoulder and spread his wings for balance as he slapped a forepaw into the center of the page she was on.

"It's not that hard, you know," the little dragon said. *"I could teach you."*

Kaylin stared at him, wide-eyed. *"You can read? I mean...the elvish, you can read it?"*

She realized that while small, her companion was much older than most of the humans around the inn and frankly had an ego that could match his age.

With this in mind, she rephrased her response. *"You could? I thought you'd spent most of your life trying to survive?"*

"I said most," the little dragon informed her. *"I didn't say what I'd spent the rest of it doing. Some of it was in a library chasing rats and silverfish."*

"And reading?" she asked hopefully.

"And reading," the dragonette confirmed. *"Why don't we begin at page one?"*

Two more weeks passed and Wivre proved an apt teacher—or maybe Kaylin was simply a very good student. Either way, she progressed slowly through the text and learned the basics of the elvish language as she translated it into her journal.

She wrote the translation on one page and any ideas or extrapolations she had on the opposite one and linked the text to the idea by using distinctive colors.

And she worked on trying to recreate what she remembered from her time in the basement and teaching her friends at the Academy.

"You'll spend our entire hoard on colored pencils and notebooks the way you're going," the little dragon grumbled.

"I will not," she told him. *"Besides, it'll pay off in the long run."*

"The long run is all well and good," the dragon told her, *"but we need to eat and have a safe place to sleep in the short run."*

Kaylin groaned and turned to look at her hoard location. *"Let me guess, more cleaning?"*

"We will need to barter tomorrow to keep the room," Wivre confirmed and she wondered how she'd lost track of the time. At least the

dragonette kept his eye on it but bacon was life for the creature after all.

Reluctantly, she laid the book aside and took out the sleeping roll and cleaning cloths. They'd amassed a number of items that needed to be cleaned, and she'd realized she'd neglected her housekeeping in favor of her books.

Isn't that always the way? she thought and settled cross-legged onto the sleeping roll.

To her surprise, Wivre lifted a cloth and a candlestick and started to clean.

Her mouth was open at least half a minute before she shut it. *"I didn't know you could do that,"* she told him, and he responded with a draconic grin.

"I learn quickly." He flexed his forepaws and waggled his claws. *"And these are more useful than they look."*

"I'll keep that in mind." She wondered if his claws were flexible enough to pick locks. After all, they were as sturdy as any lock pick she'd seen.

Not every lock was immediately opened using magic.

She didn't mention it and they worked quietly until the moon shone through the window and dimmed the lamplight with its glow.

"I think that should be enough, don't you?" she asked, and Wivre examined the pile of cleaned salvage.

"It should be," he agreed, *"and there'll be enough left over for an extra bath and a pencil. A pencil—only one. Not two or three or four, okay?"*

Kaylin giggled at the sternness of his tone. *"All right,"* she told him. *"A pencil."* She glanced at her desk. *"A blue pencil since that's the shortest."* She set her cleaning rag aside, gathered the salvage they had yet to clean, and dumped it in the chest. *"It's time to sleep."*

She looked around when Wivre didn't reply and frowned when she didn't see the little dragon on the sleeping roll. It took her a moment to notice him curled in a deep bronze bowl, the dark red of his scales a perfect complement to the dish.

"You know we have to sell that, don't you?" she asked and felt almost sorry for the dragon.

"Do we have to?" he asked and raised an eyelid. *"It fits me perfectly."*

Kaylin had to agree that it did, so she returned to the chest and rummaged through it until she found an ornate scroll case, another lamp base, and some kind of stamp.

"Do you think these would cover it?" she asked and carried them to the sleepy dragonette.

Again, Wivre raised an eyelid to make a quick study of the items.

"They should do," he murmured, his mind voice muffled.

With a sigh, she took the cleaning cloth and polish out and settled beside the bowl.

"Then you can keep your bowl until you grow out of it."

"I don't grow very fast," he replied smugly and snuggled deeper into it.

She smiled at him and got to work, glad she didn't have to take away what looked like his new favorite sleeping place.

They could still trade it when he tired of it but until then, he might as well have something from their work to enjoy.

After all, she got the books and Clay had already hinted that elven lore was in demand.

She'd finished the scroll case and lamp base and started work on the stamp when Wivre's sleepy mind voice interrupted her again.

"Do you know what I wish?" he asked dreamily and the end of his tail twitched.

"No," she replied.

"I wish I could be like my great ancestors and sleep on a proper hoard..." he mumbled before she was sure he was out.

Had he meant to share that with her?

The little dragon's words haunted Kaylin. After all, what she wanted was to find the elven library and become a great mage, and Wivre was already helping her work toward it, but a hoard? She went to sleep thinking about how she could help him to achieve it.

He was only a little dragon, so maybe there was something they could do.

Her dreams were filled with dragons and heaps of shining coins. They were also full of fire and magic and running—a fearful amount of running. She woke drenched in sweat with the sheets and blankets tangled around her.

Wivre, on the other hand, woke refreshed. He stretched lazily in his bowl and his claws scratched against the sides and the tips of his toes stuck up over the edge. The little dragon flicked himself onto all fours, arched his back, and stretched again so that his tail stuck out behind him.

"That was the best night's sleep so far," he told her, hopped nimbly out of the bowl, and nudged it over to the chest with his nose.

Kaylin gave him a sleepy nod before she packed his "bed" away. After that, she dressed, gathered their loot, and hurried downstairs to catch Clay before the breakfast rush. As she descended the stairs, she planned how to make Wivre's wish a reality.

It was possible, but only if she was willing to start very, very small —which seemed somehow fitting, given that he was a very, very small dragon.

Her generosity in letting the dragonette keep his sleeping bowl paid off. The lamp base had a signature matching the first, and Clay couldn't keep his ecstatic response well-enough hidden to escape her notice.

"So that's a match then?" she asked.

The innkeeper wrinkled his brow in mild consternation when he realized he had allowed his excitement to show. He shrugged before he gave in to a broad smile.

"It is," he admitted and set the lamp base to one side, but not before he'd retrieved its matching partner.

The smile lingered and reappeared now and then whenever his gaze strayed to the pair.

"And you have a buyer for them?" she asked.

He gave her a sharp glance and retrieved one of the lamps. "See this signature?" he asked and turned the base so she could see the sigil etched in the bottom. "Find me more of these and I'll pay you double for them."

Which probably meant he was getting triple, but Kaylin didn't care. Double for what was already one of her best-paying items of salvage was a major step forward in getting herself established at the inn.

She wondered if he'd take such items in place of the tartalium objects he'd mentioned as part of their deal.

Oblivious to her thoughts, Clay moved to the stamp-like object. At first, he treated it like any other object she brought him but suddenly, he pulled his loupe out and took a closer look.

"Do you remember where you got this?" he asked with sudden interest.

Kaylin darted a glance at Wivre.

"Of course, I do," the dragonette assured her. *"It is one of the places we need to go back to."*

"I think so," she told him, sure the innkeeper had noted her exchange with Wivre.

He paused, studied her face, then shrugged and put the stamp to one side. "Well, if you do, go through it with a fine-tooth comb. I'll take any more items like this at three times the price." His gaze drifted to the stamp again. "Maybe four," he corrected, then leaned toward her and lowered his voice. "Unless you tell someone else about it. In which case, all you'll get is the base. Understood?"

Four times the price? Kaylin nodded, wide-eyed, and laid her finger lengthwise along her lips.

Again, Clay studied her face as though trying to read her mind. After a few heartbeats, he nodded like he was satisfied and laid her payment on the table. It was far more than she'd expected, and Wivre's soft hiss confirmed the dragonette's surprise.

He mantled his wings before he flipped them close to his back and sat again. The innkeeper chuckled. "He likes his gold, that one," the man observed and she smiled.

"You should see what he's like when I have to pay for our room," she quipped although her face heated at how close to the truth the innkeeper seemed to be.

She scooped their earnings into her coin pouch and looked expectantly at him.

"So…are you open for business?" she asked.

"Anything to get a little of my gold back," he told her, although the smile softened his words.

Wivre scampered up Kaylin's arm and onto her shoulder.

"He sounds cross but he's very happy," the little dragon informed her. *"Something we found has pleased him greatly."*

Kaylin nodded and followed Clay into the storeroom that served as a miniature supply shop. There, she bought *one* pencil as promised —blue—but also bought a stout leather satchel and slung it crossways across her chest.

"For lunch," she said and patted it when Wivre gave her a look of reproach. "You get extra bacon today."

It wasn't the truth but the dragonette was so taken with the idea of extra bacon that he didn't seem to notice, and he was content to cling to her shoulder as they headed into the ruins to see what else they could find from the building that had yielded the stamp.

"It was a seal, you know," Wivre informed her. *"An elven seal."*

"Is that important?" she asked him.

"Clay seemed to think so."

"Then let's see what else we can find for him," she decided as they trotted to the building they'd been salvaging the day before.

The two of them remained vigilant as they left but this time, no one tried to follow them.

Kaylin didn't reveal what the satchel was for until they were settled on her sleeping roll, cleaning and polishing the remainder of the haul. She left Wivre to sort the objects into groups according to their metals, took the satchel, and wiped it clean of crumbs.

When she'd shaken her coin pouch onto the desk, she sorted the coins into their different denominations and tried to remember how much they'd earned between them. In the end, she couldn't remember so she took all but a handful of the lowest-denomination coins and layered them in the bottom of the bag.

The clanking of metal shifting stopped but she ignored it. She'd known there was very little chance of her completing her surprise without his attention.

Hopefully, she could get most of it finished before he decided to fly up and ask what she was doing.

After a moment's silence, the clanking continued, and she selected a half-dozen silver coins and sprinkled them into the satchel before she scooped the remaining coins into the pouch. That was too much for Wivre.

The clanking stopped and he took flight with a brief swish of wings.

Kaylin grinned when he landed on her shoulder.

"What are you doing?" he asked and his tail circled her neck as he craned to look at the satchel on the desk. *"And don't tell me it's nothing. You stink of secrets."*

"A girl has to have some secrets," she told him tartly and his claws dug into her shoulder as he tightened his grasp with displeasure.

"From her partner?" the dragon demanded, and Kaylin snickered.

"No," she admitted, *"and especially not when she's making her partner a gift."*

"A gift?" The dragonette hopped off her shoulder, landed on the desk, and circled the satchel. *"This?"* He sniffed it cautiously. *"I don't smell bacon,"* he observed. *"Only a lot of coins—some copper and some silver. What is this?"*

She leaned on the desk, picked the satchel up, and lifted the flap so he could see the coins within.

"It's not much," she told him, *"but it's the start of your hoard."*

"In a bag?" he asked and sounded doubtful.

"It's a portable hoard," she explained, lifted him, and settled him inside. *"We can take it with us wherever we go and you can sleep on it if we have to camp."*

"And here?" he asked.

"Here," she told him, put the satchel on the desk, and moved to the chest to retrieve the bronze bowl.

She placed it in the cubby under the desk, picked the satchel up, and extricated the dragonette.

"Here, you can sleep on your hoard like any other dragon," she explained and emptied the satchel into the bowl.

"And you did this for me?" Wivre asked, hopped onto the bowl, and began to arrange the coins inside.

"Well, you're helping me work toward what I want," Kaylin told him and gestured at the bowl, *"so I thought I would help you start working toward what you want. It's not much but we'll add to it from now on."*

"*We*?" he asked.

"Yes," she answered. *"From everything we make from our salvage, you'll get a percentage to add to your hoard. It might take a while for it to become as big as any your ancestors had, but even they had to start somewhere."*

The little dragon cocked his head. *"You mean it?"*

"Of course," she assured him. *"That hoard is yours. Like my pencils or my journals. It's not for sale or spending on necessities but for you to sleep on to your heart's content."*

"Even if there's gold?" Wivre asked. He turned his head to look at her, then at the coins, and back to her as though he couldn't quite believe it.

"Even if there's platinum," she answered.

His tail flicked. *"And gems?"*

"We'll discuss gems," she replied, *"but there will eventually be gems or whatever else you want to add."*

"I like books," the dragon suggested slyly.

"The books are mine," she retorted, then caught the mischievous twinkle in the wyrmling's eye. "*You—*"

He chuckled. *"Books don't make a good bed but I'd like to be able to read yours if I may."*

"Fine," she agreed, *"but if there's one claw mark, or...or toothmark..."*

"Are you sure you're not a dragon?" Wivre asked, slid into the bowl, and settled with a contented sigh.

The dragonette adored his new hoard and took part in their morning trade by poking his head out from under the flap.

"For extra lunch, huh?" Clay observed when he heard coins clink as the dragonette shifted. "Well, I guess that's one way to deter pick-pockets."

Wivre hissed at the idea of anyone stealing his hoard and Kaylin laughed.

"It keeps him happy," she explained, "and everyone knows that a happy drakeling is a well-behaved drakeling."

"This much is true," the innkeeper agreed, counted their payment out, and only seemed a little puzzled when she slipped the agreed percentage into the satchel before dropping the remainder into her coin pouch.

"It's easier if I keep some separate," she told him and tapped Wivre playfully on the nose. "That way, I get to keep my fingers."

"Oh?" Clay asked. "Possessive, is he?"

She gave the little dragon a look of chagrin. "I didn't find out until I'd put some coin in there. Until then, I thought it would be the ideal way to keep my earnings safe."

Wivre hissed at that, but the man took it to be more of the drakeling's possessive behavior.

Kaylin shrugged. "Now, whenever I receive any coin, he seems to think some of it should be his."

Clay chuckled. "I'd heard some drakelings could be like that but this is the first time I've ever seen it. You'd almost think they thought of themselves as real dragons."

She tucked her hand in the satchel to prevent Wivre from bouncing out.

"Well, they are related," she said, "so I guess I should have seen it coming."

The innkeeper chuckled again before he flipped a copper into the bag.

"For your hoard," he joked and dragonette subsided, "although I thought he preferred bacon."

At the mention of his favorite food, the little dragon poked his head out of the bag but was ignored.

"Do you need anything from the stores today?" Clay asked but she shook her head.

"Not today," she told him, "although my pencils are getting low and I'll need a new journal soon."

He raised his eyebrows. "I never took you for a writer, but a mage…I suppose you have to study, right?"

"Exactly," she confirmed.

"Another journal should come in with the next caravan," he told her, "although you could see if any of the new arrivals have any for trade."

Kaylin made a note to check. Sometimes, a merchant would arrive with a group of mercenaries and they'd bring a variety of items. She hadn't taken much interest before but she hadn't been able to afford much. Now, she could.

She followed the innkeeper into the bar, ordered breakfast, and took Wivre, satchel and all, out to forage in the ruins.

The next few days followed that routine and she made sure the dragonette received his cut of the loot until the satchel started to become heavy.

"I don't think I need all my hoard today," he told her one morning. *"Perhaps only a few coins with the rest locked away here. I wouldn't want you to run too slowly to escape any goblins."*

Kaylin snorted but she had to agree. She hadn't wanted to say anything, but coins were heavy and they'd added a few more each day until the weight had started to tell. The noise was also a concern.

"But you have to protect it properly," Wivre insisted and reminded her that she had yet to add a sigil to her chest.

She thought about disagreeing, given that the chest didn't belong to her. Since it was his hoard, she decided he had a right to have a say in how it was protected and took the time to carve the locking sigil into the trunk.

When she made the gestures to activate it, the sigil lit and the dragonette sighed happily before he asked, *"Can you do another one—a different one?"*

Kaylin scratched her head in confusion but complied, although the second one was harder and took a little longer to get right. When she was finished, though, the little dragon was satisfied.

"Thank you," he said, then paused as if in thought. *"You know that library where I learned to read elvish..."*

"You might have mentioned it," she answered warily.

"Well," he continued. *"I might have remembered where there's a vault that could help us find it."*

CHAPTER TWENTY-SEVEN

Wivre's news brought about a change in their routine. Now, instead of only looking for salvage, they worked the areas leading to the mountain entrance.

They scouted through the ruins around the path usually taken by larger mercenary companies, reasoning that the path those companies took would be more dangerous than finding a lesser-known route.

It was good logic but they found the idea had a number of flaws.

Firstly, Wivre couldn't remember how he'd come out of the mountain. He only knew it wasn't "this" way. The exit he'd used had been smaller and he didn't remember any of the buildings or streets they passed through.

"I'm not sure I can find it from this angle," he admitted as they crouched on top of an overhang and looked over their newest section.

"What about once you're inside?"

"I'm still not sure. You have no idea the number of passages and tunnels in there."

"But you have a better chance of finding it once you're in there, right?" she pressed.

"This is true. I can't have come out of the mountain too far from here," he admitted as his head flicked to look both ways and up. *"It's simply that I can't remember exactly where."*

He sounded so despondent that Kaylin stroked his eye ridges to soothe him. "We'll find it somehow," she told him.

"Quiet!" the little dragon commanded and she turned before she moved into the shelter of the wall.

She wanted to ask Wivre what he'd heard or seen but didn't dare.

Whatever had caused him to order silence, the creature must be close—or the humanoid or whatever—and she didn't want to draw its attention. It didn't take long before she could hear it.

From what she could tell, it was fairly large but moved swiftly, and from the sounds it made moving through the vegetation, it had four legs, not two. Several times, the creature stopped and snuffed the air, drew in long speculative breaths, and huffed them out again.

Kaylin listened as it trotted around the base of the wall on which she was perched and she held her breath. Twice, she heard claws scrape the rock below as though it tried to find purchase on the stone. Once, she heard a frustrated growl.

The longer she listened, the more sure she became that the creature wasn't alone and that a pack was circling and sniffing where they'd left the ground to start their climb.

Something was tracking them.

Wivre slipped out of his satchel, clambered silently onto her shoulder, then down her back before he moved along the edge of the wall to peer over the ledge. She received the impression of something large and furry like a wolf but bigger.

Several somethings, the dragonette showed her.

She held her breath again and wondered how they would manage to get back to the Rest.

There was a limit to how far she could travel over the walls. Would it be enough to break the trail? And, if she returned to the ground from where she was, would the creatures be waiting?

That latter question was answered a short time later when something bolted out of the ruin and scurried through the grass and over stone blocks as fast as it could go. A yip followed and then a scrambling rush of movement.

Other smaller creatures reacted to this by racing from cover and the pack gave chase, but Wivre didn't move from his perch. He watched the events below and his tail twitched slightly in the shadow.

There was one more creature, its attention not distracted by the pack's hunt.

Kaylin waited and the dragonette watched, and the sun started to slide down the other side of the sky. A cool breeze sprang up and she grew anxious. What if dusk came and the creature hadn't gone?

A shrill squeal broke the afternoon stillness. It cut off abruptly but was followed by a series of savage growls and snarls. The monster below them huffed impatiently and, with a soft grumbling growl, loped away.

"We should go now," Wivre told her in urgent tones. *"Right now and across the walls as much as we can."*

"Are you sure there isn't anything else out there?" she asked and remembered to use her mind instead of her mouth.

"No, the dire wolves are gone, but it is nearing dusk and the goblins will be stirring soon."

Goblins. The thought made Kaylin shiver. She'd had enough of the little bat-eared monsters to last her a lifetime but she was sure the world hadn't taken her feelings into account.

"And worse," Wivre added.

"Worse?" she whispered, scrambled to the top of the wall, and trotted carefully along it before she bounded across a gap to reach another section. "What do you mean by worse?"

"I think I can smell bugbears."

"Bugbears?"

"You know, large, hairy, smelly, live in clans, what big eyes you have?" the dragon snapped.

"I thought they had big teeth," she observed, more to take her mind off the wolves and goblins and the setting sun than anything else.

"Big teeth, bad breath... I thought you said you didn't know what they were."

"I don't, but 'large, hairy, smelly, live in clans'—that's not exactly helpful, you know," she told him. "That describes almost every monster there ever was."

"Orcs aren't hairy," Wivre retorted in sulky tones, *"or hobgoblins."*

"Hobgoblins?" she demanded and used her voice in alarm. "There are hobgoblins in these ruins?"

"What do you know about hobgoblins?"

"I asked first."

"Well, of course there are hobgoblins in these ruins," the dragonette snarled. *"Now, it's your turn. What do you know about them?"*

"Me? Nothing, so you'd better start talking," Kaylin replied sharply as she dodged some of the rock that had crumbled.

They reached the end of where the walls could take them and she surveyed the ground below and beyond the closest walls carefully.

"Tell me there won't be more monsters closer to the entrance," she muttered, hung from the side of the wall, and dropped to the street below.

"More? Are you kidding?" Wivre glided down to land on her shoulder. *"Of course there will be more—and worse ones, too. I think we were unlucky to come across the dire wolves—or lucky. It could have been worgs."*

"Worgs?" A spike of alarm made her tone a little shrill. *"Worgs?"*

"Yes, like dire wolves but smarter, faster, and bigger," the dragonette informed her.

"I thought they were the same thing. You know, extra-big wolves."

"Not on your life. For one thing, worgs can be used as mounts by orcs and hobgoblins."

Kaylin shook her head and trotted more quickly down one side street and then the next.

"And they're found here?" She didn't particularly want to know but it was the kind of thing to be sure about.

"I haven't seen any yet," the dragonette admitted. *"But I hadn't seen any dire wolves, either. They usually stick to the higher slopes of the mountain."*

"So, why are they down here then?" she asked.

"More food?" Wivre suggested. *"Or maybe they chased some adventurers down."*

"But what would adventurers be doing on the higher slopes?"

"The same thing we do," he replied and his tone suggested that she should have already known it. *"Looking for treasure. The elves built right up the mountain's sides. There were gardens and temples and some of their most important buildings were up there."*

"Like the library?" she asked hopefully, but he shook his head.

"I don't think so," he replied. *"I don't think I climbed that high before I found a way out."*

"But you can't be sure."

"True," Wivre admitted. *"I cannot be sure. It's hard to work out what level you're on when nothing but earth and stone surrounds you."*

Kaylin could only imagine it was but she found another section of wall to climb and scrambled up it. The sun was much lower and the shadows were lengthening. She scanned ahead, caught sight of the Rest's walls, and hurried forward.

Behind them, a howl echoed through the buildings, distant but not far enough away for comfort.

The next few days were filled with more of the same—more ruins and yet more monsters. Each time they tried a different route, they'd only cover a limited distance before they came across something that told them it was time to turn back.

Once, it was a large pile of dung, freshly dropped and still steaming.

"Rock monitor," Wivre informed her succinctly. *"We should go now."*

"Which way?" she replied, pleased that using her mental "voice" had almost become more like second nature.

"The only way we know it hasn't been," the dragonette had replied, *"Back the way we came. It climbs and hunts by scent and is two horses long."*

"Well, crap."

"No," he corrected. *"Dung."*

Neither of them had relaxed until they'd reached the inn and even then, they hadn't settled until Kaylin had snuck onto the walls to study their back trail and seen no sign of the big creature.

"This will get us killed," she stated morosely and Wivre rested his head on her knee.

The decider came when they traveled yet another potential path and discovered a large fire pit. It was still warm, but the area surrounding it was empty of life.

Kaylin had taken to the walls immediately and her companion took to the air to see if they'd stumbled past any sentries or guards.

They had both remained tense and watchful, and she had to coax him down.

"Do you know what made it?" she asked and gestured to the fire. *"Was it adventurers?"*

The dragonette cocked his head and tilted it from side to side as he inspected the ground below.

Only when he was sure there was nowhere something could hide did he descend to inspect the ruin more carefully. She followed him along the walls and did her best to keep watch on what was going on inside the ruin's confines as well as on the other side of its walls.

Wivre inspected the fire and sniffed the ground like a dog on a scent—although she would never tell him of the resemblance. She wanted to keep her fingers intact. Instead, she curbed her impatience while he roved the area until he came to a distant corner and scraped the vines aside.

"Bones!" He sounded horrified and sent her the image of a pile of bones tucked into the natural alcove. Long scrapes marked their surfaces as though they'd been gnawed on, the strands of remaining flesh still red.

The dragonette bounded away from the grisly find, made a hasty circuit of the rest of the ruin, and stopped when he uncovered the entrance to a stairwell. He didn't go inside. It appeared that standing at the top of the stairs and sticking his snout in was enough.

"Trolls!" This time, he sounded terrified.

He lifted into the air and flew straight at her to catch hold of her backpack and pull her forward and away from the stairwell entrance.

"We need to go. We need to go right now, and we need to take the long way. And we need to stay on the walls and—"

Kaylin caught him, pulled him against her chest, and held him until he quieted. When he stopped squirming, she caught his gaze and gave him a solemn nod, then pointed the route out.

"Yes," he agreed and she released him carefully.

The retreat took the rest of the morning and most of the afternoon, but they were through the Rest's gates by dusk.

It took only a few minutes to cross the courtyard and nod to a few she recognized. She even spoke to a mercenary named Lop who seemed to come and go like her.

"We need to find more salvage," Kaylin noted later when they were up in their room. *"We're starting to run short."*

And by starting to run short, she meant they still had a month's rent set to one side but no more.

"I agree," Wivre told her. *"My bed needs more lining."*

The sentiment made her smile and she scratched his neck ridge and elicited a contented sigh.

"We'll also need help getting into the mountain," she said and the dragonette stiffened.

"You don't mean we'll hire someone, do you?" he asked.

"No, of course not. Do I look rich to you?"

The dragonette snickered. *"No, but I was beginning to think you might think you were."*

She laughed. *"What I'm thinking of doing is to see if we can join a mercenary outfit or maybe an adventuring group heading into the mountain and get in that way. They'll have an idea of where they'll be going and the manpower to reach the entrance, and we can keep an eye out for any of the tunnels you think might lead to the vault. How about that?"*

"It sounds like a plan to me," the little dragon admitted. *"I think there have been some new arrivals in the last week or so."*

"Are you sure?" She hadn't noticed as she'd been too tired and sore to pay much attention to anything more than her food, although the Rest had seemed busier of late.

"Yes, fairly sure," Wivre told her. *"Tomorrow, we can be back early enough to find out."*

Salvage proved a little difficult the next day, not because they were followed but because Wivre was right. There had been some new arrivals at the Rest and they reported that the snow had gone from around Waypoint, which meant spring had come and the road was clear.

Besides learning about the weather on the Rim, Kaylin listened to discover what their plans were. It was an education to discover that not everyone who came to the Doom headed straight into the mountain.

Some were there to hunt for monster parts to fill orders for alchemy and spell components. Others were after specific plants. Still more planned to scour the ruins for any kind of text or inscription that would reveal more about what had been located where in the Old City.

Maps could be big business.

Something had happened to spur more interest in the city's history and the lore it might contain. The bar was busy when Kaylin and Wivre descended for breakfast, and they did their best to remain inconspicuous as they collected their meal and some lunch for later. She made sure to fill her water bottle from the well before they departed via the stable gate.

From the talk around the tables, some of the groups were thinking of going into the mountain after they'd filled their commissions but at breakfast, very few were thinking of going sooner. She hoped they'd have more luck at the evening meal.

The reason for the breakfast-hour rush became apparent when she and Wivre approached their usual area. Several rabbits bolted out of one of the houses they'd already searched and the sound of crashing and disgruntled commentary floated after them.

"...been here already. All the best stuff's gone."

"What d'you think we'll get for this?"

"Three-tenths of sweet stuff all..."

Kaylin gave Wivre a wide-eyed look and decided the group didn't need any clues to search the heights. She slipped past the turn into the street and circled, moving farther than she'd gone before.

What she hoped was that this was the fastest of the newly arrived groups but what she discovered was that they were merely the most impatient. It took her several more promising leads at the base of the mountain to find a seemingly unoccupied street. Even so, she clambered up the walls of the most intact ruin and surveyed the area around them carefully.

This time, their luck held. She caught sight of another mercenary band chasing several larger somethings away in a district some distance from the mountain's foot but no one nearby.

Rather than descend, she crossed the rooftops and worked through semi-intact upper floors where she could to avoid being silhouetted against the skyline.

The last thing she wanted was to be seen working on her own. She'd been at the Rest long enough to know that not all its patrons were honorable or above plucking lone adventurers for their finds.

There were no wardens in Tulon's City.

She doubted there was even a code of honor between companies. There were days when more went out than came back—and, she suspected, not because of foes they found in the mountain or ruins.

Some nights, Clay had more guards on watch in the taproom too.

Kaylin never asked him about it and he never offered to share. She took her cues from him and retired early whenever he seemed particularly on edge—not that leaving early was that much of a change to her routine.

When it came time to descend, she took one more cautious look around.

The newly arrived mercenaries weren't her only concern. She hadn't forgotten that the derelict buildings housed other sentients.

She caught the whiff of a campfire and studied the ruins in search of its source. Starting with those closest, she widened her scrutiny gradually until she located a faint gray haze that lingered over a courtyard surrounded by the tumbled remains of a large villa.

It was far enough from the road leading up the mountain to not pose a threat, especially if it was goblins. If it was orcs, on the other hand, the speed at which they could travel made the distance negligible.

"Wivre," she whispered and indicated the smoke.

He lowered his chin in acknowledgment and took flight, careful to remain low and close to the tops of the ruins to not draw attention from any roving parties—either monster or adventurer.

"Orcs," he confirmed a few moments later and her heart sank.

It looked like a day of slim pickings after all.

"All sleeping," the little dragon added helpfully. *"We should be able to go up two streets and be back before dusk."*

"Back to the inn?" Kaylin asked softly.

"All the way back," he confirmed. *"If we are quick and very, very quiet."*

The two weren't necessarily incompatible, and Kaylin descended swiftly from the walls to the more open ground of the street.

"Can you watch for anyone coming close enough to see us?" she asked and Wivre lifted from her shoulder.

She began to run. By sticking to the middle of the street, she risked being seen more easily but she was also able to move with speed. She'd reached the next level up before Wivre swooped over her head and she dropped quickly into the shelter of a wall.

"Mercs," the dragon said.

"Did they see me?"

"No. You paid attention to my warning in time," he reassured her.

"Are they headed this way?" she asked anxiously.

"I do not think so but they are on the hunt. I'm not sure if we can reach the street above."

Kaylin sighed unhappily but took heed. Instead of moving out into the street to continue her journey up, she turned into the closest villa and hoped it had been overlooked by earlier expeditions.

She and Wivre headed to the upper floors first and followed their usual routine of searching every building from the top down. They found more books but most were too eaten by time and nesting insects to be legible. A scroll case proved intact, and she stowed it in her pack in the hope that there was something inside worth reading.

A candle holder from the nightstand went into the pack, but the worn and slightly chewed candle stub did not. The bedding smelt damp and looked half-rotten, but she flipped it back anyway and checked under the pillows in case someone had left valuables there for safekeeping.

"There's metal here," Wivre informed her and his nostrils twitched. He ran over the top of the mattress, then under it. *"Here!"* he exclaimed and scrabbled at the underside of the bed.

Kaylin frowned but took hold of the edge of the mattress.

It fell apart as she lifted and pushed it away and she had to shove the remains of the stuffing to one side to see what he had found—a slender pouch containing several small gems, a few coins, and a ring.

"Yesss. Fingers crossed," she told him and stowed it in her pack.

An ornate ink bottle, ink well, and the decorative remains of a quill holder followed, as did the base of another lamp. She searched the desk twice in the hope of finding another seal but to no avail.

"They must have taken it with them," she muttered as Wivre alighted on the nearby window sill.

"We have to go soon," he informed her. *"It's past lunch."*

The little dragon's reminder made her realize how far behind them breakfast was and her stomach growled.

"I agree," he replied. *"It is well past the bell for bacon."*

"The bell for bacon?" she asked and wondered where the dragonette had learned to reference time.

"Yes." Wivre looked puzzled. *"You know, just as there is a bell for breakfast, one for lunch, and another for dinner there has to be one for bacon."*

She frowned in thought. *"You made that up."*

"Yes, and your point is?" the dragonette challenged.

He sounded so much like her that she chuckled. "Fine. It's bacon time for you and sandwich time for me."

"And then it will be time to head home," the dragon repeated.

Kaylin gave him a worried frown. *"What makes you say that?"*

"Because orcs don't wait for dusk and it's not good to have to run on a full belly. Besides"—he nudged the pack—*"it would be a shame to have to drop this so you could run faster. I like that big silver bowl."*

"Are you sure it's silver?"

They'd found the bowl stuffed at the back of a pantry, its insides crusted with the dark and dried remains of…well, it might have been fruit a very long time before.

"And the cups?" she asked.

They'd found four with handles that looked like they'd been intended to hang on the edges of a crystal bowl, which was probably what the glass-like shards surrounding them had been.

"Silver plating," the dragon replied, *"with a whiff of pewter beneath, although the patterns will make Clay happy."*

"I hope so," she muttered. "We didn't find much else."

She climbed to a point in the ruin where she could look over the city and studied the ruins below as she ate.

"You're right," she told Wivre when the little dragon curled beside her. *"It's time to head back."*

She studied the city a little longer, then added, *"Do you think we can try a different route back?"*

It took the little dragon a moment to catch what she'd seen and when he did, he shook his head.

"And I thought you *were clueless."*

"Clueless, yes," she agreed acerbically, focused on a small group of mercenaries that worked through the ruins, *"but not outright reckless."*

Quickly, she bundled her sandwich into her pack and scooped up the last of Wivre's bacon.

"We'll eat in our room," she promised, scrambled back from her perch, and descended rapidly into the house below. *"Do you think this street will take us into that first section we explored?"*

"The first one above the ruins?" Wivre asked.

"That one," she agreed.

"I'll scout ahead," he told her. *"You try to keep up—and don't worry about being seen. I think the mercenaries have everyone's attention and unless we run through another camp, we should get past most of those not human without being seen."*

"Aim for the stable door," she instructed. *"Everyone else will head to the front gate but I think we'll make it if we cut around the back."*

The dragonette didn't reply but launched himself into the air and flew ahead of her down the street. She watched as he zigzagged over the ruins on either side to check them for any monsters that might be waiting in ambush. Finally, he swung wide and back to scout the ground behind her.

She didn't let that distract her but continued along the road and counted the intersections from the lower levels until she reached the one that would take her over the rockslide and into more familiar territory.

By then, Wivre had rejoined her. He flew low overhead and repeated his observations of the road ahead and the ruins on either side. She followed and slipped and slid over the boulders that blocked the road, then bolted between the more intact ruins on either side.

Ever cautious, she wondered where the mercenaries from the morning had gotten to when she heard a shout from behind her.

"Hey! Hey, you!"

Kaylin gave them a wave but didn't stop. She recognized the voice from earlier. Not wanting to be shot either by accident or on purpose, she ducked into a cluster of ruins she knew would let her travel above ground level for a stretch. If they didn't think to look up, it would seem like she'd disappeared.

She didn't wait to test her theory but darted into the upper levels, ran along walls she knew were stable, and ducked so she wouldn't be seen.

Some sections were open to the sky and she traversed those as quickly as possible to avoid drawing too much attention.

When her high path came to an end, she dropped to ground level and jogged quickly toward the Rest. Only when she was in the shadow of its walls did she start to relax and passed the half-constructed building and walls she'd used on her first illicit exit from the inn's sanctuary.

She still hadn't asked Clay what it was.

The afternoon was softening into dusk by the time she reached the stable gate, and her urgent knock was answered quickly.

"I'm not sure why you don't use the front gate like everyone else," the guard remarked when she thanked him and he turned to drop the locking bar in place.

"That's why I don't use it," she told him shortly. "There's too much attention."

"Ah." He understood that and returned to his post above the gate without asking any more questions.

Kaylin took her pack and stowed it in her room before she hurried to the baths with her clothes from the day before and scrubbed them and Wivre clean.

"That's a disgusting habit," the little dragon complained when she finished scrubbing most of the dirt out of them.

"Yes, but it's cheaper than having them washed by Chloe."

"How much cheaper?" he asked and a calculating gleam slid into his eye.

"A copper per item," she told him. *"Two copper if I want them washed separately to anyone else's."*

The dragon considered two coppers and how much bacon that would buy, then watched her dress in the day's outfit. *"You'll need more,"* he told her. *"Those won't last much longer."*

She sighed. *"I know. I only...clothes are expensive out here."*

"You should have taken them from that orc you killed," Wivre suggested, a sly twinkle in his eye.

"Ew!"

The dragon's amusement rippled through her mind and she glared at him.

"You're not funny."

A pounding at the door stifled her amusement and she hurried to get dressed.

"Are you spending the night in there?"

"I'm almost done!" she called and muttered, "Impatient prick," under her breath.

"What did you say?" The voice sounded almost belligerent.

"Are you deaf?" she yelled in reply. "Keep your hair on or I'll pay for an extra hour."

"You—" The spluttered response cut off at the sound of another arrival.

"You keep bothering her and you might want to think twice about getting in the tub," a woman suggested in a hard voice.

"She wouldn't."

"Oh, I don't know if she would, but I would."

A rough sigh followed, then a soft thump as though whoever was waiting leaned against the opposite wall. Although she didn't like to be rushed, she hurried anyway and took her freshly washed clothes with her.

The merc who waited outside gave her a baleful glare, pushed off the wall as soon as she appeared, and brushed past her as she left. Kaylin bit her lip to stop herself from saying anything, glad she'd remembered to drop one hand over her purse as they'd passed.

She was sure she'd felt the light touch of his fingers on hers as he'd slid past her. A glance over her shoulder confirmed it when she caught him watching her, a wry smile twisting his lips. Kaylin resisted the urge to stick her tongue out.

He was good.

It wouldn't do to antagonize someone she might need later and she didn't want to put money on not needing him. She hurried to her room and hung her freshly laundered clothes on hooks from her wardrobe and draped them around the room.

Come summer, she would need new and cooler clothing. She tried to work out how long she had before she had to worry. It was, as best as she could work out, early spring and the days were noticeably warmer than when she'd first arrived.

She spread the bedroll out and emptied the backpack onto its water-proof cover.

"Ugh." Once she'd gathered the cleaning materials, she dropped beside the meager pile of salvage and hoped that what they'd found would be enough to cover the next month.

Clay might like her—as much as he liked anyone—but business was business. She needed to cover her expenses and she had to get into the mountain to begin her search.

It crossed her mind that getting into the mountain would also bring her more salvage and make it easier to pay her way, and that put the task even higher on her priority list.

"Food." Wivre's voice penetrated her thoughts, his hunger plain.

Reluctantly, she pulled the bacon and her sandwich out.

"Real food, not leftovers," the dragonette persisted and turned partly away. *"The dinner bell has rung."*

"I didn't hear it," she retorted as the bell chimed a distinctive chorus of notes.

"I'm prescient," he replied smugly.

"You're a smartass," she replied and he smirked.

"The sun is almost gone," he explained. *"We always eat when the sun is almost gone."*

Kaylin had to give him that. They did always eat at this time of day and the journey back had taken longer than she would have liked, thanks to her insisting that they take the stable gate.

"I wonder if the others made it back," she said and Wivre flew up to settle on her shoulder.

"If they did not, they had more experience in the field than you and no excuse to delay," he stated unsympathetically.

She had nothing to say to that. It seemed cold but the dragon had a point.

"Besides," he added, *"you can see for yourself when we go downstairs to eat."*

That last was said with enough emphasis that she laughed.

"Fine," she agreed. *"Let's go eat."*

The taproom was busy when they arrived but she was relieved to notice the colors of the mercenaries she'd seen stumble into the orc encampment. They seemed a little disheveled and were smeared with blood and dirt but at least she knew they'd survived.

With Wivre riding her shoulder, his tail wound around her upper arm, she headed to the bar.

"The usual?" Clay asked when she caught his eye.

Kaylin nodded and took the dark ale he poured for her to a table at the edge of the room. The places closest to the fire had been taken and she didn't blame them. It was cold out, even without snow.

While she waited for her meal to arrive, she listened to the conversations that ebbed and flowed around her. Wivre stayed on her shoulder and looked for all the world like a drakeling discomforted by the noise.

She slid her gaze around the room and noticed several new faces—hard faces of men and women seasoned by adventure and the road. Some met her gaze, assessed her, and returned to their vigilant watch of their surroundings.

At first, she wondered what they had to be nervous about. They were safe behind the Rest's walls and not likely to be attacked, so why were they still watchful?

Why are you still watchful? she chided herself and decided the mercs around her were no different.

Even in safety, the unexpected could still happen.

She leaned back in her seat to watch and listen.

"We have to have out in a few days," one woman said, her elbows on her table and a mug of something hot with a spicy aroma in her hands.

Kaylin's nostrils twitched at the sweet, tart scent and she made a note to ask Clay what it was. It smelt delicious.

"Mulled wine," Wivre stated as though reading her mind. *"Now why didn't I think of that?"*

"Because you've never had it?" she suggested.

"That doesn't mean I don't know what it is," the little dragon told her. *"It smells good."*

"How do you know what it is?" she asked in mock disbelief.

"I heard her order more," he informed her succinctly.

"You're incorrigible," she whispered as their meal arrived.

Wivre surveyed the taproom, then hopped off her shoulder and onto the table beside his bowl.

Another conversation drifted to her ears.

"The demand for the fur is high right now. If we can get them back to the city by the end of the month, they'll fetch a good price," a female merc stated.

"We've got to find them first," another replied.

"They're still down at this time of year. The snow won't have cleared from higher up."

The second mercenary didn't sound convinced. "Well, good luck with it."

"Are you going in?" the fur hunter asked.

"To the Mountain?"

"Anywhere else you can think of?"

The second voice laughed. "No...and no. Like you, we're on a hunting expedition."

She snorted. "Do I need to think of you as a rival?"

He laughed. "No. We're going after books, anything we think might be salvageable if the text was transcribed and then translated. Things with diagrams will fetch a higher price."

"And why are you telling me this?"

"I thought we could come to an agreement. You know, I hand you any pelts we find. You hand me the equivalent value in books."

"Or scrolls?" The hunter's voice sharpened with interest.

"Provided most of it's intact."

"How will we work the value out?"

"Uh..." It seemed the book scavenger hadn't thought that far.

The woman chuckled. "Let's make it one for one, then. I'll give you whatever scrolls we stumble across in our hunt for whatever complete carcass you bring back."

"You know that's—" he began but she cut him off.

"More than fair," she told him, "given that you don't know what monsters you'll encounter and I don't know what books I'll find. We both know some things fetch more than others depending on how the market's running at the time. Agreed values shift."

It took only a moment before the man answered, "Done."

Kaylin caught the word "mountain" and shifted focus.

"We don't go into the mountain at this time of year. It's safer and more profitable to take what comes to the valley and whatever else we find when we're chasin' it," a grizzled dwarf in chain mail stated.

"Fair call," a human dressed in hunting leathers replied. "Are you going for a particular quarter?"

That question earned him a wry smile. "We've a fair idea," the dwarf replied, "but we're not sayin'."

The man returned the smile.

"And we don't want company," the dwarf added, a hint of warning in his voice.

The human spread his hands. "I'm not looking to be companionable—"

"That's what I'm afraid of," the short, stocky merc muttered and turned pointedly away.

Kaylin frowned. There were other conversations but they all seemed to be along the same lines. No one was going into the mountain. They all seemed to be planning a prolonged hunt through the ruins.

Her spirits fell. Not only did that mean she had no way to continue her search for the vault—unless she was prepared to face the mountain depths alone—but the mercenaries would scour the closer ruins clean, meaning she'd have to start thinking about overnighting when she went foraging.

Unless they make the assumption that all the areas nearby are stripped clean and take themselves farther afield.

She listened to more conversations as she ate and once she'd finished, wandered casually around the room in the hope that she'd find someone amidst the groups doing something different. When she found what she was looking for, she'd almost given up hope.

"It should be an easy trip in," a man stated in a hard voice. "Hunters have worked out that the beasts hang around the entrance, so they'll keep those off our backs. We'll only have to deal with what we find once we get inside."

"Or what finds you." A woman chuckled.

"That too," the man agreed, "but we're prepared for that."

He stopped, and Kaylin became aware of two sets of eyes raised to study her. She'd been so interested in the conversation that she'd leaned closer to the table and stared at them.

"What d'you want, girl?"

She started and was about to stammer out that there was nothing she was interested in when she decided to come clean.

"I heard you're going into the mountain," she began,and he rolled his eyes.

"Sorry, kid, we're not recruiting."

"But—"

The man's brows pulled into a fierce frown and he moved his hand to his dagger hilt.

"That's final, girl. Now move along. No one likes an eavesdropper."

Her face heated and she moved away. Wivre's tail twitched against her spine and she hoped the little dragon wouldn't do something reckless. She made another slow turn through the taproom but without any luck. No one else, it seemed, was going into the mountain.

"We'll try again tomorrow," she told the dragonette as she wandered disconsolately upstairs.

"To find a way to get ourselves into the mountain? Without a mercenary group?" he asked in disbelief.

Kaylin shook her head. *"To see if someone can be convinced to take us."*

"Good luck with that," he retorted with a snort.

"Well, what if we talked to that old mage?" she asked. *"The one from the wall."*

"I didn't see him around," he reported, *"or smell that stench he likes to breathe."*

"That doesn't mean he's not around," she argued.

"It does, you know." The dragonette flicked his tail in irritation.

She ignored him and settled to clean the day's haul. *"We'll see Clay in the morning,"* she promised as she packed it away.

When she turned to the bed, her gaze fell on the pile of books and scrolls on her desk. She recalled the conversations she'd overheard downstairs, scooped them up, and locked them in her trunk before she made sure both sigils were activated. There might be a mage who could deactivate them, but she hoped that most mercs couldn't—even if they could pick the lock to her room—which she hoped they wouldn't.

It made her wonder if there were some way she could add extra defenses to the sigil. Could she tie a piece of lightning to it? Or fire? Either one would help her identify any would-be thief.

Leaving that as a question to answer on another day, she added another log to the fire and went to bed.

Once she'd moved their trade loot to the backpack, Kaylin made sure she hadn't missed any books the night before she locked her chest and reactivated the sigils. She took a moment to check her room to confirm that she'd left nothing out.

Granted, most of the mercenaries should head out into the ruins for at least the day, but she didn't want to take the chance. When she was sure everything was secure, she locked her door behind her and headed downstairs.

"What do you think our chances are of finding someone who'll let us travel with them into the city?" she asked Wivre.

"We could always offer to pay them," the little dragon suggested but sounded reluctant.

"Pffft. Where do you think we'd get enough to do that?" she asked.

"Well, in that case, I'd say our chances were very—"

The door to the inn was thrust open as they reached the bottom of the stairs and Kaylin stopped dead and moved instinctively to one side of the stairwell to study the woman who strode into the taproom.

She was whip-thin, her body cord-wire strong, and her face was lean and eyes hard. Dark chain mail hung over black leather armor and hide trousers and warrior's boots encased her calves. A longsword hung from one hip and a short-hafted ax dangled from the other.

They were complemented by the short bow and quiver barely visible above her shoulders.

As the girl studied her, the woman's gaze swept over the room and she noted Kaylin with a slight turn of her head. She wove between the tables and reached the bar as Clay emerged hurriedly from the kitchen, wiping his hands on a dishtowel.

His gaze drifted over Kaylin as he came in and a faint frown creased his forehead, but he didn't give any indication that she should leave.

"Lonne!" he cried and slung the dishtowel over his shoulder. "I take it your journey was successful?"

The woman favored him with a sharp grin and hefted the bulging sack she carried in one hand.

"It was," she agreed and nodded toward the room in which he carried out his trades. "Shall we?"

Her gaze flicked over Kaylin and although she didn't say anything, it was clear she wanted to continue their conversation somewhere private. Clay followed her gaze and noticed the bag the girl carried in one hand.

"This afternoon," he told her shortly to indicate that he wouldn't have time to see her.

She nodded and returned to her room. When she and Wivre returned, empty-handed save for the dragonette's satchel and the coins she slipped into a pocket, Lonne and Clay were nowhere to be seen—and neither was the older mage from the walls, whom she'd hoped to see.

That didn't mean the taproom was empty, however. A dozen men and women occupied the tables around the fire. They didn't say much and simply sat, tired and quiet. Some watched the flames while others gazed idly at their surroundings. Occasionally, their stares strayed to the kitchen door. When she entered, their attention flicked to her and away like she was of no consequence.

The only one who did more than note her presence was an older warrior who'd positioned himself in a corner from which he could see most of the room and its exits and entries. He looked idly in her direction but paused for a moment to assess her.

His gaze raked her from head to toe and noted the dragonette on her shoulder, the dagger at her belt, and the satchel hung slantwise across her chest. He didn't look very impressed by what he saw but he watched her cross the room to the kitchen and place her order with the cook.

"Same?" the woman asked and gestured at Wivre when she nodded. "And for him?"

"Please," she confirmed and her voice rasped nervously.

"Chloe will bring it."

"Thanks, Hanne."

"Get out of my kitchen."

The message was delivered without venom and she smiled as she stepped into the taproom again, then decided to risk Hanne's wrath a little more.

"That mage with the pipe..." she began and drew a sharp glance.

"Gevitter?"

"I don't know his name but he used lightning to save me the day I arrived," Kaylin explained.

"Gevitter," Hanne said matter of factly. "What about him?"

"Is he... Is he around?" she asked but the cook shook her head briskly.

"He headed out yesterday," the woman informed her. "Said he had 'mage business' to attend to and not to expect him back until he returned." She shrugged. "As long as his room's paid up, Clay will hold it." Her gaze sharpened. "Why?"

She took a step back. "Just wondering," she answered and Hanne harrumphed impatiently and returned to her cooking.

Kaylin risked a glance at the older mercenary but he'd lost interest in her and was focused on the two men who had seated themselves opposite him.

His dark eyes were intense as he tapped the table but his soft words didn't carry to where she stood. He flicked a single glance at her but it was no more than to note that she'd left the kitchen. Indifferent to her presence, he turned his attention quickly to his companions and tapped the tabletop again as though to emphasize a point.

They both nodded and leaned toward him, and one spoke quietly in response.

Unfortunately, she couldn't catch what he said either.

She wondered if the group intended to go into the mountains and decided it couldn't hurt to ask. After all, they could only say no. If she was lucky, maybe she'd be able to convince them to take her on as a junior mage or something.

The door to Clay's office opened and Lonne stepped out.

"A pleasure doing business with you," she stated cheerfully as the proprietor followed, a sour look on his face.

"You drive a hard bargain," he grumbled and the woman smiled.

She stepped into the tavern and around the bar and caught the eye of the older mercenary. He rapped the table in front of him and the other two men rose from their seats to leave the table clear for her arrival.

Kaylin stared unabashedly for a moment before she lowered her gaze quickly. Fortunately, none of the mercenaries seemed to notice. She scanned the group for a mage and her heart sank when she didn't see one.

How could she persuade them to take her on as a junior mage if they didn't have a senior mage to start with?

She contented herself with watching Lonne under the guise of paying Wivre some attention and noticed the woman's smile fade as she reached the end of the bar.

"And you're sure you'll have the supplies in the next two days?" Lonne asked as she looked over her shoulder.

Clay nodded. "Or three. It depends on what the weather's been like on the heights."

The heights. Kaylin had heard the term used to refer to the upper edge of the valley where the hills rose to meet the cliffs. The mercenaries who came from Waypoint were often asked if they'd grown tired of "life on the heights" or sometimes, "the high life." They were always asked what the news was from "on high."

They seemed to think they were making a joke and Clay had laughed when he'd explained what they'd meant. She had simply shaken her head, taken her ale, and returned to her table.

Lonne's snort drew her attention to the mercenary leader's exchange with Clay.

"And if it's late?" she demanded.

The innkeeper regarded her speculatively. "That's up to you," he stated. "You can take what I've got to hand or you can delay."

The woman scowled. "It's not the kind of mission that should wait," she replied.

"And yet you're not leaving until the end of the week." He cocked his head. "So it can't be that important."

She stilled and lowered her hand to the ax as she turned slightly to face him.

"It's important enough that we're taking time to prepare," she told him sharply, "and I'll thank you to not talk about it."

Clay's lips curled into the smile he used when he was both angry and amused and Kaylin wondered why. The mercenary leader seemed no better and no worse than any other who arrived, but he treated her as though what she said or thought was important enough to pay attention to.

Chloe bustled in from the kitchen, balancing a tray of bread rolls and another tray of bacon. She set these on the center table and hurried away to return with a stack of plates and cutlery. On her third trip, she brought two jars of pickles and two spoons.

"Ale's coming," she told the group tartly and cast a glance at Clay.

He caught her eye and nodded. With a glance at the group, he asked, "Dark or light?"

Kaylin listened to the cacophony of replies and wondered how he could tell who wanted what as she knew he never got an order wrong.

"I'll take a wine," Lonne told him. "You know the label."

Again, a slight twist of his lips indicated that the innkeeper wasn't happy.

"How could I forget?"

The woman chuckled and continued to the table where the older warrior sat. She slid onto the bench seat opposite him and rapped on the table and the two leaned toward each other. One of the other mercenaries brought two plates containing bread rolls loaded with bacon and placed them at the edge of the table.

The older mercenary nodded in thanks but the woman didn't even look up. She continued to speak softly and tapped the table with her forefinger to gain the older merc's attention. It seemed the now somewhat irritating action was a habit with the group. He turned his scarred face toward Lonne and they resumed their conversation.

Before Kaylin could ask Wivre to listen in, Chloe came to a halt beside their table.

"And here's yours," the girl told them. "Eat up and stop staring. If you want to speak to them, go over and speak to them but don't stare. Someone's likely to take offense."

She nodded and her cheeks reddened at being noticed—again. Had being mostly alone for the winter caused such a decline in her skills?

Wivre blew a raspberry in her head and she pretended she hadn't heard.

The little dragon hopped onto the table and settled in front of his bacon.

"Breakfast first," he informed her. *"Business second."*

"Business?" she asked softly.

"Sure. They're going under the mountain and you want them to take us with them."

"Do you think they need an apprentice?" She made sure to keep her question firmly in their heads.

"I think you can convince them."

Kaylin wished she shared his confidence but she didn't argue. There was no point in either voicing her doubts or indulging in false bravado. Wivre was right. With no sign of the mage she'd seen from the wall, she would ask if she could join their company—as soon as she worked out what she should say.

Most of the company had left by the time she had finished her breakfast and had enough of an idea of how she would introduce herself. By the time she'd settled on what to say and gathered the courage to approach them, only Lonne and the scar-faced warrior remained.

They rose at the same time she did.

Kaylin's heart jerked to her mouth and she almost ran into a table as she hurried to intercept them. Her movement drew their attention and they both turned toward her.

"Are you looking for us?" The woman's voice was sharp and her face hard and unforgiving.

That impression didn't fade as the girl drew closer.

The male mercenary gave his leader an uncertain look and she placed a hand in the center of his chest and focused on Kaylin. He scowled and the expression did nothing to make him look any less grizzled or disgruntled.

As his leader took two steps forward to meet the girl, he took a step back and remained in place.

Kaylin couldn't help but notice the sword he carried at his hip. Its hilt gleamed and sparks of color glittered in the smooth black surface, and the cross-guard glinted with an outline of gold. It looked somehow out of place in its plain leather scabbard.

Wivre's claws tightened on her shoulder, and she returned her attention to the woman.

"Well, girl?" Lonne demanded.

"I heard you was recruitin'," she told her.

She'd meant to say it in the more upper-class tones she'd heard at the Academy but nerves and the demand in the mercenary's voice made her revert to those of her youth.

The woman came to a halt before her and scrutinized her intently. "We don't need any more thieves."

"I'm not a thief." This time, she used her correct accent and Lonne stilled.

Her scrutiny deepened to note the dagger, the satchel, and the drakeling on the girl's shoulder. Wivre stared in return and his tail twitched behind Kaylin's back as his claws tightened. She hoped he wasn't about to change his mind because she hadn't. As unpleasant as the woman seemed, she still intended to join her company.

"What are you, then?" Lonne snapped impatiently.

"Mage," she told her and received another doubtful assessment in reply.

"Not likely."

"Private tutelage and a year at the Academy to fill some gaps," she explained and put more confidence in her words than she felt. "I came here for what the Academy couldn't teach me."

"Couldn't?" the woman asked and a mocking smile curled her lips. "Or wouldn't?"

Kaylin fought to keep her expression neutral. She wanted to appear like she didn't care and could accept the mercenary's decision either way. Casually, she hitched one shoulder in a shrug.

"Take your pick," she answered and added, "So, are you recruiting?"

"I've got no place for a half-baked mage with no adventuring experience," the woman answered shortly.

She opened her mouth to protest but Lonne inclined her head and looked speculative.

"But the company mage is a little over-worked."

A soft snort greeted that and Lonne glanced over her shoulder.

"Now, Claude, you know it's true. Thibault's run off his feet between research and getting his components together. He could do with a hand."

"He could do with—"

"Claude!"

At the woman's sharp reprimand, he closed his mouth.

Wivre growled softly in Kaylin's head. *"I don't like her. We can—"*

Kaylin shook her head and Lonne's eyebrows rose.

"No?" she asked mockingly. "Too good to be an apprentice." She turned to leave. "It's your loss, girl. The Claws is one of the better outfits you'll find around here."

The girl darted a glance at Claude and noted that his face was carefully blank. The Claws were something, she decided, but their leader might be exaggerating when she said they were one of the better companies.

"Lonne..." he warned and didn't flinch when the woman glared at him. "Are you sure we want to pick up an untried stray for this?"

Lonne shrugged. "She said—"

"I'll take it!" Kaylin blurted before the mercenary could finish. Her voice slipped to street tones as she added. "Best offer I've had all week."

The mercenary reacted with a scornful laugh but she turned to give her another assessing stare.

"I'll bet it is," the woman remarked and gestured to the man behind her. "Claude's my second in command. If I'm not giving orders, he is. Beyond that, you'll answer to the company mage when he gets back."

"Thank you!" She couldn't keep the excitement and relief out of her voice and Lonne's lips twitched into a brief, mocking smile.

The expression was quickly followed by a brief flash of disgust and the woman turned away.

"Now, get out of my sight," she ordered and turned to Claude. "I'll have Clay tell you when we need you."

It wasn't exactly the welcome she had expected and she stared in surprise.

Lonne ignored her and stalked to the inn door.

"Claude!" she snapped and after he'd studied her disapprovingly and shaken his head, the older mercenary followed.

Neither of them looked back.

"Well, he doesn't seem to like me," Kaylin muttered and wondered what they'd do if she insisted on tagging along.

"Don't be so quick to judge," Wivre told her. *"It might not be you he's unhappy with."*

"Pfft," she responded, then sighed. *"Well, we're in. What should we do in the meantime?"*

"Do?" he asked. *"You might not have noticed, but we're low on funds and our stock in treasure isn't exactly overflowing. We are going out to salvage."*

"And not try to meet our new teammates?"

"Not until their leader introduces us," the dragonette replied.

"And when do you think that might be?"

"Just before we leave. I'm still not sure why she hired you."

"Thanks," Kaylin grumbled.

"No. I mean, she didn't seem to like you, her company already has a mage, her second in command wasn't happy about something, and she didn't ask for proof of anything you said. For all she knows, you could be claiming to be something you're not. She didn't even ask you to show her a spell, for the hoard's sake!"

Now that she thought about it, Kaylin realized the little dragon was right. Lonne hadn't asked her for proof. The woman had merely studied her thoroughly, disliked what she'd seen, and hired her.

She frowned.

"That *does* seem weird," she admitted, then shrugged. "Maybe she had another reason?"

"I'm sure she did," he agreed, *"and I don't think we'll like it."*

It would take a few days to find out if Wivre had been right or not. At a loss as to what to do regarding the mercenaries, she focused on finding enough salvage to secure her room while she was gone.

Despite her fears, most of the mercenary companies had moved farther afield and the buildings closest to the inn were devoid of armored figures stirring up the local monster population. When she climbed one of her high points to look for them, she saw one company in the distance but they moved purposefully in a squad.

It looked like they were trying to gain some distance before they began their search.

"Suits me fine," she muttered, still disgruntled by the conversation she'd had that morning. They had enough to keep them occupied and if they scavenged alone, they wouldn't run the risk of having to share it.

She was even more disgruntled by events that night.

Contrary to her expectations, Lonne called to her when she and Wivre descended to the taproom for their evening meal.

"Girl!" Wivre dug his claws into her armor at the peremptory tone.

The woman smiled when she looked at her, and Kaylin managed

to return the expression, albeit with some misgivings. If her worry showed on her face, the mercenary leader didn't seem to notice. Her smile turned to welcome and she gestured for the girl to join them.

"This is Kaylin, Thibault's new apprentice." She placed a hand on the newcomer's arm and ignored Wivre's lifted lip.

Someone snickered. "Does Thibault know?"

Lonne glared in the speaker's direction and the amusement faded.

"He will as soon as he gets back," Lonne snapped and her grip tightened.

Kaylin wondered why she seemed to be so tense but the woman continued.

"She'll come with us into the mountain and I'd like you to make sure she feels like she belongs," she told the group and turned the girl toward an empty seat. "You'll eat with us from now on."

The mercenary leader made that sound like an order—partly to her and partly to the mercenaries around her. She heard stifled laughter and the company's members returned to the conversations they'd been having when she'd entered.

It was like she'd vanished the minute Lonne took her hand from her arm. Wivre growled softly in his throat.

"I wonder what they know that we don't," the little dragon muttered.

It was a good question, and one whose answer gradually became clear over the next few days. Kaylin was grateful when she arrived at the taproom on the second night and Lonne didn't seem to notice. The mercenary leader continued her conversation with Claude as if the girl didn't exist.

As was her custom, she ordered her meal at the counter, ignored Clay's worried look, and slipped quietly into a distant corner. There, at least, she could be alone but not unwelcome—and that wasn't the case when she was with the company.

"I'm very sure this isn't how it's meant to be," she muttered quietly and Wivre rubbed his face gently along her cheek.

"It isn't," he told her, *"but it shouldn't take us long to work out what's going on."*

"Before or after we get ourselves killed? Maybe I should wait."

He shifted restlessly on her shoulder and she sighed.

"You're right. This deep into the season, there won't be anyone else."

She slumped in her chair, stared glumly at the table, and let her mind drift as she listened to the conversations around her. Over the last few weeks, she'd learned much that way.

Most people assumed she was daydreaming or tired from a day in the ruins. As long as she didn't look like she was listening, they tended to forget she was there. Once the ale started to flow, most of them did forget.

Kaylin had learned of monsters, of plans for ambush, of hunts, and even a little news of the magisters and the goings-on in Waypoint. She'd also learned how to retain most of it until she reached her room and could record it in her journals.

She now kept those locked safely in her trunk, hidden under a layer of board she'd fitted to look like the bottom of her chest. It wouldn't fool anyone who looked closely, but it would fool someone who merely attempted a fast raid.

Combined with the sigils and the more conventional lock, she assumed her belongings were safe from all but the most determined thief—or someone who knew exactly what they were looking for.

"We should see Clay in the morning," she told Wivre.

"Yes," the little dragon agreed. *"If I didn't know any better, I'd have said you were avoiding the man. He looks very much like he wants to talk to you."*

"Funny you should mention that," she replied and sighed. *"I think it's because I know what he'll say and I know it won't change my mind."*

"At least you can admit that," he said approvingly. *"It's half the battle."*

Kaylin wanted to ask him what it was half the battle for but Chloe arrived with their meals. She waited for the girl to say something but she merely set their plates on the table and bustled away to take another order.

"She looked worried, too," the dragonette observed and she frowned.

"It makes me want to know what they're aware of and I'm not." She took a bite of a roll.

"You could simply ask them," he suggested sarcastically.

"I'll do that tomorrow during the trade." She picked her spoon up.

Around her, the conversation had mostly discussed who was still out in the ruins and who had been expected back or was camping. It was enlightening to know that many of the companies hunting or searching for lost lore and treasure had planned to travel half a day's hard march away from the inn before they started their quests.

"We got some good pelts from 'em too." The female fur hunter she'd seen the other evening talked business with a man Kaylin didn't recognize. "I don't know what dire wolves were doing so far down but there's still snow on the upper slopes and the gods know they're hungry beasts."

"Always," the man agreed. "Did you find anything else?"

That last was asked with such wistful hopefulness that the girl almost laughed.

"Well, now," the woman began and lowered her voice so what she said next was inaudible.

Kaylin took another spoonful of Hanne's rich stew followed by a mouthful of bread and let her ears siphon the tumult of words and cutlery clatter around her. It didn't take her long before she heard something else of interest.

"The Claws are going into the mountain tomorrow," one gruff voice declared.

"Oh, yeah? What is it this time? A quick treasure run or a monster hunt?"

"I haven't managed to get any of them to say yet," the first man admitted, "and it's not for want of tryin'."

"I heard they took on someone new," the second speaker commented and Kaylin had to force herself to keep her spoon moving to the bowl.

It was hard to behave naturally when they were talking about her, but she didn't know if they could see her and she didn't want to give the game away. This was what she'd been waiting for—hopefully, she could learn the real reason why Lonne had hired her.

"Are you sure you want to hear this?" Wivre asked and she hushed him mentally.

The voices continued obliviously and she realized they were coming from a table close by—either directly behind her or a little to one side. She didn't dare to look to find exactly where.

The gruff man's snort was not encouraging, but she forced herself to keep eating as though she hadn't heard a thing. A pause followed during which she was sure they were looking at her but she forced herself to focus on her meal.

To hazard even a glance at them would be a dead giveaway and she wanted the information.

"What?" the second man asked. "What's so funny?"

Yes. What is so funny about their new hire?

"They say they've got Thibault a new apprentice."

"That lech!"

"Yeah, whatever, but he's not that lucky. Word is that Lonne's expecting to come up against some serious opposition and she wanted to have a little insurance just in case."

After a short silence, the second man spoke. "So..." he said and sounded uncertain. "Are you saying they found someone to be what—a ransom?"

Again, the gruff man snorted with amusement. "No," he corrected and a creak suggested that he twisted in his chair to make sure no one was listening. He lowered his voice. "Bait."

"Bait?"

He laughed as though his friend had made a joke. "You heard me," he said, his voice a little louder than was necessary. "I fancy a break from all the pork Clay's been serving. Maybe I'll take a trip to one of the streams around here to see if I can catch a mess of fish. I need bait."

Kaylin could imagine the look his friend was giving him. She felt almost as bewildered except she was very sure the mercenary was merely covering until people lost interest.

She felt the attention around her shift as the voices returned to their normal volume and previous conversations. The sound of someone clapping someone else on the shoulder or arm reached her and the second man spoke again, more softly this time.

"Bait?" he repeated. "And don't feed me another line about wanting to go fishing. We both know you prefer using a roped arrow for that."

His companion chuckled. "True." His voice sobered. "But don't go shouting another's business all over the inn. The fact is, Lonne thinks they'll come up against some serious opposition and wants someone they can put between themselves and whatever it is."

"She wouldn't!"

"She bloody well would and you know it. That woman's as cold as the Twin Peaks and twice as heartless."

"You're telling me. I can't imagine Crozier likes the idea much."

"He won't go against her—he doesn't dare–and you're right. She's found some hopeful who wants into the mountain and she'll feed them to it."

The other man sighed and she forced herself to relax outwardly and not reveal the tension within.

Lonne intended to use her as bait? To gain time if she needed to… to what? Escape?

Kaylin tightened her hold on the spoon and continued to eat. There was no way she wanted either of the two men to know she'd overheard their conversation, even if they showed no sign of knowing she was the dupe under discussion.

"We don't know it's true," Wivre reminded her and she pressed her lips together and scraped the bowl with her spoon.

"There's only one way to find out," she told him firmly, pushed her clean bowl aside, and slipped what was left of her roll into the satchel.

She pushed away from the table, stood, and looked around for the mercenary leader.

Lonne wasn't hard to find and she took one look at the girl's face and jerked her head toward the door. Kaylin followed the flick of the woman's eyes and realized that maybe she didn't want the entire inn privy to this conversation.

With a shrug, she changed direction and followed her out the door.

The merc didn't stop once they reached the front courtyard but turned and marched into the shadowier area along one side of the inn. Kaylin knew it well enough to know it was far enough from the gate that their conversation wouldn't carry, either to the guards manning the walls at the front or through the inn's front door.

They'd also be out of sight of any casual spectators.

She didn't wait for the woman to stop. "You plan to use me as *bait?*" she demanded as soon as they'd turned the corner.

The woman walked a few more feet before she turned and let her catch up before she replied.

"Do you have a problem with that?" she asked coolly.

Kaylin gaped and sputtered, and Lonne gave her a cold smile.

"After that bullshit line about spending a year in the Academy, it's about all you deserve."

"I am a mage," she retorted and cast three spells in quick succession, "Avark, barda, slura."

A small fireball streaked past the woman and struck the wall before it dissipated as a shower of colored lights that flared briefly around them and vanished in a fine watery mist. Lonne laughed and scorn twisted her face.

"Is that all you've got?" she demanded. She leaned closer. "Because if that's it, little girl, bait is all you're good for. You're expendable and if you don't like it, you can stay here outside the mountain."

Kaylin opened her mouth to say something but shut it again, and mockery curled the woman's lips. "That's what I thought you'd say." She stalked past her toward the front of the inn. When she reached the edge of the shadows, she looked back.

"See you at breakfast, *bait,* and you'd better be ready to march."

Wivre hissed as she turned her back on them. She'd barely taken a stride before the older mercenary stepped out of the shadows to join her. He said something in low tones and Lonne glared at him.

"She has her uses, Claude," the mercenary leader retorted, "as do you. And as long as either of you outlive them, you can stay."

Kaylin couldn't believe it. Well, she could, but she hadn't expected the woman's brazen unrepentance. She gave herself time to calm and stalked into the inn. The voices in the taproom lowered as she entered but rose quickly as she crossed the floor and stormed up the stairs to her room.

"I'm gonna need to be up early if we want to trade this with Clay," she told Wivre and pulled their salvage out. "I have to make sure we're all paid up and our gear is safe."

The little dragon didn't argue and he didn't seem to have too much else to say.

They were going into the mountain—and they were no one's bait, regardless of what Lonne might think.

Wivre woke Kaylin early the next day, and the two of them descended to find Clay.

He took one look at her determined, angry face and sighed. "I take it you're still going," he stated and she hefted the sack.

"I came to make sure my room's still here when I get back."

The innkeeper gave her a doubtful look but didn't argue. Instead, he led the way into the trade room and closed the door behind her.

"You want to get into the mountain that badly?" he asked and settled into his chair.

She nodded and tipped her salvage onto the table. She'd been so upset the night before that it sparkled more brightly than usual and he whistled softly.

"You been holding out on me, girl?"

Kaylin blushed. "I was angry," she admitted. "I might have gone overboard on the polish."

He laughed at that and they began to negotiate.

"A pleasure doing business," he told her finally and tucked the items carefully into different boxes.

She slid half the payment across the table.

"Three months?" she asked and he glanced at the coins before he stowed the last item and scooped them into one hand.

"One and a half."

"Two." She snarled her impatience, tired of the game because she knew exactly how much her coin was worth. "And you refund me the meals I don't eat here."

"Hey, now..." Clay began and Wivre growled.

She glowered at him and he frowned in return. After a moment's stand-off, he nodded.

"Two months and I'll give you credit for any meals not eaten at the inn," he agreed and gestured at the door.

The Claws were settling around their tables as she exited with her pack in one hand and Wivre on her shoulder. From the look the woman gave her, Lonne hadn't been sure she would show up—and neither had many of the others.

Claude stared at her with his usual inscrutable expression and tossed her a small bundle of cloth.

"Put that on," he ordered and turned to Clay.

"We move out in an hour," he stated and the innkeeper nodded.

Kaylin shook the cloth out and noticed it was a black tabard with a white border and a stylized dragon's paw stitched in white. This was curled palm-upward as though clenched around an invisible heart.

Claws. She remembered the name Lonne had called her company. *Well, if that isn't delusions of grandeur.*

The entire group wore the tabard, even though they hadn't worn them in the week before.

Down time, she decided, *or maybe to save on wear and tear.*

She wondered why they bothered with them now as she set her satchel and pack on the floor beside her. Wivre alighted on the satchel and she pulled the tabard on before she retrieved her gear.

"Sitting or marching?" Clay asked as Kaylin slung the satchel across her chest and the dragonette settled on her shoulder.

"I'd prefer sitting, but we'll eat on the march if we must," the mercenary replied.

"Sit," the innkeeper told him. "I'll have Chloe bring the tea."

"Tea." Claude made the idea sound dubious.

"It'll keep your folks warm and give them a little extra pep to face the morning," Clay told him and the other man smiled.

"On the house?"

"Already paid for," the proprietor informed him with a brief glance at Lonne.

Claude grunted and turned to the table. He'd taken two steps before he turned back and addressed Kaylin.

"I take it you're joining us?"

Kaylin gave him a bright, hard smile. "I already did."

He grunted again and jerked a hand toward a thin, black-robed mage who wore a lightweight gambeson. "There's your master."

At the sound of the word "master," the mage looked up and his sallow face allowed a thin smile as he greeted her.

"Apprentice..." he all but purred and his gaze slid over her, but not in the professional assessment she'd received from Claude and Lonne.

The way this man looked at her made her feel like she was distinctly underdressed—or that he was using a spell that let him see through her armor and the tunic she wore underneath.

She blushed, then frowned.

Some of the nearby mercs chuckled and money changed hands. Several leaned closer to others and whispered, and Wivre's tail twitched violently.

"Thibault?" Kaylin asked, her mouth dry with anger and nerves.

He stood and extended his hand while the smile widened behind his greasy forked beard and mustache. His dark eyes glittered, but she couldn't tell if that was with interest or madness. Reluctantly, she took his hand.

His palm was slightly damp and his long fingers wrapped around hers in a surprisingly strong grip.

"Thibault Bardin at your service," he replied smoothly, "but you will call me Master."

Muffled snickers came from the company around them. She couldn't stop herself from blushing a deeper shade of red but she refused to acknowledge them beyond that.

"He wishes," someone close by said and she chose to ignore that too.

"Master Bardin," she replied and he scowled as though that wasn't the term of address he'd desired.

Kaylin kept her smile to herself. *Too bad,* she thought. *There's no master for you, only Master Bardin.*

After all, it wasn't as if he could correct her.

He released her hand and she resisted the urge to wipe it on her armor.

"Sit," he commanded and gestured to his table. She took the chair opposite him.

Again, he looked annoyed but she decided she'd rather see his face when she was talking to him and not have to feel him alongside her.

"So you wish to learn more magic," he began after an awkward pause.

She nodded. "I feel like I've only scraped the surface."

Bardin chuckled although she didn't see anything funny, either about what she'd said or the situation in general.

"This trip," he told her, "will be more about observation than anything else. You'll watch and learn."

"Watch and learn," the nearby commentator said knowingly, and soft laughter answered.

Bardin and Kaylin turned but neither of them could see who'd spoken. The mage shrugged, then leaned forward.

"And should you return from the mountain alive," he murmured in the smoothest of tones, "I'll have so much more to teach you."

The way he said it made her wonder what kind of magic put that particular look on his face. Before she could ask why he couldn't start teaching her on the way to the mountain or what kind of magic he specialized in, breakfast arrived, including a plate of bacon for Wivre.

The little dragon hopped onto the table and kept his plate between him and the mage's huge serving of bacon, sweet rolls, and meat-filled pastry.

"Say the word," he growled inside Kaylin's head. *"Simply say the word and I'll pluck that bastard's berries."*

CHAPTER TWENTY-EIGHT

The journey into the mountain was far more uneventful than Kaylin expected. Granted, she'd heard the night before that the dire wolves had been turned into pelts but she'd expected to see some sign of trolls, orcs, or maybe hobgoblins, and there wasn't any.

The ruins were a much quieter place than she and Wivre had investigated the week before.

"Where are all the monsters?" she asked finally.

"The hunters cleared them. They said there was more profit in it for them if they got to them before we did," one of the mercs answered and ignored Bardin's frown.

She nodded. Although she'd forgotten about the other mercs who weren't going into the mountain, now that she thought about it, the idea made sense. After all, this was the area she'd seen the most monsters in during her time exploring the Old City.

The only exception to this came when the company had climbed the broad, broken trail leading to the entrance into the mountain. As they approached the large double doors that gave entry to the tunnels and passages riddling the Spears, one of the scouts whistled softly and ran to the main body to speak to their leader.

Lonne listened, whistled, pointed to two more scouts, and gestured to the ruins around them.

Kaylin wished she could see, but a mage's position was in the middle of the march and she doubted she'd be allowed to follow the scouts.

Instead, she watched as they scrambled quickly up some nearby walls and found vantage points from which to look on the surrounding ruins. When he sensed her frustration, Wivre took flight and remained low and close to the walls until he could alight on a point higher than either scout could reach. From there, he relayed what had caused the alarm.

She got the impression of a troop of goblins—a large number and more than she'd ever seen in one place at one time. While she continued to move, she watched with rapt interest as the images in her head showed the little creatures spreading out.

Some scaled the walls for a better view like Lonne's scouts, and others found covered positions from which they could shoot anyone coming up the trail.

It looked like the little fuckers had prepared an ambush for anyone trying to enter the mountain deeps and they'd come in the numbers necessary to deal with any of the companies she had seen at the Rest.

No wonder so few ever come back if this is what's waiting for them before they enter.

Kaylin jumped when a goblin broke cover from behind a drape of vines in one of the buildings a short distance ahead of the mercenaries. An archer had his arrow nocked and his bow raised to fire, but Claude reached over and pushed the bow down gently.

"Watch," he growled. "They've seen the tabard."

She wondered what that had to do with anything, but Wivre shifted position, flew to the next building, and alighted on its top. When he showed her what else was waiting with the goblin, she gasped.

"Hill ogre," he told her when he guessed she might want to know its name. *"Smaller than a giant and closer to a cave troll in size and eating habits."*

That last was said with a wave of disgust, and she decided she didn't want to know what the creature ate. It wore what looked like roped-together beetle wings—if beetles had slate-gray wings the size of wagon beds.

Some kind of skull had been fitted over its head to make it look even more fearsome than it already was.

The goblin streaked through the front line of its troop and took a weaving path into the ruins where a slightly larger goblin wearing black leather armor and carrying a staff topped with a humanoid skull had a platform.

Some kind of chieftain, Kaylin guessed as the scout prostrated himself at the chief's feet.

She couldn't hear the report the smaller one babbled but she saw the results. The chief climbed to a slightly higher vantage point and pulled out what looked like a spyglass, through which he studied the cautiously advancing mercenaries.

After a moment, he appeared to focus on Lonne, then on Claude, and then on the leader again and almost dropped the spyglass. He caught it before it could fall, tucked it into his belt, and scrambled hastily from his perch while he shouted orders.

The sound of several horns echoed through the ruins and Wivre showed her the goblins retreating from the mountain entrance. She noticed that they didn't leave slowly either but as quickly as they could and with many fearful looks over their shoulders.

It was hard to tell how many there were, but she estimated that the creatures had the mercenaries outnumbered at least three to one.

And they're still leaving. She wondered what the company had that would make such a large group of monsters leave. *Surely they aren't that good that the monsters know them by sight and are afraid of them.*

But that seemed to be the case. It made her want to rethink her plan to travel with the group into the mountain and then sneak away.

Initially, she'd considered asking for their help to locate and enter the vault, but Lonne had changed all that. She didn't like the mercenary leader's attitude or her double-handedness and especially didn't like the woman's plan to use her as bait.

Once she'd learned that was the case, Kaylin had decided she didn't owe the mercenaries anything.

She didn't owe them an explanation and she certainly didn't owe them her sticking around until they had a monster they needed to outrun—especially since the only way to do that was to feed it their apprentice.

No, she wouldn't hang around for that.

Still, the incident with the goblins gave her pause. If they were powerful enough to scare off such a large group of goblins—and one strong enough to have a hill ogre at its command—maybe this wasn't a group she should leave in the lurch.

Not that I'd leave anyone behind who needs me, she reminded herself. *After all, who would they have thrown to a monster if I hadn't come along?*

It was a good question and one that reminded her that her fate as monster food was guaranteed if she stayed and that she had a better chance of survival without them. There wasn't any other choice she could make.

She let nothing of this show in her expression or demeanor as the company marched unmolested into the mountain.

Her thoughts were so occupied with her dilemma and the slew of questions that she didn't get a chance to discuss any of this with Wivre until Lonne called a halt to the march.

"Food," she ordered, and the mercs spread out in the small cavern they'd reached. Some settled watchfully beyond the entrances to the cavern exits but most simply sat on the floor where they stood.

Kaylin eased to the edge of the group and found a more distant corner when she thought no one was watching.

"Does any of this seem familiar?" she asked as she sat in front of Wivre and dug out the bacon scraps she'd saved from breakfast.

The little dragon hung his head despondently. *"I'm sorry,"* he told her. *"I feel like it should be familiar but I can't be sure. I was running for my life when I finally reached the surface."*

"And you don't think it was from the main doors," she concluded.

"I didn't think so," he admitted, *"but..."* He peered at the cavern around them. *"It could have been. The smell seems almost familiar."*

"How can you not be sure?" she asked, horrified that they might be trapped in the mountain without a clue as to where they were.

"It was a very long time ago and monsters were doing their best to kill each other and anything that moved near them—including me!" he snapped. *"And I hadn't eaten in a while because they'd realized that something was raiding their pantry and had started to hunt it. I had to get out. If I hadn't made it out of the caverns, I'd have died, either by monster or of starvation. I wasn't looking where I was going, I merely followed the air currents and dodged everything being aimed at me."*

"Like what?"

"Oh, you know, the usual—boots, clubs, arrows, swords, teeth, claws... That kind of thing."

"Nothing spectacular then," Kaylin teased and nudged his food toward him.

"No," he agreed, a smile in his voice, *"but I'm still sure I can find my way to the vault once we're a little deeper in."*

"Go on," she told him and nudged his food again. *"Eat. As soon as we find somewhere we can slip away, we'll leave. We'll worry about where you think we are then, okay?"*

He stilled and cocked his head. *"If you're sure..."*

She thought about the way she'd been treated and nodded. When she answered, her mental voice was hard with determination.

"I am very sure," she said.

Lonne called an end to lunch very shortly after and Kaylin returned to the group. This time, she managed to walk a little closer to the edge and away from Bardin. No one questioned why.

They moved forward and the leader allowed a single lantern at the front of the troop and another one in the center, closer to the back. The light made the girl feel uncomfortable as she remembered how brightly fires lit the dark in the ruins, but she knew they had no choice.

The lanterns might illuminate the group, but they also prevented them from tripping in the dark. Only Wivre was unaffected by the lack of light and he shared images with her of the rocks and passages around them. He showed her the rats or smaller crawling creatures that scattered into the dark or crouched, shivering, in corners as the mercenaries passed.

It was a relief when they reached a large cavern that served as a junction for several passages. Judging from the masonry still clinging to the walls and the large chunks of fallen worked stone, the area might have been something else in the past. It was merely another underground ruin now, however.

The fallen stone and chunks of masonry proved large enough that the company had to spread out as it progressed toward Lonne's designated exit. It was the best opportunity Kaylin had seen so far and she inched carefully to the edge.

As much as she wished she could use a spell to blur her figure—and wasn't she glad she hadn't chosen to reveal that ability to the mercenary leader—Kaylin didn't dare. She was fairly sure Bardin was watching her closely.

He hadn't protested when she'd moved away from him but had dropped back a little in the marching order. It worried her that he could still be watching her and might see her vanish into the shadow and alert the mercenary commander.

She drew on the skills she'd used to stay unseen on the streets of Waypoint, dropped into a crouch, and moved carefully and quietly around the fallen stone and tumbled rubble. When she'd almost reached the edge of the cavern, she realized she was no longer using lamplight to see by but the images Wivre shared of their progress.

Now, she understood why the dragon's head was pressed against her cheek. He wasn't seeking comfort or trying to give it. Rather, he was making sure that what he saw was what she should see as she moved away from the mercenaries and their lanterns.

Kaylin suppressed the urge to kiss him and moved forward quickly and quietly. She remembered to stop and check her backtrail before she committed to the tunnel beyond.

"Do you know the way?" she whispered when the cavern was far behind them and all sounds of the others had died away.

Wivre's claws clenched and she slowed. A short moment later, she heard him sniff, draw in long snuffs of air, and exhale them quickly as he sorted through the scents and his memory.

"Straight ahead," he told her and she was about to scold him for being a smartass since they were in a straight tunnel when he added, *"There should be a junction where three tunnels fan out ahead of you. Go right and we'll descend but there'll be an opening on the left."*

He paused and Kaylin waited.

"It's steep in there but straight. There are no branches until you get to the edge of whatever civilization built the vault. I don't know what it used to be,

but you can still see worked stone in parts of the wall and the tunnel underfoot. We'll have to skirt a large cavern..."

His words trailed off and he sighed.

"That's all I can remember, for now," he told her. *"I'm sorry."*

"It's more than you could remember before," she said. *"Don't give up now."*

"After what you've promised?" the little dragon reminded her. *"I won't ever give up."*

Wivre's memory proved to be mostly accurate. There were five tunnels at the junction, two of which he couldn't remember being there when he'd last passed through.

"But they could have been," he reassured her. *"I might have forgotten. They do smell familiar."*

Kaylin took his word for it and they headed down the passage to the right. The tunnel to the left was exactly where he said it would be and she felt him relax a little when he snuffed the air.

"It smells right," he told her and they continued. She stepped carefully to avoid the very real possibility that she might roll an ankle or slip and fall. Wivre hadn't been joking when he'd told her it was steep.

They both breathed a sigh of relief when the tunnel ended in a T-intersection and a much broader, flatter corridor. Exactly as the dragonette had said, some of the stone on the floor looked like the small bricks used for paving walkways, and larger blocks made up the walls on either side.

"We're almost there," he assured her, *"but we have to be quiet here. There are...things."*

"Any idea what things?" she asked.

"No."

She sighed and moved cautiously forward. While she could sense a large open area not far ahead, she still relied on Wivre's shared vision to see. The dragonette had draped himself over the top of her head and clung carefully to her temples with his forepaws while he used his hind paws to balance himself on her shoulders. He rested his chin on her forehead and watched the tunnel ahead.

They'd almost reached the arched opening to the larger cavern when Kaylin saw the first body lying at the edge of the road. She froze and stared at it, relieved when Wivre's vision showed it to be ancient and hairless, its skin long since withered until it looked like nothing more than parchment stretched over bone.

Kaylin looked around warily and noticed several more bodies, each one covered in tattered rags and slowly disintegrating armor and each one as dead as those she'd seen before. She drew a deep breath to steady her hammering heart and moved cautiously forward.

Her ears strained at the darkness as she found a path between them and turned her head to monitor them as she passed. They were dead. She was sure they were dead. They wouldn't do anything.

"One moved!" Wivre's cry of alarm came none too soon.

She lashed out with her boot as the one closest to her pulled itself onto its hands and knees. It toppled but another had started to rise. The dragonette lifted from her head and she suddenly had to rely on her eyes again.

When she wasn't plunged into blackness as she'd expected to be, she didn't have time to search for the light source. It was there but she couldn't tell exactly where and she was too busy ducking under the clawed reach of an undead arm to look.

A low moan rolled out of the mouth of one of those closest to her and a second one followed. She ducked under another swipe, drew her dagger, and slashed up and across the chest of the one facing her.

The tattered cloth parted and the parchment skin caught the blade to slow its upward momentum. The corpse didn't seem to notice and she wished she had a torch or a lit lantern. What did the old stories say? That undead were extremely flammable?

The creature reached for her and a small savage figure dropped onto its head, wrapped his claws and paws around it, and tore savagely at its scalp. She closed in and stabbed its chest with her dagger.

"It's neck!" the little dragon screamed. *"Chop its head off!"*

"With a dagger?" she demanded. *"Are you kidding me?"*

"Stop whining and start cutting. I can't hold it forever."

Not that he was doing much holding but she decided not to tell him that.

Kaylin lunged forward and ignored the fact that this put her inside its arms. With a grunt of effort, she thrust one hand under its chin to stretch its neck back and drove the dagger into its dry-skinned throat with the other.

It didn't cry out but it started to pummel her with its hands as she cut frantically at the tough, dry flesh that held it together. The force of its blows stung but it couldn't get much momentum behind its swings and stumbled back when she pushed against it.

She followed, grateful when it was stopped at the wall and she was able to use her body and legs to pin it. The cutting didn't get any easier but she was eventually able to separate its neck from its shoulders except for the skin that clung around its spine.

"Hurry!" Wivre cried and she knew it wasn't because of the corpse she was dealing with.

The images the little dragon was sharing showed a half-dozen more closing in on her from different points.

Gods! How many had she walked past without seeing? And why hadn't they attacked until she'd almost left the tunnel? They didn't seem to be able to think.

She began to stab at where the skin adhered to the bone and hacked at the joint until she was able to wedge the blade into it and use it as a lever to pry the bones apart while the edge sliced through the remaining skin.

It fell like a puppet without its strings and its body disintegrated into a fine spray of dust as the bones rattled to the floor and disappeared. With a gasp of horror, she pivoted and pushed her back against the wall.

The undead were all around her. Those from the corridor were joined by more coming from the open cavern. They shambled in under the arch and their limbs moved with a jerky lack of coordination as they approached with their arms extended toward her.

She wondered if they'd eat her or simply tear her apart.

There was nowhere to run and no gap between them large enough for her to pass through. She drew several rapid breaths and prepared to fight. Undead burned, right?

"Avark," she whispered and a small fire orb spun into being as a sheet of flame erupted out of the passage leading into the corridor.

It caught several of the undead and their bodies flared with sudden brightness before they burst into dust and ash. Her tiny orb seemed insignificant by comparison but she launched it into the rags of the nearest corpse and gave a choked laugh of relief as it caught alight.

It was short-lived relief as the creature continued toward her and threatened to roast her alive as it disintegrated. She kicked it away and it stumbled back. When it bumped into another one, the flames spread.

That meant very little, however, as four more reached for her and she couldn't see a way past them.

"Avark," she croaked, terrified of setting herself alight but even more terrified about not burning them before they grabbed her.

"He...helda..." Her voice caught and the spell flared and died. The shield provided a momentary barrier before it dissipated.

Kaylin tried again and kicked out as she cast. "Helda!"

As much as she wanted to think they wouldn't eat her, she could see their jaws stretched wide as they advanced. The shield knocked one away as its fingers tangled in her tabard and she kicked out again. It stumbled back but not very far, and more shambled closer behind it.

So this is how it ends, she thought.

A second whoosh of flame—much closer this time—was accompanied by the sound of running bootsteps and shouts. Hard blows sent echoes shuddering through the darkness and the moans grew fewer and farther between.

Kaylin kept her back to the wall and kicked the undead away from her as she fended off the hands that clawed at her throat. Wivre darted into the air and wheeled and dove in an attempt to knock her attackers off-balance.

Sometimes, he'd grab hold of them and try to pull them away.

"Run!" he cried but she couldn't. Her feet had forgotten how.

She didn't know whether to laugh or cry when a shining length of metal cleaved the closest undead in two and left its arms clutching her tabard's collar before they disintegrated with the rest of the corpse. Her mind seemed to freeze when Claude caught hold of her with one hand and pulled her behind him as he swung at the remaining corpse with the other.

Acting on instinct, she scrambled back and started to bolt down the corridor, only to have her flight cut short when a steely grasp on her collar jerked her back.

"You," Lonne all but snarled, "are one lucky little bitch."

Kaylin didn't feel lucky. As soon as the undead were cleared, she was surrounded by a company of very angry, very experienced mercenaries, none of whom were happy with her. Lonne stood with her fingers curled into the neckline of Kaylin's tabard and pinned her to the wall by sheer force of strength.

She held her there but ignored her as she looked at the company. When she saw they'd all gathered and that Claude had set the perimeter, she turned to the girl.

"So," the mercenary began in a conversational tone, "care to share?"

"Share what?" she asked and the woman pulled her away from the wall and thumped her into it again.

"What you and the drakeling are up to." Lonne turned her head to look for Wivre. "We could have done with a guide."

"I thought you knew where you were going," she retorted and received another wall pounding for her trouble.

Her captor kept her pinned and watched with lazy interest while the girl tried to catch her breath.

"We're here on a speculative mission," the woman told her. "Now if one of us knows where there's a specific treasure, it's customary for them to share it."

"There's a difference between being one of you and being bait,"

Kaylin told her acerbically. "I decided leaving before you fed me to a monster was my best bet."

Lonne favored her with a derisive smile.

"And look how well that turned out for you," she mocked. "You almost fed yourself to the monsters." She leaned closer. "By now, I'm very sure you realize your best chance of survival is with us."

She did know that but only up to a certain point. Beyond that, she also knew her very best chance of survival was to get as far away from them as she possibly could.

The mercenary leader shook her again. "So tell us where the vault is."

Kaylin's eyes widened and she stared at the woman.

"The...the vault?" she stammered.

Lonne's eyes narrowed. "The vault, girl. You know. The vault the drakeling was going to show you." Again, she glanced around and searched the tunnel for the diminutive creature. "Where is he by the way?"

"I wouldn't have a clue," she replied and made herself look into the woman's face and resisted the urge to look around in search of her friend.

The mercenary leader met her gaze and gave her a grim smile. "But you know there's a vault," she pressed.

Kaylin frowned. "I know there's a vault," she admitted, "but how do you know that's what I'm looking for?"

Lonne glanced over her shoulder in answer and Kaylin followed her gaze. The mage raised his hand and waggled his finger at her in greeting.

"But...how?" she asked in confusion.

"A little spell that lets him hear the intent inside people's heads," the woman explained and returned her attention to the girl's face. Again, she looked around. "What's in it that you would risk your life to find it?"

"I don't know," she admitted.

Lonne laughed harshly with disbelief.

"It's true," she protested. "I don't know exactly what's in the vault. I only know it's there."

"And you have to skirt the next cavern," the mercenary leader stated.

Kaylin gaped at her. Exactly how long had the mage been inside her head? She shuddered at the thought and wished she could go back to the Rest and have a long hot bath, even if it felt like no amount of scrubbing would make her clean again.

The woman ignored her and glanced instead at the small piles of dust scattered in the corridor. "At least we know why you need to skirt the cavern, although it's strange he couldn't remember."

Someone snorted and Kaylin looked up. Claude had pushed to the front of the group and stood to one side and a little behind his leader.

Lonne glanced at him.

"What?" she snapped.

"It's more unusual that he remembers being here at all," the old mercenary informed her. "Drakelings aren't known for their smarts and I don't know of any with a long-term memory."

Kaylin expected a protest from the little dragon but he remained silent and out of sight.

"Regardless," the woman responded sharply and looked into Kaylin's eyes. "You will take us to this vault."

"But I can't—" she argued but stopped when the point of a blade slid through the seams of her leather armor and dug into her side. "I don't know where it is."

The blade dug a little deeper and she hissed in pain.

"The drakeling does," Lonne reminded her.

Kaylin tore her eyes away from the mercenary's face and made a show of looking around the corridor. "I don't see him around, do you?" she asked and the blade twisted. She yelped.

Her captor sneered. "I'd say we're close enough to find it without you," the mercenary informed her, "but it would save us considerable time if you could convince him to lead us to it."

"And then what?" she wheezed and the woman gave her a savage smile.

"You're still bait."

"So? You knowing about the vault is because of me…and I still need—"

She stopped before she could say she still needed to search it for clues to the elven library. Now more than ever, she didn't want them to know about it. The thought of Thibault getting his greedy paws on elvish magic made her feel ill.

"I still need to pay for my room at the Rest. I'm almost out." she finished lamely.

From the look on Lonne's face, she didn't fully believe her story but she didn't challenge her on it. The dagger eased a little but she could still feel it against her skin.

"What makes you think you'll need it?" the mercenary leader snarled. "After this, what makes you even think you'll come out from under the mountain alive?"

Kaylin felt a flash of fear but she clenched her jaw and made herself meet the woman's eyes.

"There isn't much incentive to show you anything, is there?" she snapped. "If you're going to kill me and not share the treasure only I know about, why should I share it at all?"

The dagger dug in again and she gasped.

"Because as long as you live, you've got a chance to change my mind."

A soft growl rose from the mercenaries.

"Our minds," Lonne corrected with a slight smile. "I'm not the only one you'll have to convince."

She looked from the woman's face to the mercenaries standing beyond her. They stared in return, their faces hard and still angry—all except Claude. He gave her a nod so slight she wasn't sure the others had noticed it.

It was as if he was trying to reassure her and let her know that if she convinced him to keep her alive, he'd make sure she got back. At least that's what she hoped he was saying because she was pinning so much on that nod—and on what Wivre had said about the man.

"Don't be so quick to judge."

With a sigh, Kaylin hoped the dragonette was all right and that he'd come when she called him. She let herself sag against the stone as though defeated.

"Fine," she muttered. "I'll try to convince the drakeling to lead us to the vault."

She gasped again as the dagger slid out and away and Lonne stepped back.

"Well, girl? Best you call him, then. The day's a-wasting and I'd like to be drinking in the Rest's taproom before dawn."

Another growl greeted these words—an approving one this time—and she pushed away from the wall.

"Wivre?" she called softly and her voice whispered down the corridor.

She hoped it didn't carry too far into the cavern beyond. The little dragon hadn't said why they needed to skirt it and she didn't want to find out the hard way. At first, nothing happened and she was about to call again when the dragon swooped out of the darkness to settle a few yards from the mercenaries who guarded the perimeter of the group.

He stood in the middle of the corridor, his wings half-spread as he studied them, and let them get a good look at him.

"Wivre," Kaylin repeated and he cocked his head and took a tentative step forward.

The closest guard stepped aside and lowered his blade and the others did the same. After another cautious look at them, the dragonette trotted forward and turned his head from side to side as he tried to keep an eye on them all. The mercenaries moved so he had a clear space to walk through and he reached her unmolested.

She crouched and extended a hand to greet him, and he scrambled up her arm to perch on her shoulders. Before she could rise, Claude approached and pulled a small bottle, a pad, and a bandage out of one of the pouches at his belt.

Lonne stopped him before he got close and placed a hand on his shoulder.

"She doesn't need it," the woman told him.

To Kaylin's surprise, he looked at her hand and his mouth curled with distaste. He didn't protest when the mercenary leader kept it in place but he did lift the bottle and bandage.

"If I know you, she's bleeding. And if she's bleeding, the scent will attract something we're probably not interested in fighting—especially if the vault's occupied, as so many of them are."

"She's still bait," Lonne informed him.

Claude didn't flinch. "And you'll want to use her at a time of your choosing, not at a time chosen by some random monster who thinks it's scented a snack and walks in on a buffet."

From the startled glances he got from the closest mercenaries, Kaylin guessed none of them had thought of themselves in quite those terms before and didn't like thinking of themselves like that now. She lowered her head to hide an involuntary smile.

Lonne released his shoulder and made a sweeping gesture with her hand.

"By all means, please ensure the bait is ready to be used when I need it and not before," she instructed. "Then get it on its feet so it can try to show us it has other uses we might like to consider it for instead."

That brought a stifled snicker from one of the gathered mercs but Kaylin couldn't see who. She suspected it came from Bardin, but she couldn't see him so couldn't be sure.

Wivre snarled as Claude knelt beside her and the grizzled mercenary held up each of the items to show them to the little dragon as well as Kaylin.

"Ointment to close the blood vessels and speed healing," he said and held the bottle up before he placed it on the stone between them.

The dragonette uncurled from her shoulder and crept cautiously to the floor. As he sniffed the bottle, the mercenary held up a small square pad made of cloth stuffed with herbs and something else.

"Pad to cover the wound." He held the bandage up. "Bandage to hold it in place."

Wivre sniffed at each one, then looked at the stocky man. Claude nodded to him and turned to Kaylin.

"I need you to take your gambeson off and lift your tunic," he told her and pulled a cloth out of the pouch. "To wipe the blood off your armor."

With a doubtful glance at him, she obeyed and tried to ignore the glances she received from the mercenaries nearby. He set a lantern down beside them and tutted irritably before he took a threaded needle out of the pouch.

"I'm gonna have to stitch it closed," he told her. "It's best if you don't look and don't yell."

She nodded, pressed her lips together, and chose a spot on the far wall. Claude gave her a cursory glance and went to work, and she drew a sharp breath when the needle punctured her flesh.

With her mouth firmly closed, she held herself as still as possible while he worked. The cool feel of the tincture on her skin made her flinch but it was quickly followed by the pad and the bandage before he turned his attention to her armor.

"Done," he told her, wiped it clean with a few deft strokes, and handed it back. "Get this on and show us the way."

That last instruction was delivered in gruff tones as he pushed to his feet. He didn't move away, however, but checked her armor and laid a heavy hand on her shoulder.

"Lead on."

"I take it we have to show them all the vault," Wivre snipped and she nodded.

"Time to get moving, boy. Which way next?"

The dragonette gave her a disgusted look at being addressed like some common drakeling, but he complied and flicked his tail in her direction before he marched down the hall.

Kaylin sighed and followed.

As much as she didn't want to share her discovery with the mercenaries, she didn't have a choice. Worse, she now had to plan how to get out of the mountain alive.

She moved to the front of the group and with Claude beside her, stepped into the dark to follow Wivre around the edges of the cavern. Lonne and the rest of the mercenaries moved quietly in her wake, their presence more of a threat now that she couldn't see them.

If Wivre had planned to avoid the undead in the cavern, he'd made a mistake. They'd only traveled for an hour into the dark when stone grated in the wall alongside the group and a door appeared.

The closest mercenaries made short work of the emerging undead and looted the interior quickly.

"I take it your drakeling didn't know these people buried their dead in the walls?" Lonne demanded.

"I don't think so," Kaylin replied and pointed to where Wivre stared at the walls with wide eyes, his tail standing almost straight up.

"Lucky for you," the mercenary muttered and pushed her. "Now, quit stalling."

She stumbled forward. Wivre gave her an anxious glance but she motioned him on and noticed the little dragon took them a little farther from the cavern's edge. Now and then, he'd fly up into the broken walls of whatever structure had stood in the cavern as though trying to see what was ahead.

"Are you sure this is the way?" Kaylin asked and tried to think the question rather than say it out loud.

While she was fairly sure Bardin still had his spell running, she didn't care if he overheard her asking the dragonette for directions. It would only stand as evidence that she needed Wivre to show her the way. And if that kept the little dragon alive, it was worth it.

Again, she shuddered at the idea the mage was looking inside her head but she tried to keep the knowledge as a thought and not as speech, which Thibault might pick up. She was fairly sure he was using a conversation spell and not a mind-reading spell, which meant he'd pick up thought-speech but not thought itself. She had no idea how she could be sure but maybe he was fudging how much he could hear.

She made a note to look for ways to block mind-readers when she found the library—and also ways to know when she wasn't the only one inside or outside her head.

Another group of undead rose out of the rubble and the mercenaries surged around her to keep them at bay and destroy them.

"Keep moving," Lonne ordered. "Let us handle the monsters."

Unless you're thinking of throwing me to them, Kaylin thought sourly but didn't say it. She assumed she'd know soon enough when the woman was using her for that.

Wivre flew up so he could see the way ahead and returned to perch on her shoulder when he was done.

"Straight ahead," he told her and sounded more confident.

"Straight ahead?" she asked him. *"As in 'straight ahead where that moaning and growling is coming from?'"*

"That would be it," the dragonette assured her and flicked his tail. *"Didn't Lonne say her team could handle the monsters?"*

"Well, ye-es," Kaylin admitted, still not happy with the idea they were heading toward more.

"Besides, there isn't any part of these caverns where there aren't any monsters," he added. *"You should probably be grateful they've agreed to tag along."*

As if the mercenaries tagging along were an option they could have avoided if they'd wanted to. She frowned but resisted the urge to argue. After all, her head wasn't hers at the moment.

"There's more of them." The warning came from the mercenaries who'd moved ahead.

Sounds of fighting followed shortly thereafter and the moaning from that direction stopped. It didn't die out altogether, though, and Kaylin soon identified several new directions it was coming from.

"We're making too much noise," she muttered. "At this rate, they'll draw every monster in the cavern."

From beside her, Claude chuckled. "We can't fight quietly, girl. This was bound to happen sooner or later."

"And you're happy with it?" she demanded.

He rested his hand on the hilt of his sword and looked toward the most recent sound of battle.

"I didn't say I was happy with it," he replied. "Only that this is the way it happens. If you'd ever been under the mountain yourself, you'd know this."

She subsided to silence. The man was right but that didn't mean she had to like it.

"Wivre?" she asked, and the dragonette flicked his tail over her shoulder so it draped down her front.

"He's right," he replied, his voice worried, *"and now I am here, I remember them being here before—although I was able to avoid waking them by traveling high and not making any noise."*

The dragonette paused and she thought he'd finished, but he spoke again quickly and she realized he hadn't.

"We are close to the vault entrance," he informed her, *"but I am worried. All the undead... There was something bad in the vault I worried about but I don't remember what it is so be on your toes."*

"Wivre thinks something bad is in the vault," Kaylin relayed to Claude and the older mercenary laughed.

"When isn't there something bad in a vault?" He chuckled. "It's good that he remembers that, though. It means it's probably protecting treasure and that means a good payday for us."

He didn't say whether it meant Kaylin would end up far enough in their graces for them to consider not killing her and she didn't ask. She simply followed Wivre's directions until they stopped in front of a large squared-off portal, its stone doors shattered and lying in pieces around the entrance.

Lonne prodded her forward. "It doesn't look hopeful," the mercenary leader informed her as they walked past the doors into a large foyer.

The next set of doors looked more promising. Made of ornately carved wood overlaid with metal and banded in iron, they were closed.

"Cavill, Agarda. You're up," the woman ordered out of the gloom.

Claude drew Kaylin to one side as a man and a woman brushed past them. The man looked familiar and she recognized him from the bathhouse at the Rest—the one who'd tried to pick her pocket.

She scowled at him and he grinned but didn't stop. He even kept his hands to himself.

The woman ignored her and focused her attention on the door, the floor before it, and the walls around them. Only when she was satisfied there were no traps waiting to be triggered did she approach the door itself and examine the portion where the two sides met.

It didn't take her long to find a keyhole and to manipulate the workings inside it to produce a resounding click. Several of the mercenaries glanced nervously over their shoulders and those in the rear turned to face the cavern beyond.

Kaylin wasn't sure what they expected. They'd already killed all the undead that had approached them and she could no longer hear moans echoing off the cavern walls.

"Ready?" the woman asked as she and her partner prepared to open the doors.

The rest of the company moved out of the foyer, followed by Claude, who took Kaylin with him, and Lonne who stayed close to the girl's side.

It's almost as if she doesn't trust me, she thought and acknowledged that this was exactly the case. *Well, at least her lack of trust was earned.*

Metal creaked and wood brushed against stone and the sounds whispered past them as the doors opened. A faint stench reached her nostrils as the thieves called the all-clear.

"We're in," the man said.

It was accompanied by the woman's snort. "It doesn't look promising, boss."

Kaylin's heart sank. While it was bad that it didn't look promising for the mercenaries, she was more disappointed that it didn't look promising because that meant she might not find what she was looking for.

Lonne caught her arm and dragged her forward while Claude stayed close on her other side. When they reached the open vault doors, her heart sank.

The woman hadn't been joking.

If anything, she'd made an understatement. Not only did it not look promising but there was only one chest left whole in the entire chamber. Broken shelves lined the walls and the shattered remains of a dozen other chests lay scattered across the floor. A thick layer of dust coated broken boards, twisted pieces of metal, and small pieces of rock and stone.

She tried not to wince when the mercenary leaders' grasp tightened. The sound of the rest of the company filing into the vault and spreading out to poke at the debris was not comforting.

"I remember there being more in it than this," Wivre told her apologetically.

Kaylin looked around, partly to try to see something more to offer the mercenaries and partly to try to gauge their mood. From the expressions on the faces of those she could see, they weren't happy. Lonne's growl confirmed it, as did the dagger at her throat.

"What's the meaning of this?" the woman demanded.

She swallowed when the dagger's tip started to break skin. "I thought there'd be more."

Even to her, the words sounded weak.

"I say we take the chest and leave her behind," one mercenary suggested. "Gut her and let her contemplate her mistake as she bleeds out."

"There's no need for that," Claude interjected. He wrapped a hand around Lonne's wrist and moved the dagger away from Kaylin's throat. "The girl was following the drakeling, and who knows how long it's been since that critter was down here."

The leader wrenched her hand out of his grasp. "I agree with gutting her," she all but snarled and took a firm grip on the girl's collar.

The dagger disappeared and she drew her sword.

"Lonne—" Claude protested and she snapped a glare in his direction.

"How else do I make it clear that double-crossing us is a mistake?" she demanded and looked around the room. "It's not only the lack of treasure but not telling us about the vault and sneaking away from us once we'd got her inside. That kind of treachery needs an answer."

Several growls of approval came from around the chamber.

Lonne shook Kaylin and drew her sword back in preparation to thrust it through her gut.

"Wait!" Claude cried and she glared at him.

"That's the second time you've tried to countermand me, Crozier. Do it a third time and you'll join her."

He hesitated, then opened his mouth, but a green glow seeped into the room and a wild, dry cackle rattled through the air around them.

The mercenary leader looked around while the group moved away from the walls and closer to the center of the room.

"Get the chest!" she ordered and used her sword to point at the two men closest to it.

As they took hold of it and started to drag it toward the door, something skittered across the ceiling with the sound of cloth rustling and claws clicking as it moved.

The mercenaries glanced up, their swords drawn and faces filled with apprehension. The green glow grew stronger.

A shadow moved down the wall, a misshapen humanoid figure whose skeletal features and desiccated form became painfully clear when he moved into the lamplight. His eyes burned with sorcerous fire and he laughed again. The crackling mirth launched a wave of fear over all who heard it.

"A lich!" one of the mercenaries rasped. "A godsbedamned lich!"

That started a stampede for the door.

"Bardin! You're up!" Lonne shouted and the mage's voice raised in a spell.

Kaylin turned to watch what he was casting since she might as well learn something from this debacle.

The lich dropped to the floor and landed exactly where the chest had been. She caught sight of him from the corner of her eyes and glanced toward him as Bardin reached the end of his spell. Two orbs sizzled past her before they spiraled around the ancient undead.

He cackled again and raised his hands to catch the orbs. With a word, he spun the mage's magic together and balanced the spinning globe on one finger.

The man gasped and the lich snapped his fingers to extinguish the crackling globe.

Bardin stuttered before he began another chant but his adversary had other plans. He smiled at him, his lipless mouth leering in mockery, and he raised the hand that had held the lightning ball to his teeth and blew him a kiss.

The man screamed and took a step back, and Kaylin thought he might run. He didn't and instead, he clutched his chest. His robe began to smoke and his scream reached a higher note when his voice became shrill with agony and panic.

Lonne moved the girl to one side but kept a firm hand on her as she stared at her mage. Claude pivoted so he stood side-on to the lich and was able to both watch him and keep an eye on what was happening with the mage. The two mercenaries gasped as Bardin's chest began to smoke above where his heart was located.

They fell silent when his chest burst open to reveal the organ as it burst into flame. He dropped like a puppet whose strings had been cut, his body limp and lifeless. The lich cackled again and a familiar sound answered it.

The moans of possibly a hundred undead filled the air, reverberated through the cavern outside, and echoed around the vault itself as corpses pulled out of the floor and through the walls.

"Run!" Claude roared. "Retreat in formation."

"Fighting retreat!" Lonne ordered. "Make sure you bring that chest with you or I'll gut you myself."

Given that she'd already proven herself more than willing to do exactly that, no one argued. The two men with the chest were aided by another two as the company formed up around them and began to hack through the ranks of undead waiting outside.

"Not you!" Lonne snapped when Kaylin made to follow Claude out of the room.

She spun her around, shoved her hard, and hooked a foot around her ankles so she fell heavily. Without waiting to see what happened next, the woman pivoted and raced after Claude. She ordered the older mercenary to help her close the doors behind them.

"Bait isn't much use if it runs away!" She laughed before the vault doors slammed shut.

The girl scrambled to her feet and looked at the lich and the undead surrounding her.

"Oh, troll's turds."

CHAPTER TWENTY-NINE

Kaylin dropped into a crouch as one of the undead swiped at her, rolled between the legs of another four, and reached a clear patch before she stood. The lich laughed and his crackling cackle grated on her nerves.

As the undead turned toward her, she looked at the shelves around the wall and clawed hastily up them. The vault had been intended for storage and holding more than books and scrolls.

While she'd hoped to find some kind of mini-library there, she was glad it had turned out differently.

She scrambled up the shelves until she was out of range of the undead hands that stretched toward her. As they began to destroy the shelves and the supports below her, she scuttled along the tops to a more stable area.

The undead usually failed to notice her shift in position for a few minutes, which gave her time to catch her breath and work out where to move next. She was careful to stay where she was until her current perch became unstable. The lich watched, amused by her antics as she sought to avoid his servants.

"Tell me you know another way out of here," she said to Wivre as the little dragon scampered along ahead of her.

"I...uh..." the dragonette began but she interrupted him.

"Are you telling me that you made it through a cavern of undead, woke up a lich and all its friends, and then went back the way you came?" she demanded impatiently. *"Honestly?"*

He didn't answer immediately and the undead moved toward her and began their destruction of the shelves below. As the platform began to shudder beneath them, he took flight.

Cursing herself softly under her breath, Kaylin scrambled across two more sections. She was about to apologize to the little dragon so her friendship didn't end with a snippy comment when Wivre spoke.

"You're right. I didn't remember before but now you've said it, I do. There's a vent a way up." He looked speculatively at her as though assessing her size. *"You should fit."*

She didn't waste time being insulted. *"Where?"* she demanded and again, the dragonette took flight.

"Here!" he called with an excited chirp that reached her ears to draw her attention in the direction he needed.

A darker patch was faintly visible in the shadows that cloaked the ceiling. She frowned. It was a little farther than she thought she could jump. Maybe there was a spell she could use.

She thought hard and tried to ignore the shaking that told her she'd have to move soon. The only direction she could go would take her farther from the vent opening and the shelves that would bring her closer had collapsed under the assault of the undead.

When her perch grew perilously weak, she decided on the only spell that might work. It was usually used to make trunks lighter and had been a favorite among the students in the Academy. Mirielle had shown it to her one day when she struggled with an armful of library books.

Now, she cast it on herself.

Kaylin made her leap as soon as she was finished and propelled herself toward the opening, grateful when Wivre's teeth closed around her wrist and the little dragon attempted to pull her upward. As she struggled to find purchase on the entry, he placed her hand on the ledge where the vent changed from vertical to horizontal and seized her by the collar to haul her deeper into it.

By the time she started to fall, her torso was over the edge and she'd pulled her feet out of the chamber below and used them to push the rest of her into the narrow space.

Behind her, the lich screeched in frustration and began to cast when it looked like his toy was getting away.

"This way," the dragonette told her in urgent tones as the lich's voice reached a crescendo and green light flared brightly behind them.

The light intensified as she made an inelegant scramble through the cramped confines. An acrid scent reached her nostrils as the crackle of flames reached her ears. Heat bloomed behind her.

"Here!" Wivre's frantic instruction showed her the opening to another shaft leading down, one through which she could hear the multiple moans rising from a horde of undead. *"Hurry!"*

The stench of burning stone and intensifying heat gave her no choice. Kaylin swung her legs through the hole and used her fingers to slow her descent as she plummeted. She landed with a dull thud and barely remembered to roll to soften her fall as green flames licked out of the shaft.

They'd reached the foyer in front of the closed doors.

"I hope Lonne shut that properly," she muttered as she followed the dragonette at a sprint.

The undead had moved away from the vault entry.

Chasing the mercenaries, no doubt, she thought as the iron-bound doors creaked.

Kaylin glanced at them in alarm and saw green flame flickering around their edges.

"Run!" Wivre ordered as he flew around her head and into the cavern.

She complied and broke into a sprint when the doors burst open and the undead poured out. The lich's dry voice echoed after them in a cracked shout of victory but she didn't stop. She followed Wivre as he raced through the ruins and then into the passage beyond.

He didn't stop or turn when they came to the tunnel they'd entered through.

The moans of the undead were much louder there and drowned out the sound of those shambling in pursuit. Wivre flew past the entrance and farther down the tunnel.

"There's another tunnel farther along," he explained. *"It leads out. I'm sure of it."*

Kaylin didn't ask him if he felt more sure of this exit than he had of the last. It didn't seem fair. After all, he had found the vault and the way out.

Just because they hadn't found what she'd been hoping to find didn't mean the dragon hadn't done exactly what he'd said he would.

Grateful that he couldn't hear her thoughts, she followed him through the tunnels until they reached a second turn. The sound of the undead was much softer there and he turned up it without hesitation.

She sprinted after him.

A quick glance behind her revealed the green glow of the lich moving steadily behind them. He had ignored the tunnel the mercenaries had taken, almost as if he had chosen her to vent his ire on. Perhaps that was because she'd defied it alone and escaped.

While she had no idea what Wivre's plan might be for when they reached the surface or if they came across another group of monsters, she decided they'd work it out when they got to it. Her choices were a possible group of goblins and a freakishly large monster for their leader or a very real lich behind her and his skeletal followers.

Right now, the most important thing was to get to the surface and only then to worry about reaching the safety of the Final Rest.

Better than making my final rest here, she thought grimly and ignored the burn in her lungs and throat.

She raced up the tunnel and slowed only when she reached a cavern strewn with fallen masonry and marble blocks. It looked vaguely familiar. Wivre flew out, then back.

"We have to hurry," he urged but she could hear voices up ahead.

Shouts and curses in Lonne's all too familiar tones echoed off the cavern walls.

"Keep up!" the woman screamed. "We didn't come all this way to go back empty-handed."

Aware of the lich in pursuit, Kaylin crept into the cavern and circled away from the mercenary leader's voice until it became clear that she stood in front of the only tunnel leading out of the cavern. In front of her, the four mercenaries struggled to carry the chest and keep up.

On the other side of the cavern, the first of the undead horde that had pursued them were emerging from the tunnel leading up from the vault.

"Move your lazy asses!" Lonne screamed and earned several looks of disbelief and distaste. She moved around them. "Hurry!" she shouted and swung the flat of her blade across the closest man's legs.

He stumbled and she glared at him. "You drop it and I'll gut you and leave you to keep them occupied."

Kaylin saw no reason to disbelieve her and neither did the merc. He pushed forward and stumbled again in his haste to avoid his threatened demise. She didn't blame him and wondered why the men stayed with her.

Her answer came when Claude hurried out of the tunnel and placed a hand on the edge of the chest as he muscled in beside the others to help carry the load.

Maybe it's not her they're staying for, she thought as Claude and the mercenaries with Lonne behind them reached the tunnel leading to the exit.

"We have to go," Wivre told her. *"We have to go now!"*

She glanced back and saw the first glimmers of green in the tunnel she'd run through. It was easy to decide that the lich was far scarier than Lonne ever could be and she darted forward. Her movement caught the mercenary leader's eye.

The woman turned to face her and raised her sword. When she recognized her, she managed a greasy smile.

"So nice of you to join us," she quipped. "We could use a little more bait right now."

"So sad to be you," Kaylin retorted, thought fast, and used one of the spells she'd studied for her battle with Sylvester.

As Lonne moved toward her, she wove the components together, spoke the activation, and knew the mercenary saw her divide into three. She chuckled with satisfaction at the look of consternation on the woman's face and dodged to one side.

Even when the mercenary's expression turned from consternation to confusion and then alarm, she ignored her. The green glow grew brighter behind her and she had no desire to wait for the lich to catch her. Instead, she dodged around Lonne's initial thrust, ducked under the wild swing that followed, and leapt out of the way of the panicked backswing that might have caught her if she'd remained in one place.

Caught off-balance, Lonne over-extended and stumbled. Annoyed by the attempt to turn her into bait for a second time, the girl drew her dagger, pivoted in a low crouch, and thrust the blade into the back of the mercenary's knee.

The woman screamed and started to fall and her blade flailed. Not willing to leave her only weapon behind, Kaylin yanked the dagger sideways and sliced through tendon and muscle as she continued her turn to sprint into the tunnel. Claude and the others still struggled with the chest.

They'd heard Lonne's scream and had dropped their burden to move back to see what had happened. Kaylin didn't know why they bothered but before she bolted past them, she saw their gazes turn to horror and looked over her shoulder.

The lich had emerged from the tunnel and green flames wreathed his form as he entered the cavern. The woman's cries of pain and outrage drew his attention and he chuckled. The undead that emerged from the other tunnel had grown in number and rapidly closed the distance between their prey and themselves.

Kaylin glanced at the mercenaries. "We need to go!" she shouted at them. "You can't save her."

Claude glanced at her and seemed about to argue but the others wavered.

As she pivoted and began to move away from the cavern with Wivre on her shoulders, she couldn't help adding, "Anyone who feels like staying with the bait is welcome, but I'm getting the hell out of here!"

That earned her a startled glance from Claude and mirthless smiles from the others. They turned and followed her as Lonne hauled herself to her feet and tried to claw to the tunnel using the scattered pillars and rubble as support.

"Get back here!" the woman screamed but Claude turned away reluctantly, chivvied the men to the chest, and helped them lift it. "Don't leave me!"

The plea might have worked but the lich's voice whispered paper-thin behind them.

"It was so nice of you to wait for me, my pretty."

"No!" Lonne shrieked. "No! Don't touch me! Don't you touch meeee!"

Dry laughter acted as a counterpoint to the wordless cries that followed and neither Kaylin nor the mercenaries went back to see what caused them.

"This way," Wivre urged and she relayed the message.

"Hurry," she added as she ducked into the side tunnel and they needed no urging.

Faint screams still followed them but the moaning chorus of undead grew closer.

"This way," the dragonette urged again and paused at another small side passage. *"This way is out."*

It was a tight fit for the chest but they managed and emerged in a chamber she recognized as being not far from the mountain entrance. They were met by startled shouts and the sound of weapons being drawn, but Claude reacted swiftly.

"Stand down!" he roared and when he saw who it was, added, "Stand down. It's me."

Quiet followed as the rest of the company saw who they were.

"You made it," someone said finally and he nodded, breathing hard from the run.

He and the others moved into the chamber and Kaylin remained slightly to one side and out of sight. It took the main body a few minutes to realize someone was missing.

"Where's Irenus?"

Irenus? she wondered but Claude's response gave her the answer.

"Lonne's not coming. The lich caught her."

"Lich? But we locked him in!"

"Yeah. We left the girl to keep him busy."

The older mercenary snorted. "The girl got herself out and when Lonne tried to turn her into bait again, she turned the tables and the lich got the commander instead."

That drew all gazes to Kaylin and she readied herself to bolt. The mercenaries simply stared at her, some in surprise but most in quiet appraisal as if she'd become something new and they needed to work out where she fitted and what her presence might mean.

A low moan interrupted them and they all glanced at the chamber's entrance.

"They're still coming?" one asked in disbelief and she noticed they were all breathing as hard as she was.

Claude nodded with somber confirmation. "They're still coming," he told them.

"We thought we'd outrun them." The speaker looked crestfallen.

The older mercenary shrugged and looked around at them before his gaze swept the chamber.

"It looks like we'll have to make a stand here," he told them. "We won't make the entrance and even if we do, there'll be more monsters waiting—and they won't be on our side."

The mercenaries nodded and exhaustion and resignation marred their faces.

"They'll be here soon," one noted and looked at Claude. "How do you want to do this...boss?"

From the startled look on the erstwhile second in command's face, he hadn't expected the promotion.

"I'm not—" he began but they crowded around him.

"You are," one declared, "and you'll be a better boss than Irenus ever was."

Another moan echoed up the corridor.

"For however long that might be," another added succinctly.

"So...boss," the first mercenary pressed. "What should we do?"

Claude looked around at them.

"You know we can't beat them, right?" he asked.

"Well, I sure as shit don't want to join them, boss, so you'd better come up with something," another merc told him. "Why don't you ask the girl for a suggestion since she's already escaped them once?"

All eyes turned to Kaylin as someone murmured, "We could try running."

"No." Claude vetoed that idea with a single word. "We run and some of us might make it to the entrance but—"

That last word ended the hasty shuffle that had followed his observation.

"But," he continued, "I'd guarantee no one will survive the goblins and their cave ogre."

"Do you think they'll be waiting?" someone asked.

"They live in hope," he answered shortly. "I know they will."

Another moan rolled over them and they stilled.

"So...uh, boss, what are we going to do?"

Claude looked at Kaylin. "Do you have any ideas, girl?"

She looked around. "Is there anything we can block the tunnel with?" she asked and the mercenaries exchanged glances.

"You're too skinny," one told her sarcastically, "so that idea's out."

"No." Claude ended the nervous laughter that followed. "That's not a bad idea." When she gave him a worried look, he smiled. "You're a mage, aren't you, girl?"

Without hesitation, she nodded. She'd attended the Academy and knew enough magic that most would consider her a mage.

The new leader pointed at the cross-beams that shored up the tunnel leading to the ruined cavern. "Do you think you know enough to get a few of us up there to destroy those?"

Kaylin thought about her spell for lightening weight.

"I know enough to make—" She looked around and located a toppled pillar. "To make that light enough for you to lift so others could stand on it. Would that do?"

He frowned, glanced from the pillar to the tunnel, and focused on the group. Finally, he nodded.

"Tryptus, Denir, Elliot, you're on hammer duty. Loren, Fiddler, Enshaw, I want you to weaken the supports on either side." He looked around but was interrupted by one of the others.

"Let me guess, Hadrik, Erma, and me are on lifting duty."

Claude smiled at the man. "You're right. Now, Kaylin, if you would."

She nodded and wove the spell to make the pillar light enough for the two men and a woman to lift it. The three on hammer duty scrambled on top and linked arms to help each other balance. She held the focus on it and on keeping the pillar light as it was maneuvered into the tunnel.

As the three worked to knock the beams out of place on the ceiling line, the other three mercs went to work cutting through the uprights supporting them. Even Wivre helped and excavated around their bases until they started to wobble.

Through it all, the moaning increased and they began to hear the shuffle of a hundred footsteps moving closer to where they worked. Green light gleamed faintly in the far reaches of the corridor.

The sight made them work faster. As it grew steadily brighter and silhouetted the shambling force ahead of it, Claude fastened a rope around two of the center supports and instructed Hadrik's team to lower the pillar to the tunnel floor.

As soon as they were done, he handed them the ropes and signaled everyone out of the tunnel.

"Grab hold of the ropes," he ordered, "but wait until I give the word."

He turned to Kaylin.

"You got anything that might give them something else to think about while we pull the roof down on their heads?"

"Are they flammable?" she asked when she recalled how Bardin's balled lightning had ended.

Claude gave her a worried look. "They can be. But don't try it on the lich. I have a feeling he's got protection against that and I'm already down one mage. I can't afford to lose another."

She frowned. "What about sound?" she asked.

"Like loud noises?" She nodded, and his brow wrinkled as he thought about it. "Not in this chamber," he told her, "but farther up the tunnel, especially under the beams, it could help with the cave-in."

"We're letting them reach the beams?" The mercenary who asked it sounded alarmed.

The leader shook his head. "No. I don't want to risk any of them breaking through. We do this now." He glanced at Kaylin. "Are you ready?"

She drew a deep breath and brought up the combination of fire and sound she'd used so effectively against Sylvester. When she nodded, he surveyed the men and women who stood nervously in front of him.

"On my word," he told them, "pull as though your lives depended on it."

The mercenaries chuckled at the dark humor.

"Because they do," more than one of them replied as he looped the end of one of the ropes around his bicep and over his shoulder.

"Word!" he roared as the lich came into view at the far end of the tunnel.

His voice boomed down the corridor and the undead moaned louder in reply. The light around the lich flared, turned an iridescent green, and began to move more swiftly toward them along the ceiling.

"Pull!" Claude shouted. "And again. *Pull!*"

"Avark-tonal!" Kaylin cried, repeated the accompanying gestures three times in quick succession, and wondered if one verbal component would cover them all.

"Avark-tonal!" she repeated as the first three globes of fire streaked down the corridor to explode amidst the front ranks of the undead.

The lich shrieked in fury but several things happened at once. The support beams creaked and cracked, the boom of sound accompanying the fireballs partially drowned out the lich's cry, and the tunnel roof began to shatter and plummet as dust poured out.

With the ropes gone suddenly slack, the mercenaries tumbled back and fell in an untidy tangle. Kaylin's second set of fireballs pounded into a curtain of dust, tumbling rock, and decaying timber. They exploded early with another loud boom that reverberated around the tunnel before it rebounded into the cavern.

Coughing and cursing issued from behind them as they ducked.

Dust and small stones rattled from the ceiling and Claude scrambled to his feet, caught hold of the man next to him, and hauled him upright.

"Go!" he shouted and shoved the man toward the tunnel leading to the mountain exit.

He reached the next mercenary and repeated the action.

"Go! Go! Go!"

Kaylin's ears rang but that didn't stop her from helping Claude. As four of the mercs lifted the chest, she ran to the second line of mercs, hauled the first one to their feet, and sent her after the rest.

The woman stayed, however, and helped her to get the rest of her comrades moving toward safety. When she, Claude, and Kaylin were the only ones left, she grasped the girl's arm and began to drag her toward the exit.

"Come on!"

The leader joined them, one arm outswept to shepherd them along the tunnel beside him.

More stones rattled from the ceiling together with larger rocks before a brief moment of silence settled. Claude slowed and when Kaylin followed suit, the female mercenary let go of her arm and ran on.

The two who remained glanced over their shoulders, Kaylin partly because she was curious but mostly because she wanted to make sure the lich hadn't broken through, and Claude because he wanted to see the damage.

With a roar, the cavern ceiling gave way and filled the chamber with stone. The billow of dust and wind it created blew the lantern out, and they were plunged into darkness. To their relief, not a single shred of green broke through the shadows.

For a long moment, they stared into the black before the older mercenary laughed and clapped her on the shoulder.

"Come on," he said. "Let's get our people back to the Rest."

She created a small globe of light to brighten the path—one surprisingly free of goblins but haunted by the howls of wolves. Trollish roars broke the night and high-pitched screeches answered them.

Neither she nor the mercenaries stopped to wonder why the goblins hadn't been waiting.

CHAPTER THIRTY

"So, we're done?" Kaylin asked and pushed the bracelet across the table.

It wasn't the last thing from her share of the chest from the vault but it was almost the last. She didn't see the point in keeping everything aside when she could hoard the extra security of her living space.

Wivre, of course, had disagreed until Kaylin had bribed him with an extra serving of bacon for lunch. They'd both been down early to catch Clay before anyone else from the Claws showed up to trade.

The innkeeper lifted the bracelet carefully from the table and smiled as he turned it so he could admire it again. He pushed the small pile of coin toward her.

"Yes," he agreed and wiggled the bracelet at her. "I'll take as much of this kind of thing as you can find, but our trade today is done—unless you've got some more?"

She smiled and stood from the table.

"Not today," she told him and pushed a few coins to him. "Add another month to my room and board?"

Wivre stirred restlessly on her shoulder and she stroked the little dragon's neck. He didn't know it but he was about to get his share.

"Another month it is," Clay told her and examined the coins "And lunch as well as breakfast and dinner."

The dragonette chirped curiously and the proprietor looked at him.

"Of course that includes you," he told him. "Everything that includes Kaylin includes you. She wouldn't have it otherwise."

She fixed him with a wide-eyed stare. Granted, it was true, but she didn't remember having that discussion with him.

Clay caught her look and frowned. "That is correct, isn't it?"

"Yes," she confirmed, "but how did you know?"

"You mean you didn't ask him?" Wivre asked inside her head.

The man tapped the side of his nose. "Call it innkeeper's intuition," he told her. "Or the fact that any fool with half an eye can see you're a team."

That made Kaylin smile despite the dig of Wivre's claws on her shoulder.

"Thank you," she said and headed to her room.

"You didn't ask him to include me." The little dragon sounded almost hurt. *"Did you forget?"*

"No," she answered, unlocked her door, and slipped inside. "I could see he was including you and I didn't need to ask."

"Hmmph. It's a good thing, too," he grumbled and flitted from her shoulder to the chest.

Kaylin unlocked it and pulled his satchel out, hung it from a hook above the bed, and flipped the lid back. He flew up to it and perched momentarily on the lip.

"Wait!" she commanded as the dragonette's forequarters vanished into the bag.

She rummaged in her pouch and withdrew five gold pieces. Wivre's eyes widened when she dropped them into the bag.

"Your cut," she told him with a gentle smile. "I didn't forget."

He poked his head into the satchel and sniffed loudly as he inhaled the coins' scent. Her smile broadened and she pulled the curtains on their window back. He removed his head from the bag at the sound.

"I suppose you'll spend all day with that book again," he grumbled.

Coins clinked as he raked his claws through his portable horde and rearranged it before he descended into the bag. When she glanced at him, all she could see was his head poking out of one end while the end of his tail draped over the other.

"I won't be able to wrap my head around these spells if I don't study," she reminded him. *"Besides, I've already found one reference to another vault—or maybe a library."* Her eyes danced with excitement as she glanced at him. *"It could be the lost library of Tolan's City!"*

"Pfft! Or it could be something even greater," Wivre snarked.

Her eyes widened.

"Do you honestly think there is something greater than Tolan's library?" she asked.

The dragonette settled deeper into the satchel and his tail disappeared from view as the coins clinked under him.

"Tolan was a newcomer compared to some of the other civilizations that existed here," he told her and shifted again until only the tip of his snout was visible. He sighed happily and added, *"Gold is very comfortable."*

This was followed by a jaw-cracking yawn.

"Very comfortable..." he murmured as his snout sank out of sight.

A soft snore followed and Kaylin smiled. A moment later, she frowned as she opened the book that formed the biggest part of her share from the chest.

"Don't you dare go to sleep on me, Wivre! I will need you for this."

The snoring hiccupped and coins jangled as his head momentarily reappeared. Another jangle followed, then a sigh.

"Wake me when you do," he replied sleepily and the coins clinked softly as he settled into his bed.

Was gold an anti-stimulant—or even a sedative—to dragons? Did it cause them to want to sleep? Maybe that's why all the dragons in stories were sleeping when the adventurers arrived.

"The Dragon Queen?" Wivre asked and almost launched himself out of his satchel in alarm.

"Yes," Kaylin replied, puzzled. *"This clue seems to point to there being more elvish lore in the fabled treasure cave of the Dragon Queen. What does it mean by that? What Dragon Queen? And how old does she have to be for her treasure cave to be fabled amongst elves?"*

He settled deeper into his bag and shivered his skin clean of the coins that clung to it.

"Very old," he told her and yawned again. *"Wake me if you find something useful."* He raised his head to peer at her, narrowed his eyes, and looked annoyed. *"Like when you've read something that's more than a fable."* He dropped into the bag and sighed huffily.

"Well, if the Dragon Queen is a fable," she replied thoughtfully, *"how old was the elvish civilization whose knowledge ended up in her horde? Were they around before Tolan? And how long before?"*

She looked expectantly at the bag and was answered by another soft snore.

"Wivre..." she protested but another snore followed. "Ugh. Dragons..." she grumbled and returned to her book.

One thing was becoming very clear. She would have to go back into the mountain if she wanted to discover any more of its secrets and even more so if she wanted any of her questions answered.

The little dragon might have spent a couple of hundred years in its tunnels—he'd never told her specifically and she'd simply assumed this—but how much time had he had to discover its secrets if he was always hungry or running scared? She sighed.

If she had to go back into the mountain, she would need help.

Kaylin pushed that thought aside as a problem she could solve later and focused on her book.

She'd have missed lunch if Claude hadn't knocked at her door.

"Yes?" she asked after she'd checked who it was and unlocked everything. She stuck her head out and gave him a puzzled look. The grizzled mercenary seemed different and it wasn't because of the new helmet tucked under his arm.

It was the one the mercenaries had insisted he take from the chest as a sign that he was their leader. They all suspected it was magical but they wouldn't be able to determine what kind of magical until they either returned to Waypoint or a mage came through the Rest who had the spell to identify it.

Kaylin frowned. No, it wasn't the helmet that made him look different. He merely seemed happier?

"I didn't see you downstairs," he said by way of a greeting, "so I thought I'd check."

The jingle of coins drew their attention and they looked over in time to see Wivre emerge from his satchel. The man managed a small smile.

"Is that how you keep him quiet when you're studying?"

She nodded. "I decided drakelings were like small dragons and he might settle better with a few coins."

He shook his head. "I'd check his nest if I were you because that sounded like more than a few."

Kaylin shrugged. "Who knows what he's been hiding in there?" she said and hoped to deflect the old mercenary's interest. "I'm not willing to put my fingers inside to find out."

As if on cue, Wivre growled at them.

Claude laughed. "I'd think twice too," he admitted.

A moment passed and the smile slipped from his face. He raised a hand and rubbed the back of his neck awkwardly before he lowered it quickly to his side.

"Look," he began, "I was hoping to catch up with you over lunch, but I—"

"No." She stopped him when her stomach rumbled and gestured toward her desk. "I'll clear a few things away and be right down."

"Good. I'll meet you there."

He turned away and the dragonette emerged from his nest as she hurried into her room. She packed the book, her journal, and Wivre's satchel into the chest and secured them.

Once she was finished, she inspected the room again and headed to the taproom.

When she arrived, she found Claude seated at a table in one of the corners not far from the fire. The rest of the Dragons Claws were at the tables around them to form a barrier between their leader and the rest of the inn. From where she stood, it looked like they were making sure no one got close to their leader or his discussions.

She paused at the bar, ordered hers and Wivre's meals, and remembering the extra bacon for the little dragon before she crossed the room to talk to Claude. He smiled when he saw her and indicated she should take the seat opposite him.

"You doing anything at the moment?" he asked as she sat.

Kaylin smiled. "Talking to you?"

"No," he answered with a frown. "I mean do you have any plans for what you want to do next?"

"As in my future, you mean?"

He shrugged. "Something like that."

"I was thinking of doing more exploring," she hedged and wondered where the conversation was going.

They'd been back two days but she hadn't had time to speak to them. When they'd appeared downstairs, it was for meals and they'd been fairly quiet and subdued and watched Claude as if he'd either tear their heads off or abandon them. Why he'd do either, she wasn't sure.

She did know they'd taken most of the floor below hers on what looked like a semi-permanent basis and it had made her feel happy to know they were still around and recovering from their trip into the mountain.

"Into the mountain?" Claude asked and his eyes sharpened with interest.

"It depends," she told him warily.

"See," he stated, "I was impressed with your quick thinking down there and with the way you handled yourself."

Kaylin assumed he was mostly impressed because she hadn't left him behind when she'd had the chance, but that wasn't the case.

"You might not have finished at the Academy and I'm not asking why. I think that's a story for another day, but the fact is I liked what I saw and the way you used what you had in a way that made a difference."

She opened her mouth to protest that they would have made it without her help but he held his hand up and shook his head.

"We were done," he told her. "We'd never have brought the tunnel down without your help, and if you'd left us—which you had every right to do after the way you'd been treated. If you'd left us, we'd have all ended up the same way Lonne did."

Soft murmurs from the nearest tables told her the mercenaries were not only listening but they agreed. Claude looked around.

"I guess what I'm trying to do is ask if you'd like to join us—permanently—as our company mage and not as bait," he added hastily and his face reddened.

Someone snorted nearby and a couple of others chuckled.

Kaylin gaped at him before she covered her surprise. "Do you mean that?"

He glared at her. "No, girl. I've got all the time in the world to spend almost apologizing, saying thank you, and pulling cruel pranks! Of course I meant it."

"And there's the boss we all know and love," someone muttered and was quickly hushed.

"What would I need to do?" she asked and Claude scowled.

"Mage things," he answered. "Whatever it is you need to do to be the best damned mage the Claws can have."

"So I could still study?" Kaylin asked, and his scowl deepened. What was she missing aside from the knowledge of how a mercenary group worked?

"Could?" he almost bellowed. "Girl, if you don't, I'll chain you to that desk and ram spell books down your throat until you bleed spells through your skin."

Someone muttered, "Hear, hear," and she looked around.

"And I'll have help," Claude added when she couldn't find who'd said it. "We want— No, we need a mage who can get us through situations like the one in the vault and help us get out of them again—

someone who can follow the leads they find and bring them to us so we can follow them too. We need a proper spell-slinger."

This time, the rumbles of agreement from around them were louder.

"And you think I'll fit the bill?" she asked, not quite able to believe it.

He rolled his eyes. "I wouldn't be askin' if we didn't."

Kaylin thought about it for all of another second before she extended her hand across the table.

"Then I'd be glad to be your mage."

Claude's smile as he took her hand was expected but the sudden jubilation from the tables around her was not. The older mercenary smiled at her confusion.

"You saved their lives, girl," he explained, "so they're happy to have you along." He sobered. "And they'll be expectin' you to do it again."

"So, no pressure then," she stated but she couldn't help a smile.

She was wanted again and her skills were needed, and that meant they'd help her to at least find more resources to learn from.

Perhaps her search for the "fabled" elven library wasn't so hopeless after all.

As the group around her focused on their meals, she realized that the stories of the Thief-Mage Kaylin Knight and her dragon companion Wivre had started for real.

Where they would end was waiting to be written.

Her inner contemplation was broken when her sarcastic friend's mental voice interrupted her thoughts.

"More bacon!"

AUTHOR NOTES - MICHAEL ANDERLE

SEPTEMBER 24, 2021

First, thank you for not only reading this story but these author notes in the back as well.

If you have never read any of the books I'm a part of (in some way or another as the writer, creator, collaborator, publisher, etc.), I will drop a bit of the expected "About Me" down below. First, I'd like to explain how I decided to release a few stories on another world (is it?) with those who touch the magic of the universe...

"Go West, young man, for there is GOLD in those hills!" said some idiot who wasn't about to strap themselves into an archaic wood and iron wagon to travel for months and get shot with arrows. *But, he was willing to tell someone else to do it.*

And claim the credit if they became something BIG in the future!

My own version of this is my younger self decrying that I didn't have any sword & sorcery tales that I was enjoying (as I did as a teenager and in my twenties. This would have been the 80s and 90s. I'm kinda old, now.) This was all of last year (2020).

However, the older me (the guy above pushing his other self) decided, "What the hell! I'm a publisher, and I'm a writer. I can get a team together, and by golly by gum, we can write Sword & Sorcery stories (and Fantasy), and the gold will be there!"

That was the publisher in me (talking about the gold). The reader in me was thinking, "We don't see any rich sword & sorcery writers much anymore. I don't think there is gold. Maybe a bit of silver."

(Sure as hell no platinum, I figured. Hey, I read all sorts of stories before LitRPG was EVER a thing. This is NOT a LitRPG story (as you could tell—no stats.) Now, this series could be worth a platinum or two, but that's up to you, the readers, to decide whether these stories are worth telling your friends about.

But the reader in me *WANTED* to push the author side of myself and allow the conniving (and lying-his-ass-off-publisher-side-of-me) to convince everyone that we needed to have more Sword & Sorcery. "Sure, it will sell!" he said…and then Fantasy (this series) and also some good ol' fashioned other stuff. Because…screw it. If we are going to go and build a set of stories, *I don't do it half-assed.*

So, I did.

After I worked on Skharr, I started dreaming about something a bit more epic. This genre (Epic Fantasy) has a much larger reading (read, "income") base than a barbarian running around fighting in dungeons, following gods, and generally kicking ass. Personally, I believe these genres are evergreen. They don't age, so the income might not be amazing at first, but it should be steady for a few years.

You will find that the *Skharr DeathEater* series (eight books at the moment), *The Barbarian Princess* (three books), *The Royal Outcast* (three books, with Aaron Schneider), *Dwarvish Dirty Dozen* (coming in 2022, six books also with Aaron Schneider) which makes it twenty-six (26) books so far we have published or will publish.

Not a bad start, and an investment of over $160,000 to make it happen.

So, I have gone to where the sun meets the water and the land stops (the west). We have planted our Fantasy / Sword & Sorcery flag and flipped the finger to those who think we were stupid to write these stories.

We might not make a shit-ton of money all at once, but by God, *we* love them and screw the rest. We will be propelling a fantastic genre where barbarians brawl, warriors fight for friends, paladins have a bit of heartache, gods walk among the heathen, and young women decide the mountain is the place she wants to be.

Because like Kaylin, the safer path was to stay in Urban Fantasy, a genre I know and can successfully publish books in for the rest of my life. But, the barbarian in me must be released...

Every once in a while.

Ok, now a little about me if you've never met me.

I wrote my first book *Death Becomes Her* (*The Kurtherian Gambit*) in September/October of 2015 and released it November 2, 2015. I wrote and released the next two books that same month and had three released by the end of November 2015.

So, just under six years ago.

Since then, I've written, collaborated, concepted, and/or created hundreds more in all sorts of genres.

My most successful genre is still my first, Paranormal Sci-Fi, followed quickly by Urban Fantasy. I have multiple pen names I produce under.

Some because I can be a bit crude in my humor at times or raw in my cynicism (Michael Todd). I have one I share with Martha Carr (Judith Berens, and another (not disclosed) that we use as a marketing test pen name.

In general, I just love to tell stories, and with success comes the opportunity to mix two things I love in my life.

Business and stories.

I've wanted to be an entrepreneur since I was a teenager. I was a very *unsuccessful* entrepreneur (I tried many times) until my publishing company LMBPN signed one author in 2015.

Me.

I was the president of the company, and I was the first author published. Funny how it worked out that way.

It was late 2016 before we had additional authors join me for publishing. Now we have a few dozen authors, a few hundred audiobooks by LMBPN published, a few hundred more licensed by six audio companies, and about a thousand titles in our company.

It's been a busy five plus years.

Ad Aeternitatem,

Michael Anderle

BOOKS BY MICHAEL ANDERLE

For a complete list of books by Michael Anderle, please visit

www.lmbpn.com/ma-books/

All LMBPN Audiobooks are Available at Audible.com and iTunes. For a complete list of audiobooks visit:

www.lmbpn.com/audible

CONNECT WITH THE AUTHORS

Michael Anderle Social

Website: http://lmbpn.com

Email List: http://lmbpn.com/email/

Facebook:
www.facebook.com/TheKurtherianGambitBooks

CPSIA information can be obtained
at www.ICGtesting.com
Printed in the USA
BVHW031356021221
622774BV00023B/552/J